Henry Miller was born in New York in 1891 and raised in Brooklyn. He attended the City College of New York for just two months, then did a variety of jobs. In 1924 he left work to write full-time, moving to Paris in 1930, where he wrote *Tropic of Cancer* (1934), the 'fictional autobiography' of his first months in Paris as a struggling writer. The obscene language of *Cancer* was revolutionary for its time and brought Miller considerable notoriety. His other works include *Tropic of Capricorn*, *Black Spring*, *Quiet Days in Clichy*, and the 'Rosy Crucifixion' trilogy – *Sexus*, this, the second volume, *Plexus*, and *Nexus*. An early work, *Crazy Cock*, was rediscovered in 1988 and published for the first time in 1991.

In 1939 Henry Miller left Paris for Greece, and returned to the USA in 1940. In 1944 he moved to Big Sur, California, where he lived until his death, aged 90, in 1980.

PLEXUS
'Henry Miller's work is one long autobiographical wrestle with world, flesh, devil and angel.'   *Daily Telegraph*

'It is the measure of Miller's genius as a writer that he can fashion this mass of material into a shape of great literary richness. Is there any other living author who could have risen to such a level? It is not easy to think of one.'

Bookman

By the same author

Tropic of Cancer
Tropic of Capricorn
Black Spring
Quiet Days in Clichy
Nexus
Sexus
Crazy Cock

HENRY MILLER

Plexus

Grafton

An Imprint of HarperCollins*Publishers*

Grafton
An Imprint of HarperCollins*Publishers*
77–85 Fulham Palace Road,
Hammersmith, London W6 8JB

Published by Grafton 1965
Reprinted nine times
9 8 7 6 5 4 3 2

First published in Great Britain by
Weidenfeld & Nicholson Ltd 1963

Copyright © Henry Miller 1963

The Author asserts the moral right to
be identified as the author of this work

ISBN 0 586 01942 1

Set in Plantin

Printed in Great Britain by
HarperCollins Manufacturing Glasgow

1

IN HER TIGHT-FITTING PERSIAN dress, with turban to match, she looked ravishing. Spring had come and she had donned a pair of long gloves and a beautiful taupe fur slung carelessly about her full, columnar neck. We had chosen Brooklyn Heights in which to search for an apartment, thinking to get as far away as possible from every one we knew, particularly from Kronski and Arthur Raymond. Ulric was the only one to whom we intended giving our new address. It was to be a genuine '*vita nuova*' for us, free of intrusions from the outside world.

The day we set out to look for our little love-nest we were radiantly happy. Each time we came to a vestibule and pushed the door-bell I put my arms around her and kissed her again and again. Her dress fitted like a sheath. She never looked more tempting. Occasionally the door was opened on us before we had a chance to unlock. Sometimes we were requested to produce the wedding ring or else the marriage licence.

Towards evening we encountered a broad-minded, warmhearted Southern woman who seemed to take to us immediately. It was a stunning place she had to rent, but far beyond our means. Mona, of course, was determined to have it; it was just the sort of place she had always dreamed of living in. The fact that the rent was twice what we had intended to pay didn't disturb her. I was to leave everything to her—she would 'manage' it. The truth is I wanted the place just as much as she did, but I had no illusions about 'managing' the rent. I was convinced that if we took it we would be sunk.

The woman we were dealing with had no suspicion, of course, that we were a poor risk. We were comfortably seated in her flat upstairs, drinking sherry. Presently her husband arrived. He too seemed to find us a congenial couple. From Virginia he was, and a gentleman from the word go. My position in the Cosmodemonic world evidently impressed them. They expressed sincere amazement that one as young as myself should be holding such a

7

responsible position. Mona, to be sure, played this up for all it was worth. To hear her, I was already in line for a superintendent's job, and in a few more years a vice-presidency. 'Isn't that what Mr Twilliger told you?' she said, obliging me to nod affirmatively.

The upshot was that we put down a deposit, a mere ten-spot, which looked a little ridiculous in view of the fact that the rent was to be ninety dollars a month. How we would raise the balance of that first month's rent, to say nothing of the furniture and other paraphernalia we needed, I hadn't the slightest idea. I looked upon the deposit as ten dollars lost. A face-saving gesture, nothing more. That Mona would change her mind, once we were out of their ingratiating clutches, I was certain.

But I was wrong, as usual. She was determined to move in. The other eighty dollars? That we got from one of her devoted admirers, a room clerk at the Broztell. 'And who is *he*?' I ventured to ask, never having heard his name mentioned before. 'Don't you remember? I introduced you to him only a couple of weeks ago—when you and Ulric met us on Fifth Avenue. He's perfectly harmless.'

Seemingly they were all 'perfectly harmless'. It was her way of informing me that never would they think of embarrassing her by suggesting that she spend a night with them. They were all 'gentlemen', and usually nit-wits to boot. I had quite a job recalling what this particular duffer looked like. All I could recollect was that he was rather young and rather pale. In brief, *nondescript*. How she ever managed to prevent these gallant lovers from looking her up, ardent and impetuous as some of them were, was a mystery to me. No doubt, as she had once done with me, she gave them to believe that she was living with her parents, that her mother was a witch and her father bed-ridden, dying of cancer. Fortunately, I rarely took much interest in these gallant suitors. (Better not pry too deeply, I always said to myself.) The important thing to bear in mind was—'perfectly harmless'.

One had to have something more than the rent money to set up house. I discovered, of course, that Mona had thought of everything. Three hundred dollars she had extracted from the poor sap. She had demanded five hundred but he had protested that his bank account was almost exhausted. For being so improvident she had made him buy her an exotic peasant dress and a pair of expensive shoes. That would teach him a lesson!

Since she was obliged to go to a rehearsal that afternoon I decided to select the furniture and other things myself. The idea of paying cash for these items, when the very principle of our country was founded on the instalment plan, seemed foolish to me. I thought at once of Dolores, now a buyer for one of the big department stores on Fulton Street. Dolores, I was certain, would take care of me.

8

It took me less than an hour to choose all that was necessary to furnish our luxurious dove-cote. I chose with taste and discretion, not forgetting to include a handsome writing desk, one with plenty of drawers. Dolores was unable to hide a measure of concern regarding our ability to meet the monthly payments, but I overcame this by assuring her that Mona was doing extraordinarily well at the theatre. Besides, was I not still on the job at the Cosmococcic whorehouse?

'Yes, but the alimony,' she murmured.

'Oh *that*! I won't be paying *that* much longer,' I replied smilingly.

'You mean you're going to run out on her?'

'Something of the sort,' I admitted. 'We can't have a millstone round our necks forever, can we?'

She thought this typical of me, bastard that I was. She said it, however, as if she thought bastards were likeable people. As we were parting she added: 'I suppose I ought to know better than to trust you.'

'Tut tut!' said I. 'If we don't pay they'll call for the furniture. Why worry?'

'I'm not thinking of the store,' she said, 'I'm thinking of myself.'

'Come, come! I won't let *you* down, you know that.'

Of course I did let her down, but unintentionally. At the time, despite my first misgivings, I really and sincerely believed that everything would turn out beautifully. Whenever I became a victim of doubt or despair I could always rely on Mona to give me a hypodermic. Mona lived entirely on the future. The past was a fabulous dream which she distorted at will. One was never to draw conclusions from the past—it was a thoroughly unreliable way of gauging things. The past, in so far as it spelled failure and frustration, simply did not exist.

It took no time to feel perfectly at home in our stunning new quarters. We learned that the house had been owned formerly by a wealthy judge who had remodelled it to suit his fancy. He must have been a man of excellent taste, and something of a Sybarite. The floors were of inlaid wood, the wall panels of rich walnut; there were rose silk tapestries and bookcases roomy enough to be converted into sleeping bunks. We occupied the front half of the first floor, looking out onto the most sedate, aristocratic section in all Brooklyn. Our neighbours all had limousines, butlers, expensive dogs and cats whose meals made our mouths water. Ours was the only house in the block which had been broken up into apartments.

Back of our two rooms, and separated by a rolling door, was one enormous room to which had been added a kitchenette and a bath. For some reason it remained unrented. Perhaps it was too cloistral. Most of the day, owing to the stained glass windows, it

9

was rather sombre in there, or should I say—subdued. But when the late afternoon sun struck the windows, throwing fiery patterns on the highly polished floor, I enjoyed going in there and pacing back and forth in a meditative mood. Sometimes we would strip off our clothes and dance in there, marvelling at the riant patterns which the stained glass made on our naked bodies. In more exalted moods I would shuffle into a pair of slippery slippers and give an imitation of an ice-skating star, or I would walk on my hands whilst singing falsetto. Sometimes, after a few drinks, I would try to repeat the antics of my favourite zanies from the burlesque stage.

The first few months, during which all our needs were met providentially, it was just ducky. No other word for it. Not a soul popped in on us unexpectedly. We lived exclusively for each other—in a warm, downy nest. We had need of no one, not even the Almighty. Or so we thought. The wonderful Montague Street Library, a morgue of a place but filled with treasures, was hard by. While Mona was at the theatre I read. I read whatever pleased my fancy, and with a double awareness. Often it was impossible to read—the place was just too wonderful. I can see myself all over again closing the book, rising slowly from the chair, and wandering serenely and meditatively from room to room, filled with absolute contentment. Truly, I wanted nothing, unless it were a continuous, uninterrupted muchness of the sameness. Everything I owned, everything I used, everything I wore, was a gift from Mona: the silk bathrobe, which was more suited for a matinee idol than yours truly, the beautiful Moroccan slippers, the cigarette holder which I never used except in her presence. When I flicked the ashes on to the tray I would stoop over to admire it. She had bought three of them, all unique, exotic, exquisite. They were so beautiful, so precious, we almost worshipped them.

The neighbourhood itself was a remarkable one. A short walk in any direction brought me to the most diverse districts: to the fantastic area beneath the fret-work of the Brooklyn Bridge; to the sites of the old ferries where Arabs, Turks, Syrians, Greeks and other peoples of the Levant had flocked; to the docks and wharves where steamers from all over the world lay at anchor; to the shopping centre near Borough Hall, a region which at night was phantasmal. In the very heart of this Columbia Heights stood stately old churches, club houses, mansions of the rich, all part of a solid, ancient core which was gradually being eaten into by the invading swarms of foreigners, derelicts and bums from the outer edge.

As a boy I had often come here to visit my aunt who lived over a stable attached to one of the more hideous old mansions. A short distance away, on Sackett Street, had once lived my old friend Al Burger, whose father was captain of a tug-boat. I was about fifteen when I first met Al Burger—on the banks of the Neversink River. It was he who taught me how to swim like a fish, dive in shallow water, wrestle Indian fashion, shoot with bow and arrow, use my dukes, run without tiring, and so on. Al's folks were Dutch and, strange to say, they all had a marvellous sense of humour, all but his brother Jim, who was an athlete, a dandy, and a vain, stupid fool. Unlike their ancestors, however, they kept a disgracefully slovenly house. Each one, it seemed, went his own sweet way. There were also two sisters, both very pretty, and a mother who was rather sluttish in her way but also beautiful, and what's more, very jolly, very indolent, and very generous. She had been an opera singer once. As for the old man, 'the captain', he was seldom to be seen. When he did appear he was usually three sheets to the wind. I have no recollection of the mother ever cooking us a decent meal. When we got hungry she would fling us some change and tell us to go shop for ourselves. We always bought the same bloody victuals—frankfurters, potato salad, pickles, pie and crullers. Ketchup and mustard were used liberally. The coffee was always weak as dishwater, the milk stale, and never a clean plate, cup, or knife and fork in the house. But they were jolly meals and we ate like wolves.

It was the life in the streets that I remember best and enjoyed most. Al's friends seemed to belong to another species of boys from the ones I knew. A greater warmth, a greater freedom, a greater hospitality reigned in Sackett Street. Though they were about the same age as myself, his friends gave me the impression of being more mature, as well as more independent. Parting from them I always had the feeling of being enriched. The fact that they were from the waterfront, that their families had lived here for generations, that they were a more homogeneous group than ours, may have had something to do with the qualities which endeared them to me. There was one among them I still remember vividly, though he is long dead. Frank Schofield. At the time we met, Frank was only seventeen, but already man size. There wasn't anything at all that we had in common, as I look back on our strange friendship. What drew me to him was his easy, relaxed, jovial manner, his utter flexibility, his unequivocal acceptance of whatever was offered him, whether it was a cold frankfurter, a warm handclasp, an old penknife, or a promise to see him again next week. He grew up into a great hulking figure, tremendously overweight, and capable in some queer, instinctive way, enough so to become the right hand man of a very prominent newspaper man with whom he travelled far and wide and for whom he performed all manner of thankless tasks. I probably never saw him more than three or four times after the good old days in Sackett Street. But I had him always in mind. It used to do me good just to revive his image, so warm he was, so good-natured, so thoroughly trusting and believing. All he ever wrote were postcards. You could hardly read his scrawl. Just a line to say he was feeling fine, the world was grand, and how the hell were you?

Whenever Ulric came to visit us, which was usually on a Saturday or Sunday, I would take him for long walks through these old neighbourhoods. He too was familiar with them from childhood. Usually he brought a sketch pad along with him, 'to make a few notes,' as he put it. I used to marvel then at his facility with pencil and brush. It never once occurred to me that I might be doing the same myself one day. He was a painter and I was a writer—or at least I *hoped* to be one some day. The world of paint appeared to me to be a realm of pure magic, one utterly beyond my reach.

Though he was never, in the intervening years, to become a celebrated painter, Ulric nevertheless had a marvellous acquaintance with the world of art. About the painters he loved no man could talk with more feeling and understanding. To this day I can hear the reverberations of his long, felicitous phrases concerning such men as Cimabue, Uccello, Piero della Francesca, Botticelli, Vermeer and others. Sometimes we would sit and look at a book of reproductions—always of the great masters, to be sure. We could sit and talk for hours—*he* could, at least—about a single painting. It was undoubtedly because he himself was so utterly humble and reverent, humble and reverent in the true sense that Ulric could talk so discerningly and penetratingly about 'the masters'. In spirit he *was* a master himself. I thank God that he never lost this ability to revere and adore. Rare indeed are the born worshippers.

Like O'Rourke, the detective, he had the same tendency to become, at the most unexpected moments, absorbed and enrapt. Often during our walks along the waterfronts he would stop to point out some particularly decrepit façade or broken-down wall, expatiating on its beauty in relation to the background of skyscrapers on the other shore or to the huge hulls and masts of the ships lying at anchor in their cradles. It might be żero weather and an icy gale blowing, but Ulric seemed not to mind. At such moments he would shamefacedly extract a faded little envelope from his pocket and, with the stub of what had been once a pencil, endeavour to make 'a few more notes'. Little ever came of these note takings, I must say. Not in those days, at least. The men who doled out commissions—to make bananas, tomato cans, lamp shades, etc—were always hard on his heels.

Between 'jobs' he would get his friends, more especially his women friends, to pose for him. He worked furiously during these intervals, as if preparing for an exhibition at the Salon. Before the easel he had all the gestures and mannerisms of the 'maestro'. It was almost terrifying to witness the frenzy of his attack. The results, strange to say, were always disheartening. 'Damn it all,' he would say, 'I'm nothing but an illustrator.' I can see him now standing over one of his abortions, sighing, wheezing, spluttering, tearing his hair. I can see him reach for an album of Cézanne, turn to one of his favourite paintings, then look with a sick grin at his own work. 'Look at this, will you?' he would say, pointing to some particularly successful area of the Cézanne. 'Why in hell can't I capture something like that—*just once*? What's wrong with me, do you suppose? Oh well . . .' And he'd heave a deep sigh, sometimes a veritable groan. 'Let's have a snifter, what say? Why try to be a Cézanne? I know, Henry, what it is that's wrong. It's not just *this* painting, or the one before, it's my whole life that's wrong. A man's work reflects what he is, what he's thinking the livelong day, isn't that it? Looking at it in that light, I'm just a piece of stale cheese, eh what? Well, here's how! *Down the hatch!*' Here he would raise his glass with a queer, wry twist of the mouth which was painfully, too painfully, eloquent.

If I adored Ulric because of his emulation of the masters, I believe I really revered him for playing the role of 'the failure'. The man knew how to make music of his failings and failures. In fact, he had the wit and the grace to make it seem as though, next to success, the best thing in life is to be a total failure.

Which is probably the truth. What redeemed Ulric was a complete lack of ambition. He wasn't hankering to be recognized: he wanted to be a good painter for the sheer joy of excelling. He loved all the good things of life, and only the good things. He was a sensualist through and through. In playing chess he preferred to play with Chinese pieces, no matter how poor his game might be. It gave him the keenest pleasure merely to handle the ivory pieces. I remember the visits we made to museums in search of old chess boards. Could Ulric have played on a board that once adorned the wall of a medieval castle he would have been in seventh heaven, nor would he have cared ever again whether he won or lost. He chose everything he used with great care—clothes, valises, slippers, lamps, everything. When he picked up an object he caressed it. Whatever could be salvaged was patched or mended or glued together again. He talked about his belongings as some people do about their cats; he gave them his full admiration, even when alone with them. Sometimes I have caught him speaking to them, addressing them, as if they were old friends. What a contrast to Kronski, when I think of it. Kronski, poor, wretched devil, seemed to be living with the discarded bric-à-brac of his ancestors. Nothing was precious to him, nothing had meaning or significance for him. Everything went to pieces in his hands, or became ragged, torn, splotched and sullied. Yet one day—how it came about I never learned—this same Kronski began to paint. He began brilliantly, too. Most brilliantly. I could scarcely believe my eyes. Bold, brilliant colours he used, as if he had just come from Russia. Nor were his subjects lacking in daring and originality. He went at it for eight and ten hours at a stretch, gorging himself before and after, and always singing, whistling, jiggling from one foot to another, always applauding himself. Unfortunately it was just a flash in the pan. Petered out after a few months. After that never a word about painting. Forgot, apparently, that he had ever touched a brush. . . .

It was during the period when things were going serenely with us that I made the acquaintance of a rum bird at the Montague Street Library. They knew me well there because I was giving them all kinds of trouble asking for books they didn't have, urging them to borrow rare or expensive books from other libraries, complaining about the poverty of their stock, the inadequacy of their service, and in general making a nuisance of myself. To make it worse I was always paying huge fines for books overdue or for books lost (which I had appropriated for my own shelves), or for missing pages. Now and then I received a public reprimand, as if I were still a schoolboy, for underlining passages in red ink or for writing comments in the margins. And then one day, searching for some rare book on the circus—*why*, God knows—I fell into conversation with a scholarly looking man who turned out to be one of the staff. In the course of conversation I learned that he had been to some of the famous circuses of Europe. The word *Médrano* escaped his lips. It was virtually Greek to me, but I remembered it. Anyway, I took such a liking to the fellow that there and then I invited him to visit us the next evening. As soon as I got out of the library I called Ulric and begged him to join us. 'Did you ever hear of the Cirque Médrano?' I asked.

To make it short, the next evening was given over almost exclusively to the Cirque Médrano. I was in a daze when the librarian left. 'So that's Europe!' I muttered aloud, over and over. Couldn't get over it. 'And that guy was there . . . he saw it all. *Christ!*'

The librarian came quite frequently, always with some rare books under his arm which he thought I would like to glance at. Usually he brought a bottle along too. Sometimes he would play chess with us, seldom leaving before two or three in the morning. Each time he came I made him talk about Europe: it was his 'admission fee'. In fact, I was getting drunk on the subject; I could talk about Europe almost as if I had been there myself. (My father was the same. Though he had never set foot outside of New York, he could talk about London, Berlin, Hamburg, Bremen, Rome as if he had lived abroad all his life.)

One night Ulric brought over his large map of Paris (the Métro map) and we all got down on hands and knees to wander

14

through the streets of Paris, visiting the libraries, museums, cathedrals, flower stalls, slaughter-houses, cemeteries, whorehouses, railway stations, bals musette, *les magasins* and so on. The next day I was so full up, so full of Europe, I mean, that I couldn't go to work. It was an old habit of mine to take a day off when I felt like it. I always enjoyed stolen holidays best. It meant getting up at any old hour, loafing about in pyjamas, playing records, dipping into books, strolling to the wharf and, after a hearty lunch, going to a matinee. A good vaudeville show was what I liked best, an afternoon in which I would burst my sides laughing. Sometimes, after one of these holidays, it was still more difficult to return to work. In fact, impossible. Mona would conveniently call the boss to inform him that my cold had gotten worse. And he would always say: "Tell him to stay in bed another few days. Take good care of him!'

'I should think they would be on to you by this time,' Mona would say.

'They are, honey. Only I'm too good. They can't do without me.'

'Never answer the door bell, that's all. Or tell them I've gone to see the doctor.'

Wonderful while it lasted. *Just ducky.* I had lost all interest in my job. All I thought of was to begin writing. At the office I did less and less, grew more and more slack. The only applicants I bothered to interview were the suspects. My assistant did the rest. As often as possible I would clear out of the office on the pretext of inspecting the branch offices. I would call on one or two in the heart of town—just to establish an alibi—then duck into a movie. After the movie I would drop in on another branch manager, report to headquarters, and then home. Sometimes I spent the afternoon in an art gallery or at the 42nd Street Library. Sometimes I called on Ulric or else visited a dance hall. I got ill more and more often, and for longer stretches at a time. Things were definitely riding to a fall.

Mona encouraged my delinquency. She had never liked me in the role of employment manager. 'You should be writing,' she would say. 'Fine,' I would retort, secretly pleased but putting up a battle to salve my conscience. 'Fine! but what will we live on?'

'Leave that to *me*!'

'But we can't go on swindling and bamboozling people for-ever.'

'*Swindling?* Anybody I borrow from can well afford to lend the money. I'm doing them a favour.'

I couldn't see it her way but I would give in. After all, I had no better solution to offer. To wind up the argument I would always say: 'Well, I'm not quitting *yet.*'

Now and then, on one of these stolen holidays, we would end

up on Second Avenue, New York. It was amazing the number of friends I had in this quarter. All Jews, of course, and most of them cracked. But lively company. After a bite at Papa Moskowitz's we would go to the Café Royal. Here you were sure to find anyone you were looking for.

One evening as we were strolling along the Avenue, just as I was about to peer into a bookshop window to have another look at Dostoievsky—his photo had been hanging in this same window for years—who should greet us but an old friend of Arthur Raymond. Nahoum Yood, no less. Nahoum Yood was a short, fiery man who wrote in Yiddish. He had a face like a sledge-hammer. Once you saw it you never forgot it. When he spoke it was always a rush and a babble; the words literally tripped over one another. He not only spluttered like a fire-cracker but he dribbled and drooled at the same time. His accent, that of the 'Litvak', was atrocious. But his smile was golden—like Jack Johnson's. It gave his face a sort of Jack-o'-Lantern twist.

I never saw him in any other condition but effervescent. He had always just discovered something wonderful, something marvellous, something unheard of. In unloading himself he always gave you a spritz bath, *gratis*. But it was worth it. This fine spray which he emitted between his front teeth had the same stimulating effect that a needle bath has. Sometimes with the spritz bath came a few caraway seeds.

Snatching the book which I was carrying under my arm, he shouted: 'What are you reading? Ah, *Hamsun*. Good! Beautiful writer.' He hadn't even said, 'How are you' yet. 'We must sit down somewhere and talk. Where are you going? Have you had dinner? I'm hungry.'

'Excuse me,' I said, 'but I want to have a look at Dostoievsky.'

I left him standing there talking excitedly to Mona with both hands (and feet). I plunked myself in front of Dostoievsky's portrait, as I had done before many a time, to study his familiar physiognomy anew. I thought of my friend Lou Jacobs who used to doff his hat every time he passed a statue of Shakespeare. It was something more than a bow or salute I made to Dostoievsky. It was more like a prayer, a prayer that he would unlock the secret of revelation. Such a plain, homely face, he had. So Slavic, so moujik-like. The face of a man who might pass unnoticed in a crowd. (Nahoum Yood looked much more the writer than did the great Dostoievsky.) I stood there, as always, trying to penetrate the mystery of the being lurking behind the doughy mass of features. All I could read clearly was sorrow and obstinacy. A man who obviously preferred the lowly life, a man fresh from prison. I lost myself in contemplation. Finally I saw only the artist, the tragic, unprecedented artist who had created a veritable pantheon of characters, figures such as had never been heard of before and never would be again, each one of them more real, more potent, more mysterious, more inscrutable than all the mad Czars and all the cruel, wicked Popes put together.

Suddenly I felt Nahoum Yood's heavy hand on my shoulder. His eyes were dancing, his mouth ringed with saliva. The battered derby which he wore indoors and out had come down over his eyes, giving him a comical and an almost maniacal look.

'*Mysterium!*' he shouted. '*Mysterium! Mysterium!*'

I looked at him blankly.

'You haven't read it?' he yelled. What looked like a crowd began to gather round us, one of those crowds which spring up from nowhere as soon as a hawker begins to advertise his wares.

'What are you talking about?' I asked blandly.

'About your Knut Hamsun. The greatest book he ever wrote —*Mysterium* it is called, in German.'

'He means *Mysteries*,' said Mona.

'Yes, *Mysteries*,' cried Nahoum Yood.

'He's just been telling me all about it,' said Mona. 'It does sound wonderful.'

'More wonderful than *A Wanderer Plays on Muted Strings?*'

Nahoum Yood burst in: '*That*, that is nothing. For *Growth of the Soil* they gave him the Nobel Prize. For *Mysterium* nobody even knows about it. Look, let me explain. . . .' He paused, turned half-way round and spat. 'No, better not to explain. Go to your Carnegie chewing gum library and ask for it. How do you say it in English? *Mysteries?* Almost the same—but *Mysterium* is better. More *mysterischer, nicht?*' He gave one of his broad trolley track smiles and with that the brim of his hat fell over his eyes.

Suddenly he realized that he had collected an audience. 'Go home!' he shouted, raising both arms to shoo the crowd away. 'Are we selling shoe laces here? What is it with you? Must I rent a hall to speak a few words in private to a friend? This is not Russia. Go home . . . *shoo*!' And again he brandished his arms.

No one budged. They simply smiled indulgently. Apparently they knew him well, this Nahoum Yood. One of them spoke up in Yiddish. Nahoum Yood gave a sad complacent sort of smile and looked at us helplessly.

'They want that I should recite to them something in Yiddish.'

'Fine,' I said, 'why don't you?'

He smiled again, sheepishly this time. 'They are like children,' he said. 'Wait, I will tell them a fable. You know what is a fable, don't you? This is a fable about a green horse with three legs. I can only tell it in Yiddish . . . you will excuse me.'

The moment he began talking Yiddish his whole countenance changed. He put on such a serious, mournful look that I thought he would burst into tears any moment. But when I looked at his audience I saw that they were chuckling and giggling. The more serious and mournful his expression, the more jovial his listeners grew. Finally they were doubled up with laughter. Nahoum Yood never so much as cracked a smile. He finished with a dead pan look in the midst of gales of laughter.

'Now,' he said, turning his back on his audience and grasping us each by the arm, 'now we will go somewhere and hear some music. I know a little place on Hester Street, in a cellar. Roumanian gypsies. We will have a little wine and some *Mysterium*, yes? You have money? I have only twenty-three cents.' He smiled again, this time like a huge cranberry pie. On the way he was constantly tipping his hat to this one and that. Sometimes he would stop and engage a friend in earnest conversation for a few minutes. 'Excuse me,' he would say, running back to us breathless, 'but I thought maybe I could borrow a little money. That was the editor of a Yiddish paper—but he's even broker than I am. You have a little money, yes? Next time *I* will treat.'

At the Roumanian place I ran into one of my ex-messengers, Dave Olinski. He used to work as a night messenger in the Grand Street office. I remembered him well because the night the office was robbed and the safe turned upside down, Olinski had been beaten to within an inch of his life. (As a matter of fact, I had taken it for granted that he was dead.) It was at his own request that I had put him in that office; because it was a foreign quarter, and because he could speak about eight languages, Olinski thought he would earn a lot in tips. Everybody detested him, including the men he worked with. Every time I ran into him he would chew my ear off about Tel Aviv. It was always Tel Aviv and Boulogne-sur-Mer. (He carried about with him post cards of all the ports the boats had stopped at. But most of the cards were of Tel Aviv.) Anyway, before the 'accidents', I once sent him to Canarsie, where there was a '*plage*'. I used the word '*plage*' because every time Olinski spoke of Boulogne-sur-Mer, he mentioned the bloody '*plage*' where he had gone bathing.

Since he left our employ, he was telling me, he had become an insurance salesman. In fact, we hadn't exchanged more than a few words when he began trying to sell me a policy. Much as I disliked the fellow, I made no move to shut him off. I thought it might do him good to practise on me. So, much to Nahoum Yood's disgust, I let him babble on, pretending that perhaps I would also want accident, health and fire insurance too. Meanwhile, Olinski had ordered drinks and pastry for us. Mona had left the table to engage the proprietress in conversation. In the midst of it a lawyer named Mannie Hirsch walked in—another friend of Arthur Raymond. He was passionate about music, and particularly passionate about Scriabin. It took Olinski, who had been drawn into the conversation against his will, quite a while to understand who it was we were talking about. When he learned that it was only a composer he showed profound disgust. Shouldn't we go maybe to a quieter place, he wondered. I explained to him that that was impossible, that he should hurry up and explain everything to me quickly before we left. Mannie Hirsch hadn't stopped talking from the time he sat down. Presently Olinski launched into his routine talk, switching from one policy to another; he had to talk quite loudly in order to drown out Mannie Hirsch's voice. I listened to the two of them at the same time. Nahoum Yood was trying to listen with one ear cupped. Finally he broke into an hysterical fit of laughter. Without a word he began reciting one of his fables—in Yiddish. Still Olinski kept on talking, this time very low, but even faster than before, because every minute was precious. Even when the whole place began to roar with laughter Olinski kept on selling me one policy after another.

When I at last told him that I would have to think it over, he acted as if he had been mortally injured. 'But I have explained everything clearly, Mr. Miller,' he whined.

'But I already have two insurance policies,' I lied.

'That's all right,' he retorted, 'We will cash them in and get better ones.'

'That's what I want to think about,' I countered.

'But there is nothing to think about, Mr Miller.'

'I'm not sure that I understood it all,' I said. 'Maybe you'd better come to my home tomorrow night,' and therewith I wrote down a false address for him.

'You're sure you will be home, Mr Miller?'

'If I'm not I will telephone.'

'But I have no telephone, Mr Miller.'

'Then I will send you a telegram.'

'But I already made two appointments for tomorrow evening.'

'Then make it the next night,' I said, thoroughly unperturbed by all this palaver. 'Or,' I added maliciously, 'you could come to see me after midnight, if that's convenient. We're always up till two or three in the morning.'

'I'm afraid that would be too late,' said Olinski, looking more and more disconsolate.

'Well, let's see,' I said, looking meditative and scratching my head. 'Supposing we meet right here a week from today? Say half-past nine sharp.'

'Not here, Mr Miller, please.'

'O.K. then, wherever you like. Send me a postcard in a day or so. And bring all the policies with you, yes?'

During this last chit-chat Olinski had risen from the table and was holding my hand in parting. When he turned round to gather up his papers he discovered that Mannie Hirsch was drawing animals on them. Nahoum Yood was writing a poem—in Yiddish—on another. He was so disturbed by this unexpected turn of events that he began shouting at them in several languages at once. He was getting purple with rage. In a moment the bouncer, who was a Greek and an ex-wrestler, had Olinski by the seat of the pants and was giving him the bum's rush. The proprietress shook her fist in his face as he went through the doorway head first. In the street the Greek went through his pockets, extracted a few bills, brought them to the proprietress who made change for him and threw the remaining coins at Olinski who was now on his hands and knees, behaving as if he had the cramps.

'That's a terrible way to treat a person,' said Mona.

'It is, but he seems to invite it,' I replied.

'You shouldn't have egged him on—it was cruel.'

'I admit it, but he's a pest. It would have happened anyway.' Thereupon I began to narrate my experience with Olinski. I explained how I had humoured him by transferring him from one office to another. Everywhere it was the same story. He was always beng abused and mistreated—'for no reason at all,' as he always put it. 'They don't like me there,' he would say.

'You don't seem to be liked anywhere,' I finally told him one day. 'Just what is it that's eating you up?' I remember well the look he gave me when I fired that at him. 'Come on,' I said, 'tell me, because this is your last chance.'

To my amazement, here is what he said: 'Mr Miller, I have too much ambition to make a good messenger. I should have a more responsible position. With my education I would make a good manager. I could save the company money. I could bring in more business, make things more efficient.'

'Wait a minute,' I interrupted. 'Don't you know that you haven't a chance in the world to become a manager of a branch office? You're crazy. You don't even know how to speak English, let alone those eight other languages you're always talking about. You don't know how to get along with your neighbour. You're a nuisance, don't you understand that? Don't tell me about your grand ideas for the future . . . tell me just one thing . . . how did you happen to become what you are . . . *such a damned unholy pest*, I mean.'

Olinski blinked like an owl at this . . . 'Mr Miller,' he began 'you must know that I am a good person, that I try hard to. . . .'

'Horseshit!' I exclaimed. 'Now tell me honestly, why did you ever leave Tel Aviv?'

'Because I wanted to make something of myself, that's the truth.'

'And you couldn't do that in Tel Aviv—or Boulogne-sur-Mer?'

He gave a wry smile. Before he could put in a word I continued: 'Did you get along with your parents? Did you have any close friends there? Wait a minute'—I held up my hand to head off his answer—'did anybody in the whole world ever tell you that he liked you? *Answer me that!*'

He was silent. Not crushed, just baffled.

'You know what you should be?' I went on. 'A stool pigeon.'

He didn't know what the word meant. 'Look,' I explained, 'a stool pigeon makes his money by spying on other people, by informing on them—do you understand that?'

'And *I* should be a stool-pigeon?' he shrieked, drawing himself up and trying to look dignified.

'Exactly,' I said, not batting an eyelash. 'And if not that, then a hangman. You know—' and I made a grim circular motion with my hand—'the man who strings them up.'

Olinski put on his hat and made a few steps towards the door. Suddenly he wheeled around, walked calmly back to my desk. He took off his hat and held it with his two hands. 'Excuse me,' he said, 'but could I have another chance—in Harlem?' This in a tone of voice as if nothing untoward had occurred.

'Why certainly,' I replied briskly, 'of course I'll give you another chance, but it's the last one, remember that. I'm beginning to like you, do you know that?'

This baffled him more than anything I had said before. I was surprised that he didn't ask me why.

'Listen, Dave,' I said, leaning towards him as if I had something very confidential to propose, 'I'm putting you in the worst office we have. If you can get along up there you will be able to get along anywhere. There's one thing I have to warn you about . . . don't start any trouble in that office or else'—and here I drew my hand across my throat—'*you understand?*'

'Are the tips good up there, Mr Miller?' he asked, pretending not to be affected by my last remark.

'No one gives a tip in that neighbourhood, my good friend. And don't try to extract one either. Thank God each night when you go home that you're still alive. We've lost eight messengers in that office in the last three years. Figure it out for yourself.'

Here I got up, grasped him by the arm and escorted him to the stairs. 'Listen, Dave,' I said, as I shook hands with him, 'maybe I'm a friend of yours and you don't know it. Maybe you'll thank me one day for putting you in the worst office in New York. You've got so much to learn that I don't know what to tell you first. Above all, try to keep your mouth shut. Smile once in a while, even if it's painful. Say thank you even if you don't get a tip. Speak just one language and as little of that as possible. Forget about becoming a manager. Be a good messenger. And don't tell people that you came from Tel Aviv because they won't know what the hell you're talking about. You were born in the Bronx, do you understand? If you can't act decently, be a dope, a Schlemiel, savvy? Here's something to go the movies with. See a funny picture for a change. And don't let me hear from you again!'

Walking to the subway that night with Nahoum Yood brought back vivid memories of my midnight explorations with

O'Rourke. It was to the East Side I always came when I wanted to be stirred to the roots. It was like coming home. Everything was familiar in a way beyond all knowing. It was almost as if I had known the world of the ghetto in a previous incarnation. The quality that got me most of all was the pullulation. Everything was struggling towards the light in glorious profusion. Everything burgeoned and gleamed, just as in the murky canvases of Rembrandt. One was constantly being surprised, often by the homeliest trifles. It was the world of my childhood wherein common everyday objects acquired a sacred character. These poor despised aliens were living with the discarded objects of a world which had moved on. For me they were living out a past which had been abruptly stifled. Their bread was still a good bread which one could eat without butter or jam. Their kerosene lamps gave their rooms a holy glow. The bed always loomed large and inviting, the furniture was old but comfortable. It was a constant source of wonder to me how clean and orderly were the interiors of these hideous edifices which seemed to be crumbling to bits. Nothing can be more elegant than a bare poverty-stricken home which is clean and fully of peace. I saw hundreds of such homes in my search for vagrant boys. Many of these unexpected scenes we came upon in the dead of night were like illustrated pages from the Old Testament. We entered, looking for a delinquent boy or a petty thief, and we left feeling that we had broken bread with the sons of Israel. The parents had no knowledge whatever, usually, of the world which their children had penetrated in joining the messenger force. Hardly any of them had ever set foot in an office building. They had been transferred from one ghetto to another without even glimpsing the world in between. The desire sometimes seized me to escort one of these parents to the floor of an Exchange where he could observe his son running back and forth like a fire engine amid the wild pandemonium created by the crazy stockbrokers, an exciting and lucrative game which sometimes permitted the boy to make seventy-five dollars in a single week. Some of these 'boys' still remained boys though they had reached the age of thirty or forty and were the possessors, some of them, of blocks of real estate, farms, tenement houses or packs of gilt-edge bonds. Many of them had bank accounts running above ten thousand dollars. Yet they remained messenger boys, would remain messenger boys until they died. . . . What an incongruous world for an immigrant to be plunged into! I could scarcely make head or tail of it myself. With all the advantages of an American upbringing had I not (in my twenty-eighth year) been obliged to seek this lowest of all occupations? And was it not with extreme difficulty that I succeeded in earning sixteen or seventeen dollars a week? Soon I would be leaving this world to make my way as a writer, and as such I would become even more helpless than the lowliest of these immigrants. Soon I would be begging furtively in the streets at night, in the very purlieus of my own home. Soon I would be standing in front of restaurant windows, looking enviously and desperately at the good things to eat. Soon I would be thanking newsboys for handing me a nickel or a dime to get a cup of coffee and a cruller.

Yes, long before it came to pass I was thinking of just such eventualities. Perhaps the reason I loved the new love nest so much was because I knew it could not last for long. Our 'Japanese' love nest, I called it. Because it was bare, immaculate, the low divan placed in the very centre of the room, the lights just right, not one object too many, the walls glowing with a subdued velvety fire, the floor gleaming as if it had been scraped and polished every morning. Unconsciously we did everything in ritualistic fashion. The place impelled one to behave thus. Made for a rich man, it was tenanted by two devotees who had only an inner wealth. Every book on the shelves had been acquired with a struggle, devoured with gusto, and had enriched our lives. Even the tattered Bible had a history behind it. . . .

One day, feeling the need for a Bible, I had sent Mona out to search for one. I cautioned her not to *buy* one. 'Ask some one to make you a present of his copy. Try the Salvation Army or go to one of the Rescue Missions.' She had done as I asked and been refused everywhere. (Damned strange! I thought to myself.) Then, as if in answer to a prayer, who pops up out of a clear sky but Crazy George! There he is, waiting for me, when I arrive home one Saturday afternoon. And Mona serving him tea and cake. I thought I was looking at an apparition.

Mona of course didn't know that it was Crazy George, a figure out of my childhood. She had seen a man with a vegetable wagon standing on the dashboard preaching the word of God. The children were jeering at him, throwing things in his face, and he was blessing them (with whip in hand), saying: 'Suffer the little children to come unto me. . . . Blessed are the meek and lowly. . . .'

'George,' I said, 'don't you remember me? You used to bring us coal and wood. I'm from Driggs Avenue—the 14th Ward.'

'I remember all God's children,' said George. 'Even unto the third and fourth generation. Bless you, my son, may the Holy Spirit abide with you forever.'

Before I could say another word George had begun to pontificate in the old fashion. 'I am one that bears witness of myself, and the Father that sent me beareth witness of me. . . . Amen! Hallelujah! Praise the Lord!'

I got up and put my arms around George. He had become an old man, a cracked, peaceful, lovable old man, the last man in the world I expected to see seated in my own home. He had been a terrifying figure to us boys, always cracking that long whip in our faces, and threatening eternal damnation, fire and brimstone. Lashing his horse furiously when it slipped on the icy pavement, raising his fist to heaven and imploring God to punish us for our wickedness. What misery we inflicted on him in those days! 'Crazy George! Crazy George!' we shouted until we were blue in the face. Then we would fling snow-balls at him, icy, packed snow-balls, which sometimes struck him between the eyes and made him dance with rage. And while he chased one of us like a demon another would steal his vegetables or fruit, or dump a sack of potatoes into the gutter. Nobody knew how he had become that way. He had been preaching the word of God from his wagon ever since he was born, it seemed. He was like one of the prophets of old, and as filthy as some of the great Biblical prophets.

Twenty years had passed since I last saw George Denton. And here he was again, telling me about Jesus, the Light of the World. 'And He that sent me,' said George, 'is with me! the Father hath not left me alone; for I do always those things that please Him . . . Ye shall know the Truth, and the Truth shall make you free. Amen, brother! May God's grace abide in you and protect you!'

There was little sense asking a man like George what had happened to him during all these years. His days had probably passed like a dream. It was plain to see that he took no thought for the morrow. He was still roaming about the city with his horse and wagon, quite as if the automobile did not exist. The whip was lying beside him on the floor—it was inseparable from him.

I thought I would offer him a cigarette. Mona had a bottle of port in her hand.

'The Kingdom of God,' said George, raising his hand in protest, 'is not meat and drink; but righteousness, and peace, and joy in the Holy Ghost. . . . It is good neither to eat flesh, nor to drink wine, not any thing whereby thy brother stumbleth, or is offended or is made weak.'

Pause whilst Mona and myself take a sip of port.

Continuing as if he saw not nor heard me, George spouted: 'Know ye not that your body is the temple of the Holy Ghost which is in you, which ye have of God, and ye are not your own? Ye are bought with a price: therefore glorify God in your body, and in your spirit, which are God's. Amen! Amen!'

Not derisively but softly and easily I began to laugh—out of intoxication with the Holy Writ. George didn't mind. He went on babbling, just as of old. Never addressed us as persons but rather as vessels into which he was pouring the blessed milk of the Holy Virgin. Of the material objects which surrounded him his eyes saw nothing. One room was like another to him, and none better than the stable to which he led his horses. (He probably slept with them.) No, he had a mission to fulfil and it brought him joy and forgetfulness. From morn to midnight he was busy spreading God's word. Even in buying his produce he continued to spread the Gospel.

What a beautiful, untrammelled existence, I thought to myself. *Mad?* Sure he was mad, mad as a bedbug. But in a good way. George never really hurt anyone with that whip. He loved to crack it, just to convince nasty little urchins that he was not altogether a helpless old idiot.

'Resist the devil,' said George, 'and he will flee from you. Draw nigh to God, and He will draw nigh to you. Cleanse your hands, ye sinners; and purify your hearts, ye double-minded. . . . Humble yourselves in the sight of the Lord, and He shall lift you up.'

'George,' I said, quelling the bubble of laughter, 'you make me feel good. It's so long. . . .'

'Salvation to our God which sitteth upon the throne, and unto the Lamb. . . . Hurt not the earth, neither the sea, nor the trees, till we have sealed the servants of our God in their foreheads.'

'O.K.! Listen, George, do you remem. . . .'

'They shall hunger no more, neither thirst any more; neither shall the sun light on them, nor any heat. The Lamb which is in the midst of the Throne shall feed them, and shall lead them unto living fountains of waters: and God shall wipe away all tears from their eyes.'

With this George took out a huge, filthy red poker-dot kerchief and wiped his eyes, then blew his nose vigorously. 'Amen! Praise God for His saving and keeping power!'

He got up and went to the fireplace. On the mantel there was lying an unfinished manuscript weighted down by a figurine representing a dancing Hindu goddess. George veered round quickly and spake: 'Seal up those things which the seven thunders uttered, and write them not. . . . In the days of the voice of the seventh angel, when he shall begin to sound, the mystery of God shall be finished, as He hath declared to His servants and the prophets.'

Just then I thought I heard the horses stirring outside. I went to the window to see what was up. George had raised his voice. It was almost a shout now which went up from his throat. 'Who shall not hear Thee, O Lord, and glorify Thy name? for Thou only art holy.'

The horses were tugging the wagon off, the urchins screaming with delight and helping themselves as of yore to the fruit and vegetables. I beckoned to George to come to the window. He was still shouting. . . . 'The waters which thou sawest, where the whore sitteth, are peoples, and multitudes, and nations, and tongues. And the ten horns. . . .'

'Better hurry, George, or they'll get away from you!'

Quick as a flash George ducked for his whip and dashed out into the street. 'Whoa there, Jezebel,' I heard him shout. 'Whoa there!'

He was back in a jiffy offering us a basket of apples and some cauliflower. 'Accept the blessings of the Lord,' he said. 'Peace be with you! Amen, brother! Glory, sister! Glory to God in the Highest!' Then he made for his wagon, flicked the horses with his long whip, and waved blessings in all directions.

It was only after he had been gone some time that I discovered the worn-out Bible which he had forgotten. It was greasy, thumb-marked, fly-bitten; the covers were gone and pages were missing here and there. I had asked for the Bible and I had received it. 'Seek and ye shall find. Ask and it shall be given unto you. Knock and it shall be opened.' I began spouting a bit myself. The Scriptures are headier than the strongest wines. I opened the Book at random and it fell open to one of my favourite passages:

'And upon her forehead was a name written, MYSTERY, BABYLON THE GREAT, THE MOTHER OF HARLOTS AND ABOMINATIONS OF THE EARTH.

'And I saw the woman drunken with the blood of the saints, and with the blood of the martyrs of Jesus; and when I saw her, I wondered with great admiration.

'And the angel said unto me, Wherefore didst thou marvel? I will tell thee the mystery of the woman, and of the beast that carrieth her, which hath the seven heads and ten horns.

'The beast that thou sawest was, and is not; and shall ascend out of the bottomless pit, and go into perdition: and they that dwell on the earth shall wonder, whose names were not written in the Book of Life from the foundation of the world, when they behold the beast that was, and is not, and yet is.'

Listening to religious zealots always makes me hungry and thirsty—I mean for the so-called good things of life. A full spirit creates an appetite throughout all parts and members of the body. George had no sooner left than I began to wonder where in this bloody aristocratic quarter I could find a bakery that sold streusel küchen or jelly doughnuts (Pfann Küchen) or a good rich cinnamon cake which would melt in one's mouth. After a few more glasses of port I began to think of more substantial comestibles, such as sauer-braten and potato dumplings with fried bread crumbs swimming in a rich spicy black gravy; I thought of a tender roast shoulder of pork with fried apples on the side, of scallops and bacon as an hors d'oeuvre, of crêpes Suzette, of Brazil nuts and pecans, of charlotte russe, such as they make only in Louisiana. I would have relished anything at that moment which was rich, succulent and savoury. Sinful food, that was what I craved. Sinful food and wines that were aphrodisiac. And some excellent Kümmel to top it off.

I tried to think of some one at whose house we could be certain of getting a good meal. (Most of my friends ate out.) The ones that came to mind lived too far away or else were not the sort you could bust in on unannounced. Mona of course was all for eating in some excellent restaurant, eating until we were ready to burst, after which I was to sit and wait until she could find some one to pay for the meal. I didn't relish the idea at all. Had done it too often. Besides, it had happened to me once or twice to sit like that all night waiting for some one to show up with the dough. No sir, if we were going to eat well I wanted the money for it right in my pocket.

'How much have we, anyway?' I asked. 'Have you looked everywhere?'

About seventy-two cents was all that could be mustered, it seemed. Pay day was six days off. I was in no mood—and too hungry—to start making the rounds of the telegraph offices just to gather in a few shekels.

'Let's go to the Scotch bakery,' said Mona. 'They serve food there. It's very simple but it's substantial. *And cheap.*'

The Scotch bakery was near Borough Hall. A dismal place, with marble table tops and sawdust on the floor. The owners were dour Presbyterians from the old country. They spoke with an accent which reminded me unpleasantly of MacGregor's parents. Every syllable they uttered had the clink of small coin, the resonance of the bone-yard. Because they were civil and proper one was supposed to be grateful for the service they rendered.

We had a concoction of horse's hocks and bloated porridge with buttered scones on the side and a thin leaf of unseasoned lettuce to garnish it. There was no taste to the food whatever; it had been cooked by a sour-faced spinster who had never known a day of joy. I would rather have had a bowl of barley soup with some matzoth balls in it. Or fried frankfurters and potato salad, such as Al Burger's family indulged in.

The meal had a most sobering effect. But it left me with the aura of intoxication. Somehow I began to get that light, extra-clearheaded feeling, that hollow bones and transparent veins set-up, in which I knew an insouciance that was always extra-ordinary. Every time the door opened a hideous jangle and jumble assailed our ears. There were two sets of trolley tracks in front of the door, a phonograph shop and a radio shop just opposite, and at the corner a perpetual congestion of traffic. The lights were just going on as we rose to leave. I had a toothpick in the corner of my mouth which I was chewing complacently, my hat was cocked over one ear, and as I stepped towards the curb I was aware that it was a wonderfully balmy evening, one of the

27

last days of Summer. Queer fragments of thought assailed me. For example, I kept harking back to a Summer's day about fifteen years previous when, at that very corner where all was now pandemonium, I had boarded a street car with my old friend MacGregor. It was an open trolley and we were headed for Sheepshead Bay. Under my arm was a copy of *Sanine*. I had finished the book and was about to lend it to my friend MacGregor. As I was ruminating on the pleasurable shock which this forgotten book had made upon me I caught a burst of strangely familiar music from the loudspeaker in the radio shop across the way. I stood there as if rooted to the spot. It was Cantor Sirota singing one of the old synagogue tunes. I knew it only too well because I had listened to it dozens of times. Once I had owned every record of his which was available. And I had purchased them 'at a price!'

I looked at Mona to see what effect the music had produced. Her eyes were moist, her face strained. Quietly I took her hand and held it. We stood thus for several minutes after the music had ceased, neither of us attempting to say a word.

Finally I mumbled—'You recognize that?'

She made no answer. Her lips were quivering. I saw a tear roll down her cheek.

'Mona, dear Mona, why hold it back? I know everything. I've known for a long time. . . . Did you think I would be ashamed of you?'

'No, no Val. I just couldn't tell you. I don't know why.'

'But didn't it ever occur to you, my dear Mona, that I love you more just because you *are* a Jew? Why I say this I don't know either, but it's a fact. You remind me of the women I knew as a boy—in the Old Testament. Ruth, Naomi, Esther, Rachel, Rebecca . . . I always wondered as a child why no one I knew was called by such names. They were golden names to me.'

I put my arm around her waist. She was half sobbing now. 'Don't let's go yet. There's something more I want to say. What I tell you now I mean, I want you to know that. I'm speaking from the bottom of my heart. It isn't something that's just occurred to me, it's something I've wanted to broach for a long time.'

'Don't say it, Val. Please don't say any more.' She put her hand over my mouth to stop me. I permitted it to rest there a few moments, then I gently withdrew it.

'Let me,' I begged. 'It won't hurt you. How could I possibly hurt or wound you *now*?'

'But I know what you're going to say. And . . . And I don't deserve it.'

'Nonsense! Now listen to me. . . . You remember the day we got married . . . in Hoboken? You remember that filthy ceremony? I've never forgotten it. Listen, here's what I've been thinking. . . . Supposing I become a Jew——. Don't laugh! I mean it. What's so strange about it? Instead of becoming a Catholic or a Mohammedan I'll become a Jew. And for the best reason in the world.'

'And that is?' She looked up into my eyes as if completely mystified.

'Because you're a Jew and I love you—isn't that reason enough? I love everything about you . . . why shouldn't I love your religion, your race, your customs and traditions? I'm no Christian, you know that. I'm nothing. I'm not even a Goy. . . . Look, why don't we go to a rabbi and get married in true orthodox style?'

She had begun to laugh as if her sides would burst. Somewhat offended, I said: 'You don't think I'm good enough, is that it?'

'Stop it!' she cried. 'You're a fool, a clown, and I love you. I don't want you to become a Jew . . . you could never be one anyhow. You're too . . . too something or other. And anyway, my dear Val, I don't want to be a Jew either. I don't want to hear anything about the subject. I beg you, don't ever mention it again. I'm *not* a Jew. I'm not anything. I'm just a woman—and to hell with the rabbi! Come, let's go home. . . .'

We walked home in absolute silence, not a hostile silence but a rueful one. The wide, handsome street on which we lived seemed more than ever prim and respectable, a thoroughly bourgeois Gentile street such as only Protestants could inhabit. The big brownstone stoops, some with heavy stone balustrades, some with delicate wrought iron banisters, gave a solemn, pompous touch to the buildings.

I was deep in thought as we entered the love nest. Rachel, Esther, Ruth, Naomi—those wonderful old Biblical names kept flitting through my head. Some ancient memory was stirring at the base of my skull, trying to voice itself. . . . 'Whither thou goest, I will go; and where thou lodgest, I will lodge; thy people shall be my people, and thy God my God.' The words rang in my ears, but I couldn't place them. The Old Testament has this peculiar lilt, this repetitive quality so seductive to the Anglo-Saxon ear.

Suddenly came this phrase: 'Why have I found grace in thine eyes, that thou shouldst take knowledge of me, seeing I am a stranger?'

With this I saw myself again as a tiny boy seated in a little chair by the window in the old neighbourhood. I had been ill and was slowly recuperating. One of the relatives had brought me a large, thin book with striking illustrations. It was called *Stories from the Bible*. There was one I read over and over again —about Daniel in the lions' den.

I see myself once more, a little older now, wearing short pants still, sitting up front in the Presbyterian Church where I had learned to be a soldier. The minister is a very old man named the Reverend Dr Dawson. A Scot, but a warm, tender-hearted soul beloved of his flock. He reads long passages from the good book to his congregation before starting his sermon. He takes a long time to begin, too, first blowing his nose vigorously, then tucking the handkerchief away in the tail of his frock coat, then taking a deep draught of water from the pitcher beside the lectern, then clearing his throat and looking heavenward, and so on and so forth. He is not much of an orator any more. He is ageing and he rambles a good deal. When he loses the thread, he picks up the Bible and re-reads a verse or two to refresh his memory. I am very conscious of his failings; I twitch and turn in my seat during his moments of forgetfulness. I encourage him silently as best I can.

But now, sitting in the soft light of the immaculate love nest, I suddenly realize where all these phrases which have come to my lips stem from. I go to the bookcase and get out the battered old Bible which Crazy George left with us. I skim the pages absent-mindedly, thinking tenderly of old man Dawson, thinking of my little pal, Jack Lawson, who died so young and such a horrible death, thinking of the basement of the old Presbyterian Church and the dust we raised drilling in squads and battalions every night, all fitted up with stripes and chevrons, with epaulettes, with swords, leggings, flags, the drums deafening us, the bugles splitting our ear-drums. And as these memories pass to and fro there ring in my ears the melodious verses from the Bible which the Reverend Dr Dawson spooled off like an eight-reel film.

The book is lying open on the table, and behold, it is open at the chapter called Ruth. In large letters it reads: THE BOOK OF RUTH. And just above it, the last and 25th verse of Judges, a glorious verse whose source lies far behind childhood, so far back into the past that no man can remember anything but the wonder of it:

'In those days there was no king in Israel: every man did that which was right in his own eyes.'

In what days? I ask myself. When ever was this glorious period and why had man forgotten it? *In those days there was no king in Israel.* This is not from the history of the Jews, this is out of the history of Man. That is how man began, in high estate, in dignity, honour and wisdom. *Every man did that which was right in his own eyes.* Here in a few words is the secret of a decent, happy human society. Once upon a time the Jews knew such a condition of life. Once upon a time the Chinese knew it, too, and the Minoans, and the Hindus, and the Polynesians, and the Africans, and the Eskimos.

I began reading The Book of Ruth, wherein it speaks of

Naomi and of the Moabites. At the 20th verse I was electrified: 'And she said unto them, Call me not Naomi, call me Mara: for the Almighty hath dealt very bitterly with me.' And in the 21st verse it continues: 'I went out full, and the LORD hath brought me home again empty. . . .'

I called to Mona, who had once been Mara, but there was no answer. I looked for her but she was not there. . . . I sat down again, with tears in my eyes, thumbing through the worn and tattered pages. There would be no bridge, no heavenly synagogue music . . . not even an ephah of barley. *Call me not Naomi, call me Mara!* And Mara had disowned her people, had disowned the very name they had given her. It was a bitter name, but she had not even known what it meant. *Thy people shall be my people, and thy God my God.* She had left the fold and had been afflicted by the Lord.

I got up and walked about. The atmosphere of the place was one of elegance, simplicity and serenity. I was deeply roused but not in the least sad. I felt like the chambered nautilus walking the sands of time. I threw back the rolling doors which separated our apartment from the vacant one in the rear. I lit a candelabra at the far end of the vacant apartment. The stained glass windows gave off a smouldering glow. I moved about in the shadows, letting my mind wander freely. My heart was at rest. Now and then I wondered dreamily where she had gone. I knew she would return soon and be at ease. I hoped that she would remember to rustle up a bit of food. I was in a mood to break bread again and sip a little wine. It was in such a mood, I thought to myself, that one ought to sit down to write. I was mellow and open, fluid, solvent. I could see how easy it was, given the right ambiance, to pass from the life of a paid employee, a hack, a slave, to that of an artist. It was such a delicious thing to be alone, to revel in one's thoughts and emotions. It hardly occurred to me that I would have to write about something; all I thought of was that one day, in just such a mood as this, I would write. The important thing was to be perpetually what I now was, to feel as I did, to make music. From childhood on that had been my dream, to sit still and make music. It was just dawning on me that to make music one had first to make himself into an exquisite, sensitive instrument. One had to stop living and breathe. One had to take off the roller skates. One had to unhitch all connections with the world outside. One had to speak privately, with God as his witness. Oh yes, that was it. Indeed yes. Suddenly I became unalterably certain of what I had just quietly realized. . . . *For the Lord thy God is a jealous God.* . . .

The strange thing was, I reflected, that most everybody I knew already considered me a writer, though I had done little to prove it. They assumed I was not only because of my behaviour, which

31

had always been eccentric and unpredictable, but because of my passion for language. From the time I learned to read I was never without a book. The first person to whom I ventured to read aloud was my grandfather; I used to sit at the edge of his work bench where he sat sewing coats. My grandfather was proud of me but he was also somewhat alarmed. I remembered him warning my mother that she would do better to take the books away from me. . . . Only a few years later and I am reading aloud to my little friends, Joey and Tony, on my visits to them in the country. Sometimes I read to a dozen or more children gathered around me. I would read and read until they fell asleep one by one. If I took the trolley or the subway I would read standing up, even outside on the platform of the elevated train. Leaving the train I would still be reading . . . reading faces, reading gestures, reading gaits, reading architecture, reading streets, passions, crimes. Everything, yes everything, was noted, analysed, compared and described—for future use. Studying an object, a face, a façade, I studied it the way it was to be written down (later) in a book, including the adjectives, adverbs, prepositions, parentheses and what not. Before I had even planned the first book my mind was teeming with hundreds of characters. I was a walking, talking book, an encyclopaedic compendium which kept swelling like a malignant tumour. If I bumped into a friend or an acquaintance, or even a stranger, I would continue the writing while conversing with him. It was the work of only a few seconds to steer the conversation into my own groove, to fix my victim with a hypnotic eye and inundate him. If it were a woman I encountered I could do it even more easily. Women responded to this sort of thing better than men, I noticed. But with a foreigner it went best of all. My language always intoxicated the alien, first because I made an effort to speak clearly and simply to him, second because his greater tolerance and sympathy brought out the best in me. I always spoke to a foreigner as if I were acquainted with the ways and customs of his country; I always left him with the impression that I valued his country more than my own, which was usually the truth. And I always planted in him a desire to become better acquainted with the English language, not because I deemed it the best language in the world but because no one I knew used it with its full potency.

If I were reading a book and happened to strike a wonderful passage I would close the book then and there and go for a walk. I hated the thought of coming to the end of a good book. I would tease it along, delay the inevitable as long as possible. But always, when I hit a great passage, I would stop reading immediately. Out I would go, rain, hail, snow or ice, and chew the cud. One can become so full with the spirit of another being as to be literally afraid of bursting. Every one, I presume, has had the experience. This 'other being', let me observe, is always a sort of *alter ego*. It isn't a mere matter of recognizing a kindred soul, it is a matter of recognizing yourself. To come suddenly face to face with yourself! What a moment! Closing the book you continue the act of creation. And this procedure, this ritual, I should say, is always the same: a communication on all fronts at once. No more barriers. More alone than ever, you are nevertheless glued to the world as never before. *Incorporated in it.* Suddenly it becomes clear to you, that when God made the world He did not abandon it to sit in contemplation—somewhere in limbo. God made the world and He entered into it: that is the meaning of creation.

2

It was only a few months of bliss we enjoyed in the Japanese love nest. Once a week I paid my visit to Maude and the child, brought the alimony, went for a stroll in the park. Mona had her job in the theatre and from her earnings took care of her mother and two healthy brothers. About once every ten days I ate at the French-Italian grocery, usually without Mona because she had to be at the theatre early. Occasionally I visited Ulric to play a quiet game of chess with him. The session usually ended in a discussion of painters and how they painted. Sometimes I simply went for a stroll in the evening, generally to the foreign quarters. Often I stayed home and read or played the gramophone. Mona usually arrived home about midnight; we would have a little snack, talk for a few hours, and then to bed. It was getting more and more difficult to get up in the morning. To say good-bye to Mona was always a tussle. Finally it came about that I remained away from the office three days handrunning. It was just a sufficient break to make it impossible for me to return. Three glorious days and nights, doing exactly what I pleased, eating well, sleeping long, enjoying every minute of the day, feeling immeasurably rich inside, losing all ambition to battle with the world, itching to begin my own private life, confident of the future, done with the past, how could I go back into harness? Besides, I felt that I had been doing Clancy, my boss, a great injustice. If I had any loyalty or integrity I ought to tell him that I was fed up. I knew that he was constantly defending me, constantly making excuses for me to *his* boss, the right holy Mr Twilliger. Sooner or later, Spivak, always on my trail, would get the goods on me. Of late he had been spending a great deal of time in Brooklyn, right in my own precincts. No, the jig was up. It was time to make a clean breast of it.

On the fourth day I got up early as if in preparation for work.

I waited almost until ready to leave before broaching my thought to Mona. She was so delighted at the idea that she begged me to resign at once and be back for lunch. It seemed to me likewise that the quicker it was over the better. Spivak would undoubtedly find another employment manager in jig time.

When I got to the office there was an unusual swarm of applicants waiting for me. Hymie was at his post, his ear glued to the telephone, frantically operating the switchboard as usual. There were so many new vacancies that if he had had an army of waybills to manipulate he would still have been helpless. I went to my desk, emptied it of my private effects, gathered them up in a brief-case, and beckoned Hymie to approach.

'Hymie, I'm quitting,' I said. 'I'll leave it to you to notify Clancy or Spivak.'

Hymie looked at me as if I had taken leave of my wits. There was an awkward pause and then in a matter of fact tone he asked me what I was going to do about my pay. 'Let them keep it,' I said.

'*What?*' he yelled. This time, I could see, he knew definitely I was nuts.

'I haven't got the heart to ask for my pay since I'm leaving without notice, don't you see? I'm sorry to leave *you* in the lurch, Hymie. But you won't be here long either, I take it.' A few more words and I was off. I stood outside the big show window a few moments to observe the applicants stewing and milling about. It was over with. Like a surgical operation. It didn't seem possible to me that I had spent almost five years in the service of this heartless corporation. I understood how a soldier must feel on being mustered out of the army.

Free! Free! Free!

Instead of ducking immediately into the subway I strolled up Broadway, just to see how it felt to be on one's own and at large at that hour of the morning. My poor fellow-workers, there they were scurrying to their jobs, all with that grim, harried look I knew so well. Some were already grinding the pavement, hopeful even at that early hour of receiving an order, selling an insurance policy, or placing an ad. How stupid, meaningless, idiotic it appeared now, the rat race. It always had seemed crazy to me but now it appeared diabolical as well.

If only I were to run into Spivak! If only he were to ask me what I was doing strolling about so leisurely!

I walked about aimlessly for the sheer thrill of tasting my new-found freedom; it gave me a perverse pleasure to watch the slaves fulfilling their appointed rounds. A whole lifetime lay ahead of me. In a few months I would be thirty-three years of age—and 'my own master absolute.' Then and there I made a vow never to work for any one again. Never again would I take orders. The work of the world was for the other blokes—I would have no part in it. I had talent and I would cultivate it. I would become a writer or I would starve to death.

On the way home I stopped off at a music shop and bought an album of records—a Beethoven quartet, if I remember rightly. On the Brooklyn side I bought a bunch of flowers and wangled a bottle of Chianti out of the private stock of an Italian friend. The new life would begin with a good lunch—and music. It would take a lot of good living to wipe out all remembrance of the days, months, years I had wasted in the cosmococcic tread-mill. To do absolutely nothing for a stretch, to idle the days away, what a heavenly pastime that would be!

It was the glorious month of September; the leaves were turning and there was the smell of smoke in the air. It was hot and cool at the same time. One could still go to the beach for a swim. There were so many things I wanted to do all at once that I was almost jumping out of my skin. First of all I would get a piano and start playing again. Perhaps I would even take up painting. Letting my mind roam at will, suddenly it came to rest on a beloved image. The bike! How wonderful it would be if I could get my old racing wheel back again! It was only about two years ago that I had sold it to my cousin who lived nearby. Perhaps he would sell it back to me. It was a special model which I had picked up from a German cyclist at the end of a six-day race. Made in Chemnitz, Bohemia. Ah, but it was a long time since I had taken a spin to Coney Island. Autumn days! Just made for cycling. I prayed that my fool cousin hadn't changed the saddle; it was a Brooks saddle and well broken in. (And those straps that fitted round the toe-clips, I hoped he hadn't discarded *them*.) Recalling the feel of my foot slipping into the toe-clip, I re-experienced the most delicious sensations. Riding now along the gravel path under the archway of trees that runs from Prospect Park to Coney Island, my rhythm one with the machine, my brain thoroughly emptied, only the sensation of rushing through space, fast or slow, according to the dictates of the chronometer inside me. The landscape to either side falling away like the leaves of a calendar. No thoughts, no sensations even. Just everlasting movement forward into space, one with the machine. . . . Yes, I would go cycling again—every morning —just to get my blood up. A spin to Coney Island and back, a shower and rub-down, a delicious breakfast, and then to work. At my writing desk, of course. Not work, but play. A whole life-time ahead of me and nothing to do but write. How wonderful! It seemed to me that all I had to do was to sit down, turn on the tap, and out it would flow. If I could write twenty and thirty page letters without a halt, surely I could write books with the same ease. Everybody recognized the writer in me: all I had to do was to make it a fact.

As I hurried up the stoop I caught a glimpse of Mona moving

about in her kimono. The big window with the stone ledge was wide open. I swung myself over the balustrade and entered by the window.

'Well, I did it!' I exclaimed, handing her the flowers, the wine, the music. 'Today we begin a new life. I don't know what we're going to live on, but we're going to live. Is the typewriter in good shape? Have you food for lunch? Should I ask Ulric to come over? I'm bursting with effervescence. Today I could go through a trial by ordeal and come out of it in ecstasy. Let me sit down and look at you. Go on, move about as you were a minute ago. I want to see how it feels to sit here and do nothing.'

A pause to give Mona a chance to collect herself. Then spilling over again.

'You weren't sure I would do it, were you? I never would have if it weren't for you. You know, it's easy to go to work every day. What's difficult is to stay free. I thought of everything under the sun that I would like to do, now that I'm footloose and free. I want to *do* things. It seems to me I've been standing still for five years.'

Mona began to laugh quietly. 'Do things?' she echoed. 'Why, you're the most active person in creation. No, dear Val, what you need is to do nothing. I don't want you to even think about writing . . . not until you've had a long rest. And don't worry about how we're going to get along. Leave that to me. If I can keep that lazy family of mine I can certainly keep you and me. Anyway, don't let's think of such things now.'

'There's a wonderful bill at the Palace,' she added in a moment. 'Roy Barnes is there. He's one of your favourites, isn't he? And there's that comedian who used to be in burlesque— I forget his name. It's just a suggestion.'

I sat there in a daze, my hat on, my feet sprawled out in front of me. Too good to be true. I felt like King Solomon. Better than King Solomon, in fact, because I had cast off all responsibilities. Sure I would go to the theatre. What better than a matinee on a lazy day? I'd call Ulric later on and ask him to have dinner with us. A red letter day like this had to be shared with some one, and what better than to share it with a good friend? (I knew too what Ulric would say. 'You don't think that maybe it would have been better . . . ? Oh, what the hell am I saying? You know best. . . .' Et cetera.) I was prepared for anything from Ulric. His dubiety, his cautiousness, would be refreshing. I was almost certain that before the evening ended he would be saying—'Maybe I'll throw up the sponge myself!' Not meaning it, of course, but toying with it, flirting with it, just to titivate me. As though to say that if he, Ulric, the greatest stick-in-the-mud ever, could entertain such a notion why then it was self-evident that a man like his friend Henry Val Miller must act on it, that not to act would be suicidal.

37

'Do you think we might be able to afford to buy my bicycle back?' This out of a clear sky.

'Why of course, Val,' she answered, without a moment's hesitation.

'You don't think it funny, do you? I've got a tremendous desire to ride the bike again. I gave it up just before I met you, you know.'

It was the most natural desire in the world, she thought. But it made her laugh, just the same. 'You're still a boy, aren't you?' she couldn't resist saying.

'Yep! But it's damned sight better than being a zombie, what?'

After a few moments I spoke up again. 'Do you know what? There's another thing I thought of this morning. . . .'

'What's that?'

'A piano. I'd like to get a piano and start playing again.'

'That would be wonderful,' she said. 'I'm sure we can rent one cheaply—and a good one, too. Would you take lessons again?'

'No, not that. I want to amuse myself, that's all.'

'Maybe you could teach *me* to play.'

'Of course! If you really want to learn.'

'It's always good to know, especially in the theatre.'

'Nothing easier. Just get me the piano.'

Suddenly, getting up to stretch, I burst out laughing. 'And what are *you* going to get out of this new life?'

'You know what I'd like,' said Mona.

'No I don't. *What?*'

She came over to me and put her arms around me. 'All I would like is for you to become what you want to be—a writer. A great writer.'

'And that's all you would like?'

'Yes, Val, that's all, believe me.'

'And what about the theatre? Don't you want to become a great actress some day?'

'No, Val, I know I'll never be that. I haven't enough ambition. I took up the theatre because I thought it would please you. I don't really care what I do—so long as it makes you happy.'

'But you won't make a good actress if you think that way,' I said. 'Really, you must think about yourself. You must do what you like best, no matter what *I* do. I thought you were crazy about the theatre.'

'I'm only crazy about one thing, *you.*'

'Now you're acting,' I said.

'I wish I were, it would be easier.'

I chucked her under the chin. 'Well,' I drawled, 'you've got me now for good and all. We'll see how you like it a month from now. Maybe you'll be sick of seeing me around before then.'

'Not I,' she said. 'I've prayed for this ever since I met you. I'm jealous of you, do you know that? I want to watch your every move.' She came very close and as she spoke she tapped my forehead lightly. 'Sometimes I wish I could get inside there and know what you're thinking about. You seem so far away at times. Especially when you're silent. I'll be jealous of your writing too —because I know you won't be thinking of me then.'

'I'm already in a spot,' I said laughingly. 'Listen, what are we doing? What's the use of all this—the day is slipping by. Today is one day we don't try to read the future. Today we're going to celebrate. . . . Where's that Jewish delicatessen you were telling me about? I think I'll go and get some good black bread, some olives and cheese, some pastrami, some sturgeon, if they have any—and what else? This is a wonderful wine I bought—It needs good food to go with it. I'll get some pastry too—how about apple strudel? Oh, have you any money—I'm cleaned out. Fine. A five dollar bill? I hope you've got more? Tomorrow we'll think things out, yes? You know, *the spondulix*: how and where to get it.'

She put her hand over my mouth. 'Please, Val, don't talk about it. Not even jokingly. You're not to think about money . . . *not ever*, do you understand?'

There exists a curious book by an American anarchist, Benjamin R. Tucker, entitled INSTEAD OF A BOOK BY A MAN TOO BUSY TO WRITE ONE. The title describes my new-found situation to a T. My creative energy suddenly released, I spilled over in all directions at once. Instead of a book, the first thing I sat down to write was a prose poem about Brooklyn's back-yard. I was so in love with the idea of being a writer that I could scarcely write. The amount of physical energy I possessed was unbelievable. I wore myself out in preparation. It was impossible for me to sit down quietly and just turn on the flow; I was dancing inside. I wanted to describe the world I knew and be in it at the same time. It never occurred to me that with just two or three hours of steady work a day I could write the thickest book imaginable. It was my belief then that if a man sat down to write he should remain glued to his seat for eight or ten hours at a stretch. One ought to write and write until he dropped from exhaustion. That was how I imagined writers went about their task. If only I had known then the programme which Cendrars describes in one of his books! Two hours a day, before dawn, and the rest of the day to one's self. What a wealth of books he has given the world, Cendrars! All *en marge*. Employing a similar procedure—two or three hours a day regularly every day of one's life—Rémy de Gourmont had demonstrated, as Cendrars points out, that it is possible for a man to read virtually everything of value which has ever been written.

But I had no order, no discipline, no set goal. I was completely at the mercy of my impulses, my whims, my desires. My frenzy to live the life of the writer was so great that I overlooked the vast reservoir of material which had accumulated during the years leading up to this moment. I felt impelled to write about the immediate, about what was happening outside my very door. *Something fresh,* that's what I was after. To do this was compulsive because, whether I was aware of it or not, the material which I had stored up had been chewed to a frazzle during the years of frustration, doubt and despair when everything I had to say was written out in my head. Add to this that I felt like a boxer or wrestler getting ready for the big event. I needed a workout. These first efforts then, these fantasies and fantasias, these prose poems and rambling divagations of all sorts, were like a grand tuning up of the instrument. It satisfied my vanity (which was enormous) to set off Roman candles, pin-wheels, sputtering fire-crackers. The big cannon crackers I was reserving for the night of the Fourth of July. It was morning now, a long, lazy morning of a holiday that was to last forever. I had elected to occupy a choice seat in Paradise. It was definite and certain. I could therefore afford to take my time, could afford to dawdle away the glorious hours ahead of me during which I would still be part of the world and its senseless routine. Once I ascended to the heavenly seat I would join the chorus of angels, the seraphic choir which never ceases to give forth hymns of joy.

If I had long been reading the face of the world with the eyes of a writer, I now read it anew with even greater intensity. Nothing was too petty to escape my attention. If I went for a walk—and I was constantly seeking excuses to take a walk, 'to explore', as I put it—it was for the deliberate purpose of transforming myself into an enormous eye. Seeing the common, everyday thing in this new light I was often transfixed. The moment one gives close attention to anything, even a blade of grass, it becomes a mysterious, awesome, indescribably magnified world in itself. Almost an 'unrecognizable' world. The writer waits in ambush for these unique moments. He pounces on his little grain of nothingness like a beast of prey. It is the moment of full awakening, of union and absorption, and it can never be forced. Sometimes one makes the mistake or commits the sin, shall I say, of trying to fix the moment, trying to pin it down in words. It took me ages to understand why, after having made exhaustive efforts to induce these moments of exaltation and release, I should be so incapable of recording them. I never dreamed that it was an end in itself, that to experience a moment of pure bliss, of pure awareness, was the end all and be all.

Many is the mirage I chased. Always I was over-reaching myself. The oftener I touched reality, the harder I bounced back to the world of illusion, which is the name for everyday life. 'Experience! More experience!' I clamoured. In a frantic effort to arrive at some kind of order, some tentative working programme,

I would sit down quietly now and then and spend long, long hours mapping out a plan of procedure. Plans, such as architects and engineers sweat over, were never my forte. But I could always visualize my dreams in a cosmogonic pattern. Though I could never formulate a plot I could balance and weigh opposing forces, characters, situations, events, distribute them in a sort of heavenly lay-out, always with plenty of space between, always with the certitude that there is no end, only worlds within worlds *ad infinitum*, and that wherever one left off one had created *a* world, a world finite, total, complete.

Like a finely trained athlete, I was easy and uneasy at the same time. Sure of the final outcome, but nervous, restless, impatient, fretful. And so, after I had set off a few fireworks, I began to think in terms of light artillery. I began to align my pieces, so to speak. First of all, I reasoned, to have any effect my voice must be heard. I would have to find some outlet for my work—in newspapers, magazines, almanacs or house organs. Somewhere, somehow. What was my range, what my firing power? Though I wasn't one to bore my friends with private readings, now and then in moments of unbridled enthusiasm I was guilty of such misconduct. Rare as they were, these lapses, they had a tonic effect on me. It was seldom, I noticed, that any of my friends grew intoxicated over my efforts. This silent criticism which friends often give is, I believe, worth infinitely more than the belaboured, hostile shafts of the paid critic. The fact that my friends failed to laugh uproariously at the right moment, the fact that they did not applaud vociferously when I terminated my readings, conveyed more than a torrent of words. Sometimes, to be sure, I salved my pride by thinking of them as obtuse or too reserved. Not often, however. To Ulric's appraisals I was particularly sensitive. It was foolish of me, perhaps, to give such keen attention to his comments, since our tastes (in literature) were widely different, but he was so very, very close to me, the one friend I had whom it was imperative to convince of my ability. He was not easy to please either, my Ulric. What he enjoyed most was the fireworks, that is to say, the unusual words, the striking references, the fine brocades, the senseless jeremiads. Often he would thank me, in parting, for the string of new words I had added to his vocabulary. Sometimes we would spend another evening, an entire evening, looking up these bizarre words in the dictionary. Some we never found—because I had made them up.

But to get back to the grand plan. . . . Since I was convinced that I could write about anything under the sun, and excitingly, it seemed the most natural thing in the world to make up a list of themes which I thought of interest and submit them to editors of magazines in order that they might select what appealed to them. This entailed writing dozens and dozens of letters. Long,

41

fatuous letters they were, too. It also meant keeping files as well as observing the idiotic rules and regulations of a hundred and one editorial bodies. It involved altercations and disputes, fruitless errands to editorial offices, vexation, disgruntlement, rage, despair, ennui. *And postage stamps!* After weeks of turmoil and effervescence there might appear one day a letter from an editor saying that he would condescend to read my article if and if and if and but. Never daunted by the ifs and buts, I would regard such a letter as a bona fide pledge, a commission. Good! So I was at liberty, let us say, to write something about Coney Island in winter. If they liked it it would appear in print, my name would be signed to it, and I could show it to my friends, carry it about with me, put it under my pillow at night, read it surreptitiously, over and over, because the first time you see yourself in print you're beside yourself, you've at last proved to the world that you really are a writer, and you *must* prove it to the world, at least once in your life, or you will go mad from believing it all by yourself.

And so to Coney Island on a wintry day. Alone, of course. It wouldn't do to have one's reflections and observations diverted by a trivial-minded friend. A new pad in my pocket and a sharp pencil.

It's a long, dreary ride to Coney Island in mid-winter. Only convalescents and invalids, or demented ones, seem to be trekking there. I feel as though I were slightly mad myself. Who wants to hear about a Coney Island which is all boarded up? I must have put this theme down in a moment of exaltation, believing that nothing could be more inspiring than a picture of desolation.

Desolation is hardly the word for it. As I walk along the boardwalk, the icy wind whistling through my breeches, everything closed tight, it dawns on me that I couldn't possibly have chosen a more difficult subject to write about. There is absolutely nothing to take note of, unless it be the silence. I see it better through Ulric's eyes than my own. An illustrator might have a good time of it here, what with the bleak, crazy, tumbling edifices, the snarling piles and planks, the still, empty Ferris wheel, the noiseless roller coasters, rusting under a feeble sun. Just to assure myself that I am on the job, I make a few notes about the crazy look of the razzle-dazzle, the yawning mouth of George C. Tilyou, and so forth. . . . A hot frankfurter and a cup of steaming hot coffee would do me good, I think. I find a little booth open on a side street off the boardwalk. There is a shooting gallery open a few doors away. Not a customer in sight: the owner is shooting at the clay pigeons himself, for practise, no doubt. A drunken sailor comes lurching along; a few feet away from me he doubles up and lets go. (No need to take note of this.) I go down to the beach and watch the seagulls. I'm looking at the seagulls and thinking about Russia. A picture of Tolstoy seated at a bench mending shoes obsesses me. What was the name of his abode again? Yasna Polyana? No, Yasnaya Polyana. Well, anyway, what the hell am I speculating on this for? Wake up! I shake myself and push forward into the icy gale. Driftwood lying all about. Fantastic forms. (So many stories about bottles with messages inside them.) I wish now I thought to ask MacGregor to come along. That idiotic, pseudo-serious line of his sometimes stimulated me in a perverse way. How he would laugh to see me pacing the beach in search of material! 'Well, you're working anyhow,' I can hear him chirping. 'That's something. But why in hell did you have to pick this for a subject? You know damned well nobody will be interested in it. You probably just wanted a little outing. Now you've got a good excuse, haven't you? Jesus, Henry, you're just the same as ever—*nuts*, completely nuts.'

As I board the train to go home I realize that I have made just three lines of notes. I haven't the slightest idea what I shall say when I sit down to the machine. My mind is a blank. A frozen blank. I sit staring out the window and not even the tremor of a thought assails me. The landscape itself is a frozen blank. The whole world is locked in snow and ice, mute, helpless. I've never known such a bleak, dismal, gruesome, lack-lustre day.

That night I went to bed rather chastened and humbled. Doubly so, because before retiring I had picked up a volume of Thomas Mann (in which there was the Tonio Krüger story) and had been overwhelmed by the flawless quality of the narrative. To my astonishment, however, I awoke the next day full of piss and vinegar. Instead of going for my usual morning stroll —'to get my blood up'—I sat down at the machine immediately after breakfast. By noon I had finished my article on Coney Island. It had come without effort. Why? Because instead of forcing it out I had gone to sleep—after due surrender of the ego, *certes*. It was a lesson in the futility of struggle. Do your utmost and let Providence do the rest! A petty victory, perhaps, but most illuminating.

The article, of course, was never accepted. (Nothing was ever accepted.) It went the rounds from one editor to another. Nor did it make the rounds alone. Week after week I was turning them out, sending them forth like carrier pigeons, and week after week they came back, always with the stereotyped rejection slip. Nevertheless, nothing daunted, as they say, 'always merry and bright', I adhered rigidly to my programme. There it was, the programme, on a huge sheet of wrapping paper, tacked up on the wall. Beside it was another big sheet of paper on which were listed the exotic words I was endeavouring to annex to my vocabulary. The problem was how to hitch these words to my texts without having them stick out like sore thumbs. Often I tried them out beforehand in letters to my friends, in letters to 'all and sundry'. The letter writing was for me what shadow boxing is to a pugilist. But imagine a pugilist spending so much time fighting his shadow that when he hooks up with a sparring partner he has no fight left! I could spend two or three hours writing a story, or article, and another six or seven explaining them to my friends by letter. The real effort was going into the letter writing, and perhaps it was best so, now that I look back on it, because it preserved the speed and naturalness of my true voice. I was far too self-conscious, in the early days, to use my own voice. I was the literary man through and through. I made use of every device I discovered, employed every register, assumed a thousand different stances, always confusing the mastery of technique with creation. Experience and technique, those were the two goads that drove me on. To triumph in the world of experience as I formulated it, I would have to live at least a hundred lives. To acquire the right, or shall I say the complete, technique, I would have to live to be a hundred, not a day less.

Some of my more honest friends, brutally candid as they often were, would occasionally remind me that in talking to them I was always myself but that in writing I was not. 'Why don't you write like you talk?' they would say. At first blush the idea struck me as absurd. In the first place I never considered myself a remarkable talker, though they insisted I was. In the second place, the written word seemed so much more eloquent to me than the spoken one. When you talk you can't stop to polish a phrase, to search for precisely the right word, nor can you go back and expunge a word, a phrase, a whole paragraph. It seemed like an insult to have them tell me, who was struggling for mastery of the word, that I succeeded better without thought than with thought. Poisonous as the idea was, though, it bore fruit. Now and then, after an exhilarating evening with my friends, after I had spouted my head off, had made them drunk with my speeches, I would sneak home and silently review the performance. The words had tumbled out of my mouth in perfect order and with telling effect; there was not only continuity, form, climax and denouement, but rhythm, volume, sonority, aura and magic in the performance. If I stumbled or faltered I went ahead nevertheless, later to double back on my tracks, erase the wrong word, expunge the inept phrase, magnify the sense of a swelling cadence through repetition, innuendo and implication, through detour and parentheses. It was like juggling: the words were alive like balls, could be recalled, could be made to obey, could be changed for other balls, and so on. Or, it was like writing on an invisible slate. One heard the words instead of seeing them. They did not disappear because they had never truly appeared. Hearing them, one had an even keener sense of appreciation, of participation rather, as if viewing a sleight of hand performance. The memory of the ear was just as reliable as the memory of the eye.

One might not be able to reproduce a lengthy harangue, even three minutes afterwards, but one could detect a false note, a wrong emphasis.

Often I have wondered, after reading about evenings with Mallarmé, or with Joyce, or with Max Jacob, let us say, how these sessions of ours compared. To be sure, none of my companions of those days ever dreamed of becoming a figure in the world of art. They loved to discuss art, all the arts, but they themselves had no thought of becoming artists. Most of them were engineers, architects, physicians, chemists, teachers, lawyers. But they had intellect and they had enthusiasm, and they were all so sincere, so avid, that sometimes I wonder if the music we made might not have rivalled the chamber music which issued from the sacred quarters of the masters. Certainly there was never anything pompous or ordained about these sessions. One spoke as he pleased, was criticized freely, and never bothered his head to wonder if what he had said would please 'the master'.

There was no master among us: we were equals, and we could be sublime or idiotic, as we pleased. What brought us together was a mutual hunger for the things we felt deprived of. We had no burning desire to reform the world. We were seeking to enrich ourselves, that was all. In Europe such gatherings often have a political, cultural, or aesthetic background. The members of the group perform their exercises, so to speak, in order later to spread the leaven among the masses. *We* never thought of the masses—we were too much a part of them. We talked of music, painting, literature because, if one is at all intelligent and sensitive, one naturally ends up in the world of art. We did not come together expressly to talk about such matters, it simply happened thus.

I was probably the only one in the group who took himself seriously. That is why I became such a cantankerous idiot of a pest at times. Secretly I *did* hope to reform the world. Secretly I *was* an agitator. It was just this little difference between myself and the rest which made our evenings so lively. In every sentence I uttered there was always an extra ounce of sincerity, an extra grain of truth. It wasn't playing cricket. I would stir them up —expressly, it seemed—to draw heaps of coal on my head. No one ever fully agreed with me. No matter how I worded my thought, what I said always struck them as far-fetched. They would confess, at moments, that they just loved to hear me talk. 'Yes,' I would say, 'but you never listen.' This would provoke a titter. Then someone would say: 'You mean we don't always agree with you.' More titters. 'Shit!' I would answer, 'I don't expect you to agree with me *always*. . . . I want you to think . . . to think for yourselves.' *Hear! Hear!* 'Look,' I would say, making ready to deliver another long tirade, 'look. . . .' 'Go on,' someone would pipe up, 'go on, give it to us! Blow your top!' Here

45

I would sit down, sullen, silent, apparently squelched. 'Come on now, don't take it to heart, Henry. Here's a fresh drink. Come on, get it off your chest!' Knowing what they wanted of me, yet hoping that by some extraordinary effort I might alter their attitude, I would give in, melt, then deliver a veritable fusillade. The more desperate and sincere I grew the more they enjoyed themselves. Realizing that the game was up I would slide off into a burlesque performance. I'd say any bloody thing that came into my head, the more absurd and fantastic, the better. I'd insult them royally—but no one took offence. It was like fighting phantoms. Shadow-boxing again. . . .

(I doubt, of course, that anything like this ever went on in the rue de Rome or the rue Ravignan.)

Following out the plan I had laid down for myself I was busier than the busiest executive in the industrial world. Some of the articles I had elected to write demanded considerable research work, which was never an ordeal for me because I loved going to the library and have them dig up books that were hard to find. How many wonderful days and nights I spent at the 42nd Street Library, seated at a long table, one among thousands, it seemed, in that main reading room. The tables themselves excited me. It was always my desire to own a table of extraordinary dimensions, a table so large that I could not only sleep on it but dance on it, even skate on it. (There *was* a writer, once, who worked at such a table, which he had placed in the centre of a huge, barren room—my ideal as a work place. His name was Andreyev, and needless to add, he was one of my favourites.)

Yes, it gave one a good feeling to be working amidst so many other industrious students in a room the size of a cathedral, under a lofty ceiling which was an imitation of heaven itself. One left the library slightly dazed, often with a holy feeling. It was always a shock to plunge into the crowd at Fifth Avenue and 42nd Street; there was no connection between that busy thoroughfare and the peaceful world of books. Often, while waiting for the books to come up from the mysterious depths of the library, I would stroll along the outer aisles glancing at the titles of the amazing reference books which lined the walls. Thumbing those books was enough to set my mind racing for days. Sometimes I sat and meditated, wondering what question I could put to the genius which presided over the spirit of this vast institution that it could not answer. There was no subject under the sun, I suppose, which had not been written about and filed in those archives. My omnivorous appetite pulled me one way, my fear of becoming a book-worm the other way.

It was also enjoyable to make a trip to Long Island City, that most woe-begone hole, to see at first hand how chewing gum was manufactured. Here was a world of sheer lunacy—efficiency, it is usually called. In a room filled with a choking powder of sickenly sweet stench hundreds of moronic girls worked like butterflies packing the slabs of gum in wrappers; their nimble fingers, I was told, worked more accurately and skilfully than any machine yet invented. I went through the plant, a huge one, under an escort, each wing as it opened up to view presenting the aspect of another section of hell. It was only when I threw out a random query about the chicle, which is the base of chewing gum, that I stumbled on to the really interesting phase of my research. The *chicleros*, as they are called, the men who toil in the depths of the jungles of Yucatan, are a fascinating breed of men. I spent weeks at the library reading about their customs and habits. I got so interested in them, indeed, that I almost forgot about chewing gum. And, of course, from a study of the *chicleros* I was drawn into the world of the Mayans, thence to those fascinating books about Atlantis and the lost continent of Mu, the canals which ran from one side of South America to another, the cities which were lifted a mile high when the Andes came into being, the sea traffic between Easter Island and the western slope of South America, the analogies and affinities between the Amerindian culture and the culture of the Near East, the mysteries of the Aztec alphabet, and so on and so forth until, by some strange detour I came upon Paul Gauguin in the centre of the Polynesian archipelago and went home reeling with *Noa Noa* under my arm. And from the life and letters of Gauguin, which I had to read *at once*, to the life and letters of Vincent Van Gogh was but a step.

No doubt it is important to read the classics; it is perhaps even more important to first read the literature of one's own time, which is enormous in itself. But more valuable than either of these, to a writer at least, is to read whatever comes to hand, to follow his nose, as it were. In the musty tomes of every great library there are buried articles by obscure or unknown individuals on subjects ostensibly of no importance, but saturated with data, ideas, fancies, moods, portents of such a calibre that they can only be likened, in their effect, to rare drugs. The most exciting days often began with the search for the definition of a new word. One little word, which the ordinary reader is content to pass over unperturbed, may prove (for a writer) to be a veritable gold mine. From the dictionary I usually went to the encyclopaedia, not just one encyclopaedia but several; from the encyclopaedia, to all manner of reference books; from reference books to hand-books, and thence to a nine day debauch. A debauch of digging and ferreting, digging and ferreting. In addition to the reams of notes I made I copied out pages and pages of excerpts. Sometimes I simply tore out the pages I needed most. Between times I would make forays on the museums. The officials with whom I dealt never doubted for a moment that I was

47

engaged in writing a book which would be a contribution to the subject. I talked as if I knew vastly more than I cared to reveal. I would make casual, oblique references to books I had never read or hint of encounters with eminent authorities I had never met. It was nothing, in such moods, to give myself scholastic degrees which I had not even dreamed of acquiring. I spoke of distinguished leaders in such fields as anthropology, sociology, physics, astronomy, as though I had been intimately associated with them. When I saw that I was getting in too deep I had always the wit to excuse myself and pretend to go to the toilet, which was my word for 'exit'. Once, deeply interested in genealogy, I thought it a good idea to take a job for a space in the genealogy division of the public library. It so happened that they were short a man in this division the day I called to make application for a job. They needed a man so badly that they put me to work immediately, which was more than I had bargained for. The application blank which I had left with the director of the library was a marvel of falsification. I wondered, as I listened to the poor devil who was breaking me in, how long it would take for them to get on to me. Meanwhile my superior was climbing ladders with me, pointing out this and that, bending over in dark corners to extract documents, files, and such like, calling in other employees to introduce me, explaining hurriedly as best he could (whilst messengers came and went as in a Shakespearean play) the most salient features of my supposed routine. Realizing in a short time that I was not in the least interested in all this jabberwocky, and thinking of Mona waiting for me to lunch with her, I suddenly interrupted him in the midst of a lengthy exposition of something or other to ask where the toilet was. He looked at me rather strangely, wondering, no doubt, why I hadn't the decency to hear him out before running to the lavatory, but with the aid of a few grimaces and gestures, which conveyed most patently that I had been caught short, might do it right there on the floor or in the waste basket, I managed to get out of his clutches, grab my hat and coat which fortunately were still lying on a chair near the door, and run as fast as I could out of the building. . . .

The dominant passion was the acquisition of knowledge, skill, mastery of technique, inexhaustible experience, but like a sub-dominant chord there existed steadily in the back of my head vibration which meant order, beauty, simplification, enjoyment, appreciation. Reading Van Gogh's letters I identify myself with him in the struggle to lead a simple life, a life in which art is all. How glowingly he writes about this dedication to art in his letters from Arles, a place I am destined to visit later though reading about it now I don't even dream of ever seeing it. To give a more *musical* expression to one's life—that is how he puts it. Over and over again he makes reference to the austere beauty

48

and dignity of the life of the Japanese artist, dwelling on their simplicity, their certitude, their naturalness. It is this Japanese quality which I find in our love-nest; it is this bare, simple beauty, this stark elegance, which sustain and comfort me. I find myself drawn to Japan more than to China. I read of Whistler's experience and fall in love with his etchings. I read Lafcadio Hearn, everything he has written about Japan, especially what he gives of their fairy tales, which tales impress me to this day more than those of any other people. Japanese prints adorn the walls; they hang in the bathroom as well. They are even under the glass on my writing table. I know nothing about Zen yet, but I am in love with the art of Jujitsu which is the supreme art of self-defence. I love the miniature gardens, the bridges and lanterns, the temples, the beauty of their landscapes. For weeks, after reading Loti's *Madame Chrysanthemum*, I really feel as if I were living in Japan. With Loti I travel from Japan to Turkey, thence to Jerusalem. I become so infatuated with his *Jerusalem* that I finally persuade the editor of a Jewish magazine to let me write something about Solomon's Temple. More research! Somewhere, somehow, I succeeded in finding a model of the temple, showing its evolution, its changes—until the final destruction. I remember reading this article I wrote on the Temple to my father one evening; I recall his amazement that I should possess such a profound knowledge of the subject. . . . What an industrious worm I must have been!

My hunger and curiosity drive me forward in all directions at once. At one and the same time I am interested and absorbed in Hindu music (having become acquainted with a Hindu composer I met in an Indian restaurant), in the ballet russe, in the German expressionist movement, in Scriabin's piano compositions, in the art of the insane (thanks to Prinzhorn), in Chinese chess, in boxing and wrestling bouts, in hockey matches, in medieval architecture, in the mysteries connected with the Egyptian and Greek underworlds, in the cave drawings of the Cro-Magnon man, in the trade guilds of former times, in everything pertaining to the new Russia, and so on and so forth, from one thing to another, sliding from one level to another as naturally and easily as if I were using an escalator. But was it not in this fashion that the artists of the Renaissance acquired the knowledge and material for their amazing creations? Were they not reaching out into all avenues of life at once? Were they not insatiable and devouring? Were they not journeymen, tramps, criminals, warriors, adventurers, scientists, explorers, poets, painters, musicians, sculptors, architects, fanatics and devotees all in the same stride? Naturally I had read Cellini, Vasari's *Lives*, the history of the Inquisition, the lives of the Popes, the story of the Medici family, the Italian, German and English dramas of incest, the writings of John Addington Symonds, Jacob Buckhardt, Funck-Brentano, all on the Renaissance, but never did I read that curious little book by Balzac, called *Sur Catherine de Medici*. There was one book I was constantly dipping into in moments of peace and quiet: Walter Pater's book on the Renaissance. Much of it I read aloud to Ulric, marvelling over Pater's sensitive use of the language. Glorious evenings these, especially when having finished a long passage I would close the book and listen to Ulric expatiate lovingly on the painters he adored. The mere sound of their names put me in ecstasy: Taddeo Gaddi, Signorelli, Fra Lippo Lippi, Piero della Francesca, Mantegna, Uccello, Cimabue, Piranesi, Fra Angelico, and such like. The names of towns and cities were of equal fascination: Ravenna, Mantua, Siena, Pisa, Bologna, Tiepolo, Firenze, Milano, Torino. Thus one evening, continuing our festal bouts on the splendours of Italy at the French-Italian grocery, Ulric and I, joined later by Hymie and Steve Romero, got into such a state of exaltation that two Italians who were seated at the end of the table stopped conversing with each other and listened in open-mouthed admiration as we moved rapidly from one figure to another, one town to another. Hymie and Romero, equally intoxicated by a language which was as foreign to them as it was to the two Italians, remained silent, contenting themselves with replenishing the drinks. Exhausted finally, and about to pay up, the two Italians suddenly began to clap their hands. 'Bravo! Bravo!' they exclaimed. 'So beautiful!' We were embarrassed. The situation demanded another round of drinks. Joe and Louis joined us, offering us a choice liqueur. Then we began to sing. Fat Louis, moved to the guts, began to weep joyously. He begged us to stay a little longer, promising to fix us a beautiful rum omelette with some caviar on the side. In the midst of it who should walk in but that extraordinary Senegalese, Battling Siki, who was also a client of the establishment. He was a bit high and playful in a dangerous way. He amused us by doing little tricks with matches, cards, saucers, cane, napkins. He was jolly and disgruntled at the same time. Something was irking him. It took the greatest finesse on the part of the proprietors to prevent him, in his playfulness, from wrecking the place. They had to ply him with drinks, stroke his back, salve him with compliments. He sang and danced, all by himself, applauding himself, slapping his thighs, patting us on the shoulder—playful little pats that jolted our vertebrae and made our heads spin. Then, for no reason at all, he suddenly scooted off, knocking over a few cases of beer in his boyish enthusiasm. With his departure every one breathed more easily. Came the omelette and the caviar. Some whitefish too, washed down with a golden white wine, followed by some excellent black coffee and another rare liqueur. Louis was in ecstasy. 'Have some more!' he kept saying. 'Nothing too good for you, Mr Miller.' And Joe: 'When you go to Europe,

Mr Miller? You no stay here long, I see it. Ah, *Fiesole!* By God, one day I go back too!'

I rolled home in a cab, singing like a man under anaesthesia. Unable to navigate the stoop, I sat on the bottom steps laughing to myself, hiccupping, mumbling and muttering crazily, orating to the birds, the alley cats, the telephone poles. Finally I made my way up the steps, slowly, painfully, sliding back a step or two and starting up again, reeling from one side to the other. A veritable Sisyphian ordeal. Mona hadn't come home yet. I fell on the bed fully dressed and went sound asleep. Towards dawn I felt Mona tugging away at me. I awoke to find myself in a pool of vomit. Phew! What a stench! The bed had to be remade, the floor scrubbed, my clothes removed. Still groggy, I staggered and reeled about. I was still laughing to myself, disgusted yet happy, remorseful but gay. To stand under the shower was a feat requiring the most extraordinary skill. What amazed me throughout was Mona's gentle acceptance. Not a word of complaint from her. She moved about like a ministering angel. The one pleasurable thought which kept recurring to mind, as I made ready to go to bed again, was that I would not have to go to work when I got up. No more excuses. No remorse. No guilt. I was a freewheeler. I could sleep as long as I pleased. There would be a good breakfast awaiting me and, if I were still groggy, I could go back to bed and sleep the rest of the day. As I closed my eyes I had a vision of Fat Louis standing at the blazing stove, his eyes wet with tears, his heart pouring out into that omelette. Capri, Sorrento, Amalfi, Fiesole, Paestum, Taormina. . . . Funiculi, funicula. . . . And Ghirlandajo. . . . And the Campo Santo. . . . What a country! What a people! You bet I'd go there one day. Why not? *Long live the Pope!* (But I'll be damned if I kiss his ass!)

Week-ends took a different tenor. The usual visit to Maude, a stroll in the park with her and the child, perhaps a round on the caroussel, or rigging up a kite, or a row in the lake. Chitchat, gossip, trivialities, recriminations. She was growing a bit daffy, it seemed to me. The alimony which we raked up with such effort was being pissed away on trifles. Worthless knickknacks everywhere. Drivel about sending the child to a private school, the public school being unfit for our little princess. Piano lessons, dancing lessons, painting lessons. The price of butter, turkey, sardines, apricots. Melanie's varicose veins. No parrot any more, I noticed. No pet poodle, no dog biscuits, no Edison phonograph. More and more furniture piling up, more empty candy boxes lying on the floor of the closet. Leaving her, it was the same old tug of war. Frightful scenes. The child screaming and clinging to me, begging me to stay and sleep with mamma. Once, in the park, seated on a beautiful knoll with the child, watching her fly the kite I had bought her, Maude meanwhile meandering about on her own in the offing, the child suddenly came up to me and put her arms around my neck, began kissing me tenderly, calling me daddy, dear daddy, and so on. In spite of all my efforts, a sob broke loose, then another and another and with it a flood of tears fit to drown a horse. I staggered to my feet, the child clinging to me for dear life, and looked blindly about for Maude. People stared at me in horror and walked on. Grief, grief, unbearable grief. The more so because all about me there was nothing but beauty, order, tranquillity. Other children were playing with their parents. They were happy, radiant, bursting with joy. Only *we* were miserable, alienated, forever alienated. Every week the child was growing older, more comprehending, more sensitive, more reproachful in her own silent way. It was criminal to live thus. Under another system we might have continued to live together, all of us, Mona, Maude, the child, Melanie, the dogs, cats, umbrellas, everything. At least so I thought in moments of desperation. Any situation was better than these heart-rending reunions. We were all being wounded, lacerated, Mona as much as Maude. The more difficult it got to raise the weekly alimony, the more guilty I felt towards Mona who was bearing the brunt of it all. What good was it to lead the life of a writer if it entailed such sacrifices? What good was it to life a live of bliss with Mona if my own flesh and blood had to suffer? At night, awake or in dream, I could feel the child's little arms about my neck, pulling me towards her, pulling me homeward. Often I wept in my sleep, groaned and whimpered, reliving these scenes of anguish. 'You were weeping in your sleep last night,' Mona would say. And I would say: 'Was I? I don't remember.' She knew I was lying. It made her miserable to think that my presence alone was not sufficient to make me happy. Often I would protest, though she hadn't said a word. 'I *am* happy, can't you see? I don't want a blessed thing.' She would be silent. Awkward pauses. 'You don't think I'm worried about the child, do you?' I would blurt out. And she would answer: 'You haven't been there for several weeks now, do you know that?' It was true. I had taken to staving off the regular weekly visits, would send the money by mail or messenger boy. 'I think you ought to go this week Val. After all, she's your own child.' 'I know, I know,' I would say. 'Yes, I'll go.' And then I would give a groan. And still another groan when I'd hear her say: 'I bought something for the little one for you to take this time.' Why did I not buy anything myself? Often I stood looking into shop windows, choosing in my mind all the things I would like to buy, not just for the child, but for Mona, for Melanie, even for Maude. But I didn't think it was right of me to buy things when I wasn't earning anything myself. The money Mona earned at the theatre was not enough for our needs, not nearly enough. She was constantly gold-digging, week in and week out. Sometimes she came home with staggering gifts for

52

me, after an unusual touch, I suppose. I begged her not to get me things. 'I have everything,' I said. And it was true. (Except for the bicycle and the piano. Somehow, I had forgotten all about these items.) Things piled up so fast, that even if I had received them, I doubt that I would have used them. It would have been more sensible to give me a mouth organ and a pair of roller skates. . . .

Sometimes strange nostalgic fits assailed me. I might wake up with the hang-over of a dream and decided that it was most imperative to revive certain strong recollections, as of that fat tub I called 'Uncle Charlie', who used to sit me on his lap and regale me with stories of his exploits during the Spanish-American war. It meant a long ride, by elevated line and trolley, to a little place called Glendale, where Joey and Tony had once lived. (Uncle Charlie was *their* uncle, not mine.) After all the years which had passed, the sleepy little hamlet still wore a quaint air to me. The houses where my little friends had lived were still standing, hardly altered, fortunately. The tavern with its stables, where friends and relatives used to gather of a summer's evening, were also there. I could recall running from table to table as a tiny tot, sipping the dregs from the beer mugs, or collecting pennies and dimes from the tipsy revellers. Even the maudlin German songs, which they sang with iron lungs, ran in my ears: '*Lauderbach, lauderbach, hab' ich mein Strumpf verlor'n.*' I see them suddenly sobered, dead serious now, gathered in hollow square, like the last remnants of a gallant regiment, men, women and children, shoulder to shoulder, all members of the Kunst Verein (a nucleus of the great ancestral Saengerbund), waiting solemnly for the leader to sound the tuning fork. Like faithful warriors standing at the border of a foreign land, their chests heaving, their eyes bright and liquid, they raise their powerful voices in a heavenly choir, intoning some deeply moving Lied which stirs them to the depths of their souls. . . . Moving along. Now the little Catholic church where Mr Imhof, the father of Tony and Joey (the first artist I was to meet in the flesh) had made the stained glass windows, the frescoes on the walls and ceiling, and the carved pulpit. Though his children were fearful of him, though he was stern, tyrannical, aloof, I was always strongly drawn to this sombre man. At bed-time we were always led to his study in the garret to bid him goodnight. Invariably he was sitting at his table, painting water colours. A student's lamp threw a soft light on the table, leaving the rest of the room in chiaroscuro. He looked so earnest and tender then, distraught, and ever remote. I used to wonder what impelled him to remain long hours of the night glued to his work table. But what registered most of all was that he was *different*: he was of another breed. . . . Still strolling about. At the railroad tracks now, where we used to play in the ravine: a sort of no man's land between the edge of the village and the cemeteries on the other side of the tracks. Somewhere hereabouts there had lived a distant relative whom I called Tante Grussy, a youngish woman of great beauty, with large grey eyes and black hair, who even then, even though I was but a child, I sensed to be an unusual person. No one had ever known her to raise her voice in anger; no one had ever heard her speak ill of another; no one had ever asked her for help in vain. She had a contralto voice, and when she sang she accompanied herself on the guitar; sometimes she dressed in masquerade and danced to the tambourine, fluttering a long Japanese fan. Her husband became a drunkard; he used to beat her up, it was said. But Tante Grussy only became sweeter, gentler, more compassionate, more charming and gracious. And then, after a time it began to be rumoured about that she had become religious— this was always said in whispers, as if to imply that she had gone mad. I wanted so much to see her again. I searched and searched for the house but no one seemed to have any knowledge of it. It was hinted that she may have been committed to the asylum. . . . Strange thoughts, strange remembrances, walking about in the sleepy village of Glendale. This adorable, this saintly Tante Grussy, and the jovial sensual tub of flesh whom I called Uncle Charlie—I loved them both. The one spoke of nothing but torturing and killing the Igorotes, of tracking down Aguinaldo in the swamps and mountain fastnesses of the Philippines; the other hardly spoke at all, she was a presence, a goddess in earthly guise who had elected to stay with us and illumine our lives through the divine radiance which she shed.

When he left for the Philippines as a lance corporal, this Charlie boy was a normal sized individual. Some eight years later, when he returned as commisary sergeant, he weighed almost four hundred pounds and was constantly perspiring. I remember vividly a gift he made me one day—six dumdum bullets for which he had had a blue linen case made. These, he maintained, had been taken from one of Aguinaldo's men; for being guilty of using these bullets (which the Germans had furnished the Filipinos) they had executed the rebel and stuck his head on a pole. Stories such as this, together with horripilating tales about the 'water-cure' which our soldiers administered to the Filipinos, made me sympathize with Aguinaldo. I used to pray every night that the Americans would never capture him. Unwittingly, Uncle Charlie had made him my hero.

Thinking of Aguinaldo, I suddenly recalled a banner day on which I was dressed in my best Lord Fauntleroy outfit and taken early in the morning to a beautiful brown stone house on Bedford Avenue, where, from a balcony, we were to watch 'the parade'. The first contingent of our heroes had just returned from the Philippines. Teddy Roosevelt was there—'up front'—

leading his Rough Riders. There was tremendous excitement over this event; people wept and cheered, flags and bunting everywhere, flowers showered from the windows. People kissed one another and shouted Alleluias. I had a grand time, but it was a bit confusing to me. I couldn't grasp the reason for such extravagant emotions. What impressed me were the uniforms—and the horses. That evening a cavalry officer and an artillery man came to our home for dinner. This was the beginning of a romance to my two aunts. Nipped in the bud, however, because my grandfather, who hated the military, wouldn't hear of having them for sons-in-law. I can still remember his scorn and contempt for the whole Philippine campaign. To him it was just a skirmish. 'It should have been over in thirty days,' he snorted. And then he talked of Bismark and Von Moltke, of the battle of Waterloo and the siege of Austerlitz. He had come to America during the days of our Civil War. *That* was a war, he kept asserting. To lick helpless savages, anybody could do that. Just the same, he was obliged to give a toast to Admiral Dewey, the hero of Manila Bay. 'You're an American now,' said someone. 'And I'm a *good* American,' I can hear my grandfather saying. 'But that doesn't mean that I like to kill. Put away the uniforms, get back to work!'

This grandfather, Valentin Nieting, was a man whom everybody respected and admired. He had spent ten years in London as a master tailor, had acquired a beautiful English accent there, and always spoke affectionately of the English. He said they were a *civilized* people. All his life he retained many English mannerisms. His crony, whom he met on Saturday nights at a saloon on Second Avenue, run by my Uncle Paul, was a skinny, fiery sort of man named Mr Crow, an Englishman from Birmingham. No one in our family liked Mr Crow, except grandfather. The reason was that Mr Crow was a Socialist. He was always making speeches, too, and full of vitriol. My grandfather, whose memory extended back to the days of '48, relished and applauded these speeches. He too was against the 'bosses'. And of course against the military. It's strange, when I think back, what an unholy fear the word Socialism inspired in those days. None of our family would have anything to do with a man calling himself a Socialist; he was worse than a Catholic or a Jew. America was a free country, the land of opportunity, and it was one's duty to become successful and rich. My father, who hated his own boss —'a bloody, blimey Englishman', he always called him—was soon to become a boss tailor himself. My grandfather had to accept work from my father. But he never lost that dignity, that assurance and integrity which always made him a trifle superior to my father. Before long all the 'boss tailors' were to become woefully impoverished, forced to band together to share expenses, to keep in steady employment a small crew of workmen. The wages of the workmen—cutter, bushelman, coat maker, pants maker—would continue to rise, would represent more per week than the boss's own share. Eventually—last act in the drama—these little workmen, all foreigners, usually despised, but envied too sometimes, would be lending the bosses money in order to keep their businesses going. Maybe all this was the result of those pernicious Socialist doctrines which agitators like Mr Crow had sponsored. Maybe not. Maybe there was something inherently disastrous in that 'Get-Rich-Quick' Wallingford doctrine with which the young men of my generation had been inoculated.

My grandfather died before the First World War broke out. He left a sizeable estate, as did the other émigrés in that old neighbourhood, all of whom had come to America at the same time and from all parts of Europe. They did far, far better in this glorious land of the free than did their sons and daughters. They had started from scratch, like that butcher boy from Germany, my namesake—Henry Miller 'the cattle king'—who ended by owning an enormous slice of California. It's true, there may have been more opportunity in those days, but there was also the fact that these men were made of sterner stuff, that they were more industrious, more persevering, more resourceful, more disciplined. They began in some humble trade—butcher, carpenter, tailor, shoemaker—and the money they saved they earned by the sweat of their brow. They lived modestly always, and quite comfortably, despite the absence of all the comforts, all the labour-saving devices now deemed indispensable. I remembered the toilet in my grandfather's home. First it was just an outhouse in the yard; later he had a cubbyhole built in upstairs. But even after gas had been introduced there was no illumination in that toilet except for a little taper floating in sweet oil. My grandfather would never have considered it of importance to have a gas light in the toilet. His children ate well and were clothed; they were taken to the theatre occasionally, they went with him to outings and picnics—glorious affairs!—and they sang with him when he attended the reunions of the Saengerbund. A simple, wholesome life, and far from dull. In Winter, when the snow and ice came, he would sometimes take them for a ride in an open sleigh drawn by horse. He himself would go ice-boating occasionally. And in Summer there would be those unforgettable trips, by excursion boat, to places like Glen Island, for example, or New Rochelle. I can think of nothing offered the child today which can rival those outings. Nor can I think of anything to rival the magical festival grounds of Glen Island. The only thing approaching it is the atmosphere of certain paintings of Renoir and Seurat. Here again we have that golden ambiance, that gaiety and ripeness, that plushy, carnal opulence so characteristic of the somnolescent, yawning, indolent period between the end of the Franco-Prussian war and the outbreak of the First World War. Undoubtedly it was a bourgeois efflorescence, infected with the taint of a rotting order, but the men who epitomized it, the men who glorified it in word and pigment, were not tainted. I can never think of my grandfather as being tainted, nor can I think of Renoir and Seurat in that way. I think that my grandfather, in his way of life, had more affinities with Seurat and Renoir than with the new American way of life which was then germinating. I think he would have understood these men and their art, had he been permitted. My parents never. Nor the boys I grew up with in the street.

I ramble on, touched by memories of old. It was thus my mind wandered as I made the rounds of the old haunts. No wonder the days were so full, so savoury. Starting out for Glendale I would finish up in 'the old neighbourhood'. Couldn't resist walking by the old ancestral house again. Wouldn't dream, however, of calling on my relatives, who still lived there. On the other side of the street I would take a stand—look up to the third floor where we once lived, try to recreate the image of the world I had known as a boy of five or six. That front window, where I used to sit, will go with me into the beyond, will frame the memories which I shall relive while waiting to be born into a new body. I recall the panic and terror that invaded me when my mother first forced me to wash the windows for her; sitting on the sill, my body hanging outside, three stories from the pavement—an immense height to a child of seven or eight—my knees gripping the sill for dear life. The window rested on my legs like a leaden weight. Fear of raising the window, fear of losing my grip. My mother insisting that there were still some specks of dirt to be washed off.(Later, when quite grown up, my mother would tell me how I loved to wash the windows for her. Or how I loved to hang the awnings. How I loved this, how I loved that. . . . All bloody lies!)

Standing there in a deep reverie, I wonder to myself if perhaps I hadn't been a bit of a sissy in those days. No boy in the neighbourhood was better dressed than I. No one had better manners. No one was more alert and intelligent. I won all the prizes, got all the applause. So certain were they that I knew how to take care of myself, it never dawned on my parents that my playmates were already steeped in sin and vice. Even the fondest mother should have been able to detect in little Johnnie Ludlow the makings of a criminal. Even the most negligent parent should have been able to discern that little Alfie Betcha was already a gangster and a hoodlum. The pride of the Sunday School, such as I was, always chose for his boon companions the worst urchins in the neighbourhood. Wasn't my darling mother aware of this? Able to recite the catechism backwards, intelligent little monkey that I was, I had also, when with my comrades, a tongue that could reel off such filth, abuse and male-diction as would do honour to a gallows bird. It was the older boys who instructed us, to be sure. Not overtly or deliberately either. We were always hanging about, listening in on their arguments and disputes. They were not so much older than us, either, when I think of it. Twelve years of age at the most, they were. But words like whore, bitch, cock-sucker, bastard, shit-ass, fuck, prick, and so forth were constantly on their lips. When we younger ones employed these words they would laugh hilariously. I remember one day, elated by some new vocable I had acquired, going up to a girl of fifteen or so, and calling her vile names. When she got hold of me to spank me I swore at her like a trooper. I probably bit her hand too, and kicked her in the shanks. At any rate, I remember that she was boiling with rage and mortification. 'I'll teach you, you little brat,' she said, and with that she took me by the ear and dragged me to the police station around the corner. Led me right up the big steps, opened the door, and shoved me into the centre of the room. There I was, a tiny urchin, facing the desk sergeant seated high above me, only his head visible above the desk top.

'What's the meaning of this?' His stern, thundering voice scared the wits out of me.

'Tell him,' commanded the girl. 'Tell him what you called me!'

I was too terrified to open my mouth. I just gasped.

'I see,' said the sergeant, raising his bushy black eyebrows and glaring at me threateningly. 'He's been using dirty language, has he?'

'Yes, your honour,' said the girl.

'Well, we'll see about that.' He rose from his throne and made as if to descend.

I began to whimper, then to bellow.

'He's really a good boy,' said the girl, coming over to me and patting my head affectionately. 'His name is Henry Miller.'

'*Henry Miller?*' said the sergeant. 'Why I know his father and his grandfather. You don't mean to tell me *this* little shaver is using bad language?'

With this he came down from his high place and, stooping over me, he took me by the hand. 'Henry Miller,' he said, 'I'm surprised at you. Why. . . .'

(The mention of my name in this public place, in the police station of all places, had a tremendous effect upon me. I already regarded myself as a criminal, saw my name being heralded all over the street, printed in headlines five feet tall. I trembled to think what my parents would say when I got home, for I sur-mised that the news would have travelled ahead of me. Perhaps the sergeant had already detailed a man to inform my mother of the predicament. Perhaps she would have to come to bail me out. Together with such fears and forebodings there was a certain pride, too, in hearing my name ring out in that empty police station. I had a status now. No one had ever called me by both names at once. I was always just Henry. Now I had become Henry Miller, a full-fledged personage. The man would write my name and address down in the big book. They would have a record of me. . . . I grew ten years older in that fearful moment.)

A few minutes later, safe on my own street, the girl having released me with a promise never to use such words again, I felt heroic. I sensed that it was all a game, that no one had any intention of prosecuting me, or even of telling my parents. I was ashamed of myself for bawling like a sissy in front of the sergeant. The fact that he was such a good friend of my father and grandfather meant that he would never do me harm. Instead of thinking of him as some one to be feared, I began to look upon him as my protector and confidential ally. It had impressed me enormously that my family was in good standing with the police, perhaps on intimate terms with them. Then and there I developed a contempt for the powers that be. . . .

Before tearing myself away from the old haunts I just had to sneak through the hall and out into the backyard where the outhouse had once stood. On the side where the old smoke house used to be was a figure—painted on the fence—of a woman leading a little dog. It had been done in black paint and tar. It was almost obliterated now. This crude piece of art haunted me as a child. It was so to speak, my private Egyptian tomb painting. (Curiously, later on, when I myself took up painting, I often made figures which reminded me of this stark delineation. Instinctively my hand traced the same stiff outline; for years, it seemed, I could never do anything full on, but always in this same archaic profile. My heads always had a hawk or witch-like expression; people thought I was deliberately trying to be nightmarish but I wasn't, it was the only way I could represent the human figure.)

Returning to the street I involuntarily raised my eyes, as if to greet Mrs O'Melio, who used to harbour all the stray cats of the neighbourhood on her flat roof. There were over a hundred which she fed twice daily. She lived alone, and my mother always hinted that she must be cracked. Such Gargantuan solicitude was beyond my mother's comprehension.

I walk slowly towards the South side where I will catch the crosstown trolley for home. Every store front is rich with memories. After twenty-five years, despite all the changes, all the work of demolition, the old dwellings are still there. Faded, illkept, crumbling, like sturdy old teeth they still 'do their work.' The light that once animated them, the radiance they once shed, are gone. It was in Summer that they were especially redolent: they actually perspired, like human beings. The owners felt a pride in keeping their homes neat and trim; the glow of fresh paint, the deep shadows thrown by the awnings, were the reflections of their own humble spirits. The homes of the physicians were always a little better than the others, a little more pretentious. In the Summer one entered the doctor's office through beaded curtains which tinkled as one swished through. The doctor always seemed to be a connoisseur of art; on the walls there were usually sombre oil paintings framed in heavy gilt. The subject matter of these paintings was thoroughly alien to me. We had nothing like these on our walls; our pictures were given us by tradesmen at holiday times, bright, vile chromos which we looked at every day and forgot instantly. (Whenever my mother felt obliged to give something away to some poor neighbour she always chose a picture from the wall. 'Thank God we're rid of that,' she would murmur. Sometimes I would run to her with an offering of my own, a bright new toy, a pair of boots, a drum, because I too was surfeited with possessions. 'Oh, no, Henry, not *that!*' I can hear her say. 'That's too new!' 'But I don't want it any more,' I would insist. 'Don't talk that way,' she would answer, 'or God will punish you.')

Passing the old Presbyterian Church. At two o'clock the Sunday School class used to meet. How delightfully cool it was down there in the basement where we congregated! Outside the heat danced from the pavement. Big flies buzzed away, darting in and out of the shadows. When I think of what *Summer* then meant to me, the tangible, earth-born Summer which shimmered and vibrated throughout the long, festive days, I think of Debussy's music. Was he a lion of the Midi, I wonder? Did he have an African strain in his blood? Or were those plangent melodies studded with clustered chords an expression of yearning for a sun he had never known?

Every joyous period I have known seems to be connected with the sun. Thinking of Mr Roberts, our Sunday School superintendent, I think not only of that blazing orb in the sky but of the celestial warmth which this queer old Englishman radiated. His long flowing moustache, the colour of corn, his cheery, ruddy face, what health and confidence they imparted! He always appeared in the same cutaway suit with grey spats and an ascot under his chin. Like the minister and the deacons of the church, he was a wealthy man. They ought to have moved to better quarters long ago, but they were attached to the old neighbourhood and, besides, they enjoyed patronizing the poor and humble. At Christmas time they were truly bountiful with their gifts. My mother was frightfully impressed by this largesse; it was probably on this account that I grew up a Presbyterian instead of a Lutheran.

That evening, rehearsing my boyhood days with Mona, it suddenly occurred to me that it would a good touch to send the old minister, who was still alive, a sample of my work. I thought it might make him feel good to know that one of his 'little boys' was now a writer. God knows what it was I sent him but it had anything but the desired effect. Almost by return mail I received my manuscript back together with a letter couched in impeccable English, telling me of his sorrow and bewilderment. That I, who had been nurtured in the shelter of the fold, should descend to such crude, realistic means of expression, pained him. There was something in his letter about the garbage can, I remember. That riled me. Without wasting time, I sat down and replied in the most abusive terms, informing him that he was a fool and a dotard, that my one aim in life was to live down the stupid nonsense he had tried to implant. I added something about our Lord and Saviour which, though apt, was intended to upset him still more. As a crowning insult, I advised him to clear out of the old neighbourhood, which he did not and never had belonged to. I added that I hoped to see the star of David supplanting the Cross next time I passed the venerable old edifice. (My wish, incidentally, was soon thereafter gratified. The place did become a synagogue! And the rectory, where our dear minister once lived, was taken over by an aged rabbi with a flowing white beard.)

After I sent the letter I was of course repentant. What a silly thing to do! Still playing 'the bad boy'. It was just like me, though, to revere the past and to spit on it. I was doing the same thing with friends—and with authors. I accepted and cherished out of the past only what I could convert to creative ends. . . .

Did I mention Van Gogh whose *Letters* I was then reading and recently reread after a lapse of twenty years? What excited me was Vincent's flaming desire to live the life of an artist, to be nothing but the artist, come what may. With men of his stripe art becomes a religion. Christ long dead to the Church is born again. The passionate Vincent redeems the world through the miraculous use of pigment. The despised and forsaken dreamer re-enacts the drama of crucifixion. He rises from his grave to triumph over the unbelievers.

Over and over again Van Gogh speaks of desiring nothing more than to lead the simple life. He is extravagant only in the use of his materials. Everything goes into his art. It is such a thorough sacrifice that, by comparison, the lives of most painters seem pale and worthless. Van Gogh knows that he will never be recognized in his lifetime; he knows that he will never reap the harvest of his toil. But the artists to come—perhaps his renunciation will make it easier for them! That is his most profound wish. In a thousand different ways he says: 'For myself I expect nothing. *We* are doomed. *We* live outside our time.'

How he sweats and struggles to get together fifty good canvases which his brother is to exhibit to a scornful, contemptuous world! The last few years of his life he is truly a madman. But a madman in the proper sense of the word. All flame and spirit, he overflows with creative energy. He is the cup which runneth over. And he is alone.

It is difficult to get women to pose, at Arles. His paintings are atrocious, people say. 'They are just full of paint!' I laugh and weep when I read this. *Full of paint!* How terrifyingly true! How ironic that this wonderful thing which had come to pass (the saturation of canvas with colour, with pure riotous colour) that this dream of all the great painters (at last realized) should be used against him! Poor Van Gogh! Rich Van Gogh! Almighty Van Gogh! What a cruel, blasphemous jest! As if to say of a man of God—'*But he is too full of God!*'

I should like to paint in such a way, says Van Gogh, that every one who has eyes may see clearly what is there. It was in this way that Jesus spoke and lived. But the blind and the deaf are with us always. Only they see, only they hear, only they act who are filled with the precious holy spirit.

We know that for a long time Van Gogh abstained from using colour, that he forced himself to work with pencil, charcoal, ink We know too that he began by studying the human figure, that he sought to learn from Nature. Yes, he was training himself to read what was hidden beneath the shell. He consorted with the poor and humble, with down-trodden workers, with outcasts. He adored the peasant, extolling *him* rather than the man of culture. He studied the shapes of things, the feel of objects. He familiarized himself with all that was common and everyday so that later, when he would have acquired the necessary skill and technique, he could render this world of the ordinary, the commonplace, the everyday in the light of a reality divine. What Van Gogh desired was to make this all too familiar world familiar in a new sense —in an everlasting sense, so to speak. He wanted to show that it was not clothed in evil and ugliness, that it was never dull or boring, that we have only to look at it with loving eyes to recognize its splendour and magnificence. And when he had accomplished this, when he had given us a new earth, he found that he was no longer able to cope with the world: he voluntarily sought out an asylum.

It took almost fifty years for the man in the street to realize that a Christ, manifesting himself as painter, had lately been in our midst. Suddenly, due to the immense popularity of a sensational book, thousands upon thousands take to visiting the museums and galleries; they converge like a Niagara upon the intoxicating masterpieces of that despised and forlorn genius, Vincent Van Gogh. Reproductions of his work are to be seen everywhere; they sprout in the most unexpected places. Van Gogh at last arrives. At last 'the great failure' comes into his own. His faith was justified, apparently. His sacrifice was not in vain.

For, not only does he reach the masses, what is more important, he influences the painters.

In one of the letters—back in 1888!—he writes: 'Painting promises to become more subtle—more musical and less sculptural—*enfin elle promet la couleur*.' He underlines the word colour. How prophetic his insight! What is modern painting if not a hymn to colour? Tantamount to revelation, the free, audacious use of colour precipitated a liberation undreamed of. Centuries of painting are annihilated overnight. Unbelievable vistas open up.

In those wonderful letters in which Van Gogh relates his discoveries about the laws of colour (most of which were formulated by Delacroix), he dwells at some length on the use of black and white. One should not eschew the use of black, he writes. There is black and there is black. Did not Rembrandt and Franz Hals employ black, he asks? And Velasquez too? Not just black either, but twenty-seven different kinds of black. It all depends what kind of black, and how one employs it. The same for white. (Soon Utrillo is to demonstrate the validity of Van Gogh's apperceptions. Is not his white period still the best?)

I speak of black and white because it was inevitable that this revolutionary in the world of colour should dwell on first and last things. In this he reminds us of those true sons of God who fear not evil or ugliness but embrace and incorporate them in their world of goodness and beauty.

When the nineteenth century crumbled on the field of Armageddon the old barriers were burst asunder. The demonic artists who dominated that century contributed as much to the undermining of the past as did the statesmen and militarists, the financiers and industrialists, the revolutionaries and the propagandists who had paved the way for the débâcle. The war of 1914 seemed like the end of something; it was however only the culmination of something long overdue. Actually, it opened up vast new horizons. Through its work of demolition it afforded outlet to vast new fields of energy. The period between the first and second World Wars is rich in artistic production. It is in this period, when the world is about to be shaken to its foundations a second time, that I was taking form. It was a difficult period primarily because one had to rely so exclusively upon himself, upon his own unique powers. Society, torn by all manner of dessension, offered the artist even less support and encouragement than in Van Gogh's time. The very existence of the artist was challenged. *But was not everyone's existence menaced?*

Emerging from the Second World War, there is a vague feeling that the earth itself is threatened with extinction. We have entered into another Apocalyptic era. The spirit of man is being convulsed as was the earth itself in ancient geologic periods. It is death we are shaking off—the rigidity of death. We deplore the spirit of violence which is prevalent, but to burst the bonds of death the spirit of man must be driven. The most dazzling possibilities enfold us. We are infused and invested with powers and energies heretofore undreamed of. We are about to live again as human beings, in the full majesty which the word human implies. The heroic work of our forerunners seems now like the work of sacrificial victims. It is not necessary for us to repeat their sacrifices. It is for us to enjoy the fruits. The past lies in ruins, the future yawns invitingly. Take this everyday world and embrace it! That is what the spirit urges. What better world can there be than this in which we have full responsibility, each and every one of us? Labour not for the men to come! Cease labouring altogether and create! For creation is play, and play is divine.

That is the message I get whenever I read the life of Van Gogh. His final despair, ending in madness and suicide, could be interpreted as divine impatience. 'The Kingdom of Heaven is here,' he was shouting. 'Why do ye not enter?'

We weep crocodile tears over his lamentable end, forgetting the burst of splendour which preceded it. Do we weep when the sun sinks into the ocean? The full magnificence of the sun is revealed to us only in the few moments preceding and following its disappearance. It will appear again at dawn, another magnificence, another sun perhaps. All during the day it nourishes and sustains us, but we scarcely give heed to it. We know it is there, we count on it, but we offer no thanks, no devotion. The great luminaries, like Nietzsche, like Rimbaud, like Van Gogh, are human suns which suffer the same fate as the celestial orb. It is only when they are sinking, or have sunk from sight, that we become aware of the glory that was theirs. In mourning their passing we blind our eyes to the existence of other new suns. We look backwards and forwards but never does our gaze pierce direct to the heart of reality. If we do occasionally worship the solar body which gives us warmth and light we reflect not on the suns which have been blazing since eternity. We accept unthinkingly the fact that all space is studded with suns.

Verily, the universe swims in light. Everything is alive and alight. Man too is the recipient of inexhaustible radiant energy. Strange, only in the mind of man is there darkness and paralysis.

A little too much light, a little too much energy (here on earth), and one is rendered unfit for human society. The reward of the visionary is the mad-house or the cross. A grey, neutral world is our natural habitat, it would seem. It has been so for a long time now. But that world, that condition of things, is passing. Like it or not, with blinkers-and-blinders or without, we stand on the threshold of a new world. We shall be forced to understand and accept—because the great luminaries whom we cast out of our midst have convulsed our vision. We shall be witness to splendours and horrors, alternately and simultaneously. We shall see with a thousand eyes, like the goddess Indra. The stars are moving in on us, even the most distant ones.

With our instruments we now detect worlds of whose existence ancient man had not the slightest inkling. We are able to plot realms of worlds beyond our present ken, because our minds are already receptive to the light which emanates from them. At the same time we are also able to visualize our own wholesale destruction. But are we frozen in our tracks? No. Our faith is greater than we dare admit. We sense the magnificence of that life eternal which is man's and which we have ever denied. Despite all our pride and vanity, we behave as if we knew nothing of our true heritage. We protest that we are only human, all-too-human. But if we were truly human we would be capable of all things, ready for all exigencies, know all conditions of being. We ought to remind ourselves daily, repeat it like a litany, that in our being lies concealed the whole gamut of existence. We should cease worshipping and inspire worship. Above all, we should cease postponing the act of becoming what in fact and essence we are.

'I prefer,' wrote Van Gogh, 'to paint men's eyes than to paint cathedrals, because there is something in men's eyes which is not in cathedrals, however majestic and imposing the latter may be. . . .'

3

IT IS ONLY FOR a few brief months that this heavenly period lasts. Soon it will be nothing but trouble, nothing but want, nothing but frustration. Until I get to Paris only three short scripts will ever be published—the first in a magazine dedicated to the advancement of the coloured people, the second in a magazine sponsored by a friend and which has but one issue, and the third in a magazine revived by good old Frank Harris.

Thereafter everything I submit for publication will bear my wife's signature. (Only one freakish exception, of which more later.) It is agreed that I can do nothing on my own. I am simply to write and leave the rest to Mona. Her job at the theatre has already petered out. The rent has been long overdue. My visits to Maude have become less and less regular and the alimony is paid only now and then, when we make a haul. Soon Mona's wardrobe gives out, and I, like a dolt, make vain efforts to beg a dress or a suit off my old sweethearts. When it gets bitter cold she wears my overcoat.

Mona is for taking a job in a cabaret, but I refuse to hear of it. With each mail I look forward to a letter of acceptance accompanied by a cheque. I must have between twenty and thirty manuscripts floating about; they come and go like trained carrier pigeons. It is getting to be a problem to raise the money for the postage. Everything is becoming a problem.

In the midst of this first set-back we are rescued for a brief spell by the arrival of my old friend O'Mara who, after quitting the Cosmodemonic Telegraph Company, had gone on a long cruise with some fishermen in the Caribbean. The adventure had earned him some money.

We had hardly embraced one another when, in characteristic fashion, O'Mara emptied his pockets, placing the money in a heap on the table. 'The kitty,' he called it. It was to be for our common use. A few hundred dollars in all, enough either to pay our debts or to live on for a month or two.

'Have you anything to drink around here? No? Let me run out and get something.'

He came back with a few bottles and a bag full of food. 'Where's the kitchen here? I don't seem to see it.'

'There is no kitchen; we're not supposed to cook.'

'What?' he yelled. '*No kitchen?* What do you pay for this joint?'

When we told him he said we were crazy, plumb crazy. Mona didn't relish that in the least.

'How the hell do you manage, then?' he asked, scratching his head.

'To be frank,' I said, 'we don't.'

Mona was almost in tears now.

'Neither of you working?' he continued.

'Val's working,' was Mona's prompt reply.

'You mean writing, I suppose,' said O'Mara, implying that that was just a pastime.

'Certainly,' said Mona with asperity, 'what would you want him to do?'

'I? I don't want him to do anything. I was just wondering how you lived . . . you know, where you got the dough?'

He was silent a moment, then he said: 'By the way, that chap who let me in, was he the landlord? Looked like a swell guy.'

'He is too,' I said. 'He's a Virginian. Never pesters us for the rent. A real gentleman, I'll say.'

'You ought to treat him right,' said O'Mara. 'Listen, why don't we let him have something on account?'

'No,' said Mona quickly, 'don't do that, please. He won't mind waiting a little longer. Besides, I expect to have some money soon.'

'You do?' said I, ever suspicious of these rash statements.

'Well, the hell with that,' said O'Mara, pouring out the sherry. 'Let's sit down and have a drink. I brought some ham and eggs, and some good cheese. Too bad we have to throw it away.'

'What do you mean, throw it away?' said Mona. 'We have a little two-burner gas stove in the bathroom.'

'Is that where you cook? Christ!'

'No, we just keep it there, out of sight.'

'But they must smell the cooking upstairs, don't they?' By they O'Mara meant the landlord and his wife.

'Of course they do,' I said, 'but they're discreet. They pretend that they smell nothing.'

'Wonderful people,' said O'Mara. He meant by this that only Southerners could display such tact.

The next moment he was suggesting that we look for a cheaper place, with conveniences. 'That money's going to vanish in no time the way you people live. I'll look around for a job, of course, *but you know me.* Anyway, I'd like to take it easy for a while.'

I smiled. 'Don't worry,' I said, 'everything will be hunky dory. Just having you around will make things easier.'

'But where will he sleep?' asked Mona, not too pleased with this idea.

'We can buy a cot, can't we?' I pointed to the money lying on the table.

'But the landlord?'

'We won't tell him right away. Besides, we're privileged to have a guest, aren't we He doesn't need to know that Ted is a boarder.'

'I can sleep just as well on the floor,' said O'Mara.

'I wouldn't dream of it! We'll go out after lunch and get a second-hand cot. We'll sneak it in after dark, eh?'

I saw that it was time to say something to Mona. She hadn't taken so well to O'Mara, that was obvious. He was a little too blunt and forthright.

'Listen, Mona,' I began, 'you're going to like Ted when you get to know him. We've known each other since we were kids, isn't that right, Ted?'

'But I have nothing against him,' said Mona. 'I don't want him telling us what we should do, that's all.'

'She's right, Ted,' I said, 'you are a bit forward, you know that. A lot of things have happened since I last saw you. We're in a different world now. It's been wonderful until just recently. All due to Mona. Listen, if you two don't get to like one another it's going to be too bad.'

'I'll clear out any time you give the sign,' said O'Mara.

'I'm sorry,' said Mona, 'if I gave the wrong impression. If Val says you're a friend there must be something to you. . . .'

'What's this *Val* business?' said O'Mara, interrupting her.

'Oh, she prefers Val to Henry, that's all. You'll soon get used to it.'

'The hell I will. You're Henry to me.'

'I can see we're going to get along swell,' I chuckled. I got up to inspect the food. 'Do you suppose we could have lunch soon?' I asked.

'It's only eleven o'clock,' said Mona.

'I know, but I'm getting hungry. Ham-and-eggs sounds enticing. Besides, we haven't had too much to eat lately. Let's make up for lost time.'

O'Mara couldn't restrain himself. 'As long as I'm around you're going to eat well. If we only had a regular kitchen! I could dish up some swell meals.'

'Mona knows how to cook,' I said. 'We have wonderful meals —when we eat.'

'You mean to say you don't eat every day?'

'He exaggerates,' said Mona. 'If he misses one meal he thinks he's starving.'

'That's true,' I said, pouring out another glass of sherry. 'I'm thinking of the future all the time. Something tells me it's going to be a long, hard grind.'

'Haven't you sold anything yet?' asked O'Mara.

I shook my head.

'That's really tough,' he said. 'Listen, (an afterthought) let me look at your stuff later, will you? Maybe I can peddle it for you —if it's any good.'

'*If it's any good?*' Mona blazed. 'What do you mean?'

O'Mara burst out laughing. 'Oh, I know he's a genius. That's what's wrong, perhaps. You can't give it to 'em straight, you know. It's got to be watered down. *I know Henry.*'

With every crack he made O'Mara put his foot in deeper. I had a presentiment things were not going to work out at all. However, as long as the money held out we would enjoy a respite. After that he'd probably get a job and fend for himself.

Ever since I knew O'Mara he had been making these stories and coming back with a little jack which he always divvied up with me. There never had been a period when he had found me in good straits. Our friendship dated from the time we were seventeen or eighteen. We met for the first time in the dark at a railway station in New Jersey. Bill Woodruff and I were spending a vacation on the shores of a beautiful lake. Alec Walker, their boss, who had come to visit us, had brought O'Mara along as a surprise. It was a long drive from the station to the farm house where we were boarding. (We were travelling by horse and carriage.) About midnight we got back to the farm house. No one felt like going to bed immediately. O'Mara wanted to see the lake we had talked so much about. We got into a row-boat and headed towards the centre of the lake, which was about three miles across. It was black as pitch. On an impulse O'Mara peeled off his clothes. Said he wanted to have a swim. In a jiffy he had dived overboard. It seemed an endless time before he came up to the surface; we couldn't see him, we could only hear his voice. He was panting and puffing like a walrus. 'What happened?' we asked. 'I got stuck in the bulrushes,' he said. He turned over on his back and floated a while to get his breath. Then he started swimming, with strong, vigorous strokes. We followed in his wake, calling to him from time to time, begging him to get back in the boat before he got cold and exhausted.

That was how we met. His performance made a deep impression on me. His manliness and fearlessness won my admiration. During the week we spent together at the farm house we got to know one another inside out. Woodruff seemed more than ever a sissy to me now. He was not only full of qualms and misgivings but he was mercenary too. O'Mara, on the other hand, always gave recklessly. He was a born adventurer. At ten he had run away from the orphan asylum. Somewhere in the South, while

69

working in a carnival, he had run across Alec Walker who immediately took a fancy to him and brought him North to work for him. Later Woodruff was also taken into the office. We were to see and hear a lot of Alec Walker soon. He was to become the sponsor of our club, our patron saint virtually. But I am getting ahead of myself. . . . What I wanted to say was that it was impossible for me to ever refuse O'Mara anything. He gave all and he expected all. Among friends this was the natural, spontaneous way to behave, he believed. As for morals, he had no moral sense whatever. If he were hard up for a woman he would ask you if he couldn't sleep with your wife—that is, until he found himself 'a piece of tail'. If he lacked the money to help you out in a pinch he would do a little thieving on the side or he would forge a cheque. He had no scruples, no compunctions whatever. He liked to eat well and sleep long. He hated work but when he undertook something he went at it whole-heartedly. He always wanted to make money quickly. 'Make a haul and clear out,' that was the way he put it. He was fond of all the sports and loved to hunt and fish. When it came to cards he was a shark: he played a mean game, entirely out of keeping with his character. His excuse was that he never played for the fun of it. He played to win, to make a killing. He was not above cheating either, if he felt he could get away with it. He had formed a romantic notion of himself as a clever gambler.

Best of all was his talk. To me, at least. Most of my friends found him tiresome. But I could listen to O'Mara without ever desiring to open my own trap. All I did was to ply him with questions. I suppose the reason his talk was so stimulating to me was because it dealt with worlds I had never entered. He had been over a good part of the globe, had lived a number of years in the Orient, particularly China, Japan and the Philippines. I liked the picture he drew of Oriental women. He always spoke of them with tenderness and reverence. I liked too the way he spoke about fish, big fish, the monsters of the deep. Or about snakes, which he handled like pets. Trees and flowers also figured heavily in his talks: he knew every variety, it seemed to me, and he could dwell on their particularities endlessly. Then too he had been a soldier, even before the war broke out. A top sergeant, no less. He could talk about the qualities of a top sergeant in a way that would make one believe this little tyrant to be far more important than a colonel or a general. Officers he always spoke of with contempt and derision, or else with bitter hatred. 'They tried to push me up the ladder,' he said once, 'but I wouldn't hear of it. As top sergeant I was king, and I knew it. Any horse's ass can become a lieutenant. You have to be *good* to be top sergeant.'

He gave himself plenty of elbow room when talking. Never in a hurry to finish. Not O'Mara. Talked just as well when sober as when drunk. Of course he had a wonderful listener in me. An *ideal* listener. All anyone had to do in those days were merely to mention China, Java or Borneo, and I was all ears. Mention anything foreign and remote and I was a willing victim.

The surprising thing about a guy like O'Mara was that he also read a great deal. Almost the first thing he would do, on looking me up, would be to survey the books on hand. One by one he would go through them, savouring them slowly and delectably. The books also entered into our talks. Somehow I preferred O'Mara's impressions of a book to those of my other friends who were more widely read or more critical. Like myself, O'Mara was all appreciation, all enthusiasm. He had no critical sense. If the book held his interest it was a good book, or a great book, or a marvellous book. We would live as vividly in the books we devoured together as in our imaginary peregrinations through China, India, Africa. It was at the dinner table these jags often began. Over the coffee O'Mara would suddenly recall some incident out of his checkered past. We would egg him on. At two or three in the morning we would still be sitting there at table. By that time we would be ready for a little snack—to revive ourselves. Then a bit of a walk to get some clean fresh air into our lungs, as he always phrased it. Of course the next day was always shot. None of us thought of stirring out of bed before noon. Breakfast and lunch combined was always a leisurely affair. None of us was geared to start going first thing out of bed. And, since the day was already shot, we would immediately begin thinking about the theatre or a movie.

As long as the money lasted it was wonderful. . . .

I suppose it was O'Mara's practical turn of mind which gave me the idea one day of getting my little prose poems printed and selling them myself. After looking through my 'stuff', O'Mara was of the opinion that I would never get an editor to take them. I knew he was right. I began to turn it over in my mind. I had loads of friends and acquaintances, and they were all eager to help me, so they said. Why not sell my work direct to them, to begin with? I broached the idea to O'Mara. He thought it excellent. I would sell by mail and he would go around on foot, from one office building to another. Besides, he had lots of friends. Well, we found a little printer who gave us a very reasonable estimate; he had a good quantity of stiff coloured paper which he would use for the purpose. I was to bring out one a week, printing five hundred at a time. *Mezzotints* we called them, owing to the influence of Whistler. Signed: Henry V. Miller.

The most amazing thing, when I look back on it now, is that the first prose poem I wrote for this project was inspired by the Bowery Savings Bank. It was the architecture of their new building, not the gold in the vaults, which kindled my enthusiasm. 'The Bowery Phoenix', I called it. My friends weren't very enthusiastic but they coughed up. After all, it was only the price of a meal I was charging for these dithyrambs. Had we sold the five hundred we would have made a tidy little sum.

Among other things we tried to get yearly subscriptions, at a reduced rate. A dozen subscriptions per week and our problem would have been solved. But even my best friends were dubious that I could keep it up for a year. They knew me well. In a month or two I would be broaching another scheme. At best I was able to persuade them to take a month's subscription —mere chicken feed. O'Mara was incensed with my friends, said he could do better with utter strangers. Every morning he got up early and began plugging for me. He went all over town— Brooklyn, Manhattan, the Bronx, Staten Island—wherever he had a hunch that he would be welcome. He was trying to bag subscriptions.

After I had turned out two or three *Mezzotints* Mona came forward with another plan. She would sign her name to them and peddle them from place to place in the Village. The night spots, she meant. People who were half-drunk weren't very critical, she thought. Besides, it would be hard to resist a beautiful looking woman. O'Mara didn't take to her scheme—it was too unbusinesslike for him—but Mona insisted that there was no harm in trying. We had an assortment of back issues, all in different colours; my name had to be blacked out and hers printed below it. No one would know the difference.

The first week she did famously. They went like hot cakes. Some bought the whole series, others paid her triple and quintuple for a single *Mezzotint*. It seemed as though she had hit on the right idea. Now and then we got orders in the mail. Now and then O'Mara got a subscription, for six months or for a year. I had all sorts of ideas for the coming issues. The hell with editors—we could do better on our own.

While Mona made the rounds of the Village nightly, O'Mara and I went in search of material. We couldn't have gone about our task more energetically had we been hired by a big syndicate. We went everywhere, looked into everything. One night we would be sitting in the press box at the Six Day Bike Race, the next night we would have ringside seats at a wrestling bout. Some nights we would start out on foot, to explore Chinatown more thoroughly, or the Bowery, or we would go to Hoboken or some other God-forsaken town in New Jersey, 'just for a change. . . .' One afternoon, while O'Mara was plugging away for me in the Bronx, I called up Ned and induced him to go with me to the Burlesque on Houston Street, to write it up. I wanted Ned as my illustrator. We invented a yarn, of course, about the magazine which had requested the article. Cleo was no longer there, unfortunately, but there was a young, racy-looking blonde, who had replaced her, who was a seething mass of sex from head to foot.

72

After a little chat with her in the wings we persuaded her to have a drink with us after the show. She was one of those witless-shitless bitches who grow up in places like Newark or Sandusky. Had the laugh of a hyena. She had promised to introduce me to the comedian, who was her boy friend, but he never turned up. A few of the girls from the chorus straggled in, looking even more horrible with their clothes on, poor wretches. I got into conversation with one of them at the bar. Discovered that she was studying to be a violinist, of all things. She was as homely as sin, hadn't an ounce of sex in her, but was intelligent and sympathetic. Ned went to work on the blonde, hoping against hope to get her to go to the studio with him for a quick one. . . .

To make a *Mezzotint* of an afternoon like that was like working out a jig-saw puzzle. It would take me days to whittle my prose-poem down to the required length. Two-hundred and fifty words was the maximum that could be printed. I used to write two or three thousand, then reach for the axe.

Mona, of course, never got home till about two in the morning. It was a bit wearing on her, I thought. Not the hours, but the atmosphere of the night clubs. Now and then, to be sure, she ran into an interesting person. Like Alan Cromwell, for example, who claimed to be a banker from Washington D.C. A man of this calibre always invited her to sit down and talk to him. In Mona's opinion this Cromwell was a cultured individual. He had begun by buying everything she had with her. Seventy-five or eighty dollars he had handed over for a pile of *Mezzotints*, and in leaving he had forgotten to take them with him, purposely no doubt. A gentleman, what! He had come to New York on business once very ten days or so. Was always to be found at the Golden Eagle or at Tomtit's Nest. Though he drank heavily he was ever 'the perfect gentleman'. Never parted from her without leaving a fifty dollar bill in her palm. 'Just for keeping him company.' There were lots of lonely souls like Alan Cromwell floating about, Mona maintained. All these lonely souls were well heeled, what's more. Soon I would hear of the others, like that lumber king who kept a suite of rooms the year round at the Waldorf; like Moreau, the professor from the Sorbonne, who took her to the most exotic places whenever they happened to meet; like Neuberger, the oil man from Texas, who had so little conception of the value of money that, whether it was a long haul or a short haul, he always tipped the taxi-driver a five spot. Then there was the retired brewer from Milwaukee, who was passionate about music. He always notified Mona in advance of his coming so that she might accompany him to the concert which he came expressly from Milwaukee to hear. The little tributes which Mona exacted of these types represented so much more than anything we might have hoped to earn legitimately that O'Mara and I stopped thinking about subscriptions altogether. Any *Mezzo-*

tints which were left over at the end of the week we sent out gratis to people we thought would like to read them. Sometimes we sent them to editors of newspapers and magazines, or to the members of the Senate at Washington. Sometimes we sent them to the heads of large industrial organizations—just for the fun of it, just to see what might happen. Sometimes, and this was even more fun, we would go through the telephone book and pick out names at random. Once we telegraphed the contents of a *Mezzotint* to the director of an insane asylum on Long Island. We signed a fishy name, of course. A crazy name, like Aloysius Pentecost Onega. *Just to throw him off the track*(*!*)

An idea like this last would come to us after an evening with Osiecki who had now become a frequent visitor. He was an architect who lived in the neighbourhood; we had met him at a bar one evening just as it was closing. In the beginning his talk was fairly rational—the usual humdrum stuff about life in a big architect's office. Fond of music, he had bought himself a beautiful player piano and, after getting quietly soused all by himself he would start playing his records—until the neighbours pounded at the door.

Nothing unusual about such behaviour. We used to visit him now and then and help him listen to his bloody records. He always had a good supply of liquor in the house. Little by little, however, we observed a strange note creeping into his conversation. It was his hatred for his boss. Or rather, his *suspicions* about the boss.

It required a little coaxing at first to draw him out. He was coy about revealing the full extent of his misgivings. But when he saw that we swallowed his remarks without a murmur of surprise or disapproval, he unlimbered remarkably fast.

Apparently the boss wanted to get rid of him. But since he had nothing on Osiecki, he was at a loss how to do it.

'So that's why he puts the lice in your desk every night, eh?' piped O'Mara, slipping me the horse wink.

'I don't say that *he* does it. All I know is that they're there every morning,' and with this our friend would begin scratching himself.

'He doesn't have to do it himself, of course,' said I. 'Maybe he pays the janitor to do it for him.'

'I'm not saying *who* does it. I'm not making any accusations, not publicly anyway. All I know is that it's a dirty trick. If he were a man he would hand me my walking papers and be rid of me.'

'Why don't you turn the tables on him?' said O'Mara maliciously.

'How do you mean?'

'Why, just this . . . put the lice in *his* desk, see!'

'I'm in enough trouble,' said poor Osiecki.

74

'But you're going to lose your job anyway.'

'Don't be too sure of that. I've got a good lawyer who's promised to defend me.'

'You're certain you're not imagining all this?' I asked quite innocently.

'*Imagining it?* Listen, see those glass cups under your chairs? He's got them running around in here now.'

I looked casually around. Even the piano legs were standing in glass cups filled with kerosene.

'Jesus,' said O'Mara, 'I'm getting itchy myself. You'll go cuckoo if you don't quit that job soon.'

'All right,' said Osiecki smoothly and toneless, 'all right, I'll go cuckoo then. But I won't give him the satisfaction of handing in my resignation. *Never.*'

'Man,' I said, 'you must be a bit nuts already to talk like that.'

'I am,' said Osiecki. 'Who wouldn't be? Can you lie awake all night scratching yourself and act normal the next day?'

There was no answer to make to that. On the way home O'Mara and I began to discuss ways and means of helping the poor devil. 'Let's talk to his girl,' said O'Mara. 'That might help.' We agreed that we would get Osiecki to introduce us to his girl friend. We'd invite them both for dinner one evening.

'Maybe she's nuts too,' I thought to myself.

It was by accident we made the acquaintance shortly thereafter of Osiecki's bosom friends, Andrews and O'Shaughnessy, also architects. Andrews, a Canadian, was a short, cocky little fellow, well mannered, highly intelligent, and a loyal friend, as we soon discovered. He had known Osiecki since boyhood. O'Shaughnessy was quite another type, big, brawny, full of health and vitality, reckless, carefree, happy-go-lucky. Always looking for a good time. Always ready to go on a drinking bout. He had a mind, too, but he suppressed it. He liked to talk about food, women, horses, suspension bridges. The three of them at a bar were quite a sight—like something out of Du Maurier or Alexandre Dumas. Inseparable companions. Always took good care of one another. The reason we hadn't met them before was because Andrews and O'Shaughnessy had been away on a business trip.

They were quite pleased, it turned out, to learn that Osiecki had made friends with us. They were worried about him but had been unable to decide what to do about the situation. The boss was a fine chap, they said. Couldn't understand what had got into their friend to change him so—unless it was his girl.

'What's the matter with *her?*' we asked.

Andrews, who was doing the talking, was reluctant to say much about her. 'I know her only a short time,' he said. 'There's something fishy about her, that's all I can say. She gives me the creeps.' And with that he shut up. O'Shaughnessy simply laughed heartily over the whole affair. 'He'll come out of it,' he said. 'He's drinking too much, that's all. After you've seen snakes and cobras climbing into your bed the itch is nothing. I'll admit, though, I'd almost rather go to bed with a cobra than with that gal of his! There's something inhuman about her. I think she's a succubus, if you know what I mean.' Here he a gave a hearty guffaw. 'In plain English—a blood-sucker. Do you get it?'

While it lasted it was wonderful. I mean the walks, the talks, the books we read, the food we ate, the excursions and explorations, the characters we bumped into, the plans we made. Everything was fizzing, or else purring like a smooth-running machine. Nights when nobody showed up, nights when it was mean outdoors or we were a little short of dough, O'Mara and I would get into one of those conversations which would last the whole night. Sometimes it began over a book we had just read, such as *The Imperial Purple* or *The Eternal Husband*. Or that wonderful story about a carrier pigeon—*Gay Neck*.

Around midnight O'Mara always got a bit nervous and fidgety. He was concerned about Mona, what she was doing, where she was, could she take care of herself.

'Don't worry,' I would say, 'she knows how to take care of herself. She's had lots of experience.'

'I know,' he would say, 'but Jesus. . . .'

'Listen, Ted, if I were to start worrying about such things I'd go nuts.'

'You sure have a lot of confidence in her.'

'Why shouldn't I?'

O'Mara would hem and haw. 'Well, all I can say is, if she were my wife . . .'

'You'll never have a wife, so what the hell's the use of talking? She'll be home at ten after one sharp, wait till you see. Come on, forget about it.'

Sometimes I couldn't refrain from smiling to myself. You would think, b'Jesus, that it was *his* wife and not mine, the way he took it to heart. My friends were always behaving in this fashion to me. *They* always did the worrying.

The way to get him off the subject was to get him reminiscing. O'Mara was the greatest 'reminiscer' ever. He went to it like a cow chewing its cud. Whatever lay in the past was fodder.

The person he loved most to talk about was Alec Walker, the man who had picked him up during a carnival at Madison Square Garden and put him to work in his office. Alec Walker always remained a mystery to O'Mara. He spoke of him affectionately, with admiration and with gratitude, but there was something in Alec Walker's make up which baffled him. One night I tried to get to the bottom of it with him. Apparently, what bothered O'Mara most was that Alec Walker seemed to have no use for women. And he was such a handsome man! He could have had any woman he laid eyes on.

'You said you didn't think he was queer. If he's not queer then he's a celibate, that's all there is to it. The way I see it, he's a saint who's missed his calling.'

O'Mara wasn't at all satisfied with this cut-and-dried explanation.

'The only thing that bothers me,' I added, 'is the way he allowed Woodruff to twist him about his fingers. If you ask me, there's something fishy there.'

'Oh, that's nothing,' said O'Mara quickly, 'Alec's a softy. Anybody can twist him about his little finger. He's got too big a heart.'

'Listen,' I said, determined to have done with the subject once and for all, 'I want you to tell me the truth . . . did he ever make a pass at you?'

O'Mara gave a loud guffaw. '*A pass at me?* You don't know Alec at all or you'd never ask a question like that. Why, even if he were a queer, Alec would never do a thing like that, don't you realize that?'

'No, I don't. Unless you mean he's too much of a gentleman— Is that it?'

'No, no, not at all,' said O'Mara vehemently. 'I mean that if Alec Walker were starving to death he would never ask you for a crust of bread.'

'Then it's pride,' I said.

'It's not pride either. It's a martyr complex. *He enjoys suffering.*'

'It's lucky for him he's not poor.'

'He'll never be poor,' said O'Mara. 'He'd steal first.'

'That's quite a statement. What gives you that idea?'

O'Mara hesitated a few moments. 'I'll tell you something,' he blurted out, 'but don't ever tell it to a soul. Alec Walker once stole a big sum of money from his brother; his brother, who's a real son of a bitch, was going to send him up the river. But Sister what's her name paid it back. Where *she* got it I have no idea. It was a considerable sum.'

I said not a word to this. I was floored.

'And you know who got him into that scrape, don't you?' O'Mara continued.

I looked at him blankly.

'That little rat, Woodruff.'

'You don't say!'

'I always told you that Woodruff was no good, didn't I?'

'Yeah, but I don't get it. You mean to tell me that Alec Walker squandered all that money on our little friend Bill Woodruff?'

'That's exactly what I mean. Look, you remember that little tart Woodruff was so crazy about? He married her later, didn't he?'

'You mean Ida Verlaine?'

'That's it, *Ida*. Christ, it was Ida this and Ida that all day long. I remember because we were working together at the time. You haven't forgotten that trip to Europe Alec and Woodruff took?'

'You mean Alec was jealous of the girl?'

'Christ no! How could Alec be jealous of a little slut like that? He was trying to save Woodruff from himself, that's all. He saw that she was a no-good bitch and he tried to break it up. And Woodruff, the bastard, never satisfied with anything—I don't have to tell you what he's like!—had Alec running all over Europe. Just to keep his dirty little heart from breaking.'

'Go on,' I said, 'it's getting interesting.'

'The long and the short of it is that when they got to Monte Carlo Woodruff began to gamble—with Alec's money, of course. Alec never said a word. It went on for weeks, Woodruff losing steadily. That little bout cost Alec a fortune. He was cleaned out. But Woodruff wasn't ready to go home. He wanted to see the Queen of Roumania's winter palace; he wanted to visit the Pyramids; he wanted to go ski-ing at Chamonix. I tell you, Henry, when I talk about that guy my blood boils. You think women are gold-diggers. Listen, that guy Woodruff is worse than any whore I ever met. He'd take the pennies off a dead man's eyes.'

'In spite of it all he went back to his Ida—that's the best part of it,' I commented.

'Yeah, and she fucked him good and proper, I hear.'

I laughed. Suddenly I stopped laughing. A thought struck me.

'You know what just occurred to me, Ted? I think Woodruff was queer.'

'You *think* he was! I *know* he was. I can forgive him that, but not his meanness, not his miserliness.'

'I'll be damned,' I muttered. 'That explains why he made such a mess of it with his Ida. Well, well! To think I've known him all these years and never suspected it. . . . And you still don't think that there's anything queer about Alec?'

'I know there isn't,' said O'Mara. 'He's crazy about women. He trembles when they come within reach of him.'

'Beats me.'

'I told you before that he's ascetic. He once studied for the priesthood. Then he fell in love with a girl who jilted him. He never got over it. . . . I'll tell you something else about him you never suspected. Get this! You never saw him angry, did you? You wouldn't think he *could* get angry, eh? So soft, so suave, so gentle, so considerate. He's made of steel, that guy. Always in trim, always in fighting condition. I saw him clean up a whole bar one night, single-handed. He was magnificent. Of course we had to run for it, but once we got out of reach he was as cool and collected as could be. Asked me to brush him off while he fixed his tie. There wasn't a scratch on him. We went to a hotel where he

78

smoothed his hair and washed his hands. Then he suggested having a bite to eat—at Reisenweber's, I think it was. He looked immaculate, as always, and talked in a calm, steady voice as though we had just come from the theatre. It wasn't pose either: he was really calm, really quiet inside.

'I remember the meal too—just the sort of spread that Alec knew how to order. We dawdled over that meal for hours, it seems to me. Alec was in a mood to talk. He was trying to make me understand what a truly Christ-like figure St. Francis was. He hinted that he had once aspired to be a sort of St Francis himself. I used to make fun of Alec, you know, for being so damned pious. I used to call him a dirty Catholic—to his face, I mean. No matter what I said, though, I could never rile him. He would give me that sort of wistful, comprehending smile—you know what I mean—and I would grow ashamed of myself.'

'I never could dope out that smile,' I interrupted. 'It always made me uncomfortable. I never knew whether he was being superior or playing the innocent one.'

'Righto!' said O'Mara. 'In a way he *knew* he was superior—not just to us kids, but to most people. In another way he felt himself to be less than any one. His humility was tinged with arrogance. Or was it elegance? You remember how he wore his clothes. And then the way he spoke—that soft Irish tongue of his, the impeccable English he used . ∴ no slouch, that guy! But when he grew silent, that was something. If anything could make me uncomfortable it was the way he could shut up like a clam. It used to give me the creeps. He was always silent, if you noticed, when other people were ready to explode. He'd shut up at the critical moment and leave you suspended in mid-air. It was a way of letting you blow yourself up, know what I mean? Then's when I spotted the monk in him.'

'Listen, Ted,' I said, cutting him short, 'I still can't figure out what made him take to a guy like Woodruff.'

'That's easy,' was O'Mara's airy rejoinder. 'He wanted to redeem the poor sap. It gave him pleasure to work on a worthless little prick like Woodruff. It was a test of his powers. Don't think he didn't know Woodruff. He had him figured out to a hair. What appealed to him most about Woodruff, strangely enough, was the mercenary streak. Like the martyr he was, he just kept shelling out and shelling out, until there was nothing left. . . . Woodruff never knew that Alec had stolen for him. He wouldn't believe it, if you told him it, the little rat.'

'Did I tell you I ran into Woodruff lately? Yeah, going down Broadway.'

'What's he doing now?'

'I never asked him.'

'Probably a pimp,' said O'Mara.

'But I do know what happened to Ida. She's an actress now.

79

Saw the billboards with her name plastered all over them. We ought to go and see her some time, what?'

'Not me,' said O'Mara. 'I'll see her in hell first. . . . Listen, the hell with her and the hell with Woodruff! I don't know what set me talking about such shits. Tell me, have you seen anything of O'Rourke lately?'

'O'Rourke? No, I haven't. Strange you should think of *him*. No, to tell the truth, I haven't even thought of him since I quit the job. . . .'

'Henry, you ought to be ashamed of yourself. O'Rourke is a prince. I don't see how you could possibly forget a man like that. Why shit, he was a real father to you—and to me too. I'd certainly like to know what's become of him.'

'We could look him up some night, that wouldn't be hard.'

'I'd like nothing better,' said O'Mara. 'It would give me a clean feeling just to be in his presence again.'

'You're a funny guy,' I said. 'Towards some people you're almost worshipful. It's like you're looking for your father all the time."

'That's just what I *am* doing—you hit it on the head. That son of a bitch who calls himself my father, you know what I think of *him*! Know what he's afraid of, that crud? That I'm going to rape my own sister one day. We're too close, he says. And that's the bastard who had me sent to the orphan asylum. He's another guy, talking of no-good pricks like Woodruff, whose balls I could bite off with relish. Except I'll bet he hasn't got any! Tries to palm himself off as a Russian. He's just a kike from Galicia. Sure, if I had had a father like O'Rourke I'd have made something of myself by this time. As it is, I don't know what I'm cut out for. I'm just drifting. Fighting the Church all the time. . . . By the way, I almost did put the boots to my sister, that's a fact. It was the old man who put the idea in my head. What the hell, it was only natural; I hadn't seen her for twelve years. She wasn't a sister any more, she was just a goodlooking dame, very lovable and very lonely. I don't know what the hell held me back. I must look her up sometime. She got married not long ago, I hear. Maybe it wouldn't be so bad now—I mean to have a whack at it. . . . Jesus, Alec would be horrified if he heard me talking this way.'

We went on in this fashion, from one reminiscence to another, until one ten sharp when, just as I had predicted, Mona walked in. She had a bundle of good things to eat in one arm and a bottle of Benedictine in the other. It was one of those kindly souls again who had bestowed his favours upon her. This time a retired baker from Weehawken, of all places. A man of culture too. Somehow, all her admirers had a tinge of culture, whether they were lumbermen, ex-pugilists, tanners or retired bakers from Weehawken.

Immediately Mona entered our talk became dispersed. O'Mara

had a way of grinning at her, when she began her yarns, which irritated her. In the beginning he used to interrupt her frequently. He could ask the most insultingly straightforward questions. 'You mean he didn't even try to put his arms around you?' Things like that, which were strictly taboo with Mona. But by now he had learned to hold his tongue and listen. Only occasionally would he come out with some sly remark, some subtle innuendo, which Mona took no notice of whatever. Now and then her exaggerations were so absurd that the two of us would burst into a fit of uncontrollable laughter. The curious thing was that Mona would also laugh her head off. Even stranger than her laughter, though, was her way of picking up again right where she had left off, as though nothing unusual had occurred.

Sometimes she would ask me to corroborate one of her outlandish statements, which I would do with a straight face, to O'Mara's astonishment. I would even embellish her statement with some fanciful facts of my own. To this she would nod her head gravely, as if it were God's truth I were recounting, as if we had spoken of it time and again—or as though we had rehearsed it together.

In the realm of make-believe she was thoroughly at home. She not only believed her own stories, she acted as if the fact that she had related them were proof of their veracity. Whereas, of course, everybody assumed quite the opposite. Everybody, I say. Which only made her more secure in her ways. Hers was distinctly a non-Euclidian logic.

I spoke of laughter. There was only one sort of laughter she ever indulged in—an hysterical laughter. Actually, she was almost devoid of humour. Those who aroused her sense of humour were usually people who were themselves devoid of humour. With Nahoum Yood, who was truly a humorist, she smiled. It was a good-natured smile, indulgent, affectionate, the sort one gives to a wayward child. Her smile, as a matter of fact, was quite a different thing from her laugh. Her smile was genuine and warming. It sprang from her sympathetic nervous system. Her laugh, on the other hand, was off-key, raucous, disconcerting. The effect was harsh. I had known her for a long time before I ever heard her laugh. Between her laughter and her weeping there was scarcely any difference. At the theatre she had learned how to laugh artificially. A terrifying thing to hear! It used to send shudders up my spine.

'You know what you two remind me of sometimes?' said O'Mara, snickering. 'You remind me of a pair of confederates. All that's lacking is the old shell game.'

'It's nice and toasty here though, eh what?' I answered.

'Listen,' said O'Mara, his face utterly serious, 'if we could stick it out here for a year or two I'd say it was worth while. We're in

81

clover now, and don't I know it! I haven't relaxed this way for years. The funny thing is, I feel as if I were hiding away, as if I had committed a crime which I can't remember. It wouldn't surprise me at all if one day the police knocked at the door.'

Here we all laughed uproariously. The police! Too funny for words.

'Once I was rooming with a guy,' said O'Mara, beginning one of his never-ending stories, 'and he was plain cuckoo. I didn't know it until someone from the asylum called for him. I swear to God he was the most normal-looking person you ever saw, and he talked normal, and acted normal. In fact, that's what was the matter with him—he was too god-damned normal. I was on my uppers at the time, too disheartened to even look for work. He had a job as a motorman—on the Reid Avenue carline. On his swings he'd come back to the room and rest up. He'd always bring a bag of doughnuts along and soon as he took off his things he'd make coffee. He never said much. Mostly he'd sit by the window and manicure his nails. Sometimes he'd take a shower and a rub down. If he was in high spirits he'd suggest playing a game of pinochle. We'd always play for small stakes and he'd always let me win, though he knew I was cheating him. I never asked him any questions about his past and he never volunteered anything on his own. Every day was a new day. If it was cold he talked about the weather, how cold it was; if it was warm, he talked about how warm it was. He never complained about a thing, not even when his pay was reduced. That in itself ought to have made me suspicious, but it didn't. He was so kind and considerate, so unobtrusive and delicate, that the worst I could think of him was to call him dull. Yet I couldn't very well complain about that, seeing as how he was taking care of me. Never once did he suggest that I ought to be up and stirring. All he ever wanted to know was if I were comfortable or not. I understood that he needed me, that he couldn't live alone—but that didn't make me suspicious either. Lots of people hate to live alone. Anyway, and why the hell I'm telling you all this I don't know, anyway, as I was saying before, one day there came a knock at the door and there stood the man from the asylum. Not a bad sort either, I must say. He mouseyed in quiet-like, sat down, and started talking to my friend. In that quiet, easy way he says—"Are you ready to go back with me?" Eakins, that was the guy's name, says, "Yes, of course," in the same easy, quiet way. After a few minutes Eakins excused himself to go to the bathroom and pack his things. The officer, or whatever the hell he was, didn't seem at all uneasy about letting the fellow out of his sight. He started talking to me. (It was the first time he had addressed a word to me.) It took me a few minutes to realize that he took me for a nut too. I got wise when he began asking me all sorts of funny, queasy questions—"Do you like it here? Does he feed you

82

well? Are you sure you're comfortable?" And so on. I was taken so unawares that I fell into the part as if it were made for me. Eakins had been in the bathroom a good fifteen minutes. I was getting fidgety, wondering how I would prove myself sane should the officer decide to take me along too. Suddenly the bathroom door opened softly. I looked up and there's Eakins stark naked, his hair completely shaved off and a douche bag hanging from his neck. He had a grin on his face that I had never seen before. I got a cold chill instanter.

' "Ready, sir," he says, just as smooth as butter.

' "Come now, Eakins," said the officer, "you know better than to dress that way."

' "But I'm *not* dressed," says Eakins blandly.

' "That's what I mean," said the officer. "Now go back and put your clothes on. That's a good fellow."

'Eakins didn't budge, didn't move a muscle.

' "What suit would you like me to wear?" he asks.

' "The one you had on," said the officer tartly.

' "But it's all torn," says Eakins, and with that he steps inside the bathroom. In a jiffy he's back in the doorway, holding the suit in his hands. It's in shreds.

' "That's all right," said the officer, trying not to appear disturbed, "your friend here will lend you a suit, I'm sure."

'He turns to me. I explain that the only suit I've got is the one I'm wearing.

' "That will do nicely," he chirps.

' "*What?* I yelled. "What am *I* goin' to wear?"

' "A fig leaf," he says, "and see that it don't shrink!" '

Just at this point there came a tapping on the window pane.

'The police, I bet!' shouted O'Mara.

I went to the window and drew up the shade. It was Osiecki, grinning that sheepish grin of his and gesticulating with his fingers.

'It's Osiecki,' I said, going to the door. 'He's probably lit up.'

'Where are your companions?' I asked as I shook his hand.

'They deserted me,' he said. 'Too many lice, I guess. . . . Is it O.K. to come in?' He hesitated at the doorway, not certain if he were welcome.

'Come in!' shouted O'Mara.

'Am I busting in on something?' He looked at Mona, not knowing who she was.

'This is my wife, Mona. Mona, this is a new friend of ours, Osiecki. He's had a little trouble lately. You don't mind if he stays a few minutes, do you?'

Mona immediately poured out a glass of Benedictine and offered him a piece of cake.

'What's this?' he asked, sniffing the liqueur. 'How do you get

83

it?' He looked from one to the other of us as if we were in possession of some dark secret.

'How are you feeling?' I asked.

'Right now, fine!' he answered. 'A little too good maybe. Can you smell it?' He blew his breath in our faces, grinning even more widely this time, like a rhododendron in full bloom.

'How are the lice coming along?' asked O'Mara in a casual tone.

At this Mona began to titter, then laughed outright.

'That's his trouble . . .' I started to explain.

'You can tell everything,' said Osiecki. 'It's no secret any more. We'll get to the bottom of it soon.' He raised himself up. 'Excuse me, but I can't drink this stuff. Too much turpentine in it. Have you any coffee?'

'Of course,' said Mona. 'Would you like a sandwich perhaps?'

'No, just some black coffee. . . .' He hung his head blushingly. 'I've just had a tiff with my pals. They're getting fed up with me, I guess. I don't blame them either. They're taken a lot these last few months. You know, sometimes I think I *am* a bit screwy.' He paused to note the effect this might have on us.

'That's all right,' I said, 'we're all a bit screwy. O'Mara here was just telling us a yarn about a nut he used to live with. You can be as whacky as you like, so long as you don't start breaking up the furniture.'

'You'd get queer yourself,' said Osiecki, 'if you had those things sucking your blood all night—and all day too.' He rolled up his trousers to show us the marks they had left. His legs were a mass of scratches and blood clots. I felt damned sorry for him, sorry I had twitted him.

'Perhaps if you moved to another apartment . . .' I ventured to suggest.

'No use,' he said, looking ruefully at the floor. 'They'll keep after me till I quit—or until I catch them red-handed.'

'I thought you were going to bring your girl around for dinner some evening?' said O'Mara.

'Sure, I am,' said Osiecki. 'Right now, though, she's busy.'

'Busy doing what?' asked O'Mara.

'I don't know. I've learned not to ask unnecessary questions.' He gave us another big grin. This time his teeth wobbled a little. I noticed that his mouth was full of braces.

'I dropped in,' he continued, 'because I saw the lights burning. I hate to go home, you know. (Grin: meaning more lice.) You don't mind my staying a few minutes, do you? I like this place—it's cheerful.'

'It should be,' said O'Mara, 'we're living on velvet.'

'I wish I could say the same,' droned Osiecki. 'Drawing plans all day and playing the pianola at night is no fun.'

'But you've got a girl,' said O'Mara. 'That ought to give you a little fun.' He chortled.

Osiecki's ferret-like eyes grew small as pin points. He looked at O'Mara sharply, almost hostilely. 'You're not trying to pump me, are you?' he asked.

O'Mara smiled good-naturedly and shook his head. He was just about to open his mouth when Osiecki spoke up again.

'She's another tribulation,' he began.

'Please,' said Mona, 'don't feel that you have to tell us everything. I think we've been asking altogether too many questions.'

'Oh, that's all right, I don't mind being grilled. I just wondered how he knew about my girl.'

'I don't know a thing,' said O'Mara. 'I just made a simple remark. Skip it!'

'I don't want to skip it,' said Osiecki. 'It's better to get it off one's chest.' He paused with head down, not forgetting however to munch his sandwich. After a few moments he looked up, smiling like a cherub, finished eating his sandwich, stood up and reached for his hat and coat. 'I'll tell you some other time,' he said. 'It's getting late.'

At the door, as we were shaking hands, he grinned again and said: 'By the way, any time you're hard pressed, just let me know —I can always lend you a little something to tide you over.'

'I'll walk you home, if you like,' said O'Mara, not knowing how else to express appreciation of this unexpected kindness.

'Thanks, but I'd rather be alone now. You never can tell . . .' and with that Osiecki took off at a trot.

'What about that guy Eakins you were telling us about?' I said, soon as the door had closed behind Osiecki.

'I'll tell you some other time,' said O'Mara, giving us one of Osiecki's grins.

'There wasn't a word of truth in it,' said Mona, tripping to the bathroom.

'You're right,' said O'Mara. 'I just imagined it.'

'Come on,' I said, 'you can tell *me*.'

'All right,' he said, 'since you want the truth, I'll give it to you. To begin with, there was no guy Eakins—it was my brother. He was hiding away for a while. You remember I told you once how we ran away from the orphan asylum together? Well, it was ten years—maybe more—before we met again. He had gone to Texas where he became a cow-puncher. A good guy, if ever there was one. Then he got into a brawl with someone—he must have been drunk—and he killed the guy.'

He took a sip of Benedictine, then continued: 'It was all like I told you, except of course he wasn't batty. The man who came for him was a Ranger. He scared the shit out of me, I can tell you. Anyway, I undressed, like he told me to, and I handed the clothes to my brother. He was taller and bigger than me in every way,

85

and I knew he'd never get into that suit. But I handed it to him and he went back to the bathroom to get dressed. I hoped he'd have sense enough to climb out by the bathroom window. I couldn't understand why the Ranger was giving him such leeway, but then I figured being from Texas he had his own way of doing things. Anyway, suddenly I got the bright idea to dash out into the street naked and yell "Murder! Murder!" at the top of my lungs. I got as far as the stairs and there I tripped on the rug. The big guy was right on top of me. He held one hand over my mouth and dragged me back to the room. "Pretty cute, mister, ain't you?" he said, giving me a gentle cuff in the jaw. "Now if that brother of yours gets out the window he won't get very far. My men are waiting for him right outside."

'At that moment my brother walked into the room just as quiet and easy as ever. He looked like a circus freak in that suit—and his hair all shaved off.

' "No use, Ted," he said, "they've got me." '

' "What am I going to do for clothes?" I bawled. '

' "I'll mail the suit back to you when we get to Texas," he said. Then he put his hand in his pocket and pulled out some crumpled bills. "Maybe this will hold you a while," he said. "It was good to see you again. Take care of yourself." And with that they left.'

'And what happened after that?'

'They sent him up for life.'

'No!'

'Yep! And you can lay that to that son of a bitch of a step-father. If he hadn't sent us to the orphan asylum it would never have happened.'

'Jesus, man you can't lay everything to that orphan asylum.'

'The hell I can't! Everything bad that happens to me dates from the orphan asylum.'

'But you haven't had it so bad, God-damn it! I really can't see why you're griping all the time. Shit, many people get worse deals and come out tip-top. You've got to stop blaming your step-father for all your ills and failings. What'll you do when he croaks?'

'I'll go on blaming him and cursing him just the same. I'll make him miserable even in the grave.'

'But listen, man, what about your mother? She had a hand in it too, don't forget. You don't seem to be sore at her.'

'She's a half-wit,' said O'Mara bitterly. 'I can only feel sorry for her. She did as she was told, probably. No, I don't hate her. She was a good-natured slob, in a way.'

'Listen, Henry,' he said, suddenly changing front, 'you'll never understand the situation. You were born with a silver spoon in your mouth. You've had it easy all your life. You've been lucky too. And you've got talents. Me, I'm nobody. A misfit. I've got a grudge against the world. . . . Maybe I could have been a writer too, if I had had a chance. As it is, I don't even know how to spell.'

'But you sure know how to figure.'

'Naw,' he said, 'don't try to sweeten it. I'm all wronged up. No matter what I do I end up by hurting people. You're the only guy I ever treated decently, do you know that?'

'Come off it,' I said, 'you're getting maudlin. Have another drink!'

'I'm going to bed,' he said. 'I'm going to dream it off.'

'Dream it off?'

'Sure, don't you ever do that—*dream it off*? You close your eyes and then you fix it like you want it to be. You fall asleep and you dream it true. When morning comes there's no bad taste in your mouth. . . . I've done it thousands of times. Learned it in the orphan asylum.'

'*The orphan asylum!* Man, will you ever forget it? It's finished, done with . . . it happened centuries ago. Can't you get that through your nut?'

'It's never stopped happening, you mean.'

For a few minutes neither of us spoke. O'Mara undressed quietly and slipped into bed. I switched out the lights and lit a candle. As I was standing there at the table, reflecting on all that had passed between us, I heard him softly say: '*Listen*. . . .'

'What is it?' I said. I thought for a moment he was going to sob.

'You don't know the half of it, Henry. The worst part was waiting for my mother to come and see me. Weeks went by, then months, then years. No sign of her. Once in a blue moon I got a letter or a little package. Always promises. She was going to come at Christmas or Thanksgiving, or some other holiday. But she never came. I was only three years old when we were packed off, remember that. I needed affection. The nuns weren't too bad. Some of them were adorable, as a matter of fact. But it wasn't the same kissing them as kissing one's mother. I used to beat my brains out trying to figure a way to escape. All I thought of was to run home and fling my arms around my mother. She was a good sort, you know, but weak. Weak in an Irish way, like me. Easy come, easy go. Nothing bothered her. But I loved her. I loved her more and more as time went on. When I got the chance to make a getaway I was like a wild colt. My instinct was to rush home, but then I thought—maybe they'll send me back to the asylum! So I just kept travelling—until I got to Virginia and met up with Dr McKinney . . . you know, the ornithologist.'

'Listen, Ted,' I said, 'you'd better get to sleep and dream it off. I'm sorry if I seemed a bit insensitive. I guess I'd feel the same way if I had been in your boots. Shit, tomorrow's another day. Think of what Osiecki's up against!'

'That's exactly what I was doing. He's a lonely bastard too. *And wanting to lend us money!* Jesus, he *must* be in a bad way!'

I went to sleep that night with the determination to knock the bloody orphan asylum out of O'Mara's head. All during the night, however, I was riding my old Chemnitz bicycle like mad, or else playing the piano. In fact, I would sometimes dismount and play a tune right in the street. In dreams it's not difficult to have a piano with you while riding a bicycle—it's only in waking life that you have difficulty managing such things. It was at a place called Bedford Rest, which I conveniently transposed in the dream, that I experienced the most delicious moments. This spot, the half-way mark to Coney Island along the famous cycle path which began at one end of Prospect Park, was where all the cyclists halted to take a brief rest either coming from or going to the island. Here, under arbours and trellises, with a fountain playing in the centre of the clearance, we lounged about, examining one another's wheels, feeling one another's muscles, rubbing one another down. The wheels were stacked up against the trees and fences, all in excellent condition, all gleaming, all well oiled. Pop Brown, as we called him, was the grand arbiter. He was the oldest among us—double the age of most of us—but he could keep up with the best of us. He always wore a heavy black sweater and tight-fitting black stocking cap; his face was gaunt, lined, and so wind-burned as to be almost black. I always thought of him as 'The Night Rider'. He was a machinist by trade and his passion was bike-racing. A simple man, a man of few words, but loved by all. It was he who had induced me to join the militia in order to be able to race on the flat floor of the armoury. Saturdays and Sundays I was always sure to meet Pop somewhere along the cycle path. He was my racing father, so to speak.

I suppose that the delicious aspect of these reunions resided in the fact that we all shared the same passion. I don't remember ever discussing anything but cycling with these fellows. We could eat, drink and sleep on the bike. Many a time, at unexpected hours of the day or night, I would encounter a solitary cyclist who, like myself, had stolen an hour or two in order to fly along that smooth gravel path. Now and then we passed a man on horseback. (There was another path for equestrians running parallel to the bicycle path.) These apparitions from another world were completely removed from us, as were the fools who rode in automobiles. As for motorcyclists, they were simply *non compos mentis*.

As I say, I was reliving it all again in dream. Even down to those equally delicious moments at the end of the ride when, as a good wheelman, I would turn the bike upside down and clean and oil it. Every spoke had to be wiped clean and made to shine; the chain had to be greased and the oil cups filled. If the wheels were out of line they were trued. That way, she was always in condition to ride at a moment's notice. This cleaning and polishing always took place in the yard, right by the front window. I had to lay newspapers on the ground in order to appease my mother who disapproved of grease spots on our stone flagging.

In the dream I'm riding sort of nice and easy by the side of Pop Brown. It was customary for us to fall into a slow pace for a mile or two, in order to chat and also to get our wind up for the terrific spurt to follow. Pop is telling me about the job he's going to get me, as mechanic. He promises to teach me all I need to know. I am amused at this because the only tool I know how to handle is the bicycle wrench. Pop says he's been observing me lately and has come to the conclusion that I'm an intelligent guy. He's disturbed because I always seem to be out of work. I try to tell him that I'm glad to be out of work because then I can ride the wheel more often, but he brushes this aside as irrelevant. He's determined to make me a first-class machinist. It's better than being a boiler-maker, he assures me. I haven't the slightest idea what it is to be a boiler-maker. 'You ought to get in trim for that road race next month,' he then cautions. 'Drink lots of water, all you can hold.' His heart, I learn, is giving him trouble lately. The doctor thinks he ought to give up the bike for a while. 'I'd rather die than do that,' says Pop. We flit from one thing to another, homely little topics, just right for a rolling conversation. There's a teasing breeze stirring and the leaves are beginning to fall; brown, gold, red leaves, dry as tinder, which make a most soothing crackle as we roll lightly over them. We're just getting nicely warmed up, nicely unlimbered.

Suddenly Pop shoots forward on the tail of another bike going at a fast clip. Turning his head he shouts: 'It's Joe Folger!' I'm off like a bat out of hell. *Joe Folger!* Why, that's one of the old six-day riders. I wonder what sort of pace he'll set us. Soon, to my astonishment, Pop shoots forward, dragging me along, and Joe Folger is tailing *me*. My heart is beating wildly. Three great riders: Henry Val Miller, Pop Brown, and Joe Folger. Where is Eddie Root, I wonder, and Frank Kramer? Where's Oscar Egg, that valiant Swiss champion? My head is tucked down like a ball between my shoulders; my legs have no feeling, I'm all pulse and beat. Everything is co-ordinated, moving smoothly, harmoniously, like an intricate clock.

Suddenly we've come to the ocean front. A dead heat. We're panting like dogs, but fresh as daisies just the same. Three great veterans of the track. I dismount and Pop introduces me to the great Joe Folger. 'Quite a lad,' says Joe Folger, sizing me up and down. 'Is he training for the big grind?' Suddenly he feels my thighs and calves, grabs my forearms, squeezes my biceps. 'He'll make the grade all right—good stuff.' I'm so thrilled that I'm blushing like a schoolboy. All I need now is to meet up some morning with Frank Kramer; I'll give him the surprise of his life.

We saunter about a bit, pushing our wheels along with one hand. How steady a wheel when directed by a skilled hand! We sit down to have a beer. Of a sudden I'm playing the piano, just to please Joe Folger. He's a sentimental cuss, I discover; I have to scratch my bean to think what will suit his fancy. While tickling the ivories we're transported, as happens only in dreams, to the training grounds somewhere in New Jersey. The circus folk are here for the Winter. Before we know it, Joe Folger is practising the loop-the-loop. A terrifying spectacle, especially when one is sitting up so close to the big incline. Clowns are walking around in full regalia, some playing the harmonica, others skipping rope or practising falls.

Soon a group has collected around us, taking our bicycles apart and performing tricks, à la Joe Jackson. All in pantomime, to be sure. I'm almost weeping because I'll never to able to put my bike together again, it's in so many pieces. 'Never mind, kid,' says the great Joe Folger, 'I'll give you *my* wheel. You'll win many a race with that!'

How Hymie comes into it I don't remember, but he's there of a sudden and looking terribly downcast. There's a strike on, he wants me to know. I ought to get back to the office as quickly as possible. They're going to marshal all the taxi-cabs in New York City to deliver the telegrams and cables. I apologize to Pop Brown and Joe Folger for quitting them so unceremoniously and dive into a car which is waiting. Going through the Holland Tunnel I doze off only to find myself on the cycle path once more. Hymie beside me riding a miniature bike. He looks like the fat man of the Michelin tyres. He can hardly push the thing, he's so winded. Nothing easier than for me to lift him by the scruff of the neck, bike and all, and carry him along. Now he's pedalling in the air. He seems happy as a dog. Wants a hamburger and a malted milk shake. No sooner said than done. As we ride along the boardwalk I grab off a hamburger and a milk shake, flipping the man a coin with my other hand. At Steeplechase we ride straight up the shoot-the-shoots, as easy as soaring into the blue. Hymie looks a bit bewildered now, but not frightened. Just bewildered.

'Don't forget to send some waybills to AX office in the morning,' I remind him.

'Watch it, Mr. M,' he begs, 'you almost went into the ocean that time.'

And now, by God, whom should we run into, drunk as a pope, but my old friend Stasu! He's just gotten out of the army, and his legs are still bow-legged from the cavalry drills.

'Who's that little runt with you?' he demands surlily.

Just like Stasu to begin with fiery words. Always had to be mollified before you could begin talking to him.

'I'm leaving for Chattanooga tonight,' he says. 'Must get back to the barracks.' And with that he waves good-bye.

'Is he a friend of yours, Mr M?' asks Hymie innocently.

'HIM? He's just a crazy Pole,' I answer.

'I don't like Poloks, Mr M. I'm scared of them.'

'What do you mean? We're in the U.S.A., remember that!'

'Makes no difference,' says Hymie. 'A Polok is a Polok any-where. You can't trust 'em.' His teeth were actually beginning to rattle.

'I ought to be getting home now,' he adds disconsolately. 'The wife'll be wondering where I am. Have you the time on you?'

'O.K. let's take the subway then. It'll be a little faster.'

'Not for *you*, Mr M!' says Hymie, giving me a wild flattering smirk.

'You said it, kid. I'm a champ, I am. Watch me do a spurt. . . .' And with that I shoot forward like rocket, leaving Hymie stand-ing there with arms up yelling for me to return.

The next thing I know, I'm directing taxi-cabs, a whole fleet of them, from the saddle. I've got on a loud-striped sweater, and with megaphone in hand I'm directing traffic. The whole city seems to give way, no matter in which direction I press. It's like riding through vapour. From the top of the American Tel. & Tel. Building the president and the vice-president are sending out messages; streams of ticker tape float through the air. It's like Lingbergh coming home again. The ease with which I circle around the cabs, darting in and out and always a leap ahead of them, is due to the fact that I'm riding Joe Folger's old bike. That guy sure knew how to handle a wheel. *Training?* What better training than this? Frank Kramer himself couldn't do better.

The best part of the dream was the return to Bedford Rest. There they were again, the boys all in different accoutre, the wheels bright and gleaming, the saddles just right, all with noses upturned, as if sniffing the breeze. It was good to be with them again, feel their muscles, examine their equipment. The leaves had grown thicker, the air was cooler now. Pop was rounding them up, promising them a good work-out this time. . . .

When I got home that night—it was always the same night no matter how much time had elapsed—my mother was waiting up for me. 'You've been a good boy today,' she said, 'I'm going to let you take your bicycle to bed with you.'

'Really?' I exclaimed, hardly able to believe my ears.

'Yes, Henry,' she said, 'Joe Folger was here a few minutes ago. He told me you would be the next world's champion.'

'*He said that, mamma? No, really?*'

'Yes, Henry, every word of it. He said I should fatten you up a little first. You're under weight.'

'Mamma,' I said, 'I'm the happiest man alive. I want to give you a big kiss.'

'Don't be silly,' she said, 'you know I don't like that.'

'I don't care, mamma, I'm going to kiss you just the same.' And with that I gave her a hug and squeeze that nearly split her in two.

'You're sure you meant it, mamma—about taking the bike to bed with me?'

'Yes, Henry. But don't get any grease on the sheets!'

'Don't worry, mamma,' I yelled. I was beside myself with joy. 'I'll spread some old newspapers in between. *How's that?*'

I woke up feeling around for the bicycle. 'What are you trying to do?' cried Mona. 'You've been clawing me for the last half hour.'

'I was looking for my wheel.'

'Your wheel? What wheel? You must be dreaming.'

I smiled. 'I *was* dreaming, a delicious dream too. All about my bike.'

She began to titter.

'I know, it sounds foolish, but it was a grand dream. I had a wonderful time.'

'Hey Ted,' I yelled, 'are you there?'

No answer. I called again.

'He must have left,' I mumbled. 'What time is it?'

It was high noon.

'I wanted to tell him something. Too bad he's left already.' I turned over on my back and stared up at the ceiling. Wisps of dream floated through my brain. I felt mildly seraphic. And somewhat hungry.

'You know what,' I mumbled, still dream-logged, 'I think I ought to go see that cousin of mine. Maybe he'll lend me the wheel for a space. What do you think?'

'I think you're just a little goofy.'

'Maybe, but I sure would love to ride that bike again. It used to belong to a six-day rider; he sold it to me at the track, you remember?'

'You've told me that several times.'

'What's the matter, aren't you interested? You never rode a wheel, I guess, did you?'

'No, but I've ridden horseback.'

'That's nothing. Unless you're a jockey. Well, shit, I guess it's silly to be thinking about that bike. Them days are done for.'

Suddenly I sat up and stared at her. 'What's the matter with you this morning? What's got you?'

'Nothing, Val, nothing.' She gave me a feeble smile.

'There is too,' I insisted. 'You're not yourself.'

She sprang out of bed. 'Get dressed,' she said, 'or it'll be dark before long. I'll fix breakfast.'

'Fine. Can we have bacon and eggs?'

'Anything you like. Only hurry!'

I couldn't see what there was to be hurrying about, but I did as she said. I felt marvellous—and hungry as a wolf. Between times I wondered what was eating her. Maybe her period coming on.

Too bad O'Mara had skipped off so early. There was something I wanted to tell him, something that had leaped to mind as I was coming out of the dream. Well, no doubt it would keep.

I threw back the curtains and let the sun stream in. The place was more beautiful than ever this morning, it seemed to me. Across the street a limousine was standing at the kerb, waiting to take milady on her shopping tour. Two big greyhounds were seated in the rear, quiet and dignified, as always. The florist was just delivering a huge bouquet. What a life! I preferred my own, however. If only I had that wheel again everything would be tops. Somehow the dream clung to be tenaciously. *The champ!* What a quaint idea!

We had hardly finished breakfast when Mona announced that she had to go somewhere for the afternoon. She would be back in time for dinner, she assured me.

'That's all right,' I said, 'take your time. I can't help it, but I feel too wonderful for words. It wouldn't matter what happened today, I'd still feel fine.'

'Stop it!' she begged.

'Sorry, girlie, but you'll feel better too once you step outdoors. Why, it's like Spring.'

In a few minutes she was gone. I felt so full of energy I couldn't decide what to do. Finally I decided not to do anything—just hop into the subway and get out at Times Square. I'd stroll about and let what happens happen.

By mistake I got out at Grand Central. Walking along Madison Avenue the notion seized me to look up my friend Ned. Ages it was since I last saw him. (He was back again in the advertising and promoting racket.) I'd drop in and say hello, then scram.

'*Henry!*' he blurts out, 'it's as if God himself sent you. *Am I in a mess!* There's a big campaign on and everybody's home ill. This damned thing (he flourished some copy) has got to be finished by tonight. It's life and death. Don't laugh! I'm serious. Wait, let me explain. . . .'

I sat down and listened. The long and short of it was that he was trying to write a piece of copy about the new magazine they were putting on the market. He had just the bone of an idea, nothing more.

'You can do it, I'm sure,' he implored. 'Write anything, so long as it makes sense. I'm in a fix, I tell you. Old man McFarland —you know who I mean, don't you?—is behind this business.

He's pacing up and down in there. Threatens to give us all the sack if something doesn't happen soon.'

The only thing to do was to say yes. I got what little dope he had to offer and sat down to the machine. Soon I was pounding away. I must have written three or four pages when he tiptoed in to see how I was doing. He began reading the copy over my shoulder. Soon he was clapping his hands and shouting Bravo! Bravo!

'Is it that good?' I asked, looking up at him with twisted neck.

'*Is it good*? It's superb! Listen, you're better than the guy who does this stuff. McFarland will go nuts when he sees this. . . .' He stopped abruptly, rubbing his hands and giving little grunts. 'You know what? I've an Idea. I'm going to introduce you to McFarland as the new man I've hired. I'm going to tell him that I persuaded you to take the job. . . .'

'But I don't want a job!'

'You don't have to take it. Of course not. I want to quiet him, that's all. Besides, the main purpose is to have you talk to him. You know who he is and all he's done. Can't you give him a little salve? Flatter the pants off him! Then go into a little spiel—you know what I mean. Give him some pointers on how to launch the magazine, how to appeal to the reader, and all that shit. Lay it on thick! He's in the mood to swallow anything.'

'But I hardly know anything about the damned thing,' I remonstrated. 'Listen, you'd better do it yourself. I'll stand behind you, if you like.'

'No you don't,' said Ned. 'You're going to do the talking. Just talk a blue streak . . . anything that comes into your head. I'm telling you, Henry, when he sees what you've written he'll listen to anything you say. I haven't been in this racket for nothing. I know a good thing when I see it.'

There was only one thing to do. I said O.K. 'But don't blame *me* if I ball things up,' I whispered, as we tiptoed towards the sanctum sanctorum.

'Mr McFarland,' said Ned in his best manner, 'this is an old friend of mine whom I wired the other day. He's been down in North Carolina working on a book. I begged him to come up and give us a hand. Mr Miller, Mr McFarland.'

As we shook hands I unconsciously made obeisance to the great figure of the magazine world. For a moment or two no one spoke. McFarland was sizing me up. I must say I took to him immediately. Man of action, there was in McFarland a brooding poetic streak which dyed all his gestures. 'He's no slouch, that's certain,' I thought to myself, wondering at the same time how it was that he could permit himself to be surrounded by nit-wits and half-wits.

Ned quickly explained that I had arrived only a few minutes ago and in that brief space of time, with scarcely any knowledge

94

of the project, had written the pages which he now proceeded to hand over.

'You're a writer, are you?' asked McFarland, glancing up at me and trying to read at the same time.

'You're the best judge of that,' I replied, employing the diplomatic style.

Silence for a good few minutes as McFarland carefully perused the copy. I was on pins and needles. To hoodwink a bird like McFarland wasn't simple. I forgot, incidentally, what I had written. Couldn't remember a single line.

Suddenly McFarland looked up, smiled warmly, and remarked that what I had written looked promising. I felt that a great deal more was implied. It was almost affection which he now inspired in me. The last thing in my mind was to deceive him. He was a man I would have enjoyed working for—if I were going to work for any one. Out of the corner of my eyes I observed Ned giving me the high sign.

For a fleeting moment, whilst gathering myself for the fling, I wondered what Mona would say if she were witness to the show. ('And don't forget to tell O'Mara about the fathers!' I whispered to myself.)

McFarland was speaking. He had begun so quietly and smoothly that I was hardly aware of it. Right from the start I had again the conviction that he was no man's dupe. People had said of him that he was finished, that his ideas were out-dated. Seventy-five he was, and still going strong. A man of his stamp could never be licked. I listened to him attentively, nodding now and then, and beaming with admiration. He was a man after my own heart. A gambler and a dare-devil. . . . I wondered if I shouldn't seriously consider working for him.

It was quite a long speech the old boy was making. Despite all the signalling from Ned, I couldn't determine where to bust in. McFarland had obviously welcomed our intrusion; seething with ideas, he had been pacing back and forth, champing at the bit. Our entrance upon the scene enabled him to let off steam. I was all for letting him go on. Now and then I nodded my head more vigorously or made some little exclamation of surprise or approval. Besides, the more he talked the better prepared I would be when it came my turn.

He was on his feet now, shifting restlessly about, pointing to the charts, the maps, and what not which ranged the walls. He was a man at home in the world, a man who had traversed the globe many times and could speak from first-hand knowledge of it. As I understood it, he was trying to impress me with the fact that he wanted to reach all the peoples of the world, the poor as well as the rich, the ignorant as well as the educated. The periodical was to come out in many languages, many formats. It was to produce a revolution in the magazine world.

95

Suddenly he stopped, out of weariness. He sat down at the big desk and poured himself a glass of water from the beautiful silver pitcher.

Instead of trying to show him how smart I was, I took the occasion after a respectful silence, to tell him how much I had always admired him and the ideas he had championed. I said it sincerely, and it was the right thing to say at the moment, I was sure of it. I could feel Ned growing more and more fidgety. All he could think of was the big spiel I was to pull off. Finally he couldn't hold back any longer.

'Mr Miller would like to tell you a few things he thought of in connection with. . . .'

'Not at all,' said I, jumping to my feet. Ned looked bewildered. 'I mean, Mr McFarland, that it would be silly of me to advance my half-baked ideas. It seems to me you've covered the ground quite thoroughly.'

McFarland was visibly pleased. Suddenly recalling the reason for my presence, he picked up the copy lying before him and pretended to study it again.

'How long have you been writing?' he asked, giving me a long, penetration look. 'Have you done this kind of work before?'

I confessed that I hadn't.

'I thought so,' he said. 'Maybe that's why I like this. You've got a fresh view of things. And an excellent command of language. What are you working on now, if I may ask?'

He had me in a corner. Since he was so frank and direct there was nothing to do but return the fire pointblank.

'The truth is,' I stammered, 'I've only just begun to write. I try my hand at most everything, but nothing takes shape yet. I did write a book a few years ago, but I guess it was a pretty poor one.'

'It's better that way,' said McFarland. 'I don't care for brilliant young writers. A man needs something under his belt before he can express himself. Before he really has anything to say, I mean.' He drummed on the desk top, ruminating. Then he resumed: 'I'd like to see one of your yarns some time. Are they realistic or imaginative?'

'Imaginative, I hope.' I said it timidly.

'Good!' he said. 'All the better. Maybe we can use something of yours soon.'

I didn't know quite what to say to this. Fortunately Ned came to my rescue.

'Mr Miller is being modest, Mr McFarland. I've read almost everything he's written. He's got real talent. In fact, I might even say I think he has genius.'

'*Genius*, hum! That's even more interesting,' said McFarland.

'Don't you think I had better finish that copy?' I put in, addressing the old man.

'Take it easy,' he said, 'we have lots of time. . . . Tell me, what did you do before you began writing?'

I gave him a brief account of my youthful adventures. When I began relating my experiences in the cosmococcic realm he sat up. From here on it was one interruption after another. He kept forcing me to go into more and more detail. Presently he was on his feet again, moving about with tigerish strides. 'Go on, go on!' he urged, 'I'm listening.' He swallowed avidly every word. He demanded more and more. 'Bully, bully!' he kept exclaiming.

Suddenly he stopped dead in front of me. 'Have you written about this yet?'

I shook my head.

'Good! Now, supposing you were to write a serial for me. . . . Do you think you could write it the way you were telling it a moment ago?'

'I don't know, sir. I could try.'

'*Try?* Shucks! Do it, man. Do it right away. . . . *Here!*' and he handed Ned the pages I had written. 'Don't let this man waste his time on this nonsense. Get somebody else to do it.'

'But there's nobody to do it,' said Ned, delighted and crestfallen at the same time.

'Go out and find some one, then,' bellowed McFarland. 'Copywriters aren't hard to find.'

'Yes sir,' said Ned.

Once again McFarland drew close to me, this time pointing his finger right in my face. 'As for you, young man,' he said, almost snorting now, 'I want you to go home and start that serial tonight. We'll start you off in the first issue. But don't get literary on me, do you understand? I want you to tell your story just as you related it to me a minute ago. Can you dictate to a stenographer? I suppose not. Too bad. That would be the best way to get it out of you. Now listen to me. . . . I'm not a spring chicken any more. I've had lots of experience and I've met lots of men who thought themselves geniuses. Don't worry about whether you're a genius or not. Don't even think of yourself as a writer. Just pour it out—easy and natural—as if you were telling it to a friend. You'll be telling it to *me*, see? I'm your friend. I don't know if you're a great writer or not. You've got a story to tell, that's what interests me. . . . If you do this chore satisfactorily, I'll have something more exciting for you to tackle. I can send you to China, India, Africa, South America—wherever you please. The world is big and there's room in it for a lad like you. By the time I was twenty-one I had been around the world three times. By the time I was twenty-five I knew eight languages. By the time I was thirty I owned a string of magazines. I've been a millionaire twice over. Doesn't mean a thing. Don't let money occupy your thoughts! I've been broke too—*five times*. I'm broke now.' He tapped his bean. 'If you have courage and imagination there'll always be people to lend you money. . . .'

He looked at Ned sharply. 'I'm getting hungry,' he said. 'Could you send someone for sandwiches? I forgot all about lunch.'

'I'll go myself,' said Ned, starting for the door.

'Bring enough for all of us,' shouted McFarland. 'You know what I like. And bring some coffee too—*strong coffee.*'

When Ned returned he found us carrying on like old pals. A glow of delight swept his features.

'I've just been telling Mr McFarland that I wasn't in North Carolina at all,' I said. Ned's face fell. 'Besides, he knows the very house I'm living in. The judge who used to own the apartment—well, they're old friends.'

'I think,' said McFarland, 'I'm going to send this young man to Africa, after he writes that serial for us. *To Timbuktu!* He says he's always had a hankering to go there.'

'That sounds wonderful,' said Ned, spreading the food on the big desk and serving the coffee.

'The time to travel is when you're young,' McFarland continued. 'And with little money. I remember my first trip to China. . . .' Here he began munching a sandwich. 'When you forget to eat you know you're alive.'

It was an hour or so later when I left the office. My head was spinning. Ned had made me promise to finish the copy at home, on the q.t. He said the old man had sure fallen for me. In the hall, as I was waiting for the elevator, he caught up with me. 'You won't let me down, will you? Mail it to me tonight special delivery. Stay up all night if you have to. Thanks!' He squeezed my hand.

The place was in darkness when I arrived home. I was so drunk with excitement that I had to swallow a few tumblers of sherry to calm myself. I wondered what Mona would say on hearing about my splurge. I forgot all about the copy in my coat pocket—all I could think of was Timbuktu, China, India, Persia, Siam, Borneo, Burma, the great wheel, the dusty caravan routes, the odours and sights of the Far East, boats, trains, steamers, camels, the green waters of the Nile, the Mosque of Omar, the souks of Fez, outlandish tongues, the jungle, the veldt, the *bled*, beggars and monks, jugglers, mountebanks, temples, pagodas, pyramids. My brain was in such a whirl that if someone didn't appear soon I would go mad.

There I sat, in the big chair at the front window. The light of a candle flickered unsteadily. Suddenly the door opened softly. It was Mona. She came over to me, put her arms around me and kissed me tenderly. I felt a tear run down her cheek.

'You're still sad? What on earth's the matter?'

For answer she threw herself in my lap. In a moment her arms

98

were about me. She was sobbing. I let her weep for a while, comforting her silently.

'Is it so very terrible?' I asked after a time. 'Can't you even tell *me*?'

'No, Val, I can't. It's too ugly.'

Little by little I succeeded in worming it out of her. Her family again. She had been to see her mother. Things were more desperate than ever. Something about a mortgage—had to be paid at once or they would lose the house.

'But it isn't that,' she said, still sniffling, 'it's the way she treats me. As though I were dirt. She doesn't believe I'm married. She called me a whore.'

'Then for Christ's sake let's stop worrying about her,' I said angrily. 'A mother who talks like that is no god-damned good. Anyway, it's fantastic. Where would we get three thousand dollars in a hurry? She must be out of her mind.'

'Please don't talk that way, Val. You only make it worse.'

'I despise her,' I said. 'I can't help it if she's your mother. To me she's just a leech. Let her go drown herself, the stupid old bitch!'

'Val! Val! *Please.* . . .' She began to weep again, more violently than before.

'All right, I won't say another word. I'm sorry I let my tongue run away with me.'

Just then the bell rang, followed by a few quick taps on the window-pane. I jumped up and ran to the door. Mona was still weeping.

'Well, I'll be damned,' I exclaimed, when I saw who stood there.

'You ought to be damned, hiding away from a bosom friend all this time. Here I am living around the corner and neither hide nor sight of you. Same old bastard, aren't you? Well, how are you anyway? Can I come in?'

He was the last person I wanted to see at that moment—MacGregor.

'What's up . . . someone die?' he exclaimed, seeing the candle and Mona huddled in the big chair, the tears streaming down her face. 'Been having a tiff, is that it?' He went up to Mona and held out his hand, thought better of it, and stroked her head. 'Don't let him get you down,' he mumbled, trying to display a little sympathy. 'A nice thing to be doing at this time of day. Have you folks had dinner yet? I thought I'd stop by and invite you out. I didn't dream I was going to enter a house of mourning.'

'For God's sake, can it!' I begged. 'Why don't you wait till I explain things.'

'Please don't say anything, Val,' said Mona. 'I'll be all right in a moment.'

'That's the way to talk,' said MacGregor, sitting down beside

99

her and putting on a professional air. 'Nothing is ever as bad as you imagine it to be.'

'For Christ's sake, must we listen to that crap? Can't you see she's in trouble?'

At once his manner altered. Rising to his feet he said solemnly: 'What is it, Hen, is it something serious? I'm sorry if I put my foot in it.'

'It's all right, just don't say anything for a while. I'm glad you came. Maybe it would be a good idea to go out for dinner.'

'You two go, I'd rather stay here,' pleaded Mona.

'If there's anything I can do . . .' MacGregor began.

I burst out laughing. 'Sure there's something you can do,' I said. 'Raise three thousand dollars for us by tomorrow morning!'

'Jesus, man, is that what's worrying you?' He pulled a big cigar from his breast pocket and bit the end off. 'I thought it was something tragic.'

'I was kidding you,' I said. 'No, it's got nothing to do with money.'

'I can always lend you ten bucks,' said MacGregor cheerily. 'When it comes to thousands you're talking a foreign language. Nobody has three thousand dollars to hand out right off the bat, don't you know that yet?'

'But we don't want three thousand dollars,' I said.

'Then what's she crying for—the moon?'

'Please go and leave me alone, won't you?' said Mona.

'We couldn't do that,' said MacGregor, 'it wouldn't be sporting. Listen girlie, whatever it is, I swear it isn't as bad as you think. There's always a loophole, remember that. Come on, wash your face and put your duds on, eh? I'll take you to a *good* restaurant this time.'

The door suddenly swung open. There stood O'Mara, slightly boiled. He looked as though he were delivering manna from above.

'How did *you* get in?' was MacGregor's greeting. 'The last time I laid eyes on you was at a poker game. You swindled me out of nine bucks. *How are you?*' He stuck out a paw.

'O'Mara's living with us,' I hastened to explain.

'That settles it,' said MacGregor. 'Now you've really got something to worry about. I wouldn't trust this guy even in a straitjacket.'

'What's up?' said O'Mara, suddenly aware of Mona all hunched up in the big chair, her face streaked with tears. 'What's wrong?'

'Nothing serious,' I said. 'I'll tell you later. Have you had dinner?'

Before he could say yes or no MacGregor piped up: 'I didn't invite *him*. He come if he pays his own way, sure. But not as my guest.'

O'Mara simply grinned at this. He was in too good a mood to be upset by a little plain talk.

'Listen, Henry,' he said, making a bee line for the sherry, 'I've got lots to tell you. Wonderful things. I had a great day today.'

'So did I,' said I.

'Do you mind if I help myself to a drink too?' said MacGregor. 'Seeing as how it was such a good day for you guys, maybe a drink will do me good.'

'Are we going out for dinner?' asked O'Mara. 'I don't want to spill the beans till we get set somewhere. There's too much to tell, I don't want to spoil it going off half-cocked.'

I went over to Mona. 'You're sure you don't want to come with us?'

'Yes, Val, I'm sure,' she said weakly.

'Oh come on,' said O'Mara, 'I've got grand news for you.'

'Sure, pull yourself together,' said MacGregor. 'It's not every-day I invite people to eat with me—especially in a *good* res-raurant.'

The upshot was that Mona finally consented to go. We sat down to wait for her while she tidied up. We drank some more sherry.

'You know, Hen,' said MacGregor, 'I have a hunch I may be able to do something for you. What are you doing these days? Writing, I suppose. And broke, eh? Listen, we need a typist in our office. It doesn't pay much, but it may tide you over. *Until you're recognized*, I mean.' He finished this off with a leer and a chuckle.

O'Mara laughed in his face. '*A typist!* Haw Haw!'

'That's mighty white of you, Mac,' I said, 'but right now I don't need a job. I just landed a big one today.'

'*What?*' yelled O'Mara. 'Cripes, don't tell me that! I just fixed one up for you myself—a beauty too. That's what I wanted to tell you about.'

'It isn't really a job,' I explained, 'it's a commission. I'm to write a serial for a new magazine. After that I may be going to Africa, China, India. . . .'

MacGregor couldn't restrain himself. 'Forget it, Henry,' he burst out, 'somebody's been taking you for a ride. The job I'm talking about pays twenty a week. *Real money*. Write your serial on the side. If it turns out O.K. nothing's lost. Right? But honest, Henry, aren't you old enough to know that you can't count on such things? When are you going to grow up?'

Mona now joined in. 'What's this I hear about a job? Val doesn't want a job. You're talking nonsense, all of you.'

'Come on, let's go,' urged MacGregor. 'The place I'm taking you to is in Flatbush. I've got a car outside.'

We piled in and drove to the restaurant. The proprietor seemed to know MacGregor well. Probably a client of his.

I was astounded to hear MacGregor say: 'Order anything you like. And how about a cocktail first?'

'Has he any good wine?' I asked.

'Who's talking about wine?' said MacGregor. 'I asked you if you'd like a cocktail first.'

'Sure I would. I'd like to see the wine card too.'

'Just like you. Always making it difficult for me. Sure, go ahead, order wine if you must. I never touch it. Makes my stomach sour.'

They served us a good soup first and then came a luscious roast duckling. 'I told you it was a good place, didn't I?' crowed MacGregor. 'When did I ever let you down, tell me, you bastard. . . . So a typist's job isn't good enough for you, is that it?'

'Val's a writer, not a typist,' said Mona sharply.

'I know he's a writer,' said MacGregor, 'but a writer has to eat once in a while, doesn't he?'

'Does he look as though he were starving?' she retorted. 'What are you trying to do, bribe us with your good meal?'

'I wouldn't talk that way to a good friend,' said MacGregor, his dander rising. 'I merely wanted to make sure he was O.K. I've known Henry when he wasn't sitting so comfortably.'

'Those days are past,' said Mona. 'As long as I'm with him he'll never starve.'

'Fine!' snapped MacGregor. 'Nothing better I'd like to hear. But are you sure you'll always be able to provide for him? Supposing something were to happen to you? Supposing you become an invalid?'

'You're talking nonsense. I couldn't possibly be an invalid.'

'Lots of people have thought that way, but it happened just the same.'

'Stop croaking,' I begged. 'Listen, give us the truth. Why are you so eager for me to take that job?'

He broke into a broad grin. 'Waiter!' he shouted, 'some more wine!' Then he chuckled. 'Can't put anything over on you, can I Henry? *The truth*, you say. The truth is I wanted you to take the job just to have you around. I miss you. Fact is, the job pays only fifteen a week; I was going to add the other five out of my own pocket. Just for the pleasure of having you near me, just to listen to you rave. You can't imagine how dull these bastards are in the law business. I don't know what they're talking about half the time. As for work, there's not much to do. You could write all the stories you like—or whatever the hell it is you're doing. I mean it. You know, it's over a year since I last saw you. At first I was sore. Then I figured, hell, he's just got married. I know how it is. . . . So you're serious about this writing business, eh? Well, you must know your own mind. It's a tough game, but maybe you can beat 'em at it. I toy with the idea myself sometimes. Of course I never considered myself a *genius*. When I see the crap that's peddled around I figure nobody's looking for genius anyway. It's as bad as the law game, believe it or not. Don't think I've got a cinch of it! The old man had more sense than either of us. He became an iron moulder. He'll outlive all of us, that old buzzard.'

'I say, you guys,' O'Mara broke in, 'can I get a word in edgewise? Henry, I've been trying to tell you something for the last hour or more. I met a chap today who's nuts about your work. He coughed up a year's subscription for the *Mezzotints*. . . .'

'*Mezzotints?* What's he talking about?' MacGregor exclaimed. 'We'll tell you later. . . . Go on, Ted!'

It was a long story, as usual. Apparently, O'Mara hadn't been able to fall asleep after our talk about the orphan asylum. He had got to thinking about the past, and then everything under the sun. Despite the lack of sleep he arose early, filled with a desire to do something. Packing my scripts—the whole caboodle —in his brief case, he set out with the intention of tackling the first man he should bump into. To change his luck he had decided to go to Jersey City. The first place he stumbled into was a lumber yard. The boss had just arrived and was in a good mood. 'I fell on him like a ton of bricks, just swept him off his feet,' said O'Mara. 'I don't know what I was saying, to tell you the truth. I knew only that I had to sell him.' The lumber man turned out to be a good egg. He didn't know what it was all about either, but he was disposed to help. Somehow O'Mara had managed to transpose the whole thing to a very personal level. He was selling the man his good friend Henry Miller, whom he believed in. The man wasn't much for books and that sort of thing but the prospect of aiding a budding genius, oddly enough, appealed to him. 'He was writing out a cheque for the subscription,' said O'Mara, 'when the idea came to me to make him do something more. I pocketed the cheque first, of course, and then I dug out your manuscripts. I put the whole pile on his desk, right in front of him. He wanted to know immediately how long it had taken you to write such a slew of words. I told him six months. He nearly fell off his chair. Naturally, I kept talking fast so that he wouldn't start reading the bloody things. After a while he leaned back in his swivel chair and pressed a button. His secretary appeared. 'Get out the files on that publicity campaign we had last year,'' he ordered.'

'I know what's coming,' I couldn't help remarking.

'Wait a minute, Henry, let me finish. Now comes the good news.'

I let him ramble on. As I anticipated, it was a job. Only I wouldn't be obliged to go to the office every day; I could do the work at home.

'Of course you'll have to spend a little time with him occasionally,' said O'Mara. 'He's dying to meet you. And what's more, he's going to pay you handsomely. You can have seventy-five a week on account, to begin with. How's that? You stand to make between five and ten thousand before you're through with the job. It's a cinch. I could do it myself, if I knew how to write. I brought some of the crap he wants you to look over. You can write that stuff with your left-hand.'

'It sounds fine,' I said, 'but I just had another offer today. Better than that.'

O'Mara wasn't too pleased to hear this.

'Seems to me,' said MacGregor, 'that you guys are doing pretty well without my help.'

'It's all foolishness,' Mona put in.

'Listen,' said O'Mara, 'why don't you let him earn some money honestly? It's only for a few months. After that you can do as you please.'

The word honestly rung in MacGregor's ears. 'What's he doing now?' he asked. He turned to me. 'I thought you were writing. What is it, Hen, what are you up to now?'

I gave him a brief resumé of the situation, making it as delicate as I could for Mona's sake.

'For once I think O'Mara's right,' he said. 'You'll never get anywhere this way.'

'I wish you people would mind your own business,' blurted Mona.

'Come, come,' said MacGregor, 'don't stand on your high horse with us. We're old friends of Henry's. We wouldn't be giving him bad advice, would we now?'

'He doesn't need advice,' she replied. 'He knows what he's doing.'

'O.K. sister, have it your way then!' With this he turned abruptly to me again. 'What was that other proposition you started to tell about? You know—China, India, Africa. . . .'

'Oh *that*,' I said, and I began to smile.

'What are you shying off for? Listen, maybe you'll need me for a secretary. I'd give up the law in a minute if there was anything to grab hold of. I mean it, Henry.'

Mona excused herself to make a telephone call. That meant she was too disgusted to hear a word about the 'proposition'.

'What's griping her?' said O'Mara. 'What was she weeping for when I came home?'

'It's nothing,' I said. 'Family troubles. *Money*, I guess.'

'She's a queer girl,' said MacGregor. 'Don't mind my saying that, do you? I know she's devoted to you and all that, but her ideas are all wet. She'll be getting you into a jam if you don't watch out.'

O'Mara's eyes were glistening. 'You don't know the half of it,' he chirped. 'That's why I was so keen to do something this morning.'

'Listen, you guys, stop worrying about me. I know what I'm doing.'

'The hell you do!' said MacGregor. 'You've been telling me that as long as I know you—*and where are you?* Every time we meet you're in a new predicament. One of these days you'll be asking me to bail you out of jail.'

'All right, all right, but let's talk about it some other time. Here she comes—let's change the subject. I don't want to rile her more than necessary—she's had a hard day of it.'

'And so you've really got many fathers,' I continued without a pause, looking straight at O'Mara. Mona was lowering herself into her seat. 'It's like I was saying a moment ago . . .'

'What is this—double talk?' said MacGregor.

'Not for *him*,' I said, never moving a muscle. 'I should have explained the talk we had the night before, but it's too long. Anyway, as I was saying, when I came out of the dream I knew exactly what I had to tell you.' (Looking steadfastly at O'Mara all the while.) 'It had nothing to do with the dream.'

'What dream?' said MacGregor, slightly exasperated now.

'The one I just explained to you,' I said. 'Listen, let me finish talking to him, will you?'

'Waiter!' called MacGregor, 'Ask these gentlemen what they would like to drink, will you?' To us—'I'm going to take a leak.'

'It's like this,' I said, addressing O'Mara, 'you're lucky you lost your father when you were a kid. Now you can find your real father—and your real mother. It's more important to find your real father than your real mother. You've found several fathers already, but you don't know it. You're rich, man. Why resurrect the dead? Look to the living! Why shit, there are fathers everywhere, all around you, better fathers by far than the one who gave you his name or the one who sent you to the asylum. To find your real father you first have to be a good son.'

O'Mara's eyes were twinkling. 'Go on,' he urged, 'it *sounds* good even though I don't know what the hell it all means.'

'But it's simple,' I said. 'Now look—*take me*, for instance. Did you ever think how lucky you were to find *me*? I'm not your father, but I'm a damned good brother to you. Do I ever ask you any embarrassing questions when you hand me money? Do I urge you to look for a job? Do I say anything if you lie in bed all day?'

'What's the meaning of all this?' demanded Mona, amused in spite of herself.

'You know very well what I'm talking about,' I replied. 'He needs affection.'

'We all do,' said Mona.

'We don't need a thing,' said I. 'Not really. We're lucky, all three of us. We eat every day, we sleep well, we read the books we want to read, we go to a show now and then . . . and we have one another. *A father?* What do we need a father for? Listen, that dream I had settled everything—for me. I don't even need a bike. If I can have a dream ride now and then, O.K.! It's better than the real thing. In dreams you never puncture a tyre; if you do, it doesn't matter a straw. You can ride all day and all night without getting exhausted. Ted was right. One has to learn to dream it off. . . . If I hadn't had that dream I wouldn't have met that guy McFarland today. Oh, I haven't told you about that, have I? Well, never mind, some other time. The point is I was offered a chance to write—for a new magazine. A chance to travel, too. . . .'

'You never told me a thing about it,' said Mona, all ears now. 'I want to hear. . . .'

'Oh, it *sounded* good,' said I, 'but the chances are it would turn out to be another flop.'

'I don't understand,' she persisted. 'What were you to write for him?'

'The story of my life, no less.'

'Well. . . ?'

'I don't think I can do it. Not like he wanted me to, at any rate.'

'You're crazy,' said O'Mara.

'You're going to turn it down?' said Mona, completely mystified by my attitude.

'I'll think it over first.'

'I don't understand you at all,' said O'Mara. 'Here you've got the chance of a lifetime and you . . . why, a man like McFarland could make you famous overnight.'

'I know,' I said, 'but that's just what I'm afraid of. I'm not ready for success yet. Or rather I don't want that kind of success. Between you and me—I'm going to be damned honest with you —I don't know how to write. Not yet! I realized that immediately he made me the offer to write the damned serial. It's going to take a long time before I know how to say what I want to say. Maybe I'll never learn. And let me tell you another thing while I'm at it. . . . I don't want any jobs between times . . . neither publicity jobs nor newspaper jobs nor any kind of job. All I ask is to dawdle along in my own way. I keep telling you people I know what I'm doing. I mean it. Maybe it doesn't make sense, but it's *my* way. I can't navigate any other way, do you understand?'

O'Mara said nothing, but I sensed he was sympathetic. Mona, of course, was overjoyed. She thought I had underrated myself but she was terribly pleased that I wasn't going to take a job. Once again she repeated what she had always been telling me: 'I want you to do as you please, Val. I don't want you to think about anything but your work. I don't care if it takes ten years or twenty years. I don't care if you never succeed. Just write!'

'If *what* takes ten years?' asked MacGregor, returning just in time to catch the tail end.

'To become a writer,' I said, giving him a good-natured grin.

'You're still talking about that? Forget it! You're a writer now, Henry, only nobody knows it but you. Have you finished eating? I've got to go somewhere. Let's get out of here. I'll drop you off at the house.'

We cleared out in a hurry. He was always in a hurry, MacGregor, even to attend a poker game, as it turned out. 'A bad habit,' he said, half to himself. 'I never win either. If I really had something to do I suppose I'd get over such nonsense. It's just a way of killing time.'

'Why do you have to kill time?' I asked. 'Couldn't you hang on with us? You could kill time just as well by chewing the fat. If you *must* kill time, I mean.'

'That's true,' he answered soberly, 'I never thought of that. I don't know, I've got to be on the go all the time. It's a weakness.'

'Do you ever read a book any more?'

He laughed. 'I guess not, Henry. I'm waiting for you to write some. Maybe then I'll read again.' He lit a cigarette. 'Oh, now and then I do pick up a book,' he confessed rather sheepishly, 'but it's never a good one. I've lost all sense of taste. I read a few lines to send myself to sleep, that's the truth of it, Henry, I can no more read Dostoievsky now, or Thomas Mann, or Hardy, than I can cook a meal. I haven't the patience . . . nor the interest. You get stale grinding away in an office. Remember, Hen, how I used to study when we were kids? Jesus, I had ambition then. I was going to burn up the world, wasn't I? *Now* . . . aw well . . . it doesn't matter a damn. In our racket nobody gives a shit whether you've read Dostoievsky or not. The important thing is—*can you win the case?* You don't require much intelligence to win a case, let me tell you that. If you're really clever, you manage to stay out of court. You let somebody else do the dirty work. Yeah, it's the old story, Henry. I get sick of harping on it. Nobody should take up law who wants to keep his hands clean. If he does he'll starve. . . . You know, I'm always twitting you about being a lazy son of a bitch. I guess I envy you. You always seem to be having a good time. You have a good time even when you're starving to death. I *never* have a good time. Not any more. Why I ever got married I don't know. To make someone else miserable, I suppose. It's amazing the way I gripe. No matter what she does for me it's wrong. I do nothing but bawl the shit out of her.'

'Oh come,' I said, to egg him on, 'you're not as bad as all that.'

'Ain't I, though? You should live with me for a few days. Listen, I'm so god-damned ornery I can't even live with myself —*how do you like that?*'

'Why don't you cut your throat?' I said, giving him a broad

smile. 'Really, when things get that bad, there's no alternative.'

'You're telling *me*?' he cried. 'I have it out with myself every day. Yes sir' and he banged the wheel emphatically—'every day of my life I ask myself whether I should go on living or not.'

'The trouble is you're not serious,' I said. 'You only have to ask yourself that question once and you know.'

'You're wrong, Henry! It's not as easy as all that,' he remonstrated. 'I wish it were. I wish I could toss a coin and have done with it.'

'That's no way to settle it,' I said.

'I know, Henry, I know. But you know *me*! Remember the old days? Christ, I couldn't even decide whether to take a crap or not.' He laughed in spite of himself. 'Have you noticed, as you get older things seem to take care of themselves. You don't debate what to do every step of the way. You just grouse.'

We were pulling up to the door. He lingered over the farewell. 'Remember, Henry,' he said, feathering the gas pedal, 'if you get stuck there's always a job for you at Randall, Randall and Randall's. Twenty a week regular. . . . Why don't you look me up once in a while? Don't make me run after you all the time!'

4

'I FEEL IN MYSELF a lift so luminous,' says Louis Lambert, 'that I might enlighten a world, and yet I am shut up in a sort of mineral.' This statement, which Balzac voices through his double, expresses perfectly the secret anguish of which I was then a victim. At one and the same time I was leading two thoroughly divergent lives. One could be described as 'the merry whirl', the other as the contemplative life. In the role of active being everybody took me for what I was, or what I appeared to be; in the other role no one recognized me, least of all myself. No matter with what celerity and confusion events succeeded one another, there were always intervals, self-created, in which through contemplation I lost myself. It need only a few moments, seemingly, of shutting out the world for me to be restored. But it required much longer stretches—of being alone with myself—to write. As I have frequently pointed out, the business of writing never ceased. But from this interior process to the process of translation is always, and was then very definitely, a big step. Today it is often hard for me to remember when or where I made this or that utterance, to remember whether I actually said it somewhere or whether I intended to say it some time or other. There is an ordinary kind of forgetting and a special kind; the latter is due, more than likely, to the vice of living in two worlds at once. One of the consequences of this tendency is that you live everything out innumerable times. Worse, whatever you succeed in transmitting to paper seems but an infinitesimal fraction of what you've already written in your head. That delicious experience with which every one is familiar, and which occurs with haunting impressiveness in dreams—I mean of falling into a familiar groove: meeting the same person over and over again, going down the same street, confronting the identically same situation—this experience often happens to me in waking moments. How often I rack my brains to think where it was I made use of a certain thought, a certain situation, a certain character! Frantically I wonder if 'it' occurred in some manuscript thoughtlessly destroyed. And then, when I've forgotten all about 'it', suddenly it dawns on me that 'it' is one of the perpetual themes which I carry about inside me, which I am writing in the air, which I have written hundreds of times already, but never set down on paper. I make a note to write it out at the first opportunity, so as to be done with it, so as to bury it once and for all. I make the note—and I forget it with alacrity. . . . It's as though there were two melodies going on simultaneously: one for private exploitation and the other for the public ear. The whole struggle is to squeeze into that public record some tiny essence of the perpetual inner melody.

It was this inner turmoil which my friends detected in my comportment. And it was the lack of it, in my writings, which they deplored. I almost felt sorry for them. But there was a streak in me, a perverse one, which prevented me from giving the essential self. This 'perversity' always voiced itself thus: 'Reveal your true self and they will mutilate you.' 'They' mean not my friends alone but the world.

Once in a great while I came across a being whom I felt I could give myself to completely. Alas, these beings existed only in books. They were worse than dead to me—they had never existed except in imagination. Ah, what dialogues I conducted with kindred, ghostly spirits! Soul-searching colloquies, of which not a line has ever been recorded. Indeed, these 'excriminations', as I chose to style them, defied recording. They were carried on in a language that does not exist, a language so simple, so direct, so transparent, that words were useless. It was not a silent language either, as is often used in communication with 'higher beings'. It was a language of clamour and tumult—the heart's clamour, the heart's tumult. But noiseless. If it were Dostoievsky whom I summoned, it was 'the complete Dostoievsky', that is to say, the man who wrote the novels, diaries and letters we know, *plus* the man we also know by what he left unsaid, unwritten. It was type and archetype speaking, so to say. Always full, resonant, veridical; always the unimpeachable sort of music which one credits him with, whether audible or inaudible, whether recorded or unrecorded. A language which could emanate *only* from Dostoievsky.

After such indescribably tumultuous communions I often sat down to the machine thinking that the moment had at last arrived. 'Now I can say it!' I would tell myself. And I would sit there, mute, motionless, drifting with the stellar flux. I might sit that way for hours, completely rapt, completely oblivious to everything about me. And then, startled out of the trance by some unexpected sound or intrusion, I would wake with a start, look at the blank paper, and slowly, painfully tap out a sentence, or perhaps only a phrase. Whereupon I would sit and stare at these words as if they had been written by some unknown hand. Usually somebody arrived to break the spell. If it were Mona, she would of course burst in enthusiastically (seeing me sitting there at the machine) and beg me to let her glance at what I had written. Sometimes, still half-drugged, I would sit there like an automaton while she stared at the sentence, or the little phrase. To her bewildered queries I would answer in a hollow, empty voice, as if I were far away, speaking through a microphone. Other times I would spring out of it like a Jack-in-the-box, hand her a whopping lie (that I had concealed 'the other pages', for instance), and begin raving like a lunatic. Then I could really talk a blue streak! It was as if I were reading from a book. All to convince her—and even more myself!—that I had been deep in work, deep in thought, deep in creation. Dismayed, she would apologize profusely for having interrupted me at the wrong moment. And I would accept her apology lightly, airily, as though to say—'What matter? There's more where that came from . . . I have only to turn it on or off . . . I'm a prestidigitator, I am.' And from the lie I would make truth. I'd spool it off (my unfinished opus) like a man possessed—themes, sub-themes, variations, detours, parentheses—as if the only thing I thought about the live-long day was creation. With this of course went considerable clowning. I not only invented the characters and events, I acted them. And poor Mona exclaiming: 'Are you really putting all that into the story? or the book?' (Neither of us, in such moments, ever specified *what* book.) When the word book sprang up it was always assumed that it was *the* book, that is to say, the one I would soon get started on—or else it was the one I was writing secretly, which I would show her only when finished. (She always acted as if she were certain this secret travail was going on. She even pretended that she had searched everywhere for the script during my periods of absence.) In this sort of atmosphere it was not at all unusual, therefore, that reference be made occasionally to certain chapters, or certain passages, chapters and passages which never existed, to be sure, but which were 'taken for granted' and which, no doubt, had a greater reality (for us) than if they were in black and white. Mona would sometimes indulge in this kind of talk in the presence of a third person, which led, of course, to fantastic and often most embarrassing situations. If it were Ulric who happened to be listening in, there was nothing to worry about. He had a way of entering into the game which was not on y gallant but stimulating. He knew how to rectify a bad slip in a humorous and fortifying way. For example, he might have forgotten for a moment that we were employing the present tense and begun using the future tense. ('I know you *will* write a book like that some day!') A moment later, realizing his error he would add: 'I didn't mean *will write* —I meant the book you *are* writing—and very obviously wrting, too, because nobody on God's earth could talk the way you do about something in which he wasn't deeply engrossed. Perhaps I'm being *too* explic:t—forgive me, won't you?' At such junctures we all enjoyed the relief of letting go. We would indeed laugh uproariously. Ulric's laughter was always the heartiest— and the dirtiest, if I may put it that way. 'Ho! Ho!' he seemed to laugh, 'but aren't we all wonderful liars! I'm not doing so bad myself, by golly. If I stay with you people long enough I won't even know I'm lying any more. Ho Ho Ho! Haw Haw! Haw! Ha Ha! Hee Hee!' And he would slap his thighs and roll his eyes like a darkie, ending with a smacking of the lips and a mute request for a wee bit of schnapps. . . . With other friends it didn't go so well. They were too inclined to ask 'impertinent' questions, as Mona put it. Or else they grew fidgety and uncomfortable, made frantic efforts to get back to terra firma. Kronski, like Ulric, was one who knew how to play the game. He did it somewhat differently from Ulric, but it seemed to satisfy Mona. *She could trust him.* That's how she put it to herself, I felt. The trouble with Kronski was that he played the game too well. He was not content to be a mere accomplice, he wanted to improvise as well. This zeal of his, which was not altogether diabolical, led to some weird discussions—discussions about the progress of the mythical book, to be sure. The critical moment always announced itself by a salvo of hysterical laughter—from Mona. It meant that she didn't know where she was any more. As for myself, I made little or no effort to keep up with the others, it being no concern of mine what went on in this realm of make believe. All I felt called upon to do was to keep a straight face and pretend that everything was kosher. I would laugh when I felt like it, or make criticism and correction, but under no circumstances, neither by word, gesture or implication did I let on that it was just a game. . . .

Strange little episodes were constantly occurring to prevent our life from becoming monotonously smooth. Sometimes they happened one, two, three, like fire-crackers going off.

To begin with, there was the sudden and mysterious disappearance of our love letters, which had been hidden away in a big paper shopping bag at the bottom of the wardrobe. It took us a week or more to discover that the woman who cleaned house for us occasionally had thrown the bag in the rubbish. Mona almost collapsed when she heard the news. 'We've simply *got* to find them!' she insisted. But how? The rubbish man had already made the rounds. Even supposing we could find the place where he had dumped them, they would by now be buried under a mountain of refuse. However, to satisfy her, I inquired where the disposal dump was located. O'Mara offered to accompany me to the place. It was the hell and gone, somewhere in the Flatlands, I believe, or else near Cararsie—a Godforsaken spot over which hung a thick pall of smoke. We endeavoured to find precisely the spot where the man had dumped that day's rubbish. An insane task, to be sure. But I had explained the whole situation to the driver and by sheer force of will aroused in his brute conscience a spark of interest. He did his damnedest to remember, but it was hopeless. We got busy, O'Mara and I, and with rather elegant looking canes began poling things around. We uncovered everything under the sun but the missing love letters. O'Mara had all he could do to dissuade me from bringing home a sackful of odds and ends. For himself he had found a handsome pipecase, though what he intended to do with it I don't know, as he never smoked a pipe. I had to content myself with a bone-handled pocket knife the blades of which were so rusty they wouldn't open. I also pocketed a bill for a tombstone, from the directors of Woodlawn Cemetery.

Mona took the loss of the letters tragically. She looked upon the incident as a bad omen. (Years later, when I read what happened to Balzac in connection with the beloved Madame Hanska's letters, I relived this episode vividly.)

The day after our visit to the dumps I received a most unexpected call from a police lieutenant in our precinct. He had come in search of Mona who fortunately was not home. After a few politenesses I asked what the trouble might be. No trouble, he assured me. Merely wanted to ask a few questions. Being the husband, I wondered aloud if I couldn't answer them for her. He seemed reluctant to comply with this polite suggestion. 'When do you expect her back?' he asked. I told him I couldn't say. Was she at work, he ventured to ask. 'You mean does she have a job?' said I. He ignored this. 'And you don't know where she went?' He was boring in, obviously. I replied that I hadn't the slightest idea. The more questions he asked the more tight-lipped I became. I still had no inkling of what was on his mind.

Finally, however, I caught a clue. It was when he asked if she were an artist perchance that I began to get the drift. 'In a way,' I said, waiting for the next question. 'Well,' said he, extracting a *Mezzotint* from his pocket and laying it before me, 'maybe you can tell me something about this.'

Vastly relieved, I said—'Certainly! What would you like to know?'

'Well,' he began, settling back to enjoy a lengthy palaver, 'just what is this? *What's the racket*, I mean?'

I smiled. 'There's no racket. We sell them.'

'To whom?'

'Anybody. Everybody. Anything wrong with that?'

He paused to scratch his poll.

'Have you read this one yourself?' he asked, as if firing point-blank.

'Of course I have. I wrote it.'

'What's that? *You* wrote it? I thought *she* was the writer?'

'We're both writers.'

'But her name's signed to it.'

'That's true. We have our own reason for that.'

'So that's it?' He twiddled his thumbs, trying to think hard. I waited for him to spring the big surprise.

'And you make a living selling these . . . uh, these pieces of paper?'

'We try to. . . .'

At this point who should burst in but Mona. I introduced her to the lieutenant who, by the way, was not in uniform.

To my amazement she exclaimed: '*How do I know he's Lieutenant Morgan?*' Not a very tactful way to start off.

The lieutenant, however, was not at all put out; in fact, he behaved as if he thought it smart of her to explain the nature of his call. He did it with tact and civility.

'Now, young lady,' he said, ignoring what I had volunteered, 'would you mind telling me just why you wrote this little article?'

Here we both spoke up at once. 'I told you I wrote it! 'I exclaimed. And Mona, paying no heed to my words: 'I see no reason why I should explain that to the police.'

'Did you write this, Miss . . . or rather Mrs Miller?'

'I did.'

'She did not,' said I.

'Now which is it?' said the lieutenant in a fatherly way. 'Or did you write it together?'

'He had nothing to do with it,' said Mona.

'She's trying to protect me,' I protested. 'Don't believe a word she tells you.'

'Maybe you're trying to protect *her!*' said the lieutenant.

Mona couldn't contain herself. '*Protect?*' she cried. 'What are you getting at? What's wrong with this . . . *this* . . . ?' She was stumped what to call the incriminating piece of evidence.

'I didn't say that you had committed a crime. I'm merely trying to find out what impelled you to write it.'

I looked at Mona and then at Lieutenant Morgan. 'Let *me* explain, won't you? I'm the one who wrote it. I wrote it because I was angry, because I hate to see an injustice done. I want people to know about it. Does that answer the question?'

'So, then you didn't write this?' said Lieutenant Morgan, addressing Mona. 'I'm glad to know that. I couldn't imagine a fine looking young lady like you saying such things.'

Again Mona was stumped. She had expected quite another response.

'Mr Miller,' he continued, with a slight change of tone, 'we've been having complaints about this diatribe of yours, if I may call it that. People don't like the tone of it. It's inflammatory. You sound like a radical. I know you're not, of course, or you wouldn't be living in a place like this. I know this apartment very well. I used to play cards here with the Judge and his friends.'

I began to relax. I knew now that it would end with a pleasant little piece of advice about not becoming an agitator.

'Why don't you offer the Lieutenant a drink?' I said to Mona. 'You don't mind having a drink with us, do you, lieutenant? I take it you're off duty?'

'I wouldn't mind at all,' he responded, 'now that I know the sort of people you are. We have to look into these things, you know. Routine. This is a sedate old neighbourhood.'

I smiled as though to say I understood perfectly. Then, like a flash, I thought of that officer of the law before whom I had been hauled when I was a mere shaver. The recollection of this incident gave me an inspiration. Downing a glass of sherry, I took a good look at Lieutenant Morgan and was off like a mud-lark.

'I'm from the old 14th Ward,' I began, beaming at him in mellow fashion. 'Perhaps you know Captain Short and Lieutenant Oakley? Or Jimmy Dunne? Surely you remember Pat McCarren?'

Bull's eyes! 'I come from Greenpoint,' he said, putting out his hand.

'Well, well, what do you know!' We were in the clear.

'By the way,' I said, 'would you have rather had whiskey? I never thought to ask you.' (We had no whiskey but I knew he would refuse.) 'Mona, where's that Scotch we had around here?'

'No, no!' he protested. 'I wouldn't think of it. This is just fine. 'So you're from the old 14th Ward . . . and you're a writer? Tell me, what do you write besides these . . . uh . . . these. . . . ? Any books?'

'A few,' I said. 'I'll send you the latest one as soon as it's off the press.'

'That would be kind of you. And send me something of your wife's too, won't you? You picked a clever little lady, I must say that. She certainly knows how to defend you.'

We chatted awhile about the old days and then Lieutenant Morgan decided he had better go.

'We'll just file this under . . . what did you say you call these things?'

Mezzotints,' said Mona.

'Good. Under M, then. Good-bye, and good luck with the writing! If you're ever in trouble you know where to find me.'

We shook hands on that and gently closed the door after him.

'Whew!' I said, flopping into a chair.

'The next time any one asks for me,' said Mona, 'remember that *I* write the *Mezzotints*. It's lucky I came when I did. You don't know how to deal with such people.'

'I thought I did pretty well,' I said.

'You should never be truthful with the police,' she said.

'It all depends,' I said. 'You've got to use discrimination.'

'They're not to be trusted,' she retorted. 'You can't afford to be decent with them. . . . I'm glad O'Mara wasn't here. He's a worse fool than you in such matters.'

'I'm damned if I can see what you're complaining about.'

'He wasted our time. You shouldn't have offered him a drink, either.'

'Listen, you're going off on a tangent. The police are human, too, aren't they? They're not all brutes.'

'If they had any intelligence they wouldn't be on the police force. They're none of them any good.'

'O.K. Let's drop it.'

'You think it's ended—because he was nice to you. That's their way of taking you in. We're on the books now. The next thing you know we'll be asked to move.'

'Oh, come, come!'

'All right, you'll see. . . . *The pig*, he almost finished the bottle!'

The next disturbing incident took place a few days later. I had been going to the dentist the last few weeks, to a friend named Doc Zabriskie whom I had met through Arthur Raymond. One could spend years sitting in his waiting room. Zabriskie believed in doing only a little work at a time. The truth was, he loved to talk. You'd sit with mouth open and jaws aching while he chewed your ear off. His brother Boris occupied an adjoining niche where he made bridges and sets of false teeth. They were great chess players, the two of them, and often I had to sit down and play a bit of chess before I could get any work done on my teeth.

Among other things Doc Zabriskie was crazy about boxing and wrestling. He attended all the bouts of any importance. Like so many Jews in the professional world, he was also fond of music and literature. But the best thing about him was that he never pressed you to pay. He was especially lenient with artists, for whom he had a weakness.

One day I brought him a manuscript I had just written. It was a glorification, in the most extravagant prose, of that little Hercules, Jim Londos.* Zabriskie read it through while I sat in the chair, mouth wide open and jaws aching like mad. He went into ecstasies over the script: had to show it immediately to brother Boris, then telephone Arthur Raymond about it. 'I didn't know you could write like that,' he said. He then intimated that we ought to get better acquainted. Wondered if we couldn't meet somewhere of an evening and go into things more thoroughly.

We fixed a date and agreed to meet at the Café Royal after dinner. Arthur Raymond came, and Kronski and O'Mara. We were soon joined by friends of Zabriskie. We were just about to

* The Greek wrestler.

116

adjourn to the Roumanian Restaurant, down the street, when a bearded old man came up to our table, peddling matches and shoe-laces. I don't know what possessed me, but before I could check myself I was making sport of the poor devil, baiting him with questions which he couldn't answer, examining the shoe-laces minutely, stuffing a cigar in his mouth, and in general behaving like a cad and an idiot. Everyone looked at me in amazement, and finally with stern disapproval. The old man was in tears. I tried to laugh it off, saying that he probably had a fortune hidden away in an old valise. A dead and stony silence ensued. Suddenly O'Mara grabbed me by the arm. 'Let's get out of here,' he mumbled, 'you're making a fool of yourself.' He turned to the others and explained that I must be drunk, said he'd walk me around the block. On the way out he stuffed some money in the old man's hand. The latter raised his fist and cursed me.

We had hardly reached the corner when we ran full tilt into Sheldon, Crazy Sheldon.

'Mister *Miller!*' he cried, holding out both hands and smiling with a full set of gold teeth. 'Mister *O'Mara!*' You would think we were his long lost brothers.

We got on either side of him, locked arms and started walking towards the river. Sheldon was bubbling over with joy. He had been searching all over town for me, he confided. Was doing well now. Had an office not far from his home.

'And what are *you* doing, Mister *Miller?*'

I told him I was writing a book.

With this he disengaged himself and took up a position in front of us, his arms folded over his chest, his expression ludicrously serious. His eyes were almost shut, his mouth pursed. Any moment now I expected that peanut whistle of his to issue like steam through the tight lips.

'Mister *Miller,*' he began slowly and sententiously, as if he were summoning the whole world to listen in. 'I always wanted you to write a book. Sheldon understands. Yes indeed.' He said this raspingly, his lower lip thrust out, his head jerking back and forth in violent approval.

'He's writing about the Klondike,' said O'Mara, always ready to work Sheldon up to a lather.

'No, No!' said Sheldon, fixing us with a cunning smile, at the same time waving his index finger back and forth under our noses. 'Mister *Miller* is writing a *great* book. Sheldon knows.' Suddenly he grasped me by the forearm, relaxed his grip and put his index finger to his lips. 'Sh—h—h— !' He looked round as if to make sure we were out of earshot. Then he started walking backwards, his finger still raised. He moved it back and forth, like a metronome. 'Wait,' he whispered, 'I know a place. . . . Sh—h—h !'

'We want to walk,' said O'Mara brusquely, shoving him aside as he pulled me along. 'He's drunk, can't you see that?'

Sheldon looked positively horrified. 'Oh no!' he cried, 'No, not Mr *Miller*!' He bent over to look up into my face. 'No,' he repeated, 'Mr *Miller* would never get drunk.' He was forced to trot now, his legs stilled crooked, his index finger still wagging. O'Mara walked faster and faster. Finally Sheldon stood stock-still, allowing us to get quite a distance ahead of him. He stood there with arms folded over his chest, immobile. Then, all of a sudden, he broke into a run.

'Be careful,' he whispered, as he caught up with us. 'Poloks around here. Shhhhh!'

O'Mara laughed in his face.

'Don't laugh!' begged Sheldon.

'You're crazy!' sneered O'Mara.

Sheldon marched beside us, briskly and gingerly, as if walking with bare feet on broken glass. He was silent for a few moments. Suddenly he stopped, opened overcoat and sack coat, and quickly, furtively buttoned his inside pockets, then the outer buttons of his sack coat, then his overcoat. He thrust his lower lip forward, narrowed his gimlet-like eyes to two slits, pulled his hat well down over his eyes, and pushed onward. All this rigma-role to the tune of absolute silence. Still silent, he put forth one hand and significantly gave his gleaming rings a half turn. Then he pushed both hands deep down into his overcoat pockets. 'Quiet!' he whispered, treading even more gingerly now.

'He's gaga,' said O'Mara.

'Sh-h-h-h!'

I laughed quietly.

Now he began to talk in muffled tones, almost inaudibly, his lips scarcely moving. I could only get fragments of it.

'Open your mouth!' said O'Mara.

'Sh-h-h-h!'

More muffled flim-flam. Broken by an occasional Cooooooo or Eeeeeee. All punctuated by stifled shrieks and that infernal peanut whistle. It was getting eerie. We were now approaching the gas tanks and the dismal lumber yards. The empty streets were sinister and lugubrious. Suddenly I felt Sheldon's fingers clawing my arm. A sound like Ughhh escaped from his thin cracked lips. He was tugging at me and nodding his head. He did it like a horse tossing his mane.

I looked sharply about. There on the other side of the street was a drunk zigzagging homeward. A huge hulk of a man, with his jacket wide open, no tie on, no hat. Now and then he stopped to let out a bloody oath.

'Hurry, hurry!' muttered Sheldon, gripping me tighter.

'Shhh! It's all right,' I murmured.

'A Polok!' he whispered. I could feel him quivering all over.

'Let's get back to the Avenue,' I said to O'Mara. 'He's in torment.'

'Yes, yes,' whimpered Sheldon. 'This way is better,' and with elbow glued to his body he stuck a hand out cautiously and jerkily, like the movement of a semaphore. Once we had turned the corner his pace livened. Half running, half walking, he kept swinging his head from side to side, fearful that someone would catch us unaware. When we got to the subway station we took leave of him. Not before giving him my address, however. I had to write it out for him on the inside of a matchbox. His hands were still trembling, his teeth chattering.

'Sheldon will see you soon,' he said, as he waved good-bye. At the foot of the stairs he stopped, turned round, and put his fingers to his lips.

'SHHHHHHH!' went O'Mara as loud as he could.

Sheldon grinned solemnly. Then, without uttering a sound, he frantically moved his lips. It seemed to me he was trying to say POLOKS. He probably thought he was screaming.

'You should never have given him our address,' said O'Mara. 'That guy will haunt us. He's a pest. He gives me the creeps.' He shook himself like a dog.

'He's all right,' I said. 'I'll handle him, if he ever does show up. Besides, I rather like Sheldon.'

'You would!' said O'Mara.

'Did you notice the rocks on his fingers?'

'Rhinestones probably.'

'*Diamonds*, you mean! You don't know Sheldon. Listen, if we ever need help that guy will pawn his shirt for us.'

'I'd rather starve than have to listen to him.'

'All right, have it your way. Something tells me we may have need of Mister Sheldon one day. Jesus, how he trembled when he saw that drunken Polok!'

O'Mara was silent.

'You don't give a shit, do you?' I gibed. 'You don't know what a pogrom is like. . . .'

'Neither do you,' said O'Mara tartly.

'When I look at Sheldon I do. Yes sir, to me that poor bastard is nothing but a walking pogrom. If that Polok had started for us he would have shit in his pants.'

A few nights later Osiecki turned up with his girl. Louella was her name. Her downright homeliness almost made her beautiful. She had on a Nile-green gown and brocaded slippers of banana yellow and orange. She was quiet, self-contained, and totally humourless. Her manner was that of a nurse rather than a fiancée.

Osiecki wore the fixed grin of a death's head. His attitude was —'I promised to bring her, here she is.' The implication was that we were to get what we could out of her without his assistance. He had come to 'set' and drink what was provided. As for conversation, he listened to all that went on as if we were putting on records for him.

It was a strange conversation because all one could extract from Louella was a *Yes* or a *No* or *I think so* or *Perhaps*. Osiecki's grin widened more and more, as if to say: 'I told you so!' The more he drank the more wobbly his teeth became. His mouth was beginning to resemble a contraption of intricate wires and braces. Whatever he chewed he chewed slowly and painfully. In fact, he seemed to masticate rather than chew. Since his last visit his whole face had broken out in an eruption which did little to enhance his forlorn appearance.

Asked if things were going any better, he turned to Louella. 'She'll tell you,' he mumbled.

Louella said 'No'.

'Still the same old trouble?'

Again he looked to Louella.

This time she said 'Yes'.

Then, to our surprise, he said: 'Ask her how *she* feels.' With this he lowered his head; a few drops of saliva fell into his glass. He pulled out a handkerchief and with obvious effort wiped his mouth.

All eyes focused on Louella. No reaction except to look straight through us, one after the other. Her eyes, which were pale green, became stony and fixed. We were growing highly uncomfortable, but no one knew how to break the spell. Suddenly, of her own accord, she began to speak. She employed a low monotone, as if hypnotized. Her gaze, which never altered throughout, was riveted, to the edge of the mantelpiece, which was just above our heads. In that theatrical Nile-green gown, with those glassy green eyes, she gave the discomfiting impression of impersonating a medium. Her hair, a striking dissonance, was magnificent: a luxuriant, voluptuous auburn which fell like a cataract over her bare shoulders. For a full moment, completely bewitched, I had the odd sensation of gazing upon a corpse, an electrically warmed corpse.

What she was talking about in that dull, hollow monotone I didn't quite catch at first. It was like listening to distant surf beating against a cliff. She had mentioned no names, no places, no time. Gradually I surmised that the 'him' she was talking about was her fiancé, Osicki. Now and then I glanced at him to observe his reactions, but there were none. He was still grinning like an asbestos grill. One would hardly have suspected that she was talking about *him*.

The gist of her monologue was to the effect that she had known him for over a year now and, despite all his friends might say, she was convinced that he was really no different than he had ever been. She implied very definitely that he was cuckoo. Without the slightest modulation she added that she was certain she was also going cuckoo. No insinuation that it was his fault. No, merely as if it were an unfortunate, or perhaps fortunate, coincidence. It was his misfortune which had attracted her. She supposed she loved him, but she had no way of knowing, since both their reactions were abnormal. His friends, whom she had nothing against, regarded her as a bad influence. Perhaps she was. She had no ulterior motive in attaching herself to him. She earned her own living and, if needs be, could take care of both. She was neither happy nor unhappy. The days passed as in a dream, and the nights were the continuation of some other dream. Sometimes she thought it would be better if they left the city, other times she thought it made no difference one way or the other. She was getting less and less able to make decisions. A sort of twilight had settled over them, which, to believe her, was not at all unbearable. They were going to marry shortly; she hoped his friends wouldn't mind too much. As for the lice, she had felt them herself; it could be imaginary, of course, but she didn't see much difference between imaginary bites and real ones, especially if they left marks on one's skin. His eczema, which we had probably noticed, was only a passing thing—he had been drinking heavily. But she preferred to see him drunk than worried to death. He had his good points and his bad points, like any one else. She was sorry she didn't care much for music but she did her best to listen. She had never had any feeling for art, neither music, painting, nor literature. She had no enthusiasm for anything, really, not even as a child. Her life had always been easy and comfortable, as well as dull and monotonous. The monotony of life didn't affect her as it did others, she thought. She felt the same whether she was alone or with people. . . .

On and on she went, none of us having the heart or the wits to interrupt her. She seemed to have cast a spell over us. If a corpse could talk she was a perfect talking corpse. Except for the fact that her lips moved and emitted sounds, she was inanimate.

It was O'Mara who broke the spell. He thought he heard some one at the door. He sprang to his feet and yanked the door open. There was no one, nothing but the darkness. I noticed Louella's head jerk when he swung the door open. In a few moments her features relaxed, her eyes melted.

'Wouldn't you like another drink?' asked Mona.

'Yes,' she said, 'I would.'

O'Mara had hardly seated himself, was just about to pour himself another drink, in fact, when there was a timid knock at the door. He jumped. Mona dropped the glass she was proffering Louella. Only Osiecki remained impassive.

I went to the door and opened it quietly. There stood Sheldon, hat in hand.

'Were you here just a minute ago?' I asked.

'No,' he said, 'I just came.'

'Are you sure?' asked O'Mara.

Sheldon disregarded this and walked in. '*Sheldon!*' he said, glancing from one to another, and to each one making a slight bow. The ceremony consisted in closing the eyes and opening them quiveringly each time he returned to an erect posture.

We put him at ease as best we could and proffered him a drink.

'Sheldon never refuses,' he solemnly, his eyes glittering. Throwing his head back, he polished off the glass of sherry at one gulp. Then he loudly smacked his lips, fluttered his eyelids some more, and inquired if we were all enjoying good health. For answer we all laughed, except Louella, who smiled gravely. Sheldon tried to laugh, too, but the best he could do was to make a weird grimace, something like a wolf about to lick its chops.

Osiecki grinned hard, right in Sheldon's face. He seemed to sense a kindred spirit.

'What did he say his name was?' he asked, looking at O'Mara.

Sheldon repeated his name gravely, dropping his eyes as he did so.

'Haven't you got a first name?' he asked, this time direct.

'Just Sheldon,' said Sheldon.

'But you're Polish, aren't you?' said Osiecki, becoming more and more animated.

'I was *born* in Poland,' said Sheldon. Here he drew his words out so that there could be possibility of misunderstanding. 'But I am proud to say I am *not* Polish.'

'Well, I'm half Polish,' said Osiecki amiably, 'but I'm damned if I know whether I'm proud of it or not.'

Sheldon immediately looked away, closing his mouth tightly as if he feared to utter an ill-timed malediction. Catching my eye he gave me a painful smile. It meant—'I am doing my best to behave myself in the company of your friends, even though I smell Polish blood.'

'He won't harm you,' I said reassuringly.

'What's the matter. . . . ?' cried Osiecki. 'What did I do?'

Sheldon promptly rose to his feet, threw out his chest, frowned, then assumed his most striking histrionic pose.

'Sheldon is not afraid,' he said, sucking in air with each word he hissed. 'Sheldon does not *wish* to speak to a Polok.' Here he paused and without moving the rest of his body, turned his head around as far as it would go, then back again, exactly like a mechanical doll. In doing this he half closed his eyelids, thrust forward his under lip, and, coming to Eyes Front! slowly raised his hand, the forefinger extended—like Dr Munyon about to prate of liver pills.

'Shhhhhh!' from O'Mara.

'S-HHHHHHH!' And Sheldon lowered his hand to place the forefinger over his lips.

'What *is* this?' cried Osiecki, thoroughly elated by the performance.

'Sheldon will speak. *Afterwards the Poloks may speak*. This is not the place for hooligans. Am I right, Mr Miller? Quiet, please!' Again he twisted his head around, like a mechanical doll. 'There has happened once a very terrible thing. Excuse me if I must mention such things in the presence of ladies and gentle-men. But this man'—he glowered fiercely at Osiecki—'has asked me if I am a Pole. Pfui! (He spat on the floor.) That *I* should be a Pole—pfui! (He spat again.) Excuse me, Madame Mrs Miller—he made an ironic little bow—'but when I hear the world Pole I must spit. *Pfui!*' (And he spat a third time.)

He paused, taking a deep breath in order to inflate his chest to the proper degree. Also to gather up the venom which his glands were secreting. His lower jaw trembled, his eyes darted black rays of hate. As if made of compression rings, his body began to tighten: he had only to uncoil himself to spring to the other side of the street.

'He's going to throw a fit,' said Osiecki in genuine alarm.

O'Mara jumped to his feet to offer Sheldon a glass of sherry. Sheldon knocked it out of his hand, as if brushing away a fly. The sherry spilled over Louella's beautiful Nile-green gown. She took no notice of it whatever. Osiecki was getting more and more agitated. In distress he turned to me imploringly.

'Tell him I didn't mean anything by what I said,' he begged.

'A Pole never apologizes,' said Sheldon, looking straight ahead. 'He murders, he tortures, he rapes, he burns women and children —but he never says "I *am* sorry". He drinks blood, human blood —and he prays on his knees, like an animal. Every word from his mouth is a lie or a curse. He eats like a dog, he makes caca in his pants, he washes with filthy rags, he vomits in your face. Sheldon prays every night that God should punish them. As long as there is one Pole alive there will be tears and misery. Sheldon has no mercy on them. They must all die, like pigs . . . men, women and children. Sheldon says it . . . *because he knows them.*'

His eyes, which were half-closed when he began, were now shut tight. The words escaped his lips, each one pressed forth as if by a bellows. At the corners of his mouth the saliva had collected, giving him the appearance of an epileptic.

'Stop him, Henry, *please*,' begged Osiecki.

'Yes, Val, please do something,' cried Mona. 'This has gone far enough.'

'Sheldon!' I yelled, thinking to startle him.

He remained impassive, eyes front! as if he had heard nothing. I got up, took him by the arms, and shook him gently. 'Come,

Sheldon,' I said quietly, 'snap out of it!' I shook him again, more vigorously.

Sheldon's eyes opened slowly, flutteringly; he looked around as if he had just come out of a trance.

A sickly smile now spread over his face, as though he had succeeded in sticking his finger down his throat and vomiting up a poisonous dose.

'You're all right now, aren't you?' I asked, giving him a sound thwack on the back.

'Excuse me,' he blinking and coughing, 'it's those Poloks. They always make me sick.'

'There are no Poloks here, Sheldon. This man'—pointing to Osiecki—'is a Kanuck. He wants to shake hands with you.'

Sheldon stuck out his hand as if he had never seen Osiecki before, and making a low bow, he said: '*Sheldon!*'

'Glad to know you,' said Osiecki, also making a slight bow. 'Here, have a drink, won't you?' and he reached for a glass.

Sheldon held the glass to his lips and sipped slowly, cautiously, as if not quite convinced it was harmless.

'Good?' beamed Osiecki.

'*Ausgezeichnet!*' Sheldon smacked his lips. He smacked them not from genuine relish but to show his good manners.

'Are you an old friend of Henry's?' asked Osiecki, trying lamely to worm his way into Sheldon's good graces.

'Mister *Miller* is everybody's friend,' was the answer.

'He used to work for me,' I explained.

'Oh, I see! Now I get it,' said Osiecki. He seemed inordinately relieved.

'He's got a business of his own now,' I added.

Sheldon beamed and began twiddling the jewelled rings on his fingers.

'A *legitimate* business,' said Sheldon, rubbing his hands together like a pawnbroker. Hereupon he slipped one of his rings off and held it under Osiecki's nose. It held a large ruby. Osiecki examined it appraisingly and passed it over to Louella. Meanwhile Sheldon had slipped another ring off and handed it to Mona to examine. This time it was a huge emerald. Sheldon waited a few moments to observe the effects of this procedure. Then he ceremoniously took two rings off the hand, both diamonds. These he placed in my hand. Then he put his fingers to his lips and went Shhhhh!

While we were exclaiming how wonderful the stones were Sheldon reached into his vest pocket and brought out a little package wrapped in tissue paper. He undid this over the table, opening it out flat in the palm of his hand. Five or six cut stones gleamed forth, all small ones but of extraordinary brilliance. He laid them carefully on the table and reached into his other vest pocket. This time he brought forth a string of tiny pearls, exquisite pearls, the like of which I had never seen.

When we had feasted our eyes on all these treasures, he again assumed one of his mystifying poses, held it for an impressive length of time, then dove into his inside coat pocket and extracted a long wallet of Moroccan make. He unfolded this in mid air, like a prestidigitator, then, one by one, he drew forth bills of all denominations in about a dozen different currencies. If it was real money, as I had good reason to believe it was, it must have represented several thousand dollars.

'Aren't you afraid to walk around with all this stuff in your pockets?' someone inquired.

Fluttering his fingers in the air, as if touching little bells, he replied sententiously: 'Sheldon knows how to manage.'

'I told you he was nuts,' cackled O'Mara.

Oblivious of the remark, Sheldon continued: 'In this country no one bothers Sheldon. This is a civilized country. Sheldon always minds his own business. . . . Isn't that so, Mister *Miller?*' He paused to inflate his chest. Then he added: 'Sheldon is always polite, even to niggers.'

'But Sheldon. . . .'

'Wait!' he cried. '*Quiet*, please!' And then, with a mysterious twinkle in his gimlet eyes, he unbuttoned his shirt, rapidly retreated a few steps until his back touched the window, dangled a piece of black tape which was slung around his neck, and before we could say Boo! gave a terrific blast from a police whistle attached to the tape. The noise pierced our ear drums. It was hallucinating.

'Grab it!' I yelled, as Sheldon raised it to his lips again.

O'Mara clutched the whistle tightly. 'Quick! hide everything!' he yelled. 'If the cops come we'll have a hell of a time explaining this loot.'

Osiecki at once gathered the rings, the bills, the wallet and the jewels together, calmly slipped them in his coat pocket, and sat down with arms folded, waiting for the police to arrive.

Sheldon looked on scornfully and contemptuously. 'Let them come,' he said, his nose in the air, his nostrils quivering. 'Sheldon is not afraid of the police.'

O'Mara busied himself stuffing the whistle back in Sheldon's bosom, buttoning his shirt, then his vest and coat. Sheldon permitted him to do all this quite as if he were a mannikin being dressed for the show window. He never once took his eyes off Osiecki however.

Sure enough, in a few moments the bell rang. Mona rushed to the door. It was the police all right.

'Talk!' muttered O'Mara. He raised his voice as though continuing a heated argument. I responded in the same key, not caring what I said. At the same time I signalled Osiecki to join in. All I could get from him was a grin. With arms folded he placidly watched and waited. Between snatches of the mock dispute Mona could be heard protesting that we knew nothing about a police whistle. Hadn't heard a thing, I could hear her say. O'Mara was chattering away like a magpie, assuming other voices, other intonations now. In deaf-and-dumb code he was frantically urging me to follow suit. Had the police brushed their way in that moment they would have witnessed a droll piece of business. In the midst of it I broke out laughing, forcing O'Mara to redouble his efforts. Louella, of course, sat like a stone. Osiecki looked upon the performance as if from a stall in the circus. He was completely at ease; in fact he was radiant. As for Sheldon, he never budged from his position. His back was still against the window. He remained there all buttoned up, as if waiting for the window-dresser to arrange his arms and legs. Repeatedly I waved to him to speak, but he remained impervious, aloof, altogether disdainful, in fact.

Finally we heard the door close and Mona scurrying back.

'The stupid fools!' she said.

'They always come when I blow the whistle,' said Sheldon in a matter of fact tone.

'I only hope the landlord doesn't come down,' I remarked.

'They're away for the week-end,' said Mona.

'Are you sure those cops are not standing outside?' said O'Mara.

'They've gone,' said Mona. 'I'm sure of it. God, there's nothing worse than a thick mick, unless it's two thick micks. I thought I'd never convince them.'

'Why didn't you invite them in?' asked Osiecki. 'That's always the best way.'

'Yes,' said Louella, 'we always do that.'

'It was a good stunt,' grinned Osiecki. 'Do you always play games like that? He's fun, this Sheldon.' He got up leisurely and dumped the loot on the table. He went over to Sheldon and said: 'Could I have a look at that whistle?'

O'Mara was instantly on his feet, ready to fling both arms around Sheldon. 'Cripes! Don't start that again!' he begged.

Sheldon put his two hands out, palms forward, as if to ward us off. '*Quiet!*' he whispered, reaching with his right hand for the back pocket of his trousers. With one hand thus extended and the other on his hip, but concealed by his coat, he said quietly and grimly: 'If I lose the whistle I always have this.' So saying, he whipped out a revolver and levelled it at us. He pointed it at each of us in turn, no one daring to make a move or utter a sound for fear his hand would automatically press the trigger. Convinced that we were properly impressed, Sheldon slowly returned the revolver to his hip pocket.

Mona made a bee-line for the bathroom. In a moment she was

calling me to join her. I excused myself to see what she wanted. She almost dragged me in, then closed and locked the door. '*Please*,' she whispered, 'get them out of here, all of them, I'm afraid something will happen.'

'Is *that* what you wanted? All right,' I said, but half-heartedly.

'No, *please*,' she begged, 'do it right away. They're crazy, all of them.'

I left her locked in the bathroom and returned to the group. Sheldon was now showing Osiecki a murderous-looking pocket knife which he also carried with him. Osiecki was testing the blade with his thumb.

I explained that Mona was feeling ill, thought it best we break up.

Sheldon was for running out and telephoning a doctor. Finally we succeeded in ousting them, Osiecki promising to take good care of Sheldon, and Sheldon protesting that he could take care of himself. I expected to hear the whistle blow in a few minutes. I wondered what the cops would say when they emptied Sheldon's pockets. But no sound broke the silence.

As I undressed for bed my eye fell on the little brass ash-tray, from India supposedly, which I was especially fond of. It was one of the little objects which I had selected the day I bought the furniture; it was something I hoped to keep forever. As I held it in my hand, examining it anew, I suddenly realized that not a thing in the place belonged to the past, my own past. Everything was brand new. It was then I thought of the little Chinese nut which I had kept since childhood in a little iron bank on the mantelpiece at home. How I had come by this nut I no longer remember; it had probably been given me by some relative returning from the South Seas. At intervals I used to open the little bank, which never had more than a few pennies in it, get out the nut and fondle it. It was smooth as suede, the colour of light siena, and had a black band running lengthwise through the centre. I have never seen another nut like it. Sometimes I would take it out and carry it about with me for days or weeks, not for good luck, but because I liked the feel of it. It was a completely mysterious object to me, and I was content to leave it a mystery. That it had an ancient history, that it had passed through many hands, that it had travelled far and wide, I was certain. It was that which endeared it to me. One day, after I had been married to Maude for some time, I had such a longing for this little fetish that I made a special trip to my parents' home to recover it. To my amazement and disappointment I was informed that my mother had given it to some little boy in the neighbourhood who had expressed a liking for it. *What boy?* I wanted to know. But she could no longer remember. She thought it silly of me to be so concerned about a trifle. We talked of this and that, waiting for my father to arrive and have dinner together.

'What about my theatre,' I suddenly demanded. 'Did you get rid of that too?'

'Long ago,' said my mother. 'You remember little Arthur who lived in the flats across the way? He was crazy about it.'

'So you gave it to *him*?' I had never cared much for little Arthur. He was a born sissy. But my mother thought he was a grand little fellow, had such lovely manners, and so on.

'Do you suppose he still has it?' I asked.

'Oh no, of course not! He's a big fellow now, he wouldn't want to play with that any more.'

'You can't tell,' I said. 'Maybe I'll run over there and see.'

'They've moved.'

'And you don't know where to, I suppose?'

She didn't, of course, or most likely she did but wouldn't tell me. It was so foolish of me to want these old things back, she repeated.

'I know it,' I said, 'but I would give anything to see them again.'

'Wait till you have children of your own, then you can buy them new, better ones.'

'There couldn't be a better theatre than that one,' I protested vehemently. I gave her a long spiel about my Uncle Ed Martini who had spent months and months making it for me. As I talked I could see it again standing under the Christmas tree. I could see my little friends, who always dropped in during the holidays, sitting in a circle on the floor, watching me manipulate the paraphernalia which went with the theatre.

My Uncle had thought of everything, not only changes of scene and a variety of cast but footlights, pulleys, wings, backdrops, everything imaginable. Every Christmas I brought out this theatre, up until I was sixteen or seventeen years of age. I could play with it today even more passionately than when I was a child, so beautiful, so perfect, so intricate it was. But it was gone and I would never see it again. Most certainly I would never find another one like it, for this one had been made with love and with a patience which no one today seems to possess. It was strange, too, I reflected, because Ed Martini had always been regarded as a good for nothing, a man who wasted his time, who drank too much and talked too much. But he knew what would make a child happy!

Nothing from my boyhood had been preserved. The tool chest had been given to the Good Will Society, my story books to another little urchin whom I detested. What he had done with my beautiful books I could well imagine. The exasperating part of it all was that my mother would make not the slightest effort to help me recover these belongings. About the books, for instance, she averred that I had read them over so many times I must know the contents by heart. She simply could not, or would not, understand that I wanted to possess them physically. Perhaps she was unconsciously punishing me for the light-hearted way I used to accept gifts.

(The desire to strengthen the ties which bound me to the past, to my wonderful childhood, was becoming ever stronger The more insipid and distasteful the everyday world became, the more I glorified the golden days of childhood. I could see more and more clearly as time went on that my childhood had been one long holiday—a carnival of youth. It wasn't that I felt myself growing old, it was simply that I realized I had lost something precious.)

This theme became even more poignant when my father, thinking to revive pleasant memories, would tell me of the doings of my old playmate, Tony Marella. 'I just read something about him last week in *The Chat*,' he would begin. First it used to be about Tony Marella's athletic exploits, how, for example, he had won the Marathon and almost dropped dead. Then it was about the Club Tony Marella had organized, and how he was going to improve the lot of the poor boys in the neighbourhood. There was always a photo of him accompanying the article. From *The Chat*, which was just a local weekly, he soon began to be talked about in the Brooklyn dailies. He was a figure to be reckoned with, he would be heard from one of these days. Yes, it wouldn't be surprising if he were to run for Alderman soon. And so on. . . . There was no doubt about it, Tony Marella was the new star in the firmament of the Bushwick Section. He had started from the bottom, had triumphed over all handicaps, had put himself through law school; he was a shining example of what the son of a poor immigrant could make of himself in this glorious land of opportunity.

Much as I liked Tony Marella, it always sickened me to hear the way my folks raved about him. I had known Tony from grammar school; we were always in the same class and we graduated together at the head of the class. Tony had to struggle for everything, whereas for me it was the contrary. He was a tough, rebellious kid whose animal spirits drove the teachers crazy. With the boys he was a born leader. For years I lost track of him completely. Never even gave him a thought. One Winter's evening, tramping through the snow, I ran into him. He was on his way to a political meeting, and I, I was keeping a date with some dizzy blonde. Tony tried to get me to accompany him to the meeting, said it would do me good. I laughed in his face. A bit peeved, he began talking politics to me, told me he was out to reform the Democratic party of our district, our old home district. Again I laughed, this time almost insultingly. To this Tony cried: 'You'll be voting for me in a couple of years, wait and see. They need men like me in the Party.' 'Tony,' I said, 'I've never voted yet and I don't think I ever will. But if you're running for office I may make an exception. I'd like nothing better than to see you become President of the United States. You'd be a credit to the White House.' He thought I was kidding him, but I was dead serious.

In the midst of this talk Tony mentioned the name of his possible rival, Martin Malone. '*Martin Malone!*' I exclaimed. 'Not *our* Martin Malone?' 'The very one,' he assured me. Now the coming figure in the Republican Party I was that surprised your could have knocked me over with a feather. That blockhead! How had he ever come into such prominence? Tony explained that it was the father's influence. I remembered old man Malone well; he was a good man and an honest politician, rare thing. But his son! Why, Martin, who was four years older than us, was always at the foot of the class. He stuttered badly too, or he did as a boy. And this dunce was now a leading figure in local politics. 'You see why I'm not interested in politics,' I said. 'There's where you're wrong, Henry,' said Tony vehemently. 'Would you want to see Martin Malone become a Congressman?' 'Frankly,' said I, 'I don't give a damn who becomes Congressman of this district, or any district. It doesn't matter in the slightest. It doesn't even matter who's President. Nothing matters. The country isn't run by these shits.' Tony shook his head in thorough disapproval. 'Henry, you're lost,' he said. 'You're an out-and-out anarchist.' And on this we parted, not to meet again for a number of years.

The old man ceased harping on Tony's virtues. I knew, of course, that my father was only trying to put some life in me. I knew that after he had done talking about Tony Marella he would ask how the writing business was coming along, had I sold anything yet, and so on. And if I said that nothing of importance had happened yet, my mother would then give me one of those sad, sidelong looks, as if to pity me for the ignorance of my ways, perhaps adding aloud that I had always been the brightest boy in the class, that I had had every opportunity, yet here I was trying to become a foolish thing like a writer. 'If you could only write something for the *Saturday Evening Post!*' she would say. Or, to make my position even more ludicrous, this: 'Maybe *The Chat* would take one of your stories!' (Everything I wrote, incidentally, she called a story, though I had explained to her a dozen or more times that I didn't write 'stories'. 'Well, whatever they are, then,' was always her final word.)

In parting I would always say to her: 'You're sure now there are none of my old things left?' The answer always was— 'Forget it!' In the street, as she stood at the fence to wave good-bye, there'd be this Parthian shot from her: 'Don't you think you'd better give up that writing and find a job? You're not getting any younger, you know. You may be an old man before you're famous.'

I would leave filled with remorse that I hadn't made their evening more entertaining. On the way to the elevated station I had to pass Tony Marella's old home. His father still ran a cobbler's shop on the street front. Tony had blossomed right out of that hovel in which he was raised. The edifice itself had undergone no changes in the generation which had passed. Only Tony had changed, had evolved, in keeping with the times. I felt certain he still spoke Italian to his parents, still kissed his father affectionately when greeting him, was still providing for the family out of his meagre salary. What a different atmosphere reigned in that household! What a joy it must have been to his parents to see Tony making his way in the world! When he made his grand speeches they were unable to understand a word he said. But they knew he was saying the right thing. Everything he did was right in their eyes. He was indeed a good son. And, if he ever made the grade, he would be a damned good President.

As I rehearsed all this I recalled how my mother used to speak of my father, of the pride and joy he was to *his* parents. I was the thorn in their side. I brought nothing but problems. Who could say, though? One day it might all turn out different. One day, by a single stroke, perhaps I might alter the whole set-up. I might yet prove that I was not completely hopeless. But when? And how?

5

IT WAS ON A sunny day in the first rush of Spring that we found ourselves on Second Avenue. The *Mezzotint* racket was on its last legs and there was nothing new on the horizon. We had come to the East Side to make a touch but nothing had come of it. Weary and thirsty from tramping about in the blazing sun, we were wondering how to get a cool drink on no money. Passing a candy store with an inviting soda fountain we decided, on a mutual impulse, to go in, have our drink, and then pretend we had lost our money.

The owner, a homely, friendly sort of Jew, waited on us himself. His manner indicated that we obviously hailed from another world. We dawdled over the drink, drawing him into conversation in order to prepare him for the sad news. He seemed flattered that we took such notice of him. When it came time I fumbled around for change and, not finding any, asked Mona in a loud voice to look through her handbag, saying that I must have left my money at home. She of course couldn't dig up a red cent. I suggested to the man, who was calmly observing this performance, that, if he didn't mind, we would pay the next time we were in the neighbourhood. Quite affably he said that we could forget about it if we liked. Then he politely inquired what part of the city we came from. To our surprise we discovered that he knew intimately the very street we were living in. At this point he invited us to have another drink and with the drink he offered us some delicious cakes. It was plain he was curious to know more about us. Since we had nothing to lose, I decided to make a clean breast of it.

So we were broke? He had suspected that we were but he was dumbfounded, nevertheless, that two people so intelligent, speaking such beautiful English, born Americans to boot, should find it difficult to make a living in a city like New York. I of course pretended that I would welcome a job if I could find one. I hinted that it wasn't easy for me to find work because I was really incapable of doing anything but push the pen, adding that I was probably not very good at this either. He was of a different mind. Had he been able to read and write English, he informed us, he would now be living on Park Avenue. His story, a fairly common one, was that some eight years ago he had come to America with just a few dollars in his pocket. He had immediately accepted a job in a marble quarry, in Vermont. Brutal work. But it had enabled him to save up a few hundred dollars. With this money he had bought some odds and ends, put them in a sack, and set out on the road as a peddler. In less than no time (it almost sounded like an Horatio Alger story) he had acquired a pushcart, then a horse and wagon. His mind had always been set on coming to New York where he longed to open a shop of some sort. By chance he had found out that one could make a good living selling imported candies. At this juncture he reached up behind him and got down an assortment of foreign candies, all in beautiful boxes. He explained rather minutely how he had peddled these candies from door to door, beginning in Columbia Heights where we now lived. He had done it successfully, speaking only a broken English. In less than a year he had put aside enough to set up shop. The Americans, he said, 'loved' imported candies. They didn't mind the price. Here he began to reel off the prices of the various brands. Then he told us how much profit there was in each box. Finally he said: 'If I could do it, why can't you?' And in the next breath he offered to supply us with a full valise of imported candies, on credit, if we would only try it out.

The fellow was so kind, so obviously trying to put us back on our feet, that we didn't have the heart to refuse. We permitted him to fill a big valise, accepted the money he offered us for a taxi home, and said good-bye. On the way home I grew thoroughly excited over the prospect. Nothing for it but to start out fresh, the next morning, right in our own neighbourhood. Mona, I observed, wasn't nearly as elated as I, but she was game to try it. During the night, I confess, my ardour cooled off a bit.

(Fortunately, O'Mara was away for a few days, visiting an old friend. He would have ridiculed the idea mercilessly.)

The next day, at noon, we met to compare notes. Mona was already home when I arrived. She didn't appear very enthusiastic about her morning. She had sold a few boxes, yes, but it had been hard work. Our neighbours, according to her, weren't a very hospitable sort. (I, of course, hadn't sold a single box. I was already through, in my mind, with door to door canvassing. In fact, I was almost ready to take a job.)

There was a better way, Mona thought, to go about the business. Tomorrow she would tackle the office buildings where she would have to do with men, not housewives and servants. That failing, she would try the night clubs in the Village, and possibly

133

the cafés along Second Avenue. (The cafés appealed to me; I thought I might tackle them myself, on my own.)

The office buildings proved somewhat better than residences, but not much better. It was hard to get to the man behind the desk, particularly when it was candies you had to offer. And then there were all kinds of filthy propositions to put up with. One or two individuals, the better sort, had bought a half-dozen boxes at once. Out of pity, clearly. One of these was a very fine chap indeed. She was going to see him again soon. Apparently he had done his best to persuade her to abandon the racket. 'I'll tell you more about him later,' she said.

I'll never forget my first night as a peddler. I had chosen the Café Royal as my starting point because it was a familiar haunt. (It was my hope that I would run into some one I knew who would start me off on the right foot.) People were still loitering over dinner when I sailed in with my little suitcase filled with candy boxes. I took a quick glance about but saw no one I knew. Presently I caught sight of a group of merrymakers seated at a long table. I decided they were the ones to tackle first.

Unfortunately they were a little too gay. 'Imported candies, no less!' jeered one jolly fellow. 'Why not imported silks?' The man next to him wanted to inspect the candies, wanted to make sure they were imported and not domestic. He took a few boxes and passed them around. Seeing the women nibbling away I assumed everything was in order. I circulated round the table, coming finally to the man who appeared to be the master of ceremonies. He was full of talk, a wise-cracker. '*Candies*, hum! A new racket. Well dressed and speaks a good English. Probably working his way through college. . . .' *Et patati et patata*. He bit into a few, then passed the box around in the other direction, still making running comments, a monologue which kept the others in stitches. I was left to stand there like a stick. No one had as yet asked me the price of a box. Neither had any one said he would take a box. Like a game of parchesi, it was. Then, after they had all sampled the candy to their heart's content, after they had nibbled and joked at my expense, they began talking of other matters, about all sorts of things but not a word about candy, not a word about the young man, yours truly, who was standing there waiting for some one to speak up.

I stood there quite a time, wondering just how far these convivial souls intended to push their little joke. I made no effort to collect the boxes which were scattered about. Nor did I open my mouth to say a word. I just stood there and looked from one to the other questioningly, my gaze gradually changing to a glare. I could feel a wave of embarrassment pass from one to the other. Finally the man who was the jolly host, and at whose elbow I was standing mutely, sensed that something untoward was taking place. He turned half-way round, looked up at me for the first time, then, as if to brush me away, remarked: 'What, you still here? We don't want any candy. Away with it!' Still I said nothing, just scowled. My fingers were twitching nervously; I was itching to grab him by the throat. I still couldn't believe he intended to play that sort of trick on me—not me, a born white American, an artist to boot, and all the other grand things I credited myself with in a moment of wounded pride. Suddenly I recalled the scene I had put on for the amusement of my friends in this same café, when I had made such abominable sport of the poor old Jew. Suddenly I realized the irony of my situation. Now I was the poor helpless individual. The butt of the evening. It was grand sport. Grand indeed, if you happened to be seated at the table and not standing on your hind legs like a dog begging for a few crumbs. I went hot and cold. I was so ashamed of myself, so damned sorry for myself at the same time, that I was ready to murder the man who was baiting me. Far better to land in jail than tolerate further humiliation. Better to start a rumpus and break the deadlock.

Fortunately the man must have sensed what was passing through my head. However, he didn't quite know how to pass it off, his little joke. I heard him, in a rather conciliatory voice, say —'What's the matter?' Then for a few minutes I heard nothing, nothing but the sound of my own voice. What I was yelling I don't know. I know only that I was ranting like a madman. I might have continued indefinitely had not the waiters rushed up to bundle me off. Their arms about me, they were just about to throw me out bodily, when the man who had been baiting me begged them to let me go. Springing to his feet, he put his hand on my shoulder. 'I'm so sorry,' he said, 'I had no idea I was causing you such anguish. Sit down a moment, won't you?' He reached for a bottle and poured out a glass of wine. I was flushed and still glowering. My hands were trembling violently. The whole company now stared at me; it seemed as if they formed one huge animal with many pairs of eyes. People at the other tables were also staring at me. I felt the man's warm hand resting on mine; he was urging me in a soothing voice to take a drink. I raised the glass and swallowed it down. He refilled it and raised his own to his lips. 'To your health!' he said, and the other members of his party followed suit. Then he said: 'My name is Spiel-berg. What is yours, if I may ask?' I gave him my right name, which sounded intensely strange to my ears, and we clinked glasses. In a moment they were all talking at once, all trying desperately to prove to me how sorry they were for their rude behaviour. 'Won't you have some chicken?' begged a sweet young woman opposite me. She raised the platter and handed it to me. I couldn't very well refuse. The waiter was summoned. Wouldn't I like something else? Coffee, surely, and perhaps a little schnapps? I consented. I hadn't yet said a word, other than to give my name. ('What is Henry Miller doing here?' I kept repeating to myself. 'Henry Miller . . . Henry Miller.')

Out of the jumble of words which assaulted my ears I finally made out the following—'What on earth are you doing here? Is this an experiment?' By this time I was able to draw a smile. 'Yes,' I said feebly, 'in a way.'

It was my would-be tormentor who was now endeavouring to talk to me in earnest. 'What *are* you really?' he said. 'I mean, what do you do ordinarily?'

I told him in a few words.

Well, well! Now we were getting somewhere. He had suspected something of the sort all along. Could he help me, perhaps? He knew a number of editors intimately, he confided. Had once hoped to be a writer himself. And so on. . . .

I remained with them an hour or two, eating and drinking, and feeling thoroughly at home with them. Everyone present bought a box of candy. One or two went over to the other tables and induced their friends to buy too, somewhat to my embarrassment. Their manner of doing it suggested that this was the least they could do for a man who was obviously destined to be one of America's great writers. It was astonishing to me what sincerity and genuine sympathy they now displayed. And only a little while ago I had been the butt of their crude jokes. They were all Jews, it turned out. Middle-class Jews who took a lively interest in the arts. I suspected that they took me for a Jew too. No matter. It was the first time I had met any Americans for whom the word artist suggested magic. That I happened to be an artist *and* a peddler made me doubly interesting to them. Their ancestors had all been peddlers and, if not artists, scholars. I was in the tradition.

I was in the tradition all right. Shuffling about from joint to joint I wondered what Ulric would say if he were to run into me. Or Ned, who was still slaving for that grand old man McFarland. Musing thus, I suddenly noticed a Jewish friend of mine, an ear doctor, approaching. (I owed him quite a bill.) Before he could catch my eyes I ran into the street and hopped a bus going uptown. I waved to him from the platform. After I had ridden a few blocks I got off, walked wearily back to the bright lights, and began all over again, selling a box now and then, always, it seemed, to a middle-class Jew, a Jew who felt sorry, and perhaps a little ashamed, for me. It was strange to be receiving the commiseration of a down-trodden people. The reversal of roles yielded a mysterious assuagement. I shuddered to think what would happen to me should I have the misfortune to run into a gang of rowdy Irishers.

Around midnight I ducked home. Mona was already back and in a good mood. She had sold a whole valiseful of candies. And all in one spot. Had been wined and dined as well. *Where?* At

Papa Moskowitz's. (I had skipped Moskowitz's because I had seen the car doctor heading for it.)

'I thought you were going to start with the Village tonight?'

'I did,' she exclaimed, then hurriedly explained how she had run into that banker, Alan Cromwell, who was looking for a quiet place to chat. She had dragged him to Moskowitz's where they had listened to the cymbalon and so on and so on. Anyway, Moskowitz had bought a box of candy, then introduced her to his friends, all of whom insisted on buying candy. And then who should happen along but that man she had met in an office building the first morning. Mathias was his name. He and Moskowitz were friends from the old country. This Mathias of course also bought a half-dozen boxes.

Here she switched off about the real estate business. Mathias, it seems, was eager to have her learn the business. He was certain she could sell houses as eaily as imported candies. First, of course, she would have to learn how to drive a car. He would teach her himself, she said. She thought it a good idea to learn even if she never sold real estate. We could use the car to go for a spin occasionally. Wouldn't that be wonderful? *And so on.* . . .

'And how did he and Cromwell get along?' I finally managed to put in.

'Just fine.'

'No, really?'

'Why not? They're both intelligent and sensitive. Because Cromwell's a drunkard you needn't think he's a sap.'

'O.K. But what did Cromwell have to tell you that was so important?'

'Oh *that*! We never got to that. There were so many people at our table. . . .'

'O.K. I must say, though, you certainly did handsomely.' Pause. 'I sold a few myself.'

'I've been thinking, Val,' she began, as if she hadn't heard me. I knew what was coming. I made a wry grimace.

'Serious, Val, you shouldn't be selling candy. Let *me* do it! You see how easy it is for me. You stay home and write.'

'But I can't write night and day.'

'Well read then, or go to the theatre, or see your friends. You never go to see your friends any more.'

I said I would think about it. Meanwhile she had emptied her purse on the table. Quite a haul, it was.

'Our patron will certainly be surprised,' said I.

'Oh, did I tell you? I saw him tonight. I had to go back for more candy. He said if it keeps up this way we'll soon be able to open a shop of our own.

'Won't that be swell!'

Things rolled along merrily for a couple of weeks. I had made a compromise with Mona: I carried the two valises and waited outside while she cleaned up. I always took a book along and read. Sometimes Sheldon accompanied us. He not only insisted on carrying the valises but he also insisted on paying for the midnight repast which we always ate in a Jewish delicatessen on Second Avenue. A wonderful meal it was each night. Plenty of sour cream, radishes, onions, strudels, pastrami, smoked fish, all kinds of dark bread, creamy sweet butter, Russian tea, caviar, egg noodles—and Seltzer water. Then home in a taxi, always over the Brooklyn Bridge. Alighting in front of our stately brown stone house, I often wondered what the landlord would think were he to notice us coming home at that hour of the morning with our two valises.

There were always new admirers cropping up. She had a difficult time, Mona, to shake them off. The latest one was a Jewish artist—Manuel Siegfried. He hadn't much money but he had a wonderful collection of art books. We borrowed them freely, especially the erotic ones. We liked best the Japanese artists. Ulric came several times with a magnifying glass, so as not to miss a stroke.

O'Mara was for selling them and have Mona pretend they had been stolen. He thought we were overly scrupulous.

One night, when Sheldon called to accompany us, I opened one of the most sensational albums and asked him to look at it. He took one glance and turned his back to me. He held his two hands over his eyes until I had closed the book.

'What's the matter with you?' I asked.

He put his finger to his lips and looked away.

'They won't bite you,' I said.

Sheldon wouldn't answer, just kept edging towards the door. Suddenly he put his two hands to his mouth and made a beeline for the toilet. I heard him retching. When he returned he came up to me, and, putting his two hands in mine, looked into my eyes imploringly. 'Never let Mrs *Miller* see them!' he begged in a hushed voice. I put my two fingers to my lips and said: 'All right, Sheldon, on my word of honour!'

He was on hand now almost every night. When I didn't feel like talking I would let him stand beside me, like a post, while I read. After a time it struck me as foolish to be making the rounds with this blinking idiot. Mona, when she learned that I intended to stay home, was delighted. She would be able to operate more freely, she said. We would all be better off.

And so, one night while chewing the fat with O'Mara, who was also delighted that I was staying home, the idea came to me to start a mail order candy business. O'Mara, always ready for a new proposition, fairly jumped to the bait. 'Put it over in a big way,' that was his idea. We began at once to make plans: the right kind of letter-head, circular letters, follow-up letters, lists of names, and so on. Thinking of names, I began to count up all the clerks, telegraphers and managers I knew in the telegraph company. They couldn't possibly refuse to buy a box of candy once a week. That was all we intended to ask of our potential clients—a box a week. It never occurred to us that one might grow tired of eating a box of candy, even imported candy, once a week every week for fifty-two weeks of the year.

We decided that it was better not to let Mona know about our scheme for a while. 'You know how she is,' said O'Mara.

Of course nothing of any consequence developed. The stationery was beautiful, the letters perfect, but the sales were virtually nil. In the midst of our campaign Mona discovered what we were up to. She didn't approve of it at all. Said we were wasting time. Besides, she was about sick of the game. Mathias, her real estate friend, was ready to launch her any day. She already knew how to drive, she said. (Neither of us believed this.) A few good sales and we would soon have a house of our own. *And so on. . . .* And then there was Alan Cromwell. She hadn't told me of his proposition. She had been waiting for a propitious moment.

'Well, what is it?' I asked.

'He wants me to write a column—for the Hearst papers. One a day without fail.'

I jumped. '*What*! A column a day?' Whoever heard of the Hearst papers offering a column to an unknown writer?

'That's *his* affair, Val. He knows what he's doing.'

'But will they print the stuff?' I thought I smelled a rat.

'No,' she replied 'not right away. We're to do it for a few months, and if they like it . . . Anyway, that's not important! The thing is that Cromwell will pay us a hundred dollars a week out of his own pocket. He's dead sure he can sell the man who runs the syndicate. They're close friends.'

'And what am I—or *you*, excuse me!—supposed to write about every day?'

'Anything under the sun.'

'You don't mean it!'

'I certainly do. Otherwise I wouldn't have given it a moment's thought.'

I had to admit it sounded good. So . . . she'd sell real estate and I would write a daily column. Not bad. 'A hundred a week, you say? That's damned decent of him . . . *Cromwell*, I mean. He must think a lot of you.' (This with a straight face.)

'It's a mere bagatelle to him, Val. He's simply trying to be of help.'

'Does he know about *me*? I mean, has he no suspicion?'

'Of course not. Are you mad?'

'Well, I just wondered. Sometimes a guy like that . . . you

know. . . . Sometimes you can tell them most anything. I'd like to meet him some time. I'm curious.'

'That would be easy,' said Mona, smiling.

'What do you mean?'

'Why, just meet me at Moskowitz's some evening. I'll introduce you as a friend.'

'That's an idea. I'll do that some evening. It'll be fun. You can introduce me as a Jewish physician. How's that?'

'But before we give up this candy racket,' I added, 'I'd like to try out something. I have a hunch that if we were to send a couple of messenger boys to the various telegraph offices we would clean up. We might sell a couple of hundred at one stroke.'

'Oh, that reminds me,' said Mona. 'The candy store man has invited us to go to dinner with him next Saturday. He wants to give us a treat to show his appreciation. I think he'll offer to set us up in business. I wouldn't turn it down cold, if I were you —you might hurt his feelings.'

'Of course. He's a prince. He's done more for us than any of our friends ever have.'

The next days were absorbed in writing personal notes to all my old pals in the telegraph company. I even included messages to some of the men in the vice-president's office. In routing the itinerary, I realized that instead of a couple of messengers I would require a half-dozen—if the coup was to be accomplished at one stroke.

I totalled up the possible sales—came to something over $500.00. Not a bad way to retire from the candy business, I thought to myself, rubbing my hands in expectation.

The day came. I picked six bright boys, gave them explicit instructions, and sent them on their way.

Towards evening they came filing back, each one with a full valise. Not a box had been sold. Not one. I couldn't believe my eyes. I paid the boys off—a considerable sum!—and sat down on the floor with the valises all about me.

The letters, which I had attached to the candy boxes with rubber bands, were intact. I picked them up one by one and shook my head over each one. 'Incredible, incredible!' I kept repeating. Finally I came to the two addressed to Hymie Laubscher and Steve Romero. I held the envelopes in my two hands for a while, unable to comprehend the situation. If I couldn't depend on two old pals like Hymie and Steve, who then could I depend on?

Unwittingly I had opened the envelope addressed to Steve Romero. Something was written across the top of the letter head. Before reading a word I already felt relieved. At least he had given an explanation.

'Spivac intercepted your boy in the vice-president's office. Notified all hands to refuse the candy. Sorry. Steve.'

I opened Hymie's envelope. Same message. I opened Costigan's envelope. *Ditto.* By this time I was raging. 'That bastard Spivak! So that was his way of getting back at me!' I swore I would strangle him, right on the street, next time I ran into him.

I sat there with Costigan's note in my hand. Costigan the knuckle-duster. It was ages since I had seen or heard from him. What a treat it would be for him to teach Spivak a little lesson! All he needed to do was to lure the latter uptown some evening, trap him in a dark street near the river and give the works. The trouble that stinker had gone to! Telephoning each and every office in Brooklyn, Manhattan and the Bronx! I was surprised that Hymie hadn't dispatched a messenger to tip me off; it would have saved me a lot of jack. But he had probably been short-handed, as usual.

I got to thinking of all the goofy guys I knew who were always ready to do me a good turn. There was the night clerk in the 14th Street office who gambled incessantly; his boss was a eunuch who had been trying for years to induce the president to use carrier pigeons to deliver the telegrams. Never was there a more heartless, soulless individual than this *hombre* from Greenpoint; he would do anything for a few more dollars to place on the horses. There was the hunchback over in the fish market. An out-and-out fiend, a sort of Jack-the-Ripper in mufti. And that night-messenger, Arthur Wilmington. Once a minister of the gospel, he was now a filthy human wreck who made caca in his pants. There was sly little Jimmy Falzone, with the face of an angel and the instincts of a thug. There was the rat-faced lad from Harlem who peddled dope and falsified cheques. There was the drunken giant from Cuba, Lopez, who could crack a man's ribs with one gentle hug. There was Kovalski, the demented Pole, who had three wives and fourteen children: he would do anything short of murder—for a dollar.

For that matter I didn't even have to think of such riff-raff. There was Gus, the policeman, who escorted Mona from place to place in the Village whenever she was in the mood for it. Gus was one of those faithful dogs who would club a man to death if a woman merely hinted that she had been insulted by a strange man. And what about our good Catholic friend Buckley, the detective, who when drunk would take out his black crucifix and ask us to kiss it? Hadn't we done him a good turn one night by hiding his revolver when he was on a rampage?

When Mona arrived I was still seated on the floor, still in a reverie. The news didn't upset her greatly. She had expected something of the sort to happen. She was actually glad it had turned out so; perhaps it would cure me once and for all of my impracticable schemes. She was the only one who knew how to raise money and she did it without creating a fuss. When would I begin to put complete confidence in her?

'Let's quit all this,' I said. 'If Cromwell comes across with that hundred bucks a week we ought to be able to manage, don't you think?'

She wasn't sure. The hundred-a-week would take care of *us*, but what about the alimony, what about her mother and brothers, what about this and that?

'Did you ever raise that mortgage money your mother was asking for?' I inquired.

Yes, she had—weeks ago. She didn't want to go into that just now, it was too painful. She merely remarked that no matter how much money came in it just flew. There was only one solution, and that was to make a big haul. The real estate game appealed to her more and more.

'Let's stop the candy business anyway,' I urged. 'We'll go to dinner with our patron and we'll break the news to him gently. I'm sick of selling things . . . and I don't want you to be selling things either. It's disgusting.'

She appeared to agree with me. Suddenly, while creaming her face, she said: 'Why don't we call Ulric up and go out to dinner together? You haven't seen him for ages, you know.'

I thought it a good idea. It was rather late but I decided to phone and see. I put my things on and dashed out.

An hour or so later the three of us were sitting in a restaurant down near the City Hall. An Italian place. Ulric was delighted to see us again. Had been wondering what we were up to all this time. While waiting for the minestrone we had a couple of drinks. Ulric had been working like a dog on some soap campaign and was glad of the opportunity to relax. He was in a mellow mood.

Mona was giving him an earful about the candy business— just the highlights. Ulric always listened to her tales with a sort of bemused wonder. He waited to hear my side of it before passing any comments. If I seemed in a corroborative mood he would then listen with both ears, quite as if he were hearing it all for the first time.

'What a life!' he chuckled. 'I wish I had the guts to venture out a little more. But then those things never happen to me. So you peddled candies in the Cafe Royal. I'll be damned.' He wagged his head and chuckled some more.

'And is O'Mara still with you?' he asked.

'Yes, but he's leaving soon now. He wants to go South. Has a hunch he can clean up down there.'

'I suppose you won't miss him too much, what?'

'But I *will*,' I said. 'I like O'Mara, despite his faults.'

To this Ulric nodded his head, as if to say that I was over-indulgent but it was a good trait.

'And that Osiecki fella . . . what's happened to *him?*'

'In Canada now. His two friends—you remember them—are looking after his girl.'

'I see,' said Ulric, rubbing his tongue back and forth over his ripe red lips. 'Chivalrous lads, what?' and he chuckled some more.

'By the way,' he said, turning to Mona, 'doesn't it seem to you that the Village is getting rather seedy these days? I made the mistake of taking some of my Virginia friends down there the other night. We got out in a hurry, I can tell you. All I could see were dives and joints. Maybe we didn't have enough under our belts. . . . There was one spot, a restaurant, I think, over on Sheridan Square. Quite a place, I don't mind saying.'

Mona laughed. 'You mean Minnie Douchebag's hang-out?'

'Minnie Douchebag?'

'Yes, that crazy fairy who sings and plays the piano . . . and wears women's clothes. Wasn't he there?'

'Of course!' said Ulric. 'I didn't know that was his name. I must say it fits him. A real zany, by God. I thought at one point he'd climb the chandeliers. What a vile, stinking tongue he has too!' He turned to me. 'Henry, things have changed some since our time. Try to picture me sitting there with two staid, conservative Virginians. To tell the truth, they hardly understood a word he said.'

The dives and joints, as Ulric called them, were of course the places we had been haunting. Though I pretended to make fun of Ulric's squeamishness, I shared his opinion of these places. The Village had indeed deteriorated. There were nothing but dives and joints, nothing but pederasts, Lesbians, pimps, tarts, fakes and phonies of all description. I didn't see the point of telling Ulric about it, but the last time we were at Paul and Joe's the place was entirely dominated by homos in sailors' uniforms. Some lascivious little bitch had tried to bite off a piece of Mona's right breast—right in the dining room. Coming away from the place we had stumbled over two 'sailors' writhing on the floor of the balcony, their pants down and grunting and squealing like stuck pigs. Even for Greenwich Village that was going pretty far, it seemed to me. As I say, I saw no point in relaying these incidents to Ulric—they were too incredible for him to swallow. What he liked to hear were Mona's tales about the clients she shook down, those queer birds, as he called them, from Weehawken, Milwaukee, Washington, Puerto Rico, the Sorbonne, and so on. It was plausible but mystifying to him that men of good standing should prove so vulnerable. He could understand shaking them down once, but not again and again.

'How does she ever manage to hold them off?' he blurted out, then made as if he were biting his tongue.

Suddenly he switched. 'You know, Henry, that man McFarland has been asking for you repeatedly. Ned, of course, doesn't understand how you could turn down a good offer like that. He keeps telling McFarland you will turn up one day. You must have made a tremendous impression on the old boy. I suppose you have other plans, *but*—if you ever change your mind I think you could get most anything you want of McFarland. He told Ned confidentially that he would sack the whole office in order to keep a man like you. Thought I ought to tell you this. You never know. . . .'

Mona quickly diverted the talk to another trend. Soon we had drifted to the subject of burlesque. Ulric had a diabolical memory for names. He could not only recall the names of the comedians, the soubrettes, the hoochee-koochee dancers of the last twenty years, he could also give the names of the theatres where he had seen them, the songs they sang, whether it was Winter or Spring, and who had accompanied him on each occasion. From burlesque he drifted to musical comedies and thence to the various Quat'z'Arts Balls.

These pow-wows, when the three of us got together, were always rambling, hectic, diffuse. Mona, who was never able to concentrate on anything for long, had a way of listening which would drive any man crazy. Always, just when you had reached the most interesting part of your story, she was suddenly reminded of something, and it had to be communicated at once. It made no difference whether we were talking of Cimabue, Sigmund Freud or the Fratellini brothers: the things she thought so important to tell us were as remote as the asteroids. Only a woman could make such outlandish connections. Nor was she one of those who could have say and then let you have yours. To get back to the point was like trying to reach the shore directly oppostie by fording a swift stream. One always had to allow for drift.

Ulric had grown somewhat accustomed to this form of conversation, much against the grain. It was a pity to subject him to it, though, for when given free play he could rival the Irish harp. That photographic eye of his, those soft palps with which he touched things, particularly the things he loved, his nostalgic memory which was inexhaustible, his mania for detail, certitude, exactitude (time, place, rhythm, ambiance, magnitude, temperature) gave to his talk a quality such as the old masters achieved in pigment. Indeed, often when listening to him I had the impression that I was actually in the company of an old master. Many of my friends referred to him as quaint—'charming and quaint'. Which meant, 'old-fashioned'. Yet he was neither a scholar, a recluse, nor a crank. He was simply of another time. When he spoke of the men he loved—the painters—he was one with them. Not only had he the gift of surrendering himself, he had also the art of identifying himself with those whom he revered.

He use to say that my talk could send him home drunk. He

144

pretended that in my presence he could never say things the way he wanted to, the way he meant. He seemed to think it only natural that I should be a better story teller than he, because I was a writer. The truth is, it was just the other way round. Except for rare moments when I was touched off, when I went hay-wire, when I blew my top, I was a stuttering gawk by comparison.

What really roused Ulric's admiration and devotion was the raw content of my life, its underlying chaos. He could never reconcile himself to the fact that, though we had sprung from the same milieu, had been reared in the same stupid German-American atmosphere, we had developed into such different beings, had gone in such totally opposite directions. He exaggerated this divergence, of course. And I did little to correct it, knowing the pleasure it gave him to magnify my eccentricities. One has to be generous sometimes, even it it makes one blush.

'Sometimes,' said Ulric, 'when I talk about you to my friends it sounds fabulous, even to me. In the short time since we've known each other again it seems to me you've already led a dozen lives. I hardly know anything about that period in between —when you were living with the widow and her son, for example. When you had those rich sessions with Lou Jacobs—wasn't that his name? That must have been a rewarding period, even if a trying one. No wonder that man McFarland sensed something different in you. I know I'm treading on dangerous ground in opening that subject again'—he gave a quick, appealing glance at Mona—'but really, Henry, this life of adventure and move-ment which you crave . . . excuse me, I don't mean to put it crudely . . . I know you're a man of contemplation too. . . .' Here he sort of gave up, chuckled, snorted, rolled his tongue over his lips, swallowed a few drops of cognac, slapped his thighs, looked from one to the other of us, and let out a good long belly laugh. 'Damn it, you know what I mean!' he blurted out. 'I'm stuttering like a schoolboy. I think what I intended to say is just this—you need a larger scope to your life. You need to meet men who are more near your own stature. You should be able to travel, have money in your pocket, explore, investigate. In short—bigger adventures, bigger exploits.'

I nodded my head smilingly, urging him to continue.

'Of course I realize also that this life which you're now leading is rich in ways that are beyond me . . . rich to you as a writer, I mean. I know that a man doesn't choose the material of life which is to make his art. That's given, or ordained, by the cast of his temperament. These queer characters who seem attracted to you as if by a magnet, no doubt there are vast worlds to be plumbed there. But at what a cost! It would exhaust me to spend an even-ing with most of them. I enjoy listening to you telling about them, but I don't think I could cope with all that myself. What I mean,

Henry, is that they don't seem to give anything in return for the attention you bestow on them. But there I go again. *I'm wrong, of course.* You must know instinctively what's good for you and what's bad.'

Here I had to interrupt him. 'About that you *are* wrong, I think. I never think of such a thing—what's good or what's bad for me. I take what comes my way and I make the best of it. I don't cultivate these people deliberately. You're right, they're attracted to me—but so am I to them. Sometimes I think I have more in common with them than with you or O'Mara or any of my real friends. By the way, have I got any real friends, do you think? I know one thing, I never can count on you in a pinch, not any of you.'

'That's very true, Henry,' he said, his lower jaw dropping to a queer angle. 'I don't think any of us are capable of being quite the friend you should have. You deserve much better.'

'Shit,' I said, 'I don't mean to harp on that. Forgive me, that was just a random thought.'

'What's become of that doctor friend of yours . . . *Kronski?* I haven't heard you speak of him lately.'

'I haven't the slightest idea,' I said. 'He's probably hibernating. He'll show up again, don't worry.'

'Val treats him abominably,' said Mona. 'I don't understand it. If you ask me, he's a real friend. Val never seems to appreciate his real friends. *Except you, Ulric.* But sometimes I have to remind him to get in touch with you. He forgets easily.'

'I don't think he'll ever forget *you* easily,' said Ulric. With this he gave his thighs a thumping wallop and broke into a sheepish grin. 'That wasn't a very tactful remark, was it? But I'm sure you know what I mean,' and he put his hand over Mona's and squeezed it gently.

'I'll take care that he doesn't forget me,' said Mona lightly. 'I suppose you never thought we would last this long, did you?'

'To tell the truth, I didn't,' said Ulric. 'But now that I know you, know how much you mean to each other, I understand.'

'Why don't we get out of here?' I said. 'Why not come over to our place? We could put you up for the night, if you like. O'Mara won't be home tonight.'

'All right,' said Ulric, 'I'll take you up. I can afford to take a day or two off. I'll ask the *patron* to give us a bottle or two. . . . What would you like?'

When we threw on the lights in the apartment Ulric stood a moment at the threshold taking it in appraisingly. 'It sure looks beautiful,' he said, almost wistfully. 'I hope you can keep it for a long time.' He walked over to my work table and studied the disarray. 'It's always interesting to see how a writer arranges his things,' he said musingly. 'You can feel the ideas bubbling from the papers. It all seems so intense. You know'—and he put an arm around my shoulder—'I often think of you when I'm working. I see you huddled over the machine, your fingers racing like mad. There's always a marvellous look of concentration on your face. You had that even as a boy—I suppose you don't remember that. Yeah, yeah! Golly, it's funny how things turn out. I have a job, sometimes, to make myself believe that this writer I know is also my friend, and a very old friend. There's something about you, Henry—and that's what I was trying to get at in the restaurant—something legendary, I might say, if that doesn't seem too big a word. You understand me, don't you?' His voice was a pitch lower now, extremely suave and mellow, honeyed, in fact. But sincere. Devastatingly sincere. His eyes were moist with affection; he was drooling at the mouth. I had to shut off the current or we would all be in tears.

When I came back from the bathroom he and Mona were talking earnestly. He still had his hat and coat on. In his hands was a long sheet of paper with fantastic words which I kept by my side in case of need. Evidently he had been pumping Mona about my work habits. Writing was an art which intrigued him enormously. He was amazed, apparently, to see how much I had written since we last met. Lovingly he fingered the books which were stacked up on the writing table. 'You don't mind?' he said, glancing at a few notes lying beside the books. I didn't mind in the least, of course. I would have opened my skin to let him peer inside, were I able to. It tickled me to see how much he made of each little thing. At the same time I couldn't help thinking that here was the only friend I had who displayed a genuine interest in what I was doing. It was reverence for writing itself which he evinced—and for the man, whoever it might be, who had the guts to struggle with the medium. We might have stood there the whole night talking about those queer words I had listed, or about that little note I had made anent 'The Diary of a Futurist', which I was then labouring on.

So this was the man of another epoch whom my friends dubbed 'old-fashioned'! Yes, it had indeed become old-fashioned to show such naive mystification over mere words. The men of the Middle Ages were another breed entirely. They spent hours, days, weeks, months discussing minutiae which have no reality for us. They were capable of absorption, concentration, digestion to a degree which seem to us phenomenal if not pathological. They were artists through and through. Their lives were steeped in art, as well as in blood. It was one life through and through. It was this kind of life which Ulric craved, though he despaired of ever realizing it. What he secretly hoped was that perhaps *I* would recapture and bequeath to others this unitive life in which everything was woven into a significant whole.

He was walking around now with glass in hand, gesticulating, making guttural sounds, smacking his lips, as if he had suddenly found himself in Paradise. What an idiot he had been to talk that way in the restaurant! Now he could see that other side of me which he had touched on so lightly before. What richness the place exuded! The very annotations in the margins of my books spoke eloquently of an activity which was foreign to him. Here was a mind seething with ideas. Here was a man who knew how to work. And he had been accusing me of wasting my time!

'This cognac isn't too bad, is it?' he said, allowing himself time to pause. 'A little less cognac and a little more reflection—that would be the path of wisdom, for me.' He made one of those typical grimaces which only he knew how to combine into a compound of abjection, adulation, flattery, vilification and triumph.

'Man, how do you find time to do it all, will you tell me that?' he groaned, sinking into an easy chair without spilling a drop of the precious liquid. 'One thing is evident,' he added quickly, 'and that's this: you love what you're doing. *I don't!* I ought to take the hint and change my ways. . . . That sounds rather fatuous, I guess, doesn't it? Go ahead, laugh; I know how ridiculous I sound at times. . . .'

I explained that I wasn't laughing at him but with him.

'It doesn't matter one way or the other,' he said. 'I don't mind if you laugh at me. You're the one person I can count on to register real reactions. You're not cruel, you're honest. And I find damned little of that commodity among the fellows I associate with. But I'm not going to bore you with that old song-and-dance.' Here he leaned forward to ooze forth a warm, genial smile. 'Perhaps this is inapropos, but I don't mind telling you, Henry, that the only time I work with vim and vigour, with anything approaching love, is when that darkie, Lucy, poses for me. The hell of it is I can never get my end in. You know Lucy—how she lets me *manipulate* her and all that. She poses in the nude for me now, you know. Yeah! A wonderful piece of ass.' He chortled again. It was almost a whinny. 'Golly, those poses that critter strikes sometimes! I wish you were there to see it. You'd die laughing. But in the end she leaves me dangling. I have to douse the old boy in cold water. It gets me down. Oh well. . . .' He looked up at Mona, who was standing behind him, to see how she was reacting.

To his utter amazement she came out with this: 'Why don't you let me pose for you sometime?'

His eyes began to roll wildly. He looked from her to me and back again at her.

'By Jove!' he said, 'how is it I never thought of that before? I suppose this bird doesn't mind?'

The night wore on with reminiscence, talks of the future, plans for explorations into the night life, and ended as always with the names of the great painters ringing in our ears. Ulric's last remark before dropping off to sleep was: 'I must read Freud's essay on da Vinci soon. . . . Or would you say it wasn't so important after all?'

'The important thing now is to sleep well and wake up refreshed,' I replied.

He signified his assent by giving a loud fart—quite unintentionally, of course.

A few nights later we went to dinner with the man from the candy store. We sat in a cellar on Allen Street, that dreariest of all streets, where the elevated trains thunder overhead. An Arabian friend of his ran the restaurant. The food was excellent and our host was most generous. It was a genuine pleasure to talk to the man, he was so sincere, upright, plain-spoken. He talked at length about his youth which had been one long nightmare relieved only by intermittent dreams of being able one day to get to America. He described in simple, moving language his vision of America, conceived in the ghetto of Cracow. It was the same Paradise which millions of souls have fabricated in the darkness of despair. To be sure, the East Side wasn't exactly as he had imagined it, but life was good nevertheless. He had hopes now of moving to the country some day, perhaps to the Catskill Mountains, where he would open a resort. He mentioned a town where I had spent my vacations as a boy: a little community long since taken over by the Chosen Tribe, bearing no resemblance to the charming little village I once had known. But I could easily imagine what a haven it would be for him.

We had been talking thus for some time when he suddenly thought of something. He got up and searched his overcoat pockets. Beaming like a schoolboy, he handed Mona and myself two little packets wrapped in tissue paper. They were little gifts, he explained, in appreciation of the way we had worked to make the candy business a success. We opened them at once. For Mona there was a beautiful wrist watch, for myself a fountain pen of the finest make. He thought they would be useful.

Then he proceeded to tell us of his plans for our future. We were to continue working just as we had been for a while and, if we trusted him sufficiently, we were to leave with him each week a portion of our earnings, so that he could lay something aside for us. He knew that we were incapable of saving a penny. He wanted very much to set us up in business, rent a little office somewhere and have people work for us. He was certain we would make a go of it. One should always start from the bottom, he thought, and use cash instead of borrowing, as Americans do. He took out his bank book and showed us his deposits. There was over twelve thousand dollars to his credit. After selling the store there would be another five to ten thousand dollars. If we did well, perhaps he would sell his store to us.

Again we were at a loss how to disillusion him. I intimated gently, very gently, that we might have other plans for the future, but seeing the look on his face I quickly dropped the subject. Yes, we would carry on. We would become the candy kings of Second Avenue. Maybe we would move to the country too, help him run his resort in Livingston Manor. Yes, we would probably soon have children too. It was time to be getting serious. As for the writing, after we had built up a good business it would be time enough to think of that. Hadn't Tolstoy retired to write only late in life? I nodded agreement rather than disappoint him. Then, in dead earnest, he asked if I didn't think it would be a good idea to write up *his* life—how he rose from a worker in the marble quarries to the owner of a big resort. I said I thought it an excellent theme; we would talk it over when the time was ripe.

Anyway, we were hooked. For the life of me I couldn't run out on the man. He was just too damned decent. Beside, Cromwell had yet to give the final word about that column. (He wouldn't be in town again for a few weeks.) Why not stagger along in the candy business until then? As for Mona, she thought it would do no harm to try out the real estate business in the day time. Mathias was only too eager to advance her money on account until she made her first sale.

Despite all our good intentions the candy business was doomed. Mona could scarcely sell a box or two of an evening. I had taken to accompanying her again, waiting outside the joints with the two valises and myself with Elie Faure. (By now my blood was so saturated with the *History of Art* that I could close my eyes at will any time and recite whole passages, embroidering them with fantastic elaborations of my own.) Sheldon had mysteriously vanished. O'Mara had left for the South, and Osiecki was still in Canada. A dreary stretch. Tired of the Village and the East Side, we tried our luck uptown. It wasn't the same old Broadway that George M. Cohan sang of. It was a noisy, rowdy, hostile atmosphere breeding nasty encounters, threats, insults, scorn, contempt and humiliation. All during this period I had a frightful case of the piles. I can see myself now all over again as I hung by the arms from a high picket railing opposite the Lido, thinking to ease the pain by lifting the weight off my feet. The last visit to the Lido ended with an attempt by the manager, an ex-pugilist, to lock Mona in his office and rape her. *Good old Broadway!*

It was high time to quit the racket. Instead of accumulating a little nest-egg we now owed our patron money. In addition I owed Maude a good sum for the home-made candy I had induced her to make for us. Poor Maude had entered into it with a will, thinking it would help us to meet the alimony bill.

In fact, everything was going screwy. Instead of getting up at noon we would lie abed till four or five in the afternoon. Mathias couldn't understand what had come over Mona. Everything was set for her to make a killing, but she was letting it all drift through her hands.

Sometimes amusing things happened, such as a sudden attack of hiccups which lasted three days and finally forced us to summon a doctor. The moment I lifted up my shirt and felt the man's cold finger on my abdomen I stopped hiccupping. I felt a little ashamed of myself for having made him come all the way from the Bronx. He pretended to be delighted, probably because he discovered that we could play chess. He made no bones about the fact that when he wasn't busy performing abortions he was playing chess. A strange individual, and highly sensitive. Wouldn't think of taking money from us. Insisted on lending us some. We were to call on him whenever we were in a jam, whether for money or for an abortion. He promised that the next time he called he would bring me one of Sholem Aleichem's books. (At this period I hadn't heard of Moishe Nadir, else I would have asked him to lend me *My Life as an Echo.*)

I couldn't help remarking after he left, how typical it was of Jewish physicians to behave thus. Never had a Jewish doctor pressed me to pay my bill. Never had I met one who was not interested in the arts and sciences. Nearly all of them were musicians, painters or writers on the side. What's more, they all held out the hand of friendship. How different from the run of Gentile physicians! For the life of me I couldn't think of one Gentile doctor of my acquaintance who had the least interest in art, not one who was anything but the medico.

'How do you explain it?' I demanded.

'The Jews are always human,' said Mona.

'You said it. They make you feel good even if you're dying.'

A week or so later, in urgent need of fifty dollars, I suddenly thought of my dentist, also of the Chosen Tribe. In my usual roundabout way, I decided to go to the 23rd Street office, where old man Creighton was working as a night messenger, and dispatch him to my friend with a note. I explained to Mona, on the way to the telegraph office, the peculiar tie which existed between this night messenger and myself. I reminded her of how he had come to our rescue that night at Jimmy Kelly's place.

At the office we had to wait a while—Creighton was out on a route. I chinned a bit with the night manager, one of those reformed crooks whom O'Rourke had in hand. Finally Creighton appeared. He was surprised to see me with my wife. In his tactful way, he behaved as if he had never met her before.

I told the night clerk I would be keeping Creighton for an hour or two. Outside I called a cab, intending to ride over to Brooklyn with him and wait at the corner until he had made the touch for me. We started rolling. Leisurely I explained the nature of our errand.

'But it isn't necessary to do that!' he exclaimed. 'I have a little money put aside. It would be a pleasure, Mr Miller, to lend you a hundred, or even two hundred, if that will help you out.'

I demurred at first but finally gave in.

'I'll bring it to you the first thing in the morning,' said Creighton. He drove all the way home with us, chatted a while at the door, then headed for the subway. We had compromised on a hundred and fifty dollars.

The next morning, bright and early, Creighton showed up. 'You needn't be in a hurry to pay it back,' he said. I thanked him warmly and urged him to have dinner with us some evening. He promised to come on his next night off.

The following day there was a headline in the newspaper to the effect that our friend Creighton had set fire to the house he lived in and had been burned to death. No explanation for his grüesome behaviour was offered.

Well, that was one little sum we would never have to return. It was my custom to keep a little notebook in which I recorded the sums we had borrowed. That is, those I knew about. To ascertain what Mona owed her 'cavaliers' was practically impossible. However, I had firm intentions of paying the debts *I* had contracted. Compared to hers, mine were trifling. Even so, it made a staggering list. Many of the items were for five dollars or less. These little sums, however, were the important ones, in my eyes. They had been given me by people who could ill afford to part with a dime. For example, that measly three and a half which had been lent me by Savardekar, one of my ex-night messengers. Such a frail, delicate creature. Used to live on a handful of rice per day. He was undoubtedly back in India now, preparing for saint-hood. Most likely he no longer had need of that three-fifty. Just the same, it would have done me good, infinite good, to be able to send it to him. Even a saint has need of money occasionally.

As I sat there ruminating, it occurred to me that at one time or another almost every Hindu I had known had lent me money. Always touching little sums extracted from battered-looking purses. There was one item, I noticed, for four dollars and seventy-five cents. Due Ali Khan, a Parsee, who had the habit of writing me extraordinary letters, giving his observations of conditions in the telegraph business as well as his impressions of the municipality in general. He had a beautiful hand and used a pompous language. If it was not Christ's teachings, or the saying of the Buddha, which he quoted (for my edification), it was a matter of fact suggestion that I write the Mayor and order him to have the street numbers on all houses illuminated at night. It would make it easier for night messengers to find street addresses, he thought.

To the credit of one, 'Al Jolson,' as we called him, there was a total of sixteen dollars. I had fallen into the bad habit of touching him for a buck every time I ran into him on the street. I did it primarily because it made him so intensely happy to accommodate me with this little offering each time we met. The penalty I had to pay was to stand and listen to him while he hummed a new tune he had composed. Over a hundred of his ditties were floating around among the publishers of Tin Pan Alley. Now and then, on amateur nights, he appeared before the footlights in some neighbourhood theatre. His favourite song was 'Avalon', which he would sing straight or in falsetto, as you wished. Once, when I was entertaining a friend of mine—in 'Little Hungary'—I had to call for a messenger to bring me some cash. It was 'Al Jolson' who brought it. Thoughtlessly I invited him to sit down and have a drink with us. After a few words he asked if he might try out one of his songs. I thought he meant that he would hum it to us, but no, before I stop him he was on his feet in the centre of the floor, his cap in one hand and a glass in the other, singing at the top of his lungs. The patrons of course were highly amused. The song over, he went from table to table with cap in hand soliciting coins. Then he sat down and offered to buy us drinks. Finding this impossible, he slyly slipped me a couple of bills under the table. '*Your percentage,*' he whispered.

The man I already owed a considerable sum to was my Uncle Dave. Several hundred dollars it was, to be augmented as time went on. This Dave Leonard had married my father's sister. He had been a baker for years and then, after losing two fingers, had decided to try something else. Though a born American, a Yankee to boot, he had had no education whatever. He couldn't even write his own name. But what a man! What a heart! I used to lie in wait for Dave outside the Ziegfeld Follies Theatre. He had become a ticket speculator, a racket that netted him several hundred a week—and without much fuss or bother. If he wasn't at the Follies he was at the Hippodrome or at the Met. As I say, I used to hang around outside these places, waiting to catch him during a lull. Dave had only to see me coming and his hand would be in his pocket, ready to flash the roll. It was an enormous wad he carried on him. He'd peel off fifty for me just as easily as ten. Never batted an eye, never asked me what I needed the money for. 'See me any time,' he'd say, 'you know where to find me.' Or else: 'Stick around a while and we'll have a bite to eat.' *Or*— 'Would you like to see the show tonight? I'll have a ticket up front for you, it's an off night.'

A regal guy, Dave. I used to bless his soul every time I parted from him. . . . When I told him one day that I was writing he became thoroughly excited. To Dave it was like saying—'I'm going to become a magician!' His reverence for language was typical of the illiterate man. But there was more than this behind his enthusiasm. Dave understood me, understood that I was different from the rest of the family, and he approved of it. He reminded me touchingly of how I used to play the piano, what an artist I was. His daughter whom I had given lessons to, was now an accomplished pianist. He was stunned to learn that I no longer played. If I wanted a piano he would get me one—he knew where to pick one up cheap. '*Just say the word, Henry!* And then he would cross-examine me about the art of writing. Did one have to think it all out beforehand or did one just make it up as one went long? Of course, one had to be a good speller, he supposed. And one had to keep up with newspapers, eh? It was his idea that a writer had to be thoroughly informed—about everything under the sun. But the thought he loved to dwell on most was that one day he would see my name in print, either in a newspaper, a magazine, or on a book cover. 'I suppose it's hard to write a book,' he would muse. 'It must be hard to remember what you wrote a week ago, no? *And all those characters!* What do you do, keep a list of them in front of you?' And then he would ask my opinion of certain writers he had heard about. Or of some famous columnist who was rolling in money. 'That's the thing, Henry . . . if you could only be a columnist, or a correspondent.' Anyway, he was wishing me well. He was sure I'd make the grade. I had a lot on the ball, and so forth. 'You're sure now that that's enough?' (Referring to the bill he had handed me.) 'Well, if you run short come back tomorrow. I'm not worrying about it, you know.' And then, as an afterthought—'Listen, can you spare a moment? I want you to meet one of my pals. He's dying to shake hands with you. He used to work on a newspaper once.'

Thinking about Dave and his utter goodness it came to me that I hadn't seen my cousin Gene for a long long time. All I knew about him was that he had moved from Yorkville some years ago and was now living on Long Island with his two sons who were growing up.

I wrote him a post-card, saying I'd like to see him again, and asked where we might meet. He wrote back immediately, suggesting an elevated station near the end of the line.

I had fully intended to take with me a good package of groceries and some wine, but the best I could do on setting out to meet him was to rake up a little change, just about enough to get there and back. If he's working, thought I to myself, he can't be so terribly hard up. At the last minute I tried to borrow a dollar from the blind newspaperman at Borough Hall, but in vain.

It was something of a shock I experienced when I saw Gene standing on the platform with his little lunch box in his hand. His hair had already turned grey. He wore a pair of patched trousers, a thick sweater, and a peak cap. His smile, however, was radiant, his handclasp warm. In greeting me his voice trembled. It was still that deep, warm voice which he had even as a boy.

We stood there gazing into each other's eyes for a minute or two. Then he said, in that old Yorkville accent: 'You look fine, Henry.'

'You look good yourself,' said I, 'only a little thinner.'

'I'm getting old,' said Gene, and he removed his cap to show me how bald he was getting.

'Nonsense,' I said, 'you're only in your thirties. Why, you're still a youngster.'

'No,' he replied, 'I've lost my pep. I've had a hard time of it, Henry.'

That's how it began. I realized at once that he was telling me the truth. He was always candid, frank, sincere.

We marched down the elevated stairs into the middle of nowhere. Such a God-forsaken spot it was; something told me it would become more so as we journeyed onward.

I got it slowly, piecemeal, more and more heart-rending as the story progressed. To begin with, he was only working two or three days a week. Nobody wanted beautiful pipe cases any more. It was his father who had found a place for him in the factory. (Ages ago, it seemed.) His father hadn't believed in wasting time getting an education. I didn't need to be reminded of what a boor his father was: always sitting around in his red flannel undershirt, Winter or Summer, with a can of beer in front of him. One of those thick Germans who would never change.

Gene had married, two children had been born, and then, while the kids were still little tots, his wife had died of cancer, a painful, lingering death. He had used up all his savings and gone deep into debt. They had only been in the country, as he called it, a few months when his wife died. It was just at this time that they laid him off at the factory. He had tried raising tropical fish but it was no go. The trouble was that he had to find work he could do at home because there was no one to look after the kids. He did the cooking, the washing, the mending, the ironing, everything. He was alone, terribly alone. He never got over the loss of his wife whom he had loved dearly.

All this as we wended our way to his house. He hadn't yet asked me a thing about myself, so absorbed was he in the narration of his miseries. When we got off the bus, finally, there was a long walk through dingy suburban streets to what looked like a vacant lot, at the very end of which stood his little shack, shabby, woebegone, exactly like the dwellings of the poor white in the deep South. A few flowers were struggling desperately to maintain life outside the front door. They looked pathetic. We walked in and were greeted by his sons, two good-looking youngsters who seemed somewhat undernourished. Quiet, grave lads, strangely sombre and reserved. I had never seen them before. I felt more than ever ashamed of myself for not bringing something.

I felt I had to say something to clear myself.

'You don't have to tell me,' said Gene. 'I know what it's like.'

'But we're not always broke,' I said. 'Listen, I'm going to come again soon, very soon, I promise you. And I'll bring my wife along next time.'

'Don't talk about it,' said Gene. 'I'm so glad you came. We have some lentil soup on the stove, and we have some bread. We won't go hungry.'

He began again—about the days when they didn't have a crumb to eat, when he had grown so desperate that he had gone to his neighbours and begged for a little food—just for the children.

'But Dave would have helped you, I'm sure,' I said. 'Why didn't you ask him for money?'

He looked pained. 'You know how it is. You don't like to borrow from your relatives.'

'But Dave isn't just a relative.'

'I know, Henry, but I don't like to ask for help. I'd rather starve. If it weren't for the kids I guess I would have starved.'

While we were talking the kids had slipped out, to return in a few minutes with some cabbage leaves, celery and radishes.

'You shouldn't have done that,' said Gene, admonishing them gently.

'What did they do?' I asked.

'Oh, they filched those things from a neighbour of ours who's away.'

'Good for them!' I said. 'Damn it, Gene, they've got the right idea. Listen, you're too modest, or too proud, I don't know which.' I apologized at once. How could I berate him for his simple virtues? He was the essence of kindness, gentleness, true humility. Every words he uttered had a golden ring. He never blamed anybody, nor life either. He spoke as if it were all an accident, part of his private destiny, and not to be questioned.

'Maybe they could dig up a little wine too,' I said, half in joke, half in earnest.

'I forgot all about that,' said Gene blushingly. 'We've got a little wine in the cellar. It's home-made wine . . . elderberry . . . can you drink it? I've been saving it for just such an occasion.'

The boys had already slipped downstairs. They were becoming more expansive with each sally. 'They're fine boys, Gene,' I said. 'What are they going to do when they grow up?'

'They won't go into the factory, that's one thing I know. I'm going to try to send them to college. I think it's important to have a good education. Little Arthur, the youngest one, he wants to become a doctor. The big fellow is a wild one; he wants to go

West and become a cowboy. But he'll get over that soon, I guess. They read these silly Westerns, you know.'

Suddenly it occurred to him to ask if I didn't have a child.

'That was by my other wife,' I said. 'A girl.'

He was amazed to learn that I had re-married. Divorce, apparently, was something which never entered his head.

'Does you wife work too?' he asked.

'In a way,' I said. I didn't know quite how to explain the complexities of our life in a few words.

'I suppose,' he said next, 'you're still in the cement company.'

The cement company! I nearly fell off the chair.

'Why no, Gene,' I said, 'I'm a writer now. Didn't you know that?'

'*A writer?*' It was his turn to be astonished. His face lit up with pleasure. 'It doesn't really surprise me, though,' he said. 'I remember how you used to read to us kids in the old days. We always fell asleep on you, remember?' He paused to reflect, his head bowed, then looked up and remarked: 'Of course you had a good education too, didn't you?' He said it as if he had been an immigrant boy who had been denied the usual privileges of an American.

I tried to explain that I hadn't gone very far in school, that we were practically in the same boat. In the middle of it I suddenly asked if he ever read any more.

'Oh yes,' he answered brightly. 'I read quite a little. Nothing much else to do, you know.' He pointed to the shelf in back of me where his books were lodged. I turned round to glance at the titles: Dickens, Scott, Thackeray, the Bronte sisters, George Eliot, Balzac, Zola. . . .

'I don't read any of the modern trash,' he said, answering my unvoiced question.

We sat down to eat. The boys were ravenously hungry. Again I felt a pang of remorse. I realized that had I not been there they would have eaten twice as much. As soon as the soup was finished we tackled the greens. They had no oil, no dressing of any kind, not even mustard. The bread had given out too. I fished in my pocket and dug up a dime, all I had besides the carfare home. 'Let them go and get a loaf of bread,' I said.

'It's not necessary,' said Gene. 'They can go without. They're used to it by now.'

'Come on! I could stand a bit more myself, couldn't you?'

'But there's no butter or jam!'

'What's the difference? We'll eat it plain. I've done that before.' The kids ducked out to get the bread.

'Jesus,' I said, 'you really are down to nothing, aren't you?'

'This isn't bad, Henry,' he said. 'For a time, you know, we lived on weeds.'

'No, don't tell me that! It's preposterous.' I was almost angry with him. 'Don't you know,' I said, 'that you don't have to starve? This country is lousy with food. Gene, I'd go out and beg before I'd eat weeds. Damn it, I never heard of such a thing.'

'It's different with you,' said Gene. 'You've knocked around. You've been out in the world. I haven't. I've lived like a squirrel in a cage. . . . Except for that time I worked on the garbage scow.'

'*What?* The *garbage* scow? What do you mean by that?'

'I mean just that,' said Gene calmly. 'Hauling garbage to Barren Island. It was when my kids were living with my wife's parents for a time. I had the chance to do something different for a change. . . . You remember Mr Kiesling, the alderman, don't you? He got me the job. I enjoyed it too—while it lasted. Of course the smell was frightful, but you can get used to anything after a while. It paid eighty dollars a month, about twice what I earned in the pipe factory. It was fun too, sailing out into the bay, around the harbour, up and down the rivers. It was the first and only chance I ever had to get out into the world. Once we got lost at sea, during a storm. We drifted around for days. The worst of it was that we ran out of food. Yeah, we were forced to eat garbage. It was quite a wonderful experience. I must say I enjoyed it. Far better than being in a pipe factory. Even if there was a terrible stench. . . .'

He paused a moment to savour it anew. His best days! Then suddenly he asked me if I had ever read Conrad, Joseph Conrad, who wrote about the sea.

I nodded my head.

'There's a writer I admire, Henry. If you could ever write a story like him, well. . . .' He didn't know what to add to this. 'My favourite is *The Nigger of the Narcissus*. I must have read it at least ten times. Each time it seems better to me.'

'Yes, I know. I've read nearly all of Conrad. I agree with you, a wonderful writer. . . . How about Dostoievsky, have you ever read him?'

No, he hadn't. Never heard the name before. What was he, a novelist? Sounded like a Polish name to him.

'I'll send you one of his books,' I said. 'It's called *The House of the Dead*. By the way,' I added, 'I have loads of books. I could send you anything you like, as many as you like. Just tell me what you'd enjoy.'

He said not to bother, he liked reading the same books over and over.

'But wouldn't you care to know something about other writers too?'

He didn't think he had the energy to get interested in new writers. But his son, the big lad, he liked to read. Maybe I could send *him* something.'

'What sort of books does he read?'

158

'He likes the moderns.'

'Like whom?'

'Oh, Hall Caine, Rider Haggard, Henty. . . .'

'I see. Sure,' I said, 'I can send him something interesting.'

'Now the little fellow,' said Gene, 'he hardly reads at all. He's up on science. All he looks at are the scientific magazines. I think he's cut out to be a doctor. You should see the laboratory he's rigged up for himself. He's got everything in there, all cut up and bottled. It stinks in there. But if it makes him happy. . . .'

'Exactly, Gene. *If it makes him happy.*'

I stayed on until the last bus. Walking down the dark, mangy street we hardly exchanged a word. As I shook hands with them all I repeated that I would be back soon. 'We'll have a feast next time, eh kids?'

'Don't think of that, Henry,' said Gene. 'Just come . . . and bring your wife along too.'

The ride home seemed interminable. I not only felt sad, I felt morose, despondent, licked. I couldn't wait to get home and switch on the lights. Once inside the Love Nest I would feel secure again. Never had it seemed more like a cosy womb, our wonderful little apartment. Truly, we lacked for nothing. If now and then we were hungry we knew it wouldn't last forever.We had friends—and we had the gift of speech. We knew how to forage. As for the world, the real world was right inside out four walls. Everything we wanted of the world we managed to drag to our lair. It's true, now and then I grew sensitive, or shy, when it came to making a touch of some one, but these moments were rare. In a pinch I could muster the courage to tackle an utter stranger. Certainly it was necessary to swallow one's pride. But I preferred to swallow my pride rather than my own spittle.

Borough Hall never looked better to me than when I stepped out of the subway. I was already home. The passers-by wore a familiar air. They were not lost. Between the world I had just left and this one the difference was unthinkable. It was only the outskirts of the city, really, where Gene lived—but it was the wilderness to me. I shuddered to think that I might ever be condemned to such an existence.

An imperative desire to roam the streets for a while led me instinctively to Sackett Street. Filled with memories of my old friend, Al Burger, I walked past his house. It looked sadly dilapidated. The entire street, houses and all, seemed to have diminished since my last visit. Everything was shrunk and shrivelled. Despite all, it was still a wonderful street to me. *The Via Nostalgia.*

As for the suburbs, so sinister and forlorn—everyone I knew who had gone to live in the suburbs had given up the ghost. The current of life never bathed these purlieus. There could be only one purpose in retiring to these living catacombs: to breed and wither away. If it were an act of renunciation it would be comprehensible, but it was never that. It was always an admission of defeat. Life became routine, the dullest sort of routine. A humdrum job, a family with a big bosom to slink into, the barnyard pets and their diseases, the slick magazines, the comic sheets, the farmer's almanac. Endless time in which to study oneself in the mirror. One after another, regular as the noon-day sun, the brats fell out of the womb. The rent came due regularly, too, or the interest on the mortgage. How pleasant to watch the new sewer pipes being laid! How thrilling to see new streets opening up and finally covered with asphalt! Everything was new. New and shoddy. New and desolate. New and meaningless. With the new came added comforts. Everything was planned for the coming generation. One was mortgaged to the shining future. A trip to the city and one longed to be back in the neat little bungalow with the lawn-mower and the washing machine. The city was disturbing, confusing, oppressive. One acquired a different rhythm living in the suburbs. What matter if one was not *au courant?* There were compensations—such as warm house-slippers, the radio, the ironing board which sprang out of the wall. Even the plumbing was attractive.

Poor Gene, of course, had no such compensations. He had fresh air, and that was about all. True, his was not quite the suburbs. He was marooned in that in-between area, that no-man's land where one kept body and soul together in some hapless way which defied all logic. The ever-expanding city was always threatening to gobble him up, land and all. Or, the tide might recede for some quixotic reason and leave them high and dry. Sometimes a city starts to move outward in a certain direction, then suddenly changes its mind. Any improvements begun are left unfinished. The little community begins slowly to die, for lack of oxygen. Everything deteriorates and depreciates. In this atmosphere one may just as well read the same books—or the same book—over and over again. Or play the same phonograph record. In a vacuum one has no need of new things, nor of excitement, nor of foreign stimuli. One has only to maintain a bare survival, to vegetate, like a foetus in a jar.

I couldn't sleep that night for thinking of Gene. His plight was all the more disturbing to me for the reason that I had always regarded him as my twin brother. In him I always saw myself. We looked alike and we spoke alike. We had been born almost in the same house. His mother could well have been *my* mother: certainly I preferred her to my own. When he winced with pain, I winced. When he expressed a longing to do something, I felt the same longing. We were like a team in harness. I don't remember ever disputing with him, or crossing him, ever insisting on doing something he did not want to do. What he owned was mine, and vice versa. Between us there was never the least jealousy or rivalry. We were one, body and soul. . . . I saw in him now not the caricature of myself but rather a premonition of what was to come. If Fate could treat him so unkindly—my own brother who had never done anyone any harm—what might it not have in store for me? The good that was in me was the overflow of his own bottomless well of goodness; the bad was my very own. The bad had accumulated as the result of our separation. When we parted ways I had lost that echo which I depended on for self-orientation. I had lost my touchstone.

All this was slowly dawning on me as I lay awake in bed. Never before had I entertained such thought about our relationship. But how clear it seemed to me now! I had lost my true brother. I had gone astray. I had willed myself to be other than him. And why? Because I would not go down before the world. I had pride. I simply would not admit defeat. But what did I want to *give*? I doubt if I ever thought of that, that there was something to give the world as well as to take from it. Boasting to every one that I was now a writer, as if that were the end-all and the be-all of e8istence. What a farce! I regretted that I had not lied to Gene. I should have told him I was a clerk in an office, a bank teller, anything but that I was a writer. It was like giving him a slap in the face.

How strange that years later his son—'the wild one', as he called him—should come to me with his manuscripts and ask my advice. Had I set off a spark that night which inflamed the son? As the father had predicted, the boy had gone West, had led the life of an adventurer, had become a hobo, in fact, and then, like the prodigal son, he had returned, had taken up this weird business of writing in order to earn a living. I had given him what help I could, had urged him to stop writing for the magazines and do something serious. And then I never heard from him again. Now and then, when I pick up a magazine, I look for his name. *Why don't I write him a letter?* I might at least inquire if his father is still alive. Perhaps I don't *want* to know what became of my cousin Gene. Perhaps it would frighten me, even today, to know the truth.

6

I DECIDED THAT I would start writing the daily column without waiting for Alan Cromwell's O.K. To write something new and interesting each day, and keep it within the spatial limits allotted, demanded a bit of practice. I thought it well to be a few columns ahead; if Cromwell kept his word I would already be in the groove. In order to determine which had the most appeal, I tried out a variety of styles. I knew there would be days when I would be incapable of writing a word. I wasn't going to be caught napping.

Meanwhile Mona had taken a temporary job as hostess in one of the Village night clubs—Remo's. Mathias, the real estate operator, wasn't quite ready to launch her. Why, I couldn't discover. It might be, of course, that she had first to cool him off a bit. Sometimes these admirers of hers became too impetuous, wanted to marry her without delay. So she maintained.

Anyway, the job was rather in line with her temperament and previous experience. She danced as little as possible. The important thing was to make the victims drink as much as possible. The hostesses always got a percentage of the drink-money, if nothing more.

It wasn't long before young Corsi, who had a celebrated establishment of his own in the Village—one of the landmarks—fell violently in love with her. He would drop in towards closing time and escort her to *his place*. There they drank nothing but champagne. Towards daybreak he would have his chauffeur drive her home in his beautiful limousine.

Corsi was one of the impetuous ones who was set on marrying her. He had dreams of spiriting her away to Capri or Sorrento, where they would adopt a new mode of life. Evidently he was doing his utmost to persuade Mona to quit Remo's. So was I, as a matter of fact. I sometimes whiled away an idle hour wondering how it would look to see his reasoning and mine side by side. *And her replies.*

Well, Cromwell was due in town any day. With his arrival perhaps she'd take a different view of things. At any rate, she had intimated in an off moment that she might.

More disquieting to me, however, than young Corsi's violent attempts to woo her were the annoyances she was subject to at the hands of certain notorious Lesbians in the Village. Apparently they came to Remo's expressly to work on her, buying drinks just as liberally as the men. Corsi too was incensed, I learned. In desperation he begged her—if she *must* work—to work for him. This failing, he tried another tack. He tried to make her drunk each night, assuming that that would make her grow disgusted with her job. But this too failed to work.

The reason nothing would budge her, I finally learned, was because she had taken a fancy to one of the dancers, a Cherokee girl who was in bad straits—and pregnant to boot. Too decent, too frank and outspoken, the girl would have been fired long ago had she not been the main attraction. Every night, it seems, people dropped in just to see her do her number. The number always ended with the split. How long she could continue to do the split, without dropping the child, was a grave question.

A few nights after Mona had confided the situation to me the girl fainted on the floor. They carried her from the dance floor to the hospital, where she had a premature birth, the child being born dead. Her condition was so critical that she was obliged to remain in the hospital several weeks. Then an unexpected event occurred. The day she was to be released she was taken with such a fit of despondency that she jumped from the window and killed herself.

After this tragic incident Mona couldn't look at Remo's. For a while she made no attempt to do anything. To make her feel easier, also to prove to her that I could do a little gold-digging myself when I had a mind to, I sallied forth each day to make a few touches here and there. It wasn't that we were desperate; I did it to get my hand in, *and*—to convince her that if we really had to carry on like sharks I was almost as good at it as she. Naturally, I tackled the sure-fire ones first. My cousin, the one who owned my beautiful racing wheel, was number one on my list. I got a ten spot from him. He handed it to me grudgingly, not because he was a tight-wad but because he disapproved of borrowing and lending. When I inquired about the bike he informed me that he had never ridden it, that he had sold it to a chum of his, a Syrian. I went immediately to the Syrian's home —it was only a few blocks away—and made such an impression on him, talking about bike races, prize fights, football and so on, that when we parted he slipped me a ten dollar bill. He even urged me to bring my wife some night and have dinner with the family.

From Zabrowskie, my old friend the ticker-tapper at the telegraph office near Times Square, I got another ten spot and a new hat. An excellent lunch too. The usual conversation, of course. All about the horses, about working too hard, about looking for a rainy day. Eager to have me promise that I would accompany him some night when there was a good fight on. When I finally let out that I expected to write a column for the Hearst papers he looked at me goggle-eyed. As I say, he had already given me the ten spot. Now he began talking in earnest. I was to remember, if I needed any more between now and then—*then* meaning when I was in full swing as a columnist—I was to call on him. 'Maybe you'd better take twenty instead of ten,' he said. I handed him back the bill and received a twenty. At the corner we had to stop at a cigar store where he filled my breast pocket with fat cigars. It was then he noticed that the last hat he had bought for me looked rather seedy. We stopped at a haberdasher's, on the way back to the telegraph office, where he bought me another hat, a Borsalino no less. 'One has to look right,' he counselled. 'Never let them know you're poor.' He looked so happy when we parted you would have thought I was the one who had done the favours. 'Don't forget!' was his last shot, and he rattled the keys in his trousers pocket.

I felt pretty good with forty dollars in my pocket. It was a Saturday and I thought I might just as well keep up the good work. Maybe I'd bump into an old friend and shake down some more jack—just like that. Running my hands through my pockets, I realized I didn't have any small change on me. I didn't want to break a bill—a clean forty bucks or nothing.

I said I had nothing in change; I was mistaken, for in my vest pocket I found two ancient-looking pennies, white pennies. Had probably kept them for good luck.

Up on Park Avenue I came upon the showrooms of the Minerva Motor Company. A handsome car, the Minerva. Almost as good as the Rolls-Royce. I wondered if by chance my old friend Otto Kunst, who had once been a bookkeeper for them, was still there. Hadn't seen Otto for years—almost since the dissolution of our old club.

I stepped inside the swanky showroom and there was Otto, as sombre and sedate as an undertaker. He was sales manager now. Smoking Murads, as of yore. Had a couple of good-looking rocks on his fingers too.

He was glad to see me again, but in that restrained way which always irritated me.

'You're sitting pretty,' I said.

'And what are *you* doing?' He flung this at me as if to say—'what is it this time?'

I told him I was taking over a column for a newspaper shortly. '*Well!*' He arched his eyebrows. Hmmm!

I thought I might just as well try him for a ten spot—to make it an even fifty. After all, sales manager, old friend. . . . Why not?

I got a curt refusal. Didn't even bother to explain *why* he couldn't. It was out of the question, that was all. *Impossible.* I knew it was useless to prod him but I did, just to irritate him. Damn it, even though I didn't need it, he had no right to refuse. He should do it for old time's sake. Otto twiddled his watch chain as he listened. Cool as a cucumber, mind you. No embarrassment whatever. No sympathy either.

'God, you're a tightwad!' I concluded.

He smiled unperturbedly. 'I never ask a favour and I never give any,' he responded blandly. Smug as a bug in a rug, he was. As though he'd always been a sales manager—or something even more important. Didn't think, did he, that only a few years later he'd be trying to sell apples on Fifth Avenue. (Even millionaires couldn't afford Minervas during the depression.)

'Well, forget about it,' I said. 'The truth is, I've got a wad on me. I was just testing you out.' I hauled out the bills and flashed them before his eyes. . . . He looked puzzled, then frowned. Before he could say a word I added, as I extracted the two white pennies: 'What I really dropped in for was to ask you a favour. Could you lend me three cents to make up the nickel for the subway? I'll pay you back the next time I pass this way.'

His face brightened immediately. I could almost feel the sigh of relief he let drop.

'Sure I can do that,' he said. And rather solemnly he fished out three pennies.

'It's mighty white of you,' I said, and shook his hand with extra fervour, as if I were indeed grateful.

'It's nothing,' he said, quite seriously, 'and you don't need to give it back.'

'*You're sure?*' I said. At last he began to realize I was rubbing it in.

'I can always lend you a few pennies,' he said sourly, 'but not ten bucks. Money doesn't grow on trees, you know. When I sell a man a car I sweat for it. Besides, I haven't sold a car now for over two months.'

'That's really tough, isn't it? You know, you almost make me feel sorry for you. Well remember me to the wife and kids.'

He ushered me to the door the way he would a customer. 'Drop in again some time,' he said, as we parted.

'Next time I'll buy a car—just the chassis.'

He gave me a mirthless grin. As I walked towards the subway I cursed him up and down for a mean, stingy, heartless son of a bitch. And to think we had been bosom pals when we were boys! I couldn't get over it. The strange thing was, I couldn't help but reflect, that he had grown to be like his old man whom he had always detested. 'A mean, stingy, hard-hearted, pig-headed old Dutchman!' he used to call him.

Well, that was one friend I could wipe off my list. I did then and there, and with such a will that years later, when we encountered one another on Fifth Avenue, I was unable to recall who he was. I took him for a detective, no less! I can hear him now repeating asininely: '*What*, you don't remember *me?*' 'No, I don't,' I said. 'Really, I don't. *Who are you?*' The poor bugger had to give his name before I could place him.

Otto Kunst had been my closest chum in that street of early sorrows. After I left America the only boys I ever thought of were the ones I had had the least to do with. For example—the group that lived in the old farm house up the street. This was the only house in the whole wide neighbourhood which had seen other days, days when our street had been a country lane named after a Dutch settler, Van Voorhees. Anyway, in this ramshackle, tumble-down habitation lived three families. The Vosslers, made up exclusively of oafs and curmudgeons, dealt in coal, wood, ice and manure; the Laskis comprised a father who was a pharmacist, two brothers who were pugilists, and a grown-up daughter who was just a chunk of beef; the Newton family consisted of a mother, and a son whom I seldom spoke to but for whom I had a singular reverence. Ed Vossler, who was about my own age, strong as an ox and slightly demented, had a hare lip and stuttered woefully. We never had any prolonged conversations but we were friends, if not chums. Ed worked from morning till night; it was hard work, too, and because of this he seemed older than the rest of us who did nothing but play after school. As a boy I never thought of him except as a walking utility; we had only to offer him a few cents and he would perform the tasks we despised. We teased him a good deal, as boys will. It was when I got to Europe, curiously enough, that I found myself thinking occasionally about this queer oaf, Ed Vossler. I must say I always thought of him with affection. I had learned by this time how almost microscopic is that world of mortals of whom one can say: 'He's a man you can count on.' Now and then I sent him a picture post-card but of course I never heard from him. For all I knew he may have been dead.

Ed Vossler enjoyed a certain protection from his second cousins, the Laskis. Especially from Eddie Laski, who was a little older than us and a most unpleasant fellow too. His brother Tom, whom Eddie aped in every way, was rather a sweet person and already on the way to becoming a figure in the world of fisticuffs. This Tom was about twenty-two or three, quiet, well-behaved, neat in appearance, and rather handsome. He wore long spitcurls, after the manner of Terry McGovern. One would hardly have suspected that he was such a fighter had not Eddie, his brother, boasted so much about him. Now and then we had the pleasure of watching the two of them spar in the backyard where the manure pile stood.

But Eddie Laski—it was difficult to keep out of his range. As soon as he saw you coming he would block the path, his mouth spread in a wide, nasty grin which bared his big yellow teeth; pretending to shake hands he would make a few passes—like lightning!—and give you a tremendous jab in the ribs or else what he called 'a playful poke in the jaw'. The damned fool was always practising the old one-two. It was positive torture to extricate oneself from his clutches. We were all agreed that he would never make his mark in the ring. 'Some day he'll meet up with the wrong guy!' That was our unanimous verdict.

Jimmy Newton, who was vaguely related to the Vosslers and the Laskis, was a complete anomaly in their midst. Nobody could have been more silent than he, nor more well-behaved, nor more sincere and genuine. What he worked at no one knew. We saw him rarely and spoke to him even more rarely. He was the sort of fellow, however, who had only to say 'Good morning!' and you felt better. His good-morning was like a blessing. What intrigued us about him was the undefinable and ineradicable air of melancholy which he wore. It suited one who had experienced some deep, unmentionable tragedy. We suspected that his sorrow had to do with his mother whom we never saw. Was she an invalid perhaps? Was she insane? Or was she a horrible cripple? As for his father, we never knew whether he was dead or had deserted them.

To us healthy, care-free youngsters, this Laski menage was enveloped in mystery. Punctually every morning at seven-thirty the elder Mr Laski, who was blind, left the house with his dog, tapping the way with a stout cane. This in itself had a queer effect upon us. But the house itself looked crazy. Certain windows, for example, were never opened, the shades always down. At one of the other windows sat Mollie, the Laski daughter, usually with a can of beer beside her. She was there, as in a show, from the moment the curtain rose. Having absolutely nothing to do, having no desire moreover to do anything, she simply sat there the whole day long gathering up the gossip. She had the low-down on everything that went on in the neighbourhood. Now and then her figure ripened, as if she were about to have a child, but there never were any births or deaths. She simply changed with the seasons. Lazy slut that she was, we liked her. She was too lazy to even walk to the corner grocer's; she'd flip us a quarter or half dollar from the window, which was on the street level, and tell us to keep the change. Sometimes she forgot what she had sent us for and told us to keep the damned stuff.

Old man Vossler, who also ran a trucking business, was a big brute of a man who did nothing but curse and swear when you ran into him. He could lift enormous weights with ease, whether drunk or sober. Naturally we stood in awe of him. But it made our blood curl to see the way he booted his son around—he could fairly lift him from the ground with his big toe. And the way he lashed him with the horse whip! Though we didn't dare to play any tricks on the old man we often held prolonged conferences in the open lot at the corner as to how we might retaliate. It was disgraceful to see how Ed Vossler put his hand over his head and crouched when he saw his old man coming. In desperation once we summoned Ed to confer with us, but the moment he got the drift of our talk he ran off with his tail between his legs.

Curious how often these figures out of my boyhood reverted to memory. The ones I speak of belonged more to that old neighbourhood, the 14th Ward, which I was so fond of. In the street of early sorrows they were anomalies. As a mere lad—in the old neighbourhood—I had been accustomed to mixing with half-wits, incipient gangsters, petty crooks, would-be prize fighters, epileptics, drunks and sluts. Everyone in that dear ancient world was a 'character'. But in the new neighbourhood to which I had been transferred everyone was normal, matter of fact, non-spectacular. There was only one exception, apart from the members of the weird tribe inhabiting the farm house. I can no longer remember the name of this chap, but his personality is engraved in my memory. He was a newcomer to the neighbour-hood, somewhat older than the rest of us, and distinctly 'different'. One day, as we were shooting marbles, I dropped an expression which made him look up in astonishment. 'Where do *you* hail from?' he asked. 'From Driggs Avenue originally,' I said. At once he was off his knees and literally hugging me. 'Why didn't you tell me that before?' he cried. 'I'm from Wythe Avenue, corner of North Seventh.'

It was like two Masonic brothers exchanging pass words. At once a bond was established between us. Whatever game we played he was always on my side. If one of the older boys threatened to go for me he interposed himself. If he had anything important to confide he'd employ the jargon of the 14th Ward.

One day he introduced me to his sister, who was a trifle younger than I. It was almost love at first sight. She wasn't beautiful, even to my youthful eyes, but she had a way about her which I associated with the behaviour of the girls I had admired in the old neighbourhood.

One night a surprise party was given me. Every youngster in the neighbourhood was there—except this new-found friend of mine and his little sister. I was heart-broken. When I asked why they hadn't been invited I was told that they didn't belong. That settled it for me. At once I sneaked out of the house and went in search of them. I quickly explained to their mother that there had been a mistake, that it was a pure oversight, and that every-one was waiting for her son and daughter to appear. She patted me on the head with a knowing smile and told me what a good boy I was. She thanked me so profusely, indeed, that I blushed.

I escorted my two friends to the party in triumph, only to perceive, however, that I had made a grave blunder. On all sides they were given the cold shoulder. I did my best to dissipate the atmosphere of hostility but in vain. Finally I could bear it no longer. 'Either you make friends with my friends,' I announced boldly, hoding the latter by the arms, 'or you can all go home. This is *my* party and I want my own friends here.'

For this piece of bravado I got a sound slap in the face from my mother. I winced but stood my ground.

'It isn't fair!' I bellowed, almost on the point of tears now.

All at once they gave way. It was almost a miracle the way the ice broke up. In no time we were all laughing, shouting, singing. I couldn't understand why it had happened so suddenly.

During the course of the evening the girl, whose name was Sadie, got me in a corner to express her thanks for what I had done. 'It was wonderful of you, Henry,' she said, to which I blushed deeply. 'It was nothing at all,' I mumbled, feeling silly and heroic at the same time. Sadie looked around to see if anyone were observing us, then boldly kissed me on the lips. This time I blushed even more deeply.

'My mother would like you to come to dinner some evening,' she whispered. 'Will you come?'

I squeezed her little hand and said 'Sure'.

It was in the flats across the street where Sadie and her brother lived. I had never been inside a house on that side of the street. I wondered what their home was like. In calling for them I was too flustered to notice a thing. All I could recall was that it had a distinctly Catholic odour. Nearly all the people, incidentally, who lived in the flats—railroad flats they were—were members of the Roman Church. This was enough in itself to alienate them from the other people in the street.

The first discovery I made, on visiting my two friends, was that they were very very poor. The father, who had been a loco-motive driver, was dead; the mother, who was suffering from some grave malady, was unable to leave the house. They were Catholics all right. Devout ones. That was obvious at once. In every room, it seemed to me, there were rosaries and crucifixes, votive candles, chromos of the Madonna and Child or of Jesus on the Cross. Though I had seen these evidences of the faith in other homes, nevertheless each time it happened I got the creeps. My dislike of these sacred relics—if one could call them that— was purely and simply because of their morbidity. True, I didn't know the word morbid then but the feeling was definitely that. When I had first glimpsed these 'relics' in the homes of my other little friends I remember that I had mocked and jeered. It was my mother, oddly enough, my mother who despised Catholics almost as much as drunkards and criminals, who had cured me of this attitude. To make me more 'tolerant' she would force me to go to mass occasionally with my Catholic friends.

Now, however, when I described in detail the conditions in the home of my two friends, she showed little sympathy. She repeated that she didn't think it was good for me to see so much of them. *Why?* I wanted to know. She refused to answer me directly. When I suggested that she permit me to bring them fruit and candy from our sideboard, which was always overflowing with good things, she frowned. Sensing that there was no good reason behind her refusals, I decided to pinch the edibles and smuggle them over to my friends. Now and then I stole a few pennies from her pocketbook and handed them to Sadie or her brother. Always as if my mother had requested me to do so.

'Your mother must be a very kind woman,' said Sadie's mother one day.

I smiled, rather lamely.

'You're sure, Henry, it's your mother who sends us these gifts?'

'Certainly,' I said, smiling ever so brightly now. 'We have much more than we need. I can bring you other things too, if you like.'

'Henry, come here,' said Sadie's mother. She was seated in an old-fashioned rocker. 'Now listen to me carefully, Henry.' She patted my head affectionately and held me close to her. 'You're a very, very good boy and we love you. But you mustn't steal to make others happy. That's a sin. I know you mean well, but. . . .'

'It isn't stealing,' I protested. 'They would only go to waste.'

'You have a big heart,' she said. 'A big heart for such a little boy. Wait a while. Wait till you grow older and earn your own living. Then you can give to your heart's content.'

The next day Sadie's brother took me aside and begged me not to be angry with his mother for refusing my gifts. 'She likes you very much, Henry,' he said.

'But you don't have enough to eat,' said I.

'Certainly we do,' he said.

'You don't! I know because I know how much *we* eat.'

'I'll be getting a job soon,' he said. 'We'll have plenty then.' 'In fact,' he added, 'I may get a job next week.'

'What sort of job?'

'I'm going to work part time for the undertaker.'

'That's terrible,' said I.

'Not really,' he replied. 'I won't have to handle the stiffs.'

'You're sure?'

'Positive. He's got *men* for that. I'm going to run errands, that's all.'

'And how much will you get?'

'Three dollars a week.'

I left him wondering if I couldn't find a job too. Perhaps I

170

could find something to do on the sly. My thought was, of course, to turn over my earnings to them. Three dollars a week was nothing, even in those days. I lay awake the whole night thinking it over. I was certain in advance that I would never receive my mother's permission to take a job. Whatever was to be done had to be done secretly and with cunning and foresight.

Now it happened that a few doors from us lived a family in which the eldest son ran a coffee business on the side. That is to say, he had drummed up a small clientèle for a blend which he mixed himself; on Saturdays he used to deliver the packages himself. It was quite a route he covered and I wasn't too confident that I could manage it alone but I decided to ask him to give me a chance. To my surprise I found that he was only too happy to have me take over; he had been on the verge of abandoning his little enterprise.

The following Saturday I set forth with two valises filled with small packages of coffee. I was to get fifty cents as salary and a small commission on new business. Should I be able to collect on any of the bad debts I was to get a bonus. I carried a linen bag with a draw string in which I was to put the money I collected.

After coaching me as to how to approach the debtors he had warned me specifically to beware of the dogs in certain regions. I checked these spots with red pencil on the itinerary where everything was plainly indicated—brooks and culverts, viaducts, reservoirs, fence lines, government property, and so on.

That first Saturday was a huge success. My boss literally rolled his eyes when I dumped the money on the table. Immediately he volunteered to raise my salary to seventy-five cents. I had gotten him five new customers and collected a third of the bad debts. He hugged me as if he had found a jewel.

'You'll promise you won't tell my folks I'm working for you?' I begged.

'Of course not,' he said.

'No, *promise*! Promise on your word of honour!'

He looked at me strangely. Then slowly he repeated—'I promise on my word of honour.'

The next morning, Sunday, I waited outside the door of my friend's home to catch them on their way to church. I had no trouble persuading them to let me go to mass with them. They were delighted, in fact.

When we left the church of St Francis de Sales—a horrible place of worship—I explained to them what I had accomplished. I fished out the money—it amounted to almost three dollars—and handed it to Sadie's brother. To my utter amazement he refused to accept it.

'But I only took the job for your sake,' I expostulated.

'I know, Henry, but my mother would never hear of such a thing.'

'But you don't need to tell her it's from me. Tell her you got a raise.'

'She wouldn't believe that,' he said.

'Then tell her you found it in the street. Look, I'll dig up an old purse. Put it in the purse and say you found it in the gutter just outside the church. She'll have to believe *that*.'

Still he was reluctant to take the money.

I was at my wits' end. If he was not going to accept the money all my efforts were in vain. I left him the promise that he would think it over.

It was Sadie who came to my rescue. She was closer to her mother and she understood the situation in a more practical way. At any rate she thought her mother ought to know what I meant to do for them—in order to express her appreciation.

Before the week was up we had a talk together, Sadie and I. She was waiting for me outside the school gate one afternoon.

'It's settled, Henry,' she said, all out of breath, 'my mother agrees to take the money, but only for a little while—until my brother gets a full time job. Then we'll pay you back.'

I protested that I didn't want to be paid back, but that if her mother insisted on such an arrangement I would have to give in. I handed over the money which was wrapped in a piece of butcher's paper.

'Mother says the Virgin Mary will protect you and bless you for your kindness,' said Sadie.

I didn't know what to say to this. No one had ever used such language with me. Beside, the Virgin Mary meant absolutely nothing to me. I didn't believe in that nonsense.

'Do you really believe in all that . . . that Virgin Mary stuff?' I asked.

Sadie looked shocked—or perhaps grieved. She nodded her head gravely.

'Just what is the Virgin Mary?' I asked.

'You know as well as I do,' she answered.

'No I don't. Why do they call her *Virgin?*'

Sadie thought a moment, then replied most innocently:

'Because she's the mother of God.'

'Well, what *is* a Virgin anyway?'

'There's only one Virgin,' answered Sadie, 'and that's the Blessed Virgin Mary.'

'That's no answer,' I countered. 'I asked you—what *is* a Virgin?'

'It means a mother who is holy,' said Sadie, none too sure of herself.

Here I had a brilliant thought. 'Didn't God create the world?' I demanded.

'Of course.'

'Then there's no mother. God doesn't need a mother.'

'That's blasphemy,' Sadie almost shrieked. 'You'd better speak to the priest.'

'I don't believe in priests.'

'Henry, don't talk that way! God will punish you.'

'Why?'

'Because.'

'All right,' said I, '*you* ask the priest! You're a Catholic. I'm not.'

'You shouldn't say things like that,' said Sadie, deeply offended. 'You're not old enough to be asking such questions. *We* don't ask such questions. We believe. If you don't believe you can't be a good Catholic.'

'I'm willing to believe,' I retorted, '*if he will answer my questions.*'

'That's not the way,' said Sadie. 'First you have to believe. And then you must pray. Ask God to forgive your sins. . . .'

'Sins? I don't have any sins to confess.'

'Henry, Henry, don't speak that way, it's wicked. Everybody sins. That's what the priest is for. That's why we pray to the Blessed Mary.'

'I don't pray to anybody,' I said defiantly, a little weary of her moony talk.

'That's because you're a Protestant.'

'I am *not* a Protestant. I'm nothing. I don't believe in anything . . . *there!*'

'You'd better take that back,' said Sadie, thoroughly alarmed. 'God could strike you dead for talking like that.'

She was so visibly appalled by my utterance that her fear imparted itself to me.

'I mean,' said I, endeavouring to backwater, 'That we don't pray like you. We only pray in church—when the minister prays.'

'Don't you pray before you go to sleep?'

'No,' I replied, 'I don't. I guess I don't know much about praying.'

'We'll teach you then,' said Sadie. 'You must pray every day, three times a day at least. Otherwise you'll burn in Hell.'

We parted on these words. I gave her my solemn promise that I would make an effort to pray, at least before going to sleep. As I walked away, however, I suddenly asked myself what it was I was supposed to pray for. I was almost on the point of running back to ask her. The word 'sins' stuck in my crop. What sins? I kept asking myself. What had I been doing that was so sinful? I rarely lied, except to my mother. I never stole, except from my mother. What had I to confess? It never occurred to me that I had committed a sin in lying to my mother or stealing from her. I had to behave thus because she didn't know any better. Once she saw things in my light she would understand my behaviour.

That's how I viewed *that* situation.

Mulling over my conversation with Sadie, reflecting on the sombre gloom which pervaded their household, I began to think that perhaps my mother was right in distrusting Catholics. We didn't do any praying in our house yet everything went smoothly. Nobody ever mentioned God in our family. Yet God hadn't punished any of us. I came to the conclusion that Catholics were by nature superstitious, just like savages. Ignorant idol-worshippers. Cautious, timid folk who hadn't the guts to think for themselves. I decided I would never again go to mass. What a dungeon their Church was! Suddenly—a random flash—it dawned on me that maybe they wouldn't be so poor, Sadie's family, if they didn't think about God so much. Everything went to the Church, to the priests, that is, who were always begging for money. I had never liked the sight of a priest. Too oily and smirky for me. No, the hell with them! And to hell with their candles, their rosaries, their crucifixes—and their Virgin Marys!

At last I'm face to face with that man of mystery, Alan Cromwell, handing him another drink, slapping him on the back, having a grand time with him, in short. And right in our own little love nest!

It was Mona who had arranged the meeting—with the connivance of Doc Kronski. Kronski is drinking too, and shouting and gesticulating. And so is his mousey little wife who is posing for the occasion as my wife. I am no longer Henry Miller. I have been given a new monniker for the evening: Dr Harry Marx.

Only Mona is absent. She is 'supposed' to arrive later.

Things have progressed fantastically since that moment earlier in the evening when I shook hands with Cromwell. I have to admit to myself, speaking of the devil, that he is indeed a handsome chap. And not only handsome (in a Southern way) but fair-spoken and gullible as a child. I wouldn't say that he was stupid, no. Trusting, rather. Not cultured either, but intelligent. Not shrewd but capable. A man with a good heart, an outgoing man. Bubbling over with good-will.

It seemed a shame to be taking him in, to be making sport of him. I could see that the idea was Kronski's, not Mona's. Feeling guilty because we had neglected him, Kronski, so long, she had probably acquiesced without thought. That's how it looked to me.

Anyway, we were all in fine fettle. The confusion was enormous. Fortunately, Cromwell had arrived lit up like a Zeppelin. By nature unsuspecting, the drinks made him more so. He seemed not to realize that Kronski was Jewish, though it was obvious he was even to a child. Cromwell took him for a Russian. As for me, with that name Marx, he didn't know what to think. (Kronski had conceived the brilliant idea of palming *me* off as a Jew.) The disclosure of this startling fact—that I was Jewish —made no impression whatever on Cromwell. We might as well have told him I was a Sioux or an Eskimo. He was curious, however, to know what I did for a living. In accordance with our preconceived plan I informed Cromwell that I was a surgeon, that Dr Kronski and I shared offices together. He looked at my hands and nodded his head gravely.

For me the difficult thing was to remember, during the course of an endless evening, that Kronski's wife was *my* wife. This, of course, was another invention of Kronski's fertile brain—a way of diverting suspicion, he thought. Every time I looked at that mouse of his I felt like swatting her. We did our best to ply her with drinks; all she would do, however, was to take a little sip and push the glass aside. But as the evening wore on and our horseplay grew bolder and bolder, she livened up. A way of saying that she unkinked a bone or two, no more. When on one occasion she broke into a fit of hysterical laughter I thought she would be taken seriously ill. She was better at weeping.

Cromwell, on the other hand, was a hearty laugher. At times he didn't know what he was laughing about, but our own laughter was so infectious that he didn't give a damn what he was laughing about. Now and then he asked a question or two about Mona, whom it was obvious he regarded as a very strange individual, though an adorable one. We, of course, pretended that we had known her from infancy. We praised her writing outrageously, inventing a whole arsenal of poems, essay and stories which she, we were certain, was too modest to have mentioned the existence of. Kronski went so far as to express the opinion that she would be the foremost woman writer in America before long. I pretended not to be so certain of this but agreed that she possessed extraordinary talent, extraordinary possibilities.

Asked if we had seen any of the columns she had turned out, we professed to be completely ignorant, astounded in fact, that she was doing such a thing.

'We'll have to put a stop to that,' said Kronski. 'She's too good to be wasting her time that way.'

I agreed with him. Cromwell looked baffled. He couldn't see what was so terrible about writing a daily column. Besides, she needed money.

'*Money?*' shouted Kronski. '*Money?* Why, what's the matter with *us?* I'm sure Dr Marx and I can take care of her needs.' He seemed amazed to hear that Mona might be in need of money. A little hurt, in fact.

Poor Cromwell felt that he had made a faux-pas. He assured us that it was only an impression he had gathered. But, to get back on the subject, he *would* like us to glance at those columns and give him our honest opinion of them. He said he was no judge himself. If they were really good he was certain he could get her the assignment. He mentioned nothing, of course, about shelling out a hundred a week.

We had another drink on this and then diverted him to other subjects. It was easy enough to sidetrack him. He had only one thought in mind—*when would she arrive?* Every now and then he begged us to let him dash out and make a telephone call to Washington. In one way or another we always managed to frustrate these attempts. We knew that Mona would *not* arrive, not at least until we had gotten him out of the way. She had given us until one in the morning to get rid of him. Our only hope therefore was to get him so potted that we could put him in a taxi and pack him off.

I had tried several times to find out where he was staying but got nowhere. Kronski thought it of slight importance—any old hotel would do. In the midst of the goings-on I asked myself why this fool business had been arranged. It made no sense. Later I was told that Mona had thought it important to let Cromwell see that she was really living alone. There was another side to it, of course, and that was to find out if Cromwell really hoped to be more frank with us than with her. But we had dropped the subject early in the evening, thanks to Kronski. For some queer reason of his own, Kronski was obsessed with the notion of filling Cromwell with hair-raising stories about the operating ward. I of course had to chime in with him. No one in his right senses would have given the least credence to these yarns he kept inventing. They were so sensational, so utterly fantastic, and so gory and gruesome withal, that I wondered that Cromwell, dead drunk though he was, didn't see through them. Of course the more horrible and unbelievable the tale, the more we laughed, Kronski and I. Our hilarity puzzled Cromwell somewhat, but finally he accepted it as 'professional callousness'.

To believe Kronski, nine out of ten operations were pure criminal experiments. Except for a rare handful, all surgeons were born sadists. Not content with diabolical fantasies about the mistreatment of human beings, he went into long dissertations on the subject of our cruelty to animals. One of these, a harrowing story, which he told amidst gales of laughter, concerned a poor little rabbit which, after numerous injections, electric shocks, and all manner of miraculous resuscitations, was brutally butchered. To cap it all, he elaborated on how he, Kronski, had gathered the remnants of the poor little creature and made a stew of it, oblivious, until after he had swallowed a few portions, that arsenic had been injected into the poor rabbit. Over this he laughed inordinately. Cromwell, slightly sobered by the bloody tale, remarked that it was too bad Kronski hadn't died, then laughed so heartily over this thought that absentmindedly he swallowed a full glass of neat cognac. Whereupon he had such a fit of coughing that we had to stretch him out on the floor and work over him like a drowned man.

It was at this point that we found Cromwell becoming unmanageable. To give him a working-over we had stripped off his coat, vest, shirt and undershirt. Kronski, to be sure, was doing the major work; I merely pummelled Cromwell now and then, or slapped his chest. Now that he was stretched out comfortably, Cromwell didn't feel like putting on his things. He said he felt too good to budge. Wanted to take a snooze, if only for a few minutes. He reached out vaguely for the divan, wondering, I suppose, if he could transfer himself to a still more comfortable position without rousing himself.

The thought that he might go to sleep on us was alarming. We began to cut up like real jackanapes now, standing poor Cromwell on his head, dancing around him (to his utter bewilderment, of course), making grimaces, scratching ourselves like apes . . . anything to make him laugh, anything to prevent his heavy lids from closing. The harder we worked—and by now we had become positively frenetic—the more insistent he became about having his little snooze. He had reached the point now of crawling on all fours towards the coveted divan. Once there, God himself would be powerless to wake him up.

'Let's lay him out,' I said, indicating by gestures and grimaces that we could then dress him and bundle him out.

It took us almost a half hour to get his things on. Cromwell drunk and sleepy though he was refused with might and main to permit us to unbutton his trousers, which we had to do to tuck his shirt in. We were obliged to leave his fly open and his shirt sticking out. When it came time we would cover his shirt with the overcoat.

Cromwell passed out immediately. A heavy trance, punctuated by obscene snores. Kronski was radiant. Hadn't had such a good time in ages, he assured me. Then, without dropping his voice, he blandly suggested that we go through Cromwell's pockets. 'We ought at least to get back what we laid out for food and drink,' he insisted. I don't know why I suddenly became so scrupulous but I refused to entertain the notion. 'He'd never miss the money,' said Kronski. 'What's fifty or a hundred bucks to *him*?' Just to reassure himself he extracted Cromwell's wallet. To his utter amazement there wasn't a bill in it.

'Well I'll be damned!' he mumbled. 'That's the rich for you. Never carry *cash*. Pfui!'

'We'd better get him out of here soon,' I urged.

'Try and do it!' said Kronski, grinning like a billy-goat. 'What's wrong with letting him stay here?'

'Are you mad?' I shouted.

He laughed. Then he calmly proceeded to tell us how wonderful he thought it would be if we would play the farce out to the end, that is, to wake up, all five of (next morning) and continue to enact our respective roles. That would give Mona a chance to do some *real* acting, he thought. Kronski's wife wasn't at all enthusiastic over this suggestion—it was all too complicated to suit her.

After much palaver we decided to rouse Cromwell, drag him out by the heels, if necessary, and dispatch him to a hotel. We had to tussle with him for a good quarter of an hour before we succeeded in getting him to a semi-standing position. His knees simply refused to straighten out; his hat was over his eyes and his shirt-tails were sticking out from under the overcoat which we were unable to button. He looked for all the world like Snuffy the Cabman. We were laughing so hysterically that it was all we could do to descend the steps without rolling over one another. Poor Cromwell kept protesting that he didn't want to go yet, that he wanted to wait for Mona.

'She's gone to Washington to meet you,' said Kronski maliciously. 'We got a telegram while you were asleep.'

Cromwell was too stupefied to get the full import of this. Every now and then he sagged, threatening to collapse in the street. Our idea was to give him a bit of air, brace him up a bit, and then bundle him into a cab. To find a cab we had to walk several blocks. Our way led towards the river, a roundabout way, but we thought the walk would do him good. When we got near the docks we all sat down on the railroad tracks and took a breather. Cromwell simply stretched out between the tracks, laughing and hiccupping, quite as if he were a babe in the cradle. At intervals he begged for something to eat. He wanted ham-and-eggs. The nearest open restaurant was almost a mile away. I suggested that I would run back to the house and get some sandwiches. Cromwell said he couldn't wait that long, wanted his ham-and-eggs right away. We yanked him to his feet again, a job which demanded our combined strength, and started pushing and dragging him towards the bright lights of Borough Hall. A night watchman came along and demanded to know what we were doing there at that hour of the night. Cromwell collapsed at our feet. 'Whatcha got there?' demanded the watchman, prodding Cromwell with his feet as if he were a corpse. 'It's nothing, he's just drunk,' I said. The watchman bent over him to smell his breath. 'Get him out of here,' he said, 'or I'll fan the whole bunch of you.' 'Yes sir, yes sir,' we said, dragging Cromwell by the arm-pits, his feet scraping the ground. A few seconds later the watchman came running up with Cromwell's hat in his hand. We put it on him but it fell off again. 'Here,' I said, opening my mouth, 'put it between my teeth.' We were panting and sweating now from the exertion of dragging him. The watchman observed us a few moments in disgust, then he said: 'Let go of him! Here, sling him over my back . . . you guys are dubs.' Like this we reached the end of the street where the elevated line swung overhead. 'Now one of you guys fetch a cab,' said the night watchman. 'Don't pull him around any more, you'll wrench his arms out.'

Kronski skedaddled up the street in search of a cab. We sat down on the curb and waited.

The cab arrived in a few minutes and we bundled him in. His shirt tails were still hanging out.

'Where to?' asked the driver.

'The Hotel Astor!' I said.

'The Waldorf-Astoria!' shouted Kronski.

'Well, make up your minds!' said the cabby.

'The Commodore,' shouted Cromwell.

'Are you sure?' said the driver. 'This ain't a wild-goose chase, is it?'

'It's the Commodore all right, isn't it?' I said, sticking my head inside the cab.

'Sure,' said Cromwell thickly, 'anywhere suits me.'

'Has he got any money on him?' asked the cabby.

'He's got loads of money,' said Kronski. 'He's a banker.'

'I think one of you guys better go along with him,' said the driver.

'O.K.,' said Kronski and promptly hopped in with his wife.

'Hey!' shouted Cromwell, 'what about Dr Marx?'

'He'll come in the next cab,' said Kronski. 'He's got to make a telephone call.'

'Hey!' he shouted to me, 'what about your wife?'

'She's all right,' I said, and waved good-bye.

When I got back to the house I discovered Cromwell's brief-case and some small change which had dropped out of his pockets. I opened the brief case and found a mass of papers and some telegrams. The most recent telegram was from the Treasury Department, urging Cromwell to telephone someone at midnight without fail, extremely urgent. I ate a sandwich, while glancing over the legal documents, took a glass of wine, and decided to call Washington for him. I had a devil of a job getting the man at the other end; when I did he answered in a sleepy voice, gruff and irritated. I explained that Cromwell had met with a little accident but would telephone him in the morning. 'But who are you . . . who *is* this,' he kept repeating. 'He'll telephone you in the morning,' I repeated, ignoring his frantic questions. Then I hung up. Outside I ran as quickly as I could. I knew he'd call back. I was afraid he might get the police after me. I made quite detour to reach the telegraph office; there I sent a message to Cromwell, to the Commodore Hotel. I hoped to Christ Kronski had delivered him there. As I left the telegraph office I realized that Cromwell might not get the message until the next afternoon. The clerk would probably hold it until Cromwell woke up. I went to another cafeteria and called the Commodore, urging the night clerk to be sure to rouse Cromwell when he got the telegram. 'Pour a pitcher of cold water over him if necessary,' I said, 'but be sure he reads my telegram . . . it's life and death.'

When I got back to the house Mona was there cleaning up the mess.

'You must have had quite a party,' she said.

'That we did,' I said.

I saw the brief case lying there. He would need that when telephoning Washington. 'Look,' I said, 'we'd better get a cab and deliver this to him right away. I've been reading over those papers. They're dynamite. Better not be caught with them in our possession.'

'You go,' said Mona, 'I'm exhausted.'

There I was, in the street again, and just as Kronski had predicted, following in a cab. When I got to the hotel I found that Cromwell had already gone to his room. I insisted that the clerk take me to his room. Cromwell was lying fully clothed on the bedspread, flat on his back, his hat beside him. I put the brief case on his chest and tip-toed out. Then I made the clerk accompany me to the manager's office, explained the situation to that individual, and made the clerk testify that he had seen me deposit the brief-case on Cromwell's chest.'

'And may I have your name?' asked the manager, somewhat perturbed by these unusual tactics.

'Certainly,' I said, 'Dr Karl Marx of the Polytechnique Institute. You can call me in the morning if there is any irregularity. Mr Cromwell is a friend of mine, an F.B.I. agent. He had a little too much to drink. You'll look after him, I hope.'

'I certainly will,' said the night manager, looking rather alarmed. 'Can we reach you at your office any time, Dr Marx?'

'I'll be there all day, certainly,' I said. 'If I should be out, ask for my secretary—Miss Rabinovitch—she'll know where to reach me. I've got to get some sleep now . . . must be in the operating room at nine. Thank you so much. Good-night!'

The bell-hop escorted me to the revolving door. He was visibly impressed by the rigmarole. 'Cab, sir?' he said. 'Yes,' I said, and gave him the change which I had gathered from the floor. 'Thank you very very much, Doctor,' he said, bowing and scraping, as he showed me to the cab.

I told the cabby to drive to Times Square. There I got out and headed for the subway. Just as I was reaching the change booth I realized I hadn't a damned cent left over. The cab driver had gotten my last quarter. I climbed up the steps and stood at the curb, wondering where and how I could raise the necessary nickel. As I was standing there a night messenger came along. I looked twice to see if I knew him. Then I bethought me of the telegraph office at Grand Central. I was sure to know someone there. I walked back to Grand Central, swung down the ramp and sure enough, there at the desk, large as life, was my old friend

Driggs. 'Driggs, would you lend me a nickel?' I said. '*A nickel?*' said Driggs. 'Here, take a dollar!' We chatted a few moments and then I ducked back to the subway.

A phrase Cromwell had let drop a number of times during the early part of the evening kept recurring to mind: 'my friend William Randolph Hearst.' I didn't doubt in the least that they were good friends, though Cromwell was still a pretty young man to be a bosom friend of the newspaper Czar. The more I thought of Cromwell the better I liked him. I was determined to see him again soon, on my own next time. I prayed that he wouldn't forget to make that telephone call. I wondered what he would think of me when he realized I had gone through his brief-case.

It was only a few nights later that we met again. This time at Papa Moskowitz's. Just Cromwell, Mona and myself. It was Cromwell who had suggested the rendezvous. He was leaving for Washington the next day.

Any uneasiness I might have felt on meeting him the second time was quickly dispelled by his warm smile and hearty handshake. At once he informed me how grateful he was for what I had done, not specifying what I had done, but giving me a look which made it clear he knew everything. 'I always make an ass of myself when I drink,' he said, blushing slightly. He looked more boyish now than he had the first night I met him. He shouldn't have been more than thirty, it seemed to me. Now that I knew what his real job was I was more than ever amazed by his easy, carefree deportment. He acted like a man without any responsibilities. Just a bright young banker of good family—that was the impression he created.

Mona and he had been talking literature, it seemed. He pretended, as before, to be out of touch with literary events. Nothing but a plain business man with a slight knowledge of finance. Politics? Completely beyond his ken. No, the banking business kept him busy enough. Except for an occasional tear, he was a home-loving body. Hardly ever saw anything but Washington and New York. Europe? Yes, most eager to see Europe. But that would have to wait until he could afford a real vacation.

He pretended to be rather ashamed of the fact that the only language he knew was English. But he supposed one could get by if one had the right connections.

I enjoyed hearing him hand out this line. Never by word or gesture did I betray his confidence. Not even to Mona would I have dared reveal what I knew about Cromwell. He seemed to understand that I could be trusted.

And so we talked and talked, listening to Moskowitz now and then, and drinking moderately. I gathered that he had already made it clear to Mona that the column was no go. Everybody had praised her work, but the big boss, whoever that was, had concluded it was not for the Hearst papers.

'What about Hearst himself?' I ventured to ask. 'Did he say No to it?'

Cromwell explained that Hearst usually abided by the decisions of his underlings. It was all very complicated, he assured me. However, he thought that something else might turn up, something even more promising. He would know after he got back to Washington.

I of course was able to interpret this as a mere politeness, knowing full well now that Cromwell would not be in Washington for at least two months, that in seven or eight days, as a matter of fact, he would be in Bucharest, conversing in the language of that country with great fluency.

'I may be seeing Hearst when I go to California next month,' he said, never batting an eyelash. 'I've got to go there on a business trip.'

'Oh, by the way,' he added, as if it had just occurred to him at that moment, 'isn't your friend Doctor Kronski a rather strange person . . . I mean, for a surgeon?'

'What do you mean?' I said.

'Oh, I don't know . . . I would have taken him for a pawn-broker, or something like that. Perhaps he was only putting on to amuse me.'

'You mean his talk? He's always that way when he drinks. No, he's really a remarkable individual—and an excellent surgeon.'

'I must look him up when I get back here again,' said Cromwell. 'My little boy has a club foot. Perhaps Dr Kronski would know what to do for him?'

'I'm sure he would,' I said, forgetting that I was supposed to be a surgeon too.

As if divining my oversight, and just to be a bit playful, Cromwell added: 'Perhaps *you* could tell me something about such matters yourself, Dr Marx. Or isn't that your field?'

'No, it isn't really,' I said, 'though I can tell you this much, however. We *have* cured some cases. It all depends. To explain why would be rather complicated. . . .'

Here he smiled broadly. 'I understand,' he said. 'But it's good to know that you think there is some hope.'

'Indeed there is,' I said warmly. 'Now in Bucharest at the present time there's a celebrated surgeon who is reputed to have cured ninety per cent of his cases. He has some special treatment of his own which we over here are not yet familiar with. I believe it's an electrical treatment.'

'In Bucharest, you say? That's far away.'

'Yes, it is,' I agreed.

'Supposing we have another bottle of Rhine wine?' suggested Cromwell.

'If you insist,' I replied. 'I'll have just a wee drop, then I must be going.'

'Do stay,' he begged, 'I really enjoy talking with you. You know, sometimes you strike me as more of a literary man than a surgeon.'

'I used to write,' I said. 'But that was years ago. In our profession one doesn't have much time for literature.'

'It's like the banking business, isn't it?' said Cromwell.

'Quite.' We smiled good-naturedly at one another.

'But there have been physicians who wrote books, haven't there?' said Cromwell. 'I mean novels, plays, and such like.'

'To be sure,' I said, 'plenty of them. Schnitzler, Mann, Somerset Maugham. . . .'

'Don't overlook Elie Faure,' said Cromwell. 'Mona here has been telling me a great deal about him. Wrote a history of art, or something like that . . . wasn't that it?' He looked to Mona for confirmation. 'I've never seen his work, of course. I wouldn't know a good painting from a bad one.'

'I'm not so sure of that,' said I. 'I think you'd know a spurious one if you saw it.'

'Why do you say that?'

'Oh, it's just a hunch. I think you're quick to detect whatever is counterfeit.'

'You're probably crediting me with too much acumen, Dr Marx. Of course, in our business, one does get accustomed to being on the alert for bad money. But that's really not my department. We have specialists for that sort of thing.'

'Naturally,' I said. 'But seriously, Mona *is* right . . . one day you've got to read Elie Faure. Imagine a man writing a colossal *History of Art* in his spare time! Used to make notes on his cuff while visiting his patients. Now and then he would fly to some far off place, like Yucatan or Siam or Easter Island. I doubt if any of his neighbours knew that he made such flights. Led a humdrum life, outwards. He was an excellent physician. But his passion was art. I can't tell you how much I admire the man.'

'You speak about him exactly like Mona,' said Cromwell. 'And you tell me you have no time for other pursuits!'

Here Mona put in her oar. According to her, I was a man of many facets, a man who seemed to have time for everything.

Would he have suspected, for instance, that Dr Marx was also a skilled musician, an expert at chess, a stamp collector . . .?

Cromwell here averred that he suspected I was capable of many things I was too modest to reveal. He was convinced, for one thing, that I was a man of great imagination. Quite casually he reminded us that he had noticed my hands the other night

In his humble opinion they revealed much more than the mere ability to wield the scalpel.

Interpreting this remark in her own fashion, Mona at once demanded if he could read palms.

'Not really,' said Cromwell, looking as if abashed. 'Enough, perhaps, to tell a criminal from a butcher, a violinist from a pharmacist. Most any one can do that much, even without a knowledge of palmistry.'

At this point I had an impulse to leave.

'Do stay!' begged Cromwell.

'No, really, I must be off,' said I, grasping his hand.

'We'll meet again soon, I hope,' said Cromwell. 'Do bring your wife next time. A charming little creature. I took quite a fancy to her.'

'That she is,' said I, reddening to the ears. 'Well, goodbye! *And bon voyage!*'

To this Cromwell raised his glass over the brim of which I detected a slightly mocking glance of the eyes. At the door I encountered Papa Moskowitz.

'Who is that man at your table?' he asked in a low voice.

'Frankly, I don't know,' I answered. 'Better ask Mona.'

'He's not a friend of yours then?'

'That's hard to answer too,' I replied. 'Well, goodbye!' and I shook myself loose.

That night I had a very disturbing dream. It started off, as dreams often do, as a pursuit. I was chasing a small thin man down a dark street, towards the river. Behind me was a man chasing me. It was important for me to catch up with the man I was pursuing before the other man got me. The thin little man was none other than Spivak. I had been trailing him all night from place to place, and finally I had him on the run. Who the man behind me was I had no idea. Whoever he was he had good wind and was fleet of foot. He gave me the uneasy feeling that he could catch up with me whenever he had a mind to. As for Spivak, though I wanted nothing better than to see him drown himself, it was most urgent that I collar him first; he had on him some papers which were of vital importance to me.

Just as we were nearing the jetty which projected into the river I caught up with him, collared him firmly, and swung him around. To my utter amazement it wasn't Spivak at all—it was crazy Sheldon. He didn't seem to recognize me, perhaps because of the darkness. He slid to his knees and begged me not to cut his throat. '*I'm not a Polak!*' I said, and yanked him to his feet. At that moment my pursuer caught up with us. It was Alan Cromwell. He put a gun in my hand and commanded me to shoot Sheldon. 'Here, I'll show you how,' he said, and giving

Sheldon's arm a vicious twist he brought him to his knees. Then he placed the muzzle of the gun against the back of Sheldon's head. Sheldon was now whimpering like a dog. I took the gun and placed it against Sheldon's skull. 'Shoot!' commanded Cromwell. I pulled the trigger automatically and Sheldon gave a little spring, like a jack-in-the-box, and fell face forward. 'Good work!' said Cromwell. 'Now, let's hurry. We're due in Washington tomorrow morning early.'

On the train Cromwell changed personality completely. He now resembled to a T my old friend and double, George Marshall. He even talked exactly like him, although his talk at the moment was rather disconnected. He was reminding me of the old days when we used to act the clown for the other members —of the celebrated Xerxes Society. Giving me a wink, he flashed the button on the underside of his lapel, the very one we all religiously wore, the one on which was engraved in letters of gold—*Fratres Semper*. Then he gave me the old handclasp, tickling my palm, as we used to do, with his forefinger. 'Is that enough for you?' he said, giving me another slippery horse-wink. His eyes, incidentally, had expanded to formidable proportions: they were huge goiterous eyes which swam in his round face like bloated oysters. This only when he winked, however. When he resumed his other identity, alias Cromwell, his eyes were quite normal.

'Who *are* you?' I begged. 'Are you Cromwell or Marshall?'

He put his finger to his lips, in the manner of Sheldon, and went SHHHHHHHH!

Then, in the voice of a ventriloquist, and talking out of the side of his mouth, he informed me rapidly, almost inaudibly, and with more and more celerity—it made me dizzy trying to follow him!—that he had been tipped off in the nick of time, that they were proud of me at headquarters, and that I was to be given a very special assignment, yes, to go to Tokio. I was to impersonate one of the Mikado's right-hand men—in order to track down the stolen prints. 'You know,' and he lowered his voice still more, training those horrible floating oysters on me again, flipping back the lapel of his coat, clasping my hand, tickling my palm, 'you know, the one we use for the thousand dollar bills.' Here he began talking Japanese which, to my amazement, I discovered I could follow as easily as English. It was the art commissioner, he explained in chop-stick language, who had caught on to the racket. He was an expert, this guy, on pornographic prints. I would be meeting him in Yokohama, disguised as a physician. He'd be wearing an admiral's uniform with one of those funny three-cornered hats. Here he gave me a prodigious nudge with his elbow and tittered—just like a Jap. 'I'm sorry to say, Hen,' he continued, relapsing into Brooklynese, 'that they've got the goods on your wife. Yep, she's in the ring. Caught her redhanded with a big package of coke.' He nudged me again, more viciously this time. 'Remember that last meeting we staged—at Grimmy's? You know, the time they fell asleep on us? I've done that rope-and-ladder trick many times since.' Here he grasped my hand and gave me the sign once more. 'Now listen, Hen, get it straight. . . . When we get off the train you walk leisurely down Pennsylvania Avenue, as if you were taking a stroll. You'll meet up with three dogs. The first two, they'll be fake dogs. The third one will run up to you to be patted. That's the clue. Pat him on the head with one hand and with the other slip your fingers under his tongue. You'll find a pellet about the size of an oat. Take the dog by the collar and let him lead you. Should anyone stop you, just say *Ohio!* You know what that means. They've got spies posted everywhere, even in the White House. . . . Now get this, Hen'—and he began talking like a sewing machine, faster, faster, faster—'when you meet the President give him the old handclasp. There's a little surprise in store for you, but I'll skip that. Just bear this in mind, Hen, that he's the President. Don't ever forget that! He'll tell you this and that . . . he doesn't know his ass from a hole in the ground . . . but never mind, *just listen.* Don't let on that you know a thing. Obsipresieckswizi will make his appearance at the critical moment. You know *him* . . . he's been with us for years. . . .' I wanted to ask him to repeat the name for me but he couldn't be stopped, not for a moment. 'We'll be pulling in in three minutes,' he murmured, 'and I haven't told you half yet. This is the *most* important, Hen, now get this,' and he gave me another painful poke in the ribs. But there his voice had dropped to such a pitch that I could only catch fragments of his speech. I was writhing in agony. How would I ever carry on if the most important details were lost? I would remember the three dogs, of course. The message was in code, but I would be able to decipher that on the boat. I was also to brush up on my Japanese during the boat trip, my accent was a little off, especially for the Court. 'You've got it now?' he was saying, waving his lapel again and clasping my hand. 'Wait, wait a minute,' I begged. 'That last part. . . .' But he had already descended the steps and was lost in the crowd.

As I walked along Pennsylvania Avenue, trying to give the appearance of a stroller, I realized with a sinking heart that I was really completely befuddled. For a moment I wondered if I were dreaming. But no, it was Pennsylvania Avenue all right, no mistaking it. And then suddenly there was a big dog standing at the curb. I knew he was an imitation one because he was fastened to a hitching block. That reassured me even more that I was in possession of my waking mind. I kept my eyes open to spot the second dog. I didn't even turn around, though I was certain someone was on my heels, so anxious was I not to miss that second dog. Cromwell, or was it George Marshall—the two had become inextricably confused—hadn't mentioned anything about being followed. Maybe, though, he *had* said something—when he was talking under his breath. I was getting more and more panicky. I tried to think back, to recall just how I had gotten involved in this ugly business, but my brain was too fatigued.

Suddenly I almost jumped out of my skin. At the corner, standing under an arc light, was Mona. She was holding a bunch of *Mezzotints* in her hand, distributing them to passers-by. When I got abreast of her she handed me one, giving me a look which meant—'Be careful!'—I sauntered leisurely across the street. For a while I carried the *Mezzotint* without glancing at it, flapping it against my leg as if it were a newspaper. Then, pretending that I had to blow my nose, I switched it to the other hand, and as I wiped my nose I read on the slant these words: 'The end is round like the beginning. *Fratres Semper.*' I was sorely baffled. Maybe that was another little detail I had missed when he was talking under his breath. Anyway, I had the presence of mind to tear the message into tiny little bits. I dropped the bits one by one at intervals of a hundred yards or so, listening intently each time to make sure my pursuer was not stopping to pick them up.

I came to the second dog. It was a little toy dog on wheels. Looked like a plaything abandoned by a child. Just to make sure it wasn't a real dog I gave it a little kick with my toe. It crumbled to dust immediately. I pretended, of course, that this was most natural, and resumed my leisurely pace.

I was only a few yards from the entrance to the White House when I perceived the third and real dog. The man shadowing me was no longer dogging my steps, unless he had changed to sneakers without my knowing it. Anyway, I had reached the last dog. He was a huge Newfoundland, playful as a cub. He came running up to me with big bounds and almost knocked me over trying to lick my face. I stood a moment or two patting his big warm head; then I circumspectly stooped down and inserted a hand under his tongue. Sure enough there was the pellet, wrapped in silver leaf. As Marshall or Cromwell had said, it was about the size of an oat.

I was holding the dog by the collar as we ascended the steps to the White House. All the guards gave the same sign—a big wink and little flutter of the lapel. As I wiped my feet on the mat outside I noticed the words *Fratres Semper* in big red letters. The President was coming towards me. He had on a cutaway and striped trousers; a carnation was in his buttonhole. He was holding out both hands to greet me. 'Why, Charlie!' I cried, 'how on earth did you get here? I thought I was to meet . . .' Suddenly I remembered George Marshall's words. 'Mr President,' I said, making a low bow, 'it is indeed a privilege . . .' 'Come right in, come right in,' said Charlie, grasping my hand and tickling the palm with his forefinger. 'We've been expecting you.'

If he was indeed the President he hadn't changed an iota since the old days.

Charlie was known as the silent member of our club. Because his silence lent him an air of wisdom we had mockingly elected him president of the club. Charlie was one of the boys from the flats across the way. We adored Charlie but could never get very close to him—because of his inscrutable silence. One day he disappeared. Months passed but no word from him. The months rolled into years. Not one of us had ever received a communication from him. He seemed to have dropped off the face of the earth.

And now he was ushering me into his sanctum. The President of these United States!

'Sit down,' said Charlie. 'Make yourself comfortable.' He proffered a box of cigars.

I could only stare and stare. He looked exactly as he always had, except, to be sure, for the cutaway and striped trousers. His thick auburn hair was parted in the middle, as always. His finger-nails were beautifully manicured, as always. The same old Charlie. At the bottom of his vest, as always, he was wearing the old button of the Xerxes Society. *Fratres Semper.*

'You realize, Hen,' he began, in that soft, modulated voice of his, 'why I have had to keep my identity secret.' He bent forward and lowered his voice. 'She's still on my trail, you know.' (*She*, I knew, referred to his wife whom he couldn't divorce because he was a Catholic.) 'It's she who's behind all this. You know. . . .' He gave me one of those big slippery horse-winks such as George Marshall had employed.

Here he began to twiddle with his fingers, as if rolling a little ball. At first I didn't catch on, but after he had repeated the gesture a number of times I realized what he was hinting at.

'Oh, the pel. . . .'

Here he raised a finger, placed it to his lips, and almost inaudibly, went Shhhhhhhhh.

I extracted the pellet from my vest pocket and unrolled it. Charlie kept nodding his head gravely, but making not a sound. I handed him the message to read; he handed it back to me and I read it attentively. Then I passed it back to him and he quickly burned it. The message was in Japanese. Translated, it meant: 'We are now inexorably united in brotherhood. The end is the same as the beginning. Observe strict etiquette.'

There was a telephone call which Charlie answered in a low, grave voice. At the end he said: 'Show him in in a few minutes.'

'Obsipresieckswizi will be here shortly. He will go with you as far as Yokohama.'

I was just about to ask if he wouldn't be kind enough to be a little more explicit when suddenly he swung round in his swivel chair and thrust a photograph under my nose.

'You recognize her, of course?' Again he put his finger to his lips.

'The next time you see her she'll be in Tokio, probably in the inner court.' Here he reached down into the lower drawer of his desk and brought forth a candy box labelled Hopjes, the kind that Mona and I had been peddling. He opened it gingerly and showed me the contents: a Valentine greeting, a strand of what looked like Mona's hair, a miniature dagger with an ivory handle and a wedding ring. I examined them intently, without touching them. Charlie closed the box and put it back in the drawer. Then he gave me a wink, flipped his vest flap and said '*Ohio!*' I repeated it after him: '*Ohio!*'

Suddenly he whirled around again and thrust the photograph under my nose. It was a different face this time. Not· Mona, but someone who resembled her, someone of indeterminate·sex, with long hair which fell over the shoulders, like an Indian's. A striking and mysterious face, reminiscent of that fallen angel, Rimbaud. I had an uneasy feeling. As I gazed, Charlie turned it over; on the other side was a photograph of Mona dressed like a Japanese woman, her hair done up in Japanese fashion, her eyes slanted upwards, the lids heavy, giving the eyes the appearance of two dark slits. He turned the photos back and forth several times. In awesome silence. I was unable to figure out what significance to give to this performance.

At this point an attendant came in to announce the arrival of Obsipresiekswizi. He pronounced the name as if it were Obsequy. A tall, gaunt man entered swiftly, went straight up to Charlie, whom he addressed as 'Mr President', and began a voluble speech in Polish. He hadn't noticed me at all. It was lucky he hadn't because I might have made a grave slip and called him by his right name. I was just reflecting how smoothly things were going when my old friend Stasu, for it was none other than he, stopped talking as abruptly as he had begun.

'Who is *this*?' he demanded in his curt, insolent way, motioning to me.

'Take a good look,' said Charlie. He gave a wink, first at me then at Stasu.

'Oh, it's *you*,' said Stasu, extending his hand grudgingly. 'How does *he* fit into the picture?' he said, addressing the President.

'That's for you to determine,' said Charlie blandly.

'Hmm,' mumbled Stasu. 'He's never been good at anything. He's a failure through and through.'

'We know all that,' said Charlie, thoroughly unruffled, 'but just the same.' He pressed a button and another attendant appeared. 'See that these men get to the airport safely, Griswold.

Use my car.' He rose and shook hands with us. His behaviour was exactly that of one holding such a high office. I felt that he was indeed the President of our great Republic, and a very shrewd, capable President to boot. As we reached the threshold he shouted: '*Fratres Semper!*' We wheeled around, saluted in military fashion, and repeated:

'*Fratres Semper!*'

There were no lights on the plane, not even inside. Neither of us spoke for some time. Finally Stasu broke into a torrent of Polish. It sounded strangely familiar to me yet I was unable to make out a word except *Pan* and *Pani*.

'Talk English,' I begged. 'You know I don't speak Polish.'

'Make an effort,' he said, 'it will come back to you. You spoke it once, don't act dumb. Polish is the easiest language in the world. Here, do this . . .' and he began making sibilant, hissing sounds like a serpent in rut. 'Now sneeze! Good. Now gargle? Good. Now roll your tongue back like a carpet and swallow! Good. You see . . . there's nothing to it. The rudiments are the six vowels, twelve consonants and five diphthongs. If you're dubious, spit or whistle. Never open your mouth wide. Suck the air in and push your tongue against your closed lips. Like this. Speak fast. The faster the better. Raise your voice a little, as if you were going to sing. That's it. Now close your palate and gargle. Fine! You're getting it. Now say after me, and don't stutter: *Ochizkishyi seiecsuhy plaifuejticko eicjcyciu!* Excellent! You know what that means—"Breakfast is ready!"'

I was overjoyed with my own fluency. We rehearsed a number of stock phrases, such as: 'Dinner is served', 'the water is hot', 'there's a strong breeze blowing', 'keep the fire going', and so on. It was all coming back to me readily. Stasu was right. I had only to make a little effort and the words were there on the tip of my tongue.

'Where are we headed for now?' I asked in Polish, just to vary the rigmarole.

'Izn Yotzxkiueoeumasysi,' he replied.

Even that long word I seemed to remember. A strange language, this Polish. It made sense, even if one did have to perform acrobatics with one's tongue. It was good exercise, it limbered up the tongue. After an hour or two of Polish I would be more than fit to resume my study of Japanese.

'What will you do when we get there?' In Polish, of course.

'Drnzybyisi uttituhy kidjeueycmayi,' said Stasu. Which meant, in our own vernacular, 'Take it easy.'

Then he added, with a few oaths, which I had forgotten, 'Keep your mouth shut and your eyes open. Wait for orders.'

In all this time he hadn't said a word about the past, about our boyhood days on Driggs Avenue, about his good-natured old aunt who used to feed us from the ice-box. She was such a lovable creature, his aunt. Always spoke—in Polish, that is—as if she were singing. Stasu hadn't changed a bit. As sullen, defiant, morose and disdainful as ever. I recalled the fear and dread with which he inspired me as a boy—when he lost his temper. He was a veritable demon then. Would grab a knife or a hatchet and make for me like lightning. The only time he ever seemed sweet and gracious was when his aunt sent him to buy sauerkraut. We used to filch a bit on the way home. It was good, that raw sauerkraut. The Poles were extraordinarily fond of it. That and fried bananas. Bananas that were soft and over-sweet.

We were landing now. Must be Yokohama. I couldn't make out a blessed thing, the whole airport was enveloped in darkness.

Suddenly I realized that I was alone in the plane. I felt around in the darkness but no Stasu. I called to him softly, but no answer. A mild panic seized me. I began to perspire profusely.

Getting off the plane two Japs came running forward to meet me. '*Ohio! Ohio!*' they exclaimed. '*Ohio!*' I repeated. We tumbled into rickshaws and began moving towards the city proper. There was no electricity, evidently—nothing but paper lanterns, as if for a festival. The houses were all made of bamboo, neat and trim, the side-walks were paved with wooden blocks. Now and then we crossed a tiny wooden bridge, such as one sees in old prints.

It was just beginning to dawn as we entered the precincts of the Mikado's palace.

I should have been trembling now but instead I was serene, perfectly composed, prepared for any eventuality. 'The Mikado will turn out to be another old friend,' I said to myself, pleased with my sagacity.

We dismounted before a huge portal painted in fiery colours, changed into wooden clogs and kimonos, prostrated ourselves a few times, and then waited for the portal to swing open.

Noiselessly, almost imperceptibly, the big portal finally swung open. We were in the midst of a small circular court, the flagging of which was inlaid with mother of pearl and precious gems. An enormous statue of the Buddha stood in the centre of the court. The expression on the Buddha's face was grave and seraphic at once. There emanated from him a feeling of tranquillity such as I had never known before. I felt drawn into the circle of the blessedness. The whole universe seemed to have come to an ecstatic hush.

A woman was coming forward from one of the hidden archways. She was clothed in ceremonial garb and carrying a sacred vessel. As she approached the Buddha everything became transformed. She advanced now with the gait of a dancer, to the sound of weird cacophonous music, sharp staccato sounds made by wood, stone and iron. From every doorway dancers now came forth with terrifying banners, their faces concealed by hideous masks. As they circled about the statue of the Buddha they blew into huge conch shells which gave forth unearthly sounds. Suddenly they fell away and I was alone in the court, facing a huge animal which resembled a bull. The animal was curled up on an iron altar that looked somewhat like a frying pan. I could see now that it was not a bull but the Minotaur. One eye was closed peacefully, the other was staring at me, quite friendly however. Of a sudden this enormous eye began to wink at me, coyly, flirtatiously, like a woman under a street lamp in some low quarter of the city. And as it winked it curled itself up more, as if making ready to be roasted. Then it closed the enormous eye and pretended to be snoozing. Now and then it fluttered the lids of that monstrous orb which had winked so jocosely.

Stealthily, on tip-toes, and with painful slowness, I approached the dread monster. When I got within a few feet of the altar, which was shaped distinctly like a saucepan I now realized, I perceived with horror that little flames were licking it from below. The Minotaur seemed to be stirring in his own juice, pleasurably. Again he was opening and shutting that big eye. The expression was one of sheer drollery.

Approaching more closely I felt the heat given off by those little flames. I could also smell the stench of the animal's scorched hide. I was hypnotized with terror. I stood where I was, rooted, the perspiration streaming down my face in rivulets.

With one bound the monster suddenly sprang upright, balancing himself on his hind legs. I perceived with a retching horror that he had three heads. All six eyes were wide open and leering at me. Transfixed, I stared glumly as the burnt hide fell away, revealing an underlayer of skin which was pure white and smooth as ivory. Now the heads began to turn white also, except for the three noses and muzzles which were of bright vermilion. Around the eyes were circles of blue, the blue of cobalt. In each forehead there was a black star; they twinkled like real stars.

Still balancing itself on his hind legs the monster now began to sing, rearing its head still higher, tossing its mane, rolling all of its six horrible leering eyes.

'Mother of God!' I mumbled in Polish, ready to faint momentarily.

The song, which had sounded at first like some Equatorial chant, was becoming more and more recognizable. With a skill which was supernatural, the monster subtly and rapidly changed from one register to another, one key to another, until finally with a clear and unmistakable voice it was hymning the Star Spangled Banner. As the anthem progressed, the beautiful white skin of the Minotaur changed from white to red and then to blue. The black stars in the foreheads became golden; they flashed like semaphores.

My mind, unable to follow these bewildering changes, seemed to go blank. Or perhaps a real blackout had occurred. At any rate, the next thing I knew the Minotaur had disappeared, the altar with it. On the beautiful mauve flagging, mauve and pale rose really, on which the precious inlaid gems sparkled like fiery stars, a nude woman of voluptuous proportions and with a mouth like a fresh wound was dancing the belly dance. Her navel, enlarged to the size of a silver dollar, was painted a vivid carmine; she wore a tiara and her wrists and ankles were studded with bracelets. I would have recognized her anywhere, nude or swaddled in cotton wool. Her long golden hair, her wild eyes of the nymphomaniac, her super-sensual mouth told me unmistakably that she was none other than Helen Reilly. If she had not been so fiercely possessive she would now be sitting in the White-House with Charlie who had deserted her. She would have been The First Lady in the Land.

I had hardly time to reflect, however. She was being bundled into a plane with me, stark naked and reeking of sweat and perfume. We were off again—back to Washington, no doubt. I offered her my kimono but she waved it aside. She felt comfortable just as she was, thank you. There she sat opposite me, her knees drawn up almost to her chin, her legs brazenly parted, puffing a cigarette. I wondered what the President—Charlie, that is—would say when he laid eyes on her. He had always referred to her as a lascivious, no-good bitch. Well, anyway, I had made good. I was bringing her back, that was the all important. No doubt he, Charlie, intended to obtain one of those divorces which only the Pope himself could grant.

Throughout the flight she continued to smoke cigarette after cigarette, maintaining her brazen posture, leering at me, making goo-goo eyes, heaving her big boobies, even playing with herself now and then. It was almost too much for me: I had to close my eyes.

When I opened them we were ascending the steps of the White House, hemmed in by a cordon of guards who screened the naked figure of the President's wife. I followed behind her, watching in utter fascination the way she joggled her low-slung buttocks. Had I not known who she was I might well have taken her for one of Minsky's belly dancers . . . for Cleo herself.

As the door of the White House opened I got the surprise of my life. It was no longer the room I had been received in by the President of our grand republic. It was the interior of George Marshall's home. A table of staggering proportions took up almost the entire length of the room. At each end stood a massive candelabra. Eleven men were seated round it, each one holding a glass in his hand: they reminded me of the wax figures at Madame Tussaud's. Needless to say, they were the eleven members of the original 'Deep-thinkers', as we once called ourselves. The vacant chair was obviously for me.

At one end of the table sat our old President, Charlie Reilly; at the other end sat our real President, George Marshall. At a given signal they all rose solemnly, glasses upraised, and broke into a deafening cheer. 'Bravo, Hen! Bravo!' they shouted. And with this they swooped down on us, gathered Helen by the arms and legs, and tossed her on to the Communion table. Charlie grasped my hand and repeated warmly, 'Well done, Hen! Well done!' I now shook hands with each one in turn, and with each gave the old sign—tickling the palm with the forefinger. They were all exceedingly well preserved—I say 'preserved' because, despite the warmth and the cordiality of their greeting there was something artificial, something wax-like about them. It was good, nevertheless, to see them all. Like old times, I thought to myself. Becker, with his worn fiddle-case; George Gifford, pinched and shrunk, as always, and talking through his nose; Steve Hill, big and blustering, trying to make himself look even more important than ever; Woodruff, MacGregor, Al Burger, Grimmy, Otto Kunst, and Frank Carroll. I was so immensely pleased to see Frank Carroll. He had lavender-coloured eyes with enormous lashes, like a girl's. He spoke softly and gently, more with his eyes than his mouth. A cross between a priest and a gigolo.

It was George Marshall who brought us back to reality. He was rapping the table with his gavel. 'Meeting called to order!' He rapped again vigorously and we all filed to our respective places at the table. The circle was complete, the end like the beginning. United in brotherhood, inexorably. How clear it all was! Everyone was wearing his button on which was inscribed in letters of gold *Fratres Semper*. It was all just as it had always been even to George Marshall's mother who was trotting back and forth from the kitchen, her arms laden with tempting viands. Unconsciously I stared intently at her broad backside. Had he not said once, George Marshall, that the sun rose and set in her ass?

There was only one disturbing note about this gathering, and that was the presence (in the nude) of Charlie Reilly's wife. There she stood in the middle of the long table, as brazen and impudent as ever, a cigarette between her lips, waiting for her cue. However, and this was even more strange, more disturbing to me, no one seemed to give her a tumble. I looked in Charlie's direction to see how he was taking it; he seemed unperturbed, unruffled, comporting himself in much the same way as he had when impersonating the President of these United States.

George Marshall's voice now made itself heard. 'Before we go on with the reading of the minutes,' said he, 'I want to present to you fellows a new member of the club. She's our first and only female member. *A real lady*, if I must lie like a dog. Some of you may recognize her. I'm sure Charlie will, anyhow.' He gave us a slippery grimace, intended for a smile, then hurried on. 'This is an important meeting, I want you fellows to understand. Hen here has just been to Tokio and back—I won't say what for just yet. At the conclusion of this session, which is a secret one, by the way, I want you guys to present Hen with the little testimonial which we prepared for him. His was a dangerous mission and he followed it to the letter. . . . And now, before we get on with the business in hand, which is about the beer party to be held at Gifford's home next Saturday night, I'm going to ask the little lady (a leer and a smirk here) to do one of her specialities. This number, I guess I don't have to tell you, will be the well-known hoochee-koochee. She did it for the Mikado —no reason why she can't do it for us. Anyway, you'll notice she's got nothing on, not even a fig-leaf.' As an uproar threatened to break loose, he rapped sternly with his gavel. 'Before she begins her number let me say this to you fellows—I expect you to observe the performance in strict decorum. We've arranged this stunt, Hen and I, in order to arouse more interest in the activities of the club. The last few meetings were thoroughly disheartening. The real club spirit seems to have oozed away. This is a special meeting to bring out the old spirit of fellow-ship. . . .'

Here he gave three quick raps with the gavel, whereupon a phonograph in the kitchen started playing the St Louis Blues. 'Is everybody happy?' he cooed. 'O.K. Helen, do your stuff! And remember, *shake those ashes clean!*'

The candelabras were removed to a sideboard against the wall; all but two of the candles had been snuffed out. Helen began writhing and twisting in the grand manner of the ancients. On the other wall her shadow repeated her movements in exaggerated style. It was a Japanese version of the belly dance which she was giving. One would have said she had been trained to it since childhood. Every muscle of her body was under control. Even her facial muscles she used with extraordinary skill, especially when *simulating the convulsive movements of the orgasm.* Not one of us twelve members budged from his rigid upright position. We sat there like trained seals, our hands motionless, our eyes following every little movement, which, as we knew, had a meaning all its own. As the last note died away George Gifford fell off his chair in a dead faint. Helen sprang from the table and ran into the kitchen. George Marshall rapped savagely with his gavel. 'Drag him out to the porch,' he ordered, 'and douse his head in the bucket! Quick! We've got to get on with the minutes.' This precipitated some grumbling and growling. 'Back to your places!' shouted George Marshall. 'This is just the preliminary. Keep your shirts on and you'll get a real treat. By the way, any one who feels like jerking off can excuse himself and go to the can.'

All but George Marshall and myself rose in a body and exeunted.

'You see what we're up against,' said George Marshall in a tone of utter despair. 'No matter what we cook up for them it's hopeless. I'm going to make a move to dissolve the club. I want it read into the minutes in the regular way.'

'Jesus,' I begged, 'don't do that! After all, they're only human.'

'That's where you're wrong,' said George Marshall. 'They're all picked men, they should know better. Last time we didn't even have a quorum.'

'What do you mean, *they should know better.*'

'Etiquette demands that you show no emotion. Nine of them are jerking off out there. The tenth one fainted. What are we coming to?'

'Aren't you just a bit severe?'

'Have to be, Hen. We can't coddle them forever.'

'Just the same, I think. . . .'

'Listen, Hen,' and he began to speak more rapidly, lowering his voice more and more. 'Nobody knows except Charlie and me, what you went to Tokio for. You did a good job. They know all about it up above. This is just a little racket I thought up to throw dust in their eyes. After the meeting breaks up you, Charlie and me we're gonna take Helen and go on a little bust. I didn't want them to lose control or they might have pawed her to death. She's fixing herself up in there. . . .' He gave me a slippery wink. . . . 'Douching herself. . . . A little alum, some Spanish fly. You know. . . . My mother's giving her a massage now. Look!' He bent down to get something hidden under the table. 'See this?' It was an enormous rubber penis filled with water. He gave a little squirt. '*Get the idea?* That's for Charlie. Don't say a word about it, it's a surprise. Being President's no fun. He hasn't had his end in for over a year now. There's enough water in this'—he shook the rubber penis lewdly— 'enough to make her piss from ears, eyes and nose.'

'This is gonna be fun, Hen. All on the q.t., of course. My mother's in on it, but she won't squawk. I told you once, remember, that the sun rises and sets in her ass.'

Then he added something which completely dumbfounded me, so unlike George Marshall it was. 'Get this, Hen,' he said, 'it's right up your street: The man of India loves to see the waist bend under the weight of the breasts and the haunches; he likes long tapering forms and the single wave of the muscles as a movement surges through the whole body. Heroism and obscenity appear no more important in the life of the universe than the fighting or mating of a pair of insects in the woods. Everything is on the same plane.'

He gave me again that enormous, slippery horse-wink which had so terrified me. '*Do you get it, Hen?* As I was saying a moment ago, the old urge is spent; we've got to find new blood. You and I are getting along in years; we can't do these old tricks with the same verve and gusto. When the war comes I'm going to join the artillery.'

'What war, George?'

He replied: 'No more of that trapeze business for me.'

The other members were now trooping back from the can. Never in my life had I seen such haggard, spent, dilapidated looking buggers. 'He's right,' thought I to myself, 'we've got to look for new blood.'

Quietly they resumed their places at the table, their heads wilting like dead flowers. Some of them looked as if they were in a deep trance. Georgie Gifford was munching a stalk of celery —the very picture, saving the beard, of a silly old he-goat. The whole damned bunch were a disgrace for sore eyes.

A few raps of the gavel and the meeting was called to order. 'Those who are awake give heed!' George Marshall began in a stern, peremptory voice. 'Once you called yourselves The Deepthinkers. You banded together to form an enclave, the famous Xerxes Society. You are no longer worthy of membership in this secret society. You have degenerated. Some of you have atrophied. In a moment I am going to call for a vote in order to dissolve the organization. But first I have something to say to our old president, Charlie Reilly.' Here he gave the table a few vicious raps with the gavel. 'Are you awake, you miserable toad? I'm talking to you. Sit up straight! Button your fly! Now listen. . . . In consideration of services rendered, I'm sending you back to the White House where you will serve another four years, *if you're re-elected.* As soon as the meeting is over I want you to get into your cutaway and striped trousers and beat it. You have just about enough wits left to meet the demands of the War Office. By holding your tongue nobody will be the wiser. You're demoted, dissolved, discredited.' Here he turned his head and fixed my attention. '*How was that, Hen?* All according to Hoyle, what?' He lowered his voice and, speaking with terrifying rapidity again, he whispered out of the corner of his mouth: 'This is for *you,* a special. . . . Man will change nothing of his final destiny, which is to return sooner or later to the unconscious and the formless.'

With this he rose and, pulling me along, we rushed to the kitchen. A pall of smoke greeted us. 'As I was saying, Hen, we prepared a little surprise for you.' With this he blew the smoke away. On either side of the kitchen table sat Mona and that mysterious creature with the long black hair whom I had seen a photograph of.

'What's this?' I exclaimed.

'Your wife and her friend. A couple of bulldykers.'

'Where's Helen?'

'Gone back to Tokio. We're using these as substitutes.' He gave me a terrific nudge and a slippery wink.

'Cromwell will be here in a minute,' he said. 'It's him you've got to thank for this.'

Mona and her lover were too busy playing euchre to even glance at us. They seemed hilarious. The strange creature with the long hair was double-jointed; she had a fine moustache, firm breasts, and wore velvet trousers with gold braid down the sides. Exotic to the finger-tips. Every now and then they jabbed each other with the needle.

'A fine pair,' I remarked. 'They belong in the Haymarket.'

'Leave it to Cromwell,' said George Marshall, 'he's got it all arranged.'

He had no more than uttered the name when there was a rap at the door.

'That's him,' said George Marshall. 'Always on the dot.'

The door opened quietly, as if responding to a hidden spring. A man entered with a huge gory bandage wrapped around his skull. It was not Cromwell at all, it was crazy Sheldon. I gave a shriek and fainted away.

When I came to, Sheldon was seated at the table dealing out the cards. He had removed the bandage. From the tiny black hole in the back of his skull the blood trickled steadily, running over his white collar and down his back.

Again I felt that I would faint. But George Marshall, sensing my discomfiture, quickly produced a little glass stopper from his vest pocket, inserted it in the bullet wound, and the blood stopped running. Sheldon now began to whistle gaily. It was a Polish lullaby. Now and then he broke the melody by spitting on the floor, whereupon he would hum a few bars, so softly, so tenderly, as though he were a mother with an infant at the breast. After he had hummed and whistled, after he had spat in every direction, he took to chanting in Hebrew, moving his head back and forth, wailing doing the tremolo in a high falsetto, sobbing, moaning, praying. He sang in a powerful bass voice with a volume that was staggering. This went on for quite a time. He was like a man possessed. Suddenly he moved into another register, which gave his voice a peculiar metallic timbre, as though his lungs were made of sheet metal. He was singing in Yiddish now, a drunken tune filled with bloody oaths and filthy imprecations. *'Die Hutzulies, farbrent soln sei wern. . . . Die Merder, geharget soln sei wern. . . . Die Gozlonem, unzinden soln sei sich. . . .'* His voice rose to a piercing screech. *'Fonie-ganef, a miese meshine of sei!'* With this, still screaming, the foam dribbling from his mouth, he rose to his feet and began whirling like a dervish. *'Cossaken! Cossaken!'* he repeated over and over, stamping his foot and emitting a stream of blood from his pursed lips. He slowed down a little, put his hand to his back trousers pocket and brought out the miniature knife with the pearl handle. Now he whirled faster and faster, and as he shrieked '*Cossaken! Hutzulies! Gozlonem! Merder! Fonie-Ganef!*' he stabbed himself over and over, in the arms, in the legs, in the stomach, eyes, nose, ears, mouth, until he was nothing but a mass of wounds. Suddenly he stopped, grabbed the two women by the throat and knocked their heads together—again and again, as if they were two coconuts. Then he unbuttoned his shirt, raised the police whistle to his lips, and gave a blast which made the walls shiver. With this the ten members of the Xerxes Society rushed to the door; as they stepped across the threshold Sheldon, who had drawn his automatic, shot them down one by one, yelling '*A miese meshine of sei. . . . Hutzulies, Gozlonem, Merder, Cossaken!*'

Only George Marshall and I were alive and breathing. We were too paralysed to move. We stood with backs to the wall, waiting our turn. Walking over the bodies of the dead as if they were so much fallen timber, Sheldon slowly approached us with levelled gun, unbuttoning his fly with the left hand. 'Shitty dogs!' he said in Polish, 'this is your last chance to pray. Pray while I piss on you, and may my bloody piss scald your rotten hearts! Call on your Pope now, and your Virgin Mary! Call on that faker, Jesus Christ! The assassins will be geschiessen. How you stink, shitty Goyim! Fart your last fart!' And he poured over us his steaming red piss which ate into our skins like acid. Hardly had he finished when he fired point blank at George Marshall; the body fell to the floor like a sack of manure.

I put up my hand to yell Stop! but Sheldon was already firing. As I sank to the ground I began to whinny like a horse. I saw him raise his foot and then I got it in the face. I rolled over on my side. I knew it was the end.

7

IT WAS DAYS BEFORE I could shake off the after effects of the dream. In some mysterious way it had affected Mona too, though I had told her nothing of it. We were unaccountably listless and dispirited. Having dreamed so violently about him, I looked forward to seeing Sheldon pop up, but neither hide nor hair of him did we lay eyes on. Instead we received a post-card from O'Mara informing us that he was in the vicinity of Asheville where there was a boom on. Said he would notify us to join him as soon as things were properly under way.

Out of sheer boredom Mona took another job in the Village, this time at a shady joint called The Blue Parrot. From Tony Maurer, a new admirer, she learned that the Milwaukee millionaire was due in town any day.

'And who is Tony Maurer?' I asked.

'A cartoonist,' she replied. 'He was once a German cavalry officer. He's a real wit.'

'Never mind the rest,' I said. I was still in the doldrums. To summon even a flickering interest in one of her new admirers was beyond me. I was low, and I would stay that way until I hit bottom. Even Elie Faure was too much for me. I couldn't bring myself to concentrate on anything more important than a bowel movement.

As for looking up my friends, out of the question. When depressed I rarely ever visited anyone, even a close friend.

The few attempts I had made to do a little gold-digging on my own had contributed to lower my morale. Luther Goering, the last man I had hit up—for a mere five-spot—had taken the wind out of my sails. It wasn't my intention to lay siege to him, seeing how he was almost one of the family, but running into him in the subway, as I did, I thought I might as well profit by the occasion. The mistake I made was to interrupt him in the middle of one of his interminable harangues. He had been telling me of the huge success he was enjoying (as an insurance salesman) through the application of Christ's teachings. Having always looked upon me as an atheist, he was now delighted to be able to overwhelm me with proofs of the practical aspect of Christian ethics. Bored absolutely stiff, I listened for a while in cold silence, sorely tempted at moments to laugh in his face. Nearing our station I interrupted the monologue to ask if he would lend me five dollars. The request must have struck him as outrageously irrelevant for he flew into a tantrum. This time I could no longer control myself—I laughed in his face. For a moment I thought he would slap me in the face; he was livid with rage, his lips trembling, his fingers twitching uncontrollably. What *was* the matter with me, he demanded to know. Had I supposed that because he had at last succeeded in earning a good living I was at liberty to regard him as a charitable institution? True, the Bible did say: 'Ask and it shall be given, knock and it shall be opened unto you,' but one was not to infer from these words that one was to give up work and become a panhandler. 'God looks after me,' he said, 'because I look after myself. I put in fifteen and sixteen hours a day. I don't pray to God to put money in my pockets, *I beg him to bless my work!*' At this point he softened somewhat. 'You don't seem to understand,' he said. 'Let me try to explain it to you. It's really very simple. . . .'

I told him I didn't give a hoot for his explanations, that all I cared to know was—would he lend me the five dollars or not?

'Of course I won't, Henry, if you put it that way. You have to learn first to put yourself in God's good graces.'

'Fuck that!' I said.

'Henry, you're steeped in sin and ignorance!' In an effort to placate me he grasped my arm. I brushed it away. We walked down the street in silence. After a time, speaking as softly as he could, he said: 'I know it's hard to repent. I've been a sinner myself. But I wrestled with might and main. And finally, Henry, God showed me the way. God taught me how to pray. And I prayed, Henry, night and day. I prayed even when talking to a client. And God has answered my prayers. Yes, out of the bounteous goodness of His heart He forgave, He brought me back to the fold. Look, Henry . . . last year I earned a scant $1500.00. This year—and the year is not over—I've earned well over ten thousand dollars. That's the proof, Henry. Even an atheist can't contest such logic!'

In spite of myself I was amused. I'll listen, thought I to myself. I'll let him try to convert me. Maybe then I can make it ten bucks instead of five.

'You're not starved, are you, Henry?' he suddenly inquired. 'Because if you are we'll stop off somewhere and have a bite to eat. Perhaps this is God's way of bringing us together.'

I told him that I wasn't at the point of dropping in the street. The way I said it, however, implied that it was a possibility.

'That's good,' said Luther, with his customary insensitiveness. 'What you need more than earthly food is spiritual sustenance. If one has that, one can do without ordinary food. Remember this —God always provides sufficient for the day, even to sinners. He watches over the sparrows. . . . You haven't altogether forgotten the good teachings, have you?—I know your parents sent you to Sunday School . . . and they also provided you with a good education. God was looking after you all the time, Henry. . . .'

'Jesus,' I asked myself, 'how long will this continue?'

'Perhaps you remember the Epistles of St Paul?' he continued. Since I gave him a blank look he dove into his breast pocket and exhumed a worn-looking New Testament. He stopped dead and began thumbing the pages.

'Don't bother,' I said, 'give it to me from memory. I've got to get home soon.'

'That's all right,' he said, 'we're on God's time now. Nothing can be more important than the precious words of the Bible. God is our Comforter, remember that, Henry.'

'But what if God doesn't answer one's prayers?' I said, more to discourage him from looking up the Epistles of St Paul than to know the answer.

'God always answers him who seeks Him,' said Luther. 'Perhaps not the first time or the second time, but eventually. Sometimes God sees fit to try us first. He wants to be sure of our love, our loyalty, our faith. It would be too simple if we could just ask for something and have it fall into our laps, wouldn't it now?'

'I don't know,' I said, 'why not? God can do anything, can't He?'

'Always within reason, Henry. Always according to our merits. It's not God who punishes us, but we ourselves. God's heart is always open to him who seeks Him out. But it must be a real need. One must be desperate before God gives of His kindness.'

'Well, I'm pretty desperate right now,' I said. 'Honest, Luther, I need that money bad. We're going to be evicted in a day or two if something doesn't happen.'

Luther was strangely unmoved by this last piece of information. He was so well attuned to God's way, it seemed, that a little matter like eviction meant nothing to him. Perhaps God wanted it that way. Perhaps it was a preparation for something better. 'What does it matter, Henry,' he said fervidly, 'what does it matter where you are living if only you can find God? You can find Him in the street just as easily as at home. God will shelter you with His blessed wings. He watches over the homeless just as much as He does over others. His eye is on us always. No, Henry, if I were you, I would go home and pray, pray that He show you the way. Sometimes a change does us good. Sometimes we get too comfortable and we forget whence all our blessings flow. Pray to Him tonight, on your knees, and with a full heart. Ask

Him to give you work for your hands. Ask to serve Him, remember that. Serve the Lord, it is said, and keep His commandments. That is what I am constantly doing—now that I have found the light. And God rewards me abundantly, as I explained to you before....'

'But look, Luther, if God is really taking care of you so handsomely, as you say, couldn't you share just a little of your blessed reward with me? After all, five dollars isn't a fortune.'

'I *could* do that, Henry, most certainly—*if I thought it were the right thing to do* But you're in God's hands now: *He will* look after you.'

'In what way would it interfere with God's plans if you were to lend me that five bucks?' I insisted. I was getting fed up.

'The ways of the Lord are beyond our knowing,' said Luther solemnly. 'Perhaps He will have a job for you to go to in the morning.'

'But I don't want a job, damn it! I have my own work to do. What I need is five bucks, that's all.'

'That will probably be provided, too,' said Luther. 'Only you must have faith. Without faith, even the little you have will be taken from you.'

'But I haven't anything,' I protested. 'Not a God-damned thing, don't you understand? God can't take anything away from me because I have nothing. Figure that out!'

'He can take away your health, he can take your wife from you, he can take from you the power to move your limbs, do you realize that?'

'He'd be one big louse to do that!'

'God afflicted Job sorely, surely you haven't forgotten that? He also raised Lazarus from the dead. God giveth and God taketh away.'

'Sounds like a swindle game.'

'Because you are still beclouded with ignorance and folly,' said Luther. 'For each one of us God has a special lesson to teach. You will have to learn humility.'

'If I only got a bit of a break,' I said, 'I might be ready to learn my lesson. How can a man learn humility when his back is already broken?'

Luther disregarded this last completely. In restoring the New Testament to his breast pocket he came upon some forms from the insurance company which he flourished in my face.

'*What?*' I fairly shrieked, 'you don't mean to say you want to sell me a policy?'

'Not now, to be sure,' said Luther, grasping my arm again to quell my agitation, 'not now, Henry, but perhaps in a month or so. God works His wonders in mysterious ways. Who knows but that a month from now you may be sitting on top of the world? If you had one of these in your possession you could borrow from the insurance company. It would save you a lot of embarrassment.'

Here I abruptly took leave of him. He was still standing with hand outstretched, as if immobilized, when I got to the other side of the street. I gave him one parting glance and spat out a gob of juicy disgust. 'You prick!' I said to myself. 'You and your fucking Comforter! For a pair of heartless shits I've never seen the like of you. *Pray?* You bet I'll pray. I'll pray that you have to crawl on hands and knees to scratch for a penny. I'll pray that your wrists and knees give out, that you have to crawl on your belly, that your eyes will become bleary, and filled with scum.'

The house was dark when I got back. No Mona. I sank into the big chair and gave myself up to moody reflections. In the soft light of my table lamp the room looked better than ever. Even the table, which was in a state of huge disorder, affected me pleasantly. It was obvious that there had been a long interruption. Manuscripts were lying about everywhere, books lay open at pages where I had left off reading. The dictionary too was lying open on top of the book-case.

As I sat there I realized that the room was impregnated with my spirit. I belonged here, nowhere else. It was foolish of me to stir out in the manner of a householder. I should be home writing. I should do nothing but write. Providence had taken care of me thus far, why not forever? The less I did about practical matters the more smoothly things went. These forays into the world only alienated me from mankind.

Since that fantastic evening with Cromwell I hadn't written a line. I moved over to the writing table and began fiddling with the papers. The last column I had written—the very day that Cromwell had visited us—lay before me. I read it over quickly.

It sounded good to me, extraordinarily good. Too good, in fact, for the newspaper. I pushed it aside and began slowly perusing a novelette which was unfinished, that 'Diary of a Futurist', of which I had read fragments to Ulric once. I was not only favourably impressed, I was deeply moved by my own words. I must have been in good spirits to have written that well.

I glanced at one manuscript after another, reading only a few lines at a time. Finally, I came to my notes. They were as fresh and inspiring as when I had jotted them down. Some of them, which I had already made use of, were so provocative that I wanted to write the stories all over again, write them from a fresh, new angle. The more I unearthed, the more feverish I became. It was as though a huge wheel inside me had begun to revolve.

I pushed everything aside and lit a cigarette. I gave myself up to a delicious reverie. All that I had wanted to write these past fall months was now writing itself out. It oozed out like milk from a coconut. I had nothing to do with it. Someone else was in charge. I was merely the receiving station transmitting it to the blue.

Just the other day, some twenty years since this occurrence, I came upon the words of one Jean-Paul Richter, which described exactly how I felt at that moment. What a pity I did not know them then! Here is what he wrote:

'Rien ne m'a jamais ému davantage que le sieur Jean-Paul. Il s'est assis à sa table et, par ses livres, il m'a corrompu et transformé. Maintenant, je m'enflamme de moi-même.'

My reverie was broken by a gentle knock at the door. 'Come in,' I said, not moving from the spot. To my surprise Mr Taliaferro, our landlord, entered.

'Good evening, Mr Miller,' he said, in his quiet, easy Southern way. 'I hope I am not disturbing you?'

'Not at all,' I replied, 'I was just dreaming.' I motioned to him to take a seat and after a due pause I asked what I might do for him.

At this he smiled benevolently, drawing his chair a little closer. 'You look as though you were deep in work,' he said, with sincere kindliness. 'It's unfortunate that I should have disturbed you at such a moment.'

'I assure you I wasn't working, Mr Taliaferro. I'm glad indeed to see you. I've been intending to call on you for some time. You must have wondered. . . .'

'Mr Miller,' he interrupted, 'I thought it was time we had a little chat together. I know you have lots of preoccupations, besides your work. Perhaps you are not even aware that it is some months now since you last paid your rent. I know how it is with writers. . . .'

The man was so truly gentle and considerate that I simply couldn't stand on pretence with him. I had no idea how many months we were in arrears. What I admired in Mr Taliaferro was that he had never in any way made us feel uncomfortable. Only once before had he ventured to knock at our door and that was to inquire if we needed anything. It was with a feeling of great relief, therefore, that I surrendered myself to him.

Just how it happened I don't know, but in a few moments I was sitting beside him on the cot we had bought for O'Mara. He had his arm around my shoulders and was explaining to me, quite as if I were a younger brother, and in a voice so gentle, so soothing, that he knew I was a good individual, knew I had never intended to put him off so long (it was five months, I discovered) but that sooner or later I would have to come to terms with the world.

'But Mr Taliaferro, I think if you gave us just a little time. . . .'

'Son,' he said, pressing my shoulder ever so lightly, 'it's not

205

time you need, it's an awakening. Now if I were you, I would talk it over with Mrs Miller this evening and see if you couldn't find a place more suited to your income. I am not going to hurry you unduly. Look around . . . take your time . . . find the place you like, and then move. What do you think?'

I was almost in tears. 'You're too kind,' I said. 'Of course you're right. Certainly we shall find another place, and quickly too. I don't know how to thank you for your delicacy and consideration. I guess I *am* a dreamer. I never realized that it was so long since we last paid you.'

'Of course you didn't,' said Mr Taliaferro. 'You're an honest man, I know that. But don't worry about . . .'

'But I do worry about it,' I said. 'Even though we may have to move without paying you the back rent, I want you to know that I will definitely pay it back later, probably in driblets.'

'Mr Miller, if you were situated differently, I would be glad to accept your promise, but it's too much to ask of you now. If you can find another place before the first of next month I shall be quite content. Let's forget about the back rent, yes?'

What could I say? I looked at him with moist eyes, shook his hand warmly and gave him my word that we would be out on time.

As he rose to take leave of me he said: 'Don't be too discouraged about this. I know how much you like this place. I hope you were able to do good work here. Some day I expect to read your books.' Pause. 'I hope you'll always think of us as friends.'

We shook hands once more, then I closed the door softly after him. I stood a few minutes with my back to the door, surveying the room. I felt good. As though I had just come through a successful operation. Just a little dizziness from the anaesthetic. How Mona would take it I didn't know. Already I was breathing easier. Already I had visions of living among poor people, my own sort. Down to earth again. Excellent. I walked to and fro, threw open the rolling doors and strutted about in the vacant apartment in the rear. A last taste of refinement. I took a good look at the stained glass window, rubbed my hand over the rose silk tapestry, slid a few feet on the highly polished floor, looked at myself in the huge mirror. I grinned at myself and said again and again, 'Good! Good!'

In a few minutes I had made myself a pot of tea and fixed a thick, juicy sandwich. I sat down at my work table, put my feet up on a hassock, and picked up a volume of Elie Faure, opening it at random. . . . 'When this people is not cutting throats or burning buildings, when it is not decimated by famine and butchery, it has only one function—to build and decorate palaces whose vertical wall shall be thick enough to protect the Sar, his wives, his guard, and his slaves—twenty or thirty thousand persons—against the sun, invasion, or perhaps revolt. Around the great central courts are the apartments covered with terraces or with domes, with cupolas, images of the absolute vault of the deserts, which the Oriental soul will rediscover when Islam shall have reawakened it. Higher than these, observatories which are at the same time temples, the *zigurats*, the pyramidal towers whose stages painted with red, white, blue, brown, black, silver and gold, shine afar through the veils of dust which the winds whirl in spiral. Especially at the approach of evening, the warring hordes and the nomadic pillagers, who see the sombre confines of the desert streaked with this motionless lightning, must recoil in fear. It is the dwelling of the god, and resembles those steps of the plateau of Iran leading to the roof of the world, which are striped with violent colours by subterranean fire and by the blaze of the sun. The gates are guarded by terrific brutes, bulls and lions with human heads, marching. . . .'

A few blocks away, in a quiet street largely taken over by the Syrians, we found a modest furnished room situated in the rear of the house on the ground floor. The woman who rented the place was a blue-nose from Nova Scotia, a harridan who gave me the shudders every time I looked at her. Everything imaginable had been crammed into our quarters: wash tubs, cooking stove, heater, huge sideboard, old-fashioned wardrobe, extra couch, a battered rocker, a still more battered armchair, a sewing machine, a horsehair sofa, a what-not filled with five-and-ten-cent store knick-knacks, and an empty bird cage. I suspected that it was this room the old witch herself had inhabited prior to our arrival.

To put it pleasantly, an atmosphere of dementia reigned.

The saving thing was the garden outside our back door. It was a long rectangular garden enclosed by high brick walls, reminding me for some unaccountable reason of the garden in *Peter Ibbetson*. At any rate, it was a place in which to dream. Summer had just begun and in the late afternoons I would drag out a big armchair and read. I had just discovered Arthur Weignall's books and was devouring them one after another. After reading a few pages I would fall into a reverie. Here in the garden everything was conducive to dream and reverie—the soft, fragrant air, the humming of insects, the lazy flight of the birds, the swishing of foliage, the murmur of foreign voices in the gardens adjoining.

An interlude of peace and privacy.

It was during this period that purely by chance I ran into my old friend Stanley one day. Forthwith Stanley began to visit us at frequent intervals, usually accompanied by his two boys, one five, the other seven. He had grown very fond of his youngsters and took great pride in their appearance, their manners, their speech. From Stanley I learned that my daughter was not attending a private school. His elder son, also named Stanley, had quite a crush on her, he informed me. This last he imparted with great relish, adding that Maude viewed the situation with alarm. As to how 'they' were getting along, that I had to drag out of him. It was nothing to worry about, he assured me, but the tone in which he said it conveyed that their circumstances were none too good. Poor old Melanie was still slaving away at the hospital, hobbling to work now with a cane; her nights she spent coddling her varicose veins. She and Maude were more than ever at odds. Maude, of course, was still giving piano lessons.

It was just as well I didn't visit them any more, was Stanley's summing up. They had given me up as hopeless and irresponsible. Only Melanie, apparently, had a good word to say for me but then Melanie was just a doddering idiot. (Always subtle and tactful, Stanley.)

'Can't you sneak me in there some time when no one's home?' I begged. 'I want to see how the place looks. I'd like to see the child's toys, if nothing more.'

Stanley couldn't see the wisdom of this but promised to think it over.

Then he added quickly: 'You'd better forget about them. You've made a new life for yourself, stick to it!'

He must have sensed that we didn't have enough to eat, for every time he came he brought food, usually the remnants of some Polish concoction his wife had made—soups, stews, puddings, jam. Good gruel, the sort we needed. In fact, we began to look forward to these visits.

There wasn't much change in Stanley, I noticed, except that his nose was now pressed closer to the grindstone. He was working nights in a big printing establishment in lower New York, he told me. Now and then, standing up over the kitchen tubs, he would try to write. He found it almost impossible to concentrate —too many domestic worries. Usually they were broke before the week was up. Anyway, he was more interested in his children now than in writing. He wanted them to have a good life. Soon as they were old enough he would send them to college. And more of the same. . . .

Though he found it impossible to write, he did read. Now and then he brought along one of the books which entranced him. It was always the work of a romantic writer, usually of the 19th century. Somehow, no matter what book we were discussing, no matter what the world situation, no matter even if a revolution were impending, our talks always ended on Joseph Conrad. Or if not Conrad, then Anatole France. I had long ceased to be interested in either of these writers. Conrad bored me. But when Stanley began to sing his praise I would become intrigued despite myself. Stanley was no critic, to be sure, but, just as in the old days when we used to sit by the glowing stove in the kitchen and while the hours away, so now Stanley had a way of talking about the men he adored which infected me. He was full of yarns, usually about trivial episodes. These yarns were always humorous and spiced with malice and irony. The undercurrent, however, was freighted with tenderness, an immense, throbbing tenderness, which was almost suffocating. This tenderness of his, which he always smothered, redeemed his rancour, his cruelty, his vindictiveness. It was an aspect of his nature, however, which he rarely betrayed to others. In general he was brusque, mordant, acidulous. With a few words and gestures he could destroy any ambition. Even when silent there emanated from him a fluid which was corrosive.

In talking to me, however, he always melted. For some strange reason he saw in me an alter ego. Nothing gave him more delight, nothing could make him more charming and solicitous, than the fact I felt miserable or defeated. Then we were brothers. Then he could relax, expand, sun himself. He liked to think that we were accursed. Had he not prophesied time on end that all my efforts would not be of no avail? Had he not predicted that I would never make a good husband, nor a father, nor ever become a writer? Why did I persist? Why didn't I settle down, as he had, take some humdrum job and accept my lot? It was patent that it did his heart good to gloat thus. Ever and always he went out of his way to remind me that I was 'just a Brooklyn boy', a lad from the 14th Ward—like himself, like Louis Pirossa, like Harry Martin, like Eddie Goeller, like Alfie Betcha. (All failures.) No, none of us would ever come to aught. We were condemned in advance. I ought to be grateful, he thought, that I wasn't sitting in the penitentiary or that I hadn't become a drug addict. Lucky for me that I came of a solid, respectable family.

Just the same, I was doomed.

As he continued to rant, however, his voice became more and more soothing. There was now a wistful quality in it, a nostalgic tinge. It was so very clear that, despite all he said, he could think of no better heritage than the life we once led, the companions we once had, in the good old 14th Ward. He spoke of our mutual friends of long ago as if he had made a life's study of each separate one. They were all so diverse in character and temperament, yet each and every one had been circumscribed by his limitations, held in a vice of his own making. For Stanley there was not hope of egress, never had been, for any of them. Nor for us, to be sure. For other individuals there might be loop-holes, but not for the men of the 14th Ward. We were in jeopardy, forever. It was this very fact, this deliciously ineluctable fact, which endeared the memory of our bygone friends. Most certainly, he admitted, they possessed as great talent as men elsewhere in the world. Undisputably they possessed all the qualities which made of other men poets, kings, diplomats, scholars. And they had proved themselves capable of revealing these qualities, each on his own level, each in his own unique way. Was not Johnny Paul the very soul of a king? Was he not a potential Charlemagne? His chivalry, his magnanimity, his faith and tolerance, were they not the very attributes of a Saladin? Stanley could always wax most eloquent when it came to Johnny Paul whom neither of us had seen since we were nine or ten. What became of him, we used to ask each other. What? No one knew. By choice or by fate he had remained anonymous. He was there, somewhere, in the great mass of humanity, leavening it with the fervour of his truly regal spirit. That was sufficient for Stanley. For me too, indeed. Strange that the very mention of the name Johnny Paul could bring tears to our eyes. Was he really so near and dear to us—or had we magnified his importance with the passing years? In any case, there he stood—in the hall of memory—the incarnation of all that was good, all that was promising. One of the grand Untouchables. Whatever it was he possessed, whatever it was he purveyed, it was imperishable. We had been aware of it as boys, we were convinced of it now as men. . . .

Mona, at first rather distrustful of Stanley, rather uneasy in his presence, warmed to him more and more with each succeeding visit. Our talk of the old neighbourhood, of our wonderful playmates, our curious and brutal games, our fantastic notions (as children) of the world we inhabited, revealed to her a side of life she had never known. Occasionally she would remind Stanley of her Polish origin, or her Roumanian origin, or her Viennese origin, or telescope them all into 'the heart of the Carpathian mountains.' To these overtures Stanley always gave a lame ear, or as the Greeks say—*koutsaftis*. In his mind the fact that she couldn't speak a word of Polish was sufficient to put her in the same category as all the other 'outlanders' of this world. Besides, for Stanley's taste she was a little too glib. Out of deference to me he never contradicted her, but the devastating expressions which flitted over his features spoke volumes. Doubt and disdain were the expressions Stanley most easily summoned. More than anything else Stanley was disdainful. This disdain which never quite left his features, which at most he subdued or repressed, was concentrated in his nose. He had the rather long, fine nose with flaring nostrils which is often noticeable among the Poles. Whatever was suspect, whatever was distasteful or antipathetic, manifested itself at once through this organ. The mouth expressed bitterness, the eyes a steadfast cruelty. They were small eyes, the colour of agate; they were set wide apart and the look they gave bored clean through one. When he was merely ironical they twinkled, like cold, remote stars; when he was angry they burned like arrows dipped in poison.

What made him particularly awkward and ill at ease in Mona's presence was her fluency, her agility, her quick intelligence. They were not qualities he admired in the other sex. It was not altogether by accident that he had chosen for wife a dolt, a half-wit, who, to hide her ignorance or embarrassment, would grin fatuously or titter in a most disconcerting way. True to form, he treated her like an object. She was the vassal. Perhaps he did love her once, but if so it must have been in another incarnation. Nevertheless he felt at home with her. He knew how to cope with her faults and transgressions.

He was such a queer, queer fellow, Stanley. Such a mixture of rasping contradictions. But there was one thing he seldom did, queer gazabo that he was—he seldom asked questions. When he did, they were direct questions and they had to be answered directly. It was, of course, not tact but pride which made him act in this seemingly discreet way. He took it for granted that I would inform him of anything important which came to pass. He preferred to have me volunteer the information than to pump it out of me. Knowing him as I did, I regarded it as hopeless to explain to him our manner of life. Had I told him simply that I had taken to thieving he would have swallowed it unquestioningly. Had I told him I had become a counterfeiter he might have arched his eyebrows in quizzical approbation. But to tell him of the devious nature of our operations would have baffled and repelled him.

A rum bird, this Polski. The only trace of suavity he ever displayed was in narrating one of his quaint yarns. At table, if he asked for a piece of bread, it was like a slap in the face. He was deliberately rude and insulting. It made him feel good to see others squirm.

At the same time he had a shyness which was quixotic. If Mona were to seat herself opposite him and cross her legs he would avert his eyes. If she put her make-up on in his presence he would pretend not to be aware of it. Her beauty itself made him self-conscious. It also made him suspicious. A woman as beautiful and intelligent as Mona marrying a guy like me—there was something *louche* about it in his eyes. He knew of course where and how I had met her. Now and then he referred to it casually, but always tellingly. When she spoke of her childhood in Poland or Vienna he would watch me attentively, hoping, I suppose, that I would embellish the story, fill in the long missing details. There was a gap somewhere and it bothered him. Once he went so far as to remark that he doubted she was ever born in Poland. But that she was a Jewess, *that* he never suspected. She was American through and through, that was his private belief. But an unusual American, for a female, that is. He couldn't get over her diction, which was without the slightest trace of accent or locale. How did she ever learn to speak such a pure English? he would ask. How could I be sure of anything concerning her? 'I know you,' he would say, 'you're a Romantic . . . you prefer to have it a mystery.' Which was quite true. 'Me,' he said, 'I want to know what's what. I want things above board. No hide-and-seek games for me.' Yet it was he, Stanley, who was so enamoured of Herr Nagel, the hero of *Mysteries*. What discussions we had by the kitchen fire à propos this enigmatic figure of Hamsun's! He would have given his right arm, Stanley, to have created such a character. It was not only that Herr Nagel enveloped himself in a shroud of mystery, it was also his sense of humour, his pranks, his volte-faces which appealed to Stanley. But what he adored above all was the contradictory nature of the man. Herr Nagel's helplessness in the presence of the woman he loved, his maso-chism, his diabolism, his sentimentality, his extreme vulnerability —these qualities made him extraordinarily precious. 'I tell you, Henry, that Hamsun is a master,' Stanley would say. He had said the same of Conrad, of Balzac, of Anatole France, of de Maupassant, of Loti. He had said the same of Reymont when he finished *The Peasants*. (For quite different reasons, to be sure.) Of one thing I could be certain, he would never say it of me, even if the whole world were unanimous about it. A master of literature, from Stanley's viewpoint, had to be a type like the above-mentioned. He had first of all to be of the Old World; he had to be suave, he had to have finesse, subtlety, velleity. He had to have a style which was finished; he had to be adept with plot, character, situations; he had to command a broad knowledge of the world and of human affairs. In his opinion I would never, never be able to spin a good yarn. Even in Sherwood Anderson, whom he grudgingly admitted now and then to be an excellent story-teller, he found grave faults. His style was too fresh, too raw, too new for Stanley's taste. Yet he laughed until the tears came to his eyes when he read *The Triumph of the Egg*. He admitted it resentfully. He had laughed in spite of himself, as it were. And then he took on about Jerome K. Jerome, certainly a strange bird for a Polski to mention. In Stanley's opinion nothing funnier had ever been written than *Three Men in a Boat*. Even the Polish writers had no one equal to him. But then the Poles were seldom *funny*. 'If a Pole calls something funny,' said Stanley, 'it means that he finds it bizarre. He's too sombre, too tragic, to appreciate horseplay.' Speaking thus, the word droll would inevitably cross his lips. Droll was his favourite word, and it expressed a multitude of dissimilar things. To be droll implied a certain vein of excellence, of uniqueness, which Stanley prized exceedingly. If he said of an author—'He's a droll chap'—he meant thereby to pay him a weighty compliment. Gogol, for instance, was one of these droll chaps. On the other hand he could refer to Bernard Shaw as a droll chap too. Or Strindberg. Or even Maeterlinck.

A rum bird, Stanley. *Droll*, what!

As I say, these sessions often took place in the garden. If we had the money I would get a few bottles of beer for him. He liked only beer and vodka. Now and then we held conversation with a Syrian neighbour leaning out of a second storey window. They were friendly people and the women were ravishingly beautiful. Mona with her heavy dark tresses they had taken at first to be one of them. Our landlady, we soon learned, was violently prejudiced against the Syrians. For her they represented the scum of the earth—first, because they were dark-skinned, second, because they spoke a language which no one else understood. She made it clear to us in no uncertain terms that she was horrified by the attention we gave to them. She trusted we would have sense enough not to invite them to our quarters. After all, she put it tersely, she was running a 'respectable' rooming house.

I swallowed her remarks as best I could, always bearing in mind that we might one day need a stay-of-grace. I dismissed her as an eccentric old witch about whom the less said the better. I took the precaution to warn Mona never to leave our door unlocked when we were absent. One look at my manuscripts and we would be done for.

It was after we were here a few weeks that Mona informed me one day that she had run into Tony Maurer again. He and the Milwaukee millionaire were gadding about together. Apparently, Tony Maurer was sincerely desirous of helping Mona. He had confided that he was working on his friend to get him to write out a sizeable cheque—perhaps for a thousand dollars.

This was precisely the sort of break we had been praying for. With a sum like that we would be able to break out and see something of the world. Or we might join O'Mara. The latter was constantly sending us postcards from the sunny South telling us how smooth and easy things were down there. At any rate, we were through with little ole New York.

It was Mona who kept urging a change of scene. It disturbed her profoundly that I no longer made any effort to write. To be sure, I had half convinced her that it was all her fault, that so long as she continued to lead a double life I could do nothing. (Not that I distrusted her, I emphasized, but that she caused me too much worry.) As I say, she was only partially convinced. She knew that the trouble went deeper. In her simple, naive way she concluded that the only way to alter the situation was to alter the scene.

Then one day there came a telephone call from Tony Maurer, appraising her that everything was set for the kill. She was to meet the two of them at Times Square where a limousine would be waiting to take them up the Hudson. A good meal at an inn and the cheque would be forthcoming. (It would be for seven hundred and fifty, not a thousand.)

After she had gone I picked up a book. It was *Wisdom and Destiny*. I hadn't read a line of Maeterlinck for years: it was like getting back to a raw diet. Towards midnight, feeling somewhat restless and uneasy, I went for a stroll. Passing a department store I noticed a window crammed with camping and sporting outfits. That gave me the idea of *tramping* through the South. With knapsacks over our backs we could hitch-hike to the Virginia border and then foot it the rest of the way. I saw just the outfit I intended to don, including a magnificent pair of brogans. The idea so fascinated me that I suddenly grew hungry, hungry as a bear. I headed for Joe's restaurant at Borough Hall where I treated myself to a porterhouse steak smothered in onions. As I ate I dreamed. In a day or two we would be out of the filthy city, sleeping under the stars, fording streams, climbing mountains, sweating, panting, singing at the top of our lungs. I prolonged the reverie while putting away a huge piece of home-made apple pie (deep-dish fashion) together with a strong cup of coffee. I was about ready now to pick my teeth and saunter homeward. At the cash register I noticed the array of choice cigars. I selected a Romeo and Juliet and, with a feeling of peace and good-will toward the whole world, I bit off the tip of the cigar and spat it out.

It must have been two o'clock when I got home. I undressed and got into bed; I lay there with eyes wide open, expecting any minute to hear her footsteps. Towards dawn I dozed off.

It was eighty-thirty when she came tripping in. Not the least bit tired either. Couldn't think of going to bed. Instead, she began making breakfast—bacon and eggs, coffee, hot rolls which she had picked up on the way. Insisted that I remain in bed until the last minute.

'But where in hell have you been all this time?' I did my best to growl. I knew everything must have passed off well—she was too radiant for it to have been otherwise.

'Let's eat first,' she begged. 'It's a long story.'

'Did you get the cheque—that's all I want to know.'

She waved it before my eyes.

That afternoon we ordered a slew of things at the department store; they were to be delivered the next day, by which time we hoped to cash the cheque. The morrow came and still we hadn't cashed the cheque. The clothes, of course, went back to the department store. In despair we put the cheque through a bank, which meant a delay of several days at least.

Meanwhile a serious altercation had broken out between Mona and the blue-nosed harridan of a landlady. It seems that in the midst of a conversation with the beautiful Syrian woman next door the landlady had erupted into the garden and begun hurling names at the Syrian woman. Outraged, Mona had insulted the old bitch, whereupon the latter took to abusing her in fantastic terms, saying that she was a Syrian too, and a whore, and this and that. The fracas almost ended in a hair-pulling match.

The upshot of it all was that we were given a week's notice to get out. Since we intended to leave anyway we were not unhappy about it. There was one thought, however, which rankled in me: how to get even with the old bitch?

It was Stanley who showed me the way. Since we were clearing out for good, why not pay her back in regal style? 'Fine,' I said, 'but how?' In his mind it was simple. He would bring the kids along, as usual, on the last day; he would hand them the ketchup bottle, the mustard, the fly paper, the ink, the flour, everything with which to do the devil's work. 'Let them do whatever comes into their heads,' he said. 'How's that?' He added: 'Kids love to do whatever is destructive.'

Myself I thought it a marvellous idea. 'I'll give them a hand,' I said. 'When it comes to dirty work, I'm a bit of a vandal myself.'

The day after we planned this campaign of despoilation we received word from the bank that our cheque was no good. Frantic telephone calls to Tony Maurer—and to Milwaukee. Our millionaire had disappeared—as if the earth had swallowed him. For a change, *we* were the victims of a hoax. I had a good laugh at myself, despite my chagrin.

But what to do now?

We broached the news to Stanley. He took it philosophically. Why not move into his flat? He would take the mattress off his bed and put it on the floor in the parlour—for us. They never used the parlour. As for food, he guaranteed that we wouldn't starve.

'But where will you sleep? Or how, rather?' I asked.

'On the springs,' he said.

'But your wife?'

'She won't mind. We've often slept on the bare floor.'

Then he added: 'After all, it's only temporary. You can look for a job, and when you get one you can find a place of your own.'

'O.K.' I said, and clasped his hand.

'Get your things packed,' said Stanley. 'What have you got to take with you?'

'Two valises and a typewriter, that's all.'

'Get busy then. I'll put the kids to work.' And with this he moved the big horsehair sofa over against the door, so that no one could enter.

While Mona packed the valises I ransacked the cupboard. The kids had been looking forward to this event. They went to it with a vengeance. In ten minutes the place was a wreck. Everything that could be smeared was smeared with ketchup, vinegar, mustard, flour, broken eggs. On the chairs they pasted the fly paper. The garbage they strewed over the floor, grinding it in with their heels. Best of all was the ink work. This they splattered over the walls, the rugs and the mirrors. The toilet paper they made garlands of to festoon the bespattered furniture.

Stanley and I, for our part, stood on the table and decorated the ceiling with ketchup and mustard, with flour and cereals which we had made into a thick paste. The sheets and covers we ripped with knives and scissors. With the big bread knife we gouged out huge chunks of the horsehair sofa. Around the toilet-seat we spread some mouldy marmalade and honey. Everything which could be turned upside-down, dismantled, disconnected or torn apart we turned upside-down, dismantled, disconnected and ripped apart. Everything was done with quiet commotion. The last bit of destruction I left for the children to perform. It was the mutilation of the sacred Bible. First they doused it in the bath tub, then smeared it with filthy unguents, then tore out handfuls of pages and scattered them about the room. The woeful-looking remains of the Holy Book we then put in the bird cage which we suspended from the chandelier. The chandeliers themselves we bent and twisted into an unrecognizable shape. We hadn't time to wash the kids; we wiped them as best we could with the torn sheets. They were radiant with joy. What a job! Never again would they have a chance like this. . . . This last operation finished, we took counsel. Seating the kids on his knees, Stanley gravely instructed them what to do. They were to leave first, by the back exit. They were to walk quietly and leisurely to the front gate, quicken their steps as they moved down the street, then run as fast as they could and wait for us around the corner. As for us, if we encountered the old blue-nosed bitch, we would hand her the keys and bid her good-bye pleasantly. She would have a job to push the door open, assuming that she suspected anything amiss. By that time we would have joined the kids and hopped a taxi.

Everything went as planned. The old lady never made an appearance. I had one valise, Stanley the other, and Mona carried the typewriter. At the corner the children were waiting for us, merry as could be. We caught a taxi and drove to Stanley's home.

I thought his wife might be a bit put out when she learned what the children had done, but no, she thought it was a wonderful prank. She was delighted that they had had such a holiday. Her only complaint was that they had soiled their clothes. Lunch was waiting for us—cold meats, boloney, cheese, beer and crackers. We laughed our guts out rehearsing the morning's work.

'You see what the Poles are capable of,' said Stanley. 'When it comes to destruction we know no limits. The Poles are brutes at bottom; they're even worse than the Russians. When they kill they laugh, when they torture they get hysterical with glee. That's Polish humour for you.'

'And when they're sentimental,' I added, 'they give you their last shirt—or the mattress from their bed.'

Luckily it was Summertime, for the only covering we had was

a sheet and Stanley's winter overcoat. The place was clean, fortunately, even though poverty-stricken. No two dishes were alike; the knives, forks and spoons, all odd pieces, had been collected from junk heaps. There were three rooms, one after another, all of them dark—the typical railroad flat. There was no hot water, no bath-tub, not even a shower. We bathed in turn at the kitchen sink. Mona wanted to assist with the cooking but Sophie, his wife, wouldn't hear of it. All we had to do was to roll up our mattress each day and sweep the floor. Now and then we washed the dishes.

It wasn't bad at all, for a temporary flop. The neighbourhood was depressing, to be sure—we were living in the dumps, only a few doors from the elevated line. The worst thing about the situation was that Stanley slept in the day time. However, he slept only about five hours. He ate sparingly, I noticed. The one thing he couldn't do without was cigarettes. He rolled his own, incidentally; it was a habit which he had retained from the old days at Fort Oglethorpe.

The one thing we couldn't demand of Stanley was cash. His wife doled him out ten cents each day for carfare. When he left for work he took a couple of sandwiches with him wrapped in newspaper. From Tuesday on everything was bought on credit. A depressing routine, but Stanley had been following it for years. I don't think he ever expected things to be otherwise. So long as they ate every day, so long as the children were nourished and clothed. . . .

Every day Mona and I disappeared towards noon, went our respective ways, and returned in time for dinner. We gave the impression that we were busy scouting for jobs. Mona concentrated on raising little sums to tide us over; I floated about aimlessly, visiting the library, the art museums, or taking in a movie when I could afford it. Neither of us had the least intention of looking for work. We never even mentioned the subject to one another.

At first they were pleased to see Mona returning each day with something for the children. Mona made it a point to return with arms loaded. Besides the food we sorely needed she often brought rare delicacies which Stanley and his wife had never tasted. The children always got candy or pastry. They lay in wait for her each evening at the front door. It was quite jolly for a while. Plenty of cigarettes, wonderful cakes and pies, all kinds of Jewish and Russian bread, pickles, sardines, tuna fish, olives, mayonnaise, smoked oysters, smoked salmon, caviar, herrings, pineapples, strawberries, crab meat, charlotte russe, God knows what all. Mona pretended that they were gifts from friends. She didn't dare admit that she had squandered money on these luxuries. Sophie, of course, was dazzled. She had never seen such an array

217

of food as now graced the cupboard. It was obvious that she could support such a diet indefinitely. The children likewise.

Not Stanley however. He could think only in terms of privation. What would they do when we left? The children were being spoiled. His wife would expect miracles which it was beyond his power to perform. He began to resent our luxurious ways. One day he opened the cupboard, took down some tins and jars of the finest delicacies, and said he was going to exchange them for money. There was a gas bill to pay, long overdue. The next day he took me aside and informed me bluntly that that wife of mine was to cut out bringing candies and cakes for the children. He was getting to look more and more glum. Perhaps the restless days on the bare springs were wearing him down. Perhaps he surmised that we were making no effort to get work.

The situation was definitely Hamsunesque, but Stanley was in no mood to appreciate this quality. At table we scarcely spoke. The children acted as if they were cowed. Sophie spoke only when her Lord and Master approved. Now and then even the carfare was lacking. It was always Mona who handed out the dough. I expected to be asked point blank one day how she happened to always have ready cash on hand. Sophie, of course, never asked questions. Mona had her enchanted. Sophie followed her constantly with her eyes, observing every movement, every gesture. It was apparent that to her Mona was a sort of goddess.

I used to wonder, when I lay awake nights, how Sophie would react if she were permitted to follow Mona in her eccentric course for just one day. Let us suppose a day when Mona is keeping an appointment with the one-legged veteran from Weehawken. Rothermel, that was his name, would of course be drunk as usual. He would be waiting in the back of a beer parlour in one of those lugubrious side streets of Weehawken. He would already be drooling in his beer. As Mona enters he endeavours to rise from his seat and make a ceremonious bow, but his artificial leg hinders him. He flutters helplessly, like a big bird whose leg is caught in a trap. He splutters and curses, wiping the spittle from his vest with a dirty napkin.

'You're only two hours late this time,' he grumbles. '*How much?*' and he reaches inside his breast pocket for his fat wallet.

Mona of course—it is a scene they enact frequently—pretends to be insulted. 'Put that thing away! Do you think that's all I come for?'

He: 'I'm damned if I can think of any other reason. Certainly it's not on *my* account.'

That's how it begins. A duet which they have rehearsed a hundred times.

He: 'Well, what's the story this time? Even if I am a dope, I must say I admire your invention.'

She: 'Must I always give you a reason? When will you learn to put confidence in other human beings?'

He: 'A nice question, that. If you would stay for a half-hour sometime maybe I could answer it. When must you be going?' He looks at his watch. 'It's just a quarter to three.'

She: 'You know that I have to be back by six.'

He: 'Your mother's still an invalid, then?'

She: 'What do you suppose—that a miracle occurred?'

He: 'Thought maybe it was your father this time.'

She: 'Oh, stop it! You're drunk again.'

He: 'Fortunately for you. Otherwise I might forget to bring my wallet along. *How much?* Let's get that over with, then perhaps we can chat a bit. It's an education to talk with you.'

She: 'You'd better make it fifty today. . . .'

He: '*Fifty?* Listen, sister, I know I'm a fool, but I'm not a gold mine.'

She: 'Must we go through this all over again?'

Rothermel pulls out his wallet ruefully. He lays it on the table. 'What are you going to have?'

She: 'I told you.'

He: 'I mean what will you have to drink? You're not going to rush off without a drink, are you?'

She: 'Oh well . . . make it a champagne cocktail.'

He: 'You never drink beer, do you?' He toys with the wallet.

She: 'What are you fiddling with that for? Are you trying to humiliate me?'

He: 'That would be rather difficult, it seems to me.' A pause. 'You know, sitting here waiting for you, I was thinking of how I might give you a real thrill. You don't deserve it, but shit! If I had any sense I wouldn't be sitting here talking to you.' Pause. 'Do you want to know what I was thinking of? *How to make you happy.* You know, for a beautiful girl you're about the most unhappy creature I ever met. I'm not a bundle of optimism myself, and I'm not much to look at, and I'm getting more decrepit every day, but I can't say I'm thoroughly miserable. I still have one leg. I can hop around. I laugh now and then, even if it's at my own expense. *But*, do you know something—I've never once heard you laugh. That's terrible. In fact it's painful. I give you all you ask for but you never change. You're always set for a touch. It ain't right. You're doing yourself harm, that's what I mean. . . .'

She (cutting him short): 'Everything would be different if I married you, is that what you mean to say?'

He: 'Not exactly. Christ knows, it wouldn't be a bed of roses. But at least I could provide for you. I could put an end to this begging and borrowing.'

She: 'If you really wanted to free me you wouldn't put a price on it.'

219

He: 'It's just like you to put it that way. You never suppose for an instant. . . .'

She: 'That we could lead separate lives?'

The waiter arrives with the champagne cocktail.

He: 'Better fix another one—the lady is thirsty.'

She: 'Do we have to go through this farce every time we meet? Don't you think it's a bit boring?'

He: 'To me it isn't. I haven't any illusions left. But it's in a way of talking to you. I prefer this subject to hospitals and invalids.'

She: 'You don't believe my stories, is that it?'

He: 'I believe every word you tell—because I want to believe. I have to believe in something, if it's only you.'

She: '*Only me?*'

He: 'Come, you know what I mean.'

She: 'You mean that I treat you like a sucker.'

He: 'I couldn't express it more accurately myself. Thank you.'

She: 'What time is it now, please?'

Rothermel looks at his watch. He lies: 'It's three twenty exactly.' Then, with an air of consternation: 'You got to have another drink. I told him to fix one for you.'

She: 'You drink it, I won't have time.'

He (frantically): 'Hey, waiter, where's that cocktail I ordered an hour ago?' He forgets himself and attempts to rise from his seat. Stumbles and sinks back again, as if exhausted. 'Damn that leg! I'd be better off with a wooden stump. Damn the bloody, fucking war! Excuse me, I'm forgetting myself. . . .'

To humour him Mona takes a sip of the cocktail, then rises abruptly. 'I must be going,' she says. She starts walking towards the door.

'Wait a minute, wait a minute!' shouts Rothermel. 'I'll call a taxi for you.' He pockets his wallet and hobbles after her.

In the taxi he puts the wallet in her hand. 'Help yourself,' he says, 'You know I was only joking before.'

Mona coolly helps herself to a few bills and stuffs the wallet in his side pocket.

'When will I see you again?'

'When I need more money, no doubt.'

'Don't you ever need anything but money?'

Silence. They ride through the crazy streets of Weehawken which is in the New World, according to the atlas, but which might just as well be a wart on the planet Uranus. There are cities one never visits except in moments of desperation—or at the turn of the moon when the whole endocrine system goes haywire. There are cities which were planned aeons ago by men of the antediluvian world who had the consolation of knowing they would never inhabit them. Nothing is amiss in this anachronistic scheme of things except the fauna and flora of a lost geological age. Everything is familiar yet strange. At every corner one is disoriented. Every street spells *micmac*.

Rothermel, sunk in despair, is dreaming of the variegated life of the trenches. He remains a lawyer even though he has but one leg. He not only hates the Boches who took his leg away, he hates his own countrymen equally. Above all, he hates the town he was born in. He hates himself for drinking like a sot. He hates all mankind as well as birds, animals, trees and sunlight. All he has left of an empty past is money. He hates that too. He rises each day from a sodden sleep to pass into a world of quicksilver. He deals in crime as if it were a commodity, like barley, wheat, oats. Where once he gambolled, carolling like a lark, now he hobbles furtively, coughing, groaning, wheezing. On the morning of the fatal battle he was young, virile, jubilant. He had cleaned out a nest of Boches with his machine gun, wiped out two lieutenants of his own brigade, and was about to rifle the canteen. That same evening he was lying in his own blood and sobbing like a child.— The world of two-legged men had passed him by; he would never be able to rejoin them. In vain he howled like a beast. In vain he prayed. In vain he called for his mother. The war was over for him—he was one of its relics.

When he saw Weehawken again he wanted to crawl into his mother's bed and die. He asked to see the room where he played as a child. He looked at the garden from the window upstairs and in utter despair he spat into it. He shut the door on his old friends and took to the bottle. Ages pass during which he shuttles back and forth on the loom of memory. He has only one security —his wealth. It is like telling a blind man he may have a white cane.

And then one evening, seated alone at a table in a village dive, a woman approaches and hands him a *Mezzotint* to read. He invites her to sit down. He orders a meal for her. He listens to her stories. He forgets that he has an artificial limb, forgets that there ever was a war. He knows suddenly that he loves this woman. She does not need to love him, she needs only to be. If she will consent to see him occasionally, for just a few minutes, life will have meaning again.

Thus Rothermel dreams. He forgets all the heart-rending scenes which have sullied this beautiful picture. He would do anything for her, even now.

And now let us leave Rothermel for a while. Let him dream in his taxicab as the ferryboat gently cradles him on the bosom of the Hudson. We will meet him again, on the shores of Manhattan.

At Forty-Second Street Mona dives into the subway to emerge in a few minutes at Sheridan Square. Here her course becomes truly erratic. Sophie, if she were still on her heels, would indeed have difficulty following her. The Village is a network of laby-rinths modelled upon the corrugated reveries of the early Dutch settlers. One is constantly coming face-to-face with himself at the end of a tortuous street. There are alleys, lanes, cellars and garrets, squares, triangles, courts, everything anomalous, incongruous and bewildering: all that lacks are the bridges of Milwaukee. Certain doll's houses, squeeze between sombre tenements and morbid factories, have been dozing in a vacuum of time which could be described only in terms of decans. The dreamy, somnolent past exudes from the façades, from the curious names of the streets, from the miniature scale imparted by the Dutch. The present announces itself in the strident cries of the street urchins, in the muffled roar of traffic which shakes not only chandeliers but the very foundations of the underground. Dominating everything is the confusion of races, tongues, habits. The Americans who have muscled in are off-centre, whether they be bankers, politicians, magistrates, Bohemians, or genuine artists. Everything is cheap, tawdry, vulgar and phoney. Minnie Douchebag is on the same level as the prison warden round the corner. The fraternization, such as it is, takes place at the bottom of the melting pot. Everyone is trying to pretend that it is the most interesting locale in the city. It is the quarter full of characters; they collide like protons and electrons, always in a five-dimensional world whose fundament is chaos.

It in a world like this that Mona is at home and thoroughly herself. Every few paces she runs into someone she knows. These encounters resemble to a remarkable degree the collisions of ants in the throes of work. Conversation is conducted through antennae which are manipulated frenetically. Has some devastating upheaval just occurred which vitally concerns the entire anthill? The running up and down stairs, the salutations, the hand-shaking, the rubbing of noses, the phantom gesticulations, pourparlers, the gurgitations and regurgitations, the aerial transmissions, the dressing and undressing, the whispering, the warnings, the threats, the entreaties, the masquerades—all goes on in insect fashion and with a speed such as only insects seem capable of mustering. Even when snowbound the Village is in constant commotion and effervescence. Yet nothing of the slightest importance ever ensues. In the morning there are headaches, that is all.

Sometimes, however, in one of those houses which one notices only in dream, there lives a pale, timid creature, usually of dubious sex, who belongs to the world of du Maurier, Chekov or Alain Fournier. The name may be Alma, Frederika, Ursula, Malvina, a name consonant with the auburn tresses, the pre-Raphaelite figure, the Gaelic eyes. A creature who rarely stirs from the house, and then only in the wee hours of the morning.

Towards such types Mona is fatally drawn. A secret friendship veils all their intercourse in mystery. Those breathless errands which drive her through the runnelled streets may have for objective nothing more than the purchase of a dozen white goose eggs. No other eggs will do. *En passant* she may take it into her head to surprise her seraphic friend by buying her an old-fashioned cameo smothered in violets, or a rocking-chair from the hills of Dakota, or a snuff-box scented with sandalwood. The gifts arrive first and then a few bills fresh from the mint. She arrives breathlessly and departs breathlessly, as if between thunder claps. Even Rothermel would be powerless to suspect how quickly and for what ends his money goes. All we know, who greet her at the end of a feverish day, is that she had managed to buy a few groceries and can dispense a little cash. On the Brooklyn side we talk in terms of coppers, which in China is 'cash'. Like children we play with nickels, dimes and pennies. The dollar is an abstract conception employed only in high finance. . . .

Only once during our stay with the Poles did Stanley and I venture abroad together. It was to see a Western picture in which there were some extraordinary wild horses. Stanley, reminded of his days in the cavalry, became so excited that he decided not to go to work that evening. All through the meal he told yarns, with each yarn growing more tender, more sympathetic, more romantic. Suddenly he recalled the voluminous correspondence which we had exchanged when we were in our teens.

It all began the day after I saw him coming down 'the street of early sorrows', seated atop the hearse beside the driver. (After his uncle's death Stanley's aunt had married an undertaker, a Pole again. Stanley always had to accompany him on the burial expeditions.)

I was in the middle of the street, playing cat, when the funeral procession came along. I was certain it was Stanley who had waved to me, yet I could not believe my eyes. Had it not been a funeral procession I would have trotted alongside the vehicle and exchanged greetings. As it was, I stood rooted to the spot, watching the cortege slowly disappear round the corner.

It was the first time I had seen Stanley in six years. It made an impression on me. The following day I sat down and wrote him a letter—to the old address.

Stanley now brought out that first letter—and all the others which had followed. I was ashamed to tell him that I had long since lost his. But I could still remember the flavour of them, all written on long sheets of yellow paper, in pencil, with a flourishing hand. The hand of an autocrat. I recalled the perennial salutation he employed: 'My charming fellow !' This to a boy in short pants! They were letters, to speak of style, such as Theophile Gautier might have written to an unknown sycophant. Doped with literary borrowings. But they put me in a fever, always.

What my own letters were like I had never once thought of. They belonged to a distant past, a forgotten past. Now I held them in my hand, and my hand trembled as I read. So this was me in my teens? What a pity no one had made a movie of us! Droll figures we were. Little jackanapes, bantams, cock-o'-the-walk. Discussing such ponderous things as death and eternity, reincarnation, metampsychosis, libertinism, suicide. Pretending that the books we read were nothing to the ones we would write ourselves one day. Talking of life as if we had experienced it to the core.

But even in these pretentious exercises of youth I detected to my amazement the seeds of an imaginative faculty which was to ripen with time. Even in these fly-blown missives there were those abrupt breaks and rushes which indicate the presence of hidden fires, of unsuspected conflicts. I was moved to observe that even at this period I could lose myself, I who was hardly aware that I had a self. Stanley, I recalled, never lost himself. He had a style and in it he was fixed, as if constricted by a corset. I remember that at that period I thought of him as being so much more mature, so much more sophisticated. He would be the brilliant writer; I would be the plodding ink-slinger. As a Pole he had an illustrious heritage; I was merely an American, with an ancestry which was vague and dubious. Stanley wrote as if he had stepped off the boat only the day before. I wrote as if I had just learned to use the language, my real language being the language of the street, which was no language at all. Back of Stanley I always visualized a line of warriors, diplomats, poets, musicians. Myself, I had no ancestry whatever. I had to invent one.

Curious, but any feelings of lineage or of ephemeral connections with the past which might arise in me were usually evoked by one of three curiously disparate phenomena: one, narrow, olden streets with miniature houses; two, certain unreal types of human beings, generally dreamers or fanatics; three, photographs of Tibet, of the Tibetan landscape particularly. I could be disoriented in a jiffy, and was then marvellously at home, one with the world and with myself. Only in such rare moments did I know or pretend to understand myself. My connections were, so to speak, with man and not with men. Only when I was shunted back to the grand trunk line did I become aware of my real rhythm, my real being. Individuality expressed itself for me as a life with roots. Efflorescence meant culture—in short, the world of cyclical development. In my eyes the great figures were always identified with the trunk of the tree, not with the boughs and leaves. And the great figures were capable of losing their identity easily: they were all variations of the one man, Adam Cadmus, or whatever he be called. My lineage stemmed from him, not from my ancestors. When I became aware I was super-conscious; I could make the leap back at one bound.

Stanley, like all chauvinists, traced his arboreal descent only to the beginnings of the Polish nation, that's to say, to the Pripet marshes. There he lay bogged, like a weasel. His antennae reached only to the frontiers which were limitrophe to Poland. He never became an American, in the true sense. For him America was merely a condition or state of trance which permitted him to transmit his Polish genes to his heredity. Any differentiations from the norm, that is, from the Polish type, were to be attributed to the rigours of adjustment and adaptation. Whatever was American in him was merely an alloy which would be dissolved in the generation that was to spring from his loins.

Preoccupations of this sort Stanley never divulged overtly, but they were there and they manifested themselves in the form of insinuations. The emphasis he gave to a word or phrase always provided the clue of his real feelings. He was thoroughly anti-pathetic to the new world in which he found himself. He made only enough effort to keep alive. He went through the motions, as we say, nothing more. Though his experience of life was purely negative it was none the less potent. It was a matter of charging the battery: his children would make the necessary connections with life. Through them the racial energy of the Poles, their dreams, their longings, their aspirations, would be revived. Stanley was content to inhabit an in-between world.

All this admitted, it was nevertheless a luxury for me to bathe in the effluvium of the Polish spirit. Polonesia, I called it. An inland sea, like the Caspian, surrounded by the steppes. Over the troubled, stagnant waters, over treacherous shoals and invisible sources, flew huge migratory birds, heralds of past and future—of a Polish past and future. All that surrounded this sea was inimical and poisonous. From the language alone came the much needed sustenance.

What are the riches of English, I used to say to myself, com-pared to the melodious verdure of this Babel? When a Pole employs his native tongue he speaks not only to his friend but to his compatriots everywhere in the world. To the ear of a foreigner like myself, who was privileged to assist at these sacred per-formances, the speeches of my Polish friends seemed like interminable monologues addressed to the innumerable ghosts of the Diaspora within and without. Every Pole regards himself as the secret custodian of the fabulous repositories of the race; with his death some secret part of the accumulated intangibles, unfathomable to aliens, dies with him. But in the language nothing is lost: so long as one Pole is left to articulate, Poland will live.

When he spoke Polish he was another man, Stanley. Even when he spoke to one as insignificant as his wife Sophie. He might have been talking of milk and crackers, but to my ears it sounded as if we were back in the Age of Chivalry. Nothing is better suited to describe the modulations, dissonances and distillations of this language than the word alchemy. Like a strong dissolvent, the Polish language converts the image, concept, symbol or metaphor into a mysterious transparent liquid of camphorous odour which, by its mellifluous resonances, suggests the perpetual alternation and interchange of idea and impulse. Issuing like a hot geyser from the crater of the human mouth, Polish music—for it is hardly a language—consumes everything with which it comes into contact, intoxicating the brain with the pungent, acrid fumes of its metallic source. A man employing this medium is no longer a mere man—he has appropriated the powers of a sorcerer. The Book of Demonology could only have been written in this language. To say that this is a quality of the Slavs explains nothing. To be a Slav does not mean to be a Pole. The Pole is unique and untouchable; he is the prime mover, the original impetus personified, and his realm is the dread realm of doom. For him the sun was extinguished long ago. For him all horizons are limited and circumscribed. He is the desperado of the race, self-accursed and self-acquitted. *Make the world over?* He would rather drag it down to the bottomless pit.

Reflections of this order always rose to the surface when I would leave the house to stretch my legs. A short distance from Stanley's home lay a world akin in many respects to the one I had known as a child. Through it ran a canal black as ink whose stagnant waters stank like ten thousand dead horses. But all about the canal were winding lanes, eddying streets, still paved with cobblestones, the worn sidewalks flanked by diminutive shanties cluttered with shutters dislocated from their hinges, creating the impression, from a distance, of being enormous Hebrew letters. Furniture, bric-à-brac, utensils, implements and materials of all kinds littered the streets. *The fringe of the societal world.*

Each time I approached the confines of this Lilliputian world I changed back to a boy of ten. My senses became more acute, my memory more alive, my hunger more sharp. I could hold conversation with the self which I once was and with the self I had become. Who *I* was that walked and sniffed and explored, I knew not. An interlocutory, I, doubtless. An I suborned by a superior court of justice. . . . In this supraliminal arena Stanley always figured tenderly. He was the invisible comrade to whom I imparted those larval thoughts which elude speech. Immigrant, orphan, derelict—of these three ingredients he was composed. We understood one another because we were complete opposites. What he envied I gave him regally; what I craved he fed me from his carrion beak. We swam like Siamese fish on the glaucous surface of the lake of childhood. We knew not our Protector. We rejoiced in our imagined freedom.

What intrigued me as a child, what intrigues me to this day, is the glory and the wonder of eclosion. There are balmy days in childhood when, perhaps because of the great retardation of time, one steps outdoors into a world which is dozing. It is not the world of humans, nor is it the world of nature which is drowsing—it is the inanimate world of stones, minerals, objects. The inanimate world is in bud. . . . With the slow-motion eyes of childhood one watches breathlessly as this latent realm of life slowly reveals its pulse-beat. One becomes aware of the existence of those invisible rays which emanate perpetually from the most remote parts of the cosmos and which radiate from the microcosm as well as from the macrocosm. 'As above, so below.' In the twinkle of an eye one is divorced from the illusory world of material reality; with every step one places himself anew at the *carrefour* of these concentric radiations which are the true substance of an all-encompassing and all-pervading reality. Death has no meaning. All is change, vibration, creation and re-creation. The song of the world, registered in every particle of that specious substance called matter, issues forth in an ineffable harmony which filters through the angelic being lying dormant in the shell of the physical creature called man. Once the angel assumes dominion, the physical being flowers. Throughout all realms a quiet, persistent blossoming takes place.

Why is it that angels, whom we foolishly associate with the vast interstellar spaces, love everything which is *mignon?*

As soon as I reach the banks of the canal, where my world in miniature lies waiting, the angel takes over. I no longer scrutinize the world—the world is inside me. I see it as clearly with eyes closed as with eyes wide open. Enchantment, not sorcery. Surrender, and the bliss which accompanies surrender. What was dilapidation, decay, sordidness, is transmuted. The microscopic eye of the angel sees the infinite parts which compose the divine whole; the telescopic eye of the angel see nothing but totality, which is perfect. In the wake of the angel there are only universes to behold—size means nothing.

When man, with his pitiful sense of relativity, looks through the telescope and marvels at the immensity of creation, he means to confess that he has succeeded in reducing the limitless to the limited. He acquires, as it were, an optic lease on the boundless grandeur of a creation which is unfathomable to him. What matter if he succeed in putting a thousand universes within the focus of his microscopic telescope? The process of enlargement merely enhances the sense of the miniature. But man feels more at home in his little universe, or pretends he does, when he has uncovered what lies beyond its bounds. The thought that his universe may be no bigger than a tiny blood corpuscle entrances him, lulls his desperate anguish. But the use of the artificial eye, no matter to what monstrous proportions it be magnified, never brings him joys. The greater his physical vision, the more awed he becomes. He understands, though he refuses to believe, that with this eye he will never penetrate, still less partake of, the mystery of creation. To re-enter the mysterious world from which he sprang he realizes, in a vague, dim way, that other eyes are needed.

It is with the angelic eye that man beholds the world of his true substance.

These miniature realms, where all is sunken, muted and transformed, emerge often as not in books. A page of Hamsun frequently yield the same mysterious harmonies of enchantment as a walk by the canal. For a brief moment one experiences the same sort of vertigo as when the motorman deserts his post with the trolley in full flight. After that it is pure *volupte*. Surrender again. Surrender to the spell which has rendered the author superfluous. Immediately one's rhythm is retarded. One lingers before the verbal structures which palpitate like living houses. One knows that someone never encountered before, and never to be encountered again, will emerge and take possession of one. It may be a personage as innocuous as Sophie. It may be a question of large white goose eggs which will dominate the whole passage. No governing the cosmic fluid in which the events and situations are now bathed. The dialogue may become pure nonsense, astral in its implications. The author has made it clear that he is absent. The reader is face to face with an angelic sport. He will live this scene, this protracted moment, over and over again, and with a sharpened sense of reality verging on the hallucinatory. Only a little street—perhaps not a block long. Diminutive gardens tended by trolls. Perpetual sunshine. And remembered music, toned down to blend with the hum of insects and the rustle of leaves. Joy, joy, joy. The intimate presence of flowers, of birds, of stones which have preserved the record of similar magical days.

I think of Hamsun because it was with Stanley that I shared so often these extraordinary experiences. Our grotesque life in the street, as boys, had prepared us for these mysterious encounters. In some unknown way we had undergone the proper initiation. We were, without knowing it, members of that traditional underground which vomits forth at suitable intervals those writers who will later be called Romantics, mystics, visionaries or diabolists. It was for such as us—then mere embryonic beings—that certain 'outlandish' passages were written. It is we who keep alive these books which are constantly threatening to fall back into oblivion. We lie in wait, like beasts of prey, for moments of reality which will not only match but confirm and corroborate these literary extravaganzas. We grow like corkscrews, we become lop-sided, we squint and stammer in a vain endeavour to fit our world into the existent one. In us the angel sleeps lightly, ready at the slightest tremor to assume command. Only solitary vigils restore us. Only when we are cruelly separated do we really communicate with each other.

Often it is in dreams that we communicate. . . . I am on a familiar street searching for a particular house. The moment I set foot in this street my heart beats wildly. Though I have never seen the street it is more familiar to me, more intimate, more significant, than any street I can have known. It is the street by which I return to the past. Every house, every porch, every gate, every lawn, every stone, stick, twig or leaf speaks eloquently. The sense of recognition, compounded of myriad layers of memory, is so powerful that I am almost dissolved.

The street has no beginning nor end: it is a detached segment swimming in a fuzzy aura and complete in itself. A vibrant portion of the infinite whole. Though there is never any activity in this street it is not empty or deserted. Indeed, it is the most alive street I can think of. It is alive with memories, like an arcane grove which pullulates with its swarms of invisible hosts. I can't say that I *walk* down this street, nor can I say either that I *glide* through it. The street invests me. I am devoured by it. Perhaps only in the insect world are there sensations to match this harrowing form of bliss. To eat is wonderful, but to be eaten is a treat beyond description. Perhaps it is another, more extravagant, kind of union with the external world. An inverted sort of communion.

The end of this ritual is always the same. Suddenly I am aware that Stanley is waiting for me. He stands not at the end of the street, for there is no end . . . he stands at that fuzzy edge where light and substance fuse. His summons is always curt and brusque: 'Come on, let's go!' Immediately I adapt my pace to his. *Forward march!* The beloved street wheels softly around, like a turn-table operated by an unseen switchman, and as we reach the corner it joins neatly and inexorably with the intersecting streets which form the pattern of our childhood precincts. From here on it is an exploration of the past, but a different past from that of the memorial street. This past is an active one, cluttered with souvenirs, but souvenirs only skin deep. The other past, so profound, so fluid, so sparkling, made no separation between itself, present and future. It was timeless, and if I speak of it as a past it is only to suggest a return which is not really a return but a restoration. The fish swimming back to the source of its own being.

When the inaudible music begins, one knows for a certainty that he is alive.

Stanley's part in the second half of the dream is to rekindle the flame. I will take leave of him when he has set all the mnemonic filaments a-quiver. This function, which he performs with instinctive adroitness, might be likened to the quivering oscillations of a compass needle. He holds me to the path, a tortuous, zigzag path, but saturated with reminiscences. We buzz from flower to flower, like bees. When we have extracted our fill of nectar we return to the honeycomb. At the entrance I take leave of him, plunging into the very hub of transformation. My ears resound with the oceanic hum. All memory is stifled. I am deep in the labyrinthian shell, as secure and alive as a particle of energy adrift in the stellar sea of light. This is the deep sleep which restores the soul. When I awaken I am new-born. The day stretches before me like a velvet meadow. I have no recollection of anything. I am a freshly-minted coin ready to fall into the palm of the first-comer.

It is on such a day that I am apt to make one of those haphazard encounters which will alter the course of my life. The stranger coming towards me greets me like an old friend. We have merely to exchange a few words and the intimate stenographic language of ancient brothers replaces the current jargon. Communication is cryptic and seraphic, accomplished with the ease and rapidity of born deaf-mutes. For me it has only one purport—to bring about a re-orientation. Altering the course of my life, as I put it before, means simply—*correcting my sidereal position*. The stranger, fresh from the other world, tips me off. Given my true bearings, I cut a fresh swathe through the chartered realms of destiny. Just as the dream street swung softly into position, so I now wheel into vital alignment. The panorama against which I move is awesome and majestic. A landscape truly Tibetan beckons me onward. I know not whether it is a creation of the inner eye or some cataclysmic disturbance of the outer reality attuning itself to the profound re-orientation I have just made. I know only that I am more solitary than ever. Everything that occurs now will have the quality of shock and discovery. I am not alone. *I am in the midst of other solitaries.* And each and every one of us speaks his own unique language! It is like the coming together of distant gods, each one wrapped in the aura of his own incomprehensible world. It is the first day of the week in the new cycle of consciousness. A cycle, need I say, which may last a week or a lifetime. *En avant, je me dis. Allons-y! Nous sommes là.*

8

IT WAS MAXIE SCHNADIG who had introduced me, some years ago, to Karen Lundgren. Whatever brought these two together I can't possibly imagine. They had nothing whatever in common, nothing.

Karen Lundgren was a Swede who had been educated at Oxford, where he had made something of a stir due to his athletic prowess and his rare scholarship. He was a giant with curly blond hair, soft-spoken and excessively polite. He possessed the combined instincts of the ant, the bee and the beaver. Thorough, systematic, tenacious as a bull-dog, whatever he engaged in he pursued to the limit. He played just as hard as he worked. Work, however, was his passion. He could work standing up, sitting down, or lying in bed. And, like all hard workers, at bottom he was lazy as sin. Whenever he set out to do something he had first to devise ways and means of doing it with the least effort. Needless to say, these short cuts of his entailed much time and labour. But it made him feel good to sweat his balls off devising short cuts. Efficiency, moreover, was his middle name. He was nothing but a walking, talking, labour-saving device.

No matter how simple a project might be, Karen could make it complicated. I had had a good dose of his eccentricity while serving as his apprentice in a bureau of anthropological research some years previously. He had initiated me into the absurd complexities of a decimal system for filing which made our Dewey system seem like child's play. With Karen's system we were able to index anything under the sun, from a pair of white wool socks to haemorrhoids.

As I say, it was some years since I last saw Karen. I had always regarded him as a freak, having respect neither for his vaunted intelligence nor for his athletic prowess. Dull and laborious, those were his chief characteristics. Now and then, to be sure, he indulged in a hearty laugh. He laughed too heartily, I might say, and always at the wrong time or for the wrong reason. This ability to laugh he cultivated, just as he had once cultivated his muscles. He had a mania to be all things to all men. He had the mania, but no flair.

I give this thumb-nail sketch because it happens that once again I'm working with him, working *for* him. Mona too. We're all living together on the beach at Far Rockaway, in a shack which he has erected himself. To be exact, the house isn't quite finished. Hence our presence in it. We work without compensation, content to room and board with Karen and his wife. There's much yet to be done. Too much. Work begins from the moment I open my eyes until I drop from fatigue.

To go back a pace. . . . Running into Karen on the street was something of a God-send for us. We were literally without a cent when he happened along. Stanley, you see, had told us one evening, just as he was setting forth to work, that he was fed up with us. We were to pack our things and get out immediately. He would help us pack and see us to the subway. No words. Of course I had been expecting something of the sort to happen any day. I wasn't the least bit angry with him. On the contrary, I was rather amused.

At the subway entrance he handed over the valises, put a dime in my hand for car fare, and without shaking hands turned abruptly and stalked off. Not even a good-bye. We of course got into the subway, not knowing what else to do, and began riding. We rode back and forth two or three times trying to decide what the next step would be. Finally we got out at Sheridan Square. We had hardly walked a few steps when, to my astonishment, I saw Karen Lundgren approaching. He seemed unusually pleased to have found me again. What was I doing? Had we had dinner yet? And so on.

We accompanied him to his town flat, as he called it, and while his wife prepared the meal we unburdened ourselves. He was even more delighted to hear of our circumstances. 'I've got just the thing for you, Henry,' he said, with his insensitive cheerfulness. And he began at once to explain the nature of his work, which sounded like higher mathematics to me, meanwhile plying us with cocktails and caviar sandwiches. He had taken it for granted, when he began his discourse, that I would give assent to his project. To make things more interesting I pretended that I would have to think it over, that I had other things in mind. That of course only stimulated him more.

'Stay with us overnight,' he begged, 'and let me know what you think in the morning.'

He had explained, to be sure, that in addition to acting as his secretary and amanuensis, I might have to give him a hand with the house-building. I had warned him frankly that I wasn't much good with my hands, but he had waved this aside as unimportant. It would be fun, after working with one's brain, to devote a few more hours to more menial tasks. Recreation, he called it.

And then there was the beach: we would be able to swim, toss the ball around, perhaps even do a bit of canoeing. In passing he made mention of his library, his collection of records, his chess set, as if to say that we would have all the luxuries of a firstclass club.

In the morning I said yes, naturally. Mona was enthusiastic. She was not only willing, but eager, to help Karen's wife do the dirty work. 'O.K.,' I said, 'no harm in trying it.'

We went by train to Far Rockaway. All during the ride Karen talked incessantly about his work. I gathered that he was engaged in writing a book about statistics. According to him, it was a unique contribution to the subject. The data he had amassed was enormous, so enormous in fact that I was terrified before I had even moved a finger. In his customary way he had equipped himself with all manner of devices, machines which he assured me I would catch on to in no time. One of them was the dictaphone. He had found it more convenient, he explained, to dictate to the machine, which was impersonal, than to a secretary. There would be times, of course, when he might feel impelled to dictate direct, in which case I could take it down on the typewriter. 'You needn't worry about the spelling,' he added. My spirits dropped, I must say, when I learned of the dictaphone. However, I said nothing, just smiled and let him roll on from one thing to another.

What he had omitted to tell us about was the mosquitoes.

There was a little storeroom, just big enough to accommodate a creaky bed, which he indicated as our sleeping quarters. The moment I saw the netting over the bed I knew what we were in for. It began at once, the first night. Neither of us slept a wink. Karen tried to laugh it off by urging us to loaf for a day or two until we got adjusted. Fine, I thought. Mighty decent of him, I thought. An Oxford gentleman, what! But we didn't sleep the second night either, even though protected by the netting, even though we had greased ourselves all over, like Channel swimmers. The third night we burned Chinese punk and incense. Towards dawn, utterly worn out, our nerves frazzled, we dozed off. As soon as the sun came up we plunged into the surf.

It was after we had breakfast that morning that Karen intimated we ought to begin work in earnest. His wife took Mona aside to explain *her* duties. It took Karen almost the whole morning to explain the mechanism of the various machines he found invaluable for his work. There was a veritable mountain of records piled up which I was to transcribe on the typewriter. As for the charts and diagrams, the rulers, compasses and triangles, the slide rules, the filing system, and the thousand and one details which I was to familiarize myself with, that could wait a few days. I was to make a dent in the heap of records and then, if there were still enough light, I was to assist him on the roof.

I'll never forget that first day with the bloody dictaphone. I thought I would go mad. It was like operating a sewing machine, a switchboard and a victrola all at once. I had to use simultaneously hands, feet, ears and eyes. If I had been just a bit more versatile I could have swept out the room at the same time. Of course the first ten pages made absolutely nonsense. I not only wrote the wrong things, I missed whole sentences and began others in the middle or near the end. I wish I had preserved a copy of that first day's work—it would have been something to put beside the cold-blooded nonsense of Gertrude Stein. Even if I had transcribed correctly, the words would have made little sense to me. The whole terminology, not to speak of his plodding, wooden style, was foreign to me. I might just as well have written down telephone numbers.

Karen, like a man who is accustomed to training animals, a man of infinite patience and perseverance, pretended that I hadn't done bad at all. He even tried to joke a bit, reading over some of the screwy sentences. 'It will take a little time,' he said, 'but you'll get on to it.' And then, to add a little sauce: 'I'm really ashamed of myself for asking you to do this kind of work, Henry. You don't know how much I appreciate your assistance. I don't know what I would have done if you hadn't come along.' He would have talked much the same way if he were giving me lessons in ju-jutsu, of which he was supposedly a master. I could well visualize him picking me up, after spinning me twenty feet through the air, and saying solicitously: 'Sorry, old man, but you'll get the hang of it after a few days. Just couldn't help it, you know. Are you much hurt?'

What I wanted more than anything was a good drink. But Karen rarely drank. When he wanted relaxation he employed his energies at a different kind of work. To work was his passion. He worked while he slept. I mean it seriously. On falling off he would set himself a problem which his unconscious was to solve during the night.

The best I could wheedle out of him was a coke. Even this I couldn't enjoy in peace, for while I leisurely sipped it he was busy explaining to me the next day's problems. What bothered me more than anything was his way of explaining things. He was one of those idiots who believe that diagrams make things easier to comprehend. For me, anything in the way of a chart or a diagram means hopeless confusion. I have to stand on my head to read the simplest plans. I tried to tell him this but he insisted that I had been miseducated, that if I would just be patient I would soon learn to read charts and diagrams with ease —and enjoyment. 'It's like mathematics,' he told me.

'But I detest mathematics,' I protested.

'One shouldn't say a thing like that, Henry. How can one detest something useful? Mathematics is only another instrument

234

to serve us.' And here he expatiated *ad nauseam* on the wonders and the benefits of a science in which I had not the slightest interest. But I was always a good listener. And I had discovered already, in the space of just a few days, that one way of reducing the working time was to involve him in just such lengthy discussions. The fact that I listened so good-naturedly made him feel that he was really seducing me. Now and then I would throw in a question, in order to put off for a few more minutes the inevitable return to the grindstone. Of course, nothing he told me about mathematics made the least impression on me. It went in one ear and out the other.

'You see,' he would say, with all the seriousness of the fatuous ones, 'it's not nearly as complicated as you imagined. I'll make a mathematician of you in no time.'

Meanwhile Mona was getting her education in the kitchen. All day long I heard the dishes rattling. I wondered what in hell they were up to in there. It sounded like a spring cleaning. When we got to bed I learned that Lotta, Karen's wife, had allowed the dirty dishes to accumulate for a week. She didn't like housework, apparently. She was an artist. Karen never complained. He wanted her to be an artist—that is, after she had done the chores and assisted him in every possible way. He himself never set foot in the kitchen. He never noticed the condition of the plates or the cutlery, no more than he noticed what sort of food was being served him. He ate without relish, to stoke the furnace, and when he was through he pushed the dishes aside and began figuring on the tablecloth, or if there were no tablecloth, on the bare boards. He did everything leisurely, and with painful deliberation, which in itself was enough to drive me frantic.

Wherever he worked there was dirt, disorder and a clutter of non-essentials. If he reached for something he had first to remove a dozen obstructions. If the knife he grabbed were dirty he would slowly and deliberately wipe it clean with the tablecloth, or with his handkerchief. Always without fuss or emotion. Always bearing down, pressing onward, like a glacier in its relentless advance. Sometimes there were three cigarettes burnin at once at his elbow. He never stopped smoking, not even in bed. The butts piled up like sheep droppings. His wife was also an inveterate smoker, a chain smoker.

Cigarettes were one thing we had a plentiful supply of. *Food*, that was another matter. Food was doled out scantily and in the most unappetizing fashion. Mona, of course, had offered to relieve Lotta of the burden of cooking, but Lotta had refused to hear of it. We soon discovered why. She was stingy. She feared that Mona might prepare succulent, bounteous repasts. She was damned right about that! To take over the kitchen and stage a feast was the one thought uppermost in our minds. We kept praying that they would go to town for a few days and let us take it over. Then at last we would enjoy a good meal.

'What I would like,' Mona would say, 'is a good roast of beef.'

'Give me chicken—or a fine roast duck.'

'I'd like to have sweet potatoes for a change.'

'Suits me, honey, only make some rich gravy to go with them.'

Like Badminton it was. We shuffled the phantom food back and forth like two starved peacocks. If only they would breeze! God, but we were sick of looking at sardine tins, cans of sliced pineapple, bags of potato chips. The two of them nibbled away like mice the whole damned day. Never a hint of wine, never a drop of whiskey. Nothing but coke and sarsparilla.

I can't say that Karen was stingy. No, he was insensitive, unobservant. When I informed him one day that we were not getting enough to eat he professed to be appalled. 'What would you like?' he asked. And at once he got up from his work, borrowed a car from a neighbour, and whisked us off to town where we went from one store to another ordering provisions. It was typical of him to react in this way. Always to extremes. By going to extremes he intended, quite unconsciously, I believe, to make you slightly disgusted with yourself. 'Food? Is that all you want?' he seemed to say. 'That's easy, we'll buy heaps of it, enough to choke a horse.' There was a further implication in his exaggerated willingness to please you. 'Food? Why that's a mere trifle. Of course we can get you food. I thought you had deeper worries.'

His wife, of course, was dismayed when she saw the load of provisions we brought back with us. I had asked Karen not to say anything to his wife about our hunger. He pretended, therefore, that he was laying in a supply against a rainy day. 'The larder was getting low,' he explained. But when he added that Mona would like to fix a meal for us at dinner time her face dropped. For an instant there passed over her countenance that horrified look of the miser whose hoard is menaced. Once again Karen stepped into the breach. 'I thought, darling, that you would enjoy having some one else cook the meal for a change. Mona is an excellent cook, it appears. We're going to have filet mignon this evening—how does that sound to you?' Lotta, of course, had to feign delight.

We made the dinner an event. In addition to fried onions and mashed potatoes we had succotash, beets and brussel sprouts, with celery, stuffed olives and radishes on the side. We washed this down with red and white wine, the best obtainable. There were three kinds of cheese, followed by strawberries and rich cream. For a change we had some excellent coffee, which I prepared myself. Good, strong coffee with a bit of chicory in it. All that lacked was a good liquer and Havana cigars.

Karen enjoyed the meal immensely. He acted like a different man. He joked, told stories, laughed until his sides ached, and never once referred to his work. Toward the end of the meal he even tried to sing.

'Not bad, eh?' I said.

'Henry, we ought to do this oftener,' he responded. He looked to Lotta for approval. She gave a thin, bleak smile which caused her face to crack. It was obvious that she was desperately trying to reckon the cost of the spread.

Suddenly Karen pushed his chair back and rose from the table. I thought he was going to bring his charts and diagrams to the table. Instead he went into the next room and returned in a jiffy with a book. He waved it before my eyes.

'Ever read this, Henry?' he demanded.

I looked at the title. 'No,' I said, 'Never heard of it.'

Karen passed the book to his wife and begged her to read us a morsel. I expected something dismal, and instinctively poured out some more wine.

Lotta solemnly turned the pages, looking for one of her favourite passages.

'Read anywhere,' said Karen. 'It's good through and through.'

Lotta stopped fumbling with the pages and looked up. Her expression changed suddenly. For the first time I saw her countenance illuminated. Even her voice had altered. She had become a *diseuse*.

'It's chapter three,' she began, 'from *The Crock of Gold*, by James Stephens.'

'And a darling of a book it is!' Karen broke in gleefully. With this he pushed his chair back a bit and put his big feet on the arm of the easy chair near by. 'Now you're going to hear something, you two.'

Lotta began: 'It's a dialogue between the Philosopher and a farmer called Meehawl MacMurrachu. The two have just greeted one another.' She begins reading.

' "Where is the other one?" said he (the farmer).

' "Ah!" said the Philosopher.

' "He might be outside, maybe?"

' "He might indeed," said the Philosopher gravely.

' "Well, it doesn't matter," said the visitor, "for you have enough knowledge by yourself to stock a shop. The reason I came here today was to ask your honoured advice about my wife's washing board. She only had it a couple of years, and the last time she used it was when she washed out my Sunday shirt and her black shirt with the red things on it—you know the one?"

' "I do not," said the Philosopher.

' "Well, anyhow, the washboard is gone, and my wife says it was either taken by the fairies or by Bessie Hannigan—you know Bessie Hannigan? She has whiskers like a goat and a lame leg!"

' "I do not," said the Philosopher.

' "No matter," said Meehawl MacMurrachu. "She didn't take

it, because my wife got her out yesterday and kept her talking for two hours while I went through everything in her bit of a house—the washboard wasn't there."

' "It wouldn't be," said the Philosopher.

' "Maybe your honour could tell a body where it is then?"

' "Maybe I could," said the Philosopher; "are you listening?"

' "I am," said Meehawl MacMurrachu.

'The Philosopher drew his chair closer to the visitor until their knees were jammed together. He laid both his hands on Meehawl MacMurrachu's knees. . . .

' "Washing is an extraordinary custom," said he. "We are washed both on coming into the world and on going out of it, and we take no pleasure from the first washing nor any profit from the last."

' "True for you, sir," said Meehawl MacMurrachu.

' "Many people consider that scourings supplementary to these are only due to habit. Now, habit is continuity of action, it is a most detestable thing and is very difficult to get away from. A proverb will run where a writ will not, and the follies of our forefathers are of greater importance to us than is the well-being of our posterity." '

At this point Karen interrupted his wife to ask if we liked the passage.

'I do indeed,' I said. 'Let her continue!'

'Continue!' said Karen, settling still deeper into his chair.

Lotta read on. She had an excellent voice and could handle the brogue expertly. The dialogue got funnier and funnier. Karen began to titter and then to laugh like a hyena. The tears were rolling down his face.

'Do be careful, Karen,' begged his wife, putting the book down for a moment. 'I'm afraid you'll get the hiccups.'

'I don't care,' said Karen, 'it's worth getting the hiccups.'

'But you remember, the last time it happened we had to call a doctor.'

'Just the same,' said Karen. 'I'd like to hear the end of it.' And again he exploded into peals of laughter. It was frightening to hear him laugh. He had no control whatever. I wondered to myself if he could weep just as bravely. It would be something to unnerve one.

Lotta waited for him to subside, then resumed her reading.

' "Did you ever hear, sir, about the fish that Paudeen MacLaughlin caught in the policeman's hat?"

' "I did not," said the Philosopher. "The first person who washed was possibly a person seeking a cheap notoriety. Any fool can wash himself, but every wise man knows that it is an unnecessary labour, for nature will quickly reduce him to a natural and healthy dirtiness again. We should seek, therefore, not how to make ourselves clean, but how to attain a more unique and splendid dirtiness, and perhaps the accumulated layers of matter might, by ordinary geologic compulsion, become incorporated with the human cuticle and so render clothing unnecessary. . . ."

' "About that washboard," said Meehawl, "I was just going to say. . . ."

' "It doesn't matter," said the Philosopher. "In its proper place I . . ." '

Here Lotta had to close the book. Karen was laughing, if it could be called that, with such uncontrollable violence that his eyes were popping out of his head. I thought he would throw a fit.

'Darling, darling!' came Lotta's anxious voice, registering a concern I hadn't believed her capable of. 'Please, darling, calm yourself!'

Karen continued to be rocked by spasms which now sounded more like sobs. I got up and thumped him violently on the back. At once the commotion subsided. He looked up at me gratefully. Then he coughed and wheezed and blew his nose vigorously, wiping the tears away with his coat sleeve.

'Next time, Henry, use a mallet,' he sputtered. 'Or a sledge-hammer.'

'That I will,' I said.

He began to titter again.

'Please don't!' begged Lotta. 'He's had enough for one evening.'

'It was indeed a wonderful evening,' said Mona. 'I'm beginning to like it here. And how wonderfully you read,' she said, addressing Lotta.

'I used to be on the stage,' said Lotta modestly.

'I thought so,' said Mona. 'So was I once.'

Lotta arched her eyebrows. '*You were?*' There was a tinge of sarcasm in her voice.

'Why yes,' said Mona, unruffled, 'I played with the Theatre Guild.'

'Hear, hear!' said Karen, relapsing into his Oxford manner.

' What's so strange about that?' I demanded to know. 'Didn't you think she had any talent?'

'Why, Henry,' said Karen, clasping my arm, 'you *are* a sensitive brute, aren't you? I was congratulating myself on our good luck. We'll all take turns reading some night. I was on the stage once myself, you know.'

'And I was once a trapeze artist,' I countered.

'*Really!*' This from Lotta and Karen simultaneously.

'Didn't I ever tell you? I thought you knew.'

For some strange reason this innocent lie impressed them. If I had said I had been a cabinet minister once it could not have produced as telling an effect. It was amazing how limited was

239

their sense of humour. Naturally I expatiated at length on my virtuosity. Mona chimed in now and then to help me out. They listened as if spellbound.

When I had finished Karen soberly remarked: 'Among other things, Henry, you're not a bad story teller. You must tell us some more yarns like that when we're in the mood.'

The next day, as if to make up for the grand splurge, Karen was determined to tackle the roof. It had to be shingled and then coated with tar. And I who could never drive a nail straight was to do the job—under his directions. Fortunately it took some time to find the right ladder, the proper nails, the hammer and saw and a dozen other tools which he thought might come in handy. What followed was straight out of Laurel and Hardy. First of all I insisted on finding a pair of old gloves so as not to get any splinters in my hands. I made it clear as a Euclidian theorem that with splinters in my fingers I would be unable to type and being unable to type would mean no dictaphone work. After that I insisted on finding a pair of sneakers so as not to slip and break my neck. Karen nodded approval in dead seriousness. He was the type who, in order to get the maximum amount of work out of you, would carry you to the toilet if necessary and wipe your ass for you. It was clear by this time that I would need a lot of assistance to fix the roof. Mona was to stand by in case anything fell to the ground; she was also to fetch us some ice-cold lemonade at intervals. Karen, of course, had already drawn several diagrams explaining how the shingles were to be adjusted one to another. Naturally I profited not at all from these explanations. I had only one thought in mind—to start hammering away like a demon and let the chips fall where they would.

In order to limber up I suggested that I first practise walking along the ridge pole. Karen, still nodding approval, wanted to lend me an umbrella, but at this Mona laughed so heartily that he abandoned the idea. I scurried up the ladder as nimbly as a cat, hoisted myself up to the ridge pole and began my tight rope exercises. Lotta looked on with suppressed fright, her mind busy, doubtless, computing hospital expenses in the event I should slip and break a leg. It was a scorcher of a day, the flies out in swarms and biting like fury. I had on a huge Mexican hat much too big for me which kept falling over my eyes. When I descended I took the notion to change into my swimming trunks. Karen thought he would do likewise. This consumed a little more time.

Finally there was nothing left but to begin. I climbed up the ladder with the hammer under my arm clutching a keg of nails. It was getting on towards noon. Karen had rigged up a platform on wheels from which he unloaded the shingles and gave directions. He looked like a Carthaginian setting the defences of the city in order. The women stood below, clucking away like hens, all set to catch me if I fell.

I got the first shingle set and picked up the hammer to drive the first nail home. I missed it by an inch or two and the shingle went flying homeward like a kite. I was so surprised, so stunned, that the hammer fell out of my hands and the keg of nails tumbled to the ground. Karen, unperturbed, gave orders to remain where I was, the women would gather up the hammer and nails. It was Lotta who ran to the kitchen to get the hammer. When she returned I learned that I had broken the tea pot and a few plates. Mona was scrabling for the nails, picking them up so fast that they fell out of her hand before she could get them in the keg.

'Easy, easy!' shouted Karen. 'All right up there, Henry? Steady now!'

With this I got the giggles. The situation reminded me all too vividly of those dreadful occasions in the past when my mother and sister would aid me in putting up the awnings—parlour floor front. Nobody except an awning maker has any idea how complicated an awning can be. There are not only the rods and flaps, the bolts and screws, the pulleys and cords, there are a hundred perplexing difficulties which arise after you have mounted the ladder and anchored yourself gingerly on the edge of the double window. Somehow there always seemed to be a gale blowing when my mother decided to put up the awnings. Holding the flapping awning with one hand and the hammer with the other, my mother would then endeavour to pass the various things which were needed and which my sister had handed to her. To keep a tight grip with my legs and not permit the awning to carry me aloft was a feat in itself. My arms would grow tired before I had driven in the first screw. I would have to disentangle the damned contraption and jump down for a breathing spell. All the time my mother would be mumbling and groaning—'It's so simple, I could put them up myself in a few minutes if I didn't have the rheumatism.' Recommencing, she would be obliged to explain to me all over again which part went outside and which inside. For me it was like doing something backwards. Once in position again, the hammer would fall from my hands, and I would sit there wrestling with the belly of the awning while my sister ran below and fetched it. It would take at least an hour to put up one awning. At this point I could invariably say—'Why not leave the other ones till tomorrow?' Whereupon my mother would fly into a rage, horrified by the thought of what the neighbours would think seeing only one awning in place. Sometimes, at this point, I would suggest that we call upon a neighbour to finish the job, offering to pay him handsomely out of my own pocket. But this would enrage her even more. It was a sin, in her opinion, to pay out money for work which one could do oneself. By the time we finished I always had a few bruises. 'Serves you right,' my mother would say. 'You ought to be ashamed of yourself. You're as helpless as your father.'

Sitting astride the ridge pole, laughing quietly to myself, I congratulated myself that we were doing something other than dictaphone work. I knew that by evening my back would be so sunburned that I would be unable to work on the morrow. I would have to lie on my belly all day. Fine. It would give me a chance to read something interesting. I was growing stupid listening to nothing but statistical abracadabra. I realized that Karen would try to find something 'light' for me to do while lying on my belly, but I knew how to discourage such attempts.

Well, we bagan again, slowly and deliberately this time. The way I worked over one nail would have driven any normal person crazy. But Karen was anything but a normal individual. From his Carthaginian tower he continued to shower me with directions and encouragements. Why he didn't put the shingles up himself and let me pass them to him I couldn't understand. But he was happy only when directing. Even when it was a simple thing he had to do he could somehow break it up into a multitude of component parts which would necessitate the co-operation of several individuals. It never mattered to him how long it took to complete a job; all that mattered was that it be done his way, i.e., the longest and the most complicated way. This was what he called 'efficiency'. He had learned it in Germany while studying how to make organs. (*Why organs?* So that he could appreciate music better.)

I had only put up a few shingles when the signal came for lunch. It was a cold lunch made of the odds and ends from yesterday's banquet. 'A salad,' Lotta called it. Happily there were a few bottles of beer to make it palatable. We even had a few grapes. I ate them slowly, one by one, stretching the minutes out. Already my back looked raw. Mona wanted me to put a shirt on. I assured them that I tanned quickly. Wouldn't think of donning a shirt. Karen who wasn't altogether a fool, suggested that we lay off the roof work for the afternoon and tackle something 'light'. He began explaining that he had made some complicated charts which had to corrected and remade.

'No, let's get on with the roof,' I urged. 'I'm just getting the hang of it.'

As this sounded plausible and logical to him, Karen voted to tackle the roof again. Once more we clambered up the ladder, did a little preliminary footwork on the ridge pole, and settled down to hammering nails. In a short time the sweat was pouring off me like rain. The more I perspired the more the flies buzzed and bit. My back felt like a raw steak. I accelerated my rhythm perceptibly.

'Good work, Hank!' yelled Karen. 'We ought to be through in a day or two at this rate.'

He had no more than got the words out of his mouth when a shingle flew skyward and caught him over the eye. It made a gash from which the blood trickled into his eye.

'Oh darling, are you hurt?' cried Lotta.

'It's nothing,' he said. 'Carry on, Henry.'

'I'll get some iodine,' yelled Lotta, trotting off into the house.

Quite unintentionally I let the hammer fall from my hand. It fell through a hole in the sheathing right on Lotta's skull. She gave a shriek as if a shark had bitten her, and with that Karen scrambled down from his perch.

It was time to call a halt. Lotta had to be put to bed with a cold compress on her head. Karen had a big patch of court plaster over his left eye. He never uttered a word of complaint.

'I guess you'll have to make the dinner again tonight,' he said to Mona. It seemed to me that there was a secret note of pleasure in his voice. Mona and I had difficulty restraining our jubilation. We waited a while before broaching the subject of the menu.

'Fix anything you like,' said Karen.

'How about lamb chops?' I put in. 'Some lamb chops with French peas, some noodles and maybe artichokes too—how does it sound?'

Karen thought it would be excellent. 'You don't mind, do you?' he asked Mona.

'Not at all,' she said. 'It's a pleasure.'

Then, as if it were quite an afterthought, she added: 'Didn't we bring some Riesling yesterday? I think a bottle of Riesling would go well with the chops.'

'Just the thing,' said Karen.

I took a shower and got into my pyjamas. The prospect of enjoying another good meal revived me. I was ready to sit down and do a bit of dictaphone work to show my appreciation.

'I think you'd better rest up,' said Karen. 'You'll feel a little muscle-bound tomorrow.'

'What about those charts?' I said. 'I'd really like to do something, you know. I'm sorry I was so damned awkward.'

'Tut tut,' said Karen. 'You've done a good day's work. Take it easy till dinner time.'

'All right, if you insist. O.K.'

I opened a bottle of beer and plunked myself in the easy chair.

Thus it went *au bord de la mer*. Great sand spits, with an increasing surf which pounded in one's ears at night like the hammering of a stupendous toccata. Now and then sand storms. The sand seeped in everywhere, even through the glass panes, it seemed.

We were all good swimmers; we bobbed up and down in the

243

heavy surf like otters. Karen always seeking to improve matters, made use of an inflated rubber mattress. After he had taken a siesta on the bosom of the deep, he would swim out a mile or two and give us all a good fright.

Evenings he enjoyed playing games. He played in dead earnest always, whether it was pinochle, cribbage, checkers, casino, whist, fan-tan, dominoes, euchre or backgammon. I don't believe there was a game with which he was not conversant. Part of his general education, don't you know. The rounded individual. He could play hopscotch or tiddly-winks with the same furious zeal and adroitness. Once, when I went to town with him, I suggested that we drop into a pool parlour and play a game of pool. He asked me if I wanted to shoot first. Without thinking I said, 'No, you go ahead.' He did. He cleaned up the table four times before I had a chance to use the cue. When it finally came my turn I suggested that we go home. 'Next time you shoot first,' he said, intimating that that would be a break for me. It never occurred to him, that just because he was a shark, it would have been sporting to miss a shot occasionally. To play ping pong with him was hopeless; only Bill Tilden could have returned his serves. The only game in which I might have stood a chance to break even was craps, but I never liked rolling dice, it was boring.

One evening, after discussing some books on occultism, I reminded him of the time we had taken a trip up the Hudson on an excursion boat. 'You remember how we pushed the ouija board around?' His face lit up. Of course he did. He would like to try it again if I were willing. He'd improvise a board.

We sat up that night till two in the morning pushing the damned thingamajig around. We must have made a lot of connections in the astral realm, judging by the time which elapsed. As usual it was I who summoned the eccentric figures—Jacob Boehme, Swedenborg, Paracelsus, Nostradamus, Claude Saint-Martin, Ignatius Loyola, the Marquis de Sade and such like. Karen made notes of the messages we received. Said he would dictate them to the dictaphone the next day. To be filed under 1.352-Cz 240.(18), which was the exact index for material derived from the departed spirits by means of the ouija board on such and such an evening in the region of the Rockaways. It was weeks later when I decocted this particular record. I had forgotten all about the incident. Suddenly, in Karen's serious voice I began getting these crazy messages from the blue. . . . 'Eating well. Time hangs heavy. Coronary divertissements tomorrow. Paracelsus.' I began to shake with laughter. So the idiot really was filing this stuff away! I was curious to know what else he might have tucked away under this classification. I went to the card files first. There were at least fifty cross references indicated. Each one was battier than the previous one. I got out the folders and file boxes in which the papers were stored away. His

notes and jottings were scribbled in a minute scrawl on odds and
ends, often paper napkins, blotters, menus, tally cards. Sometimes it was nothing more than a phrase which a friend
had dropped while conversing in the subway; sometimes it was an
embryonic thought which had flitted through his head while
taking a crap. Sometimes it was a page torn from a book—the
title, author, publisher and place always carefully noted as well
as the date when he had come across it. There were bibliogra-
phies in at least a dozen languages, including Chinese and
Persian.

One curious chart interested me enormously; I intended to
pump him about it one day but never did. As best I could make
out, it represented a map of some singular region in limbo, the
boundaries of which had been given in a seance with a medium.
It looked like a geodetic survey of a bad dream. The names of
the places were written in a language which nobody could possibly understand. But Karen had given a rough translation on
separate sheets of paper. '*Notes*', it read: 'The following transla-
tions of place names in the quaternary decan of Devachan were
volunteered by de Quincey working through Madame X.
Coleridge is said to have verified them before his death but the
documents in which the testimony is given are temporarily lost.'
The singular thing about this shadowy sector of the beyond was
this: in its confines, imaginary perhaps, were gathered the shades
of such diverse and interesting personalities as Pythagoras, Hera-
clitus, Longinus, Virgil, Hermes Trismegistus, Apollonius of
Tyana, Montezume, Xenophon, Jan van Ruysbroeck, Nicolaus
of Cusa, Meister Eckhart, St Bernard of Clairvaux, Asoka, St
François de Sales, Fenelon, Chuang Tzu, Nostradamus, Saladin,
the Pope Joanna, St Vincent de Paul, Paracelsus, Malatesta,
Origen, together with a coterie of women saints. One would like
to know what had drawn this conglomeration of souls together.
One would like to know what they discussed in the mysterious
language of the departed. One would like to know if the great
problems which had tormented them on earth had been finally
resolved. One would like to know if they consorted together in
divine harmony. Warriors, saints, mystics, sages, magicians,
martyrs, kings, thaumaturgists. . . . What an assemblage! What
would one not give to be with them for just a day!

As I say, for some mysterious reason I never brought this
subject to Karen's attention. There was little, indeed, outside our
work which I did discuss with him, first because of his great
reserve, second because to introduce even a slight detail meant
listening to an inexhaustible harangue, third because I was
intimidated by the vast domain of knowledge which appeared to
be his. I contented myself with browsing through his books,
which embraced an enormous range of subject matter. He read
Greek, Latin, Hebrew and Sanskrit with apparent ease, and was

fluent in a dozen living languages, including Russian, Turkish and Arabic. The titles of his books were alone sufficient to set my head spinning. What astounded me, however, was that so little of this vast store of learning seeped into our daily talk. Sometimes I had the feeling that he regarded me as a thorough ignoramus. Other times he embarrassed me by posing questions which only a Thomas Aquinas could cope with. Now and then he gave me the impression that he was just a child with an over-developed brain. He had little humour and almost no imagination. Outwardly he appeared to be a model husband, always ready to cater to his wife's whims, always alert to serve her, always solicitous and protective, at times positively chivalric. I couldn't help but wonder at times what it would be like to be married to this human adding machine. With Karen everything proceeded according to schedule. Intercourse too, no doubt. Perhaps he kept a secret file reminding him when intercourse was due, together with notes on the results—spiritual, moral, mental and physical.

One day he caught me unawares reading a volume of Elie Faure which I had dug up. I had just read the paragraph which opens the chapter on The Sources of Greek Art. . . . 'On condition that we respect ruins, that we do not rebuild them, that, after having asked their secret, we let them be recovered by the ashes of the centuries, the bones of the dead, the rising mass of waste which once was vegetations and races, the eternal drapery of the foliage—their destiny may stir our emotion. It is through them that we touch the depths of our history, just as we are bound to the roots of life by the griefs and sufferings which have formed us. A ruin is painful to behold only for the man who is incapable of participating by his activity in the conquest of the present. . . .'

He came on me just as I had finished the paragraph. '*What!*' he exclaimed. 'You're reading Elie Faure?'

'Why not?' I was at a loss to understand his amazement.

He hesitated a moment, scratched his head, then answered falteringly: 'I don't know, Henry . . . I never thought. . . . Well, I'll be damned! Do you really find it interesting?'

'*Interesting?*' I echoed. 'I'm mad about Elie Faure.' 'Where are you at?' he asked, reaching for the book. 'Ah, I see.' He read the paragraph over, aloud. 'I wish I had the time to read that sort of book—it's too much of a luxury for me.'

'I don't follow you.'

'One has to swallow such books early in life,' said Karen. 'It's sheer poetry, you know. Makes too much of a demand on one. You're lucky you have time to spare. You're still an aesthete.'

'And you?'

'Just a work-horse, I guess. I've put my dreams behind me.'

'All those books in there. . . .' I nodded in the direction of the library. 'You've read them?'

246

'Most of them,' he answered. 'Some of them I'm reserving for leisure moments.'

'I noticed you had several books on Paracelsus. I only glanced at them—but they intrigue me.'

I hoped he would snatch at the bait, but no, he dismissed the subject by remarking, as if to himself, that one could spend a life-time struggling to grasp the meaning of Paracelsus' theories.

'And what about Nostradamus?' I asked. I was intent on getting *some* spark from him.

To my surprise his face suddenly lit up. 'Ah, that's another story,' he replied. 'Why do you ask—have you been reading him?'

'One doesn't *read* Nostradamus. I've been reading *about* him. What excites me is the Preface which he addressed to his infant son, Caesar. It's an extraordinary document, in more ways than one. Can you spare a minute?'

He nodded. I got up, brought the book back, and hunted up the page which had inflamed me just a few days before.

'Listen to this,' I said. I read in a few salient passages, then stopped abruptly. 'There are two passages in this book which . . . well, they baffle me. Perhaps you can explain them to me. The first one is this: "M le Pelletier (says the author) conceives that the *Commun Advènement*, or *l'avènement au règne des gens du commun*, which I have rendered 'The Vulgar Advent', extending from the death of Louis XVI to the reign of Antichrist, is the grand object of Nostradamus." I'll come back to this in a moment. Here's the second one: "As an accepted visionary he (Nostradamus) is perhaps less swayed by the imagination than any man of a hall kindred type that one can mention." ' I paused. 'What do you make of them, if anything?'

Karen took his time before answering. I surmised that he was conducting an inner debate, first, as to whether he could spare the time to make adequate answer to the question, second, whether it would be worth his while to waste his ammunition on a type like myself.

'You understand, Henry,' he began, 'that you're asking me to explain something highly complex. Let me ask you first, have you ever read anything by Evelyn Underhill, or by A. A. Waite?' I shook my head. 'I thought as much,' he continued. 'Naturally you wouldn't have asked my opinion if you hadn't sensed the nature of these preplexing statements. I'd like to ask you another question, if you don't mind. Do you understand the difference between a prophet, a mystic, a visionary and a seer?'

I hesitated a moment, then said: 'Not too clearly, but I see what you're driving at. I believe, however, that if given time to reflect I could answer your question.'

'Well, let's not bother now,' said Karen. 'I merely wanted to test your background.'

'Take it for granted that it's nil,' said I, growing a bit annoyed by these preliminaries.

'You must excuse me,' said Karen, 'for beginning in this fashion. It's not very kind, is it? A hang-over from schooldays, I guess. Look here, Henry . . . Intelligence is one thing—native intelligence, I mean. Knowledge is another. Knowledge and training, I should say, because they go together. What you know you've picked up in haphazard fashion. I underwent a rigorous discipline. I say this so that you will understand why I fumble about instead of answering right off the bat. In these matters we speak different languages, you and I. In a way—forgive the thought!—you're like a superior type of savage. Your I.Q. is probably just as high as mine, perhaps higher. But we approach the domain of knowledge in diametrically opposite ways. Because of my training and background I'm quite apt to underestimate your ability to grasp what I have to impart. And you, for your part, are most apt to think that I am wasting words, splitting hairs, parading my erudition.'

I interrupted him. 'It's you who fancy all this,' said I. 'I haven't any preconceived notions whatsoever. It doesn't matter to me how you proceed, so long as you give me a definite answer.'

'That's just what I expected you to say, old man. To you it's all quite simple and straightforward. Not so to me! You see, I was taught to postpone queries of this sort until convinced that I could find the answer nowhere. . . . However, all this is no answer, is it? Now let's see. . . . What was it precisely you wished to know? It's important to get that straight, otherwise we'll end up in the Pontine marshes.'

I read the second statement over again, giving emphasis to the words 'less swayed by the imagination'.

To my own astonishment I caught myself saying: 'Never mind, I understand it perfectly now.'

'You do?' cried Karen. 'Huh! Explain it to *me*, then, will you?'

'I'll try,' said I, 'though you must realise that it's one thing to understand a thing yourself and another to explain it to someone.' (That's tit for tat, thought I to myself.) Then, sincerely in earnest, I began: 'If you were a prophet instead of a statistician or mathematician, I would say that there was something of a resemblance between you and Nostradamus. I mean, in the way you go about things. The prophetic art is a gift, and so is the mathematical flair, if I may call it that. Nostradamus, it would seem, refused to exploit his natural gift in the usual way. As you know, he was versed not only in astrology but in the magic arts. He had knowledge of things hidden—or forbidden—to the scholar. He was not only a physician but a psychologist. He was many, many things all in one. In short, he had command of so many coordinates that it clipped his wings. He limited himself—

248

I say this advisedly—to what was given, like a scientist. In his solo flights he moved from one level to another with cold-blooded precision, always equipped with instruments, charts, tables and private keys. However fantastic his prophecies may sound to us, I doubt if they originated in dream and reverie. *Inspired* they were, beyond question. But one has every reason to believe that Nostradamus deliberately refused to give free rein to his imagination. He proceeded objectively, so to speak, even when (paradoxical as it may sound) he was subjugated by trance. The purely personal aspect of his work. . . . I hesitate to call it his creation . . . centres about the veiled delivery of the oracles, the reason for which he made clear in the Preface to Caesar, his son. There is a dispassionate tone about the nature of these revelations which one feels is not altogether attributable to modesty on the part of Nostradamus. He stresses the fact that it is God who deserves the credit, not himself. Now a true visionary would be fervent about the revelations disclosed to him; he would make haste either to recreate the world, according to the divine wisdom he had tasted, or he would make haste to unite himself with his Creator. A prophet, more egotistical still, would make use of his illumination to take revenge upon his fellow-men . . . I'm hazarding all this at random, you understand.' I gave him a quick keen glance to make sure I had him hooked, then continued. 'And now, suddenly, I think I begin to understand the real import of the first citation. I mean that part about the grand object of Nostradamus, which, as you recall, the French commentator would have us believe was nothing less than a desire to give predominant significance to the French Revolution. Myself, I think that if Nostradamus had any ulterior motive for dwelling on this event so markedly, it was in order to disclose to us the manner in which history is to be liquidated. A phrase like *'la fin des temps'*—what *does* it mean? Can there really be an end to time? And if so, could it possibly mean that time's end is really *our* beginning? Nostradamus predicts a millenium to come—in a time not far distant, either. I am no longer sure at the moment whether it follows upon the Day of Judgment or precedes it. Neither am I certain whether his vision extended to the end of the world or not. (He speaks of the year 3797, if I remember rightly, as though that were as far as he could see.) I don't think the two—the Judgment Day and the end of the world—were meant to be simultaneous. *Man knows no end,* that's my conviction. The *world* may come to an end, but if so, it will be the world imagined by the scientists, not the world God created. When the *end* comes we will take our world with us. Don't ask me to explain this—I just know it for a fact. . . . But to approach this end business from another angle. All it can possibly mean, as I see it now—and to be sure, this is quite enough!—is the emergence of a new and fecund chaos. Were we living in Orphic times we would speak of it as the coming of a new order of gods, meaning, if you like, the investiture of a new and greater consciousness, something even beyond *cosmic* consciousness. I look upon the Oracles of Nostradamus as the work of an aristocratic spirit. It has meaning only for true individuals. . . . To get back to the Vulgar Advent, excuse my circumlocutiousness! The phrase so widely used today—the common man—strikes me as an utterly meaningless one. There is no such animal. If the phrase has any meaning at all, and I think Nostradamus certainly implied as much when he spoke of the Vulgar Advent, it means that all that is abstract and negative, or retrogressive, has now assumed dominion. Whatever the common man is or is not, one thing is certain—he is the very antithesis of Christ or Satan. The term itself seems to imply absence of allegiance, absence of faith, absence of guiding principle—or even instinct. Democracy, a vague, empty word, simply denotes the confusion which the common man has ushered in and in which he flourishes like the weed. One might as well say—mirage, illusion, hocus-pocus. Have you ever thought that it may be on this note—on the rise and dominion of an anacephalic body—that history will end? Perhaps we will have to begin all over again from where the Cro-Magnon man left off. One thing seems highly evident to me, and that is that the note of doom and destruction, which figures so heavily in all prophecies, springs from the certain knowledge that the historical or world element in man's life is but transitory. The seer knows how, why and where we got off the track. He knows further that there is little to be done about it, so far as the great mass of humanity is concerned. History must run its course, we say. True, but only? Because history is the myth, the true myth, of man's fall made manifest in time. Man's descent into the illusory realm of matter must continue until there is nothing left to do but swim up to the surface of reality—and live in the light of everlasting truth. The men of spirit constantly exhort us to hasten the end and commence anew. Perhaps that is why they are called paracletes, or divine advocates. Comforters, if you like. They never exult in the coming of catastrophe, as mere prophets sometimes do. They indicate, and usually illustrate by their lives, how we may convert seeming catastrophe to divine ends. That is to say, they show us, those of us who are ready and aware, how to adapt and attune ourselves to a reality which is permanent and indestructible. They make their appeal. . . .'

At this point Karen signalled me to stop. 'Christ, man,' he exclaimed, 'what a pity you aren't living in the Middle Ages! You would have made one of the great Schoolmen. You're a metaphysician, by crikey. You ask a question and you answer it like a master of dialectic.' He paused a moment to draw a deep breath. 'Tell me something,' he said, putting a hand on my shoulder 'how did you come by all this? Come on now, don't feign humility with me. You know what I'm getting at.'

I hemmed and hawed.

'Come, come! he said.

His earnestness was pathetically child-like. The only response I could make was to blush deeply.

'Do your friends understand you when you talk this way? Or do you talk this way only to yourself?'

I laughed. How could one answer such queries with a straight face? I begged him to change the subject.

He nodded silently. Then: 'But don't you ever think of making use of your talents? As far as I can see, you do nothing but fritter your time away. You waste it on idiots like MacGregor and Maxie Schnagid.'

'To you it may seem that way,' I said slightly nettled now. 'To me it seems otherwise. I don't intend to be a thinker, you know. I want to write. I want to write about life, in the raw. Human beings, any kind of human beings, are food and drink to me. I enjoy talking about other things, certainly. The conversation we just had, that's nectar and ambrosia. I don't say it doesn't get anyone anywhere, not at all, *but*—I prefer to reserve that sort of food for my own private delectation. You see, at the bottom I'm just one of those common men we were talking about. Only, now and then I get flashes. Sometimes I think I'm an artist. Once in a great while I even think I may be a visionary, but never a prophet, a seer. What I have to contribute must be done in a roundabout way. When I read about Nostradamus or Paracelsus, for example, I feel at home. But I was born in another vector. I'll be happy if I ever learn to tell a good story. I like the idea of getting nowhere. I like the idea of the game for the game's sake. And above all, wretched, botched and horrible though it may be, I love this world of human beings. I don't want to cut myself adrift. Perhaps what fascinates me in being a writer is that it necessitates communion with all and sundry. Well, anyway, this is all surmise on my part.'

'Henry,' said Karen, 'I'm just beginning to know you. I had you all wrong. We've got to talk some more—another time.'

With this he excused himself and retired to his study. I sat there for a while, in a semi-trance, mulling over the shreds of our conversation. After a time I absent-mindedly reached for the book which he had put down. As absent-mindedly I picked it up and read: 'For the divine works, which are absolutely universal, God will complete; those which are contingent, or medial, the good angels direct; and the third sort come under the evil angels.' (From the Preface for Caesar Nostradamus, his son.) These few lines kept singing in my head for days. I had a vague hope that Karen would appear for another closed session in which we might discuss the probable task of the good angels. But on the third day thereafter his mother arrived with a friend of long standing. Our conversations took quite another turn.

Karen's mother! A majestic creature in whose person were combined the diverse qualities of matriarch, hetaera and goddess. She was everything that Karen was not. No matter what she was doing she radiated warmth; her ringing laugh dissolved all problems, asured one of her confidence, trust, benevolence. She was positive through and through, yet never arrogant or aggressive. Divining instantly what you were endeavouring to say, she gave her approval before the words were out of your mouth. She was a pure, radiant spirit in a most enchantingly carnal form.

The man she had brought along was a mellow sort of individual, of idealistic temperament, who ran for Governor now and then and was always defeated. He talked of world affairs with knowledge and insight, always in a dispassionate way and with sly humour. He had been in Wilson's entourage at Versailles, he knew Smuts of South Africa, and he had been an intimate friend of Eugene V. Debs. He had translated obscure works of the pre-Socratic Greeks, was an expert chess player, and had written a book on the origins and evolution of the game. The more he talked the more I was impressed by the multitudinous facets of his personality. The places he had been to!—Tibet, Arabia, Easter Island, Tierra del Fuego, Lake Titicaca, Greenland, Mongolia. And what friends he had made—of the most diverse sort—during the course of his travels! I recalled these: Kipling, Marcel Proust, Maeterlinck, Rabindranath Tagore, Alexander Berkman, the Archbishop of Canterbury, Count Keyserling, Henri Rousseau, Max Jacob, Aristide Briand, Thomas Edison, Isadora Duncan, Charlie Chaplin, Eleanora Duse. . . .

To sit down to table with him was like attending a banquet given by Socrates. Among other things he was a connoisseur of wines. He made sure that we ate well and drank well, larding the dinner talk with such comestible delicacies as the great plagues, the hidden meanings of the Aztec alphabet, the military strategy of Attila, the miracles of Apollonius of Tyana, the life of Sadakichi Hartman, the magic lore of the Druids, the inner workings of the financial clique which rules the world, the visions of William Blake, and so on. He spoke of the dead with the same intimate tenderness as of the living. He was at home in all climes, all epochs of mankind. He knew the habits of birds and snakes, he was an expert on constitutional law, he invented chess problems, he had written treatises on the drift of the continents, on international law, on ballistics, on the art of healing.

Karen's mother provided the spice. She had a ringing laugh which was infectious. No matter what the subject under discussion, she could make it appetizing by her comments. Her learning seemed almost as prodigious as her consort's, but she carried it lightly. Karen suddenly seemed like an adolescent who had not yet begun to live his own life. His mother treated him like an overgrown child. Now and then she told him plainly that he was just a fool. 'You need a vacation,' she would say. 'You ought to have had five children by now.' Or—'Why don't you go to Mexico for a few months, you're getting stale.'

As for herself, she was getting ready to make a trip to India. The year before she had been to Africa, not big game hunting either, but as an ethnologist. She had penetrated to regions where no white woman had ever set foot. She was fearless but not reckless. She could adapt herself to any circumstances, enduring hardships which made even the stronger sex flinch. She had a faith and a trust which were invincible. No one could come into her presence without being enriched. At times she reminded me of those Polynesian women of royal lineage who preserved, in the far Pacific, the last vestiges of an earthly Paradise. Here was the mother I should like to have chosen before entering the womb. Here was the mother who personified the primal elements of our being, in whom earth, sea and sky were harmonized. She was a natural descendant of the great Sybilline figures, embodying the texture of myth, fable and legend. Terrestrial to the core, she nevertheless lived in a realm of super-dimensions. Her consciousness seemed to expand or contract at will. For the greatest tasks she made no more effort than for the humblest. She was equipped with wings, fins, tail, feet, claws and gills. She was aeronautic and amphibious. She understood all languages yet spoke as a child. Nothing could dampen her ardour or mutilate her irrepressible joy. Just to look at her was to take courage. Problems became non-existent. She was anchored in reality, but a reality which was divine.

For the first time in my life, I had the privilege of gazing upon a Mother. Images of the Madonna had never meant anything to me: they were too bright, too translucent, too remote, too ethereal. I had formed an image of my own—darker, more substantial, more mysterious, more potent. I had never expected to see it concretized. I had imagined such types to exist, but only in the remote places of this world. I had sensed their existence in previous times; in Etruria, in ancient Persia, in the golden days of China, in the Malay archipelago, in legendary Ireland, in the Oberian peninsula, in far off Polynesia. But to come upon one in the flesh, in every day surroundings, to be eating, talking, laughing with her—no, that I had never believed possible. Every day I studied her anew. Every day I expected the veil to fall away. But no, each day she grew in stature, ever more wondrous, ever more real, as only dreams become when we sink deeper and deeper into their meshes. What I had understood heretofore to be human, all-too-human, became magnified to an inexhaustible degree. It was no longer necessary to await the coming of a superman. The boundaries of the human world suddenly became limitless, everything has been given, we are told again and again. All that is demanded of us, I saw it now clearly, is to realize out own nature. One speaks of man's potential nature as though it were a contradition of the one he reveals. In Karen's mother I saw the potential being flourish, I observed it expropriating the crude, external shell in which it is encased. I understood that metamorphosis is present and actual, the very sign of vitality. I saw the feminine principle usurped by the human. I understood that a greater endowment of the human element awakened a greater sense of reality. I understood that, in augmenting the life force, the being incarnating it grows ever closer to us, ever more tender, ever more indispensable. The superior being is not, as I once supposed, more remote, more detached, more abstract. Quite the contrary. Only the superior being can arouse in us the hunger which is justifiable, the hunger to surpass ourselves by becoming what we truly are. In the presence of the superior being we recognize our own majestic powers; we do not long to be that person, we merely thirst to demonstrate to ourselves that we are indeed of that same pith and substance. We rush forward to greet our brothers and sisters, knowing beyond all doubt that we are all kin . . .

The visit of his mother and her companion lasted only a few days, alas. They had hardly gone when Karen decided that we should all go back to town, where he had some matters to attend to. He thought it might do us all good to go to the theatre, hear a concert or two, and then return to the beach to work in earnest. I realized that his mother's visit had completely derailed him.

The town flat, as he called it, was one unholy mess. God knows when a broom had last been put to it. The kitchen was strewn with garbage which had lain there for weeks. Mice, ants, cockroaches, bedbugs, every sort of vermin infested the place. The tables, beds, chairs, divans, commodes were littered with papers, with open fileboxes, with cards, graphs, statistical tables, instruments of all kinds. There were at least five ink bottles uncorked. Partly eaten sandwiches lay among the heaps of letters. Cigarette butts were there by the hundreds.

The place was so filthy, indeed, that Karen and his wife decided to go to a hotel for the night. They would return the next evening after we had tidied the place up as best we could. I was to do what I could with his files.

We were so glad to be alone for a change that we didn't mind the imposition. I had borrowed a ten spot from Karen so that we could get some food. As soon as they had left we went out to eat, and we ate well. An Italian dinner with some good red wine.

Returning to the flat we noticed the odour as we ascended the stairs. 'We're not going to touch a thing,' I said to Mona. 'Let's get to bed and clear out in the morning. I'm fed up.'

'Don't you think we ought to see them at least and tell them we're quitting?'

'I'll leave a note,' I said. 'I'm too disgusted to prolong matters. I don't feel that we owe them a thing.'

It took us an hour to clean the bedroom sufficiently to be comfortable for the night. At that we had to sleep between soiled sheets. No matter what one touched, it was out of order. To pull the shade down was like working out a mathematical problem. I came to the conclusion that the two of them were suffering from a mild case of dementia. Just as I was about to turn in I noticed on the shelf above the bed a row of hat boxes and shoe boxes. On each one was written an index number, indicating the size, colour and condition of the hat or shoes. I opened them to see if they really contained hats and shoes. They did. None of them were in a condition to be worn by anyone but a panhandler. This was the last straw for me.

'I tell you,' I groaned, 'that guy's batty. Crazy as a loon.'

We rose early, unable to sleep because of the bedbugs. We took a quick shower, examined our clothes thoroughly to make sure they were not infested, and prepared to decamp. I was just in the mood to write a note. I decided it should be a good one, because I intended never to see the two of them again. I looked around for a suitable piece of paper. Catching sight of a big map on the wall, I ripped it down and, using the end of a broom handle which I dipped in a pot of paint, I scrawled a farewell in hieroglyphics tall enough to be read thirty yards away. With the back of my hand I shoved the things on the big work table on to the floor. I placed the map on the table and in the centre of it I dumped a pile of the most ancient, the most reeking, garbage. I was sure he wouldn't miss that. I took a final look about, so as to retain a lasting impression of the scene. I walked to the door, then suddenly turned back. One more thing was needed—a postscriptum to the note. Choosing a sharp-pointed pencil I wrote in a microscopic hand: 'To be filed under C, for catarrh, cleanliness, cantharides, cowbells, Chihuahua, Cochin-China, constipation, curlicues, crinology, cacchination, co-terminous, cow-flop, cicerone, cockroaches, cimex lectularius, cemeteries, crêpes Suzette, corn-fed hogs, citrate of magnesia, cowries, cornucopia, castration, crotchets, cuneiform, cistern, cognomen, Cockaigne, concertina, cotyleddons, crapulated. cosine, creasote, crupper, copulation, Clytemnestra, Czolgosz—and Blue Label catsup.'

My one regret, as we descended the stairs, was that I couldn't leave my calling card on the table too.

We had a jolly little breakfast in a lunch wagon opposite the Tombs during which we discussed our future, which was a complete blank.

'Why don't you go to a movie this afternoon?' said Mona.

'I'll run over to Hoboken or somewhere and see what I can scrape up. Let's meet at Ulric's for dinner—how's that?'

'Fine,' I said, 'but what will I do this morning? Do you realize it's only eight o'clock?'

'Why don't you go to the Zoo? Take a bus. The ride will do you good.'

She couldn't have made a better suggestion. I was in the proper mood to look at the creature world. Being foot-loose and free at that ungodly hour of the morning gave me a sense of superiority. I would sit on the upper deck and watch the busy toilers scurrying to their appointed tasks. I wondered for a moment what my mission in life might be. I had almost forgotten that I had intended to be a writer. I knew only one thing—I was not cut out to be a scavenger. Nor a drudge. Nor an amanuensis.

At the corner I parted with Mona. At Fifth Avenue I hopped a bus going north and clambered up to the top deck. Free again! I inhaled a few deep draughts of ozone. As we came alongside Central Park I took a good look at the fading mansions which flank the Fifth Avenue side. Many of them I knew from having entered through the servants' or tradesmen's door. Yes, there was the Roosevelt home where, as a boy of fourteen, I delivered cut-away suits, tuxedos, alpaca jackets for the old man. I wondered if the elder Mr Roosevelt, the banker, that is, and his four giant sons still walked five abreast to their office in Wall Street each morning—after having taken a gallop through the park, *bien entendu*. A little farther along I recognized old man Bendix's mansion. The brother, who had a penchant for fancy vest buttons, was dead a long time. But H. W. was probably still alive and probably still grousing over the fact that his tailor had forgotten that he dressed on the right side. How I loathed that man! I smiled to think of the anger I had vented on him in days gone by. He was probably a very lonely, feeble old man now, attended by a faithful servant, a cook, a butler, a chauffeur and so on. How busy he always managed to keep himself! Truly, the rich are to pitied.

So it went. . . . Reminiscence upon reminiscence. Suddenly I thought of Rothermel. I could just picture him getting out of bed with a hang-over, tripping over his own piss-pot, fuming, fussing, hopping around like a crow on one leg. Well, it would be a red-letter day for him, seeing Mona again. (I was sure she was headed in his direction.)

Thinking of Rothermel's early morning condition I got to ruminating on how various people I knew greeted the new day. It was a delightful game. From friends and acquaintances I moved over into the realm of celebrities—artists, actors and actresses, political figures, criminals, religious leaders, all classes and all levels. It grew positively fascinating when I began digging into the habits of the great historical personages. How did

Caligula greet the day? A swarm of distant personalities suddenly took possession of my brain: Sir Francis Bacon, Mohammed the Great, Charlemagne, Julius Caesar, Hannibal, Confucius, Tamerlane, Napoleon at St Helena, Herbert Spencer, Modjeska, Sir Walter Scott, Gustavus Adolphus, Friedrich Barbarossa, P. T. Barnum. . . .

Approaching Bronx Park I forgot what had led me to this spot. I was just rehearsing my first impressions of the three-ringed circus, that awesome moment in a boy's life when he sees his idol in flesh and bone. Mine was Buffalo Bill. I loved him. To see him gallop into the centre of the sawdust ring and doff his huge sombrero to the applauding spectators was something unforgettable. He has long locks, a goatee, and a big curling moustache. There is an elegance to the spectacular garb he sports. One hand holds the reins lightly, the other grasps the faithful rifle. In a moment he will display his unerring marksmanship. He is making the full circle of the arena first, his proud steed snorting fire. What a splendid figure of a man! His friends are the fierce Indian chiefs—Sioux, Commanches, Crows, Blackfeet.

What a boy admires is unostentatious strength—skill, poise, flexibility. Buffalo Bill was the epitome of all these. We never saw him except in full costume, and then only once a year—if we were lucky. In those few moments allotted to us he never missed a shot, never made an awkward move, never departed one iota from the ideal portrait we carried in our hearts. He never deceived us, never betrayed us. *Always at par.*

Buffalo Bill was to us what Saladin was to his followers—and to his enemies. A boy never forgets his idols. Well, *fuck a duck*—here we are at the Zoo. The first thing I see is a giraffe. Then a Bengal tiger, then a rhinoceros, then a tapir. Ah, here are the monkeys! Home again. Nothing cleans out the psychological system like looking at wild animals. *Tabula rasa.* The very names of their habitats are inspiring. One drifts back into the old Adamic world where the serpent reigned supreme. Evolution explains nothing. We were all there together, from the beginning of time, and we will remain together until eternity. The stars and the constellations drift, the continents drift, man drifts together with his companions of antediluvian days—the armadillo, the dodo bird, the dinosaur, the sabre-toothed tiger, the diminutive horse of upper Mongolia. Everything in the cosmos is drifting towards some drifting point in space. And God Almighty is probably drifting too, together with his Creation.

Drifting along, one with the Zoo and all its occupants, I suddenly had the clearest vision of Renée Tietjen. Renée was the sister of Richies Tietjen with whom I used to play as a boy of ten. He was like a bloodthirsty Zouave, this Richie. He would bite a piece out of you if you angered him. It was important, when choosing sides for a game of prisoner's base, to have Richie on your side. Now and then Renée, his sister, would stand at the gate and watch us. She was about six years older than him, quite a woman already, and to us youngsters utterly ravishing. When you got close to her you inhaled the perfume which she used—or was it simply the fragrance of her delicious flesh? From the time I had ceased playing in that street I had never given a thought to Renée Tietgen. Now suddenly, and for no reason I could think of, her image danced before me. She was leaning on the iron fence beside the gate and the wind moulded her thin silk dress about her limbs. I realized now what had made her so ravishing and unattainable: she was an exact replica of one of the medieval French madonnas. All light and grace, chaste, seductive, with golden tresses and sea green eyes. Always silent, always seraphic. Buffeted by the wind, she swayed back and forth like a young willow. Her breasts, which were two nubile hemispheres, and the little tuft which adorned the pelvis, seemed extraordinarily alive and sensitive. They met the wind like the bulging contour of a ship's prow. Within a few feet of her we were dashing about like mad bulls, ripping, slashing, biting, squealing, as if possessed. Renée always stood there imperturbable, her lips faintly parted in an enigmatic smile. Some said she had a lover who had jilted her. Some said she was lame. Not one of us had the courage to address her. She took her place at the railing and remained there like a statue. Now and then the wind lifted her skirt and we gasped when we caught sight of the milky flesh above her knees. Towards evening old man Tietjen would come trudging home, a long whip in his hand. Seeing Richie, his clothes torn, his face spattered with mud and blood, the old man would flick him with the whip. Richie never uttered a sound. The old man would greet his daughter surlily and disappear through the front door. A strange scene whose sequel we never knew.

All this came back to me so vividly that I felt impelled to make a few notes immediately. I rush frantically out of the park in search of paper and pencil. Now and then I stopped to make water. Finally I found a little stationery store run by an old Jewish woman. She was wearing one of those hideous wigs the colour of a cockroach's wings. For some reason she had difficulty in understanding me. I began making signs in the air. She thought I was deaf. She began to yell at me. I yelled back at her, drowning her with oaths. She grew frightened and ran to the back of the store to call for help. Baffled, I stood there a moment, then dashed into the street. A bus was standing at the corner. I got in and sat down. Beside me was a newspaper. I picked it up and began making notes, first in the margins, then across the black print. When we came to Morningside Park I furtively threw the paper out the window. I felt relieved, as relieved as if I had just had a good fuck. Renée had faded out, along with the

258

giraffes, the camels, the Bengal tigers, the peanut shells and the sullen roar of the lions. I would tell Ulric all about it, he would enjoy it. Unless he was just in the midst of a banana campaign.

9

ONCE AGAIN WE ARE living in a sedate neighbourhood, not far from Fort Greene Park. The street is as wide as a boulevard, the houses set far back from the sidewalk, most of them of brownstone and adorned with high stoops of the same material. Some of the houses are veritable mansions flanked by immense lawns studded with shrubs and statues. Ample driveways lead to the stables and servants' quarters in the rear. The whole atmosphere of this old neighbourhood is redolent of the 80' and 90's. The remarkable thing about it is its state of preservation. Even the hitching posts are intact and gleaming, as if just wiped with an oil rag. Sumptuous, elegant, somnolescent, it seems like a wonderful haven to us.

It was Mona, of course, who had found the two rooms. And once again, we had a congenial landlady, one of those witless young American widows who didn't know what to do with herself. We had taken our furniture out of storage and fitted up the two rooms. The landlady was delighted to have us as tenants. She ate with us frequently. Quite a jolly creature, with a melodious voice and the indolence of a lost soul. Things promised to go well here. The rent was cheap, the gas, water and electricity functioned perfectly, an abundance of good food, movies afternoons and evenings, if we desired it, a game of cards now and then, to please the landlady, and no visitors. Not a soul knew our address. Where the funds came from I wasn't too sure. Mathias, still in the offing, and Rothermel, more alive than ever, I knew contributed the bulk of it. But there must have been others, too, for we were living high. The landlady, of course, was liberal with food and drink, and often invited us to the theatre or took us to a cabaret. What fascinated her was that we were obviously artists —'Bohemians', as she put it. Her husband had been an insurance agent and a pretty dull bird, according to her, and she intended to make merry now that he was gone.

I rented a typewriter and began writing once more. Everything was just ducky. The beautiful silk bathrobe, the pyjamas, the Moroccan slippers I wore, all were gifts from the landlady: heirlooms. The mornings were luxurious. We would get out of bed around ten, bathe leisurely while the phonograph played, then sit down to a delicious breakfast, usually prepared by the landlady. Always fresh fruit and berries smothered in cream, muffins fresh from the oven, thick strips of bacon, marmalade, steaming coffee with whipped cream. I felt like a pasha. Though I had no use for them, I was equipped with two beautiful cigarette cases and a long cigarette holder, which I used only at mealtime, and to please the good landlady who had given me them.

I must stop calling her 'the landlady'. Her name was Marjorie, and it suited her to a T. There was something lascivious about her, as if she were always picking up the scent. She had a beautiful figure and she displayed it freely, especially in the morning when all she wore was a filmy bathrobe. It didn't take long before we were patting one another affectionately on the rump. She was the sort of woman who could grab your cock and make you laugh at the same time. One couldn't help liking her, even if she were pock-marked, which she wasn't. Everything she did was open and above-board. If you merely voiced a desire, she sought at once to appease it. Whatever she possessed was yours for the asking.

What a change from Karen's establishment! The meals alone were enough to put one in a state of divine contentment. Her rooms adjoined ours but the door between was never locked. We wandered to and fro at ease, as if we were sharing a common ménage.

After breakfast I would usually take a walk, to work up an appetite for lunch. It was early Fall and the weather was superb. Often I strolled to the Park and flopped on a bench to doze in the bright sunshine. A marvellous sense of well-being possessed me. No worries of any kind, no responsibilities, no intrusions. Completely my own master, and waited on hand and foot by two eager, beautiful women who treated me like a peacock. Faithfully each day I wrote for an hour or two; the rest of the day was —fuck, feast and fun. What I wrote must have been of slight consequence—probably dreams and fantasies. It was too good a life to inspire serious work. I wrote to keep my hand in, nothing more. Now and then I knocked out something expressly for Marjorie's benefit, something whimsical and humorous, which I would read aloud at table between sips of cognac or some precious liqueur from her inexhaustible stock. It wasn't difficult to please either of them. All they demanded of me was to go through the motions.

'I wish I knew how to write,' Marjorie would say sometimes. (To her the art of writing was sheer magic.) She wondered, for example, where I got my ideas. 'You hatch them, like eggs,' I said. 'And those big words, Henry?' She doted on them, mispronounced them deliberately, rolled them over on her tongue lasciviously. 'You sure can juggle them,' she'd say. Sometimes she made up a tune in which she introduced these jaw-breakers. What a pleasure it was to hear her hum a tune—or whistle softly! Her sex seemed to move right up into her throat. Often she burst out laughing in the midst of a tune. Such laughter! As if she were getting her ashes hauled.

Sometimes of an evening I would go for a solitary promenade. I knew the neighbourhood intimately, having lived for a time right opposite the Park. Only a few blocks away—Myrtle Avenue was the boundary line—the slums commenced. After strolling through the sedate quarters it was a thrill to cross the line, to mingle with Italians, Filipinos, Chinese and other 'undesirables'. A pungent odour invested the poor quarters: it was compounded of cheese, salami, wine, punk, incense, cork, dried fish skins, spices, coffee, stale horse piss, sweat and bad plumbing. The shops were full of nostalgic wares familiar from childhood. I loved the funeral parlours (the Italian ones especially), the religious shops, the junk shops, the delicatessen stores, the stationery stores. It was like passing from a cool, immaculate mausoleum into the thick of life. The tongues employed had a musical quality, even when it was nothing but an exchange of oaths. People dressed differently, each one in his own crazy fashion. The horse and wagon were still in evidence. Children were everywhere, amusing themselves with that lusty exuberance which only the children of the poor display. There were no longer the stereotyped wooden faces of the born American but racial types, all saturated with character.

If I kept walking in certain direction I would come eventually to United States Street. It was somewhere near here that my friend Ulric was born. Here it was easy to wander astray; in every direction fascinating detours opened up. At night one walked with dream feet. Everything appeared to be up-ended, churned, tossed about. Sometimes I found myself winding up at Borough Hall, sometimes in Williamsburg. Always within striking distance were the Navy Yard, fantastic Wallabout Market, the sugar refineries, the big bridges, roller mills, grain elevators, foundries, paint factories, tombstone yards, livery stables, glaziers, saddlers, grill works, canneries, fish markets, slaughterhouses, tin factories—a vast conglomeration of workaday horrors over which hung a pall of smoke impregnated with the stench of burning chemicals, rotting flesh and seared metals.

If I thought of Ulric on such walks I thought also of the Middle Ages, and of Breughel the Elder, and Hieronymus Bosch, or of Petronius Arbiter, Lorenzo the Magnificent, Fra Lippo Lippi . . .

to say nothing of the Seven Dwarfs, Swiss Family Robinson and Sinbad the Sailor. Only in a God-forsaken hole like Brooklyn could one assemble the monsters, freaks and anomalies of this world. At the Star Theatre, which was given over to burlesque, one rubbed elbows with the hairy denizens of this incredible region. The performance was always on a level with the almost extinct imagination of the audience. No holds were barred, no gestures considered too indecent, no filth too slimy to be rippled off the tongue of the comedian. It was always a visual and aural feast such as Peeping Tom craves. I was thoroughly at home in this broth: Smut was my maiden name.

Arriving home after one of these promenades I would usually find Marjorie and Mona waiting for me, the table spread for a light repast. What Marjorie called a 'snack' consisted of cold cuts, salami, head cheese, olives, pickles, sardines, radishes, potato salad, caviar, Swiss cheese, coffee, a German cheese cake or apple strudel, with Kummel, Port or Malago to top it off. Over the coffee and liqueurs we would sometimes listen to John Jacob Niles' recordings. Our favourite was 'I Wonder As I Wander', sung in a clear, highpitched voice with a quaver and a modality all his own. The metallic clang of his dulcimer never failed to produce ecstasy. He had a voice which summoned memories of Arthur, Merlin, Guinevere. There was something of the Druid in him. Like a psalmodist, he intoned his verses in an ethereal chant which the angels carried aloft to the Glory seat. When he sang of Jesus, Mary and Joseph they became living presences. A sweep of the hand and the dulcimer gave forth magical sounds which caused the stars to gleam more brightly, which peopled the hills and meadows with silvery figures and made the brooks to babble like infants. We would sit there long after his voice had faded out, talking of Kentucky where he was born, talking of the Blue Ridge mountains and the folk from Arkansas. Marjorie, always, a-humming and a-whistling, would suddenly break out into song, some simple folk tune which one knew from the cradle.

It was the glorious month of September, described in the Old Farmer's Almanac as the time when 'the porcupines take their fill of the ripening apples and the deer munch the fine green beans one has tended so carefully'. A lazy time and not a thing to worry about. From our window we looked down on a row of well-kept gardens studded with majestic trees. Everything in apple-pie order, everything serene. The leaves were turning gold and red, flecking the lawns and pavements with fiery splashes. Often I sat at the breakfast table, which commanded a view of the back-yards, and fell into a deep reverie. On certain days not a leaf or twig stirred; there was only the splendour of sunlight and the incessant drone of insects. It was hard to believe sometimes that not so very long ago I had lived in this neighbourhood with another wife, that I had pushed a baby carriage up and down the streets, or carried the child to the park and watched it romp in the grass. Sitting there by the window, my past grew dim and faint; it was more like another incarnation. A delicious feeling of detachment would overcome me and I would swim back, leisurely, playfully, like a dolphin, into the mysterious waters of imaginary pasts. In such moods, catching a glimpse of Mona flitting about in her Chinese shift, I would look at her as if she were a total stranger. Sometimes I even forgot her name. Looking away, I would suddenly feel a hand on my shoulder. 'What are you thinking about?' I can hear her say. (Even now I remember vividly how from far, far away her voice seemed to come.) '*Thinking . . . thinking?* I wasn't thinking of anything.' She would remark that there was such a concentrated look in my eyes. 'It's nothing,' I would say, 'I was just dreaming.' Then Marjorie would chime in: 'He's thinking about what he's going to write, I guess.' And I would say, 'That's it, Marjorie.' Whereupon they would steal away and leave me to myself. Immediately I would fall back into a state of reverie.

Suspended three storeys above the earth, I had the illusion of floating in space. The lawns and shrubs on which my gaze was riveted would vanish. I saw only what I was dreaming of, a perpetual shifting panorama as evanescent as mist. Sometimes queer figures, garbed in the costumes of the period, floated before my eyes—incredible personages such as Samuel Johnson, Dean Swift, Thomas Carlyle, Izaak Walton. Sometimes it was as if the smoke of battle suddenly rolled away and men in armour, chargers sumptuously caparisoned, stood lost and bewildered amidst the slain of the battle-field. Birds and animals also played their part in these still visions, particularly the mythological monsters, with all of whom I seemed to be on familiar terms. There was nothing too outlandish, nothing too unexpected, about these apparitions to rout me out of my nothingness. I wandered with motionless feet through the vast halls of memory, a sort of living cinematograph. Now and then I relived an experience which I had had as a child: A moment, for instance, when one sees or hears something for the first time. In such instances I was both the child experiencing this wonder and the nameless individual observing the child. Sometimes I enjoyed that rare experience of synchronizing my thought and being with the tenuous fragment of a dream long, long forgotten, and, rather than pursue it, rather than fix it objectively in image and sensation, I would toy with the fringes of it, bathe in its aura, so to say, grateful merely that I had caught up with it, that I had scented its immortal presence.

To this period belongs a night dream which I recorded with scrupulous accuracy. I feel it is worth transcribing. . . .

'It opened with a nightmarish vertigo which sent me hurtling from a dizzy precipice into the warm waters of the Caribbean. Down, down I swirled, in great spiral curves which had no beginning and promised to end in eternity. During this ceaseless descent a bewildering and enchanting panorama of marine life unrolled before my eyes. Enormous sea dragons wriggled and shimmered in the powdered sunlight, which filtered through the green waters; huge cactus plants with hideous roots floated by, followed by sponge-like coral growths of curious hues, some sullen as ox-blood, some a brilliant vermilion or soft lavender. Out of this teeming aquatic life poured myriads of animalcules, resembling gnomes and pixies; they bubbled up like gorgeous flux of star-dust in the tail-sweep of a comet.

'The roaring in my ears gave way to plangent, verdant melodies; I became aware of the tremors of the earth, of poplars and birches shrouded in ghost-like vapours, bending gracefully to the caress of fragrant breezes. Stealthily the vapours roll away. I am trudging through a mysterious forest alive with screaming monkeys and birds of tropical plumage. There is a quiver of arrows in my girdle and over my shoulder a golden bow.

'Penetrating deeper and deeper into the wood the music becomes more celestial, the light more golden; the earth is carpeted with soft, blood-red leaves. The beauty of it is such I swoon away. On awakening the forest has vanished. To my befuddled senses it seems that I am standing before a pale, towering canvas on which a pastoral scene of great dignity is depicted: it resembles one of those murals by Puvis de Chavannes in which the grave, seraphic void of dream is materialized. Sedate, sombre wraiths move to and fro with a measured, haunting elegance which made our earthly movement appear grotesque. Stepping in the canvas I follow a quiet path which leads towards the retreating line of the horizon. A full-hipped figure in a Grecian robe, balancing an urn, is directing her footsteps toward the turret of a castle dimly visible above the crest of a gentle knoll. I pursue the undulating hips until lost in a dip beyond the crest of the knoll.

'The figure with the urn has disappeared. But now my eyes are rewarded by a more mystifying sight. It is as if I had arrived at the very end of this habitable earth, at that magic fringe of the ancient world where all the mysteries and gloom and terror of the universe are concealed. I am hemmed in by a vast enclosure whose limbs are only faintly discernible. Ahead of me loom the walls of a hoary castle bristling with spears. Pennants blazoned with incredible emblems flutter ominously above the crenellated battlements. A sickly fungus growth chokes the broad sweeps leading out from the terrifying portals; the gloomy casements are bespattered with the remains of great carrion birds whose foul stench is unbearable.

'But what awes and fascinates me most is the colour of the

castle. It is a red such as my eyes have never beheld. The walls are of a warm blood-like hue, the tint of rich corpuscles laid bare by the knife. Beyond the frontier walls loom more spectacular parapets and battlements, turrets and spires, each receding rank steeped in a more awesome red. To my terrified eyes the whole spectacle takes on the proportions of a monstrous butchers' orgy dripping with gore and excrement.

'In fear and horror I avert my gaze an instant. In that fleeting moment the scene changes. Instead of poisonous fungus and the scabby carcasses of vultures there is spread before me a rich mosaic of ebony and cinnamon, shadowed by deep purple panoplies from which cascades of cherry blossoms slither away in billowy heaps on a chequered court. Within reach, almost, stands a splendid couch festooned with royal drapes and smothered in pillows of gossamer loveliness. On this sumptuous divan, as if languidly anticipating my arrival, reclines my wife Maude. It is not a wholly familiar Maude, though I recognize at once her tiny, bird-like mouth. I wait expectantly for her usual inanities. Instead there issues from her throat a flood of dark music which sends the blood hammering to my temples. It is only at this moment that I realize she is nude, feel the vague, splendid pain of her loins. I bend over to lift her in my arms but recoil immediately in full horror as I perceive a spider slowly crawling over her milky breast. As if possessed, I flee in panic towards the castle walls.

'And now a strange thing happens. To the groaning and creaking of rusty hinges the towering gates swing slowly open. Swiftly I race up the narrow path which leads to the foot of the spiral staircase. Frantically I climb the iron steps—higher and higher, without ever seeming to reach the top. Finally, when it seems as if my heart will break from exertion, I find myself at the summit. The ramparts and battlements, the casements and turrets of the mysterious castle, are no longer there beneath me. Before my eyes there unfolds a black, volcanic waste furrowed with innumberable chasms of bottomless depth. Nothing of plant or vegetable life is visible. Petrified limbs of gigantic proportions, carbuncled with glistering mineral crustations, lie sprawled about over the void. Gazing more intently I perceive with horror that there *is* a life down below there—a slimy, crawling life which reveals itself in huge coils that wind and unwind about the crazy, dead limbs.

'Suddenly I have a presentiment that the towering steeple up which I had climbed in panic is crumbling at the base, that this immense spire is teetering at the edge of the loathsome abyss, threatening at any moment to hurl me into a shattering annihilation. For just the fraction of a moment there is an eerie stillness, then faintly, so faintly as to be almost inaudible, there come the sound of a voice—a human voice. Now it rings out boldly, with a weird, moaning accent, only to die out immediately, as if it had been strangled down in the sulphurous depths below. Instantly the tower lurches violently; as it swoops out over the void, like a drunken ship, a babble of voices breaks forth. Human voices, in which there are mingled the laughter of hyenas, the shrill screams of lunatics, the blood-curdling oaths of the damned, the piercing, horror-laden cackles of the possessed.

'As the rail gives way I am catapulted into space with meteroric speed. Down, down, down, my frail body stripped of its tender flesh, the entrails clawed by leprous talons, by beaks crusted with verdigris. Down, down, down, stripped and mangled by fang and tusk.

'And then it ceases, this hurtling through the void; it gives way to a sliding sensation. I am shooting down a paraffin incline supported by colossal columns of human flesh that bleed from every pore. Awaiting me is the wide, cavernous maw of an ogre champing its teeth with fierce expectancy. In an instant I shall be swallowed alive, shall perish to the hideous accompaniment of bones, my own precious bones, being crunched and splintered. . . . But just as I am about to slide into the gaping red maw the monster sneezes. The explosion is so vast that the whole universe is snuffed out. I awake coughing like a smoking bellows.'

Was it a coincidence that the very next day I should run into my friend Ulric, that he should inform me stutteringly that Maude had been to see him the day before and had begged him to speak to me, urged me to return to her? She had been pitifully abject, he told me ruefully. She had wept unceasingly from the time she entered his studio until she left. She had even got down on her knees and begged him to promise that he would leave no stone unturned to accomplish his mission.

'I told her truthfully,' said Ulric, 'that I didn't know where to find you. She said there must be a way to track you down. She begged you to forgive her as she forgave you. She said the child was asking for you constantly. She said she didn't care what you did if only you would come back. . . . I tell you, Henry, it was an ordeal. I promised her I would do all I could, knowing though that it was futile. I know it must pain you to listen to all this.' He hesitated a moment, then added: 'There's one thing I'd like to ask of you, if it's not too much—would you mind getting in touch with her yourself? I don't think I could face another session like that. It unnerves one.'

I assured him I would handle the situation myself. I told him not to worry about either of us. 'Listen, Ulric, let's forget about this for a while. Come along with me and have a spot of lunch with us. Mona will be delighted to see you again. And I think you'll like Marjorie.' His eyes lit up at once. He rubbed his juicy lips with the tip of his tongue.

'All right,' he said, slapping his thigh, 'I'll take you up on it

By golly, it's time we had a little pow-wow. Do you know, I began to wonder if I'd ever see you again. You must have lots to tell me.'

As I had surmised, Marjorie and Ulric hit it off perfectly. We had a staggering lunch, supplemented by a couple of bottles of Rhine wine. After lunch Ulric stretched himself out on the divan and took a little snooze. He explained that he had been working hard on a pineapple campaign. When he had had a little rest he might try a sketch or two. Perhaps Marjorie would be good enough to pose for him, yes? One eye was already closed. The other, frighteningly alive, rolled and lurched under his beetling brow. 'You sure eat well around here,' he said, crossing his hands over his paunch. He raised himself on one elbow and shaded his eyes with his hand. 'I say, do you mind if we were to lower that shade just a little? That's it, that's fine.' He gave a gentle sigh and sank quietly into sleep.

'If you don't mind,' I said to Marjorie, 'we'll take a little snooze ourselves. Call us when he wakes up, won't you?'

Towards evening we found Ulric sitting on the divan sipping a cool drink. He was thoroughly refreshed and in a mellow mood.

'Golly, but it's good to be with you folks again,' he said, twisting his lips and moving that one infernal eyebrow up and down. 'I've just been giving Marjorie an earful about our life in the old days.' He beamed at us affectionately, set his drink carefully down on the tabouret beside him and took a deep breath. 'You know, when I don't see you for a long time there are so many things I want to ask you about. I make hundreds of notes—about the damnedest things—and then when I see you I forget everything. . . . I say, wasn't it somewhere around here that you once had a flat with O'Mara and—what was his name again, that crazy Hindu . . . you know, the one with the long hair and the hysterical laugh?'

'You mean Govindar,' I said.

'That it. He sure was a weird one, that fella. You thought quite highly of him, I remember. Wasn't he writing a book then?'

'Several,' I said. 'One of them, a long metaphysical treatise, was really extraordinary. I only realized how good it was years later, when I began comparing his work with the soporific tomes of our distinguished numb-skulls. Govindar was a metaphysical Dadaist, I should say. But in those days he was just a joke to us. I was a pretty insensitive brute, as you know. I didn't give a shit about Hindu philosophy then; he might just as well have written his books in Sanskrit. He's back in India now—one of Gandhi's chief disciples, I'm told. Probably the most unusual Hindu I ever met.'

'You ought to know,' said Ulric, 'you sure had a flock of them on your hands. And then there were those Egyptians—especially that cock-eyed fellow. . . .'

'Skukrullah, you mean!'

'What a memory! Yes, I do remember the name now. And the other one, who wrote those flowery epistles that never ended?'

'Mohamed Eli Sarwat.'

'Christ, what names! He was a Loulou, Henry. I hope you saved those letters.'

'I'll tell you the chap I can never forget, Ulric. That was the little Jewish boy, Sid Harris. Do you remember—"Merry Xmas, President Carmichael, and be sure to ask Santa Claus to give all the messenger boys a raise!" What a guy! I can see him all over again as he sat beside me filling out the application blank. Sid Harris, born in his mother's womb, address The East Side, religion unknown, previous occupation—errand boy, shoe shine boy, fire insurance, skeleton keys, soda water jerker, life-saver, coughdrops, and Merry Xmas from the American flag waving high over the Statue of Liberty.'

'You didn't give him a job, I suppose?'

'No, but he used to call regularly every week and fill out an application blank. Always smiling, whistling, shouting Merry Xmas to everyone. I used to throw him a quarter to go to the movies. Next day I'd get a letter telling me what he had seen, whether he had sat in the third or fourth row, how many peanuts he ate, what the next programme would be, and whether there were fire extinguishers or not. At the end he would sign his name in full: Sidney Roosevelt Harris, or Sidney R. Harris, or S. Roosevelt Harris, or S. R. Harris, or just plain Sidney—one after the other, one under the other, followed of course by the perennial Xmas greeting. Sometimes he would add a postscript saying that he preferred to be a night messenger, or a telegraph operator, or just a manager. He was a nuisance, of course, but I enjoyed his visits—they gave me a lift for the day. Once I gave him an old trumpet which I had found in a rubbish bag. It was a battered looking thing and all the stops were eaten away. He polished it up, tied it around his shoulder, with a piece of string, and came trooping into my office one morning, looking like the Angel Gabriel. Nobody had noticed him coming up the stairs. There were about fifty boys waiting to be hired, the telephones were ringing like mad—one of those days when I thought I would burst a blood vessel. Suddenly there came a tremendous blast. I nearly fell off my perch. There he stood, little Sidney, trying to blow taps. Immediately there was pandemonium. Before we could collar him, Sidney began to sing the Star Spangled Banner; the other boys joined in of course, jeering, laughing, cursing, upsetting the inkwells, throwing the pens around like darts, marking the walls with chalk, and in general raising ructions. We had to clear the office out and lock the door downstairs. Outside, that damned trumpet was blasting away. . . . He was completely cuckoo, Sidney, but in a delightful way. I could never get angry

269

with him. I tried to find out where he lived, but it was impossible. He probably didn't have a home, he probably slept in the streets. In winter he wore a man's coat that reached right to the ground —and woollen mittens, b'Jesus! He never wore a hat or a cap, unless as a joke. Once, in mid-winter, he made his appearance in that grotesque overcoat and mittens—and on his head was a huge straw hat, a sort of Mexican sombrero with a gigantic cone-like crown. He came up to my desk, made a low bow, and doffed his huge straw hat. It was filled with snow. He shook the snow out on my desk and then scurried away like a rat. At the door he stood a moment and shouted "Merry Xmas and don't forget to bless President Carmichael!"'

'I certainly remember those days,' said Ulric, swallowing the remnants of his drink. 'I never did understand how you managed to hold your job. I'm sure there wasn't another employment manager like you in all New York.'

'In all America, you mean,' said Mona.

Ulric looked around appraisingly. 'Quite another life, this. I certainly do envy you. . . . The thing I'll always remember about this fellow'—he looked from one to the other with a melting glow —'is his inextinguishable gaiety. I don't think I've seen him depressed more than once or twice in all the time I've known him. As long as there's food and a place to flop . . . *isn't that it?*' He turned his gaze on me with unmingled affection. 'Some of my friends—you know the ones I mean—ask me occasionally if you aren't just a bit touched. I always say, "Certainly he is . . . too bad we're not all touched in the same way." And then they ask me how you support yourself—and your family. There I have to give up. . . .'

We all began to laugh rather hysterically. Ulric laughed even more heartily than the rest of us. He laughed at himself—for raising such silly issues. Mona, of course, had a different reason for laughing.

'Sometimes I think I'm living with a madman,' she blurted out, tears in her eyes.

'Yes?' said Ulric, drawling the word out.

'Sometimes he wakes up in the middle of the night and begins laughing. He's laughing about something that happened eight years ago. Something tragic usually.'

'I'll be damned,' said Ulric.

'Sometimes he laughs that way because things are so hopeless he doesn't know what to do. It worries me when he laughs that way.'

'Shucks,' I said, 'it's only another way of weeping.'

'Hear that!' said Ulric. 'Golly, I wish I could see things that way.' He raised the empty glass for Marjorie to replenish.

'It sounds silly to ask, perhaps,' he continued, gulping down a good throatful, 'but when you get into a state like that isn't it usually followed by a rather painful fit of depression?'

I shook my head. 'It might be followed by anything,' I answered. 'The important thing is to first have a good meal. That usually sets me up, gives me equilibrium.'

'You never drink to drive away a mood, do you? Pshaw! don't bother answering . . . I know you don't. That's another thing I envy about you. . . . *Just a good meal*, you say. How simple!'

'You think so?' I said. 'I wish it were. . . . Well, let's skip that! now that we have Marjorie, food is no longer a problem. I never ate better in my life.'

'I can well believe that,' said Ulric, smacking his lips. 'It's strange—with me it's often a job to work up an appetite. I'm the worrying sort, I guess. A guilty conscience, probably. I inherited all the old man's bad traits. Including this'—and he tapped the glass he was holding.

'Nonsense,' I said, 'you're just a perfectionist.'

'You ought to get married,' said Mona, knowing that this would provoke a reaction.

'That's another thing,' said Ulric, making a wry grimace. 'The way I treat that girl of mine is a crime. We've been going together for five years now—but if she dares to mention the word marriage I take a fit. The very thought of it scares the life out of me. I'm selfish enough to want her all for myself and yet I'm ruining her chances. I sometimes urge her to leave me and find someone else. That only makes things worse, of course. Then I make a half-hearted promise to marry her, which I forget about the next day, to be sure. The poor girl doesn't know where she stands.' He looked at us half-sheepishly, half-roguishly. 'I'll be a bachelor all my life, I guess. I'm selfish to the core.'

At this we all laughed uproariously.

'I think we should be thinking about dinner soon,' said Marjorie. 'Why don't you men go for a walk' Come back in an hour and dinner will be ready.'

Ulric thought it a good idea.

'You might try to find a good piece of Roquefort,' said Marjorie as we sauntered out. 'And a loaf of sour rye, if you can.'

We walked aimlessly along one of the sedate, spacious streets peculiar to this neighbourhood. We had had many walks together through similar vacuums. Ulric was remined of the days long ago when we used to promenade along Bushwick Avenue of a Sunday afternoon, hoping to catch a glimpse of the shy young girls we were in love with. It was like an Easter Parade every Sunday—from the little White Church to the reservoir near Cypress Hill cemetery. Mid-way one passed the lugubrious Catholic church of St François de Sales, situated a block or two away from Trommers' beer garden. I speak of a period before the first war, the period when in France men like Picasso, Derain, Matisse, Vlaminck and others were just becoming known. It was still the 'end of the century'. Life was easy, though we weren't aware of it. The only thought in our heads was girls. If we succeeded in stopping them long enough to chat for a few minutes we were in seventh heaven. Week-days we sometimes repeated the promenade in the evening. Then we became bolder. If we had the good fortune to encounter a couple of girls—near the reservoir or in the dark lanes of the park, or even at the confines of the cemetery—we would really attempt some daring advances. Ulric could remember the names of all of them. There was one couple he particularly remembered—Tina and Henrietta. They had been in the same class with us at graduation time, but, being somewhat backward, were two or three years older than the rest of the class. Which meant they were quite mature. And not only mature but bursting with sex. Everyone knew that they were just a pair of sluts. Tina, who was really audacious, was like one of Degas' women; Henrietta was bigger, juicier, already a wench. They were always whispering smutty stories under their breath, to the amusement of the class. Now and then they drew their dresses up above their knees—to give us a look. Or sometimes Tina would grab Henrietta by the teat and squeeze it playfully—all this in class, behind the teacher's back, of course. What more natural, therefore, than to be on the look-out for them when out for a walk in the evening? Now and then it happened. Hardly any words exchanged. Pushing them back against the iron railing, or against a tomb-stone, we slobbered all over them, fingered them, mauled them—everything but the real thing. It took older, more experienced boys to get away with that. At best we could manage a dry fuck. And go home limping, our balls aching like sixty tooth-aches.

'Did I ever tell you,' said Ulric, 'how I tried to make Miss Bairnsfeather, the graduating teacher? I mean, of course, several years after we had graduated. What a gawk I must have been! Well, you know what a juicy piece of tail she was. . . . I could never get her out of mind. So one day I wrote her a note—I had just taken a little studio and thought myself quite an artist, I can tell you—and to my surprise she answered it, urging me to look her up some time. I was so excited I nearly pissed in my pants. I called her up and invited her over to the studio. Of course I had prepared for her coming—all kinds of drinks, delicious little cakes, my canvases casually strewn about, a few nudes conspicuously placed over the divan, and so on . . . you know what I mean. What I had forgotten was the difference in age. She was still appetizing, of course, but so much of a woman now that I was intimidated. It took a bit of manoeuvring to establish the right footing. I could see that she was trying to help me, but I was so damned shy, so gauche, that I nearly had nervous prostration. After all, one doesn't just rip the pants off one's favourite teacher.'

He interrupted himself to chuckle and waggle his ears.

'Did you manage it eventually?' I asked, to help him out.

'I did indeed,' said Ulric, 'but only after a heap of drinks. By that time she was so damned eager for it that she just fished my pecker out and pulled me on top of her. I had one of those eternal hard-ons that you get sometimes from drinking. We did just about everything, I can assure you, and still it wouldn't go down. She was lying on the divan with just a blouse on, panting like a bitch. I had just washed myself with cold water, hoping that would do the trick. "Come here," she said, "I want to have a good look at that tool of yours. Ulric, why didn't I know about this when you were in my class?" I looked at her in amazement. "You mean you would have let me. . . . ?" "*Let you?*" she said—"I would have eaten you alive. Didn't the other boys ever tell you about me?" I could hardly believe my ears. All the while, Henry, I was standing over her, my prick pointing heavenward. Suddenly she sat up and grabbed it; I thought she would break it in two. Soon she was on her knees, sucking me off. Even then I didn't come. I tell you, I was getting frantic. At last I turned her over, put it in from behind—until she began to moan. Then I eased it out, dragged her off the divan and, lifting her by the middle, I walked her around the studio on her hands. It was just like pushing a wheel-barrow upside down. . . . And even that had no effect. Desperate, I sat down in the big easy chair and let her straddle me. "Just let's sit and fuck," I said. "Or don't fuck—just leave it there till it melts." We had another drink, sitting there like that, and then another, and then another. It was still a brute of a bird when we unhitched. But limp. . . . *But get this Henry.* What do you suppose she says to me at that moment?'

I looked at him blankly. Then I said: 'Don't tell me! For Christ's sake, let's turn around. I'll have to tear off a piece before we sit down to eat.'

He blinked his eyes like an owl. He was just going to open his mouth again, when I said: 'By the way, have you tackled Marjorie yet? She's dying for it, you know.'

'Not a bad idea,' said Ulric. 'Do you suppose we can manage it . . . er . . . *circumspectly?*'

'Leave it to me!'

We hastened our steps. By the time we reached the door we were almost on the double trot.

I took Mona aside and broached the idea.

'Why don't you wait till after dinner?' she suggested. 'I mean, for Marjorie and Ulric.' We closed the door after us and had a quick one while Ulric and Marjorie talked it over. When we joined them Marjorie was sitting on Ulric's lap, her skirt up over her knees.

'Why don't you get into something comfortable?' said Mona. 'Something like this,' and so saying, she opened her kimono and revealed her naked flesh.

Marjorie lost no time in following suit. Ulric and I had to don pyjamas. In this fashion we sat down to eat dinner.

A meal which is going to culminate in a sexual orgy has a way of travelling direct to the parts which need nourishment, as if directed by the little switchman who regulates the traffic throughout the autonomic system. It began with oysters on the half-shell and caviar, followed by a delicious ox-tail soup, porterhouse steak, mashed potatoes, French peas, cheese, sliced peaches and cream, all to the tune of a genuine Pommard which Marjorie had unearthed. With the coffee and liqueurs we had a second dessert — French ice cream swimming in Benedictine and whiskey. Between courses Marjorie fiddled with Ulric's pecker. The kimonos were now wide open, the breasts exposed, the belly buttons gently rising and falling. Inadvertently one of Marjorie's nipples fell into the whipped cream, giving me the opportunity to suckle her breast for a brief moment or two. Ulric tried to balance a saucer on his pecker but unsuccessfully. Everything was proceeding merrily.

Still nibbling at the tarts, cream puffs, napoleons and what not which the women had provided, we fell into an easy conversation about the good old days. The women had shifted position and were now ensconced in our laps. It took quite a bit of wriggling and jiggling before they could get themselves properly adjusted. Now and then one of us had an orgasm, fell silent for a while, then recovered with the aid of ice cream, Benedictine and whiskey.

After a time we moved from the table to the divans and, between cat winks, kept up a running conversation about the most diverse subjects. It was easy, natural talk, and no one felt embarrassed if he dropped off into a snooze in the midst of a sentence. The lights had been dimmed, there was a warm, fragrant breeze sifting through the open windows, and we were all so thoroughly sated that it didn't matter in the least what was said or what answer was given.

Ulric had dropped off to sleep during a conversation with Marjorie. He hadn't been asleep more than five minutes when he awoke with a jerk, exclaiming as if to himself: 'Golly, I thought so!' Then, realizing that he was not alone, he mumbled something inaudible and raised himself on one elbow.

'Was I asleep long?' he asked.

'About five minutes,' said Marjorie.

'That's funny. It seemed to me like hours. I had one of those dreams again.' He turned to me. 'You know, Henry, those dreams in which you try to prove to yourself that you are only dreaming.'

I had to confess that I had never had one.

Ulric could always describe his dreams in great detail. They terrified him somewhat because, to his mind, they indicated that he never really fell into a state of complete unconsciousness. In the dream his mind was even more active than in the waking state. It was his logical mind which came to the fore when asleep. It was that which disquieted him. He went on to describe the endless pains he took, when dreaming, to prove to himself that he was not awake but dreaming. He would take a heavy arm-chair, for example, and lift it high in the air with two fingers, sometimes with his brother seated in the chair. And in the dream he would say to himself: 'There, nobody can do that if he's awake—it's impossible!' And then he would perform other impossible feats, some of them quite extraordinary, such as flying through a partially-opened window and returning the same way, without disarranging his clothes or mussing his hair. Everything he did led to a suspected Q. E. D. which proved nothing, so he averred, because—'Well, I'll put it this way, Henry: to prove to yourself that you are dreaming you would have to be awake, and if you are awake you can't be dreaming, can you?'

Suddenly he recalled that what had started him dreaming was the sight of a copy of 'Transition' lying on the dresser. He reminded me that I had once loaned him a copy in which there was a wonderful passage on the interpretation of dreams. 'You know the man I mean,' he said, snapping his fingers.

'Gottfried Benn?'

'Yes, that's the fellow. A rum one, that bird. I wish I could read more of him. . . . By the way, you don't have that issue here, do you?'

'Yes, I do, Ulric me lad. Would you like to see it?'

'I tell you what,' he said, 'I wish you would read that passage aloud to us—that is, if the others don't mind.'

I found the copy of 'Transition' and turned to the page.

'Let us now turn to psychological facts. "At night all leaping fountains speak with a louder tone; my soul, too, is a leaping fountain," says Zarathustra. . . . "Into the night life seems to be exiled"—these are the famous words from Freud's *Interpretation of Dreams*—"into the night life seems to be exiled what once ruled during the day." *This sentence contains the entire modern psychology*. Its great idea is the stratification of the psyche, the geological principle. The soul has its origin and is built in strata, and what we learned before in the organic field apropos of the construction of the big brain from the anatomic-evolutionary standpoint out of vanished aeons, is revealed by the dream, revealed by the child, revealed by psychosis as a still existing reality. We carry the ancient. . . .'

'Hear, hear!' exclaimed Ulric.

'We carry the ancient peoples in our souls and when the later acquired reason is relaxed, as in the dream or in drunkenness, they emerge with their rites, their pre-logical mentality, and grant us an hour of mystic participation. When the. . . .'

'Excuse me,' said Ulric, interrupting again, 'but I wonder if we could have that passage once again?'

'Sure, why not?' I reread it slowly, allowing each phrase to sink in.

'The next sentence is a honey, too,' said Ulric. 'I almost know the damned thing by heart.'

I continued: 'When the logical superstructure is loosened, when the scalp, tired of the onslaught of the prelunar states. . . .'

'Golly! What language! Excuse me, Henry, I didn't mean to interrupt again.'

'When the scalp, tired of the onslaught of the prelunar states, opens the frontiers of consciousness about which there is always a struggle, then there appears the old, the unconscious, in the magical transmutation and identification of the "I", in the early experience of the everywhere and the eternal. The hereditary patrimony. . . .'

'*Of the middle brain!*' exclaimed Ulric. 'Jesus, Henry, what a line, that! I wish you would explain that to me a little more fully. No, not now . . . afterwards, perhaps. Excuse me.'

'The hereditary patrimony of the middle brain,' I continued, 'lies still deeper and is eager for expression: if the covering is destroyed in the psychosis there emerges, driven upward by the primal instincts, from out the primitive-schizoid sub-structure, the gigantic archaic instinctive "I", unfolding itself limitlessly through the tattered psychological subject.'

'*The tattered psychological subject!* Wow!' exclaimed Ulric. 'Thanks, Henry, that was a treat.' He turned to the others. 'Do you wonder sometimes why I'm so fond of this guy? (He beamed in my direction.) There isn't a soul who comes to my studio capable of bringing me that sort of pabulum. I don't know where he gets these things—certainly *I* never stumble on them by myself. Which only goes to show, no doubt, how differently we're geared.'

He paused a moment to fill his glass. 'You know, Henry, if you don't mind my saying so, a passage like that could have been written by you, don't you think? Maybe that's why I like Gootfried Benn so much. And that Hugo Ball is another guy—he's got something on the ball, too, *what*? The curious thing, though, is this—all this stuff, which means so much to me, I'd never have known about it if it weren't for you. How I wish sometimes that you were with me when I'm with that Virginia bunch! You know they're really not untelligent, but somehow this sort of thing seems to repel them. They look upon it as unhealthy.' He gave a wry smile. Then he looked at Marjorie and

276

Mona. 'Forgive me for dwelling on these things, won't you? I know it's not the moment to indulge in windy discussions. I was going to ask Henry something about the hereditary patrimony of the middle brain, but I guess we could leave it until some more suitable occasion. How about a stirrup cup?—and then I'll be off.'

He filled our glasses, then went over to the mantelpiece and leaned against it.

'I suppose it will always be a thing of wonder and mystery to me,' he said slowly, caressing his words, 'how we ran into each other that day on Sixth Avenue after a lapse of so many years. What a lucky day it was for me! You may not believe it, but often when I was in some weird place—like the middle of the Sahara—I would say to myself: "I wonder what Henry would have to say if he were here with me." Yes, you were often in my thoughts, even though we had lost all touch with one another. I didn't know that you had become a writer. No, but I always knew that you would become *something* or *somebody*. Even as a kid you gave off something which was different, something unique. You always made the atmosphere more intense, more sparkling. You were a challenge to all of us. Maybe you never realized that. Even now, people who met you only one continue to ask me—"How is that Henry Miller?" *That Henry Miller!* You see what I mean? They don't say that about anyone else I know. Oh well . . . you've heard this a dozen times or more, I know.'

'Why don't you get a good rest and stay the night?' said Mona.

'I'd like nothing better, but. . . .' He cocked the left eyebrow and twisted his lips. 'The scalp, tired of the onslaught of the pre-lunar states. . . . Some day we'll have to go into all this more thoroughly. Right now the gigantic archaic instinctive I is struggling upward through the schizoid sub-structure.' He left off and began shaking hands with us. 'You know,' he went on, 'I'm sure to have a fantastic dream tonight. Not *a* dream but dozens of them! I'll be slithering in the primal ooze, trying to prove to myself that I'm living the Pleocene epoch. I'll probably meet up with dragons and dinosaurs—unless the covering has been entirely destroyed by previous psychoses.' He smacked his lips, as if he had just swallowed a dozen succulent bivalves. He was on the threshold now. 'By the way, I wonder if it would be imposing on you too much to borrow that Forel book from you again? There's a passage on amorous tyranny that I'd like to reread.'

As I was going to bed I opened 'Transition' at random. My eye fell on this sentence: 'Our human biological presence carries in its body two hundred rudiments: how many the soul carries is unknown.'

How many the soul carries! With this phrase on my tongue I plunged into a profound trance. In my sleep I re-enact a scene out of life. . . . I am with Stanley again. We are walking rapidly in the dark towards the house where Maude and the little one live. Stanley is saying that it is a silly, futile thing to do, but since I wish it he will go through with it. He has the key to the front door; he keeps reassuring me that no one will be home. What I want is to see what the child's room looks like. It is ages since I have seen her and I am afraid that when I next meet her—*when?* —she won't recognize me any more. I keep asking Stanley how big she is, what she wears, how she talks, and so on. Stanley answers gruffly and brusquely, as usual. He sees no point to this expedition.

We enter the house and I explore the room minutely. Her toys intrigue me—they are lying everywhere. I begin to weep silently, as I examine her toys. Suddenly I perceive a battered old stuffed doll lying on a shalf in a corner. I tuck it under my arm and motion to Stanley to clear out. I can't utter a word, I'm shaking and sputtering.

When I awake next day the dream is still vivid with me. Out of habit I get into my old clothes, a pair of faded corduroys, a torn, frayed denim shirt, a pair of busted shoes. I haven't had a shave for two days, my head is heavy, I feel restless. The weather has changed overnight; a cold, fall wind is blowing and it threatens to rain. In listless fashion I kill the morning. After lunch I don an old cardigan jacket out at the elbows, slap my wilted hat over my ear, and set out. I've become obsessed with the idea that I must see the child again, at any cost.

I emerge from the subway a few blocks from the house and with eyes peeled I edge into the danger zone. I creep nearer and nearer to the house, until I am at the corner, only half a block away. I stand there a long while, my eyes riveted to the gate, hoping to see the little one appear any moment. It's getting chilly, I put my collar up and pull my hat down over my ears. I pace back and forth, back and forth, opposite the lugubrious Catholic church made of mossgreen stone.

Still no sign of her. Keeping to the opposite side of the street, I walk rapidly past the house, hoping that I may detect a sign of life indoors. But the curtains have been pulled to. At the corner I stop and begin pacing to and fro again. This goes on for fifteen, twenty minutes, perhaps longer. I feel lousy, itchy, crummy. Like a spy. And guilty, guilty as hell.

I've almost decided to return home when suddenly a troop of youngsters swing around the far corner opposite the church. They run wildly across the street, shouting and singing. My heart is in my throat. I have a feeling that she is among them, but from where I stand it is impossible to pick her out. Now I hasten towards the other corner. When I get there I see no signs of them. I'm baffled. I stand there like a lost soul for a few minutes, then decide to wait. After a few moments I notice a grocery store a few doors beyond the church. It's just possible they are in the store. Carefully now I ease up the side street. A bit beyond the store, on the opposite side of the street, of course, I dash up a stoop and stand at the top of the stairs, my heart pounding like mad.

I'm sure now that they are all in the grocery store. Not for a second do I take my eyes off the door. Suddenly I realize that I am rather conspicuous, standing there at the top of the stairs. I lean back against the door and try to make myself inconspicuous. I am shivering, not so much with cold as with fright. What will I do if she spots me? What will I say? What *can* I say or do? I am in such a state of funk that I am almost on the point of bolting down the steps and running away.

Just then, however, the door opens with a bang and three children dash out. They dash right into the middle of the street. One of them, seeing me standing on the stoop, suddenly grabs the others by the arm and rushes back into the store with them. I have a feeling that it was my own little one who did this. I avert my gaze for a few moments, trying to appear nonchalant and disinterested in their behaviour, as though I were waiting for someone to come out of the house from above and join me. When I look again I see a little face pressed against the window pane of the door across the way. She is looking up at me. I look at her long and hard, unable to tell if it is she or not.

She withdraws and another little one presses her nose against the glass pane. Then another and another. Then they all retreat into the depths of the store.

A panicky feeling now overcomes me. It *was* her, I am certain of it now. But why are they so shy? Or is it that they are afraid of me?

Beyond the shadow of a doubt it is fear which grips them. When she looked up at me she didn't smile. She looked intently to make sure it was me, her father, and no other.

Suddenly I realize how disgraceful is my appearance. I feel my beard, which seems to have grown an inch longer. I look at my shoes and the sleeves of my jacket. Damn it, I might well pass for a kidnapper.

Kidnapper! Her mother had probably dinned it into her that if she ever ran across me in the street she must not listen to me. 'Run home immediately and tell mamma!'

I was crushed. Slowly, painfully, like one broken and bruised, I descended the steps. When I reached the foot of the stoop the door of the grocery store was suddenly flung open and out trooped the whole group, six or seven of them. They ran as if the Devil himself were pursuing them. At the corner, though cars were speeding by, they turned obliquely and ran for the house —'our' house. It seemed to me that it was my little one who stopped in the middle of the street—just for a second—and looked around. It could have been one of the others, of course.

All I could be certain of was that she was wearing a little bonnet trimmed with fur.

I walked slowly to the corner, stood there a full minute gazing in their direction, then marched rapidly towards the subway station.

What a cruel misadventure! All the way to the subway I chided myself for my stupidity. To think that my own daughter should be frightened of me, that she should run away from me, in terror! What a pass!

In the subway I stood in front of a slot machine. I looked like a bum, a derelict. And to think that maybe I would never see her again, to think that this might be the last impression of me she would retain! Her own father crouching in a doorway, spying on her like a kidnapper. It was like a horrible cheap movie.

Suddenly I recalled my promise to Ulric—to see Maude and talk things over. Now it was impossible, utterly impossible. *Why?* I couldn't say. I knew only that it *was* so. I would never see Maude again, not if I could help it. As for the little one—I would pray, yes, pray to God, to give one more chance. I *must* see her and talk to her. *When*, though? Well, some day. Some day when she would be able to see things in a better light. I begged God not to let her hate me . . . above all, not to let her fear me. 'It's too horrible, too horrible,' I kept mumbling to myself. '*I love you so, my little one. I love you so much, so much. . . .*'

The train came along, and as the doors slid open, I began to sob. I pulled a handkerchief out of my pocket and stuffed it over my mouth. I almost ran to the vestibule where I hid myself in a corner, hoping the noise of the grinding wheels would drown my convulsive sobs.

I must have been standing there like that a few minutes, unconscious of anything but my aching misery, when I felt a hand gently pressing my shoulder. Still holding the handkerchief to my mouth, I turned around. An elderly lady dressed all in black was looking at me with a most compassionate smile.

'My dear man,' she began, in a soft, soothing voice. 'My dear man, what on earth has happened to you?'

With that I literally howled. The tears were blinding me. All I could see was a compassionate blur in front of me.

'Please, please,' she begged, 'try to control yourself!'

I continued to weep and sob. And then the train came to a halt. Some passengers entered and we were crowded against the door.

'Have you lost someone dear to you?' she asked. Her voice was so gentle, so soothing.

I shook my head by way of answer.

'Poor, dear man, I know what it is.' Again I felt the pressure of her hand.

The doors were about to close. Suddenly I dropped the

handkerchief, pushed my way through the crowd, and got out. I
ran up the steps top speed and began walking like a madman. It
had begun to rain. I walked into the rain with head down, laughing and crying. I jostled into people and was jostled back. Someone gave me a shove which sent me spinning into the gutter. I
never even looked around. I kept on with head down, the rain
running down my back. I wanted to be soaked through and
through. I wanted to be cleansed of all iniquity. Yes, that's how
I put it to myself—*cleansed of all iniquity*. I wanted to be soaked
through and through, then stabbed, then thrown into the gutter,
then flattened out by a heavy truck, then ground down into the
muck and mire, obliterated. annihilated for good and all.

10

WITH THE TURN OF the solstice a new phase of existence has opened for us—not in the sunny South but in Greenwich Village. The first stage of the underground life.

To run a speakeasy, which is what we are doing, and to live in it at the same time, is one of those fantastic ideas which can only arise in the minds of thoroughly impractical individuals.

I blush when I think of the story I concocted to wheedle the money which we required to open the place from my mother.

Ostensibly I'm the manager of this joint. I also wait on tables, fill short orders, empty the garbage, run errands, make the beds, clean house and in general make myself as useful as possible. (The one thing I shall never be able to do is to clear the rooms of smoke. The windows have to be kept closed during operations, for reasons soon to be disclosed.) The place—a typical basement flat in the poor section of the Village—is composed of three small rooms, one of them a kitchen. The windows are heavily curtained, so that even in daytime the light scarcely filters through. No doubt about it, if the enterprise proves a success we'll have tuberculosis. Our intention is to open towards evening and close when the last customer leaves, which will probably be towards dawn.

There'll be no writing done here, I can see that. I'll be lucky if I can find time to stretch my legs once a day.

Only our most intimate friends are to know that we live here —and that we are married. Everything is to be veiled in secrecy. Which means that if the bell rings and Mona happens to be out, I am not to answer it. I'm to sit quiet in the shadows until the person has gone away. If possible I am to peek out and see who it is—just in case. In case what? In case it's a detective or a bill collector. Or one of the more recent, hence ignorant and intrepid, lovers. . . .

Such is the set-up, in brief. The most we shall get out of it, I know in advance, is fret and worry. Mona, of course, is full of dreams about retiring in a few months and buying a house in the country. Pipe dreams. I'm so inoculated with them, however, that I'm immune. The only way to burst the bubble is to go through with the ideal. I have *another* flock of dreams, but I've sense enough to keep them under my hat.

It's amazing the number of friends we have, all of whom have promised to be on hand for the opening night. Some who were mere names to me before—all from Mona's retinue—have been helping us put things to rights. Cedric Ross, I discover, is a fop with a monocle who pretends to be a pathobiologist; Roberto de Sundra, one of the 'heavy lovers', is a Chilian student reputed to be fabulously rich; George Innes, an artist who indulges in opium bouts occasionally, is a superb fencer; Jim Driscoll, whom I have seen in the ring, is a wrestler with intellectual pretensions; Trevelyan, an English writer with a past, is a remittance man; Caccicacci, whose parents are supposed to own a marble quarry in Italy, is a clown with a flair for telling incredible stories.

And then there's Baronyi, the most ingratiating of all, who simply cannot do enough, to make the venture a success. A publicity man, he styles himself.

To my great surprise, the night before the opening, two ancient lovers appeared simultaneously, neither knowing the other, of course. I mean Carruthers and that man Harris who had paid a princely sum for the privilege of breaking my wife's hymen. The latter arrived in a Rolls-Royce with a chorus girl on either arm. Carruthers also had two girls with him, both former friends of Mona's.

Of course all my old cronies have sworn to be on hand the opening night, including O'Mara who has just returned from the South. Cromwell is also expected, though he may only be able to stay for a few minutes. As for Rothermel, Mona is trying to persuade him to stay away—he blabbers too much. I'm wondering if Sheldon will show up—just by chance. Certainly one or two of the millionaires will make an appearance—the shoe manufacturer possibly, or the lumber king.

Will we have enough liquor to go round?—that's our primary concern. Marjorie has promised to let us tap her private stock —in a pinch.

The understanding, between Mona and myself, is this— should either of us happen to get drunk the other will remain sober. Of course neither of us is a booze artist, but just the same ... the chief problem will be—how to get rid of the drunks. The cops will be sitting on our necks, no use fooling ourselves about that. The natural thing, under the circumstances, would be to put something aside for hush money. But Mona is certain we can get better, bigger protection. Talks about Rothermel's friends from the swamp lands—judges, politicians, bankers, ammunition makers.

That Rothermel! I'm dying to set eyes on him. . . .

There's one little detail about the new establishment which pleases me no end that's the ice-box. It's filled with delicious edibles, and it's got to be kept filled no matter what happens. I keep opening and closing the damned contraption just to gaze at all the wonderful good things to eat. The bread is excellent too —Jewish bread from the East Side. When I get bored I'll sit down all by my lonesome and enjoy a little snack. What better than a caviar sandwich on black bread smeared with sweet butter—at 2.00 a.m.? With a glass of Chablis or Riesling to wash it down, *certes*. And to round it off, perhaps a dish of strawberries floating in sour cream, or if not strawberries then blackberries or huckleberries or blueberries or raspberries. I see Halvah and Baklava too. Goody goody! And on the shelf Kirschwasser, Strega, Benedictine, Chartreuse Verte. As for the whiskey—we have a dozen different brands—it leaves me cold. The beer likewise. Beer and whiskey—they're for the dogs. *C'est-à-dire —les clients.*

We also have on hand, I notice, an excellent stock of cigars, all choice brands. *For the customers.* Now and then I enjoy a cigar myself—a fine Havana, say. But I can also do without them. To really enjoy a cigar one has to be at peace with the world, that's my belief. However, I'm sure the customers will be stuffing my pockets with them.

No, we won't lack for food and drink, that's certain. But exercise, fresh air. . . . ? I'm already feeling pale about the gills.

All we lack, frankly, is a cash register. I see myself running to the bank daily with a satchel full of bills and coins. . . .

The opening night came off with a bang. We must have taken in close to five hundred dollars. For the first time in my life I was really lousy with money: every pocket, including my vest pockets, was stuffed with bills. Carruthers, who arrived with two new girls this time, must have pissed away a good hundred dollars standing treat to all our friends. Two of the millionaires showed up also, but they kept to themselves and left early. Steve Romero, whom I hadn't seen for ages, showed up with his wife; he looked as good as ever, the Spanish bull through and through. From Steve I got an earful about my cosmodemonic friends, most of them still on the job apparently, and all playing the horses on the side to make ends meet. I was delighted to hear that Spivak had fallen from favour, been transferred to some dinky place in South Dakota. Hymie, I learned, had become an insurance agent; he'd be down some night soon, some quiet night when we could have a good talk, the three of us. As for Costigan, the knuckle-duster, the poor bugger was in a sanatorium—had been taken down suddenly with galloping consumption.

Around midnight MacGregor arrived, had a few drinks on the house, and left in short order. Wasn't at all impressed. Couldn't understand, he said, how a man of my intelligence could fall for such a dumb racket. 'Too lazy to take a job but doesn't mind serving drinks all night . . . ha ha! ha ha!' On leaving he stuck a card in my mitt. 'If you get in a jam, remember, I'm a lawyer. Don't go hiring some shyster who's full of promises!'

We informed each one as he left that if he sent any friends around he was to give them the pass-word: *Fratres Semper*. (Naturally none of them remembered it.) We also warned each one all over again to park his car a block or two away.

The first thing I discovered about the new job was that it was hard on the feet—and on the eyes. The smoke was unbearable: by midnight my eyes were like two burnt cinders. When we finally got to bed and pulled back the blankets the smell of beer, wine and tobacco was overpowering. In addition to smoke and liquor I thought I detected the odour of smelly feet. However, we fell in a trance immediately. In my sleep I was still serving drinks and sandwiches, still making change for the customers.

I had intended to get up at noon the next day, but it was almost four o'clock when we tumbled out of bed, more dead than alive. The joint looked like the wreck of the Hesperus.

'You'd better take a walk and eat your breakfast out,' I urged. 'I'll fix myself something as soon as I've tidied up a bit.'

It took me about an hour and a half to create even a semblance of order. By then I was too weary to think of making breakfast for myself. I poured myself a glass of orange juice, lit a cigarette, and waited for Mona to return. The customers would be showing up any minute now. It seemed to me that the last one had left only a few minutes ago. Outdoors it was already dark.

The rooms still reeked of stale smoke and stale drinks.

I opened the windows back and front to create a draught, only to find myself coughing fit to bust a lung. The toilet was the place to repair to. I took the orange juice with me, sat down on the toilet seat, and lit another cigarette. I felt used up.

Presently there was a knock on the toilet door. Mona, of course. 'What's wrong with you?' she cried. I had resumed my seat, the glass in one hand, the cigarette in the other.

'I'm resting,' I said. 'Besides, it's too draughty out there.'

'Get your things on and take a good walk. I'll take over now. Here are some strudels for you and a charlotte russe. I'll have breakfast ready for you when you get back.'

'*Breakfast*?' I yelled. 'Do you know what time it is? It's time for *dinner*, not breakfast. Jesus, I'm all topsy-turvy.'

'You'll get used to it. It's lovely out . . . hurry! So soft and balmy. Like a second Spring.'

I made ready to go. It seemed crazy to set out for a morning walk just as the moon was coming up.

Suddenly I thought of something. 'You know what? It's too late to go to the bank.'

'The bank?' She stared at me vacantly.

'The bank, yes! That's where to put the money we rake in.'

'Oh *that*! I forgot all about the money.'

'Well I'll be damned, you forgot about *that*! That's just like you.'

'Go on, take your walk. You can bank the money tomorrow— or the day after. It won't melt.'

Strolling along I kept fingering the money. It made me itchy. Finally, like a thief I made for a quiet spot where I could disgorge. Almost five hundred dollars did I say? I had *over* five hundred! So elated was I that I almost ran back to show it to Mona.

Instead of running, however, I sauntered along at an easy pace. I forgot for a little while that I was in search of breakfast. After a time I decided that I must have miscalculated. Keeping my eyes peeled, I stopped in the shadow of an abandoned house and fished the money out again. This time I counted it out very extra careful, as they say. It came to exactly five hundred and forty three dollars and sixty-nine cents. I was electrified. And a bit frightened, too, walking around in the dark with a sum like that on me. Better make to the bright lights, I told myself. Keep moving, man, or somebody will sneak up on you from behind!

Money! And they talk about benzedrine. . . . For a shot in the arm give me money any time!

I kept myself on the move. My feet weren't touching the ground: I was rolling along on roller-skates, my eyes peeled, my ears laid well back against the sides of my head. I was that dizzy, that full of pep, that I could have counted up to a million and back without missing a digit.

Gradually a feeling of hunger overtook me. A powerful hunger it was. I broke into a dog trot as I headed back for the joint, one hand pressed against my breast pocket where the wallet was stowed away. My menu was already composed for me: a light omelette with cold lox, some cream cheese and jam, some Jewish rolls with bird-seed covered with slabs of sweet butter, coffee and thick fresh cream, a dish of strawberries with or without sour cream. . . .

At the front door I found I had forgotten the key. I rang the bell, my mouth watering with the thought of the breakfast coming. It took several minutes for Mona to answer the bell. She came to the door with a finger over her lips. 'Shhhhhh! Rothermel's inside. Wants to speak to me alone. Come back in about an hour.' She scooted off.

Dinner hour—for ordinary people—was well advanced and here was I looking for breakfast. In despair I went to a lunch wagon and ordered ham and eggs. That down, I strolled over to Washington Square, flopped on a bench and dreamily watched the pigeons gobbling up crumbs. A panhandler came along and without thinking I gave him a dollar bill. He was so astounded that he stood there, right in front of me, examining the bill as if it were counterfeit money. Convinced finally that it was the real thing, he thanked me warmly and—just like a sparrow—hopped away.

I killed a good hour and then some before returning—just to make certain the coast was clear. 'You'd better get some ice,' were the first words that greeted me. I set off again, to look for ice.

'*When*,' I asked myself, 'is the day going to begin?'

It took some scouting around to find the ice man. He lived in a cellar near Abingdon Square. A big surly brute of a Pole he was. Said he had made two attempts to deliver the ice but no one had answered the bell. Then he looked me up and down, as if to say—'how will you get it home?' His attitude told me clearly enough—crystal clear, in fact—that he had no intention of helping me deliver it a third time.

With five hundred odd bucks in my pocket I saw no reason why I shouldn't hail a cab, ice and all. . . .

During the brief trip back to the house I had some strange recollections, thoroughly irrelevant too. At any rate, there in my mind, as clear and vivid as could be, was Mr Meyer, an old friend of my parents. He was standing at the top of the stairs waiting to greet us. Looked exactly as I had known him when I was a boy of eight or nine. Only now I realized what I had never suspected then—that he was the image of 'Gloomy Gus' from the comic strip.

We shake hands, exchange greetings, and enter. Now Mr Meyer's wife enters the picture. She is coming out of the kitchen, wiping her hands on the spotless white apron she wears. A frail little woman, neat, quiet, orderly. She speaks to my parents in German, a more refined, more pleasing German than I am accustomed to hearing at home. What I can't get over is the fact that she is old enough to be Mr Meyer's mother. They stand there arm in arm, exactly like mother and son. As a matter of fact she was Mr Meyer's mother-in-law before she married him. Yes, even as a boy, that fact had registered deep. Katie, her daughter, had been a beautiful young woman. Mr Meyer had fallen in love with the daughter and married her. A year later Katie died, quietly and quickly. Mr Meyer couldn't get over it. But a year later he married his wife's mother. And to all effects they got along beautifully. Briefly, that was the situation. But there was something else connected with this remembrance which stirred me even more deeply. Why was it that every time we visited the Meyers I had the conviction that it was in their living room I once sat in a high chair reciting German verses, while above me in a cage near the window a nightingale sang. My mother always insisted that this was impossible. 'It must have been some other place, Henry!' Yet each time we visited the Meyers I walked instinctively to a certain spot in the living room, where the bird cage had once hung, and tried to reconstruct the original scene. To this very day, if I but close my eyes and concentrate, I am able to relive this unforgettable moment.

However, as Strindberg says in his *Inferno*—'there is nothing I dislike more than calf's head with brown butter.' Mrs Meyer always served parsnips with these meals. From the very first I disliked parsnips, especially buttered parsnips. Every time I taste one now I think of Mr Meyer sitting opposite me at the head of the table, his face wreathed in melancholy resignation. My mother used to say of him that he was such a good man, so quiet, thoughtful and considerate. To me he always smelled of the grave. Never one did I see him smile. His brown eyes were ever swimming in a dolorous fat. Twiddling his thumbs, he would sit motionless and expressionless with hands folded in his lap. When he spoke it was if from far off and deep down in the bowels of the earth. He must have been like that even when he was in love with Katie, his wife's daughter.

Ah, but he was indeed a strange man! Peaceful and serene as their home life appeared to be, nevertheless one day this lugubrious soul up and disappeared. Never a word from him. Not a trace did he leave behind. Naturally, everyone thought he had committed suicide. Not I. I thought then, as I do now, that he simply wanted to be alone with his sorrow. The only thing he had taken with him was the photograph of his Katie which used to stand on the dresser. Not a stitch of clothing . . . not even a handkerchief.

Strange recollection. Followed immediately by another, equally baroque. Now it's my father's sister, the one who married my Uncle Dave. Aunt Millie is lying on a couch in the middle of the room, their parlour. I am sitting on the piano stool, only a foot or two away from her, with a fat music roll on my lap. (My mother has sent me to New York to play for my Aunt Millie who is dying of cancer.) Like all my father's sisters, Aunt Millie has a sweet, beautiful nature. I ask her what she would like me to play for her. She says—'Anything'. I pick out a sheaf of music—The Orange Blossom Waltz—and I play it for her. When I turn around she is gazing up at me with a beatific smile. 'That was lovely, Henry,' she says. 'Won't you play another?' I pick out The Midnight Fire Alarm, and I rattle that off. Again the same warm look of appreciation, the same plea to continue. I go through my whole repertoire—The Chariot Race, Poet and Peasant, The Burning of Rome, and so on. What drivel to be hammering out to someone dying of cancer! But Aunt Millie is in raptures. She thinks I am a genius. 'You will be a great musician some day,' she whispers when I am leaving.

It's at this point that the cab stops and I unload the ice. The genius! ('*Il est l'afiection et l'avenir.*') Eight p.m. and the genius

288

is just about to begin the day's work—serving drinks and sandwiches. In a good mood, however. Somehow, the recollection of these odd incidents from the warm past awakens the thought that I am still a writer. I may not have time to set them down on paper now, but I will one day.

(It's now a good twenty years later. The 'genius' never forgets. '*Il est l'amour et l'éternité*.')

I am obliged to make two trips through the rooms with a block of ice on my shoulder. To the customers—there are eight or ten on hand—it seems amusing. One of them offers to help me. It's Baronyi, the promoter. Says he must} have a long talk with me soon. Buys me a drink to cement the deal. We stand there in the kitchen chatting, my eyes riveted to a spot just above his head where I have pasted a shapshot of my daughter, her head set off by a little bonnet trimmed with fur. Baronyi drones away. I nod my head and throw him a smile now and then. What is she doing at this moment, I wonder? Has she been tucked to bed already? And Maude, still practising like a madwoman, I suppose. Liszt, always Liszt, to warm her fingers up. . . . Someone asks for a pastrami sandwich on rye bread. Baronyi immediately dives into the ice-box and gets out the pastrami. Then he slices the bread. I'm still riveted to the spot.

From far away I hear him telling me that he'd like to play me a game of chess some night. I nod and absent-mindedly make myself a sandwich which I begin to much between sips of Dubonnet.

Now Mona sticks her head in. Wants to tell me that George Inness would like a few words with me—when I can spare the time. He's sitting in the bedroom with his friend Roberto, the Chilean.

'What's on his mind?' I ask. 'Why does everyone want to talk to *me*?'

'Because you're a writer, I guess.' (What an answer!)

In a corner, near the front window, Trevelyan and Caccicacci are huddled. They are having a furious argument. Trevelyan has the features of a vulture. The other is like a clown out of the Italian opera. A strange pair to be hobnobbing together.

In another corner sit Manuel Siegfried and Cedric Ross, two discarded lovers. They stare at each other gloomily. Now Marjorie comes bouncing in, her arms loaded with packages. Immediately things brighten up. In a few minutes, like trains pulling in, Ned arrives, then O'Mara, then Ulric himself. The old club spirit, what! *Frates Semper!*

Everyone has now become acquainted with his neighbour. All talking at once. And drinking! That's my job, to see that no one is without a fresh glass. Now and then I sit down to have a little chat with someone. But what I enjoy most is waiting on the customers, running to and fro, lighting their cigars, making up short orders, uncorking the bottles, emptying the ash-trays, passing the time of the day with them and that sort of thing. The constant activity enables me to enjoy my own private thoughts. Seems I'm due to write another big book in my head. I study eyebrows, the curve of a lip, gestures, intonations. It's as though I'm rehearsing a play and the customers ad-libbing. Catching a little phrase on my way to the kitchen, I round it out into a sentence, a paragraph, a page. If someone asks a question of his neighbour I answer it for him—in my head. Droll effects. Really exciting. Now and then I have a little drink or another sandwich on the q.t.

The kitchen is my realm. In there I dream away whole passages of destiny and causality.

'Well, Henry,' says Ulric, cornering me at the sink, 'how goes it? This is to your success!' He raises his glass and downs it. 'Good stuff! You must give me the address of your bootlegger later.' We have a little drink together while I fill a couple of orders. 'Golly,' he says, 'it sure does look funny to see you with that carving knife in your hand.'

'Not a bad way to pass the time,' I remark. 'Gives me a chance to think of what I will write some day.'

'You don't mean it!'

'Of course I do. It's not *me* making these sandwiches—it's someone else. This is like sleep-walking. . . . How about a nice piece of salami? You can have the Jewish kind or the Italian. Here, try these olives—*Greek* olives, what! You know, if I were simply a bartender I'd be miserable.'

'Henry,' he says, 'you couldn't be miserable no matter what you were doing. You'll always find life interesting, even when you're at the bottom. You know, you're like those mountain climbers who, when they fall into a deep crevasse, see the stars twinkling overhead . . . in broad daylight. You see stars where others see only warts or blackheads.'

He gave me one of those knowing, tender smiles, then suddenly assumed a serious mien. 'I thought I ought to tell you something,' he began. 'It's about Ned. I don't know if he's told you, but he lost his job recently. *Drink*. He can't take it. I tell you this so that you'll keep an eye on him. He thinks the world of you, as you know, and he'll probably be here frequently. Try to keep him in hand, won't you? Alcohol is poison to him. . . .'

'By the way,' he continued, 'do you suppose I might bring my chess set down some evening? I mean, when things quiet down a bit. There'll be nights when nobody will turn up. Just give me a ring. By the way, I've been reading that book you lent me—on the history of the game. An astonishing book. We must go one day to the Museum and have a look at those medieval chess boards, eh?'

'Sure,' I said, 'if we ever manage to get up by noon!'

One by one my friends filed into the kitchen to chat with me. Often they served the customers for me. Sometimes the customers came to the kitchen themselves to ask for a drink, or just to see what was going on.

O'Mara, of course, anchored himself in the kitchen. He talked incessantly about his adventures in the sunny South. Thought it might be a good idea to go back there, all three of us, and make a new start. 'Too bad you haven't got an extra bed here,' he said. He scratched his head thoughtfully. 'Maybe we could put a couple of tables together and spread a mattress over them?'

'Later, maybe.'

'Sure, sure,' said O'Mara. 'Any time. It was just a thought. Anyway, it's good to see you again. You'll like it down South. Good clean air there, for one thing. . . . *This is some dump!* What a come down from that other place! By the way, do you still see that crazy gink—what's his name again?'

'You mean Sheldon?'

'Yeah, Sheldon, that's the guy. He'll pop up again, just wait! You know what they'd do with a pest like that down South? They'd grab him by the seat of his pants and run him over the line—or else lynch him.

'By the way,' he continued, clutching my sleeve, 'who's that dame in the corner over there? Ask her in here, will you? I haven't had a good lay now in two weeks. She's not a Yid, is she? Not that I give a damn . . . only they cling too much. *You know.*' He gave a dirty little laugh and helped himself to a brandy.

'Henry, I'll have to tell you sometime about the gals I fooled around with down there. It was like a passage out of the *History of European Morals*. One of them, with a big colonial house and a retinue of flunkeys, was all set to hook me for life. I almost fell for it too—she was that pretty. That was in Petersburg. In Chattanooga I ran across a nymphomaniac. She nearly sucked me dry. They're all a bit queer, I tell you. Faulkner's got the low-down on them, no gain-saying it. They're full of death—or something. The worst of it is, they spoil you. I was pampered to death. That's why I came back. I've got to *do* something. Christ, but New York looks like a morgue! People must be crazy to stay here all their lives. . . .'

The girl in the corner, whom he had been eyeing steadily, gave him a sign. 'Excuse me, Henry,' he said, 'this is it,' and off he skedaddled.

It was when Arthur Raymond started coming regularly that things began to take a dramatic turn. He was usually accompanied by his bosom pal, Spud Jason, and Alameda, the latter's 'paramour'. Arthur Raymond liked nothing better than to argue and dispute, and, if possible, to consummate these sessions on the floor, with toe-holds and arm-locks. Nothing gave him more pleasure than to twist someone's arm or wrench it out of its socket. His idol was Jim Driscoll, who had lately turned professional. Perhaps it was because Jim Driscoll had once studied to be an organist that he adored him so.

As I say, Arthur Raymond was always itching for trouble. If he was unable to inveigle the others into argument and disputation he fell back on his comrade Spud Jason. The latter was a thorough-going Bohemian, a painter of considerable talent, who was going to seed. He was always ready to drop his work on the slightest excuse. His place was a pig-sty in which he and his little spit-fire, Alameda, wallowed. One could knock at his door any hour of the day or night. He was an excellent cook, always in good humour, amenable to any suggestion or proposal, no matter how fantastic. Too, he always had a bit of cash on him which he lent freely.

Mona didn't care for Spud Jason at all. And she detested 'the little Spanish bitch', as she called Alameda. However, they usually brought three or four other customers with them when they came. Certain people usually left when this gang arrived—Tony Maurer, for instance, Manuel Siegfried and Cedric Ross. Caccicacci and Trevelyan, on the other hand, always welcomed them with open arms. For them it meant free drinks and a spot of food. Besides, they enjoyed argument and dispute. They revelled in it.

Posing as a Florentine, though he had not seen Italy since he was two years old, Caccicacci could tell marvellous anecdotes about the great Florentines—all pure inventions, to be sure. Some of these anecdotes he repeated, with alterations and elaborations, the extent of these depending on the indulgence of his listeners.

One of these 'inventions' had to do with a robot of the twelfth century, the creation of a medieval scholar whose name he could never recall. Originally, Caccicacci was content to describe this mechanical freak (which he insisted was hermaphroditic) as a sort of tireless drudge, capable of performing all sorts of menial tasks, some of them rather droll. But as he continued to embellish the tale, the robot—which he always referred to as Picodiribibi—gradually came to assume powers and propensities which were, to say the least, astounding. For example, after being taught to imitate the human voice, Picodiribibi's master instructed his mechanical drudge in certain arts and sciences which were useful to the master—to wit, the memorizing of weights and measures, of theorems and logarithms, of certain astronomical calculations, of the names and positions of the constellations at any season for the previous seven hundred years. He also instructed him in the use of the saw, the hammer and chisel, the compass, the sword and pike, as well as certain primitive musical instruments, Picodirivivi, consequently, was not only a sort of *femme de ménage*, sergeant-at-arms, amanuensis and compendium of useful information, but a soothing spirit who could lull his master to sleep with weird melodies in the Doric mode. However, like the parrot in the cage, this Picodiribibi developed a fondness for speech which was beyond all bounds. At times his master had difficulty in suppressing this proclivity. The robot, who had been taught to recite lengthy poems in Latin, Greek, Hebrew and other tongues, would sometimes take it into his head to recite his whole repertoire without pausing for breath and, of course with no consideration for his master's peace of mind. And, since fatigue was utterly meaningless to him, he would occasionally ramble on in this senseless, faultless fashion, reeling off weights and measures, logarithmic tables, astronomical dates and figures, and so on, until his master, beside himself with rage and irritation, would flee the house. Other curious eccentricities manifested themselves in the course of time. Adept in the art of self-defence, Picodiribibi would engage his master's guests in combat upon the slightest provocation, knocking them about like ninepins, bruising and battering them mercilessly. Almost as embarrassing was the habit he had developed of joining in a discussion, suddenly flooring the great scholars who had come to sit at the master's feet by propounding intricate questions, in the form of conundrums, which of course were unanswerable.

Little by little, Picodirivivi's master became jealous of his own creation. What infuriated him above all, curiously enough, was the robot's tirelessness. The latter's ability to keep going twenty-four hours of the day, his gift for perfection, meaningless though it was, the ease and rapidity with which he modulated from one feat of skill to another—these qualities or aptitudes soon transformed 'the idiot', as he now began to call his invention, into a menace and a mockery. There was scarcely anything any more which 'the idiot' could not do better than the master himself. There remained only a few faculties the monster would never possess, but of these animal functions the master himself was not particularly proud. It was obvious that, if he were to recapture his peace of mind, there was only one thing to be done—destroy his precious creation! This, however, he was loath to do. It had taken him twenty years to put the monster together and make him function. In the whole wide world there was nothing to equal the bloody idiot. Moreover, he could no longer recall by what intricate, complicated and mysterious processes he had brought his labours to fruition. In every way Picodiribibi rivalled the being whose simulacrum he was. True, he would never be able to reproduce his own kind, but like the freaks and sports of human spawn, he would undoubtedly leave in the memory of man a disturbing haunting image.

To such a pass had the great scholar come that he almost lost his mind. Unable to destroy his invention, he racked his brain to determine how and where he might sequester him. For a time he thought of burying him in the garden, in an iron casket. He even entertained the idea of locking him up in a monastery. But fear, fear of loss, fear of damage or deterioration, paralyzed him. It was becoming more and more clear that, inasmuch as he had brought Picodiribibi into being, he would have to live with him forever. He found himself pondering how they could be buried together, secretly, when the time came. Strange thought! The idea of taking with him to the grave a creature which was not alive, and yet in many ways more alive than himself, terrified him. He was convinced that, even in the next world, this prodigy to which he had given birth would plague him, would possibly usurp his own celestial privileges. He began to realize that, in assuming the powers of the Creator, he had robbed himself of the blessing which death confers upon even the humblest believer. He saw himself as a shade flitting forever between two worlds— and his creation pursuing him. Ever a devout man, he now began to pray long and fervently for deliverance. On his knees he begged the Lord to intercede, to lift from his shoulders the awesome burden of responsibility which he had unthinkingly assumed. But the Almighty ignored his pleas.

Humiliated, and in utter desperation, he was at last obliged to appeal to the Pope. On foot he made the journey with his strange companion—from Florence to Avignon. By the time he arrived a veritable horde had been attracted in his wake. Only by a miracle had he escaped being stoned to death, for by now all Europe was aware that the Devil himself was seeking audience with his Holiness. The Pope, however, himself a learned man and a master of the occult sciences, had taken great pains to safe- guard this curious pilgrim and his offspring. It was rumoured that his Holiness had intentions of adopting the monster himself, if for no other reason than to make of him a worthy Christian. Attended only by his favourite Cardinal, the Pope received the penitent scholar and his mysterious ward in the privacy of his chamber. What took place in the four and a half hours which elapsed nobody knows. The result, if it can be called such, was that the day after the scholar died a violent death. The following day his body was publicly burned and the ashes scattered *sous le pont d'Avignon.*

At this point in his narrative Caccicacci paused, waiting for the inevitable question—'*And what happened to Picodiribibi?*' Caccicacci put on a mysterious baiting smile, raised his empty glass appealingly, coughed, cleared his throat, and, before resuming, inquired if he might have another sandwich.

'*Picodiribibi!* Ah, now you ask me something! Have any of you ever read Occam—or the *Private Papers* of Albertus Magnus?'

No one had, needless to say.

'Every now and then,' he continued, the question being wholly rhetorical, 'one hears of a sea monster appearing off the coast of Labrador or some other outlandish place. What would you say if tomorrow it were reported that a weird human monster had been glimpsed roaming through Sherwood Forest? You see, Picodiri-bibi was not the first of his line. Even in Egyptian times legends were in circulation attesting to the existence of androids such as Picodiribibi. In the great museums of Europe there are documents which describe in detail various androids or robots, as we now call them, which were made by the wizards of old. Nowhere, however, is there any record of the destruction of these man-made monsters. In fact, all the source material we have on the subject leads to the striking conclusion that these monsters always succeeded in escaping from the hands of their masters. . . .'

Here Caccicacci paused again and looked about inquiringly.

'I am not saying it is so,' he resumed, 'but there is respectable evidence to support the view that in some remote and inaccessible spot these Satanic creatures continue their unnatural existence. It is highly probable, in fact, that by this time they have established a veritable colony. Why not? They have no age, they are immune to disease—and they are ignorant of death. Like that sage who defied the great Alexander, they may indeed boast of being indestructible. Some scholars maintain that by now these lost and imperishable relics have probably created their own unique method of communication—more, that they have even learned to reproduce their own kind, *mechanically*, of course. They hold that if the human being evolved from the dumb brute why could these pre-fabricated creatures not do likewise—and in less time? Man is as mysterious in his way as is God. So is the creature world. And so is the inanimate world, if we but reflect on it. If these androids had the wisdom and the ingenuity to escape from their vigilant masters, from their horrible condition of servitude, might they not have the ability to protect themselves indefinitely, become sociable with their own kind, increase and multiply? Who can say with certitude that there does not exist somewhere on this globe a fabulous village—perhaps a resplendent city!—populated entirely by these soulless specimens, many of them older than the mightiest sequoia?

'But I am forgetting about Picodiribibi. . . . The day his master came to a violent end he disappeared. All over the land a hue and cry went up, but in vain. Not a trace of him was ever found. Now and then there were reports of mysterious deaths, of inexplicable accidents and disasters, all attributed to the missing Picodiribibi. Many scholars were persecuted, some put to the stake, because they were thought to have harboured the monster. It was even rumoured that the Pope had ordered a "replica" of Picodiribibi to be manufactured, and that he had made dark use of this spurious one. All rumour and conjecture, to be sure.

Nevertheless, it is a fact that, hidden in the archives of the Vatican, are descriptions of other robots more or less contemporaneous; none of these, however, is credited with possessing anything approaching the functional range of Picodiribibi. Today, of course, we have all sorts of robots, one of them, as you know, drawing his first breath of life, so to speak, from the radiance of a distant star. Had it been possible to do this in the early Middle Ages, think, try to think, of the havoc which would have ensued. The inventor would have been accused of employing black magic. He would have been burned at the stake, would he not? But there may have been another result, another outcome, dazzling and sinister at the same time. Instead of machines, perhaps we would not be using these star-driven menials. Perhaps the work of the world would be done entirely by these expert-work-hungry slaves. . . .'

Here Caccicacci stopped short, smiled as if bemused, then suddenly burst out with this: '*And who would arise to emancipate them?* You laugh. But do we not regard the machine as our slave? And do we not suffer just as indubitably from this false relationship as did the wizards of old with their androids? Back of our deep-rooted desire to escape the drudgery of work lies the longing for Paradise. To the man of today Paradise means not only freedom from sin but freedom from work, for work has become odious and degrading. When man ate of the Tree of Knowledge he elected to find a shortcut to Godhood. He attempted to rob the Creator of the divine secret, which to him spelled power. What has been the result? Sin, disease, death. Eternal warfare, eternal unrest. The little we know we use for our own destruction. We know not how to escape the tyranny of the convenient monsters we have created. We delude ourselves into believing that, by means of them, we shall one day enjoy leisure and bliss, but all we accomplish, to be truthful, is to create more work for ourselves, more distress, more enmity, more sickness, more death. By our ingenious inventions and discoveries we are gradually altering the face of the earth—until it becomes unrecognizable in its ugliness. Until life itself becomes unbearable. . . . That little beam of light from a remote star—I ask you, if that imperishable ray of light could thus affect a non-human being, why can it not do as much for us? With all the stars in the heavens lavishing their radiant powers on us, with the aid of the sun, the moon and all the planets, how is it that we continue to remain in darkness and frustration? Why do we wear out so quickly, when the elements of which we are composed are indestructible? *What is it that wears out?* Not that of which we are made, that is certain. We wither and fade away, we perish, because the desire to live is extinguished. And why does this most potent flame die out? For lack of faith. From the time we are born we are told that we are mortal. From the time we are able to understand words we are taught that we must kill in order to survive. In season and out we are reminded that, no matter how intelligently, reasonably or wisely we live, we shall become sick and die. We are inoculated with the idea of death almost from birth. It is any wonder that we die?'

Caccicacci drew a deep breath. There was something he was struggling to convey, something beyond words, one might say. It was evident that he was being carried away by his narrative. One felt that he was trying to convince himself of something. The impression I got was that he had told this story over and over—in order to arrive at a conclusion beyond the limits of his own comprehension. Perhaps he knew, deep down, that the tale had a significance which eluded him only because he lacked the courage to pursue it to the end. A man may be a story-teller, a fabulist, a down-right liar, but embedded in all fiction and false-hood there is a core of truth. The inventor of Picodiribibi was a story-teller too, in his way. He had created a fable or legend mechanically instead of verbally. He had defrauded our senses as much as any story-teller. However. . . .

'Sometimes,' said Caccicacci, solemnly now and with all the sincerity he was capable of mustering, 'I am convinced that there is no hope for mankind unless we make a complete break with the past. I mean, unless we begin to think differently and live differently. I know it sounds banal . . . it has been said thousands of times and nothing has happened. You see, I keep thinking of the great suns which surround us, of these vast solar bodies in the heavens of which no one knows anything, except that they exist. From one of them it is admitted that we draw our sustenance. Some include the moon as a vital factor in our earthly existence. Others speak of the beneficent or maleficent influence of the planets. *But*, if you stop to think, everything—and when I say everything I mean everything!—whether visible or invisible, known or unknown, is vital to our existence. We live amidst a network of magnetic forces which, in a variety of ways incalcu-lable and indescribable, are ceaselessly operative. We created none of these ourselves. A few we have learned to harness, to exploit, as it were. And we are puffed with pride because of our petty achievements. But even the boldest, even the proudest among our latter-day magicians, is bound to concede that what we know is infinitesimal compared to what we do *not* know. I beg you, stop a moment and reflect! Does any one here honestly believe that one day we shall know all? I go farther . . . I ask in all sincerity—do you believe that our salvation depends on *knowing*? Assuming for a moment that the human brain is capable of cramming into its mysterious fibres the sum total of the secret processes which govern the universe, what then? Yes, *what then*? What would we do, we humans, with this unthinkable know-ledge? What *could* we do? Have you ever asked yourself that question? Everyone seems to take it for granted that the accumulation of knowledge is a good thing. No one ever says—"And what shall I do with it when I have it?" No one dares believe any longer that, in the span of one short lifetime, it is possible to acquire even a minute fraction of the sum of all *existent* human knowledge. . . .'

Another breathing spell. We were all ready with the bottle this time. Caccicacci was labouring. He had derailed. It was not knowledge, or the lack of it, that he was so desperately concerned with. I was aware of the silent effort he was making to retrace his steps; I could feel him floundering about in his struggle to get back to the main line.

'Faith! I was talking about faith a moment ago. We've lost it. Lost it completely. *Faith in anything*, I mean. Yet faith is the only thing man lives by. Not knowledge, which is admittedly inexhaustible and in the end futile or destructive. But faith. Faith too is inexhaustible. Always has been, always will be. It is faith which inspires deeds, faith which overcomes obstacles—literally moves mountains, as the Bible says. *Faith in what?* Just faith. Faith in everything, if you like. Perhaps a better word would be acceptance. But acceptance is even more difficult to understand than faith. Immediately you utter the word, there is an inquisitioner which says: "*Evil too?*" And if one says yes, then the way is barred. You are laughed out of countenance, shunned like a leper. Good, you see, may be questioned, but evil—and this is a paradox—evil, though we struggle constantly to eliminate it, is always taken for granted. No one doubts the existence of evil, though it is only an abstract term for that which is constantly changing character and which, on close analysis, is often found to be good. No one will accept evil at its face value. It is, and it is not. The mind refuses to accept it unconditionally. It would really seem as is it existed only to be converted into its opposite. The simplest and readiest way to accomplish this is, of course, to accept it. But who is wise enough to adopt such a course?

'I think of Picodiribibi again. Was there anything "evil" about his appearance or existence? Yet he was held in dread by the world in which he found himself. He was regarded as a violation of nature. *But is not man himself a violation of nature?* If we could fashion another Picodiribibi, or one even more marvellous in his functioning, would we not be in ecstasy? But suppose that, instead of a more marvellous *robot*, we were suddenly confronted by a genuine human being whose attributes were so incomparably superior to our own that he resembled a god? This is a hypothetical question, to be sure, yet there are, and always have been, individuals who maintain, and persist in maintaining, despite reason and ridicule, that they have had witness of such divine beings. We can all summon suitable names. Myself, I prefer to think of a *mythical* being, someone nobody has ever heard of, or seen, or will know in this life. Someone, in brief, who *could* exist and fulfil the requirements I speak of. . . .'

Here Caciccacci digressed. He was forced to confess that he did not know what had prompted him to make such a statement, nor where he was heading. He kept rubbing his poll and murmuring over and over: 'Strange, strange, but I thought I had something there.'

Suddenly his face lit up with joy. 'Ah yes, I know now. I've got it. Listen. . . . Supposing this being, universally admitted to be superior to us in every way, should take it to address the world in this fashion: "Stop where you are, O men and women, and give heed! You are on the wrong track. You are headed for destruction." Supposing that everywhere on this globe the billions which make up humanity did stop what they were doing and listened. Even if this god-like being said nothing more than what I've just put in his mouth, what do you suppose the effect would be? Has the entire world ever stopped to listen in unison to words of wisdom? Imagine, if you can, a total, drastic silence, all ears cocked to catch the fatal words! *Would it even be necessary to utter the words?* Can you not imagine that everyone, in the silence of his heart, would supply the answer himself? There is only one response that humanity longs to give—and it can be voiced in one little monosyllable: *Love*. That little word, that mighty thought, that perpetual act, positive, unambigious, eternally effective—if that should sink in, take possession of all mankind, would it not transform the world instantly? Who could resist, if love became the order of the day? Who would want power or knowledge—if he were bathed in the perpetual glory of love?

'It is said, as you know, that in the fastnesses of Tibet there actually exists a small band of men so immeasurably superior to us that they are called "The Masters". They live in voluntary exile from the rest of the world. Like the androids I spoke of earlier, they too are ageless, immune to disease, *and indestructible*. Why do they not mingle with us, why do they not enlighten and ennoble us by their presence? Have they *chosen* to remain isolate or is it we who keep them at a distance? Before you attempt to answer, ask yourself another question—what have we to offer them which they do not already know, possess, or enjoy? If such beings exist, and I have every reason to believe they do, then the only possible barrier is consciousness. Degrees of consciousness, to be more exact. When we reach to deeper levels of thought and being *they will be there*, so to speak. We are still unready, unwilling, to mingle with the gods. The men of olden times knew the gods: they saw them face to face. Man was not removed, in consciousness, from either the higher or the lower orders of creation. Today man is cut off. Today man lives as a slave. Worse, we are slaves to one another. We have created a condition hitherto unknown, a condition altogether unique: we have become the slaves of slaves. Doubt it not, the moment we truly desire freedom we shall be free. Not a whit sooner! Now we think like machines, because we have become as machines. Craving power, we are the helpless victims of power. . . . The day we learn to express love we shall know love and have love—and all else will fall away. Evil is a creation of the human mind. It is powerless when accepted at face value. *Because it has no value in itself*. Evil exists only as a threat to that eternal kingdom of love we but dimly apprehend. Yes, men have had visions of a liberated humanity. They have had visions of walking the earth like the gods they once were. Those whom we call "The Masters" undoubtedly found the road back. Perhaps the androids have taken another road. All roads, believe it or not, lead eventually to that life-giving source which is the centre and meaning of creation. As Lawrence said with dying breath—"For man, the vast marvel is to be alive. For man, as for flower, beast and bird, the supreme triumph is to be most vividly, most perfectly, alive. . . ." In *this* sense, Picodiribibi was never alive. In *this* sense, none of us is alive. *Let us become fully alive*, that is what I have been trying to say.'

Exhausted by this unintended flight, Caccicacci took leave abruptly in embarrassment and confusion. We who had listened in silence remained seated in the corner by the window. No one seemed able to summon breath for a few minutes. Arthur Raymond, usually immune to such disquisitions, looked from one to another defiantly, ready to pounce upon the slightest provocation. Spud Jason and his 'consort' were already three sheets to the wind. No argument coming from that quarter! Finally it was Baronyi who broke the ice, remarking in a gentle, perplexed voice that he had never imagined Caccicacci to be so serious. Trevelyan groaned, as if to say—'You don't know the half of it!' Then, to our stupefaction, without the slightest preliminary, he launched into a long monologue about his own private troubles. He began by telling how his wife, who was not only pregnant but mad, mad as a hatter, had tried to strangle him in bed while asleep just the night before. He confessed, in his bland, suppressed, underdone way—he was British to the core—that he had certainly treated her abominably. He made it painfully clear that from the very beginning he had loathed her. He had married her out of pity, because the man who had made her with child had run out on her. She was a poetess and he thought highly of her work. What he couldn't abide was her moods. She would sit for hours, knitting woollen socks which he never wore, and never a peep out of her. Or, she would sit in the rocker, doing absolutely nothing, and while swaying back and forth would hum, hum for hours. Or, she would suddenly get a talking jag, corner him in the kitchen or the bedroom, and fill him with dreamy stuff which she called inspiration.

'What do you mean—dreamy stuff?' asked O'Mara, grinning maliciously.

'Oh,' said Trevelyan, 'it might be about fog, fog and rain how the trees and bushes looked when the fog suddenly drifted away. It might be about the colour of fog, all the shades of grey which she could discern with her cat-like eyes. She had lived on the coast of Cornwall during her childhood—they're all a bit loony there—and she would relive her walks in the fog, her experiences with goats and cats, or with the village idiot. In these moods she talked another language—I don't mean a dialect, I mean a language of her own which no one could understand. It used to give me the creeps. It was a sort of cat language, as best I can dscribe it. She yowled now and then, a real yowl that made your blood curdle. Sometimes she imitated the wind, all kinds of wind, from a gentle breeze to a ripping gale. And then she would snuffle and weep, trying to convince me that she mourned the flowers which had been cut down—the pansies and the lilies particularly, they were so helpless, so defenceless. Before you know it she would be walking through strange places, describing them intimately, as if she had lived there all her life. Places like Trinidad, Curacao, Mozambique, Guadeloupe, Madras, Cawnpore and such like. *Eerie?* I'll tell you, I thought for a while she had second sight. . . . *By the way, couldn't we have another drink?* I haven't a farthing, as you probably know. . . .

'She's a quéer one, all right. And a bloody, obstinate cuss, too. Get in an argument with her and you're doomed. She knows how to block all the exits. You're trapped, once you start in with that one. I never realized that women could be so utterly logical. It wouldn't matter what you were discussing—odours, vegetation, diseases or sun-spots. Her's is always the last word, no matter what the subject. Add to all that, a mania for detail, a mania for minutiae. She'll sit at the breakfast table, for example, with a broken petal in her hand, and she'll examine it for an hour. She'll ask you to concentrate on a minute piece of this petal no bigger than the merest sliver of a splinter. Claims she can see all sorts of curious and wondrous things in this piece of nothingness. All with the naked eye, mind you. Her eyes are not human eyes, by God. She can see in the dark, of course, even better than a cat. She can see with her eyes closed, believe it or not. She demonstrated that to my own satisfaction one night. *But what she can't see is the other person!* She looks right through you when she talks to you. She sees only what she is talking about, whether it's fog, cats, idiots, remote cities, floating islands or floating kidneys. In the beginning I used to grab her by the arm and shake her—I thought perhaps she was in a trance. Nothing of the sort! Just as wide-awake as you or I. Even more awake, I'd say. Nothing escapes her. "Did you hear that?" she says sometimes, right in the middle of a sentence. "Hear *what*?" Maybe a cake of ice slipped just the fraction of an inch in the ice-box. Maybe a leaf fell to the ground in the back-yard. Maybe a drop of water dripped from the kitchen faucet. "*Did you hear that?*" I'd jump whenever she said it. After a while I began to think I was growing deaf—she gave such importance to these inaudible nothings. "It's nothing," she'd say, "it's just your nerves." And with all that she has absolutely no ear for music. All she hears is the scratching of the needle: her pleasure is derived solely from detecting whether the record is an old one or a fairly new one, and how new, or how old. She can't tell the difference between Mozart, Puccini and Satie. She likes hymns. Dingy, melancholy hymns. Which she always hums with a seraphic smile, as if she were already among the angels. No, really, she's the most detestable bitch imaginable. There's not a spark of jor or gaiety in her. If you tell her a funny story she's bored. If you laugh she's outraged. If you sneeze you have bad manners. If you indulge in a drink you're a sot. . . . We've had intercourse—if you can call it that—about three times, I guess. She closes her eyes, lies rigid as a pole, and begs you to get done with it as quickly as possible. Worse than raping a martyr. When it's over she gets a pad, props herself up in bed, and writes a poem. To purify herself, I suppose. I could kill her sometimes. . . .'

'What about the brat?' O'Mara piped up. 'Does she want the child?'

'Search me!' said Trevelyan. 'She never mentions the subject. It might just as well be a tumour, for all it seems to matter. Now and then she says she's getting too stout . . . she wouldn't say "fat", that's too coarse. *Stout*. As though it were strange to be blowing up like a balloon when you're seven months along!'

'How do you know she *is* pregnant?' asked Spud Jason sleepily. 'Sometimes it's only imaginary.'

'Imaginary, huh! I only wish to Christ it were; she's pregnant alright. . . . I've felt it moving inside her.'

'It could be wind,' said someone.

'Wind doesn't have arms and legs,' said Trevelyan, getting irritated. 'Wind doesn't roll over or have conniption fits.'

'Let's get out of here,' said Spud Jason. 'You'll be giving this one ideas,' and with this he gave his sidekick a poke in the ribs that almost knocked her off the chair.

As if it were a game they played time and again, Alameda rose quietly, walked round him, then gave him a resounding thwack on the face with the palm of her hand.

'So that's it?' cried Spud Jason, leaping from his chair and twisting her arm. With his other hand he grabbed her long mane and pulled it vigorously. 'Behave yourself, or I'll blacken your eyes for you!'

'You will, will you?' Alameda was brandishing an empty bottle.

'Get out of here, the two of you!' shouted Mona. 'And don't come back again, *please*!'

'How much do I owe you?' said Spud Jason sheepishly.

'You don't owe anything,' said Mona. 'Just get out and stay out!'

11

To my surprise MacGregor dropped in one night, ordered a drink, and paid for it without a murmur. He seemed unusually mellow. Inquired solicitously how we were doing, what the prospects were, did we need any help—*legal* help—and so on. I couldn't make out what had come over him.

Suddenly, when Mona had turned her back, he said: 'Couldn't you pull yourself away for a few hours some night?'

Without waiting for me to say yes or no, he went on to tell me that he was in love again, head over heels, in fact. 'Guess you can tell it, can't you.' She was a funny gal, in a way, he explained. A divorcee, with two kids on her hands. 'How do you like *that*?' He then said that he wanted to impart something very confidential. He knew it was hard for me to keep my trap shut, but just the same. . . . 'Tess, you know, doesn't suspect a thing. I wouldn't hurt her for the world. Damn it! Don't laugh! I say it only because you might spill the beans some night in one of your chivalrous moods.'

I grinned.

So that was the set-up. Trix, the new one, lived in the Bronx. 'To hell and gone,' as he put it. He was out every night till three, four or five in the morning. 'Tess thinks I'm gambling. The way the money's going I might just as well be out shooting crap every night. But that's neither here nor there. What I'm asking you is—can you steal away some night, just for a few hours?' I said nothing, just grinned again. 'I'd like you to look her over . . . tell me if I'm cuckoo or not.' Here he paused a minute, as if embarrassed. 'To focus it a little better for you, Hen, let me tell you this: every night after dinner she gets the kids to sit in my lap, one on each knee. And what do you think *I* do? Tell them bed-time stories! *Can you picture that?*' He burst out into a loud guffaw. 'You know, Hen, I can hardly believe it myself. But it's a fact. I couldn't be more considerate of them if they were my own kids. Christ, I've already brought them a whole menagerie of toys. You know, if Tess hadn't had her insides cleaned out, we would have had three or four brats ourselves. Maybe that's one of the reasons why we've drifted apart. You know Tess, Henry—she's got a heart of gold. But she's not much to talk to. Interested in her law work and that's about all. If I stay home of a night I fall asleep. Or else I get drunk. Why the hell I ever married her I don't know. You, you bastard, you never said a word: you let me sail straight into it. Thought it would do me good, didn't you? Well, I'm drifting. . . . You know, sometimes, listening to myself, I hear my old man talking. He can't stick to the point longer than two minutes. Mother's the same way. . . . *How about another drink?* I'm paying for them, don't worry.'

There was silence for a few moments, then I asked him point-blank just why he was so eager to have me meet his new gal. 'I know damned well,' I added, 'that you don't want my approval.'

'No, Hen,' and he looked down at the table top, 'to be serious about it, I wanted you to come for dinner some night when the kids are eating with us and. . . .'

'And what?'

'And give me some pointers about these damned fairy tales. Kids take these things seriously, you know. I have a feeling I'm doing it ass-backwards. Maybe I'm telling them things they oughtn't to hear till they're five years older. . . .'

'So that's it?' I blurted out. 'Well, I'm damned! And what makes you think I know anything about this business?'

'Well, you had a kid of your own, didn't you? Besides, you're a writer. You're up on this crap, I'm not. I start a story and I don't know how to finish it. I'm all at sea, I tell you.'

'Haven't you any imagination?'

'Are you kidding? Listen, you know *me*. All I know is law, and maybe not too much of that. I've got a single-track mind. Anyway, it's not just for that I want you to come. . . . I want you to meet Trix. I think you'll like her. Boy, she's some cook! Tess, by the way—well, I don't have to tell you—but Tess can't even fry an egg. This one'll make you think you're dining at the Ritz. She does it with class. She has a bit of a cellar, too—maybe that will get you. Listen, what are you hemming and hawing about? I'd like you to have a good time, that's all. You've got to have a change once in a while. O'Mara can take over for a few hours, can't he? That is, if you trust him! Personally, I wouldn't trust him out of my sight. . . .'

Just then Tony Maurer popped in, carrying a thick book under his arm. As usual, he was extremely cordial. Took a seat at the table alongside of us and asked if we wouldn't join him in a drink. He held the book up in order for me to read the title: *Decline of the West.*

'Never heard of it,' I said.

'You will before long,' he answered. 'A great work. Prophetic. . . .'

MacGregor burst in under his breath: 'Forget it! You have no time to read anyway.'

'May I borrow it when you're through?' I asked.

'Of course,' said Tony Maurer. 'I'll make you a present of it.'

MacGregor, to excuse himself, inquired if it were a mystical work. He wasn't a damned bit interested, of course, but he saw that Tony Maurer was not an idiot.

Told that it was a philosophy of history, he mumbled: 'It's all yours!'

We had a couple of drinks with Tony Maurer, and by this time I was feeling rather high. It was just dawning on me that we might have a very good evening, or dinner at least, chez Trix. Trix Miranda was the full name. I liked the sound of it.

'Which bed-time story do they like best?' I asked.

'Something about the three bears.'

'You mean *Goldilocks and the Three Bears*? Why, Jesus, I know that thing backwards. You know, I'm just thinking . . . how would the night after next do?'

'Now you're talking, Henry. I knew you wouldn't let me down. By the way, you don't have to, of course, but if you could bring a bottle of wine along, Trix would appreciate it. A French wine if you can.'

'Easiest thing in the world! I'll bring two or three.'

He got up to go, and as he shook hands with me he said: 'Do me a favour, will you? Don't get tight before we put the kids to bed.'

'It's a bargain. And now I'll ask *you* a favour. Let *me* tell them the story about the three bears, eh?'

'O.K., Henry—but no dirty work!'

Two nights later I'm having dinner with MacGregor and Trix —in a remote corner of the Bronx. The kids are in fine fettle. The boy is five and the girl about three and a half. Charming youngsters but rather precocious. I'm doing my best not to get tight before the kids are put to bed. But we've had three Martinis while waiting for dinner and now we're sampling the Chambertin which I brought along.

Trix is a good scout, as MacGregor would say. Not a beauty, but easy to look at. Has a jovial disposition. The only drawback I detect so far is that she's hysterical.

Everything has been proceeding smoothly. I feel at home with the kids. They keep on reminding me that I've promised to tell them the story of the three bears.

'You're in for it, Henry,' says MacGregor.

Truth to tell, I haven't the least desire now to reel off that bed-time story. I stretch the meal out as long as I can. I'm a bit groggy. I can't remember how the damned story begins.

Suddenly Trix says: 'You must tell it now, Henry. It's long past their bed time.'

'All right!' I groan. 'Get me another black coffee and I'll begin.'

'I'll start it for you,' says the boy.

'You don't do anything of the sort!' says Trix. 'Henry is going to tell this story—from beginning to end. I want you to listen carefully. Now shut up!'

I swallowed some black coffee, choked on it, sputtered and stuttered.

'Once there was a big black bear. . . .'

'That's not how it begins,' piped the little girl.

'Well, how does it begin then?'

'*Once upon a time.* . . .'

'Sure, sure . . . how could I forget? All right, are you listening? Here goes. .·. . *Once upon a time* there were three bears—a polar bear, a grizzly bear, and a Teddy bear. . . .'

(Laughter and derision from the two kids.)

'The polar bear had a pelt of long white fur—to keep him warm, of course. The grizzly bear was. . . .'

'That's not the way it goes, Mommy!' screamed the little girl.

'He's making it up,' said the boy.

'Be quiet, you two!' cried Trix.

'Listen, Henry,' said MacGregor, 'don't let them rattle you. Take your time. Remember, easy does it. Here, have another drop of cognac, it'll oil your palate.'

I lit a fat cigar, took another sip of cognac, and tried to work myself back into the groove. Suddenly it struck me that there was only one way to tell it and that was fast as lightning. If I stopped to think I'd be sunk.

'Listen, folks,' I said, 'I'm going to start all over again. No more interruptions, eh?' I winked at the little girl and threw the boy a bone which still had some meat on it.

'For a man with your imagination you're certainly having a hard time,' said MacGregor. 'This ought to be a hundred dollar story, with all the preliminaries you're going through. You're sure you don't want an aspirin?'

'This is going to be a thousand dollar story,' I replied, now in full possession of all my faculties. 'But don't interrupt me!'

'Come on, come on, stop diddling! *Once upon a time*—that's the way it begins,' bawled MacGregor.

'O.K. . . . *Once upon a time.* . . . Yeah, that's it. Once upon a time there were three bears: a polar bear, a grizzly bear, and a Teddy bear. . . .'

'You told us that before,' said the boy.

'Be quiet, you!' cried Trix.

'The polar bear was absolutely bare, with long white fur which reached to the ground. The grizzly bear was just as tough as a sirloin steak, and he had lots of fat between his toes. The Teddy bear was just right, neither too fat nor too lean, neither tough nor tender, neither hot nor cold. . . .'

Titters from the kids.

'The polar bear ate nothing but ice, ice cold ice, fresh from the ice house. The grizzly bear thrived on artichokes, because artichokes are full of burrs and nettles. . . .'

'What's burrs, mommy?' piped the little girl.

'Hush!' said Trix.

'As for the Teddy bear, why he drank only skimmed milk. He was a grower, you see, and didn't need vitamins. One day the grizzly bear was out gathering wood for the fire. He had nothing on but his bearskin and the flies were driving him mad. So he began to run and run and run. Soon he was deep in the forest. After a while he sat down by a stream and fell asleep. . . .'

'I don't like the way he tells it,' said the boy, 'he's all mixed up.'

'If you don't keep quiet, I'll put you to bed!'

'Suddenly little Goldilocks entered the forest. She had a lunch basket with her and it was filled with all sorts of good things, including a bottle of Blue Label Ketchup. She was looking for the little house with the green shutters. Suddenly she heard someone snoring, and between snores a big booming voice was shouting: *Acorn pie for me! Acorn pie for me!* Goldilocks looked first to the right and then to the left. She saw no one. So she got out her compass and, facing due west, she followed her nose. In about an hour, or perhaps it was an hour and a quarter, she came to a clearing in the woods. And there was the little house with the olive drab shutters.'

'*Green* shutters!' cried the boy.

'With the green shutters, right! And then what do you think happened? A great big lion came dashing out of the woods, followed by a little man with a bow and arrow. The lion was very shy and playful. What did he do but jump on the roof and wrap himself around the chimney. The little man with the dunce cap began crawling on all fours—until he got to the doorway. Then he got up, danced a merry jig, and ran inside. . . .'

'I don't believe it,' said the little girl. 'It ain't true.'

'It is, too,' I said, 'and if you're not careful I'll box your ears.' Here I took a deep breath, wondering what next. The cigar was out, the glass was empty. I decided to make haste.

'From here on it goes still faster,' I said, resuming the narrative.

'Don't go too fast,' said the boy, 'I don't want to miss anything.'

'O.K. . . . Now then, once inside, Goldilocks found everything in apple pie order: the dishes were all washed and stacked, the clothes mended, the pictures neatly framed. On the table there was an atlas and an unabridged dictionary, in two volumes. Somebody had been moving the chess pieces around in Teddy bear's absence. Too bad, because he would have mated in eight more moves. Goldilocks, however, was too fascinated by all the toys and gadgets, especially the new can opener, to worry about chess problems. She had been doing trigonometry all morning and her little brain was too weary to puzzle out gambits and that sort of thing. She was dying to ring the cow bell which hung over the kitchen sink. To get at it she had to use a stool. The first stool was too low; the second one was too high; but the third stool was just right. She rang the bell so loud that the dishes fell out of the racks. Goldilocks was frightened at first, but then she thought it was funny, so she rang the bell again. This time the lion unwound himself and slid off the roof, his tail twisted into forty knots. Goldilocks thought this was even funnier, so she range the bell a third time. The little man with the dunce cap came running out of the bedroom, all a-quiver, and without a word, he began turning somersaults. He flipped and flopped, just like an old cart wheel, and then he disappeared into the woods. . . .'

'You're not losing the thread, I hope?' said MacGregor.

'Don't interrupt!' shouted Trix.

'Mommy, I want to go to bed,' said the little girl.

'Be quiet!' said the boy, 'I'm getting interested.'

'And *now*,' I continued, having caught my breath, 'it suddenly began to thunder and lightning. The rain came down in buckets. Little Goldilocks was really frightened. She fell head over heels off the stool, twisting her ankle and spraining her wrist. She wanted to hide somewhere until it was all over. "Nothing easier," came a tiny little voice from the far corner of the room where the Winged Victory stood. And with that the closet door opened of itself. I'll run in there, thought Goldilocks, and she made a dash for the closet. Now it so happened that in the closet were bottles and jars, heaps and heaps of bottles, and heaps and heaps of jars. Goldilocks opened a tiny little bottle and dabbed her ankle with arnica. Then she reached for another bottle, and what do you suppose was in it? *Sloan's Liniment!* "Goodness Gracious!" she said, and suiting word to action, she applied the liniment to her wrist. Then she found a little iodine, and drinking it straight, she began to sing. It was a merry little tune—about Frère Jacques. She sang in French because her mother had taught her never to sing in any other language. After the 27th verse she got bored and decided to explore the closet. The strange thing about this closet it that it was bigger than the house itself. There were seven rooms on the ground floor, and five above, with a toilet and a bath in each room, to say nothing of a fireplace and a pier glass decked with chintz. Goldilocks forgot all about the thunder and lightning, the rain, the hail, the snails and the frogs; she forgot all about the lion and the little man with the bow and arrow, whose name, by the way, was Pinocchio. All she could think of was how wonderful it was to live in a closet like this. . . .'

'This is going to be about Cinderella,' said the little girl.

'It is not!' snapped the boy. 'It's about the seven dwarfs.'

'Quiet, you two!'

'Go on, Henry,' said MacGregor, 'I'm curious to see how you get out of this trap.'

'And so Goldilocks wandered from room to room, never dreaming that the three bears had come home and were sitting down to dinner. In the alcove on the parlour floor she found a library filled with strange books. They were all about sex and the resurrection of the dead. . . .'

'What's sex?' asked the boy.

'It's not for *you*,' said the little girl.

'Goldilocks sat down and began reading aloud from a great big book. It was by Wilhelm Reich, author of *The Golden Flower* or *The Mystery of the Hormones*. The book was so heavy that Goldilocks couldn't hold it in her lap. So she placed it on the floor and knelt beside it. Every page was illustrated in gorgeous colours. Though Goldilocks was familiar with rare and limited editions, she had to admit to herself that never before had she seen such beautiful illustrations. Some were by a man named Picasso, some by Matisse, some by Ghirlandajo, but all without exception were beautiful and shocking to behold. . . .'

'That's a funny word—*behold!*' cried the little boy.

'You said it! And now just take a back seat for a while, will you? Because now it's getting really interesting. . . . As I say, Goldilocks was reading aloud to herself. She was reading about the Saviour and how he died on the Cross—for *us*—so that our sins would be washed away. Goldilocks was just a little girl, after all, and so she didn't know what it was to sin. But she wanted very very much to know. She read and read until her eyes ached, without ever discovering what it was, exactly, to sin. "I'll run downstairs," she said to herself, "and see what it says in the dictionary. It's an unabridged dictionary, so it must have sin in it." Her ankle was all healed by this time, her wrist too, *mirabile dictu*. She went skipping down the stairs like a seven day goat. When she got to the closet door, which was still ajar, she did a double somersault, just like the little fellow with the dunce cap had done. . . .'

'Pinocchio!' cried the boy.

'And then what do you think happened? She landed right in the grizzly bear's lap!'

The youngsters howled with delight.

' "All the better to eat you up!" growled the big grizzly bear, smacking his rubbery lips. "Just the right size!" said the polar bear, all white from the rain and hail, and he tossed her up to the ceiling. "She's mine!" cried the Teddy bear, giving her a hug which cracked little Goldilocks' ribs. The three bears got busy at once; they undressed little Goldilocks and put her on the platter, ready to carve. While Goldilocks shivered and whimpered, the big grizzly bear sharpened his axe on the grind-stone; the polar bear unsheathed his hunting knife, which he carried in a leather scabbard attached to his belt. As for Teddy bear, he just clapped his hands and danced with glee. "She's just right!" he shouted. "Just right!" Over and over they turned her, to see which part was the tenderest. Goldilocks began to scream with terror. "Be quiet," commanded the polar bear, "or you won't get anything to eat." "Please Mr Polar Bear, don't eat *me*!" begged Goldilocks. "Shut your trap!" yelled the grizzly bear. "We'll eat first, and you'll eat afterwards." "But I don't want to eat," cried Goldilocks, the tears streaming down her face. "You're not going to eat," screamed the Teddy bear, and with that he grabbed her leg and put it in his mouth. "Oh, oh!" screamed Goldilocks. "Don't eat me yet, I beg you. I'm not cooked." '

The children were getting hysterical.

' "Now you're talking sensible," said the grizzly bear. Incidentally, the grizzly bear had a strong father complex. He didn't like the flesh of little girls unless well done. It was fortunate, indeed, for little Goldilocks that the grizzly bear felt this way about little girls, because the other two bears were ravenously hungry, and besides, they had no complexes whatever. Anyway, while the grizzly bear stirred the fire and added more logs, Goldilocks knelt in the platter and said her prayers. She looked more beautiful than ever now, and if the bears had been human they would not have eaten her alive, they would have consecrated her to the Virgin Mary. But a bear is always a bear, and these were no exception to the rule. So when flames were giving off just the right heat, the three bears took little Goldilocks and flung her on to the burning logs. In five minutes she was roasted to a crisp, hair and all. Then they put her back on the platter and carved her into big chunks. For the grizzly bear a great big chunk; for the polar bear a medium-sized chunk, and for the Teddy bear, the cute little thing, a nice little tenderloin steak. My, but it tasted good. They ate every bit of her—teeth, hair, toe-nails, bones and kidneys. The platter was so clean you could have seen your face in it. There wasn't even a drop of gravy left. "And now," said the grizzly bear, "we'll see what she brought in that lunch basket. I'd just love to have a piece of acorn pie." They opened the basket and, sure enough, there were three pieces of acorn pie. The big piece was very big, the middlin' piece was about medium, and the little piece was just a tiny, wee little snack. "Yum yum!" sighed the Teddy bear, licking his chops.

"*Acorn pie!*" "What did I tell you?" growled the grizzly bear. The polar bear had stuffed his mouth so full he could only grunt. When they had downed the last mouthful the polar bear looked around and, just as pleasant as could be, he said: "Now wouldn't it be wonderful if there were a bottle of schnapps in that basket!" Immediately the three of them began pawing the basket, looking for that delicious bottle of schnapps. . . .'

'Do *we* get any schnapps, mommy?' cried the little girl.

'It's ginger snaps, you dope!' yelled the boy.

'Well, at the bottom of the basket, wrapped in a wet napkin, they finally found the bottle of schnapps. It was from Utrecht, Holland, a year 1926. To the three bears, however, it was just a bottle of schnapps. Now bears, as you know, never use cork-screws, so it was quite a job to get the cork out. . . .'

'You're wandering,' said MacGregor.

'That's what *you* think,' I said. 'Just hold your horses.'

'Try to finish it by midnight,' he rejoined.

'Much sooner than that, don't worry. If you interrupt again, though, I *will* lose the thread.'

'Now this bottle,' I resumed, 'was a very unusual bottle of schnapps. It had magic properties. When each bear in turn had taken a good swig, their heads began to spin. Yet, the more they drank, the more there was left to drink. They got dizzier and dizzier, groggier and groggier, thirstier and thirstier. Finally the polar bear said: "I'm going to drink it down to the last drop," and, holding the bottle between his two paws, he poured it down his gullet. He drank and drank, and finally he did come to the last drop. He was lying on the floor, drunk as a pope; the bottle upside down, the neck half-way down his throat. As I say, he had just swallowed the very last drop. Had he put the bottle down, it would have refilled itself. But he didn't. He continued to hold it upside down, getting the last drop out of that very last drop. And then a miraculous thing took place. Suddenly, little Goldi-locks came alive, clothes and all, just as she always was. She was doing a jig on the polar bear's stomach. When she began to sing, the three bears grew so frightened that they fainted away, first the grizzly bear, then the polar bear, and then the Teddy bear. . . .'

The little girl clapped her hands with delight.

'And now we're coming to the end of the story. The rain had stopped, the sky was bright and clear, the birds were singing, just as always. Little Goldilocks suddenly remembered that she had promised to be home for dinner. She gathered up her basket, looked around to make sure she had forgotten nothing, and started for the door. Suddenly she thought of the cow-bell. "It would be fun to ring it just once more," she said to herself. And with that, she climbed on to the stool, the one that was just right, and she rang with all her might. She rang it once, twice, three times—and then she fled as fast as her little legs would carry her. Outside, the little fellow with the dunce cap was waiting for her. "Quick, get on my back!" he ordered. "We'll make double time that way." Goldilocks hopped on and away they raced, up dell and down dell, over the golden meadows, through the silvery brooks. When they had raced this way for about three hours, the little man said: "I'm getting weary, I'm going to put you down." And he deposited her right there, at the edge of the woods. "Bear to the left," he said, "and you can't miss it." He was off again, just as mysteriously as he had come. . . .'

'Is that the end?' piped the boy, somewhat disappointed.

'No,' I said, 'not quite. Now listen . . . Goldilocks did as she was told, bearing always to the left. In a very few minutes she was standing in front of her own door.'

' "Why, Goldilocks," said her mother, "What great big eyes you have!"

' "All the better to eat you up!" said Goldilocks.

' "Why, Goldilocks," cried her father, "and where in hell did you put my bottle of schnapps?"

' "I gave it to the three bears," said Goldilocks dutifully.

' "Goldilocks, you're telling me a fib," said her father threateningly.

' "I'm not either," Goldilocks replied. "It's the God's truth." Suddenly she remembered what she had read in the big book, about sin and how Jesus came to wipe away all sin. "Father," she said, kneeling before him reverently, "I believe I've committed a sin."

' "Worse than that," said her father, reaching for the strap, "you've committed larceny." And without another word he began to belt and flay her. "I don't mind your visiting the three bears in the woods," he said, as he plied the strap. "I don't mind a little fib now and then. But what I do mind is not to have a wee drop of schnapps when my throat is sore and parched." He flayed her and belted her until Goldilocks was just a mass of welts and bruises. "And now," he said, putting in an extra lick for the finish, "I'm going to give you a treat. I'm going to tell you the story of the three bears—or what happened to my bottle of schnapps."

'And that, my dear children, is the end.'

The story finished, the kids were hustled off to bed. We could now settle down comfortably to drink and chew the fat. Mac-Gregor liked nothing better than to talk of old times. We were only in our thirties but we had twenty years of solid friendship between us, and besides, at that age one feels older than at fifty or sixty. Actually, both MacGregor and I were still in a period of prolonged adolescence.

Whenever MacGregor took up with a new girl it seemed imperative for him to look me up, get my approval of her, and then settle down for a long, sentimental talk-fest. We had done it so many times that it was almost playing a duet. The girl was supposed to sit there enchanted—and to interrupt us now and then with a pertinent question. The duet always began by one of us asking if the other had seen or heard anything recently of George Marshall. I don't know why we instinctively chose this opening. We were like certain chess players who, no matter who the opponent may be, always open with the Scotch gambit.

'Have you seen George lately?' says I, apropos of nothing at all.

'You mean George Marshall?'

'Yeah, it seems ages since I've seen him.'

'No, Hen, to tell you the truth, I haven't. I suppose he's still going to the Village Saturday afternoons.'

'To dance?'

MacGregor smiled. 'If you want to call it that, Henry. *You know George!*' He paused, then added: 'George is a queer guy. I think I know less about him now than ever.'

'*What?*'

'Just that, Henry. That guy leads a double life. You ought to see him at home, with the wife and kids. You wouldn't know him.'

I confessed I hadn't seen George since he got married. 'Never liked that wife of his.'

'You should talk to George about her sometime. How they manage to live together is a miracle. He gives her what she wants and in return he goes his own way. Boy, it's like skating on dynamite when you visit them. You know the sort of double talk George indulges in. . . .'

'Listen,' I interrupted, 'do you remember that night in Green-point, when we were sitting in the back of some gin mill and George began a spiel about his mother, how the sun rose and set in her ass?'

'Jesus, Hen, you sure think of strange things. Sure, I remember. I remember every conversation we ever had, I guess. And the time and place. And whether I was drunk or sober.' He turned to Trix. 'Are we boring you? You know, the three of us were great pals once. We had some good times together, didn't we, Hen? Remember Maspeth—those athletic contests? We didn't have much to worry about, did we? Let's see, were you tied up with the widow then, or was that later. *Get this*, Trix. . . . Here's this guy hardly out of school and he falls in love with a woman old enough to be his mother. Wanted to marry her, too, didn't you, Hen?'

I grinned and gave a vague nod.

'Henry always falls hard. The serious sort, though you'd never think it to look at him. . . . But about George. As I was saying

314

before, Hen, George is a different guy. He's at loose ends. Hates his work, loathes his wife, and the kids bore him to death. All he thinks of now is tail. And boy, does he chase it! Picks 'em younger and younger all the time. The last time I saw him he was in a hell of a mess with some fifteen year old—from his own school. (I still can't picture George as a principal, can you?) It began right in his office, it seems. Then he takes to meeting her at the dance hall. Finally he has the nerve to take her to a hotel— and register as man and wife. . . . The last I heard they were diddlin' one another in a vacant lot near the ball grounds. Some day, Hen, that guy's goin' to make the headlines. And boy, that won't make pleasant reading!'

At this point I had a flash of memory, so vivid and so complete, I could scarcely contain myself. It was like opening a Japanese fan. The picture was of a time when George and I were still twins, so to speak. I was then working for my father, which means I must have been twenty-two or -three. George Marshall had come down with a bad case of pneumonia which had kept him bed-ridden for several months. When he got well enough, his parents shipped him to the country—somewhere in New Jersey. It all started by my receiving a letter from him one day saying that he was recuperating fast and wouldn't I come to visit him. I was only too glad of the chance to steal a few days' vacation, and so I sent him a wire saying I'd be there the following day.

It was late autumn. The countryside was cheerless. George met me at the station, with his young cousin, Herbie. (The farm was run by George's aunt and uncle, that is, his mother's sister and her husband.) The first words out of his mouth—as I might well have expected—were to the effect that it was his mother who had saved his life. He was overjoyed to see me and appeared to be in excellent shape. He was brown and weatherbeaten.

'The grub is wonderful, Hen,' he said. 'It's a real farm, you know.'

To me it looked much like any other farm—sort of seedy, grubby and run-down. His aunt was a stout, kind-hearted, motherly creature whom George worshipped, apparently, almost as much as he did his mother. Herbie, the son, was a bit of a zany. A blabbermouth too. But what got me at once was the look of wonder in his eyes. He evidently idolized George. And then the way we talked to one another was something new for him. It was hard to shake him off our heels.

The first thing we did—I remember it so well—was to have a tall glass of milk. Rich milk. Milk such as I hadn't tasted since I was a boy. 'Drink five and six of them a day,' says George. He cut me a thick slice of home-made bread, spread some country butter over it, and over that some home-made jam.

'Did you bring any old clothes with you, Hen?'

I confessed I hadn't thought of that.

'Never mind, I'll lend you my things. You've got to wear old clothes here. You'll see.'

He looked pointedly at Herbie. 'Eh, Herbie?'

I had arrived on the afternoon train. It was now getting on to dark. 'Change your clothes, Hen, and we'll take a brisk hike. Dinner won't be ready till seven. Got to work up an appetite, you know.'

'Yeah,' said Herbie, 'we're going to have chicken tonight.'

And in the next breath he asked me if I were a good runner.

George gave me a sly wink. 'He's crazy about games, Hen.'

When I met them at the foot of the stairs I was handed a big stick. 'Better wear your gloves,' said Herbie.

He threw me a big woollen muffler.

'All set?' says George. 'Come on, let's hurry.' And he starts off at a recording-breaking clip.

'Why the hurry?' said I. 'Where are we going?'

'Down by the station,' said Herbie.

'And what's down there?'

'You'll see. Won't he, George?'

The station was a dismal, forlorn affair. A line of freight cars were standing there, waiting for milk cans, no doubt.

'Listen,' said George, slowing up a bit to keep in step with me, 'the idea is to take the lead. You know what I mean!' He talked rapidly, mumbling the words, as if there were something secretive connected with our actions. 'Up to now there's been just Herbie and me: we've had to make our own fun. Nothing to worry about, Hen. You'll get on to it quick enough. Just follow me.'

I was more than ever baffled by this quixotic piece of information. As we hopped along Herbie became positively electrified. He gabbled like an old turkey cock.

George opened the door of the station softly, stealthily, and peered inside. An old drunk was snoozing away on the bench. 'Here,' said George, grabbing my hat and stuffing an old cap in my hand, 'wear this!' He shoves a crazy looking contraption on his own head and pins a badge on his coat. 'You stay here,' he commands, 'and I'll open shop. Do just as Herbie does and you'll be all right.'

As George ducks into the office and opens the ticket window Herbie pulls me by the hand. 'This is it, Hen,' says he, going up to the window where George is already standing, pretending to make up the train schedule.

'Sir, I would like to buy a ticket,' says Herbie in a timid voice.

'A ticket to where?' says George, frowning, 'We've got all kinds of tickets here. Do you want first, second, or third class? Let's see, the Weehawken Express pulls out of here in about eight minutes. She's making a connection with the Denver and Rio Grande at Omaha Junction. *Any baggage?*'

'Please sir, I don't know where I want to go yet.'

'Whaddaya mean, you don't know where you want to go? What do you think this is—*a lottery*? Who's that man behind you? Any relation of yours?'

Herbie turns round to look at me and blinks.

'He's my great uncle, sir. Wants to go to Winnipeg, but he's not sure when.'

'Tell him to to step up here. What's the matter with him—is he deaf or just hard of hearing?'

Herbie pushed me in front of him. We look at each other, George Marshall and I, as if we had never seen each other before.

'I just *came* from Winnipeg,' says I. 'Isn't there some other place I could go to?'

'I could sell you a ticket to New Brunswick, but there wouldn't be much in it for the company. We've got to make ends meet, you know. Now here's a nice looking ticket for Spuyten Duyvil—how would that suit you? Or would you like something more expensive?'

'I'd like to go by way of the Great Lakes, if you could arrange it.'

'*Arrange it?* That's my business! How many in the party? Any cats or dogs? You know the lakes are frozen now, don't you? But you can catch the iceboat this side of Canandaigua. I don't have to draw a map for you, do I?'

I leaned forward as if to communicate something private and confidential.

'*Don't whisper!*' he shouted, banging a ruler against the counter. 'It's against the rules. . . . Now then, what is it you wished to convey to me? Speak clearly and pause for your commas and semi-colons.'

'It's about the coffin,' I said.

'The *coffin?* Why didn't you mention that right off? Hold on a minute, I'll have to telegraph the dispatch master.' He went over to the machine and tapped the keys. 'Got to get a special routing. Livestock and corpses take the deferred route. They spoil too quickly. . . . Anything in the coffin besides the body?'

'Yes sir, my wife.'

'Get the hell out of here before I call the police!' Down came the window with a bang. And then an infernal racket inside the coop, as if the new station master had run amok.

'Quick,' says Herbie, 'Let's get out of here. I know a short cut, come on!' And grabbing my hand, he pulls me out by the other door, around by the water tank. 'Flop down, quick,' he says, 'or they'll spy you.' We flopped in a puddle of dirty water under the tank. 'Shhhhh!' says Herbie, putting his finger over my lips. 'They might hear you.'

We lay there for a few minutes, then Herbie got up on all fours, cautiously, looking about as if we were already trapped. 'You lay here a minute and I'll run up the ladder and see if the tank's empty.'

'They're nuts,' I said to myself. Suddenly I asked myself why I should be lying in that cold dirty water. Herbie called softly: 'Come on up, the coast is clear. We can hide in here a while.' As I gripped the iron rungs I felt wind go through me like an icy blast. 'Don't fall in,' says Herbie, 'the tank's half-full.' I climbed to the top and hung from the inside of the tank with frozen hands.

'How long do we stay this way?' I asked after a few minutes. 'Not long,' says Herbie. 'They're changing the watch now. Hear 'em? George'll be waiting for us in the caboose. He'll have a nice warm stove going.'

It was dark when we clambered out of the tank and raced across the yard to the end of the freight train standing on the siding. I was frozen through and through. Herbie was right. As we opened the door of the caboose there was George sitting before a hot stove, warming his hands.

'Take you coat off, Hen,' he says, 'and dry yourself.' Then he reaches up to a little closet and gets down a flask of whiskey. 'Here, take a good pull—this is dynamite.' I did as instructed, passed the flask to George who took a good swig himself, and then to little Herbie.

'Did you bring any provisions?' says George to Herbie.

'A chippie and a couple of potatoes,' says Herbie, fishing them out of his pockets.

'Where's the mayonnaise?'

'I couldn't find it, *honest*,' says Herbie.

'Next time I want mayonnaise, understand?' thunders George Marshall. 'How the hell do you expect me to eat roast potatoes without mayonnaise?' Then, without transition, he continues: 'Now the idea is to crawl under the cars until we're near the engine. When I whistle, the two of you crawl from under and run as fast as you can. Take the short cut down to the river. I'll meet you under the bridge. Here Hen, better take another gulp of this . . . it's cold down there. Next time I'll offer you a cigar— but don't take it! *How do you feel now?*'

I felt so good I couldn't see the sense of leaving in a hurry. But evidently their plans had to be executed in strict timing.

'How about that chippie and the potatoes?' I ventured to ask.

'That's for next time,' says George. 'We can't afford to be trapped here.' He turns to Herbie. 'Have you got the gun?'

Off again, scrambling around under the freight trains as if we were outlaws. I was glad Herbie had given me the woollen muffler. At a given signal Herbie and I flung ourselves face downward under the car, waiting for George's whistle.

'What's the next move?' I whispered.

'Shhhhh! Someone may hear you.'

In a few minutes we heard a low whistle, crawled out from

under, and ran as fast as our legs would carry us down the ravine towards the bridge. There was George again, sitting under the bridge, waiting. 'Good work,' he says. 'We gave 'em the slip all right. Now listen, we'll rest a minute or two and then we'll make for that hill over there, do you see?' He turned to Herbie. 'Is the gun loaded?'

Herbie examined his rusty old Colt, nodded, then shoved it back in the holster.

'Remember,' says George, 'don't shoot unless it's absolutely necessary. I don't want you to be killing any more children accidentally, you understand?'

There was a gleam in Herbie's eyes as he shook his head.

'The idea, Hen, is to get to the foot of that hill before they give the alarm. Once we get there we're safe. We'll make a detour home by way of the swamp.'

We started off on a trot, crouching low. Soon we were in the bulrushes and the water coming over our shoe tops. 'Keep an eye open for tramps,' muttered George. We got to the foot of the hill without detection, rested there a few moments, then set off at a brisk pace to skirt the swamp. Finally we reached the road and settled down to a leisurely walk.

'We'll be home in a few minutes,' says George. 'We'll go in by the back way and change our clothes. Mum's the word.'

'Are you sure we shook them off?' I asked.

'Reasonably sure,' says George.

'The last time they followed us right to the barn,' says Herbie. 'What happens if we get caught?'

Herbie drew the side of his hand across his throat.

I mumbled something to the effect that I wasn't sure I wanted to be involved.

'You've got to be,' says Herbie. 'It's a feud.'

'We'll explain it in detail tomorrow,' says George.

In the big room upstairs there were two beds, one for me, and one for Herbie and George. We made a fire at once in the big-bellied stove, and began changing our clothes.

'How would you like to give me a rubdown?' says George, stripping off his under-shirt. 'I get a rubdown twice a day. First alcohol and then goose fat. Nothing like it, Hen.'

He lay down on the big bed and I went to work. I rubbed until my hands ached.

'Now you lay down,' says George, 'and Herbie'll fix you up. Makes a new man of you.'

I did as instructed. It sure felt good. My blood tingled, my flesh glowed. I had an appetite such as I hadn't known in ages.

'You see why I came here,' says George. 'After supper we'll play a round of pinochle—just to please the old man—and then we'll turn in.'

'By the way, Hen,' he added, 'watch your tongue. No cursing

or swearing in front of the old man. He's a Methodist. We say grace before we eat. Try not to laugh!'

'You'll have to do it too some night,' says Herbie. 'Say any god-damned thing that comes to mind. Nobody listens anyway.'

At the table I was introduced to the old man. He was the typical farmer—big horny hands, unshaven, smelling of clover and manure, sparse of speech, wolfing his food, belching, picking his teeth with the fork and complaining about his rheumatism. We ate enormous quantities, all of us. There were at least six or seven vegetables to go with the roast chicken, followed by a delicious bread pudding, fruits and nuts of all kinds. Everyone but myself drank milk with his food. Then came coffee with real cream and salted peanuts. I had to open my belt a couple of notches.

As soon as the meal was over the table was cleared and a pack of greasy playing cards was produced. Herbie had to help his mother with the dishes while George, the old man and I played a three-handed game of pinochle. The idea was, as George had already explained, to throw the game to the old man, otherwise he became grouchy and surly. I seemed to draw nothing but excellent hands, which made it difficult for me to lose. But I did my best, without being too obvious about it. The old man won by a narrow margin. He was highly pleased with himself. 'With your hands,' he remarked, 'I would have been out in three deals.'

Before we went upstairs for the night Herbie put on a couple of Edison phonograph records. One of them was *The Stars and Stripes Forever*. It sounded like something from another incarnation.

'Where's that laughing record, Herbie?' says George.

Herbie dug into an old hat box and with two fingers dexterously extracted an old wax cylinder. It was a record I've never heard the like of. Nothing but laughter—the laughter of a loon, a crack-pot, a hyena. I laughed so hard my stomach ached.

'That's nothing,' says George, 'wait till you hear Herbie laugh!'

'Not now!' I begged. 'Save it for tomorrow.'

I no more than hit the pillow and I was sound asleep. What a bed! Nothing but soft, downy feathers—tons of them, it seemed. It was like slipping back into the womb, swinging in limbo. Bliss. Perfect bliss.

'There's a piss-pot under the bed, if you need it,' were George's last words. But I couldn't see myself getting out of that bed, not even to take a crap.

In my sleep I heard the maniacal laugh of the loon. It was echoed by the rusty door knobs, the green vegetables, the wild geese, the slanting stars, the wet clothes flapping on the line. It even included Herbie's old man, the part of him that gave way sometimes to melancholy mirth. It came from far away, deliciously off-key, absurd and unreasonable. It was the laugh of aching muscles, of food passing through the midriff, of time foolishly squandered, of millions of nothings all harmoniously fitting together in the great jig-saw puzzle and making extraordinary sense, extraordinary beauty, extraordinary well-being. How fortunate that George Marshall had fallen ill and almost died! In my sleep I praised the grand cosmocrator for having arranged everything so sublimely. I slid from one dream to another, and from dream to a stone-like slumber more healing than death itself.

I awoke before the others, content, refreshed, motionless except for a pleasure waggle of the fingers. The farm-yard cacophany was music to my ears. The rustling and scraping, the banging of pails, the cock-a-doodle-doo, the pitter patter, the calls of the birds, the cackling and grunting, the squealing, the neighing and whinnying, the chug-chug of a distant locomotive, the crunch of hard snow, the slap and gust of the wind, a rusty axle turning, a log wheezing under the saw, the thud of heavy boots trudging laboriously—all combined to make a symphony familiar to my ear. These homely ancient sounds, these calls, cackles, echoes and reverberations of the barn-yard filled me with an earthling's joy. A starveling and a changeling, I heard again the immemorial chant of early man. The old, old song—of ease and abundance, of life where you find it, of blue sky, running waters, peace and gladness, of fertility and resurrection, and life everlasting, life more abundant, life superabundant. A song that starts in the very bowels, pervades the veins, relaxes the limbs and all the members of the body. Ah, but it was indeed good to be alive—and horizontal. Fully awake, I once again gave thanks to the Heavenly Father for having stricken my twin, George Marshall. And, whilst rendering devout thanks, praising the divine works, extolling all creation, I allowed my thoughts to drift towards the breakfast which was doubtless under way and towards the long, lazy stretch of hours, minutes, seconds before the day would draw to a close. It mattered not how we filled the day, nor if we left it empty as a gourd; it mattered only that time was ours and that we could do with it as we wished.

The birds were calling more lustily now. I could hear them winging from tree top to tree top, fluttering against the window-panes, swooshing about under the eaves of the roof.

'Morning, Hen! Morning, Hen!'

'Morning, George! Morning, Herbie!'

'Don't get up yet, Hen . . . Herbie'll make the fire first.'

'O.K. Sounds wonderful.'

'How did you sleep?'

'Like a top.'

'You see why I don't want to get well too quick.'

'Lucky guy, you. Aren't you glad you didn't die?'

'Hen, I'm never going to die. I promised myself that on my death-bed. It's just too wonderful to be alive.'

'You said it. I say, George, let's fool them all and live forever, *what?*'

Herbie got up to make the fire, then crawled back into bed and began chuckling and cooing.

'What do we do now?' I asked. 'Lie here till the bell rings?'

'Exactly,' said Herbie.

'I say, Hen, wait till you taste those corn muffins his mother makes. They melt in your mouth.'

'How do you like your eggs?' said Herbie. 'Boiled, fried or scrambled?'

'Any old way, Herbie. Who gives a damn? Eggs are eggs. I can suck them raw too.'

'The bacon, Hen, that's the thing. Thick as your thumb.'

Thus the second day began, to be followed by a dozen more, all of the same tenor. As I said before, we were twenty-two or three at the time, and still in our adolescence. We had nothing on our minds but play. Each day it was a new game, full of hair-raising stunts. 'To take the lead,' as George had put it, was as easy as drawing one's breath. Between times we skipped rope, threw quoits, rolled marbles, played leap-frog. We even played tag. In the toilet, which was an outhouse, we kept a chess board on which a problem was always waiting for us. Often the three of us took a shit together. Strange conversations in that out-house! Always some fresh tit-bit about George's mother, what she had done for him, what a saint she was, and so on. Once he started to talk about God, how there *must* be one, since only God could have pulled him through. Herbie listened reverently —he worshipped George.

One day George drew me aside to tell me something confidential. We were to give Herbie the slip for an hour or so. There was a young country girl he wanted me to meet. We could find her down near the bridge, towards dark, with the right signal.

'She looks twenty, though she's only a kid,' said George, as we hastened towards the spot. 'A virgin, of course, but a dirty little devil. You can't get much more than a good feel, Hen. I've tried everything, but it's no go.'

Kitty was her name. It suited her. A plain-looking girl, but full of sap and curiosity. Hump for the monkeys.

'Hello,' says George, as we sidle up to her. 'How's tricks? Want you to meet a friend of mine, from the city.'

Her hand was tingling with warmth and desire. It seemed to me she was blushing, but it may have been simply the abundant health which was bursting through her cheeks.

'Give him a hug and squeeze.'

Kitty flung her arms about me and pressed her warm body

tight to mine. In a moment her tongue was down my throat. She bit my lips, my ear lobes, my neck. I put my hand under her skirt and through the slit in her flannel drawers. No protest. She began to groan and murmur. Finally she had an orgasm.

'How was it, Hen? What did I tell you?'

We chatted a while to give Kitty a breathing spell, then George locked horns with her. It was cold and wet under the bridge, but the three of us were on fire. Again George tried to get it in, but Kitty managed to wriggle away.

The most he could do was to put it between her legs, where she held it like a vice.

As we were walking back towards the road Kitty asked if she couldn't visit us sometime—when we got back to the city. She had never been to New York.

'Sure,' said George, 'Let Herbie bring you. He knows his way around.'

'But I won't have any money,' said Kitty.

'Don't worry about that,' said big-hearted George, 'we'll take care of you.'

'Do you think your mother would trust you?' I asked.

Kitty replied that her mother didn't give a damn what she did. 'It's the old man: he tries to work me to the bone.'

'Never mind,' said George, 'Leave it to me.'

In parting she lifted her dress of her own accord, and invited us to give her a last good feel.

'Maybe I won't be so shy,' she said, 'when I get to the city.' Then, impulsively, she reached into our flies, took out our cocks, and kissed them—almost reverently. 'I'll dream about you tonight,' she whispered. She was almost on the point of tears.

'See you tomorrow,' said George, and we waved good-bye.

'See what I mean, Hen? Boy, if you could get that you'd have something to remember.'

'My balls are aching.'

'Drink lots of milk and cream. That helps.'

'I think I'd rather jerk off.'

'That's what you think *now*. Tomorrow you'll be panting to see her. I know. She's in my blood, the little bitch. . . . Don't let Herbie know about this, Hen. He'd be horrified. He's just a kid compared to her. I think he's in love with her.'

'What will we tell him when we get back?'

'Leave that to me.'

'*And her old man*—don't you ever think of that?'

'You said it, Hen. If he ever caught us I think he'd cut our balls off.'

'That's cheering.'

'You've got to take a chance,' said George. 'Here in the country all the gals are dying for it. They're much better than city tripe, you know that. They smell clean. *Here*, smell my fingers—ain't that delicious?'

Childish amusements. . . . One of the funniest things was taking turns riding an old tricycle which had belonged to Herbie's dead sister. To see George Marshall, a grown man, pushing the pedals of that ridiculous vehicle was a sight for sore eyes. His fanny was so big he had to be squeezed into the seat with might and main. Steering with one hand, he energetically rang a cowbell with the other. Now and then a car stopped, thinking he was a cripple in trouble: George would allow the occupants to get out and escort him to the other side of the road, pretending that he was indeed a paralytic. Sometimes he would bum a cigarette or demand a few pennies. Always in a strong Irish brogue, as if he had just arrived from the old country.

One day I espied an old baby carriage in the barn. It struck me that it would be still funnier if we took George Marshall out for a walk in that. George didn't give a shit. We got a bonnet with ribbons and a big horse blanket to cover him. But try as we would, we couldn't get him into the carriage. So Herbie was elected. We dressed him up like a kewpie doll, stuck a clay pipe in his mouth, and started down the road. At the station we ran into an elderly spinster waiting for the train. As usual, George took the lead.

'I say, Ma'am,' touching his cap, 'but would you be tellin' us where we might get a little nip? The boy's almost frozen.'

'Dear me,' said the spinster automatically. Then suddenly getting the drift of his words, she squeaked: *'What's that you said, young man?'*

Again George touched his cap respectfully, pursing his lips and squinting like an old spaniel. 'Just a wee nip, that's all. He's nigh on to eleven but it's a terrible thirst he has.'

Herbie was sitting up now, puffing vigorously at the short clay pipe. He looked like a gnome.

At this point I felt like taking the lead myself. The spinster had a look of alarm which I didn't like.

'I beg pardon, Ma'am,' said I, touching my cap, 'but the two of them are dotty. You know. . . .' I tapped my skull.

'Dear me, dear me,' she wheezed, 'how perfectly dreadful.'

'I do my best to keep them in good spirits. They're quite a trial. Quite. Especially the little one. Would you like to hear him laugh?'

Without giving her a chance to answer, I beckoned Herbie to go to it. Herbie's laugh was really insane. He did it like a ventriloquist's dummy, beginning with an innocent little smile which slowly broadened into a grin, then a chuckle and a cooing followed by a low gurgling, and finally a belly laugh which was irresistible. He could keep it up indefinitely. With the pipe in one hand and the rattle which he waved frantically in the other, he was a picture out of a Swiss joke book. Every now and then he paused to hiccup violently, then leaned over the side of the carriage and spat. To make the situation still more ludicrous, George Marshall had taken to sneezing. Pulling out a large red handkerchief with huge holes in it, he vigorously blew his nose, then coughed, then sneezed some more.

'The tantrums,' I said, turning to the spinster. 'There's no harm they be doing. Wonderful boys, the two of 'em—except they be queer.' Then, on the impulse, I added: 'Fact is, Ma'am,' touching my cap reverently, 'we're all screw-balls. You wouldn't know where we might stop for the night, seein' the condition we're in? If only you had a drop of brandy—just a thimbleful. Not for meself, you understand, but for the little ones.'

Herbie broke into a crying fit. He was so gleefully hysterical he didn't know what he was doing. He waved the rattle so assiduously that suddenly he lurched too far and the carriage tipped over.

'Goodness gracious, goodness gracious!' wailed the spinster.

George quickly pulled Herbie loose. The latter now stood up, in his jacket and long pants, the bonnet still wreathed around his head. He clutched the rattle like a maniac. Goofy was no word for it.

Says George, touching his cap, 'No hurt, Ma'am. He's got a thick skull.' He takes Herbie by the arm and pulls him close. 'Say something to the lady! Say something nice!' And he gives him a god-awful box on the ears.

'You bastard!' yells Herbie.

'Naughty, naughty!' says George, giving him another cuff. 'What do you say to ladies? Speak up now, or I'll have to take your pants down.'

Herbie now assumed an angelic expression, raised his eyes heavenward, and with great deliberation, delivered himself thus:

'Gentle creature of God, may the angels deliver you! There are nine of us in all, not counting the goat. My name is O'Connell, Ma'am. Terence O'Connell, we were going to Niagara Falls, but the weather. . . .'

The old cluck refused to hear any more. 'You're a public disgrace, the three of you,' she cried. 'Now stay here, all of you, while I look for the constable.'

'Yes, Ma'am,' says George, touching his cap, 'we'll stay right here, won't we, Terence?' With this he gives Herbie a sound slap in the face.

'Ouch!' yells Herbie.

'Stop that, you fool!' screams the spinster. 'And *you*!' she says to me, 'why don't *you* do something? Or are you crazy too?'

'That I am,' says I, and so saying, I put my fingers to my nose and began bleating like a nanny goat.

'Stay right here! I'll be back in a minute!' She ran towards the station master's office.

'Quick!' says George, 'let's get the hell out of here!' The two of us grabbed the handle of the baby carriage and started running. Herbie stood there a moment, unfastening his bonnet; then he too took to his heels.

'Good work, Herbie,' said George, when we got safely out of sight. 'Let's rehearse this tonight. Hen'll give you a new spiel, won't you Hen?'

'I don't want to be the baby any more,' said Herbie.

'All right,' said George amiably, 'we'll let Hen ride in the carriage.'

'If I can squeeze in, you mean.'

'We'll squeeze you in, if we have to use a sledge-hammer.'

But after dinner that night we got new ideas, better ones, we thought. We lay awake till midnight discussing plans and projects.

Just as we were dozing off, George Marshall suddenly sat up.

'Are you awake, Hen?' he says.

I groaned.

'There's something I forgot to ask you.'

'What's that?' I mumbled, fearing to wake myself up.

'Una . . . Una Gifford! You haven't said a word about her all this time. What's the matter, aren't you in love with her any more?'

'Jesus!' I groaned, 'what a thing to ask me in the middle of the night.'

'I know, Hen, I'm sorry. I just want to know if you still love her.'

'You know the answer,' I replied.

'Good, I thought so. O.K., Hen, good-night!'

'Good-night!' said Herbie.

'Good-night!' said I.

I tried to fall back to sleep but it was impossible. I lay there staring at the ceiling and thinking of Una Gifford. After a while I decided to get it out of my system.

'Are you still awake, George?' I called softly.

'You want to know if I saw her lately, don't you?' he said.

He hadn't closed his eyes, obviously.

'Yeah, I would. Tell me anything. Any little crumb will do.'

'I wish I could, Hen, I know how you feel, but there just isn't anything to tell.'

'Christ, don't say that! Make up something!'

'All right, Hen, I'll do that for you. Hold on a minute. Let me think. . . .'

'Something simple,' I said. 'I don't want a fantastic story.'

'Listen, Hen, this is no lie: I know she loves you. I can't explain how I know, but I do.'

'That's good,' I said. 'Tell me a little more.'

'The last time I saw her I tried to pump her about you. She pretended to be absolutely indifferent. But I could tell she was dying to hear about you. . . .'

'What I'd like to know,' I broke in, 'is this: has she taken up with someone else?'

'There *is* somebody, Hen, I can't deny that. But it's nothing to worry about. He's just a fill-in.'

'What's his name?'

'Carnahan or something like that. Forget about him! What worries Una is the widow. That hurt her, you know.'

'She can't know very much about *that*!'

'She knows more than you think. Where she gets it, I don't know. Anyway, her pride's hurt.'

'But I'm not going with the widow any more, you know that.'

'Tell it to *her*!' says George.

'I wish I could.'

'Hen, why don't you make a clean breast of it? She's big enough to take it.'

'I can't do it, George. I've thought and thought about it, but I can't screw up the courage.'

'Maybe I can help you,' said George.

I sat up with a bang. 'You think so? Really? Listen, George, I'd swear my life away to you if you could patch it up. I know she'd listen to *you*. . . . *When are you going back?*'

'Not so fast, Hen. Remember, it's an old sore. I'm not a wizard.'

'But you'll try, you promise me that?'

'Of course, of course. *Fratres Semper!*'

I thought hard and fast for a few minutes, then I said: 'I'll write her a letter tomorrow, saying I'm with you and that we'll both be back soon. That might prepare the way.'

'Better not,' said George promptly. 'Better spring a surprise on her. I know Una.'

Maybe he was right. I didn't know what to think. I felt elated and depressed at the same time. Besides, there was no prodding him into quick action.

'Better go to sleep,' said George. 'We've got lots of time to hatch up something.'

'I'd go back tomorrow, if I could get you to go with me.'

'You're crazy, Hen. I'm still convalescing. She won't get married in a hurry, if that's what's eating you up.'

The very thought of her marrying someone else petrified me. Somehow I had never visualized that. I sank back on the pillow like a dying man. I actually groaned with anguish.

'Hen. . . .'

'Yes?'

'Before I go to sleep I want to tell you something. . . . You've got to stop taking this so seriously. Sure, if we can patch it up, fine! I'd like nother better than to see you get her. But you won't if you let it get under your skin. She's going to make you miserable just as long as she can. That's her way of getting back at you. She's going to say No because you expect her to say No. You're off balance. You're licked before you start. . . . If you want a bit of advice, I'd say drop her for a while. Drop her cold. It's a risk, certainly, but you've got to take it. As long as she's got the upper hand you're going to dance like a puppet. No woman can resist doing that. She's not an angel, even if you like to think she is. She's a swell-looking girl and she's got a big heart. I'd marry her myself, if I thought I stood a chance. . . . Listen, Hen, there's plenty to pick from. For all you know, there may even be better ones than Una. Have you ever thought of *that?*'

'You're talking drivel,' I replied. 'I wouldn't care if she were the worst bitch in creation . . . she's the one I want—*and no one else.*'

'O.K., Hen, it's your funeral. I'm going to sleep. . . .'

I lay awake a long while, revolving all manner of memories. They were delicious thoughts, filled with Una's presence. I was certain George would patch it up for me. He liked to be coaxed, that was all. Through a slit in the window-shade I could see a brilliant blue star. Seemed like a good omen. I wondered, calf-like, if she were also lying awake mooning about me. I concentrated all my powers, hoping to wake her if she were asleep. Under my breath I softly called her name. It was such a beautiful name. It suited her perfectly.

Finally I began to doze. The words of an olden song came to my lips. . . .

> I wonder as I wander out under the sky
> How Jesus our Saviour did come for to die
> For poor orn'ry people like you and like I
> I wonder as I wander out under the sky

Forget all about her? How easy to say that! I could never, never forget Una, not even if I lived to have nine wives and forty-six children. George was really a sap. He would never know what it was to be in love—he was too clear-headed. I made up my mind to find out all about that guy Carnahan as soon as I got back. Taking no chances. I wondered some more as I wandered out under the sky. Then blotto—like a sheet of lead falling.

The next day it rained. We cooped ourselves up in the barn the whole day, playing one game after another—euchre, whist, backgammon, checkers, dominoes, lotto, parchesi. . . . We even played jacks. Towards evening George suggested that we try out the organ which was in the parlour. It was an ancient, wheezy contraption, just made for melancholy hymns. George and I took turns playing. We sang with full lungs, lustily, like Christian martyrs. Our favourite, which we jazzed up finally, was—'Will There be any Stars in my Crown?' Herbie could sing it to perfection, with tears in his eyes. His mother, never dreaming that we were clowning it, came in, took a seat in the corner, and murmured now and then: 'How beautiful!'

Finally the old man appeared. He too joined in the singing. Said it made him feel good. Hoped we boys would continue to live and act like good Christians. At dinner he thanked God for having inspired us to sing His praises so beautifully. He thanked Him heartily for all the blessings He had showered on them throughout the years.

It was a smoked tenderloin of pork this time, with sauerkraut and mashed potatoes, red cabbage, boiled onions, apple sauce and stewed pears. For dessert we had a cheese cake which was still warm. And, of course, the usual glass of milk rich with cream.

Oddly enough, the old man was talkative for a change. He had been reading a book, the same book, for over a year now. It was called *In Tune with the Infinite*. He wondered if George or I had ever read it. George avoided the issue, but gave me a sidelong glance which meant—'Take the lead!'

Since we had to talk, I felt we might just as well make an evening of it on a subject dear to the old man's heart. I began by pretending that I wasn't certain I had understood everything the author meant to convey. The old man was pleased by this show of modesty. He probably had understood very little himself, if the truth were known.

'I had a friend once,' I began, 'who could explain all manner of things. He carried this very book about with him night and day, wherever he went. George knows who I mean, don't you George?'

'Sure,' says George, 'you mean Abercrombie.'

(There was no such person, of course.)

'Yes, that's the name.'

'He lisped a bit, didn't he?' said George.

'No, he limped.'

The old man signalled to get on with the story. He didn't care what the man's name was nor whether he limped or stuttered.

'I met him out in California, about three years ago, it was. He was studying to be a minister of the gospel then. I say then, because he discovered a gold mine shortly after we met and he forgot all about God pretty quick.'

'Didn't he meet with an accident?' says George.

'No, that was his brother—or his half-brother, rather.'

The old man didn't relish George's interruptions, I could see that plainly. I decided to make haste.

'It was at the edge of the Mojave Desert we happened to meet,' I continued. 'I had been looking for a job with the borax people.

Abercrombie says to me: "You don't want a job, Henry, what you need is to find God. I've come to help you." He called me Henry, mind you, though I had never told him my name. He says: "I had a dream about you back in Barstow the other night. I knew you were in trouble, so I came just as quickly as I could." His talk made me just a little uneasy. I had never before met anyone who had second sight or who could communicate telepathically. I thought at first he might be spoofing me. But he was dead serious, as I soon discovered.'

'You say he had this book with him?' the old man asked, looking somewhat puzzled.

'Yes sir . . . it was by Ralph Waldo Trine, wasn't it?'

'That's right,' said the old man. 'Go on now, I'm interested.'

'I hardly know where to begin,' I faltered. 'Seems like so many things happened at once.'

'Take your time,' said the old man, 'this is very interesting indeed. Mom, let's have some more of that coffee, will you—and another cut of cheese cake.'

I was glad to have a breather because I actually didn't know what was coming next. I had started a story without any idea of how it would end. I had expected George Marshall to fill in, to help me over the humps.

'As I was saying, we were alone out there in the desert. He had come to me in the middle of the night, and he was standing there talking to me as if he had known me all his life. In fact, I might say that he seemed to know me better than my most intimate friends. He kept saying, "You're in trouble, let me help you." Now the strange thing is I didn't know I was in trouble, not any special trouble, at any rate. All I wanted was a job, and that wasn't so difficult. But the next day I realized that he knew what he was talking about, because in the afternoon I got a telegram from a friend of mine saying my mother was very ill and that I should return at once. I didn't have more than a couple of dollars in my pocket. Of course, Abercrombie knew what was in the telegram—I didn't have to read it aloud to him. "What'll I do?" I says, and he answers: "Get down on your knees and pray!" So I got down, and he got down too, right beside me, and we prayed a long time. I immediately felt better, I must say. It was a though a load had been lifted off me. That very evening a stranger knocked at our door. He was a cattleman from Wyoming. He wanted to know if we could put him up for the night. Well, we got to talking and before long he too knew all about my circumstances. We went to bed and the next morning this stranger pulls me aside. "How much would it take to get you back home?" he asks me straight off. I was flabbergasted. I didn't know what to say. "Here, take this," he says, and he shoves two bills in my hand. They were two fifty dollar bills. "I guess that'll see you through," he says, giving me a warm, friendly smile.

"I'll pay you back as soon as I can," I said gratefully. "Don't worry about that, son," he says, "I've got more than I need. Take it and give it to somebody else in need when the time comes."

'When he left, Abercrombie says to me: "Your prayer was answered. Never doubt again. I'm going back to Barstow. If you're ever in need again, send for me."

' "But where and how?" I asked.

' "Send out a call, that's all. I'll get it wherever you are. Just believe."

'About six months later I was in trouble again. This time over a woman. I was desperate. And then suddenly I remembered Abercrombie's words, and I sent out a call. Three days later he showed up at my home—all the way from Colorado.'

The old man leaned forward, his elbows on the table, his head buried in his hands. 'That *is* remarkable, Henry,' he said. 'And did he help you the second time?'

'He did indeed,' I answered. 'I didn't have to do a thing, except pray. This time, when he left, Abercrombie says to me: "You'll never have to send for me again, Henry. By now you must realize that it is not I who has the power but God. Trust in Him and your prayers will be answered. I'll probably never see you again —but I'll always be near you, in spirit." And I never did see him again. But, as he said, I know he's always near. I'd know if he were to die, for instance.'

'Well, George,' says the old man, 'what have to say for yourself? Did you ever have an experience like that?'

'No,' says George, 'but I'd like to ask Hen a question.' He turned to me with a perfectly straight face, and said: 'Isn't it true. Hen, that this Abercrombie was a jail-bird once?'

(Pure invention, of course, but I had to take it up.)

'Yes,' I replied, 'he had been in prison for ten years on a charge of manslaughter. I never knew whether he was guilty or not.'

'But how did he happen to commit the crime?'

I had to think fast.

'He was convicted of killing a man in self-defence. There were no witnesses.'

'But didn't Abercrombie have a strange reputation—before the killing?'

'Ye-e-s,' I admitted, not knowing what George's next move might be.

'Did it ever strike you, Hen, that Abercrombie was a bit queer? I don't mean crazy, but he must have had a loose tile. Didn't you tell me once that he believed he could fly?'

'Yes, he did say that—once. But he never repeated it. He wasn't boasting, either, when he said it. He was telling me of the extraordinary powers God sometimes grants us mortals when we have need of His protection. That isn't so queer, is it?'

'Maybe not, Hen . . . but there were other things.'

'Like what?'

'You said he could see in the dark, like a cat, that he heard things other people couldn't possibly hear, that he had a phenomenal memory. I think you said once that he claimed to have two fathers. *What did he mean by that?*'

This last really stumped me. I had to admit I couldn't answer the question.

'Listen, Hen, there were a lot of things about Abercrombie that were shady. I never said anything at the time, because you believed in him so implicitly. You said before that he discovered a gold mine. Are you sure of that?'

'No,' I said, 'I heard that from his half-brother.'

'Who was a notorious liar,' says George quickly.

The old man signified that he wasn't taking kindly to George's grilling.

'But Hen's gullible,' George insisted. 'He believes anything and everything.'

'Belief is God-like,' said the old man curtly.

'But it's got to be within reason,' said George. 'One can't believe anything and everything!'

'George,' said the old man, 'you're like your father. You're a doubting Thomas.'

'Now, now,' said George's aunt, 'don't say things like that!'

'I will too!' said the old man, thumping the table with his fist. 'George's father is a good man, but he has no faith. He never did have any—not an ounce. He'll die in sin, like he was born.'

The old man's wrath was rising.

'He's been good to me,' said George stubbornly, not because he cared about his father, but just to make the old man angrier.

'That doesn't matter,' said the old man, 'it's his duty to treat you right, he deserves no credit for that. *What is he doing for God?* That's what I want to know.'

George couldn't answer that. The old man continued to rant and rail. His wife tried to calm him down but succeeded only in fanning his ire. These bursts of temper obviously took the place of a good souse.

I don't know what would have happened had not little Herbie had an inspiration. Suddenly he began to sing—one of those sweet, sticky Christian hymns which make the tears flow. He sang like an angel, with eyes closed, and in a falsetto voice. We were all so astounded no one dared say a word. When he had finished, he leaned forward, bowed his head, and murmured a prayer. He begged God to restore peace and harmony in the bosom of the family, to forgive his father for losing his temper, to ease his mother's burdens, and finally with great sanctimoniousness, to look after cousin George who had been grievously stricken. When he lifted his face the tears were streaming down his cheeks.

The old man was visibly moved. Apparently Herbie had never put on an act like this before.

'You'd better go to bed now, son,' he said, his voice quivering. 'Tomorrow I'm going to get you that bicycle you've been asking for.'

'Bless you, father,' said Herbie. 'And you, too, mother. May God keep us all and preserve us from harm!'

I noticed that his mother looked rather apprehensive.

'You're not ill, are you, Herbie?' she inquired solicitously.

'No, ma, I'm just fine.'

'Well, have a good sleep,' she said, 'and don't worry too much.'

'George,' said the old man, putting his arm around George's shoulder, 'forgive my hasty words. Your father is a good man. He'll find his way to God some day.'

'We're all sinners before the Lord,' said Herbie.

I was beginning to find it difficult to keep a straight face.

'Let's take a little walk before we turn in,' I suggested.

'You go straight to bed,' said the old man to Herbie. 'It's getting late.'

Outside George and I started walking rapidly towards the river. When we got a convenient distance away from the house we exploded with laughter.

'That little Herbie's a comedian,' I said. 'I don't know how the hell I managed to keep a straight face.'

'He sure knows how to take the lead,' said George. 'I wonder if Kitty's still up?' he added impulsively.

'Jesus, don't let's try that!' I cautioned. 'It's too late.'

'You never know,' says George. 'I'd like to twine my fingers around that rose-bush before going to bed, wouldn't you?'

'I'd like a good drink, if you ask me,' said I.

'That's an idea. Let's go to the caboose and see what's there.'

We took the long way around, skirting Kitty's house. The lights were out, but George insisted on giving the signal—two low whistles—just in case. 'If she's not dead to the world,' said George, 'she'll sneak out and follow us.' We strolled leisurely to the caboose.

We put the lantern on the stove, opened the flask which still contained a few drops, and sat there with ears cocked.

'You're taking a hell of a chance, George. You can get twenty years for this.'

'If I could only get it in,' he replied, 'it would be worth it.'

'You can have her.' I said, 'I'm clearing out.'

'Don't do that, Hen. Wait a few minutes and I'll go with you.'

I waited a few minutes, then got up.

'Maybe she's down by the bridge, waiting for us,' said George.

We strolled down to the bridge. Sure enough, there she was. 'Oh, George,' she cried, 'I thought you'd never come.' She flung her arms about him passionately. I walked away, saying I'd keep

watch. I stood at the cross-roads for almost a half-hour. I had
doused the lantern, of course. 'The fool!' I thought to myself.
'He won't be happy until he knocks her up.'

Finally I heard them coming. 'Well, any luck this time?' I
asked, after we had seen Kitty off.

George groaned. 'Let's go down to the river. I think I've got
blood all over me.'

'Oi yoi!' I whistled. 'So that's it! Now you're really in for it.'

'Guess we'll have to go back to the city soon,' said George.

'What? Are you going to leave her in the ditch?'

'She won't tell on me. I made her promise.'

'I'm not thinking of you, you bastard, I'm thinking of *her*.'

'Oh, we can fix it up when she comes to the city,' said George.
'I know a medical student who'll do the trick.'

'Supposing she gets a haemorrhage?'

'She won't,' said George. 'She's too healthy.'

We didn't speak for a while.

'About Una,' says George suddenly. 'I've been thinking it over,
Hen. I think the best thing is for you to see her yourself. I might
only make a mess of it.'

'You bastard!'

Another streak of silence.

'I think I'll leave in a day or two,' I said, as we neared the
house.

'Might be a good idea,' said George. 'You don't want to wear
out your welcome.'

'I'd like to pay something for my board,' I said.

'You can't do that, Hen, they'd be insulted.'

'Well, I'll buy them something then.'

'O.K.,' said George.

After a pause, he added:

'Don't think I'm not grateful for all you've done.'

'It was nothing,' I said. 'Some day you can take care of *me*.'

'I'm sorry about Una . . . I really don't. . . .'

I cut him short. 'Forget it!'

'It would be a shame to lose her, Hen.'

'Don't let that worry you. I'm not giving her up.'

'This Carnahan . . . she's engaged to him, you know.'

'*What?* Why didn't you tell me that before?'

'I didn't want to hurt you,' said George.

'So that's it? Listen, I'm leaving tomorrow by the first train.'

'Don't get panicky, Hen! They've been engaged for three
months now.'

'*What?* Jesus, it beats me how you could keep such a thing
quiet.'

'I thought it would blow over. I'm sure she's not in love with
him.'

'But she might marry him just to spite me,' I retorted.

'That's true. . . . But she'd regret it for the rest of her life, if she did.'

'And what good would that do me? Listen, you're a chump, do you know that?'

'Don't get sore, Hen. What could I do? If I had told you, you'd have been miserable. Besides, we hadn't seen one another for a long while.'

'Why not be honest about it? You simply don't give a shit one way or the other, isn't that it?'

'Come on now, don't be foolish!'

'George,' I said, 'I like you just as much as ever, I can't help liking you, we've been so close all these years. But I'll never trust you again. You had a right to let me know.'

'All right, Hen, have it your own way.'

We said no more. We went to bed in silence—after George had washed himself thoroughly. I half hoped he'd get a good dose of clap.

In the morning I said good-bye to everyone. When I got to New York I stopped at a shop and sent the folks a huge box of chocolates, not knowing what the hell would please them.

From then on, George Marshall was no longer my twin brother. . . .

'So that's how you lost Una?' said MacGregor.

'Yep! When I got back I found that she was married. Had married just three days before.'

'Well, Hen, it was all for the best, I guess.'

'That sounds just like George.'

'No, seriously, why try to buck Fate? Supposing you *had* married her? In a year or two years you'd have separated—*if I know you.*'

'Better to separate than never to marry.'

'Hen, you're a chump! To hear you, I'd say you were still in love with her.'

'Maybe I am.'

'You're nuts. If you were to run into her tomorrow, in the street, you'd probably run away from her.'

'Maybe I would. But that has nothing to do with it.'

'You're hopeless, Hen.' He turned to Trix. 'Did you ever hear the like of it? And he calls himself a writer! Wants to write about life but doesn't know human nature.' He turned square around. 'When you get ready to write the great American novel, Hen, see me! I'll give you a few facts of life to set you straight.'

I laughed outright.

'All right, wise guy, go ahead and laugh. When your smoke dreams clear away, come to me and I'll untangle the mess for you. I'll give you two more years with this . . . this what's her name . . . yeah, *Mona*. Mona, Una . . . sort of go together, don't they? Why don't you choose a gal with an ordinary name, like Mary, Jane or Sal?'

Having delivered himself of this, MacGregor felt a little mellower. 'Hen,' he began, 'we're all saps. You're not the worst guy in the world, not by a long shot. The trouble is, we all had big ideals. But once your eyes are opened you realize that you can never change the set-up. Sure, you can make minor changes—revolutions and all that—but they don't mean a thing. People remain what they are, whether Royalists, Communists, or just plain Democrats. Everyone for himself, that's the game. When you're young it's disheartening. You can't quite believe it. The more faith you have, the greater the disillusionment. It'll take another fifty thousand years—*or more!*—before there's any fundamental change in humanity. Meanwhile we've got to make the best of it, isn't that so?'

'You talk exactly like your old man.'

'That's true enough, Henry.'

He said it soberly. 'Shows you that we're not as original as we thought we were. We're getting old, do you realize that?'

'You may be—I'm not!' I said bluntly.

Even Trix had to laugh at this. 'You're just kids, the two of you,' she said.

'Don't fool yourself, sister,' said MacGregor, going over to her and fondling her. 'Because I still have a pair of balls doesn't make me a youngster. I'm a disillusioned old man, believe it or not.'

'Then why do you want to marry me?'

'Oh, I don't know,' said MacGregor wearily. 'Maybe just to have a change.'

'I like *that*,' said Trix, slightly offended.

'*You know what I mean*,' said MacGregor. 'Jesus, do we have to become romantic—just to please this guy? I want a home, a real home, that's what! I'm sick of running around.'

Trix looked at me dumbly. She shook her head.

'Don't take him seriously,' said I comfortingly, 'He always puts things in the worst light.'

'That's it,' chirped MacGregor. 'Now let me hear you say something nice about me. Tell her not to worry, I'll settle down soon enough. Prove to her what a good husband I'll make. . . . No, hold on! Better not say anything. You have the god-damnedest way of gumming things up.'

'Let him talk!' said Trix. 'I'm curious to know what your friend Henry really thinks of you.'

'You don't think he'd tell you the truth, do you? That guy's as slippery as an eel. He talks of George Marshall but . . . well, if I didn't know him so long and so well I'd have dropped him ages ago.'

336

'Henry,' said Trix, 'do you really think I should marry him?'

'Don't ask me to answer that, *please*.' I tried to laugh it off.

'You see,' said MacGregor. 'He couldn't say yes or no, just like that. Now what *do* you mean, Henry? Is it Yes or No?'

I held my tongue.

'That means no,' said MacGregor.

'Don't be so quick!' said Trix.

'Well, Henry, nothing like being honest,' said MacGregor. 'I guess you know me too well.'

'I haven't said one thing or another,' said I. 'Why jump to conclusions? By the way, what time is it?'

'There you are! Now he wants to know the time. That's Henry to a T.'

'It's only two-thirty,' said Trix. 'Let me fix you some coffee before you go.'

'Fine,' said I. 'And is there any cake left?'

'See, now he's all alert. Always wide awake when you mention food. Jesus, Hen, you'll never change. I guess maybe that's what I like about you—you're incorrigible.' He sat down close beside me, flicked the ash off his cigar, and proceeded to unburden himself. 'Tess has all sorts of connections, you know. She'd like to see me on the bench. The thing is, I can't run for judge and start divorce proceedings—*see what I mean?* Besides, I'm not so sure I want to be a judge. Even on the bench you can't keep your skirts clear, you know that. Still, I'm not much good as a lawyer, to be frank with you. Can't work up any enthusiasm. . . .'

'Why don't you pull out and try something else?'

'Like what—selling tyres? What *can* you do, Henry? One job's as bad as another.'

'But isn't there anything you're keen about?'

'Frankly, Hen, no! I'm just a lazy bugger at heart. I want to float along with the least effort.'

'Then float!' I said.

'That's no answer. Now, if I had a hankering to write, it would be different. But I don't. I'm not an artist. And I'm not a politician. I'm not a ball of fire either.'

'Then you're licked,' I said.

'I don't know, Hen, I wouldn't say that. There must be lots of things a fellow can do without getting all heated up.'

'The trouble with you is,' I said, 'you always want someone to make up your mind for you.'

'Now you're talking,' said MacGregor, suddenly more cheerful, though why, I couldn't understand. 'That's why I want to marry Trix. I need someone to steady me. Tess is like a wet sponge. Instead of putting some back-bone in me, she lets me fall apart.'

'When are you going to grow up?' said I.

'Come on now, Henry, don't hand me that line. You're just a

big boy yourself. Running a speakeasy, think of it! And you were going to set the world on fire. Ho ho! Ho ho!'

'Give me time. I may fool you yet. At least, I know what I'd like to do. That's something.'

'*Can you do it?* That's the question.'

'That remains to be seen.'

'Henry, you've been trying to write ever since I knew you. Other writers your age have had at least a half-dozen books published already. You haven't even finished your first book—or have you? Come, come, get wise to yourself!'

'Maybe I won't begin till I'm forty-five,' I said jokingly.

'Make it sixty, Henry. By the way, who was that English writer who began at seventy?'

I couldn't remember his name either at the moment.

Trix appeared with the coffee and cake. We moved back to the table.

'Well, Hen,' he began again, helping himself to a huge slice of cake, 'all I've got to say is—*don't weaken!* You may yet be a writer. Whether you'll be a great one, I can't predict. You've got a hell of a lot to learn.'

'Don't pay any attention to him,' said Trix.

'Nothing bothers *him*,' said MacGregor. 'He's even more obstinate than I am, and that's saying a lot. The truth is, it hurts me to see him wasting his time.'

'Wasting his time?' echoed Trix. 'And what about *you*?'

'Me? I'm lazy. That's different.' He gave her a broad grin.

'If you're thinking to marry me,' she rejoined, 'you'll have to get on your toes. You don't think I'm going to support *you*, do you?'

'Will you listen to that, Henry,' howled MacGregor, chuckling as if it were a great joke. 'Now who said anything about wanting to be supported?'

'Well, how *will* we live? Not on what you earn, I'm sure.'

'Tush tush!' said MacGregor. 'Honey, I haven't begun to work yet. Just wait till the divorce is granted, then I'll get down to brass tacks.'

'I'm not so sure I want to marry you,' said Trix. This in dead seriousness.

'Now, do you hear that?' said MacGregor. 'How do you like that? Well, honey, it's your loss. In ten years I may be sitting on the Supreme Court bench.'

'But in the meantime?'

'Don't cross any bridges before you come to them, that's my motto.'

'He can always make a living as a public stenographer,' said I.

'And a damned good living at that,' said MacGregor.

'I don't want to marry a public stenographer.'

338

'You're marrying *me*,' said MacGregor. 'Who knows *what* I am?'

'Right now you're just a misfit,' said Trix.

'That's true, honey,' said MacGregor lightly, 'but so were lots of men before they climbed to the top of the ladder.'

'But you're not a climber!'

'Right again,' said MacGregor. 'I was only using a figure of speech. Look, you two, you don't honestly think I'm a failure, do you? I'm only working on two cylinders now. I need inspiration. I need a good wife, a home, and one or two real friends. Like this bloke, for example. How about it, Henry, am I talking sense?'

Without waiting for a reply, he continued: 'You see. Trix, guys like Henry and me are out of the common run. We've got *quality*. If you get me for a husband, you're getting a jewel. I'm the most tolerant guy in the world. Henry will vouch for that. I can work as hard as anyone . . . *if I have to!* Only I don't see the sense of killing myself. It's stupid. Now, I haven't told you anything about this, but I've got several bright schemes up my sleeve. More than that—I'm actually carrying them out. I didn't want to tell you until they panned out successfully. If only one of them comes through, we can sit back and breathe easy for the next ten years. *How does that strike you?*'

'You're a dear,' said Trix, suddenly melting.

I don't think she believed in his schemes one bit, but she was eager to clutch at any straw.

'There!' said MacGregor, beaming, 'you see how simple it is?'

On my way home, an hour or so later, I got to thinking of all the wild projects he had hatched, beginning from the time I first knew him—when he was still going to prep school. How he had always complicated his life trying to make things easier for himself. I thought of the hours he had spent doing drudge work, so that 'later' he might be free to do as he pleased, though he never knew precisely what it was he would do when he would be able to do only what he pleased. To do nothing at all, which he always pretended was the *summum bonum*, was thoroughly out of the question. If we went to the beach for a holiday he was sure to bring his note-book along, and a law-book or two, or even a few pages from the unabridged dictionary which he had been reading, a page at a time, for years. If we flung ourselves into the water he would have to race someone to the raft or propose that we swim around the point or suggest we play water polo. Anything but float quietly on our backs. If we stretched out on the sand he would suggest we shoot craps or play cards. If we started a pleasant conversation he would turn it into an argument. He was never able to do anything in peace or contentment. His mind was always on the next thing, the next move.

Another peculiar thing I remembered about him was that he always had a bad cold—'a chest cold', as he put it. Winter or summer, it made no difference. A summer cold was worse, ashe always said. With the colds he often got hay fever. In short, he was usually in a miserable condition, always ailing, griping, sneezing, and always blaming it on the cigarettes which he swore he would cut out next week or next month, and which sometime he did do, to my great amazement, but only to go back to them, only to smoke more heavily. Sometimes it was the drinking which he felt was putting him 'on the bum', and he would lay off the stuff for a while, maybe six or eight months, but only to return to it, only to drink still more heavily. He did everything in this on-and-off fashion. When he studied he studied for eighteen and twenty hours a day, until he almost got congestion of the brain. He might break the study routine by playing cards with the boys, which he considered relaxation. But he played cards in the same way he studied, smoked and drank—always to excess. He was a bad loser, moreover. As for the women—if he was chasing a girl he would keep after her, no matter how many times she refused him, until he almost drove her crazy. The moment she relented, or succumbed, he was through with her. Then no more women for a period. Taboo. Absolutely. It was better to live without women: it was saner and healthier: he ate better, slept better, felt better: he'd rather have a good shit than a good fuck. And so on—to ninety-six decimal places. *Until he ran into another girl*, someone simply too irresistible for words. Then it would be another long goose chase, night and day, week after week, until he got his end in, and then she was just like all the rest, not a bit better, not a bit worse. '*Just cunt, Hen . . . just cunt!*'

There were always twenty or more hefty tomes stacked up on his desk: he would read them as soon as he could get round to it. Often years went by before he ever opened one, and by then of course the book had lost all its flavour. He would try to sell me them at half price; if I refused he would reluctantly make me a present of them. 'But you've got to promise you'll read them!' he would say. He had copies of magazines ten and fifteen years old, and newspapers too, which were treated in the same manner. Occasionally he would take a batch of these with him, open them up on the trolley or the train, skim through them rapidly, then fling them out the window. 'That's that!' he would say, smiling ruefully. He had cleared his conscience.

Now and then, meeting me accidentally, he'd say: 'Why don't we go to the theatre? I hear there's a good play on at the Orpheum.' We'd get to the theatre a half-hour late, stay a few minutes, then rush out as if the very atmosphere were poisonous. 'That's five bucks gone to hell,' he'd say. 'How much have you on you, Hen? Oh shit, don't bother to look, I know the answer. When will you ever have any money in your pocket?' Then he'd steer me to a bar up some dismal side street, a bar where he knew the proprietor or the waiter or someone, and he'd try to borrow a few dollars; if he couldn't get the money he'd make them stand us treat for a few rounds. 'Have you got a nickel at least?' he'd ask petulantly. 'I want to phone that little bastard Woodruff— he owes me a few bucks. I don't care if he's in bed or not. We'll take a taxi and make him pay for it, what say?' He'd make one telephone call after another. Finally he'd think of some girl he had thrown over years ago, some good-natured slob, as he put it, who would be only too glad to see him again. 'We'll have a few drinks and beat it. Maybe I can make a touch. But don't start any funny work—she's always getting over the clap.' Thus the night would pass, running from place to place, getting no-where, getting tired, getting crotchety, getting disgusted. Even-tually we would wind up in Greenpoint, at his parents' home, where there was sure to be some beer on the ice. It had to be filched stealthily, noiselessly, because he was always on the outs with his old man, or else with his ma, sometimes with the whole family. 'They don't have much love for you, Henry, I don't mind telling you. I don't know why it is, but they've got it in for you. I guess that business with the widow was just too much for them. To say nothing of that dose of clap you used to brag about.'

Though he had left home years ago, his room was always there for him, exactly as he had left it, which is to say, in thorough disorder and smelling as if a corpse were rotting in it. 'You'd think they'd have the decency to clean it up occasionally, wouldn't you?' he'd say, throwing open the windows. 'I suppose they're still trying to teach me a lesson, the damned idiots. You know, Henry, no one could have more stupid parents than you and me. No wonder we don't get anywhere. We got off to a bad start.' After rummaging around a bit he'd add: 'I suppose I *could* clean it up myself, but I never get round to it. I guess I *am* a lazy son-of-a-bitch. Just the same. . . .' And he'd trail off with oaths and curses.

Over a bottle of beer. . . . 'Do you remember, Hen, when we put that advertising campaign over for your old man? Right in this room, wasn't it? Imagine, writing a thousand letters by hand! But we had a good time, didn't we? I can still see all those bottles standing on the floor beside us. We must have consumed a truck-load of beer. We never got paid for the job, either—that's what I can't forget. Jesus, I can see what a chip off the old block you are! Never a cent on you. By the way, how *is* the old boy these days? Has he still the same twelve customers—or have they all died off? What a goofy business that was! I'm glad my old man was nothing but an iron moulder. Wonder how *we'll* wind up, eh? You'll probably be begging in the street in your old age. Your old man had some pride, but *you*, Jesus, you haven't an ounce of pride, faith, loyalty or anything, as far as I can see. Just day by day, that's it, eh Hen? *What a life!*'

He could ramble on this way indefinitely. Even when we turned in, the lights out, the covers over our heads, he would carry on. Often he lay in bed with a cigar in his mouth and a beer bottle in his hand, talking, talking, flitting from memory to memory, like the ghost of a butterfly.

'Don't you ever brush your teeth?' I would ask. He liked such interruptions.

'Hell no! I used to, Hen, but it's too much bother. They'll fall out anyway some day.'

'But don't you have a bad taste in your mouth?'

'Of course I do. *Terrible!* But I'm used to it.' (Chuckling softly to himself.) 'Sometimes it's so bad I can hardly stand it myself. Now and then I've had a girl remind me of it. That makes you feel a bit ashamed, of course. But you get over it. You've got to keep their minds concentrated on the other thing. Once you get it in, it doesn't matter what your breath smells like. *Right?*'

Lighting his stale cigar and sitting bolt upright . . . 'What does bother me, though, I'll tell you honestly, is to have a dirty crotch. I don't know, Hen, but I have the bad habit of wearing my shorts until they fall off. You know how often I take a bath! *Once in a blue moon.*' He chuckled. 'I guess I don't know how to wipe my ass. There's always something clinging to the short hairs—dilberries, I guess. Sometimes I clip them off with the scissors.'

Still running on . . . 'We should have come home early and had a good talk, instead of running around that way. What's the matter with me, do you suppose? I've been chasing around like this since I was a kid. Sometimes I get so feverish I think I've got St Vitus' dance. It gives me the jitters. I tell you, I can tremble like a dipso. Now and then I stutter too. That scares the shit out of me. . . . *How about some more beer?*'

'Let's sleep, for Christ's sake!'

'Why, Hen? You'll sleep a long time when you're dead.'

'Save something for tomorrow.'

'*Tomorrow!* Did you ever think, Henry, that there may be no tomorrow? You may die in your sleep—ever think of that?'

'So what?'

'Well, think of all you'd be missing.'

'I won't miss a damned thing,' I said irritably. 'All I ask is a good ten hours' sleep—and a good breakfast when I wake up! Did you ever think of breakfast in heaven?'

'There you go—thinking of breakfast already. And who's to buy it, tell me that?'

'We'll worry about that tomorrow.'

Silence for a while.

342

'I say, Hen, just how much have you in your pocket? Tell me, will you, I'm curious.'

'I don't know . . . fifteen or twenty cents maybe.'

'You're sure it's not thirty-five?'

'It could be. Why? Do you want to borrow some?'

'Borrow from *you*? Christ no! You're a pauper. No, Hen, I was just curious, like I said. You start out with fifteen or twenty cents in your pocket—and not a wrinkle in your brow. You bump into someone—*like me, for instance*—and you go to the theatre, you drink, you take taxis, you make telephone calls. . . .'

'So what?'

'*And it never disturbs you.* . . . I'm not speaking for myself, Hen. But supposing it were someone else?'

'What a thing to worry about!'

'I suppose it's all a matter of temperament. If it were me, I'd be miserable.'

'You like to feel miserable.'

'I guess you're right there. I must have been born that way.'

'And you'll die that way.'

He coughed violently, then reached for a box of cigars. '*What about a cigar, Hen?* They're a bit dry but they're Havanas.'

'You're mad. I'm going to sleep. Good-night!'

'O.K. You don't mind if I read a while, do you?' He held up a few large pages torn from the dictionary. My eyes were closed, I was almost out, but I could hear him droning away.

'I'm on page 1504 now,' he was saying. 'The unabridged. *Mandelic*. What a word! If I live to be another Methusaleh maybe I'll make use of a word like that sometime. *Are you asleep?* It's queer, though, what you do retain out of all this shit and verbiage. Sometimes the simplest words are the strangest. A word like corpse, for instance. Cadaver is natural and easy, but *corpse*! Or take Easter—I'll bet you never thought where that comes from. English is a crazy language, do you know that? Imagine words like Michaelmas and Whitsuntide—or wassail or syndrome or nautch or whangdoodle. Wait a minute, here's a funnier one —prepollent. Or *parlous*—isn't that a strange one? Or take acne or cirrhosis—it's hard to imagine anyone *inventing* words like that, what? Language is sheer mystery. The more etymological I get the less I know. *Are you awake?* Listen, Hen, you were always a stickler for words. I'm surprised you haven't read the dictionary through yet. Or have you? I know you tried to read the Bible through. The dictionary's more fun, I think. It's even crazier than the Bible. . . . You know, just to look at some words, just to roll them around in your mouth, makes you feel good. Here's a few off-hand—old favourites: anacoluthon, sesquipedalian, apotheosis, which, by the way, you always mispronounce. It's apotheosis. Some mean exactly what they look like or how they sound: gimcrack, thingamajig, socdolager, gazabo, yammer.

The Engles and the Jutes were responsible for the worst ones, I guess. Do you ever have a look at a Swedish book? There's a mad language for you! And to think we once talked that way.... Listen, I don't want to keep you awake all night. Forget it! I have to do this every night because I promised myself I would. It won't get me anywhere, I know that god-damn well. But there's one thing about this job, Hen—when I'm through I'm through. Yes sir! When I finish a page I wipe my ass with it. How do you like that? It's like putting *Finis* to a book....'

12

IT DOESN'T TAKE LONG for the speakeasy to become a sort of private club and recreation centre. On the kitchen wall is a long list of names. Beside the names is chalked up the sums owed is by our friends, our only steady customers.

Roberto and George Inness sometimes come to fence in the afternoon. If not, O'Mara, Ned and I play chess in the backroom near the window. Should an important client, like Mathias, turn up, we duck through the window into the back-yard, hop the fence and out into the next street through a narrow lane. Occasionally Rothermel comes for a couple of hours in the late afternoon, to talk to Mona privately. He pays her ten or twenty dollars for the privilege.

If it's an off night, we drive the paying customers out early, put the tables together, and settle down to play ping pong. We hold regular tournament bouts. Cold snacks in between of course. Always washed down with beer, gin or wine. If we run out of liquor we go to Allen Street for sacramental wine. Usually the 'championship matches' are between Arthur Raymond and myself. We run up fantastic scores. In the end I usually throw the game to him because he's such a hard loser. . . . Always day-break before we turn in.

One evening Rothermel turns up with several of his bosom pals from the Jersey swamps. All judges and politicians. They order the best of everything, of course.

Everything was going smoothly until Tony Maurer turned up with a beautiful model. For some reason Rothermel instantly took a violent dislike to him, partly because his hair was cropped close, partly because, in Rothermel's opinion, he was too glib. I happened to be serving Tony Maurer when Rothermel left his table in the backroom, determined to pick a quarrel. He was already quite crocked, to be sure. A nasty bird, even when sober. I stood to one side for a while, observing with admiration the cool way in which Tony Maurer parried Rothermel's thrusts.

But when the latter grew outrageously insulting I decided it was time to intervene.

'You'd better get back to your table,' I said quietly and firmly. 'Who are you?' he snarled.

Boiling inside but outwardly cool as a cucumber, I said: 'Me? I'm the boss here.'

Rothermel sniffed and snorted. I took him by the arm and turned him round, in the direction of the other room. 'Don't manhandle me!' he yelled.

Fortunately at this juncture his friends came to my rescue. They dragged him back to the other room, as if he were a sack of wood. Then they returned to make apologies to Tony Maurer and to Mona.

'We'll get them all out of here soon,' I whispered to Tony Maurer.

'Please don't!' he begged. 'I can handle the situation. I'm used to it, you know. He thinks I'm a Hun, that's what bothers him. Sit down a moment, won't you? Have a drink. You mustn't let these things disturb you.' Here he tailed off into a long anecdote about his experience during the war—first as an intelligance officer, then as a spy. As I listened to him I could hear Rothermel's voice rising higher and shriller. It sounded as if he were having the tantrums. I signalled to Ned and O'Mara to quiet him.

Suddenly I heard him scream: 'Mona! Mona! Where *is* that bitch? I'll fuck her yet, by Christ!'

I rushed to his table and shook him, none too gently. I looked quickly at his friends to see if they were going to make trouble. They seemed embarrassed and disconcerted.

'We'll have to get him out of here,' I explained.

'Certainly,' said one of them. 'Why don't you call a cab and send him home? He's a disgrace.'

Ned, O'Mara and myself bundled him into his overcoat and pushed him out into the street. A light sleet had fallen; it was now covered with a thin coat of snow. Rothermel was unable to stand without support. While Ned went in search of a cab, O'Mara and I half-dragged, half-shoved him towards the corner. He was fuming and cussing; he was particularly venomous towards me, naturally. In the scramble he lost his hat. 'You don't need a hat,' said O'Mara. 'We'll use it to piss in.' Rothermel was now blind with rage. He tried to unhitch his arms in order to take a swing at us, but we held him tight. Suddenly and instinctively we both let go at once. Rothermel stood swaying lightly, not daring to make a move for fear his legs would give way. We retreated a few steps and then, moved by a common impulse, we began dancing around him like goats, making faces at him, taunting him, thumbing our noses, scratching our behinds like monkeys, capering and cavorting like zanies. The poor bugger was beside himself. He was actually bellowing now. Fortunately the street was deserted. Finally he could stand it no longer. He made a lunge for us, lost his footing and slid into the gutter. We picked him up, stood him safely on the sidewalk, and repeated our antics, this time to the tune of a little ditty in which we made shameful use of his name.

The cab pulled up and we bundled him in. We told the driver that he had the D.T.s, gave him a phoney address in Hoboken, and waved good-bye. When we returned his friends thanked us and apologized all over again. 'He belongs in the asylum,' said one of them. With that he ordered a round of drinks and insisted on buying us steak sandwiches. 'If you ever have any trouble with the flat-footed guys, just call on us,' said the bald-headed politician. He handed me his card. Then he suggested the name of a bootlegger from whom we could get credit, if we ever needed credit. And so we had a second round and a third round, always of the best Scotch, which could have been horse piss for all I cared about it.

Shortly after they left, Arthur Raymond fell into a violent quarrel with some young chap whom I had never seen before, insisting that the latter had insulted Mona. Duffy was the lad's name. Seemed like a decent chap, even if a little under the weather. 'He'll have to apologize publicly,' Arthur Raymond kept insisting. Duffy thought this a great joke. At last Arthur Raymond could stand it no longer. He got up, twisted Duffy's arm, and threw him on the floor. Then he sat on Duffy's chest and banged his head against the floor. '*Will you or won't you?*' he repeated, banging the poor fellow's head mercilessly. At last Duffy mumbled a thick apology and Arthur Raymond lifted him to his feet. There was a dead silence, an unpleasant one for Arthur Raymond. Duffy searched for his coat and hat, paid his bill, and left—without a word. Arthur Raymond sat alone at his table, head down, looking glum and shame-faced. In a few moments he got up and stalked out.

It was not until a few nights later, when he showed up with a pair of black eyes, that we learned that Duffy had waited for him outside and given him a good beating. Oddly enough, Arthur Raymond appeared to be happy over the trouncing he had received. It turned out that after the fracas Duffy and he had become good friends. With his usual false modesty he added that he had been somewhat at a disadvantage, always was when it came to fisticuffs, because he couldn't afford to ruin his hands. Anyway, it was the first time in his life that he had taken a beating. It had given him a thrill. With a touch of malice he concluded: 'Everybody seems to be happy about it. Maybe I deserved it.'

'Maybe it will teach you to mind your own business,' said Mona.

Arthur Raymond made no reply.

'And when are you going to pay your bill?' she added.

To everyone's astonishment, Arthur Raymond replied: 'How much is it?' Fishing into his pocket he brought up a roll of bills and peeled off the amount due.

'Didn't expect that, did you?' he said, looking around like a bantam cock. He got up, went to the kitchen, and crossed his name off the list.

'And now I've got another surprise for you,' he said, requesting that drinks be served all around. 'A month from today I'm giving a concert. Bach, Beethoven, Mozart, Ravel, Prokofieff and Stravinsky. You're all invited to come—it's on me. My last appearance, so to say. After that I'm going to work for the Communist Party. And I don't care what happens to my hands. I'm through with this sort of life. I'm going to do something constructive. *Yes sir!*' and he banged his fist on the table. '*From now on I disown you all.*'

As he sailed out he turned round to deliver this: 'Don't forget the concert! I'll send you seats up front.'

From the time that Arthur Raymond delivered himself of this declaration things took a definite turn for the worse. All our creditors seemed to descend on us at once, and not only the creditors but the police and the lawyer whom Maude had engaged to collect the back alimony. It would begin, in the early morning with the iceman pounding furiously on our door and we pretending to be sound asleep or out. Afternoons, it would be the grocer, the delicatessen man or one of the bootleggers rapping on the front window. In the evening, trying to pass himself off as a client, would come a process server or a plain clothes man. Finally the landlord began to dun us for the rent, threatening to haul us to court if we didn't pay up. It was enough to give one the jitters. Sometimes we felt so done up that we would close the joint and go to a movie.

One night the old trio—Osiecki, O'Shaughnessy and Andrews —arrived with three girls from the Follies. This was towards midnight and they were already lit up like ocean liners. It was one of those nights when just our intimate friends were on hand. The Follies girls, beautiful, brittle, and extraordinarily vulgar, insisted on putting the tables together so that they could dance on the table tops, do the split, and that sort of thing. Osiecki, imagining himself to be a Cossack, kept spinning like a top, to our utter amazement. Hadn't improved a whit in the interim, of course. But he was jollier than usual, and for some queer reason fancied himself to be an acrobat. After a few chairs had been broken and some crockery smashed, it was suddenly decided that we all go to Harlem. Mona, Osiecki and I got into a cab with Spud Jason and his Alameda who was carrying on her lap a mangy little dog called Fifi. By the time we reached Harlem it had peed over everyone. Finally Alameda peed in her pants from excitement.

At Small's, which was then the rage, we drank champagne, danced with the coloured folk and ate huge steaks smothered with onions. Dr Kronski was in the party and seemed to be enjoying himself hugely. Who was paying for it all I had no idea. Probably Osiecki. Anyway, we got home toward dawn and tumbled into bed exhausted. Just as we were falling asleep Alan Cromwell rapped at the window, begging to be allowed in. We paid no attention to him. 'It's me, Alan, let me in!' he kept shouting. He raised his voice until it sounded as if he were screaming. Obviously he was soused to the gills and in a bad way. Finally a cop came along and dragged him away, giving him a few love taps with his night stick as he did so. Kronski and O'Mara, who were sleeping on the tables, thought it a hell of a good joke. Mona was worried. However, we soon fell back into a dead slumber.

The next evening Ned, O'Mara and myself hatched an idea. We had taken to sitting in the kitchen with a ukelele, humming and talking softly while Mona took care of the customers. It was the time of the Florida boom. O'Mara, always restless, always itching to strike it rich, got the idea that the three of us ought to light out for Miami. It was his belief that we could make enough in a few weeks to send for Mona and lead a new life. Since none of us had money to invest in real estate we would have to get it from those who had made it. We would offer our services as waiters or bell hops. We were even willing to shine shoes. Anything for a start. The weather was still good, and it would get better the farther south we travelled.

O'Mara always knew how to make the bait attractive.

Naturally Mona wasn't very keen about our project. I had to promise that I would telephone her every night, no matter where we might be. All I needed was a nickel to drop in the slot; the charges could be reversed. By the time the telephone bill arrived the speak-easy would be closed and she would be with us.

Everything was set to decamp in a few days. Unfortunately, two days before starting the landlord served us with a summons. In desperation I tried to raise at least part of the money we owed him. On an impulse I looked up the son of one of my father's bosom friends. He was quite a young man but making good in the steamship business. I don't know what on earth possessed me to tackle him—it was like grasping at a straw. The moment I mentioned money he turned me down cold. He even had the cheek to ask me why I had singled *him* out. He had never asked me for any favours, had he? (Already a hard-boiled business man. In a few years he would be a 'success'.) I swallowed my pride and bored in. Finally after being thoroughly humiliated, I succeeded in extracting a ten spot from him. I offered to write

349

out a promissory note but he spurned this derisively. When I got back to the joint I felt so wretched, so beaten, that I almost set fire to the place. However. . . .

It was a Saturday afternoon when O'Mara and I set forth for Miami. It was high time. The air was thick with wet, heavy snow-flakes—the first snow-fall of the season. Our plan was to get on the highway outside Elizabeth, there to catch a car as far as Washington where we were to meet Ned. For some reason of his own Ned was going to Washington by train. He was taking the ukelele along—for morale.

It was almost dark when we bundled into a car outside Elizabeth. There were five darkies in the car and they were all liquored up. We wondered why in hell they were driving so fast. Before long we found out—the car was full of dope and the Federal men were on their tail. Why they had stopped to pick us up we couldn't figure out. We felt vastly relieved when a little this side of Philadelphia they slowed down and dumped us out.

The snow was falling heavily now and a stiff gale was blowing, an icy gale. Moreover, it was pitch dark. We walked a couple of miles, our teeth chattering, until we struck a gas station. It was hours before we got another lift, and then only as far as Wilmington. We decided to spend the night in that God-forsaken hole.

Mindful of my promise I called Mona. She held me on the phone for almost fifteen minutes, the operator butting in every so often to remind us that the toll was rising. Things were pretty black at her end: she was to appear in court the following day.

When I hung up I had such a fit of remorse that I was of a mind to turn back in the morning.

'Come on,' said O'Mara, 'don't let it get you down. You know Mona, she'll find a way out.'

I knew that myself but it didn't make me feel any better.

'Let's get started bright and early tomorrow,' I said. 'We can be in Miami in three days, if we try.'

The next day, around noon, we walked in on Ned who had installed himself in a broken-down hotel for a dollar a night. His room was like a setting for Gorky's *Night Lodging*. Every other window-pane was broken; some were stuffed with rags, some with newspapers.

The faucets didn't work, the bed had a straw mattress, and the springs had completely given way. There were cobwebs hanging everywhere. The smell of dust was so thick it almost choked us. And this was a hotel for 'white people'. In our glorious capital no less.

We bought some cheese, wine and salami, a good loaf of bread and some olives, and moved across the bridge, into Virginia. Once across the line, we sat down on the grass under a shady tree and filled our bellies. Then we stretched out in the warm sunshine, smoked a cigarette or two, and finally sang a little tune. This tune was to become our theme song—something about looking for a friendly face.

We were in high spirits when we got up on our hind legs. The South looked good—warm, inviting, gracious, spacious. We were already in another world.

Entering the South is always inspiring. By the time one hits Maryland and starts going over the roller coaster curves everything has undergone moderation, softening. When you come to the 'Old Dominion' you are definitely in a new world, no mistaking it. People have manners, grace, dignity. The State that gave us the most Presidents, or at least the best ones, was a great State in its day. It still is, in many ways.

Many times I left New York, not caring in what direction I was wafted, so long as I could put some distance between myself and the city I loathed. Often I wound up in North Carolina or Tennessee. Passing through Virginia was like rehearsing a motif from a familiar symphony or quartet. Occasionally I would stop in a little burg and ask for a job because I liked the looks of the place. Of course I never took the job. I would linger for a while in an effort to imagine what it would be like to pass the rest of my days there. Hunger always routed me out of my reverie. . . .

From Washington we got to Roanoke not without difficulty, since we were three; not many drivers are willing to pick up three vagabonds, especially from the North. We decided that night that it would be better to split up. We looked at the map and decided that we would all meet the next evening at the Post Office in Charlotte, N.C. The plan worked out beautifully. One by one we arrived at our destination, the last one only a half hour later than the first. Here we again changed plans, since Ned had discovered that he might have gone all the way through to Miami with the man who had picked him up. We decided that our next rendezvous would be in Jacksonville. O'Mara and I were to stick together; Ned would travel alone. It was a drizzling rain we faced next morning, shortly after dawn, standing on the highway outside of Charlotte, for an hour or more no one gave us a tumble. Fed up, we decided to stand in the middle of the road. It worked. The next car in sight came to a stop with a screech.

'What in Christ's name's the matter with you?' shouted the driver.

'Where are you headed?' we shouted.

'Jacksonville!'

The door opened and we tumbled in. We were off again, at a record breaking clip. Not a word out of the driver for several minutes. When he did open his trap it was to say—'Lucky I didn't run you down.' We said nothing. 'I didn't know whether to shoot or to run you over,' he continued. O'Mara and I exchanged glances. 'Where are you from?' he asked. 'What's your racket?' We told him. He looked at us searchingly, decided, I suppose, that we were speaking the truth, then slowly, painfully, related to us that he had accidentally killed a friend of his at a bar in a drunken brawl. He had hit him over the head with a bottle, in self-defence. Terrified and panic-stricken, he had fought his way out of the place, piled into his car, and skipped. He had two guns in his pockets and was ready to use them should anyone attempt to bar his way. 'You had a narrow escape,' he said.

After a while he confided that he was making for Tampa, where he could safely hide away for a while. At least he thought he could. 'I'll probably go back and take what's coming to me. I've got to collect myself first,' he said. Again and again he repeated: 'It wasn't my fault, I never meant to *kill him*.' Once he broke down and wept like a child.

When we stopped for lunch he insisted on paying the bill. He paid for dinner too. In Macon (Georgia) we took a room with two beds, for which he also footed the bill. At the far end of the wide hall, seated in a rocker under a red light, sat a whore. As we were undressing our friend laid his revolvers out on the dresser, together with his wallet, remarking quietly that whoever got to them first would be the lucky man.

Early next morning we set out again. Our friend should have gone straight on to Tampa but no, he insisted on depositing us first in Jacksonville. Not only that, but we had to accept the ten dollar bill he handed us—'for good luck'.

'You'd better get the lay of the land before you go any farther,' he warned. 'I have a hunch the boom is over.' We wished him good luck and watched him take off again, wondering how long it would be before the law caught up with him. He was a simple, honest chap with a good heart, a mechanic by trade. One of those people of whom one says—'He wouldn't hurt a fly.'

It was indeed fortunate for us that we had met up with him. Aside from the ten dollars he had handed us we had just about four dollars between us. Ned had most of the money and he had forgotten to divvy up. Well, we went to the Post Office, as agreed upon. Sure enough, there was Ned. Had been there some two hours or more. The man who picked him up in Charlotte had driven him straight through, and what's stranger still, he had also paid for his meals and put him up in the same room with him.

All in all we hadn't done so bad. The next thing was to get the feel of the land.

It didn't take us long to find out what the situation was, Jacksonville was filled to overflowing with poor dopes like ourselves, all returning from the boom country below. If we had had any sense we would have turned about immediately and trekked homeward, but pride made us determined to stick it out for a while. 'There must be *something* we can do,' we kept telling one another. But there was not only nothing to do, there wasn't even a place to sleep. In the daytime we hung around at the Y.M.C.A., which had come to resemble a Salvation Army shelter. No one seemed to be making any effort to find work. Everyone was waiting for a letter or a telegram from the folks back home. Waiting for a train ticket, a money order, or just a plain dollar bill. It went on like that for days. We slept in the park (until the cops caught up with us), or on the floor of the jail, in the company of a hundred or more filthy bodies wrapped in newspapers, some vomiting, some shitting in their pants. Now and then in an effort to create work, we would wander off to a neighbouring village and try to invent a job which would at least keep us in food. On one of these forays, not having eaten for thirty-six hours and having walked eight miles to the mythical job, we had to walk back again on empty bellies, our legs creaking, our guts rumbling, so dog-tired, so utterly weary and dejected that, like Indians, we walked single file, one behind the other, heads down, tongues hanging out. That night we tried to storm the Salvation Army. Useless. One had to have a quarter to be allowed to sleep on the floor. In the toilet there my guts began to fall out. The pain was so great I keeled over. Ned and O'Mara had to carry me out of the place. We inched our way to the railroad yards where the freight trains were loaded with rotting fruit for the North. There we ran into a sheriff who drove us away with a gun in our backs. He wouldn't even permit us to gather a few rotten oranges which were lying on the ground. 'Get back where you belong!' Always the same cry.

By great luck the next day Ned ran into a weird old chap named Fletcher whom he had known in the advertising business in New York. The man was a commercial artist, had a studio, as he called it, and, though utterly broke, promised to make us a meal that evening. It seems he was celebrating his silver anniversary. For the occasion he had managed to get his wife released from the insane asylum.

'It won't be very merry,' he informed Ned, 'but we'll make it as cheerful as we can. She's a sweet creature, perfectly harmless. She's been this way for the last fifteen years.'

It was one of the longest days I ever put in, waiting for that promised meal. I lolled about the Y.M.C.A. the whole day, trying to conserve my energies. Most of the fellows passed the time playing cards or checkers—dice was forbidden. I read the newspapers, the Christian Science magazines, and all the other trash that was lying about. If a revolution had broken out in New York it wouldn't have excited me in the least. I had only one thought —food!

353

The moment I set eyes on poor Fletcher I felt an immense sympathy for him. He was a man approaching seventy, with watery blue eyes and a big moustache. He looked for all the world like Buffalo Bill. On the walls were examples of his work—from the old days—when he had been handsomely paid to do ponies and cowboys for the magazine covers. A small pension helped him to eke out a bare existence. He lived in hopes of getting a fat commission some day. Between times he painted little signs for tradespeople, anything that would bring in a few pennies. He was thankful to be living in the South where the days at least were warm.

To our surprise he brought out two bottles, one half-filled with gin, the other containing about a fingerful of rye. With the help of a lemon, some orange peels and a generous quantity of water, we managed to make his stock go a few rounds. His wife meanwhile was reposing in the next room. Fletcher said he would bring her out when it came time to eat. 'It makes no difference to her,' he said. 'She has her own world and her own rhythm. She doesn't remember me any more, so don't be surprised at what she says. She's usually very quiet—and fairly cheerful, as you'll see.'

He then set about preparing the table. The dishes were broken and chipped, nothing matched of course, and the cutlery was of tin. He laid the 'couvert' on the bare table, and in the centre of the table he placed an immense bowl of flowers. 'It'll only be a cold snack,' he said apologetically, 'but it may help to quiet the wolf.' He put out a bowl of potato salad, some rat cheese, some bologna and liverwurst, together with a loaf of white bread and some margarine. There were a few apples and nuts, for dessert. Not an orange in sight. After he had set a glass of water at each place he put a pot of coffee up to boil.

'I guess we're about ready now,' he said, looking towards the other room. 'Just a minute and I'll bring Laura in.'

The three of us stood in silence as we waited for the two of them to issue from the next room. We could hear him rousing her from her slumber; he was speaking to her softly, gently, as he helped her to her feet.

'Well,' he said, smiling desperately through his tears, as he led her to the table, 'here we are at last. Laura, these are my friends —*your friends too*. They're going to eat with us—isn't that lovely?'

We approached in turn, shook hands first with her, then with him. We were all in tears as we raised the water glasses and drank to their twenty-fifth anniversary.

'Well, this is almost like old times,' said Fletcher, looking first at his poor demented wife, then at us. 'Do you remember, Laura, that funny old studio I had in the Village years ago? We weren't very rich then either, were we?' He turned to us. I won't say grace, though tonight I would like to. I've lost the habit. But I want to tell you how grateful I am that you are sharing this little celebration with us. It might have been very sad, just the two of us alone.' He turned to his wife.

'Laura, you're still beautiful, do you know it?' He chucked her under the chin. Laura looked up wistfully and gave the flicker of a smile. 'You see?' he exclaimed. 'Ah yes, Laura was the belle of New York once. Weren't you, Laura?'

It didn't take us long to plough through the victuals, including the apples and nuts and a few stale cookies which Fletcher had dug up by chance while searching for the canned milk. Over a second cup of Java Ned got out the ukulele and we took to singing, Laura too. We sang homely ditties, such as 'O Susanna', 'A bull-frog sat on a railroad track', 'Annie Laurie', 'Old Black Joe'. . . . Suddenly Fletcher rose and said he would sing 'Dixie', which he did with gusto, ending up with the blood-curdling Rebel yell. Laura, highly pleased with the performance, demanded that he sing another tune. He got up again and sang 'The Arkansas Traveller', topping it off with a little jig. My, but we were merry. It was pathetic.

After a time I got hungry again. I asked if there wasn't any stale bread around. 'We might make French pancakes,' I said.

We searched high and low but there wasn't even a crust to be found. We did find some mouldy zwieback though and, dipping this in the coffee, we got a new lease of energy.

If it weren't for the vacant look in her eyes one wouldn't have thought Laura to be insane. She sang heartily, responded to our quips and jokes, and ate her food with relish. After a while, however, she dozed off, just like a child. We carried her into the bedroom and put her back to bed. Fletcher leaned over her and kissed her brow.

'If you boys will wait a few minutes,' he said, 'I think I may be able to dig up a wee bit more gin. I'm going to see my next-door neighbour.'

In a few minutes he was back with a half bottle of bourbon. He also had a little bag of cakes in his hand. We put up another pot of coffee, poured the bourbon, and began to chat. Now and then we threw a short log into the old pot-bellied stove. It was the first comfortable, cheery evening we were spending in Jacksonville.

'I was in the same fix when I came here,' said Fletcher. 'It takes time to get acquainted. . . . Ned, why don't you go down to the newspaper office. I've got a friend there, he's one of the editors. Maybe he can dig up something for you.'

'But I'm not a writer,' said Ned.

'Hell, Henry will write your stuff for you,' said O'Mara.

'Why don't you both go?' said Fletcher.

We were so elated with the prospect of getting a job that we all did a jig in the middle of the room.

'Let's have that one about looking for a friendly face,' begged Fletcher. We took to humming and singing again, not too loud because of Laura.

'You mustn't worry about her,' said Fletcher, 'she sleeps like an angel. In fact, she *is* an angel. I honestly think that's why she's —you know. She didn't fit in our world. Sometimes I think it's a blessing she's the way she is.'

He showed us some of his work which he had stored away in big trunks. It wasn't too bad. At least he was a good draughtsman. He had been all over Europe in his youth—Paris, Munich, Rome, Prague, Budapest, Berlin. He had even won a few prizes.

'If I had my life to live all over again,' he said, 'I'd do nothing at all. I'd keep tramping around the world. Why don't you fellows go west? There's still lots of room in that part of the world.'

That night we slept on the floor of Fletcher's studio. Next morning Ned and I went to see the newspaper man. After a few words I was voted out. But Ned was given a chance to write a series of articles. Naturally, I would do the dirty work.

All we had to do now was to pull our belts in until pay-day. Pay-day was *only* two weeks off.

That same day O'Mara led me round to the home of an Irish priest whose address someone had given him. We immediately got the cold shoulder from the Sister who opened the door. Descending the stoop we noticed the good Father easing his Packard out of the garage. O'Mara tried to plead with him. For encouragement he got a puff of heavy smoke from the Father's Havana cigar. 'Be off with yer and don't be disturbin' the peace'. That was all Father Hoolihan deigned to say.

That evening I wandered off by my lonesome. Passing a big synagogue I heard the choir singing. It was a Hebrew prayer and it sounded enchanting. I stepped inside and took a seat far back As soon as the service was over I went up front and collared the rabbi. 'Reb,' I wanted to say, 'I'm in a bad way. . . .' But he was a solemn looking cuss, utterly devoid of bonhomie. I told him my story in a few words, winding up with an appeal for food, or meal tickets, and a place to flop, *if possible*. I didn't dare mention that we were three.

'But you're not a Jew, are you?' said the Reb. He squinted as if he couldn't make me out clearly.

'No, but I'm hungry. What difference does it make what I am?'

'Why don't you try the Christian churches?'

'I have,' I replied. 'Besides, I'm not a Christian either. I'm just a Gentile.'

Grudgingly he wrote a few words on a slip of paper, saying that I was to present the message to the man at the Salvation

Army. I went there immediately, only to be told that they had no room.

'Can you give me something to eat?' I begged.

I was informed that the dining room had been closed hours ago.

'I'll eat anything,' I said, clinging to the man at the desk. 'Haven't you got a rotten orange or a rotten banana?'

He looked at me strangely. He was unmoved.

'Can you give me a dime—just a dime?' I begged.

Disgustedly he fished into his pocket and flung me the dime.

'Now clear out of here!' he said. 'You loafers belong up North where you came from.'

I turned on my heel and walked away without a word. On the main street I saw a pleasant looking fellow selling newspapers. Something about his looks encouraged me to address him.

'Hullo,' I said, 'how goes it?'

'Not too badly. Where are you from—*New York?*'

'Yeah, and you?'

'Jersey City.'

'Shake!'

A few moments later I was hawking the few papers he had given me. It took me about an hour to get rid of them. But I had earned a few pennies. I hurried back to the 'Y' and found O'Mara dozing behind a newspaper in a big arm-chair.

'Let's go and eat,' I said, shaking him vigorously.

'Yeah,' he responded derisively, 'Let's go to Delmonico's.'

'No, seriously,' I said, 'I just made a few cents, enough for coffee and doughnuts. Come on.'

At once he was on his feet. As we hurried along I told him briefly what had happened.

'Let's find that guy,' he said, 'he sounds like a friend. From Jersey City, eh? Swell!'

Mooney was the name of the newsie. He knocked off to have a bite with us.

'You can sleep in my room,' said Mooney. 'I've got an extra couch. It's better than sleeping in the jail.'

The next day, towards noon, we followed his advice and went to the rear of the newspaper office to get a bundle of papers. Our friend Mooney of course had lent us the money to buy the papers. There were about fifty kids milling around, all trying to get their bundles first. I had to bend over a window-sill and haul them out through the iron bars. Suddenly I felt someone crawling up my back. It was a little darkie, trying to reach over my head for his bundle. I got him off my back and he crawled between my legs. The kids were all laughing and jeering. I had to laugh myself. Anyway, we were soon loaded and marching up the main street. It was the hardest thing in the world for me to open my mouth and yell. I tried shoving the papers at the passers-by. That didn't work at all.

I was standing there, looking rather foolish, I suppose, when Mooney came along. 'That's no way to sell papers,' he said. 'Here, watch me!' And with this he whirls around, flashing the paper and yelling 'Extra! Extra! All about the big broo . . . siiis. . . .' I wondered what the great news was, unable to catch the important word at the end of his phrase. I looked at the front page to see what the headline was. There was no headline. There didn't seem to be any news at all, in fact.

'Yell anything,' said Mooney, 'But yell it at the top of your lungs! And don't stand in one spot. *Keep moving!* You've got to hustle if you want to get rid of them before the next edition is out.'

I did my best. I hustled up and down the main street, then ducked into the side streets. Soon I found myself in the park. I had sold only three or four papers. I put the bundle on the ground and sat down on a bench to watch the ducks swimming in the pond. All the invalids, recuperationists and valetudinarians were out sunning themselves. The park seemed more like the recreation grounds of an Old Soldiers' Home. An old codger beside me asked to borrow a paper to see what the weather report was like. I waited drowsily and blissfully while he read the paper from front to back. When he handed it back to me I tried to fold it neatly so that it wouldn't look shopworn.

On my way out of the park a cop stopped me to buy a paper. That almost unnerved me.

By the time the next edition was due on the streets I had sold exactly seven papers. I hunted up O'Mara. He had done a little better, but nothing to brag about.

'Mooney's going to be disappointed,' he said.

'I know it. I guess we're not cut out to peddle papers. It's a job for kids—or for a hustler like Mooney.'

'You said it, Henry.'

We had coffee and doughnuts again. Better than nothing. It was food and food was what we needed. All that walking up and down, and with a heavy bundle, gave one a furious appetite. I wondered just how long I would be able to stick it out.

Later in the day we ran into Mooney again. We apologized for our inability to do better.

'Forget about it,' he said. 'I understand. Listen, let me lend you five bucks. Scout around for something better. You're not cut out for this kind of thing. I'll see you tonight at the lunch counter. O.K.?' He hustled off, waving his hand cheerily.

'That's what you call a swell guy,' said O'Mara. 'Now, b'Jesus, we've really got to land something. Come on, let's strike out!'

We set off straight ahead, neither of us having the faintest notion what we were looking for or how to find it. A few blocks farther on we met up with a cheerful looking guy who tried to hit us up for a dime.

He was a coal miner from Pennsylvania. Trapped, like us. Over a coffee and doughnut we got to exchanging ideas.

'Tell you what,' he said, 'Let's go down to the redlight district tonight. You're always welcome if you can buy a drink. You don't have to go upstairs with the gals. Anyway, it's cosy and comfortable—and you can hear some music. Damned sight better than sitting around in the morgue.' (Meaning the 'Y'.)

That evening, over a few drinks, he asked us whether we had ever been converted.

Converted? We wondered what he was driving at.

He explained. Seems there were always a few guys hanging around 'the morgue' who were eager to win converts to the church. Even the Mormons had their scouts out. The thing was, he explained, to listen innocently and appear interested. 'If the fool thinks he's hooking you, you can worm a meal out of him easy as pie. Try it sometime. They're on to me—I can't work it any more.'

We stayed in the whorehouse as long as we possibly could. Every so often a new girl showed up, made a few passes at us, and gave up.

'It's not exactly Paradise for them,' said our friend. 'A dollar a crack, and the house gets the best part of it. Still, some of them don't look so bad, do they?'

We looked them over appraisingly. A pathetic bunch, even more pathetic looking than the Salvation Army lassies. All of them chewing gum, humming, whistling, trying to look appealing. One or two, I noticed, were yawning, rubbing their bleary eyes.

'At least they eat regularly.' This from O'Mara.

'Yeah, there's something to that,' said our friend. 'I'd rather go hungry, myself.'

'I don't know,' said I. 'If I had to choose . . . if I were a woman . . . I'm not sure but what I'd take a crack at it. At least till I got fattened up a bit.'

'You *think* so,' said our friend, 'but you're mistaken. You don't get fat on this job, let me tell you that.'

'How about that one?' said Mara, pointing out a ton of lard.

'She was born fat, anyone can see that. Besides, she's a booze artist.'

That night, on the way back to nowhere, I got to wondering about Mona. Only one little note from her since our arrival. True, she wasn't much of a letter writer. Nor was she ever very explicit about anything. All I had gleaned from her note was that she was going to be dispossessed any day. And then what? I wondered.

The next day I hung around the 'Y' most of the day, hoping,

or praying rather, that someone would start working on me. I was ready and willing to be converted to anything, even to Mormonism. But no one gave me a tumble. Towards evening I got a bright idea. It was so simple a stunt that I wondered why it hadn't occurred to me sooner. However, one has to get truly desperate before one thinks of such simple solutions.

What was the bright idea? To go from shop to shop asking only for foodstuffs which they were ready to throw out: stale bread, spoiled fruit, sour milk. . . . I never realized at the time how similar was my plan to the begging tactics of St Francis. He too had demanded only what was unfit to eat. The difference was, of course, that he had a mission to perform. I was merely trying to keep afloat. A grand difference!

Nevertheless, it worked like a charm. O'Mara took one side of the street, I the other. By the time we met at the end of the block our arms were full. We rushed over to Fletcher's place, got hold of Ned, and prepared for a feast.

To be truthful, the scraps and the waste which we had gathered was far from being repugnant. We had all eaten tainted meat before, though not intentionally; the vegetables needed only to be trimmed; the stale bread made excellent toast; the sour milk gave the overripe fruit a delicious quality. A Chinese coolie would have regarded our repast as a luxurious one. All that lacked was a bit of wine to wash down the stale rat cheese. However, there was coffee on hand and a bit of condensed milk. We were elated. We ate like wolves.

'Too bad we didn't think of inviting Mooney,' said O'Mara.

'Who's Mooney?' asked Ned.

We explained. Ned listened with mouth open.

'Jesus, Henry,' he said, 'I can't get over it. And me sitting upstairs in the front office all the while. Selling *your* stuff under *my* name—and you guys peddling papers! I'll have to tell Ulric about it. . . . By the way, have you seen the stuff you wrote? They think it's pretty good, did I tell you?'

I had forgotten all about the articles. Perhaps I read them, during those comas at the 'Y', and never realized that it was I who wrote them.

'Henry,' said Fletcher, 'you ought to get back to New York. It's all right for these lads to waste their time, but not you. I have a hunch you're cut out for something big.'

I blushed and tried to pass it off.

'Come,' said Fletcher, 'don't be so modest. You've got qualities, anyone can see that. I don't know what you're going to become—saint, poet, or philosopher. But you're an artist, that's definite. And what's more, you're unspoiled. You have a way of forgetting youself that tells me a lot about you.'

Ned, who was still feeling guilty, applauded Fletcher warmly. 'As soon as I get my check, Henry,' he said, 'It'll give you the train fare back home. That the *least* I can do. O'Mara and I will stick it out. Eh, Ted? You're a veteran: you've been on the bum since you were ten years old.'

O'Mara grinned. Now that he had found a way to get food his spirits rose.

Besides, there was Mooney, to whom he had taken quite a fancy. He was certain that between them they could cook up something.

'But who'll write the articles for the paper?'

'I've already taken care of that,' said Ned. 'They're making me lay-out man next week. That's right up my alley. The chances are I'll be making real dough soon.'

'Maybe you'll be able to throw something my way,' said Fletcher.

'I've thought of that too,' said Ned. 'If Ted here will take care of the food problem I'll answer for the rest. It's only a few days now till pay day.'

Again we slept at Fletcher's place. I passed a sleepless night, not because the floor was hard but because of Mona. Now that there was a chance to return I couldn't get back quickly enough. The whole night long I racked my brain to find a quick way out. Towards dawn it occurred to me that possibly the old man would send me part of the fare at least. If only I got as far as Richmond it would help.

Bright and early I went to the telegraph office to wire the old man. By nightfall the money had arrived—for a full trip. I borrowed an extra five bucks from Mooney, so as to eat, and that same evening I was off.

The moment I boarded the train I felt like a new man. Before half an hour had passed I had completely forgotten Jacksonville. What luxury to doze off in an upholstered seat! The strange thing was that I found myself writing again—in my head. Yes, I was positively itching to get to the machine. It seemed like a century ago that I had written the last line. . . . I wondered vaguely, dreamily, where I would find Mona, what we would do next, where we would live, and so on. Nothing was of too great consequence. It was so damned good to be sitting in that comfortable coach—with a five dollar bill in my pocket. . . . Maybe a guardian angel *was* looking after me! I thought of Fletcher's parting words. Was I really an artist? Of course I was. But I had yet to prove it. . . . Finally I congratulated myself on having had such a bitter experience. 'Experience is golden,' I kept repeating to myself. It sounded a bit silly, but it lulled me into a peaceful slumber.

13

Back to the old homestead, or to put it another way—back to the street of early sorrows. Mona lives with her family, I with mine. The only way—*pro tem*—to solve the economic problem. As soon as I've sold a few stories we'll find a place of our own again.

From the time the old man leaves for the tailor shop until he returns for dinner I'm hard at it—every day. Every day we talk to each other, Mona and I, over the phone; sometimes we meet at noon to have a bite together in some cheap restaurant. Not often enough, however, to please Mona. She's going mad with fear, doubts, jealousy. Simply can't believe that I'm writing day in and day out from morn to dusk.

Now and then, of course, I knock off to do 'research work.' I have a hundred different ideas to exploit, all of them demanding investigation and documentation. I'm running on all eight cylinders now: when I sit down to the machine it just flows off my fingers.

At the moment I'm putting the finishing touches to a self-portrait which I'm calling 'The Failure'. (I haven't the remotest suspicion that a man named Papini, a man living in Italy, will soon produce a book by this very title.)

I wouldn't say it was an ideal place to work—my parents' home. I sit at the front window, hidden by the lace curtains, one eye open for callers. The rule of the house is—if you see a visitor coming, duck! And that's exactly what I do each time—duck into the clothes closet, with typewriter, books, papers and everything. Fantastic! I call myself 'the family skeleton'. Sometimes I get brilliant ideas hidden away in the dark folds of the clothes closet—induced no doubt by the acrid smell of camphor balls. My thoughts come so fast that it is almost unbearable to wait until the visitor leaves. In utter darkness I make illegible notes on odd bits of paper. (Just key words and phrases.) As for breathing, no trouble at all. I can hold my breath for three hours, *if necessary*.

Coming out of the hole my mother is sure to exclaim: 'You shouldn't smoke so much!' The smoke has to be explained, you see. Her line is: 'Henry was just here.' Hearing her give this feeble explanation to a caller I sometimes stuff my mouth with a coat sleeve for fear of breaking loose with a chortle.

Now and then she hands me this: 'Can't you make your stories shorter?' Her thought—poor soul!—is that the sooner I finish them the quicker I will be paid. She doesn't want to hear about rejection slips. Acts almost as though she didn't believe in them.

'What are you writing about now?' she asks one morning.

'Numismatics,' I tell her.

'What's that?'

I explain in a few words.

'Do you think people really want to read such things?'

I wonder to myself what she would say if I were to tell her the truth, tell her about 'The Failure'.

The old man is more amenable. I sense that he doesn't expect anything to come of all this nonsense, but he's curious and at least pretends to be interested in what I'm doing. He doesn't quite know what to make of the fact that he has a son twice married, and the father of a child, who sits in the dining room day after day tapping away on a typewriter. At bottom he has confidence in me. He knows I'll get somewhere some day somehow. He's not uneasy in his soul.

Around the corner, where I trot each morning to get the paper and a pack of cigarettes, is a little store run by a newcomer—a Mr Cohen. He's the only person, this Mister Cohen, who seems at all interested in my doings. He thinks it remarkable that he has a writer, even if only an embryonic one, for a customer. All the other tradespeople, be it said, know me of old; not one of them suspects that I've grown a new soul. To them I am still the little boy with the corn-coloured hair and the innocent smile.

Mister Cohen, however, is of another world, another epoch. He doesn't 'belong' any more than I. In fact, being a Yid, he's still suspect. Especially to the old-timers. One bright and lovely morning the dear Mister Cohen confesses to me that he too once had ambitions to be a writer. With genuine feeling he informs me how much our little conversations mean to him. It is a privilege, he says, to know someone who is 'on the bias'. (Of the same stripe, I suppose he meant.) Lowering his voice, he confides with huge disgust his low opinion of the neighbouring shopkeepers. Ah, dear Mister Cohen, darling Mister Cohen, come forth, come forth, wherever you are, and let me kiss your waxen brow! What was it, now, we had in common? A few dead authors, fear and hatred of the police, scorn for the Gentiles and a passion for the aroma of a good cigar. You were no virtuoso, and neither was I. But your words came to me as if they were played on the celesta. Step forth, pale sprite, step forth from the divine telesma and let me embrace you once again!

My mother, of course, is not only surprised but shocked to discover that I have become friends with 'that little Jew'. What on earth do we talk about? *Books?* Does *he* read? Yes, mother dear, he reads in five languages. Her head swings back and forth unbelievingly, and again back and forth disapprovingly. Anyway, Hebrew and Yiddish, which are one and the same to her, don't count: only Jews understand such gibberish. (Ech! Ech!) Nothing of importance, says she, could possibly be written in such outlandish tongues. *And the Bible,* mother dear? She shrugs her shoulders. She meant books, not the Bible. (*Sic.*)

What a world! Not one of my old pals left. I used to wonder if I wouldn't run into Tony Marella some day. His father still sat by the window mending shoes. Every time I passed the shop I greeted him. But I never had the courage to inquire about Tony. One day, however, reading the local newspaper—*The Chat*—I discovered that my old friend was running for alderman in another district, where he now lived. Maybe he *would* become President of the United States one day! That would be something, what!—a President out of our obscure little neighbourhood. Already we could boast of a colonel and a rear-admiral. The Grogan brothers, no less. They had lived only a few doors away from us. 'Grand boys!' as the neighbours all said. (A little later and, by God! one of them actually becomes a general; as for the other, the rear-admiral, blast me if he isn't sent to Moscow on a special mission—and by none other than the President of our Holy Roller Empire. Not so bad for our little insignificant Van Voorhees Street!)

And now, thinks I to myself (*de la part des voisins*), we have little Henry with us. Who knows? Maybe he'll become another O'Henry. If Tony Marella is slated to become a President one day, surely Henry, our little Henry, can become a famous writer. *Dixit.*

Just the same—a slightly different key now—it was too bad we hadn't produced at least one good prize-fighter. The Laski brothers had faded out. Lacked the stuff that champs are made of. No, it wasn't the neighbourhood to breed John L. Sullivans or James J. Corbetts. The old 14th Ward, to be sure, had turned out a dozen good pugilists, not to speak of politicians, bankers, and good old 'con' men. I had the feeling that, were I back in the old neighbourhood, I would be writing more vividly. If only I could say hello to chaps like Lester Reardon, Eddie Carney, Johnny Paul, I'd feel like a new man.

'Shit!' I said to myself, rapping my bare knuckles against the iron spike of a fence, 'I'm not done for yet. Not by a long shot. . . .'

And so one morning I woke full of piss and vinegar. Decided to bust out into the world and make my presence. No set plan or project in mind. Tucking a sheaf of manuscripts under my arm, I made a dash for the street.

Playing a hunch, I make my way into the inner sanctum of an editorial office where I find myself face to face with one of the editors of a five cent magazine. My thought is to ask for an editorial position.

The curious thing is that the man is one of the Miller tribe. Gerald Miller, no less. A good omen!

I don't have to exercise my charms because he's already predisposed in my favour. 'No doubt about it,' says he, 'you're a born writer.' In front of him is a slew of manuscripts; he's glanced here and there, enough to convince himself that I have the goods.

'So you would like a job on the magazine? Well, it's just possible I can make room for you. One of the editors is leaving in a week or so; I'll speak to the boss and see what can be done. I'm certain you could fill the bill, even if you've had no training for it.' Follows this up with a few discerning compliments.

Then, apropos of nothing, he suddenly says: 'Why don't you write something for us meanwhile? We pay well, you know. I imagine you could use a cheque for $250.00, couldn't you?'

Without waiting for a reply, he continues: 'Why don't you write about words? I don't have to read very far to see that you're in love with words. . . .'

I wasn't sure I understood what exactly he wished me to say on this subject, especially to a five cent audience.

'I don't quite know myself,' he said. 'Use your imagination. Don't make it too long, either. Say five thousand words. And remember, our readers are not all college professors!'

We sat there a while, chinning, and then he escorted me to the elevator. 'See me in about a week,' he said. Then diving into his pocket, he fished out a bill and stuffed it in my fist. 'You might need that to hold you over.' He smiled. It was a twenty dollar bill, as I discovered when I hit the street. I felt like running back and thanking him again, but then I thought no, perhaps they're used to treating their writers that way.

'The snow was softly falling all over Ireland. . . .' The words were running like a refrain through my head as I skipped lightly over the cobble-stones homeward bound. Then came another line—why, I had no idea: 'In my Father's house are many mansions. . . .' They blended perfectly, the snow falling gently, softly, steadily (*all over Ireland*), and the jewelled mansions of bliss, of which the Father kept an infinite number. It was St Patrick's day for me, and no snakes in sight. For some weird reason I felt Irish to the core. A bit of Joyce, a bit of the

Blarney Stone, a few shenanigans—and *Erin Go Bragh*; (Every time the teacher's back was turned one of us would steal to the blackboard and scrawl out in flaming chalk: *Erin Go Bragh!*) It's Brooklyn I'm walking through and the snow is softly falling. I must ask Ulric to recite the passage for me again. He's got just the voice for it, has he. It's a beautiful melodious voice. And that he has, Ulric!

'The snow was softly falling over Ireland. . . .'

Nimble as a goat, thin as air, wistful as a faun, I wend my way over the lovely bubbly cobble-stones.

If only I knew what to write! Two hundred and fifty dollars was not to be sneezed at. And an editorial position to boot! My, but I had risen suddenly! Mister Cohen must hear of this. (*Sholem Aleichem!*) Five thousand words, A cinch. Once I knew what to say I could write it at one sitting. Words, words. . . .

Believe it or not, I don't put a damned word to paper. My favourite subject and here I am, tongue-tied. Curious. Worse than that—*depressing*.

Maybe I ought to do a little research work first. After all, what do I know about the English language? Almost nothing. To use it is one thing; to write about it intelligently quite another.

I have it! Why not go straight to the source? Why not call on the editor-in-chief of the famous unabridged dictionary? Which one? Funk & Wagnall's. (The only one I ever used.)

Next morning bright and early I'm sitting in the ante-room, waiting for Dr Vizetelly himself to appear. (It's like asking Jesus Christ to help you, think I to myself.) However, the cards are on the table. All I pray for is not to make a damned fool of myself, as I did years ago when I called on a famous writer and asked him straight out: 'How does one begin to write?' (The answer is: 'By writing.' That's exactly what he said, and that was end of the interview.)

Dr Vizetelly is standing before me. A live, genial man, full of sparkle and verve. Puts me at ease immediately. Urges me to unburden myself. Draws up a comfortable chair for himself, listens attentively, then begins. . . .

For a full hour or more this kind, gracious soul, to whom I shall always feel indebted, delivers himself of all that he thinks may serve me. He speaks so rapidly and fulsomely that I haven't the chance to make a single note. My head is spinning. How will I remember even a fraction of all this exciting information? It's as though I had put my head under a fountain.

Dr Vizetelly, conscious of my dilemma, comes to the rescue. He orders a page to bring me folders and pamphlets. Urges me to look them over at my leisure. 'I'm certain you'll write an excellent article,' he says, beaming at me like a godfather. Then he asks if I will be good enough to show him what I've written before submitting it to the magazine.

Without warning he now puts me a few direct questions about myself: how long have I been writing? what else have I done? what books do I read? what languages do I know? One after another—tic, tac, toc. I feel like less than nobody, or as they say in Hebrew—*efesefasim*. What indeed *have* I done? What indeed *do* I know? Smoked out at last, what is there to do but humbly confess my sins and omissions. I do so, exactly as I would to a priest, were I a Catholic and not the miserable spawn of Calvin and Luther.

What a virile, magnetic individual, this man! Who would ever dream, meeting him in the street, that he was the editor of a dictionary? The first erudite to inspire me with confidence and admiration. *This is a man.* I say it over and over to myself. A man with a pair of balls as well as a think-tank. Not a mere fount of wisdom but a living, rushing, roaring cataract. Every particle of his being vibrates with an electric ardour. He not only knows every word in the English language (including those in 'cold storage', as he put it) but he knows wines, horses, women, food, birds, trees; he know how to wear clothes, knows how to breathe, knows how to relax. And he also knows enough to take a drink once in a while, Knowing all, he loves all. *Now we touch him!* A man rushing forward—*on all fours*, I almost said—to greet life. A man with a song on his lips. Thank you, Dr Vizetelly! Thank you for being alive!

In parting he said to me—how can I ever forget his words? —'Son, you have all the makings of a writer, I'm sure of it. Go along now and do what you can. Call on me if you need me.' He placed one hand on my shoulder affectionately and with the other gave me a warm hand-clasp. It was the benediction. Amen!

No longer falls the soft white snow. It is raining, raining deep inside me. Down my face the tears stream—tears of joy and gratitude. I have beheld at last the face of my true father. I know now what it means—the Paraclete. Good-bye, Father Vizetelly, for I shall never see you again. May thy name be hallowed forever more!

The rain ceases. Just a thin drizzle now—down there under the heart—as if a cess-pool were being strained through fine gauze. The whole thoracic region is saturated with the finest particles of this substance called H_2O which, when it falls on the tongue, tastes salty. Microscopic tears, more precious than fat pearls. Sifting slowly into the great cavity ruled over by the tear ducts. Dry eyes, dry palms. The face absolutely relaxed, open as the great plains, and ripening with joy.

('Is it snowing again, Mr Conroy?')

It's wonderful to speak one's own idiom, to have it rebound in your face, become again the universal language. Of the 450,000 words locked up in the unabridged dictionary, Dr Vizetelly had assured me I must know at least 50,000. Even the shit-pumper has a vocabulary of at least 5,000 words. To prove it, all one had to do was to go home, sit down, and look around. Door, knob, chair, handle, wood, iron, curtain, window, sill, button, legs, bowl. . . . In any room there were hundreds of things with names, not to mention the adjectives, the adverbs, the prepositions, the verbs and participles that accompanied them. And Shakespeare had a vocabulary hardly bigger than a moron's of today!

So what does it add up to. What will we do with more words? ('And haven't you your own language to keep in touch with?')

Aye, the own language! *Langue d'oc*. Or—*huic, huic, huic.* In Hebrew one says 'How are you?' in at least ten different ways, according to whether one is addressing a man, a woman, men, women, or men and women, and so on. To a cow or a goat nobody in his right senses says 'How are you?'

Wending homeward, toward the street of early sorrows. Brooklyn, city of the dead. Return of the native. . . .

('And haven't you your own land to visit?')

Aye, dismal Brooklyn I have, and the neighbouring terrain— the swamps, the dumps, the stinking canals, the ever vacant lots, the cemeteries. . . . Native heath.

And I am neither fish nor fowl. . . .

The drizzle ceases. The innards are lined with wet lard. The cold drifts down from the north. Ah, but it's snowing again!

And now it comes to me, fresh from the grave, that passage which Ulric could recite like a born Dubliner. . . . 'It had begun to snow again. He watched sleepily the flakes, silver and dark, falling obliquely against the lamplight. The time had come for him to set out on his journey westward. Yes, the newspapers were right: snow was general all over Ireland. It was falling on every part of the dark central plain, on the tireless hills, falling softly upon the Bog of Allen and, farther westward, sofly falling into the dark mutinous Shannon waves. It was falling, too, upon every part of the lonely churchyard on the hill where Michael Furey lay buried. It lay thickly drifted on the crooked crosses and head-stones, on the spears of the little gate, on the barren thorns. His soul swooned slowly as he heard the snow falling faintly through the universe and faintly falling, like the descent of their last end, upon all the living and the dead.'

In this snowy realm, with language chanting its own sweet litany, I sped homeward, ever homeward. Between the covers of the giant lexicon, amid ablatives and gerundives, I curled up and fell fast asleep. Between Adam and Eve I lay, surrounded by a thousand reindeer. My warm breath, cooled by living waters enveloped me in a refulgent mist. In *la belle langue d'Oc*, I was out to the world. The caul was about my neck, strangling me, but ever so gently. And the name of the caul was Nemesh. . . .

It took me a solid month or more to write the article for my namesake, Gerald Miller. When I finished I found that I had written fifteen thousand words instead of five. I squeezed out half and brought it to the editorial offices. A week later I had my cheque. The article, by the way, was never published. 'Too good,' was the verdict. Nor did the editorial job ever materialize. I never found out why. Probably because I was 'too good'.

However, with the 250 we were able to resume life together once more. We picked ourselves a furnished room on Hancock Street, Brooklyn, city of the dead, the near dead, and the deader than the dead. A quiet, respectable street: row after row of the same nondescript frame houses, all adorned with high stoops, awnings, grass plots and iron railings. The rent was modest; we were permitted to cook over gas-burners tucked away in an alcove next to an old-fashioned sink. Mrs Henniker, the landlady, occupied the ground floor; the rest of the house was let out to roomers.

Mrs Henniker was a widow whose husband had grown rich in the saloon business. She had a mixture of Dutch, Swiss, German, Norwegian and Danish blood. Full of vitality, idle curiosity, suspicion, greed and malice. Could pass for a whore-house keeper. Always telling risqué stories and giggling over them like a schoolgirl. Very strict with her roomers. No monkey business! No noise! No beer parties! No visitors! Pay on the dot or you go!

It took this old geezer some time to get used to the idea that I was a writer. What stupefied her was the way the keys clicked. She had never believed anyone could write at such speed. But above all she was worried, worried for fear that, being a writer, I would forget to pay the rent after a few weeks. To allay her fears we decided to give her a few weeks' rent in advance. Incredible how a little move like that can solidify one's position!

At frequent intervals she would knock at the door, offer some flimsy excuse for interrupting me, than stand at the threshold for an hour or more pumping me. Obviously it excited her to think that anyone could pass the whole day at the machine, writing, writing, writing. What *could* I be writing? Stories? What kind of stories? Would I permit her to read one some day? Would I this and would I that? It was inconceivable the questions the woman could ask.

After a time she began dropping in on me in order, as she said, to give me ideas for my stories: fragments out of her life in Hamburg, Dresden, Bremen, Darmstadt. Innocent little doings which to her were daring, shocking, so much so that sometimes her voice dropped to a whisper. If I were to make use of these incidents I was to be sure to change the locale. And of course give her a different name. I led her on for a while, glad to receive her little offerings—cheese cake, sausage meat, a left-over stew, a bag of nuts. I wheedled her into making us cinnamon cake,

369

streusel kuchen, apple cake—all in approved German style. She was ready to do most anything if only she might have the pleasure of reading about herself some day in a magazine.

One day she asked me point blank if my stories really sold. Apparently she had been reading all the current magazines she could lay hands on and had not found my name in one of them. I patiently explained to her that sometimes one had to wait several months before a story was accepted, and after that another few months before one got paid. I at once added that we were now living on the proceeds of several stories which I had sold the year before—at a handsome figure. Whereupon, as though my words had no effect whatever upon her, she said flatly: 'If you get hungry you can always eat with me. I get lonely sometimes.' Then, heaving a deep sigh: 'It's no fun to be a writer, is it?'

It sure wasn't. Whether she suspected it or not, we were always hungry as wolves. No matter how much money came in, it always melted like snow. We were always trotting about, looking up old friends with whom we could eat, borrow carfare, or persuade to take us to a show. At night we rigged up a washline which we stretched across the bed.

Mrs Henniker, always over-fed, could sense that we were in a perpetual state of hunger. Every so often she repeated her invitation to dine with her—'if you're ever hungry.' She never said: 'Won't you have dinner with me this evening, I have a lovely rabbit stew which I made expressly for you.' No, she took a perverse pleasure in trying to force us to admit that we were ravenous. We never did admit it of course. For one thing, to give in meant that I would have to write the sort of stories Mrs Henniker wanted. Besides, even a hack writer has to keep up a front.

Somehow we always managed to borrow the rent money in time. Dr Kronski sometimes came to the rescue, and so did Curley. But it was a tussle. When we were really desperate we would walk to my parents' house—a good hour's walk—and stay until we had filled our bellies. Often Mona fell asleep on the couch immediately after dinner. I would do my utmost to keep up a running convrsation, praying to God that Mona wouldn't go on sleeping until the last horn.

These post-prandial conversations were sheer agony. I tried desperately to talk of everything but my work. Inevitably, however, there would come the moment when either my father or my mother would ask—'How is the writing going? Have you sold anything more since we saw you last?' And I would lie shamefacedly: 'Why yes, I sold two more recently. It's going fine, really.' Then would come a look of joy and astonishment and they would ask simultaneously: 'To which magazines did you sell them?' And I would give the names at random. 'We'll be watching for them, Henry. When do you think they will appear?' (Nine months later they would remind me that they were still on the look-out for those stories I said I had sold to this and that magazine.)

Towards the end of the evening, my mother, as if to say, 'Let's get down to earth!' would ask me solemnly if I didn't think it would be wiser to crop the writing and look for a job. 'That was such a wonderful position you had with. . . . How could you ever have given it up? It takes years to become a good writer—and maybe you will never succeed at it.' And so on and so forth. I used to weep for her. The old man, on the other hand, always pretended to believe that I would come through with flying colours. He fervently hoped so, that I was certain of. 'Give him time, give him time!' he would say. To which my mother would reply—'But how will they live in the meantime?' Then it was *my* cue. 'Don't worry, mother, I know how to get along. I've got brains, you know that. You don't think we're going to starve, do you?' Just the same, my mother thought, and she would repeat it over and over, as if to herself, that it would really be wiser to take a job and do the writing on the side. 'Well, they don't look as though they were starving, do they?' This was the old man's way of telling me that, if we really were starving, all I had to do was to call on him at the tailor shop and he'd lend me what he could. I understood and he understood. I would thank him silently and he would acknowledge my thanks silently. Of course I never called on him. Not for money. Now and then, out of a clear sky, I would drop in on him just to cheer him up. Even when he knew I was lying—I told him outrageous cock-and-bull stories—he never let on. 'Glad to hear, son,' he'd say. 'Great! You'll be a best seller yet, I'm sure of it.' Sometimes, on leaving him, I would be in tears. I wanted so much to help him. There he sat in the back of the shop, a sort of collapsed wreck, his business shot to hell, no hopes whatever, and still acting cheerful, still talking optimistically. Perhaps he hadn't seen a customer for several months, but still 'a boss tailor'. The frightful irony of it! 'Yes,' I would say to myself, walking down the street, 'the first story I sell I'm going to hand him a few greenbacks.' Whereupon I myself would wax optimistic, persuaded by some crazy logic that some editor would take a fancy to me and write out a check, in advance, for five hundred or a thousand dollars. By the time I reached home, however, I'd be willing to settle for a five-spot. I'd settle for anything, in fact, that meant another meal, or more postage stamps, or just shoe laces.

'Any mail today?' That was always my cry on entering. If there was fat envelopes waiting for me I knew it was my manu-scripts coming home to roost. If they were thin envelopes it meant rejection slips, with a request to forward postage for the return of the scripts. Or else it was bills. Or a letter from the lawyer, addressed to some ancient address and forwarded to me in some miraculous fashion.

The back alimony was piling up. I would never be able to foot the bill, never. It looked more than ever certain that I would end my days in Raymond Street jail.

'Something will turn up, you'll see.'

Whenever anything did turn up it was always by her contrivance. It was Mona who ran into the editor of 'Scurrilous Stories', and got a commission to write a half-dozen stories for them. Just like that. I wrote two, under her name, with great effort, with heroic effort really; then I got the bright idea to look up their old files, take their own published stories, change the names of the characters, the beginnings and endings, and serve them up rehashed. It not only worked—they were enthusiastic about these forgeries. *Naturally*, since they had already savoured the stew. But I soon grew weary of making potpourris. Just so much time wasted, it seemed to me. 'Tell them to go to hell,' I said one day. She did. But the kick-back was wholly unanticipated. From being 'our editor', his nibs now became a heavy lover. We got five times the money we used to get for the damned stories. What *he* got I don't know. To believe Mona, all he demanded was a half hour of her time in a public place, usually a tea room. Fantastic! More fantastic still was this—he confessed one day that he was still a virgin. (At the age of forty-nine!) What he omitted to say was that he was also a pervert. The subscribers to the bloody magazine, we learned, included a respectable number of perverted souls—ministers, rabbis, doctors, lawyers, teachers, reformers, congressmen, all sorts of people whom one would never suspect of being interested in such trash. The vice crusaders were undoubtedly the most avid of their readers.

As a reaction to this phoney slush I wrote a story about a killer. I wrote it as if I had known the man intimately, but the truth is I had gleaned all the facts from little Curley who had spent a night in Central Park with this 'Butch' or whatever he was called. The night Curley told me the story I had one of those bad dreams in which you are pursued endlessly and relentlessly, escaping death only by coming awake.

What interested me about this 'Butch' was the discipline he imposed on himself in plotting his hold-ups. To plot a job accurately required the combined powers of a mathematician and a yogin.

There he was, right in Central Park, and the whole nation searching high and low for him. Telling his story, like a fool, to a young lad like Curley. Even divulging a few sensational aspects of the job he was then plotting.

He might as well have stood on the corner of Times Square as prowl about Central Park late at night.

A reward of fifty thousand dollars was coming to the man who got him, dead or alive.

According to Curley, the man had locked himself in his room for weeks; he had spent hours upon hours lying on the bed with a bandage over his eyes, rehearsing in detail every step, every move that was to be made. Everything had been thought out thoroughly, even the most trifling details. But, like an author or a composer he would not undertake the execution of his plans until they were perfect. He not only took into account all possibilities of error and accident, but like an engineer, he allowed a margin of safety to meet unexpected stress and strain. He might have been dead certain himself, he might have tested the ability and the loyalty of his confederates, but in the end he could count only on himself, on his own brains, his own fore-sight. He was alone against thousands. Not only was every copper in the country on the alert, but so were the civilians throughout the land. One careless little move and the jig was up. Of course he never intended to let himself be caught alive. He would shoot it out. But there were his pals—he couldn't let them down.

Perhaps, when he strolled out to get a breath of air that evening, he was so chockful of ideas, so certain that nothing could go amiss, that he simply couldn't contain himself any longer. He would collar the first comer and spill the beans, trusting to the fact that his victim would be reduced to such a state of terror that he would be paralysed. Perhaps he enjoyed the thought of brushing elbows with the guardians of the law, asking them for a light, maybe, or for directions, looking them straight in the eye, touching them, *thanking them*, and they none the wiser. Maybe he needed such a thrill to steady himself, to get the cold feel of things—because it's one thing to think it out intensely all by yourself, securely locked in a room, and quite another thing to start moving about outdoors, with every pair of eyes examining you, with every man's hand raised against you. Athletes have to warm up first. Criminals probably have to do something similar. . . . Butch was the sort who enjoyed courting danger. He was an A-1 criminal, a guy who might have made a great general, or a wily corporation lawyer. Like so many of his kind, he had assured Curley not once but several times, that he had always given his man a fair chance. He was not a coward, neither was he a sneak, and certainly not a traitor. He was against Society, that was all. Playing a lone hand, he had reason to be proud of his success. Like a movie star, he was vain about his following. Fans? He had millions of them. Now and then he had done something off the record, just to let them know his calibre. Playing to the gallery. Sure. Why not? One had to get a little fun out of it too. He didn't particularly relish the killings, though he didn't have a bad conscience about them either. What he liked more than anything was to put it over on the soft shoe blokes.

They always thought themselves so god-damned smart!

Curley was still trembling with excitement, fear, anguish, admiration and God knows what. He could talk of nothing else. He urged us to watch the papers. It would be a sensational affair. Even to us he refused to reveal the nature of it. He was still frightened, still hypnotized. 'His eyes!' he exclaimed over and over. 'I felt as if I were turning to stone.'

'But you met in the dark.'

'Doesn't matter. They glowed like coals. They gave off sparks!'

'Don't you think maybe you imagined it, knowing he was a killer?'

'Not me! I'll never forget those eyes. They'll haunt me to my dying day.' He shuddered.

'Do you really think, Curley,' asked Mona, 'that a criminal's eyes are different from other people's?'

'Why not?' said Curley. 'Everything else about them is different. Why not their eyes? Don't you think eyes change when the personality changes? They all have "other" personalities. I mean, they're not themselves. They're something plus—or less, I don't know which. They're another breed, that's all I can say. Even before he told me who he was I felt it. It was like getting a vibration from another world. His voice was unlike any human voice I know. When he shook hands with me I thought I had hold of an electric current. I got a shock, I can tell you—I mean a physical shock. I would have run away from him, then and there, but those eyes kept me rooted to the spot. I couldn't budge, couldn't lift a finger. . . . I begin to understand now what people mean when they talk of the Devil. There was a strange smell about him—did I mention that? Not sulphur and brimstone. More like some concentrated acid. Maybe he had been working with chemicals. But I don't think it was that. *It was something in his blood. . . .*'

'Do you think you would recognize him if you saw him again?'

Here Curley paused, to my surprise. He seemed baffled.

'Frankly,' he answered, and with great hesitation, 'I don't think I would. Strong as his personality was, it also had the power to erase itself from one's consciousness. Does that sound fishy? Let me put it another way.' (Here I was genuinely astounded. Curley had indeed made strides.) 'Supposing St Francis appeared before you tonight in this very room. Supposing he spoke to you. Would you remember what he looked like tomorrow or the day after? Wouldn't his presence be so overwhelming as to wipe out all remembrance of his features? Maybe you've never thought

374

of such an eventuality. I have because I knew someone once who had visions. I was only a kid at the time but I can remember the look on the person's face when she told me of her experiences. I know that she saw more than the physical being. When some-one comes to you from above he brings something of heaven with him—and that's blinding. Anyway, that's how it seems to me. . . . Butch gave me a similar feeling, only I knew he didn't come from above. Wherever he came from, it was all about him. You could sense it. And it was terrifying.' He paused again, his face brightened. 'Listen, you're the one who urged me to read Dostoievsky. You know what it is, then, to be dragged into a world of unmitigated evil. Some of his characters talk and act as if they inhabited a world absolutely unknown to us. I wouldn't call it Hell. Something worse. Something more complex, more subtle than Hell. Nothing physical can describe it. You sense it from their reactions. They have an unpredictable approach to everything. Until he wrote about them, we'd never known people who thought as his characters do. And that reminds me—with him the criminal, the idiot, the saint are not so very far apart, are they? How do you figure that out? Did Dostoievsky mean that we're all of one substance? What is evil, and what divine? Maybe you know. . . . I don't.'

'Curley, you really surprise me,' said I. 'I mean it.'

'You think I'm so very different now?'

'*Different?* No, not so very, but certainly more mature.'

'What the hell, you don't remain a kid all your life.'

'True. . . . Tell me honestly, Curley, if you could get away with it, would you be tempted to lead the life of a criminal?'

'Possibly,' he answered, lowering his head ever so little.

'You like danger, don't you?'

He nodded.

'And you don't have many scruples either, when the other fellow gets in your way?'

'I guess not.' He smiled. A rather twisted smile.

'And you still hate your step-father?'

Without waiting for a reply I added: 'Enough to kill him, if you could get away with it?'

'Right!' said Curley. 'I'd kill him like a dog.'

'Why? Do you know why? Now think, don't answer me straight off.'

'I don't have to think,' he barked. '*I know.* I'd kill him because he stole my mother's love. It's as simple as that.'

'Doesn't that sound slightly ridiculous to you?'

'I don't give a damn if it does. It's the truth. I can't forget it a d, what's more, I'll never forgive him. *There*'s a criminal for you, if you want to know.'

'Maybe you're right, Curley, but the law doesn't recognize him as one.'

'Who cares about the law? Anyway, there are other laws—and more important too. We don't live by legal codes.'

'Right you are!'

'I'd be doing the world a service,' he continued heatedly. 'His death would purify the atmosphere. He's of no use to anyone. Never was. I ought to be honoured for doing away with him and his kind. If we had an intelligent society, I would be. In literature men who commit such crimes are regarded as heroes. Books are as much a part of life as anything else. If authors can think such thoughts, why not me or the other fellows? My grievances are real, not imaginary. . . .'

'Are you so sure of that, Curley?' It was Mona who spoke.

'Dead sure,' said he.

'But if you were the central character in a book,' said she, 'the important thing would be what happened to *you*, not your step-father. A man who kills his father—in a book—doesn't become a hero just on that account. It's the way he behaves that counts, the way he faces the problem—and resolves it. Anyone can commit a crime, but some crimes are of such stupendous import that the doer becomes something more than a criminal. Do you see what I'm getting at?'

'I follow you all right,' said Curley, 'but I don't give a damn about all those subtleties and complexities. *That's literature!* I'm telling you honestly that I still hate his guts, that I'd kill him without compunction, if I could get away with it.'

'I see one big difference already. . . .' Mona began.

'What do you mean?' he snapped.

'Between you and the hero of a book.'

'I don't want to be a hero!'

'I know,' said Mona gently, 'but you do want to remain a human being, don't you? If you go on thinking this way, who knows, some day you may get your wish. Then what?'

'Then I'd be happy. No, not exactly happy, but relieved.'

'Because he was out of the way, you mean?'

'No! *Because I had done away with him.* There's a difference there.'

Here I felt impelled to break in. 'Look, Curley, Mona got off the track. I think I know what she meant to say. It's this—the difference between a criminal who commits a crime and the hero of a book who commits the same crime is that the latter doesn't care whether he will get away with it or not. He's not concerned about what happens to him afterwards. He must accomplish his purpose, that's all. . . .'

'Which only proves,' said Curley, 'that I'll never make a hero.'

'Nobody's asking you to become a hero. But if you see the distinction between the two then you'll realize that you're hardly much better than the man you hate and despise so much.'

'Even if that's true I don't give a damn!'

376

'Let's forget it then. The probabilities are that he'll die a peaceful death and that you'll end up on a ranch in sunny California.'

'Maybe it'll be the griffs and the grinds—how do you know?'

'Maybe. And maybe not.'

Before he left that night Curley imparted a piece of information which gave us quite a shock. Tony Maurer, he told us, had committed suicide. He had hanged himself in the bathroom during the course of a party he was giving his friends. They had found him with a sardonic smile on his lips and a pipe hanging from his mouth. No one, apparently, knew why he had done it. He was never in lack of money and he was deeply in love with the woman he lived with, a beautiful Javanese girl. Some said he had done it out of sheer boredom. If so, it was in keeping with his character.

The news affected me strangely. I kept thinking what a pity it was that I had not gotten to know Tony Maurer more intimately. He was the sort of man I would have been proud to call a friend. But I was too bashful to make advances, and he was too surfeited to recognize my need. I always felt a little uncomfortable in his presence. Like a schoolboy, to be precise. Everything I wanted to do he had done already. . . . Perhaps there was something else which had drawn me to him all unconsciously: his German blood. For once in my life I had had the pleasure of knowing a German who did not remind me of all the other Germans I knew. The truth is, he wasn't really a German—he was a cosmopolite. The perfect example of that 'late-city man' whom Spengler has so well described. His roots were not in German soil, German blood, German tradition, but in those end periods which distinguished the late-city man of Egypt, Greece, Rome, China, India. He was rootless and 'at home' everywhere —that is, where there was culture and civilization. He might just as well have fought on the Italian, French, Hungarian or Rumanian side as ours. He had a sense of loyalty without being patriotic. No wonder he had spent six months (by accident) in a French prison camp—and enjoyed it. He liked the French even more than the Germans—or the Americans. He liked good conversation, that was it.

All these aspects of the man, plus the fact that he was debonair, adroit, thoroughly sophisticated, utterly tolerant and forgiving, had endeared him to me. Not one of my friends possessed these qualities. They had better and worse traits, traits all too familiar to me. They were too much like myself *au fond*, my friends. All my life I had wanted, and still crave, as a matter of fact, friends whom I could look upon as being utterly different from myself. Whenever I succeeded in finding one I also discovered that the attraction necessary to maintain a vital relation-

377

ship was lacking. None of these individuals ever became more than 'potential' friends.

Anyway, that night I dreamed. An interminable dream, as I said before, and full of hair-raising escapades. In the dream Butch and Tony Maurer had exchanged personalities. In some mysterious way I was in league with them, or him, for sometimes this mysterious, baffling confederate of mine would split into two distinct personalities, never however being clearly Tony Maurer or clearly Butch, but always a composite of the two, even when split. This sort of double play was sufficient in itself to cause me extreme anguish, to say nothing of the fact that I was never certain whether he or they were with me or against me.

The theme of this disturbing dream centred about a job we were pulling off in some strange city which I had never visited, a remote place like Sioux Falls, Tonopah or Ludlow. I played the role of stooge, a most uncomfortable role, since I was always exposed, always left in the lurch. Over and over again it was impressed on me that one false move, one little mistake, and I would be so much horse meat. The instructions were always garbled, always given in a code which it took me hours to decipher. Of course the job was never pulled off. Instead we were on the run continuously, driven from pillar to post, badgered like wild game, When we were obliged to hide away—in caves, cellars, swamps, mineshafts—we played cards or rolled dice. The stakes were always for grand sums. We paid one another off in I.O.U's, or else in Confederate money which we had seized in rifling a bank. This Butch-Maurer wore a monocle, wore it even in public, despite all my entreaties. His language was a mixture of thieves' argot and Oxford slang. Even when explaining the devious complexities of a perilous undertaking he had a bad habit of wandering off the track, of telling stories which were long-winded and pointless. It was excruiating to follow him. Eventually the three of us were cornered, or pocketed rather, in a narrow defile (in the Far West, it seemed) by a band of vigilantes. We were all killed outright, shot down like wild boars. I only realized that I was still alive when I came awake. Even then I could scarcely believe it. I was already sprouting wings.

Such was the gist of the dream. I tried to condense this raw material into a tale of pursuit, with a strict plot and a definite locale. The manhunt part of it I captured quite well, I thought, but the choppy, fantastic, episodic dream substance of flight and incident refused to be converted into intelligible narrative. I fell between two stools. Still, it was a brave attempt, and it gave me the courage to tackle more imaginative stories. Perhaps I might have succeeded, in this latter vein, had we not received a telegram from O'Mara urging us to join him in North Carolina, the seat of another big real estate boom. As usual, he intimated that he was holding down a big job: 'they' had need of me on the publicity end.

I wired back immediately to send us the train fare and advise what my salary would be. The answer I received read as follows: 'Don't worry everything jake borrow the fare.'

Mona immediately suspected the worst. It was just like him, she thought, to be vague, non-committal and utterly unreliable. It was nothing more than loneliness that had made him wire us.

Defending him instinctively, I worked myself up to such a pitch of enthusiasm that, despite the fact that I had a sinking feeling about the whole business, I could no longer back out.

'Well,' she said, 'and where will we get the fare?'

I was stumped. For a minute only. Suddenly I had a bright thought. 'The money? Why, from that little Lesbian you met the other day in the department store, remember? The Tansy perfume girl. *That's where.*'

'Preposterous!' That was her first reaction.

'Come, come,' I said, 'she'll probably bless you for asking her.'

She continued to assert that it was out of the question, but it was obvious that whe was revolving the suggestion in her mind. By the morrow, I was certain she'd display a different attitude.

'I tell you what,' said I, as if to dismiss the subject, 'let's go to a show tonight, what do you say? Let's see something funny.'

She thought it an excellent idea. We ate out, picked a good show—at the Palace—and came home laughing our heads off. We laughed so much in fact that it took us hours to fall asleep.

The next morning, as I had anticipated, she was off to see her little Lesbian friend. No trouble at all borrowing fifty smackers. Her difficulty had been to shake the girl off.

I suggested that we hitch-hike instead of taking the train. That would leave something over on arriving. 'You never know about O'Mara. It may be all a smoke dream.'

'You talked differently yesterday,' said Mona.

'I know, but now it's today. I'd rather play safe.'

She acquiesced readily enough. Agreed that we would probably see more of the country by hitch-hiking. Besides, with a woman by one's side it was always easier to get a lift.

The landlady was a bit put out by the suddenness of our decision but when I explained that I had been commissioned to do a book she took it with seeming good nature and wished us well.

'What sort of book?' she asked, clutching my hand in farewell.

'About the Cherokee Indians,' I said, quickly closing the door behind us.

We got lifts easily enough but to my amazement Mona registered nothing but disappointment. By the time we reached Harper's Ferry she was plainly disgusted—with the landscape, the towns, the people we met, the meals and everything.

It was late afternoon when we reached Harper's Ferry. We sat high up on a rock overlooking three States. Below us the Shenandoah and the Potomac. A hallowed spot, if for no other reason than the fact that here John Brown, the great Liberator, met his fate. Mona, however, wasn't at all interested in the historic aspects of the place. As for the splendour of the vista, that she couldn't repudiate. But it filled her with desolation. To tell the truth, I felt much the same, but for different reasons. It was impossible to pull myself away. Too much had happened here to permit the obtrusion of one's private worries. I read with moist eyes what Thomas Jefferson had said of this particular spot: the words were carved on a tablet fastened to the rock. There was sublimity in Jefferson's words. But there was even more sublimity in the action of John Brown and his faithful followers. 'No man in America,' said Thoreau, 'has ever stood up so persistently for the dignity of human nature, knowing himself for man and equal of any and all governments.' A fanatic? Possibly. Who else but a just man could plan to overthrow the stable, conservative government of these United States, with a mere handful of men? Glory to John Brown! Glory on high! 'I believe in the Golden Rule, sir, and the Declaration of Independence. I think they both mean the same thing. Better that a whole generation should pass off the face of the earth—men, women and children —by a violent death, than that one jot of either should fall in this country.' (The words of John Brown in the year 1857.) Let us not forget that the number of Liberators who took possession of the town of Harper's Ferry was only twenty-two, of whom seventeen were whites. 'A few men in the right, and knowing they are, can overturn a king,' said John Brown. With twenty men in the Alleghanies he was certain he could smash Slavery in two years. 'Who would be free, themselves must strike the blow.' There you have John Brown in a nut-shell. A fanatic? more than likely. The sort who said: 'A man dies when his time comes, and a man who fears is born out of time.' If he was indeed a fanatic, he was a unique one. Is this the language of a fanatic? —'Do not allow anyone to say that I acted from revenge. I claim no man has a right to revenge himself. It is a feeling that does not enter into my heart. What I do, I do for the cause of human liberty, and because I regard it as necessary.'

Compromise was not in his nature. Nor palliation. He was a man of vision. And it was a great, great vision which inspired his 'mad' behaviour. Had John Brown taken over the helm the slaves would really be free today—not only the black slaves but the white slaves and the slaves of the slaves, which is to say, he slaves of the machine.

The ironic thing is that the great Liberator came to a disastrous end because of his overwhelming sense of consideration for the enemy. (That was where his real madness lay!) After forty days in chains, after a mock trial during which he lay on the floor of the court-room in his blood-soaked, sabre-torn clothes, he went to the gallows, with his head erect, standing there on the trap blindfolded, waiting, waiting (though his one and only request had been to get done with it quickly), while the gallant military men of Virginia performed their interminable and asinine parade manoeuvres.

To those who had written him towards the end, asking how they might aid him, John Brown had replied: 'Please send fifty cents a year to my wife in North Elba, New York.' As he made his way to the gallows he shook hands in turn with each of his comrades, handing them each a quarter with his blessing. That's how the great Liberator went to meet his Maker. . . .

The gateway to the South is Harper's Ferry. You enter the South by way of the Old Dominion. John Brown had entered the Old Dominion to pass into life eternal. 'I acknowledge no master in human form,' he said. Glory! Glory be!

One of his contemporaries, almost as famous in his own way, said of John Brown: 'He could not have been tried by his peers, for his peers did not exist.' Amen! Alleluia! And may his soul go marching on!

14

I'M NOW GOING TO sing of 'The Seven Great Joys'. This
is the refrain:

> Come all ye out of the wilderness
>   And glory be,
> Father, Son and the Holy Ghost
>   Through all eternity.

We will sing it often as we writhe like snakes in the sultry
bosom of the South. . . .

Asheville. Thomas Wolfe, who was born here, was probably
composing *Look Homeward, Angel!* at the time of our entry. I
had not even heard of Thomas Wolfe. A pity, because I might
have looked at Asheville with different eyes. No matter what anyone says of Asheville, the setting is magnificent. In the very heart
of the Great Smokies. Ancient Cherokee land. To the Cherokees
it must have been Paradise. It is still a Paradise, if you can view
it with a clear conscience.

O'Mara was there to usher us into Heaven. But once again we
were too late. Things had taken a bad turn. The real estate boom
was over. There was no publicity job awaiting me. No job of any
sort. To tell the truth, I felt relieved. Learning that O'Mara had
put a little money aside, enough to tide us over a few weeks, I
decided that it was as good a place as any to stay a while and
write. The only drawback was Mona. The South was not to her
liking. I had hopes however, that she would adjust herself. After
all, she had rarely set foot outside New York.

According to O'Mara, there was a ranger's cabin which we
could make use of indefinitely, rent free, if we liked the place.
An ideal spot, he thought, for me to write in. Only a short
distance out of town it was, up in the hills. He seemed eager to
see us move in immediately.

It was nightfall when we got to the foot of the hill, where we were to obtain the keys for the cabin. With the aid of an over-grown idiot we rode up on mule-back, in pitch darkness. Just Mona and myself, that is. As we slowly and laboriously ascended we listened to the roar of the mountain torrent rushing beside us. It was that dark you couldn't see your hand in front of you. It took us almost an hour to get to the clearing where the cabin stood. Hardly had we dismounted when we were assailed by swarms of flies and mosquitoes. The idiot, a gangling, gawky lad who never opened his mouth, pushed the door in and hung the lantern on a cord dangling from a rafter. Obviously the place hadn't been inhabited for years. It was not only filthy, it was infested with rats, spiders and all manner of vermin.

We stretched out on the two cots side by side; the idiot lay on the floor at our feet. I was aware of the unpleasant sound of bats swooping about over our heads. The flies and mosquitoes, disturbed by our intrusion, attacked us mercilessly.

Despite everything, however, we succeeded in falling asleep.

It seemed to me I had hardly closed my eyes when I felt Mona clutching my arm.

'What is it?' I muttered.

She leaned over and whispered in my ear.

'Nonsense,' I said, 'you were probably dreaming.'

I tried to fall back to sleep. In an instant I felt her clutching me again.

'It's him,' she whispered, 'I'm sure of it. He's feeling my leg.'

I got up, struck a match, and took a good look at the idiot. He was lying on his side, his eyes closed, still as a stick.

'You're imagining things,' I said, 'he's sound asleep.'

Just the same I thought it better to be on the alert. A dumb gawk like that had the strength of a brute. I struck another match and took a quick look about to see what I might use as a weapon should he really get out of hand.

At daybreak we were all wide awake and scratching like mad. The heat was already stifling. We sent the boy to fetch a pail of water, dressed hurriedly, and decided without delay to clear out. While waiting for the goon to pack we inspected the spot more closely. The cabin was literally smothered by trees and brush. No view whatever. Just the sound of running water and the insane twittering of birds. I recalled O'Mara's parting words when we started up the goat path—'Just the place for you . . . an ideal retreat!'

Descending, again on mule-back, we observed with a shudder what a narrow escape we had had. One little slip and we would have been done for. Before we had gone very far we dismounted and followed on foot. Even thus it was a ticklish feat to keep from slipping.

At the bottom we were presented to all the members of the family. There were over a dozen kids running about, most of them half-naked. We inquired if we might have breakfast with them. We were told to wait, they'd call us when ready. We sat down on the steps of the porch and waited glumly. By now—it was not yet seven—the heat was almost intolerable.

When they called us in we found the whole family congregated about the table. For a moment I could scarcely believe my eyes: all those black spots that peppered the food, were they really flies? At each end of the table stood two youngsters busily engaged in brushing away the flies with dirty towels. We sat down, all together, and the flies settled in our ears, eyes, nose, hair and teeth. We sat in silence for a moment while the venerable patriarch said grace.

> The very first blessing that Mary had
> Hit was the blessing of one,
> To think her little Jesus
> Was God's only Son,
> Was God's only Son.

The repast was a bounteous one—grits, bacon and eggs, corn bread, coffee, ham, flapjacks, stewed pears. All for twenty-five cents per head. No extra charge for the flies.

O'Mara was a bit put out to see us back so quick. 'No guts,' he said glumly.

'You know I hate flies,' was all I could say.

As luck would have it, we went to a restaurant that evening which had just opened. In West Asheville. The owner, Mr Rawlins, had been a schoolteacher. For some reason he took a fancy to us instantly. On leaving he gave us a letter of introduction to a man and wife who had a comfortable room to let and at a very small sum. We paid a week's rent in advance and the next day turned over to Mr Rawlins sufficient to pay for a week's supply of meals.

From this point on we saw almost nothing of O'Mara. No quarrel. Going different ways, that's all.

I borrowed a typewriter from Mr Rawlins, who displayed a touching eagerness to be of service to 'a man of letters'. To be sure, I had handed him quite a line regarding the books I had written, as well as about the magnum opus which was in progress. We ate well in his cosy little restaurant. There were all sorts of side dishes which he thrust upon us gratis, in further recognition, no doubt, of 'the man of letters'. Now and then he put a good cigar in my breast pocket or insisted that we accept a pint of ice cream to eat when we got home.

It turned out that Rawlins had been a professor of English at the local High School. Which explains the royal sessions we held over the Elizabethan writers. But what endeared me to him most, I do believe, was my love of the Irish writers. The fact that I had read Yeats, Synge, Lord Dunsany, Lady Gregory, O'Casey, Joyce, led him to accept me as a boon companion. He was dying to read my work, but I had sense enough to keep it out of sight. Besides, there was really nothing to show him.

At the rooming house we struck up an acquaintance with a lumber man from West Virginia, Matthews was his name. He was a Scot through and through, but a gallant one. It gave him the utmost pleasure, a sincere pleasure, to drive us about the country in his beautiful car on his off days. He had a liking for good food and good wines, and he knew where they were to be found. It was at Chimney Rock one day that he blew us to a meal of which I can truthfully say that only twice since have I enjoyed anything like it. I must say this of Matthews, that from the very beginning he divined our true situation; from the very beginning of our relationship he made it clear that, whenever we were with him, we were never to put our hands into our pockets.

To say only this about him would be to give a false impression of the man. He was not a wealthy man, nor was he what we call a 'sucker'. He was a sensitive, highly intelligent individual who knew almost nothing about books, music or painting. But he knew life—and of nature, animals particularly, he was extremely fond. I said that he was not wealthy. Had he wished to, he could have become a millionaire in no time. But he had no desire to become rich. He was one of those rare Americans who is content with his lot. To be in his company was like being with your own brother. Often, in the evening, we sat on the front porch and talked for five and six hours at a stretch. Easy talk. Restful talk. . . .

But the writing. . . . Somehow it wouldn't come. To finish a simple story, a bad one at that, took me several weeks. The heat had something to do with it. (In the South the heat explains almost everything, except lynching.) Before I could get two lines written my clothes would be drenched with perspiration. I'd sit at the window and stare at the chain gang—all Negroes—working away with pick and shovel, chanting as they worked, the sweat rolling down their backs in rivulets. The harder they worked the less effort I was able to make. The singing got into my blood. But what disturbed me even more was the looks of the guards; just to glance into the faces of these human bloodhounds sent the shivers up my spine.

To vary the monotony Mona and I would make an excursion on our own occasionally, selecting some distant spot, any old spot, which we would get to by hitch-hiking. We made these excursions merely to kill time. (In the South time flies like lead.) Sometimes we took the first car that came along, not caring which direction it was taking. Like that, observing one day that we were headed for South Carolina, I suddenly recollected the name of an old schoolchum who, from last reports, was teaching music in a little college in South Carolina. I decided that we would pay him a visit. It was a long ride and, as usual, we had not a cent in our pockets. I was sure, however, that we could count on having a good lunch with my old friend.

It was a good twenty years since I had last seen this good old chum. He had left school ahead of us in order to study music in Germany. He became a concert pianist, travelled all over Europe, and then returned to America to accept an insignificant post in this little Southern town. I had had a few cards from him—and then silence. As I mused I began to wonder if he could have forgotten who I was. Twenty years is a long time.

Every day, on our way home from school, I would stop at his home to listen to him play. He played all the compositions I was later to hear in concert halls, and he played them (to my youthful mind) as well as the maestros. He had the size and the reach to command attention. On his forehead was a budding growth which, when he grew inspired, looked almost like a short horn. He towered over me by a good foot. He looked like a foreigner and he spoke like a European of the upper class who had learned English with his mother tongue. Add to this that he usually wore striped trousers and a soft black coat. It was in the German class that we struck up a friendship. He had taken German, which he knew perfectly, in order to have that much less to study. The teacher, a delightful, flirtatious young woman with a keen sense of humour, was really taken by him. She pretended, however, to be annoyed with him. Every now and then she gave him a sly dig. One day, incensed by the perfect translation he had just delivered aloud, and without preparation, she asked him why he hadn't chosen to learn some other language. Hadn't he any desire to learn something new? And so on. Putting on a malicious smile, he replied that he had better things to do with his time.

'Oh, you have, have you? Like what, may I ask?'

'I have my music.'

'So! You're a musician? A pianist—or perhaps a composer?'

'Both,' he said.

'And what have you composed thus far?'

'Sonatas, concertos, symphonies and operas . . . plus a few quartets.'

The class burst into an uproar.

'You're even more of a genius than I thought you were,' said she, after the hubbub had died down.

Before the lesson was over he handed me a note which he had hastily scribbled and folded up. I had no more than read it when I was ordered up front. I handed it to her face open. She read the message, blushed crimson, and threw it into the waste basket. All it said was: '*Sie ist wie eine Blume.*'

I thought of other things in connection with this 'genius'.

How he despised everything American, for example, how he detested our literature, how he mimicked the professors, how he loathed any form of exercise. But above all, I remembered the freedom he enjoyed in his own home and the respect shown him by his parents and brothers. There wasn't another chap like him in the whole school. How delighted I was when I got my first letter from him, dated Heidelberg. He was thoroughly at home, he wrote, even more of a German than the Germans. Why was I staying in America? Why didn't I join him and become a good German poet?

I was just thinking how odd it would be if he should say—'I don't remember you'—when I realized that we had entered the town. It took less than no time to learn that my old friend had left the day before to tour the East. What luck! We were famished, it being long after noon. In desperation I held on to the Dean, a brittle, querulous old lady, trying to impress upon her the fact that we had made a tremendous detour, on our way to Mexico—our car having broken down some miles away—expressly for the purpose of greeting my dear boyhood friend of long ago. By dint of holding on, chewing her ear off, I managed to get across to her (telepathically) that we were in need of refreshment. With bad grace she eventually ordered up tea and scones for us.

We walked to the edge of the town, to stretch our legs. Here we caught a lift homeward in a battered Ford. The driver, a veteran and somewhat cracked, also a bit spifflicated—in the South everyone drinks like a fish—said he would be passing through Asheville. He didn't seem to know very definitely where he was going, except northward. The conversation which we carried on during the long ride back to Asheville was absolutely crazy. The poor devil had not only been banged up in the war, had not only lost his wife to his best friend, but had been in several bad accidents since. To make it worse, he was a dunce and a bigot, one of those ornery cusses who become even more ornery when they happen to be Southerners. We flitted from subject to subject like grasshoppers, nothing apparently being of interest to him except his own woes and miseries. As we neared Asheville he became more cantankerous than ever. He made it plain that he thoroughly and heartily disliked everything about us, including our manner of speech. When he finally deposited us on the sidewalk in Asheville he was fuming.

We stuck out our hands to thank him for the lift and, without wasting words, said—'Goodbye!'

'*Goodbye?*' he cried. 'Aren't you going to pay me?'

Pay? I was dumbfounded. Whoever heard of paying for a ride?

'You didn't expect to ride for nothing, did you?' he shouted 'What about the gas and oil I bought?' He leaned out of the car belligerently.

387

I had to do some tall explaining and fast. He looked at us incredulously, then shook his head and mumbled: 'I though as much when I set eyes on you.' As an afterthought: 'I've a good mind to run you in.' Then something I would never had expected happened: he burst into tears. I leaned forward to say a comforting word, my heart completely melted. 'Go way from me!' he yelled. 'Go way!' We left him sitting huddled up over the steering wheel, his head in his arms, weeping to break his heart.

'What in Christ's name do you make of that?' I said, somewhat shaken.

'You were lucky he didn't pull a knife on you,' said Mona. The experience confirmed the conviction she had always held about Southerners—that they were absolutely unpredictable. It was time we thought of returning home, she thought.

The next day, as I sat at the machine with a vacant stare, I began to wonder how longer we could carry on in sunny Carolina. Several weeks had passed since we last paid a cent towards our room. What we owed the good Mr Rawlins for meals I didn't dare think.

The following day, however, to our utter astonishment we received a telegram from Kronski informing us that he and his wife were on their way, would see us that very evening. A windfall!

Sure enough, just a little before dinner time they blew in.

> Come all ye out of the wilderness
> And glory be, the
> Father, Son and Holy Ghost
> Through all eternity.

Almost the first thing we asked, disgraceful as it sounds, was whether they had any money to spare.

'Is that all that's eating yez?' Kronski was fairly beaming. 'That's easy. How much would you like? Would fifty do?'

We hugged one another for joy. '*Money*,' he said—'why didn't you wire me?' And in the next breath—'Do you really like it here? Kinda scares me, to tell you the truth. This ain't no country for niggers—nor for Jews. Makes me creepy. . . .'

Over the meal he wanted to know what I had written, whether I had sold anything, and so on. He had suspected, so he said, that things weren't going well with us. 'That's why we hopped down sort of sudden like. I've got thirty-six hours to spend with you.' He said this with a smile which meant—you won't have to put up with me a minute longer.

Mona was all for going back with them, but for some perverse reason I insisted that we stick it out a little longer. We argued about this rather heatedly but got nowhere.

'The hell with that question,' said Kronski. 'Now that we're here, what can you show us before we leave?'

Promptly I replied: 'Lake Junaleska.' I didn't know why I said it, it just popped out of my mouth. But then suddenly I did know. It was because I wanted to see Waynesville again.

'Every time I get near this place—Waynesville—I feel as though I would like to settle down. I don't know what it is about the place, but it gets me.'

'You'll never settle down in the South,' said Kronski. 'You're a born New Yorker. Listen, why don't you stop roaming through the hinterland and go abroad? The place for you is France, don't you know that?'

Mona agreed most enthusiastically.

'You're the only one who talks sense to him,' said she.

'If it were me,' said Kronski, 'I'd pick Russia. But I don't have the wanderlust. I don't find New York so bad, would you believe that?' Then, in characteristic fashion, he added: 'Once I set up practice I'll stake you two to a trip to Europe. I'm serious about it. I've had the thought many a time. You're getting stale here. You don't belong in this country, neither of you. It's too small, too petty . . . it's too god-damned prosaic, that's what. As for you, *Mister* Miller, quit writing those damned things for the magazines, do you hear me? You're not meant to write that stuff. You're cut out to write books. *Write a book*, why don't you? You can do it. . . .'

The next day we went to Waynesville and to Lake Junaleska. Neither place made the least impression on any of them.

'Funny,' said I, as we were riding back, 'you can't picture a guy like me spending the rest of his days in a spot like that—like Waynesville, I mean. Why? Why does it seem so fantastic?'

'You don't belong, that's all.'

'I don't, eh?' Where *do* I belong, asked myself. France? Maybe. Maybe not. Forty million Frenchmen was a lot to swallow in one dose. If anything, I preferred Spain. I took instinctively to Spaniards, as I did to Russians.

Somehow the conversation had got me to pondering the economic question again. That was always a nightmare. In a weak moment I found myself wondering if we hadn't better return to New York after all.

The next day, however, I was of a different mind. We accompanied Kronski and his wife to the edge of the town where they quickly got a lift. We stood there a moment waving good-bye, then I turned to Mona and mumbled thickly: 'He's a good egg, that Kronski.'

'The best friend you've got,' said she quick as a flash.

With the fifty from Kronski we paid something on our debts, and, trusting that Kronski would send us a little more when he got back to New York, we made another stab at it. By sheer force of will I succeeded in finishing another story. I tried to begin another, but it was hopeless: I hadn't an idea in my bean. So instead I wrote letters to all and sundry, including that kind editor who had once offered to give me a job as his assistant. I also looked up O'Mara, but found him in such a despondent mood that I didn't have the heart to mention money.

There was no doubt about it, the South was getting us down. The landlord and his wife did everything to make us comforable; Mr Rawlins, too, did his best to encourage us. Never a word from any of them about the money we still owed them. As for Matthews, his trips to West Virginia were becoming more frequent and more protracted. Besides, we simply couldn't bring ourselves to borrow from him.

The heat, as I have already said, had a great deal to do with our lowered morale. There is a heat which warms and vitalizes, and there's another kind which enervates one, saps one's strength, one's courage, even one's desire to live. Our blood was too thick, I suppose. The general apathy of the natives only added to our own apathy. It was like somnolescing in a vacuum. Never did one hear the word art: it was absent from the vocabulary of these people. I had the feeling that the Cherokees had produced more art than these poor devils ever would. One missed the presence of the Indian whose land, after all, it was. One felt the overpowering presence of the Negro. A heavy, disturbing presence. The 'tar heel', as the native is called, is certainly no nigger lover. He's not much of anything, in fact. As I say, it was a vacuum, a hot, smouldering vacuum, if one can imagine such a thing.

It made me itchy at times to walk up and down the desolate streets. Walking the road was no fun either. On every side a gorgeous setting presented itself to the eye, yet inwardly one felt nothing but despair and desolation. The beauty of the surroundings only served to ravage one. God had certainly meant for man to lead a different life here. The Indian had been much closer to God. As for the Negro, he would have thrived here had the white man given him a chance. I used to wonder, and I wonder still, whether eventually the Indian and the Negro will not get together, drive the white man out, and re-establish Paradise in this land of milk and honey. Ah well——

> The very next blessing that Mary had
> Hit was the blessing of two
> To think her little Jesus
> Could read the Bible through
> Read the Bible through.

A few contributions dribbled in—pin money, no more! as a result of the letters I had sent out 'to all and sundry'. Not a word from Kronski, though.

We held out a few more weeks, then totally discouraged, we decided one night to get up at the crack of dawn and sneak away. We had only two little grips to lug. After a sleepless night we rose with the first streak of light and, carrying our shoes in one hand and a grip in the other, we eased out as noiseless as mice. We walked several miles before a car came along. It was noon by the time we reached Winston-Salem, where I decided to send my father a collect message asking for a few dollars. I suggested he wire the money to Durham, where we planned to spend the night.

Towards evening we entered Durham. A telegram was waiting for me, sure enough. It read: 'Sorry son but I haven't a cent in the bank.' I felt like weeping, not over our own plight but because of the humiliation it must have caused the old man to send a message like that.

Thanks to a stranger, we had had a sandwich and coffee around noon. We were now famished, more famished than ordinarily, of course, because of the impossible distance still to go on an empty stomach. There was nothing to do but to take to the road again, which we did—like automatons.

As we were standing on the highway, too tired and defeated to trudge another step, as we stood there blankly watching the sun go down like a burst tomato, all of a sudden a rather snazzy car pulled up and a cheery voice called out—'Want a lift?' It was a couple headed for some little town about two hours distant. The man was from Alabama, and spoke with the accent of a man of the deep South, the woman was from Arkansas. There were cheerful, lively individuals who seemed not to have a care in the world.

On the way we had car trouble, one little thing after another. Instead of making it in two hours it took almost five. By the time we reached our destination, thanks to the delays, we had become firm friends. We had told them the truth about ourselves, the whole truth and nothing but the truth, and it had gone straight to their hearts. I shall never, never forget the way that good woman, immediately we entered the house, rushed to the bath-room, filled the tub with hot water, had out the soap and towels, and begged us to relax while she scared up a meal. When we reappeared, clothed in their bathrobes, the table was set; we sat down at once to an excellent meal of hash and fried eggs with hot muffins, coffee, preserves, fruit and pie. It was about three in the morning when we turned in. At their request we slept in their bed, never realizing until we awoke that our kind hosts had improvised a bed for themselves by removing the seats from the car.

When we got up, around noon, we had a hearty breakfast, after which the man showed me around his huge backyard where the remains of cars were strewn about. Wrecks were his livelihood. He was certainly a happy-go-lucky sort of fellow, and his wife even more so. Our unexpected visit seemed to make them slaphappy. Why we didn't stay with them a few days, as they begged us to to, I don't know.

As we made ready to leave, the woman took Mona to one side and furtively pressed a few bills in her hand, while the husband shoved a carton of cigarettes under my arm. They insisted on driving us out of town a little distance so that we might get a lift more easily. When we finally parted they had tears in their eyes.

It was getting on and we were bent on making Washington that day. We would have made it too, were it not for the fact that we got nothing but short hauls. By the time we sailed into Richmond it was nightfall. And again we were broke. The few dollars the woman had given us had disappeared—the purse with it. Had someone robbed us of those miserable few dollars? If so, it was a grim joke. However, we felt too good, too near our goal, to be depressed over the loss of our little fortune.

Time to eat again. . . .

With a calculating eye we scanned the various restaurants and finally decided on a Greek one. We would eat first, then explain our predicament. We put away a good meal, with extra helpings of dessert, and then gently broke the news to the proprietor. Our story made no impression on him whatever, or rather, it made the wrong impression. All he could think of—hardly a solution! —was to call the police. In a few minutes a motorcycle cop appeared. After the usual grilling he asked us point blank what we intended to do about the situation. I said that if he would pay for the wire we would send a message to New York, that undoubtedly the money would be forthcoming in the morning. He thought this a reasonable idea and volunteered to put us up in a hotel nearby. He then turned to the Greek and informed him that he would be responsible for us. All of which struck me as damned decent.

I dispatched a message to Ulric, not without misgivings. The cop escorted us to our room and said he would be round to see us early the next morning. Despite that fact that we were from New York, he showed us uncommon consideration. A New York cop, I couldn't help but reflect, was a horse of another colour.

During the night I got up to make sure the proprietor hadn't locked us in. I found it impossible to close my eyes. As the night wore on I felt more and more certain that there would be no answer to our telegram.

To slip out without the night clerk spying us was impossible. I got up, went to the window, and looked out. It was a drop of about six feet to the ground. That settled it: we'd leave by the window at dawn.

As the sun came up we were again standing on the highway a mile or two outside the town. We still had our two little grips.

Instead of making a bee-line for Washington we headed for Tappahannock—just in case the cop might be on our trail. As luck would have it we got a lift in jig time. No breakfast, of course, and no lunch. En route we ate a few green apples, which gave us the colic.

A little distance out of Tappahannock a lawyer en route to Washington picked us up. A charming fellow, well read, easy to talk to. We gave him an earful in the time allotted us. It must have taken effect as we were saying good-bye to him in Washington, he insisted on lending us twenty dollars. He said he was 'lending' it, but what he meant very plainly was that we were to spend it and forget about it. As he toyed with the brake he mumbled over his shoulder:

'I once tried to be a writer myself.'

We were so elated we couldn't get home fast enough. Around midnight we landed in the big city. The first thing we did was to phone Kronski. Could he put us up for the night? Certainly. We drove into the subway and made for the Bronx where he was again living.

The subway was a doleful sight to our eyes. We had forgotten how pale and worn the people looked, we had forgotten what a stench the city gave off. The treadmill. Trapped again.

Well, at least we were on familiar ground. Maybe someone would be glad to see us after the lapse of a few months. Maybe I'd look for a job in real earnest.

The sixth joy goes like this—how appropriate!

> The very next joy Mary had
> It was the joy of six
> To see her little Jesus
> On the crucifix.

And here is Dr Kronski. . . .

'Well well! Back again! I told you so. But don't think you can camp out on us. No sir! You can stay the night, but that's all. Have you eaten? I've got to get up early. There are no clean towels, don't ask for any. You'll have to sleep in the raw. And don't expect your breakfast served in bed. Goodnight!' All in one breath.

We cleared the cots of medical books and scraps of food, pulled back the grey sheets, noticed the blood stains but said nothing, and crawled in.

O COME ALL YE OUT OF THE WILDERNESS AND GLORY BE!

15

In a buddhist magazine not long ago I read something like this: 'If we could only get what we want when we think we need it life would present no problem, no mystery, and no meaning.' I was a trifle indisposed the morning I read this. I had decided to spend the day in bed. Reading these words, however, I began to howl with laughter. In less than no time I was up and out of bed, chirping away as merrily as usual.

If I had come across this piece of wisdom in the period I am writing of I doubt if it would have had any effect upon me. It was just impossible for me to take a detached view of things. The day was full of problems, full of complications. There was mystery in everything, irritating mystery. The mystery surrounding the universe—that was sheer intellectual luxury. The whole meaning of life was wrapped up in the solution of how to keep afloat. It sounds simple, but we knew how to complicate even such a simple problem.

Disgusted with our haphazard way of life, I made up my mind to take a job. No more gold-digging. No more chasing rainbows. I was determined to earn sufficient for the daily necessities, come what may. I knew it would be a blow to Mona. The very thought of taking a job was anathema to her. Worse than that, it was sheer black treachery.

Her response; when I broached my resolution, was characteristic. 'You're undermining everything I've done!'

'I don't care,' I answered, 'I've got to do it.'

'Then I'll take a job too,' said she. And that very day she hired herself out as a waitress at The Iron Cauldron.

'You're going to regret this,' she informed me. By this she meant that it was fatal ever to leave one another's side.

I had to promise her that while looking for work I would have my meals at The Iron Cauldron twice a day. I went once, for lunch, but the sight of her waiting on tables discouraged me so that I couldn't go back again.

394

To get regular employment in an office was out of the question. In the first place there was nothing I could do really well, and in the second place I knew I would never be able to stand the routine. I had to find something which would give me the semblance of freedom and independence. There was only one job I could think of which filled the bill—and that was the book racket. Though it wouldn't offer me a regular salary my time would be my own, and that meant a great deal to me. To get up every morning on the dot and punch a clock was out of the question.

I couldn't go back to work for the Encyclopaedia Britannica again—my record was too shady. I'd have to find another encyclopaedia to handle. It didn't take long to discover the loose leaf encyclopaedia. The sales manager, to whom I had applied for a job, didn't have much difficulty convincing me that it was the best encyclopaedia on the market. He seemed to think I had excellent possibilities. As a favour he gave me some of his own personal leads to start with. They were 'pushovers', he assured me. I left the office with a brief case filled with specimen pages, various types of binding, and the usual paraphernalia which the book salesman always carries about with him. I was to go home and study all this crap and then start out. I was never to take 'No' for an answer. *Soit.*

I made two sales the first day, netting me quite a handsome commission since I had managed to sell my customers the most expensively bound sets. One of my victims was a Jewish physician, a charming, considerate individual who not only insisted on my staying to dinner with the family but who gave me the names of several good friends of his whom he was certain I could sell. The next day I sold three sets, thanks to this kind Jew. The sales manager was secretly elated but pretended that I had the usual beginner's luck. He warned me not to let this quick success go to my head.

'Don't be satisfied because you sell two or three a day. Try to sell five or six. We have men who sell as many as twelve sets a day.'

'You're full of shit,' I thought to myself. 'A man who can sell twelve sets of encyclopaedias a day wouldn't be selling encyclopaedias, he'd be selling the Brooklyn Bridge.'

Nevertheless I went about my work conscientiously. I followed up every lead religiously, even though it meant journeying to such outlandish towns as Passaic, Hoboken, Carnarsie and Maspeth. I had sold three of those 'personal' leads the sales manager had given me. He thought I should have sold the entire seven, the idiot. Each time we met he became more friendly, more conciliatory. The publishers were going to have a big show at the Garden soon, he informed me one day. If I kept on my toes he might arrange to have me work with him in the booth which the firm was renting. He implied that there, at the Garden, the sales fell into your lap like ripe plums. It would be a clean-up. He added that he had been studying me; he liked the way I spoke. 'Stick with me,' he added, 'and we may give you a big piece of territory to handle—out West, perhaps. You'll have a car and a crew of men under you. How does that appeal to you?'

'Marvellous!' I said, though the mere thought of it terrified me. I didn't want to be that successful. I was quite content to sell one a day—*if I could.*

Anyone who tries to sell books soon learns that there is one type of individual who takes the wind out of your sails. This is the fellow who seems so pliant and yielding that you almost feel sorry for him when first you sink your hooks into him. You feel certain that he'll not only buy a set for himself but that he'll bring you signed orders from his friends in a day or two. He agrees with everything you say, and goes you one better. He marvels that every intelligent person in the land is not already in possession of the books. He has innumerable questions to ask, and the answers always incite him to greater enthusiasm. When it comes to the last touch—the bindings—he fingers them lovingly, dwelling with exasperating elaboration on the relative advantages of each. He even shows you the niche in the wall where he believes the set will show up to best advantage. A dozen times you make ready to hand him the pen in order to sign on the dotted line. Sometimes you rouse these birds to such a pitch that nothing will do but call up a neighbour and have him look at the books too. If the friend comes, as he usually does, you rehearse the programme all over again. The day wears on and you find yourself still talking, still expounding, still marvelling over the wonders contained in this beautiful and practicable set of books. Finally you make a desperate effort to pull in the line. And then you get something like this: 'Oh, but I can't buy the books *now*—I'm out of work at the moment. I sure would love to own a set, though. . . .' Even at this point you feel so certain the guy is sincere that you offer to stake him to the first instalment. 'You can pay me later, when you get a job. Just sign here!' But even here the type I speak of will manage to squirm out. Any bare-faced excuse serves him. Only at this point do you realize that he never had the least intention of buying the books, it was just a way of passing the time. He may even tell you blandly, as you take leave, that he never enjoyed anything so much as hearing the way you talked. . . .

The French have an expression which sums it up neatly: '*il n'est pas serieux.*'

It's a great business, the book racket. You learn something about human nature if nothing else. It's almost worth the time wasted, the sore feet, the heartaches. One of the striking features about the game, though, is this—once you're in it you can think of nothing else. You talk encyclopaedias—if that happens to be the line—from morn to midnight; you talk it every chance you get, and when there is no one else to talk to you talk to yourself. Many's the time I sold myself a set in an off moment. It sounds preposterous, if you're not in the grind, but actually you get to believe that everyone on God's earth must possess the precious book you have been given to dispense. Everyone, you tell yourself, has need of more knowledge. You look at people with just one thought in your mind—is he a prospect or not? You don't give a damn whether the person will ever make use of the damned set: you think only of how you can convince him that what you have to offer is a *sine qua non*. As for other commodities—shoes, socks, shirts, etc.—what fun would there be in selling a man something he has to have? No sir, you want your victim to have a sporting chance. You'd almost prefer him to turn his back on you—then you could really put on your song and dance with gusto. A good salesman doesn't enjoy taking money from a 'push-over'. He wants to *earn* his money. He wants to delude himself that, if he were really put to it, he could sell books to an illiterate —or to a blind man!

It's a game, moreover, which throws interesting characters across your path, some of them having tastes similar to your own, some being more alien than the heathen Chinese, some admitting that they had never owned a book, and so on. Sometimes I came home so elated, so hilarious, that I couldn't sleep a wink. Often we lay awake the whole night talking about these truly 'droll' characters whom I had encountered.

The ordinary salesman, I observed, had sense enough to clear out quick when he saw that there was little prospect of making a sale. Not me. I had a hundred different reasons for clinging to any man. Any crackpot could hold me till the wee hours of the morning, recounting the history of his life, spinning out his crazy dreams, explaining his mad projects and inventions. Many of these witless ones reminded me strongly of my cosmococcic messenger boys; some, I discovered, had actually been in the service. We understood one another perfectly. Often, in parting from them, they would make me little gifts, absurd trifles which I usually threw away before reaching home.

Naturally I was bringing in less and less orders. The sales manager was at a loss to understand; according to him, I had all the requisites for making an A-1 salesman. He even offered to take a day off and make the rounds with me, to prove how simple it was to get orders. But I always managed to dodge the issue. Occasionally I hooked a professor, a priest or a prominent lawyer. These strikes tickled him pink. 'That's the sort of clientele we're after,' he would say. 'Get more like them!'

I complained that he rarely gave me a decent lead. Most of the time he was handing me children or imbeciles to call on. He pretended it didn't matter much what the intelligence or station in life of the prospect might be—the important thing, the *only* thing, was to get inside the house *and stick*. If it was a child who had fallen for the ad, then I was to talk to the parents, convince them that it was for the child's good. If it was a nit-wit who had written in for information, so much the better—a moron had no resistance. And so on. He had an answer for everything, that guy. His idea of a good salesman was one who could sell books to inanimate objects. I began to loathe him with all my heart.

Anyway, the whole damned business was nothing more than an excuse to keep active, a means of bolstering the pretence that I was struggling to make a living. Why I bothered to pretend I don't know, unless it was guilt which prompted me. Mona was earning more than enough to keep the two of us. In addition she was constantly bringing home gifts, either of money or of objects which could be converted into cash. The same old game. People couldn't resist thrusting things on her. They were all 'admirers', of course. She preferred to call them 'admirers' rather than 'lovers'. I wondered very often what it was they admired in her, particularly since she handed out nothing but rebuffs. To listen to her carry on about these 'dopes' and 'saps' you would think that she never even smiled at them.

Often she kept me awake nights telling me about this new swarm of hangers-on. An odd lot, I must say. Always a millionaire or two among them, always a pugilist or wrestler, always a nut, usually of dubious sex. What these queer ones saw in her, or hoped to get out of her, I could never fathom. There were to be plenty of them, as time went on. Right now it was Claude. (Although, to be truthful, she never referred to Claude as an admirer.) Anyway, Claude. Claude what? Just *Claude*. When I inquired what this Claude did for a living she became almost hysterical. He was only a boy! Not a day over sixteen. Of course he *looked* much older. I must meet him some day. She was certain I would adore him.

I tried to register indifference, but she paid no heed. Claude was unique, she insisted. He had roamed all over the world— *on nothing*. 'You should hear him talk,' she babbled on. 'You'll open your eyes. He's wiser than most men of forty. He's almost a Christ. . . .'

I couldn't help it, I burst out laughing. I had to laugh in her face.

'All right, laugh! But wait till you meet him, you'll sing a different tune.'

It was from Claude, I learned, that she had received the beautiful Navajo rings, bracelets and other adornments. Claude had spent a whole summer with Navajos. He had even learned to talk their language. Had he wished it, she said, he could have lived the rest of his life with the Navajos.

I wanted to know where he came from originally, this Claude. She didn't know for sure herself. From the Bronx, she thought. (Which only made him all the more unique.)

'Then he's Jewish?' I said.

Again she wasn't sure. One couldn't tell a thing about him from his looks. He didn't look anything. (A strange way to put it, I thought.) He might pass for an Indian—or for a pure Aryan. He was like the chameleon—depended when and where you met him, the mood he was in, the people surrounding him, and so on.

'He was probably born in Russia,' I said, taking a wide swing.

To my surprise she said: 'He speaks Russian fluently, if that means anything. But then he speaks other languages too—Arabic, Turkish, Armenian, German, Portuguese, Hungarian. . . .'

'Not Hungarian!' I cried. 'Russian, O.K. Armenian, O.K. Turkish ditto, though that's a bit hard to swallow. But when you say Hungarian, I balk. No, by crikey, I'll have to hear him talk Hungarian before I believe that one.'

'All right,' she said, 'come down some night and see for yourself. Anyhow, how could you tell—you don't know Hungarian.'

'Righto! But I know this much—anyone who can talk Hungarian is a wizard. It's the toughest language in the world—except for the Hungarians, of course. Your Claude may be a bright boy, but don't tell me he speaks Hungarian! No, you don't ram that one down my throat.'

My words hadn't made a dent in her, obviously because the next thing out of her mouth was—'I forgot to tell you that he also knows Sanskrit, Hebrew, and. . . .'

'Listen,' I exclaimed, 'he's not *almost* a Christ, he *is* the Christ. Nobody but Christ Almighty could master all those tongues at his age. It's a wonder to me he hasn't invented the universal tongue. I'll be down there mighty soon, don't fret. I want to see this phenomenon with my own eyes. I want him to talk six languages *at once*. Nothing less will impress me.'

She looked at me as if to say—'You poor doubting Thomas!'

The steadiness of her smile finally nettled me. I said: 'Why do you smile like that?'

She hesitated a full minute. 'Because, Val . . . because I was wondering what you'd say if I were to tell you that he also had the power to heal.'

For some queer reason this sounded more plausible and consonant with his character than anything she had told me about him. But I had to maintain my attitude of doubt and mockery.

'How do you know this?' I said. 'Have you seen him heal anyone?'

She refused to answer the question squarely. She insisted, however, that she could vouch for the truth of her statement.

To taunt her I said: 'What did he cure—a sick headache?'

Again she took her time in responding. Then, rather solemnly, almost too solemnly, she replied: 'He's cured cancer, if that means anything.'

This made me furious. 'For Christ's sake,' I yelled, 'don't stand there and tell me a thing like that! Are you a gullible idiot? You might just as well tell me he's raised the dead.'

The flicker of a smile passed over her countenance. In a voice no longer solemn, but grave, she said: 'Well, Val, believe it or not, he's done that too. Among the Navajos. That's why they love him so. . . .'

'O.K. girlie, that's enough for tonight. Let's change the subject. If you tell me any more I'll think you've got a screw loose.'

Her next words took me completely by surprise. I nearly jumped out of my skin.

'Claude says he has a rendezvous with you. He knows all about you . . . knows you inside out, in fact. And don't go thinking *I* told him, because I didn't! Do you want to hear more?' She went right on. 'You have a tremendous career ahead of you: you'll be a world figure one day. According to Claude, you're playing blind man's bluff now. You're *spiritually* blind, as well as dumb and deaf. . . .'

'Claude said that?' I was thoroughly sober now. 'All right, tell him I'll keep the rendezvous. Tomorrow night, how's that? But not at that damned joint of yours!'

She was overjoyed by my complete surrender. 'Leave it to me,' she said, 'I'll choose a quiet spot where the two of you can be alone.'

Of course I couldn't resist inquiring how much he had told her about me. 'You'll learn all that tomorrow,' she kept repeating 'I wouldn't want to spoil it for you.'

I fell asleep with difficulty. Claude kept reappearing, like a vision, each time in a different aspect. Though he always had the figure of a boy, his voice sounded like the voice of the ancient one. No matter what language he spoke I was able to follow him. I wasn't the least amazed, curiously enough, to hear myself talk Hungarian. Nor was I amazed to find myself riding a horse, riding bareback with bare feet. Often we carried on our discussions in foreign lands, in remote places such as Judea, the Nubian desert, Turkestan, Sumatra, Patagonia. We made use of no vehicles; we were always there where our thoughts roamed, without effort, without the use of the will. Aside from certain sexual dreams I don't believe I had ever had such a pleasant dream. It was more than pleasant—it was instructive in the highest sense. This Claude was more like an *alter ego*, even though at times he did strikingly resemble the Christ. He brought me great peace. He gave me direction. More than that— he gave me reason for being. I was at last something in my own right and no need to prove it to anyone. I was securely in the world yet not a victim. I was participating in a wholly new way, as only a man can who is free from conflict. Strangely, the world had grown much smaller than I thought it to be. More intimate, more understandable. It was no longer something against which I was pitted; it was like a ripe fruit which I was inside of, which nourished me, and which was inexhaustible. I was one with it, one with everything—that's the only way I can put it.

As luck would have it, I failed to meet Claude the next night. It so happened that I was in Newark or some such place when evening came on, talking to a prospect whom I found fascinating. He was a black man who was working his way through law school as a stevedore. He had been out of work for several weeks and was in a receptive mood to listen to me expound the advantages of the loose-leaf encyclopaedia. Just as he was on the verge of signing his demiquivers for a set his aged mother poked her head through the doorway and begged me to stay for dinner. She apologized for intruding on us, explaining that they were going to a meeting after dinner and that she had to remind her son to change his clothes. The latter dropped the pen which he had been holding and escaped to the bathroom.

Waiting for him to reappear my eye fell upon an announcement. It was to the effect that the great Negro leader, W. E. Burghardt Dubois, was to speak in the town-hall that very evening. I could hardly wait for the lad to return. I paced up and down the room in a fever. Well I knew this Dubois. Years ago, when I was keen about attending lectures, I had heard Dubois speak on the great heritage of the black race. It was in some little hall on the lower East Side; the audience, oddly enough, was mostly Jewish. I had never forgotten the man. He was handsome, thoroughly Aryan in features, and of an imposing figure; he wore a goatee then, if I remember rightly. I learned later that he had been born in New England; his ancestors were of mixed blood, French, Dutch and other strains. What I remembered best about him was his impeccable diction and his vast erudition. He had a challenging, straightforward way of speaking which won me over to him immediately. He struck me at once as a superior being. And was it not he, I thought to myself, who had accepted and published the first article of mine ever to appear in print?

At the dinner table I met the other members of the family. The sister, a young woman of about twenty-five, was strikingly beautiful. She had decided to go to the lecture too. That settled it for me—Claude could wait. When I made known to them that I had heard Dubois before and that I had an unbounded admiration for him, they insisted that I come along as their guest. The young man now suddenly recalled that he had not signed his name on the dotted line; he begged me to let him do so before he forgot a second time. I felt embarrassed, as though I had tricked him.

'Think it over first,' I said. 'If you really want the books you can mail me the slip later.'

'No, no!' cried his mother and sister at once. 'He'll sign up right now, 'cause if he don't he never will. You know how we folks are.'

Now the sister was becoming interested in the subject. I had to explain the whole business to her hurriedly.

'Sounds wonderful,' she said. 'Leave me some blanks, I think I can get you a few orders.'

We hurried through the meal, then piled into their car. A goodlooking car, it seemed to me. On the way to the hall they told me of Dubois' activities since I had last heard of him. He had assumed an educational post in the South, a world not too congenial for one of his temperament and upbringing. He had grown somewhat bitter, they thought, and more caustic in his speech. Impulsively I told them that he reminded me, in some strange, undefinable way, of Rabindranath Tagore whom I also had heard years ago. What I was thinking of probably was that neither of these men minced words when it came to telling the truth.

By the time we reached the hall I was in the midst of a long drawn-out rhapsody about another Negro, my quondam idol, Hubert Harrison. I was telling them of all I had learned standing at the foot of his soap-box in Madison Square in the days when one could discuss anything freely and publicly. There was no one in those days, I told them candidly, who could hold a candle to Hubert Harrison. With a few well-directed words he had the ability to demolish any opponent. He did it neatly and smoothly too, 'with kid gloves', so to speak. I described the wonderful way he smiled, his easy assurance, the great sculptured head which he carried on his shoulders like a lion. I wondered aloud if he had not come of royal blood, if he had not been the descendant of some great African monarch. Yes, he was a man who electrified one by his mere presence. Beside him the other speakers, the white ones, looked like pygmies, not only physically but culturally, spiritually. Some of them, the ones who were paid to foment trouble, carried on like epileptics, always wrapped in the stars and stripes, to be sure. Hubert Harrison, on the other hand, no matter what the provocation, always retained his self-possession, his dignity. He had a way of placing the back of his hand on his hip, his trunk tilted forward, his ears cocked to catch every last word the questioner, or the heckler put to him. Well he knew how to bide his time! When the tumult had subsided there would come that broad smile of his, a broad, good-natured grin, and he would answer his man—always to the point, always fair and square, always full on, like a broadside. Soon everyone would be laughing, everyone but the poor imbecile who had dared to put the question. . . .

I was rattling on in this vein as we entered the hall. The place was crowded; this time the audience was mainly Negro. As every white man who's not prejudiced can testify, it's a privilege to be with a crowd of Negroes. The atmosphere is always super-charged. At intervals there are hearty guffaws, weird ejacula-tions, genuine peals of laughter such as you never hear from the throats of white people. White people lack spontaneity. When they laugh it seldom comes from the guts. Usually it's a mocking sort of laughter. The black man's laugh comes to him as easily as breathing.

It was quite a time before Dubois appeared on the platform. When he did it was with the air of a sovereign mounting his throne. The very majesty of the man silenced any would-be demonstration. There was nothing of the rabble-rouser in this leonine figure—such tactics were beneath him. His words, how-ever, were like cold dynamite. Had he wanted to, he could have set off an explosion that would rock the world. But it was obvious that he had no intention of rocking the world—not yet, at any rate. As I listened to his speech I pictured him addressing a body of scientists in much the same way. I could imagine him unleash-ing the most devastating truths, but in such a manner that one would be left stunned rather than moved to action.

What a pity, I thought, that a man of his ability, his powers, should be obliged to narrow his range. Because of his blood he was doomed to segregate himself to restrict his horizon, his activities. He could have remained in Europe, where he was freely accepted and honoured; he could have made a bigger place for himself there. But he had elected to remain with his own kinsmen, to raise them up, and, if possible, to make a better world for them to live in. He must have known from the begin-ning that it was a hopeless task, that nothing of any importance could be accomplished for his brethren in the space of one short lifetime. He was too intelligent a man to have any illusions on the subject. I didn't know whether to admire or deplore his vain, courageous, stubborn persistence. Involuntarily I was making comparisons in my mind between him and John Brown. One had intelligence, the other blind faith. John Brown, in his passionate hatred of injustice and intolerance, had not hesitated to set himself up against the holy government of these United States. Had there been just a few hundred souls like himself in this big broad land, I doubt not but that he would have over-thrown the existent government of these United States. When John Brown was executed a commotion pervaded this country which has never truly subsided. It is possible that John Brown may have set back the cause of the Negro in America. The fiasco at Harper's Ferry may have made it forever impossible for the Negro to obtain his just rights by direct action. The amazing deeds of the great Liberator may have made any form of insurrection unthinkable—in the minds of later generations. (Just as the memory of the French Revolution makes a Frenchman quake). Since John Brown's day it seems to be silently agreed that the only way to permit a Negro to take his place in our world is through a long and dolorous education. That this is only a pretext for delaying the true event no one wishes to face. Imagine Jesus the Christ advocating such a policy!

The blessing of freedom! Are we to wait forever until we are fit for it before we receive it? Or is freedom something to be wrested from those who tyrannically withhold it? Is there any-one great enough, wise enough, to say how long a man should remain a slave?

Dubois was no rabble-rouser. No, but to a man like myself it was all too obvious that what his words implied were—'Assume the spirit of liberty and you will be free!' *Education?* As I saw and felt it, he was saying almost bluntly: 'I am telling you that it is your own fear and ignorance which keep you in slavery. There is only one kind of education, that which leads you to assert and maintain your own freedom.' What other purpose could he have had, in citing all the marvellous examples of African culture, *before the white man's intrusion,* than to indicate the Negroes' own self-sufficiency? What need had the Negro of the white man? None. What difference was there between the two races, what real, fundamental, vital difference? None. The paramount fact, the only fact worth consideration, was that the white man, despite all his grand words, all his tortuous principles was still holding the Negro in subjection. . . . I am not quoting his words. I am recording my reactions, my interpretation of his speech. 'First get off our backs!' that's what I could hear him screaming—though he scarcely raised his voice, though he made no dramatic gestures, though he never said anything of the kind. 'I'm telling you tonight about the glories of the past, of *your* past, *of our common past,* as Negroes. What of the future? Are you going to wait until the white man has sucked your blood dry? Will you wait meekly until he has filled our veins with his own poisonous blood? Already you are nothing but half-baked imitations of the white man. You ridicule him and you mimick him, at the same time. With every day that passes you are losing your own precious heritage. You are forfeiting it to your keepers who have not the least intention of granting you equality. Educate yourselves, if you wish. Improve your lot, if you can. But remember this—unti you stand free and equal with your white neighbours nothing will avail. Don't delude yourselves that the white man is your superior *in any way.* He isn't. His skin may be white. but his heart is black. He is guilty before God and before his fellowman. He is bringing the world down about his ears in his pride and arrogance. The day is coming when he will rule no more. He has sown hatred throughout the world. He has pitted brother against brother. He has denied his own God. No, this miserable specimen of humanity is not the superior of the black man. This breed of man is doomed. Awake, my brothers! Awake and sing! Shout the white man down? Shut him out of your sight! Seal his lips, bind his limbs, bury him where he belongs—on the dung heap!'

I repeat, nothing of the sort passed Dubois' lips. He would undoubtedly have held me in contempt had I voiced such an interpretation of his speech. But words mean little. What's back of them—that's what counts. I almost felt ashamed of Dubois for using other words than the ones I heard in my mind. Had his words created a bloody insurrection he would have been the most bewildered man in the whole Negro community. And yet I persisted in believing that in his heart the message I have just given was recorded, recorded in blood and tears. If he were truly a wit less ardent he would not, could not, be the noble figure he was. I blushed to think that a man of such gift, such powers, such insight, should be obliged to muffle his voice, to throttle his own true feelings. I admired him for all that he had done, for all that he was, and it was indeed much—but if only he possessed a spark of that passionate spirit of John Brown! If only he had a touch of the fanatic! To speak of injustice and to remain cool—only a sage can act thus. (It must be granted, however, that where the ordinary man sees injustice the sage perhaps detects another kind of justice.) The just man is hard, merciless, in-human. The just man will set fire to the world, will destroy it with his own hands, if he can, rather than see injustice perpetuated. John Brown was that sort of man. History has forgotten him. Lesser men have come forward, have upset the world, thrown it into a panic—and for nothing even approaching that which we call justice. . . . Give him a little more time and the white man will destroy himself and the pernicious world he has created. He has no solutions for the ills he has foisted upon the world. None whatever. He is empty, disillusioned, without a grain of hope. He pines for his own miserable end.

Will the white man drag the Negro down with him? I doubt it. All those whom he has persecuted and enslaved, degenerated and emasculated, all whom he has vampirized will, I believe, rise up against him on the fateful day of judgment. There will be no succour for him, not one friendly alien hand raised to avert his doom. Neither will he be mourned. Instead there will come from all corners of the earth, like the gathering of a whirlwind, a cry of exultation. 'White man, your day is over? Perish like the worm! And may the memory of your stay on earth be effaced!'

Curiously enough, it was only quite recently that I discovered that Dubois had written a book on John Brown in which he predicted much that has already befallen the white race and much that has yet to come to pass. Strange that, knowing nothing of his passion and admiration for the great Liberator, I should have linked their names. . . .

The next morning, I was having breakfast in a coffee shop on Pineapple Street, I felt a hand on my shoulder. A voice from behind was quietly asking if I was not Henry Miller. I looked up to find Claude at my elbow. Not a possible doubt that it could be anyone else.

'I was told you usually took breakfast here,' he said. 'Too bad you didn't come last night; I had a friend with me whom you would have enjoyed meeting. He was from Teheran.'

I offered apologies and urged him to have a second breakfast with me. It was nothing for Claude to eat two or three breakfasts in a row.

He was like a camel—he tanked up whenever he had the chance.

'You *are* a Capricorn, aren't you?' he asked. 'December 26th, is that right? About noon?'

I nodded.

'I don't know too much about astrology,' he continued. 'It's simply a point of departure for me. I'm like Joseph in the Bible —I have dreams. Prophetic dreams, sometimes.'

I smiled indulgently.

'You're going to travel soon—perhaps in a year or two. An important voyage. Your life will be radically altered.' He paused a moment to gaze out of the window, as if trying to concentrate. 'But that's not important now. I wanted to see you for another reason.' He paused again. 'You'll have a harrowing time of it, this next year or so. I mean, before you begin your journey. It will take all your courage to survive. If I didn't know you so well I would say there was a danger of your going mad. . . .'

'Excuse me,' I interrupted, 'but how do you happen to know me so well?'

It was Claude's turn to smile. Then, without the slightest hesitation, he answered:

'I've known you for a long while—in my dreams. You come back again and again. Of course I didn't know it was *you* until I met Mona. Then I realized it could be no other.'

'Strange,' I murmured.

'Not so very,' said Claude. 'Many men have had the same experience. Once, when I was in a little village in China, a man met me on the street and, taking me by the arm, he said: "I've been waiting for you to come. You arrived exactly on time." He was a magician. He practised the black arts.'

'Are you a magician too?' I asked jokingly.

'Hardly,' said Claude. And in the same tone he added: 'I practise divination. It's a gift I was born with.'

'But it doesn't help *you* much, does it?'

'True,' he replied, 'but it permits me to help others. That is, if they wish to be helped.'

'And you want to help *me*?'

'If I can.'

'Before you go any further,' said I, 'supposing you tell me a little about yourself. Mona has told me something of your life, but it all sounds rather confusing. Tell me this, if you don't mind—do you know where you were born and who your father and mother were?'

Claude looked straight into my eyes. 'That's what I'm trying to find out,' he said. 'Perhaps you can be of help. You wouldn't have appeared in my dreams so often if you weren't of importance in my life.'

'Your dreams? Tell me, how do I appear to you in dream?'

'In various roles,' said Claude promptly. 'Sometimes as a father, sometimes as a devil, and sometimes as a ministering angel. Whenever you appear it's to the strain of music. Celestial music, I would say.'

I was at a loss what to say to this.

'You are aware, of course,' Claude continued, 'that you have power over others. Great power. You seldom employ it, however. When you do you usually misuse it. You're ashamed of your better self, if I may put it that way. You'd rather be thought wicked than good. And you *are* wicked at times—wicked and cruel—especially to those who are fond of you. That's what you've got to work out. . . . But you'll soon be put to the test!'

'There's something eerie about you Claude. I begin to suspect that you do have second sight, or whatever you choose to call it.'

To this Claude replied: 'You're essentially a man of faith. A man of great faith. The sceptic in you is a transitory phenomenon, a heritage from the past, from some other life. You've got to throw off your doubts—self doubts, above all—they're suffocating you. A being like yourself has only to throw himself on the world and he will float like a cork. Nothing truly evil will ever touch you or affect you. You were made to walk through the fires. But if you shun your true role, and you alone know what that is, you will be burned to a cinder. That's the clearest thing I know about you.' I admitted quite frankly that what he had just said was neither vague nor unfamiliar to me. 'I've had inklings of such things a number of times. At the moment, however, nothing is altogether clear to me. Go on, if you will, I'm all ears.'

'What's brought us together,' said Claude, 'is that we are both seeking our true parents. You asked me where I was born. I was a foundling; my parents left me on a stoop somewhere in the Bronx. I have a suspicion that my parents, whoever they were, came from Asia. Mongolia perhaps. When I look into your eyes I am almost convinced of it. You have Mongol blood, beyond a doubt. Has no one ever remarked it before?'

I now took a deep look at the young man who was telling me all this. I took him in as you would a tall drink of water when you're very thirsty. *Mongol blood!* Of course I had heard it before! And always from the same sort of people. Whenever the word Mongol came up it registered on me like a password. 'We're on to you!' is what it usually conveyed. Whether I admitted or denied it, I was 'one of them'.

The Mongol business was, of course, more symbolical then genealogical. The Mongols were the bearers of secret tidings. At some remote period in the past, when the world was one and when its real rulers kept their identity hidden, 'we Mongols' were *there*. (Strange language? Mongols talk only this way.) There was something physical, or physiological, or physiognomical at least, which characterized all who belonged to this strange clan. What distinguished them from 'the rest of humanity' was the expression about the eyes. It was neither the colour, shape or look of the eye: it was the way the eyes were set off, or set in, the way they swam in their mysterious sockets. Veiled ordinarily, in talk these veils peeled off, one after another, until one had the impression of peering into a deep black hole.

Studying Claude, my gaze came to rest on the two black holes in the centre of his eyes. They were fathomless. For a full minute or two not another word was exchanged. Neither of us felt embarrassed or uncomfortable. We simply stared at each other like two lizards. The Mongol look of mutual recognition.

It was I who broke the spell. I told him that he reminded me slightly of Deerslayer—of Deerslayer and Daniel Boone combined. With a just a touch of Nebuchadnezzar!

He laughed. 'I've passed for many things,' he said.' The Navajos thought I had Indian blood in my veins. Maybe I have too. . . .'

'I'm sure you have a drop of Jewish blood,' said I. 'Not because of the Bronx!' I added.

'I was raised by Jews,' said Claude. 'Until I was eight years of age I heard nothing but Russian and Yiddish. At ten I ran way from home.'

'Where was that—what you call home?''

'A little village in the Crimea, not far from Sevastopol. I had been transplanted there when I was six months old.' He paused a moment. He started to say something about memory, then dropped it. 'When I first heard English,' he resumed, 'I recognized it as a familiar tongue, though I had heard it only during the first six months of my life. I learned English almost instinctively, in less than no time. As you notice, I speak it without a trace of accent. Chinese also came easy to me, though I really never became proficient in it. . . .'

'Excuse me,' I interrupted, 'but how many languages *do* you speak, would you mind telling me?'

He hesitated a moment, as if making a quick calculation·
'Frankly,' he replied, 'I can't tell. I know at least a dozen,
certainly. It's nothing to be proud of; I have a natural flair for
language. Besides, when you knock about the world you can't
help but pick up languages.'

'But *Hungarian*!' I exclaimed. 'Surely that didn't come easy to
you!'

He gave me an indulgent smile. 'I don't know why people
think Hungarian is so difficult. There are Indian tongues right
here in North America which are far more difficult—from the
standpoint of pure linguistics, I mean. But no language is difficult if you're living it. To know Turkish, Hungarian, Arabic or
the Navajo tongue you have to become as one of them, that's all.'

'But you're so young! How could you have had time to . . .?'

'Age means nothing,' he interrupted. 'It isn't age which
makes us wise. Nor even experience, as people pretend. It's the
quickness of the spirit. *The quick and the dead*. . . . You, of all
people should know what I mean. There are only two classes in
this world—*and in every world*—the quick and the dead. For
those who cultivate the spirit nothing is impossible. For the
others, everything is impossible, or incredible, or futile. When
you live day after day with the impossible you begin to wonder
what the word means. Or rather, how it ever came to mean what
it does. There's a world of light, in which everything is clear and
manifest, and there's a world of confusion, where all is murky
and obscure. The two worlds are really one. Those in the world
of darkness get a glimpse now and then of the realm of light, but
those in the world of light know nothing of darkness. The
men of light cast no shadow. Evil is unknown to them. Nor
do they harbour resentment. They move without chains or
fetters. Until I returned to this country I associated only with
such men. In some ways my life is stranger than you think. Why
did I go among the Navajos? To find peace and understanding.
If I had been born in another time I might have been a Christ or
a Buddha. Here I'm a bit of freak. Even *you* have difficulty not to
think that way about me.'

Here he gave me a mysterious smile. For a full moment I felt
as though my heart had stopped.

'Did you feel something strange then?' said Claude, his smile
now transformed into a more human one.

'I did indeed,' said I, unconsciously placing a hand over my
heart.

'Your heart stopped beating for a moment, that was all,' said
Claude. 'Imagine, if you can, what it would be like if your heart
began to beat with cosmic rhythm. Most people's hearts don't
even beat with human rhythm. . . . There will come a time when
man will no longer distinguish between man and god. When the
human being is raised to his full powers he will be divine—his

human consciousness will have fallen away. What is called death will have disappeared. Everything will be altered, *permanently altered*. There will be no further need for change. Man will be free, that's what I mean. Once he becomes the god which he is, he will have realized his destiny—which is freedom. Freedom includes everything. Freedom converts everything to its basic nature, which is perfection. Don't think I am talking religion or philosophy. I disclaim them both, utterly. They are not even stepping stones, as people like to think. They must be hurdled, at one jump. If you put something outside you, or above you, you become victimized. There is only the one thing, *spirit*. It's all, everything, and when you realize it you're it. You're all there is there is nothing more . . . do you understand what I'm saying?'

I nodded my head affirmatively. I was a little dazed.

'You understand,' said Claude, 'but the reality of it escapes you. Understanding is nothing. The eyes must be kept open, constantly. To open your eyes you must relax, not strain. Don't be afraid of falling backwards into a bottomless pit. There is nothing to fall into. You're in it and of it, and one day, if you persist, *you will be it*. I don't say you will *have it*, please notice, because there's nothing to possess. Neither are you to be possessed, remember that! You are to liberate yourself. There is no exercises, physical or spiritual, to practise. All such things are like incense—they awaken a feeling of holiness. We must be holy without holiness. We must be whole . . . complete. That's being holy. Any other kind of holiness is false, a snare and a delusion. . . .'

'Excuse me for talking to you this way,' said Claude, hastily swallowing another mouthful of coffee, 'but I have the feeling that time is short. The next time we meet it will most likely be in some remote part of the world. Your restlessnes may lead you to the most unexpected places. *My* movements are more determined; I know the pattern set down for me.' He paused to take another tack. 'Since I've gone thus far let me add a few more words.' He leaned forward, and his face took on a most earnest expression. 'Right now, Henry Miller, nobody in this country knows anything about you. Nobody—and I mean it literally— knows your true identity. At this moment I know more about you than I shall probably ever know again. What I know, however, is only of importance for *me*. This is what I wanted to tell you— that you should think of me when you are in distress. Not that I can help you, don't think that! Nobody can. Nobody will, probably. You—(and here he spaced his words)—you will have to solve your own problems. But at least you will know, when thinking of me, that there is one person in this world who knows you and believes in you. That always helps. The secret, however, lies in not caring whether anyone, not even the Almighty, has confidence in you. You must come to realize, and you will undoubtedly, that you need no protection. Nor should you hunger after salvation, for salvation is only a myth. *What* is there to be saved? Ask yourself that! And if saved, saved from *what*? Have you thought of these things? Do! There is no need for redemption, because what men call sin and guilt have no ultimate meaning. *The quick and the dead!*—just remember that! When you reach to the quick of things you will find neither acceleration nor retardation, neither birth nor death. *There is* and *you are*—that's it in a nutshell. Don't break your skull over it, because to the mind it makes no sense. Accept it and forget it—or it will drive you mad. . . .'

When I walked away I was floating in the clouds. I had my brief-case with me, as usual, but all thought of calling on prospects was gone. I got into the subway automatically and out again automatically—at Times Square. Whenever I had no set destination I would get out automatically at Times Square. There I always came upon the *rambla*, the Nevsky Prospekt, the souks and bazaars of the damned.

The thoughts and emotions which possessed me were almost frighteningly familiar. They were the same which I experienced when I first heard my old friend Roy Hamilton talk, when first I listened to Benjamin Fay Mills, the Evangelist, when first I glanced at that strange book, *Esoteric Buddhism*, when I read at one gulp the *Tao Teh Ch'ing*, or—whenever I picked up *The Possessed*, *The Idiot*, or *The Brothers Karamazov*. The cow-bells which I carried under my ribs began clanking wildly; in the belfry above it it was as if all the stars in the heavens had come together to make a celestial bonfire. There was no weight to my body, none whatever. I was at the 'six extremes' simultaneously.

There was a language which never failed to set me off—and it was always the same language. Boiled to the size of a lentil, its whole scope and purport could be expressed in two words: *Know thyself!* Alone with myself, and not only alone but dis-connected, discalibrated, I ran up and down the harmonica, talking the one and only language, breathing only the pure in-effable spirit, looking upon everything with new eyes and in an absolutely new way. *No birth, no death?* Of course not! What more, what else, could there be than was at this moment? Who said that everything was fucked up? Where? When? On the seventh day God rested from his labours. And He saw that all was good. *D'accord.* How could it have been otherwise? Why should it be otherwise? According to reason, that fat wingless slug, humanity was slowly, slowly evolving from the primordial slime. A million years hence we would begin faintly to resemble the angels. What rot! Is the mind encysted, then, in the ass-hole of creation? When Roy Hamilton spoke, though he possessed not a shred of learning, he spoke with the sweet authority of the

411

angels. He was all instantaneity. The wheel flashed and you were immediately at the hub, in the centre of that empty space without which not even the constellations can wheel and flash their secret codes. Ditto for Benjamin Fay Mills, who was not an Evangelist but a hero who had abandoned Christianity in order to be a Christ. And Nirvana? Not tomorrow but now, forever and eternally *now*. . . .

This language was ever bright and clear to me. The language of reason, which is not even the language of common sense, spelled gibberish. When God lets go the arm that hold the pen the author no longer knows what he is writing. Jacob Boehme used a language all his own, a language direct from the Maker. Scholars read it one way, men of God another. The poet speaks only to the poet. Spirit answereth spirit. The rest is hog-wash.

A hundred voices are speaking at once. I am still on the Nevsky Prospekt, still toting the brief-case. I could as well be in limbo. I am most assuredly 'there,' wherever that may be, and nothing can derail me. Possessed, yes. But by the great Manitou this time.

Now I've gotten below the *rambla*. I'm approaching the old Haymarket. Suddenly a name juts out from a billboard, cuts my eye-ball just as clean as a razor-blade. I have just passed a theatre which I thought had been torn down long ago. Nothing remains in the retina but a name, her name, an utterly new name: MIMI AGUGLIA. This is the important thing, her name. Not that she is Italian, not that the play is an immortal tragedy. Just her name: MIMI AGUGLIA. Though I keep walking steadily ahead, and then round and about, though I keep scudding through the clouds like a three-quarter moon, her name will draw me back punctually at 2.15 p.m.

From the celestial realm I slide to a comfortable seat in the third row orchestra. I am about to witness the greatest performance I shall probably ever witness. And in a language of which I know not a word.

The theatre is packed—and with Italians exclusively. An awesome hush precedes the rising of the curtain. The stage is semi-dark. For a full minute not a word is spoken. Then a voice is heard: the voice of Mimi Aguglia.

Only a few moments ago my head was seething with thought; now all is still, the great swarm gathered in a honey-comb at the base of the skull. Not even a buzz issues from the hive. My senses sharpened to a diamond point, are fully concentrated on the strange creature with the oracular voice. Even were she to speak a language I know, I doubt that I could follow her. It is the sounds she makes, the immense gamut of sound, which enthrals me. Her throat is like an ancient lyre. So very, very ancient. It has the ring of man before he ate of the tree of knowledge. Her gestures and movements are mere accompaniments to the voice. The features, monolithic in repose, express the most subtle modulations with her ceaseless change of mood. When she throws her head back, the oracular music from her throat plays over her features like lightning playing over a bed of mica. She seems to express with ease emotions which we can only stimulate in dream. All is primordial, effulgent, annihilating. A moment ago she was sitting in a chair. It is no longer a chair; it has become a thing, an animated thing. Wherever she moves, whatever she touches, things become altered. Now she stands before a tall mirror, ostensibly to catch her own reflection. Illusion! She is standing before a gap in the cosmos, answering the Titan's yawn with an inhuman shriek. Her heart, suspended in a crevice of ice, suddenly glows—until her whole being shoots forth flames of ruby and sapphire. Another instant and the monolithic head turns to jade. The serpent confronting chaos Marble returning in horror to the void. Nothingness. . . .

She is pacing back and forth, back and forth, and in her wake a phosphorescent glow. The very atmosphere thickens, impregnated by the impending horror. She is unveiling now, but as if in warm oil, as if still drugged by the fumes of the sacrificial altar. A phrase gurgles from her tortured lips, a strangled phrase which causes the man beside me to groan. Blood oozes from a burst vein in her temple. Petrified, I am unable to make a sound, though I am screaming at the top of my lungs. It is no longer theatre, it is the nightmare. The walls close in, twisting and twining like the dread labyrinth. The Minotaur is breathing upon us with hot and evil breath. At precisely this moment, and as if a thousand chandeliers had been shattered at once, her mad, fiendish laugh splits the ear. She is no longer recognizable. One sees only a human wreck, a tangle of arms and limbs, a mass of twisted hair, a gory mouth, and this, this *thing*, gropes, staggers, grapples, blindly suddenly, towards the wings. . . .

Hysteria sweeps the audience. Men with jaws locked are hanging limp in the seats. Women scream, faint, or tear their hair convulsively. The whole auditorium has become like the bottom of the sea—and pandemonium struggling like a crazed gorilla to remove the heavy liquid stone of fright. The ushers gesticulate like puppets, their shouts smothered in the screeching roar which gradually swells like a typhoon. And all this in total darkness, because something has gone wrong with the lights. Finally from the pit comes the sound of music, a blare and a blast, which is met by an angry roar of protest. The music fades out, silenced as if by a hammer. The curtain rises slowly to reveal a stage still in darkness. Suddenly she comes forth from the wings, a lighted taper in her hand, bowing, bowing, bowing. She is mute, absolutely mute. From the boxes, from the balconies, from the pit itself flowers rain down upon the stage. She is standing in a sea of flowers, the taper burning brightly. Suddenly the theatre is

flooded with light. The crowd is screaming her name—MIMI...
MIMI ... MIMI AGUGLIA. In the midst of the uproar she
calmly blows the taper out and walks swiftly back to the
wings. . . .

With the brief-case still under my arm I start ploughing
through the *rambla* again. I feel as if I had come down from Mt
Sinai by parachute. All about me are my brothers, *humanity*,
as they say, still marching on all fours. I have an overpowering
desire to kick out in all directions, speed the poor buggers into
Paradise. Just at this 'precise chronological moment' when I'm
fizzing like champagne, a man tugs at my sleeve and shoves a
dirty post-card under my nose. I keep walking straight ahead
with him clinging to me, and as we move on, trancelike, he
keeps changing the cards and muttering under his breath: 'A
honey, what! Dirt cheap. Take the whole pack—for two bits.'
Suddenly I stop dead in my tracks; I begin to laugh, a frightening
laugh which grows louder and louder. I let the cards slide from
my fingers, like snow-cakes. A crowd begins to gather, the
peddlar takes to his heels. People are beginning to pick up the
cards; they keep crowding in on me, closer and closer, curious to
know what made me laugh so. In the distance I spy a cop
approaching. Pivoting round abruptly, I yell: 'He's gone in there.
Get him!' Pointing to a shop near the corner I push forward
eagerly with the crowd; as they press forward and ahead of me I
turn quickly and walk as fast as my legs will carry me in the
opposite direction. At the corner I swing round, moving like a
kangaroo now, until I come to a gin-mill.

At the bar two men are in the midst of a violent dispute. I
order a beer and make myself as inconspicuous as possible.

'I tell you he's off his nut!'

'You'd be too if you had had your balls cut out.'

'He'll make you look like a horse's ass.'

'The Pope's ass he will!'

'*Look*, who made the world? Who made the stars, the sun,
the rain drops? Answer me that!'

'*You* answer it, since you're so bloody learned. *You* tell me
who made the world, the rainbows, the piss-pots and all the other
cocksucking devices.'

'You'd like to know, lad? Well, let me say this—it wasn't made
in a cheese factory. And it wasn't evolution made it either.'

'Oh no? What was it then?'

'It was the Almighty Jehovah himself, Lord of Creation, Be-
getter of the Blessed Mary, and Redeemer of lost souls. That's a
fair answer for you. Now what have you to say?'

'I still say he's nuts.'

'You're a dirty infidel, that's what. You're a pagan.'

'I'm not neither. I'm Irish through and through. And what's

more, I'm a Mason . . . yeah, a bloody Mason. Like George Abraham Washington and the Marquis of Queensbury. . . .'

'And Oliver Cromwell and Bloody Bonesapart. Sure, I know your breed. It was a black snake that borned you and it's his black venom you've been spreading ever since.'

'We'll never take orders from the Pope. Put that in your pipe and light it!'

'And *this* for you! You've made a Bible out of Darwin's crazy preachings. You make a monkey of yourself and you call it evolution.'

'I still say he's nuts.'

'Can I ask you a simple question? *Can I now?*'

'That you can. Fire away! I'll answer anything that has sense to it.'

'Perfect! . . . Now what makes worms crawl and birds to fly? What makes the spider spin his crazy web? What makes the kangaroo . . .?'

'Hold it, man! One question at a time. Now which is it—the bird, the worm, the spider or the kangaroo?'

'Why do two and two make four? Maybe you can answer that! I don't ask you to be an anthroposophagist, or whatever the devil they're called. Plain arithmetic . . . two plus two equals four. WHY? Answer that and I'll say you're an honest Roman. Go on, how, give it to me!'

'Bugger the Romans! I'd rather be a monkey with Darwin, b'Jasus! *Arithmetic!* Bah! Why don't you ask me if red-eyed Mars ever wobbled in her funicular orbit?'

'The Bible answered that long ago. So did Parnell!'

'In the pig's ass he did!'

'There isn't a question but was answered once and for all—by somebody or other.'

'You mean the Pope!'

'Man, I've told you a hundred times—the Pope is but a Pontifical interlocutor. His Holiness never asserted that he was the risen Christ.'

'Lucky for him, because I'd deny it to his treacherous face. We've had enough of Inquisitions. What the sad, weary world needs is a bit of common sense. You can rave all you like about spiders and kangaroos, but who's going to pay the rent? Ask your friend that!'

'I told you that he joined the Dominicans.'

'And I said that he was nuts.'

At this point the bartender, thinking to quiet them, was about to offer drinks on the house when who walks in but a blind man playing a harp. He sang in a tremulous falsetto which was woefully false. He wore dark blue glasses and over his left arm was slung a white cane.

'Come give us a bawdy song!' cried one of the disputants.

415

'And none of your shananigans! . . .' cried the other.

The blind man removed his glasses, slung the harp and cane over a peg in the wall, and shuffled to the bar with an alacrity that was amazing.

'Just a wee drop to wet the palate,' he whined.

'Give him a drop of Irish whiskey,' he whined.

'And a bit of brandy,' said the other.

'To the men of Dublin and County Kerry,' said the blind man, raising both glasses at once. 'Down with all Orangemen!' He looked around, bright as a bob-o-link and took a swallow from each of the tumblers.

'When will you get any shame in you?' said the one.

'He's wallowing in gold' said the other.

'It's loike this,' said the blind man, brushing his lips with his sleeve, 'when me owld mother died I promised her I'd never do another stroke of work. I've kept to me bargain, and so has she. Every time I pluck the strings she calls to me softly; "Patrick, are you there? It's grand, me boy, it's grand," Before I can ask her a question she's gone again. *The fair grounds*, I call it. She's been there for thirty years now—and she's kept to her bargain.'

'You're dotty, man. What bargain?'

'It's long to explain and my throat's parched. . . .'

'Another brandy and whiskey for the scoundrel!'

'You're kind, the two of you. *Gentlemen*, that's what you are?' Again he raises both glasses. 'To the Blessed Mary and her prodigal son!'

'Did you hear that now? That's blasphemy or I'll eat me hat.'

'It's not either. Tush tush!'

'The Blessed Mary had only one son—*and by the holy Patrick he was no prodigal!* He was the Prince of Paupers, that's what he was. I'll take an oath on it.'

'This is no court. Easy with your oaths! Go on, man, tell us of your bargain!'

The blind man pulled his nose meditatively. Again he looked about—bright and merry, chipper as could be. Like an oily sardine.

'It's loike this . . .' he began.

'Don't *say* that, man! On with yer! Out with it!'

'It's a long, long story. And me throat's still dry, if yer don't mind me saying so.'

'Get on with it, man, or we'll be fleeing your bottom!'

The blind man cleared his throat, then rubbed his eyes.

'It's loike I wuz sayin' . . . Me owld mother had the gift of sight. She could see through a door, her gimlicks were that strong. Wanst, when the dadda was late for supper. . . .'

'Your dadda be damned! You're a creepy old counterfeiter!'

'I am that too,' screeched the blind man. 'I've every little weakness.'

'And a throat that's always parched.'

'And a pocketful of gold, eh, you rascal!'

Suddenly the blind man became terrified. His face blanched.

'No, no!' he screamed, 'not me pockets. You wouldn't do that to me? You wouldn't do that. . . .'

The two cronies began to laugh uproariously. Pinning his arms to his sides, they went through his pockets—pants, coat and vest. Dumping the money on the bar, they piled it neatly in bills and coins of every denomination, putting the bad money to one side. It was a stunt they had evidently rehearsed more than once.

'Another brandy!' called the one.

'Another Irish whiskey—*the best!*' called the other.

They dished out some coins from the pile, and then a few more, to make a generous tip for the barman.

'And is your throat still parched?' they asked solicitously.

'And what will *you* have?' says the one.

'And *you*?' says the other.

'My throat's getting dryer and dryer.'

'Aye, and so is mine.'

'And did you ever hear about the bargain Patrick made with his owld mother?'

'It's a long story,' says the other, 'but I've a mind to hear it to the end. Would you tell it now, while I down a goblet to your health and virility?'

The other, raising his goblet: 'I could tell it till the Day of Judgement, it's that good. A corkin' yarn. But let me wet me throat first.'

'They're a bunch of thieves, the three of 'em,' said the barkeep as he filled my glass. 'Would you believe it, one of 'em was a priest once. He's the biggest faker of the lot. Can't put 'em out—they own the building. See what I mean?'

He busied himself with the empty glasses, rinsed them, wiped them, polished them, lit himself a cigarette. Then he ambled over to me again.

'All shandy-gaff,' he mumbled confidentially. 'They can talk sense, if they want to. They're as smart as steel traps. Like to put on an act, that's all. Beats me why they pick this place to do it in.' He leaned backward to spit a gob in the spitoon beside his feet. '*Ireland!* They never saw Ireland, none of them. They were born and raised a block away from here. They love to put it on. . . . You'd never think it, would you, but the blind fellow was a great little fighter once. Until he got knocked cold by Terry McGovern. He's got the eyes of an eagle, that bird. Comes in here to count his money every day. It burns him up to get wooden money. You know what he does with the bad coins? Passes them off on real blind men. *Ain't that nice?*'

He left me a moment to beg them to quiet down. The champagne was beginning to have its effect.

'Know what the big news is now? They're planning to hire a hansom and take a ride through Central Park. Time to feed the pigeons, they say. How's that for you?' He leaned backwards again to use the cuspidor. 'That's another one of their acts—feeding the pigeons. They throw out some crumbs or peanuts, and when they've collected a crowd they begin throwing away the wooden money. Gives them a great kick. After that Blind Ben does a little number and they pass the hat around. As if they hadn't a cent in the world! I'd like to be there sometime and put a nice lump of shit in the kitty. . . .'

He looked around to eye them disdainfully. Turns back to me again and starts sprouting.

'Maybe you thought they were really arguing about something? I've listened time and again to find out how it begins—but I never can. Before you know it they're in the thick of it. They say any old thing—to get wound up. It's gab they like. The argumentation is just dirt in the eye. The Pope, Darwin, Kangaroos—you heard it all. It never makes sense, no matter what they're talking about. Yesterday it was hydraulic engineering and how to cure constipation. The day before it was the Easter Rebellion. All mixed up with a lot of horse shit—the bubonic plague, the Sepoy mutiny, Roman aqueducts and horse feathers. *Words, words.* . . . It drives me nuts sometimes. Every night I'm arguin' in my sleep. The hell of it is I don't know what I'm arguin' about. Just like them. Even my day off is ruined. I keep wondering if they're goin' to show up somewheres. . . . Some people think they're funny. I've seen guys split their sides laughing at 'em. It ain't funny to *me*, no sir! By the time I finish here I'm standing on my head. . . . *Listen*—I did a stretch once—for six months—and a coloured guy had the cell next to mine . . . *Can I freshen it up for you?* . . . He sang all day long, and nights too. Got me so mad I wanted to throttle him. Funny hah? Shows you how sensitive you can get. . . . Brother, if I ever get out of this racket I'm headin' for the Sierra Nevadas. What I need is peace and quiet. I don't even want to look at a cow. It might go MOO-ooo-ooo—*see what I mean?* Trouble was, when I got back my wife was gone. Yeah! Ran out on me—and with my best friend, of course. Just the same, I can't forget that month of peace and quiet. It was worth everything that happened afterwards . . . you get sensitive, working like a slave all day long. I was cut out for somethin' else. Never could find out what. I've been off beat for a long time. . . . *Can I freshen it up for you?* It's on the house, what the hell! You *see* . . . now I'm talking like a blue streak That's what happens to you. You see a sympathetic puss and you spill the beans. . . . I haven't told you anything yet.' He reached up and took down a bottle of gin. Poured himself a thimbleful, a good one. 'Here's how! And let's hope they get the hell out of here soon. *Where was I?* Yeah, the bad news. . . . What do you think my parents wanted me to be? *An insurance agent.* Can you beat that? They thought it was refined like. The old man was a hod-carrier, you see. From the old country, sure enough. A brogue as thick as mulligatawney. Yeah, the insurance racket. Can you picture me goin' through a routine like that? So I joins the Marines. After that the horses. Lost everything. Then I take up plumbing. No go. Too clumsy. Besides, I hate filth, believe it or not. So what? Well, I bummed around a bit, got wise to myself and borrowed a little from the old man so as I could open a hash joint. Then I make the mistake of gettin' hitched up. A battle royal from the day we were spliced. Except for that vacation I was telling you about. So help me God, one experience wasn't enough. Before you know it, I'm hooked up with another one—a cute little bitch too. Then the real agony starts. She was a screwball, this last one. She got me so bitched up I didn't know whether I was goh' or comin'. That's how I landed in the clink. When I came out I was that low I was ready for religion. Yes sir, those six months in the clink put the fear of Christ in me. I was ready to toe the line. . . .' He poured himself another thimbleful of gin, spat again, and resumed where he had left off. 'Listen, I was that careful you could have offered me a gold ingot and I wouldn't touch it. That's how I got inter this business. I asked for somethin' to keep me busy. It was the old man who got me the job'. He leaned over to whisper the words: 'He coughed up five hundred clam to get this break! That's kindness, *what!'*

Here I begged off to take a leak.

When I came out the bar was full.

The trio had disappeared, I noticed. I shook myself like a dog and headed back for the Gay White Way. Everything had fallen back into its normal aspect. It was Broadway once again, not the *rambla*, not the Nevsky Prospekt. A typical New York throng, no different from what it was in the year One. I bought a paper at Times Square and ducked into the subway. The workers were wending their weary way homeward. Not a spark of life in the whole train. Only the switchboard in the motorman's compartment was alive, crackling with electricity. You could add up all the thoughts that were being thought, put a decimal in front of them, and add twenty-six digits to make it even less than nothing.

On the seventh day God rested from His labour and saw that all was good. *Put that in your pipe and smoke it!*

I wondered vaguely about the pigeons. And from that to the Sepoy Mutiny. Then I dozed off. I fell into such a stupor that I never woke up till we got to Coney Island. The brief case was

419

gone. So was my wallet. Even the newspaper was gone. . . . Nothing to do but stay in the train and ride back again.

I felt hungry. Voraciously hungry. And in excellent spirits. I decided I might as well eat at The Iron Cauldron. It seemed as if I hadn't seen my wife for ages.

Fine! Giddy-ap, horsey! To the Village!

16

THE IRON CAULDRON was one of the landmarks of the Village. Its clientele was drawn from far and near. Among the many interesting characters who frequented the place were the inevitable freaks and eccentrics who made the Village notorious.

To believe Mona, it would seem that all the nuts congregated at her tables Almost every day I heard of some new figure, each one, of course, more extravagant than the last.

The latest was Anastasia. She had blown in from the Coast and was having a time of it to keep going. She had had a few hundred dollars with her on arriving in New York but it had vanished like smoke. What she hadn't given away had been stolen. According to Mona, she was an extraordinary looking person. She had long black hair which she wore like a mane, violet blue eyes, beautiful strong hands and large sturdy feet. She called herself Anastasia simply. Her last name, Annapolis, she had invented. Apparently she had wandered into The Iron Cauldron in search of work. Mona had overheard her talking to the proprietor and had come to her rescue. Wouldn't hear of her washing dishes or even waiting on tables. She had divined at once that this was an unusual person, had invited her to sit down and eat, and after a long conversation had loaned her some money.

'Imagine, she was walking around in overalls. She had no stockings and her shoes were worn through. People were making fun of her.'

'Describe her again, will you?'

'I really can't,' said Mona, whereupon she launched into an extravagant description of her friend. The way she said 'my friend' gave me a queer feeling. I had never heard her refer to

421

any of her other acquaintances in quite this way. There was a fervour to her words which suggested veneration, adoration and other undefinable things. She had made of this meeting with her new-found friend an event of the first magnitude.

'How old is she?' I ventured to ask.

'How old? I don't know. Maybe twenty-two or three. She has no age. You don't think of such things when you look at her. She's the most extraordinary being I've ever met—outside of yourself, Val.'

'An Artist, I suppose?'

'She's everything. She can do anything.'

'Does she paint?'

'Of course! She paints, sculpts, makes puppets, writes poetry, dances—and with it all she's a clown. But a sad clown, like you.'

'You don't think she's nuts?'

'I should say not! She does queer things, but only because she's unusual. She's about as free a person as I've ever seen, and tragic to boot. She's really unfathomable.'

'Like Claude, I suppose.'

She smiled. 'In a way,' she said. 'Funny you mentioned him. You ought to see the two of them together. They look as if they hailed from another planet.'

'So they know each other?'

'I introduced them to one another. They get along splendidly, oo. They talk their own private language. And do you know, they even resemble one another physically.'

'I suppose she's a bit on the mannish side, this Anapopoulos or whatever it is?'

'Not really,' said Mona, her eyes glistening. 'She prefers to dress in men's clothes because she feels more comfortable that way. She's more than a mere female, you see. If she were a man, I'd speak the same way. There's some added quality in her which is beyond sexual distinction. Sometimes she reminds me of an angel, except that there's nothing ethereal or remote about her. No, she's very earthy, almost coarse at times. . . . The only way to explain it to you, Val, is to say that she's a superior being. You know how you felt about Claude? Well . . . Anastasia is tragic buffoon. She doesn't belong in this world at all. I don't know where she belongs, but certainly not here. The very tone of her voice will tell you that. It's an extraordinary voice, more like a bird's than a human being's. But when she gets angry it becomes frightening.'

'Why, does she fly into rages frequently?'

'Only when people insult her or make fun of her.'

'Why do they do that?

'I told you—*because she's different*. Even her walk is unique. She can't help it, it's her nature. But it makes me furious to see

422

the way she's treated. There never was a more generous, reckless soul. Of course she has no sense of reality. That's what I love about her.'

'What do you mean by that exactly?'

'Just what I said. If someone came along who needed a shirt she'd take hers off—right in the street—and give it to the person. She'd never think about the fact that she was indecently exposed. She'd take her pants off too, if necessary.'

'You don't call that mad?'

'No, Val, I don't. For her it's the natural, sane thing to do. She never stops to think of consequences; she doesn't care what people think of her. She's genuine through and through. And she's as sensitive and delicate as a flower.'

'She must have had a strange bringing up. Did she tell you anything about her parents, anything about her childhood?'

'A little.'

I could see that she knew more than she cared to reveal.

'She was an orphan, I believe. She said the people who adopted her were very kind to her. She had everything she wanted.'

'Well, let's get to bed, what do you say?'

She went to the bathroom to go through the usual interminable routine. I got in bed and waited patiently. The door to the bathroom was open.

'By the way,' I said, thinking to divert her mind, 'how is Claude these days? Anything new?'

'He's leaving town in a day or two.'

'Where to?'

'He wouldn't say. I have a notion he's heading for Africa.'

'*Africa*? Why would he be going *there*?

'Search me! It wouldn't surprise me, though, if he said he were going to the moon. You know Claude. . . .'

'You've said that several times now, and always the same way. No, I don't know Claude, not like *you* mean. I know only what he chooses to tell me, nothing more. He's an absolute conundrum to me.'

I heard her chuckling to herself.

'What's so funny about that?' I asked.

'I thought you understood one another perfectly,'

'No one will ever get to understand Claude,' said I. 'He's an enigma, and he'll remain an enigma.'

'That's just the way I feel about my friend.'

'Your *friend*,' said I a little testily. 'You hardly know her and you speak of her as if she were a life-long friend.'

'Don't be silly. She *is* my friend—the only friend I've ever had.'

'You sound as if you were infatuated. . . .'

423

'I am! She appeared at the right moment.'

'Now what does that mean?'

'That I was desperate, lonely, miserable. That I needed someone I could call a *friend*.'

'What's come over you anyway? Since when have you needed a friend? *I'm your friend*. Isn't that enough for you?' I said it mockingly, but I was half in earnest.

To my astonishment she replied: 'No, Val, you're not my friend any more. You're my husband, and I love you. . . . I couldn't live without you, but. . . .'

'But what?'

'I had to have a friend, a woman friend. Someone I can confide in, someone who understands me.'

'Well I'll be damned! So that's it? And you mean you can't confide in *me*?'

'Not like I can in a woman. There are some things you just can't tell a man, even if you love him. Oh, they're not *big* things, don't worry. Sometimes little things are more important than big things, you know that. Besides, look at you . . . you've got loads of friends. And when you're with your friends you're a different person entirely. I used to envy you sometimes. Maybe I was jealous of your friends. Once I thought that I could be everything to you. But I see I was wrong. Anyway, now I have a friend—*and I'm going to keep her*.'

Half teasingly, half seriously, I said: 'Now you want to make *me* jealous, is that it?'

She came out of the bathroom, knelt beside the bed and put her head in my arms. 'Val,' she murmured, 'you know that isn't true. But this friendship is something very dear and very precious to me. I don't want to share her with anyone, not even with you. Not for a while, at least.'

'All right,' I said. 'I get it.' My voice sounded a trifle husky, I noticed.

Gratefully she burbled: 'I knew you'd understand.'

'But what is there to understand?' I asked. I said it softly and gently.

'That's it,' she answered, 'nothing, nothing. It's only natural.' She bent forward and kissed me affectionately on the lips.

As she got to her feet to put out the lights I said impulsively: 'You poor girl! Wanting a friend all this time and I never knew it, never suspected it. I guess I must be a dumb, insensitive bugger.'

She switched off the lights and crawled into bed. There were twin beds but we used only one.

'Hold me tight,' she whispered. 'Val, I love you more than ever. Do you hear me?'

I said nothing, just held her tight.

'Claude said to me the other day—are you listening?—that you were one of the few.'

'One of the elect, is that it?' I said jokingly.

'The only man in the world for me.'

'But not a friend. . . .'

She put her hand over my mouth.

Every night it was the same theme song—'My friend 'Stasia'. Varied, of course, to add a little spice, with tall tales of the annoying attentions lavished upon her by an incongruous quartette. One of them—she didn't even know his name—owned a string of book stores; another was the wrestler, Jim Driscoll; the third was a millionaire, a notorious pervert, whose name—it sounded incredible—was Tinkelfels; the fourth was a mad individual who was also somewhat of a saint. Ricardo, this last-named, appealed to me warmly, assuming that her description of him tallied with reality. A quiet, sober individual who spoke with a strong Spanish accent, had a wife and three children whom he loved dearly, was extremely poor but made lavish gifts, was kind and gentle—'tender as a lamb'—wrote metaphysical treatises which were unpublished, gave lectures to audiences of ten or twelve, *et patati et patata*. What I liked about him was this—each time he accompanied her to the subway, each time he said good-night, he would clutch her hands and murmur solemnly: 'If I can't have you, nobody will. *I will kill you.*'

She came back to Ricardo again and again, saying how much he thought of Anastasia, how 'beautifully' he treated her, and so forth. And each time she brought up his name she would repeat his threat, laughing over it as if it were a great joke. Her attitude began to annoy me.

'How do you know he won't keep his word some day?' I said one night.

She laughed even harder at this.

'You think it's so impossible, do you?'

'You don't know him,' said she. 'He's one of the gentlest creatures on earth.'

'That's precisely why I think he's capable of doing it. He's serious. You'd better watch yourself with him.'

'Oh, nonsense! He wouldn't hurt a fly.'

'Maybe not. But he sounds passionate enough to kill the woman he loves.'

'How can he be in love with *me*? It's silly. I don't show him any affection. I hardly listen to him, in fact. He talks to Anastasia more than to me.'

'You don't have to *do* anything, you only need to *be*. He's got a fixation. He isn't mad. Unless it's madness to fall in love with an image. You're the physical image of his ideal, that's obvious.

425

He doesn't need to plumb you, or even to get a response from you. He wants to gaze at you eternally—because you've incarnated the woman of his dreams.'

'That's just the way *he talks*,' said Mona, somewhat taken aback by my words. 'You two would get on wonderfully together. You speak the same language. I know he's a sensitive creature, and a most intelligent one, too. I like him enormously, but he gets in my hair. He has no sense of humour, none whatever. When he smiles he looks even sadder than usual. He's a lonely soul.'

'It's a pity I don't know him,' I said. 'I like him more than anyone you've talked about. He sounds like a real human being. Besides, I like Spaniards. They're *men*. . . .'

'He's not a Spaniard—he's Cuban.'

'Same thing.'

'No, it isn't, Val. Ricardo told me so himself. He despises the Cubans.'

'Well, no matter. I'd like him even if he were a Turk.'

'Maybe I could introduce him to you,' said Mona suddenly. 'Why not?'

I reflected a moment before answering.

'I don't think you'd better,' said I. 'You couldn't fool a man like that. He's not a Cromwell. Besides, even Cromwell isn't the fool you take him to be.'

'I never said he was a fool!'

'But you tried to make me believe so, you can't deny that.'

'Well, you know why.' She gave me one of her faun-like smiles

'Listen, sister, I know so much more about you and your wiles than you'd ever give me credit for that it hurts to even mention the subject.'

'You have a great imagination, Val. That's the reason why I sometimes tell you so little. I know how you build things up.'

'But you must admit I build on a firm foundation!'

Again the faun-like smile.

Then she busied herself with something, in order to hide her face.

A pleasant sort of pause intervened. Then, out of a clear sky I suddenly remarked—'I suppose women are obliged to lie . . . it's in their nature. Men lie too, of course, but so differently. Women seem to have an unholy fear of the truth. You know, if you could stop lying, if you could stop playing this foolish, unnecessary game with me, I think. . . .'

I noticed that she had halted whatever it was she was pretending to be doing. Maybe she'll really listen, I thought to myself. I could see only the side of her face. The expression was one of intense alertness. Of wariness too. Like an animal.

'I think I would do anything you asked of me. I think I would even surrender you to another man, if that was what you wished.'

These unexpected words of mine gave her intense relief, or so it seemed. What it was she had imagined I would say I don't know. A weight had fallen off her shoulders. She came over to me—I was sitting on the edge of the bed—and sat beside me. She put a hand on mine. The look which stole into her eyes was one of utter sincerity and devotion.

'Val,' she began, 'you know I would never make such a demand of you. How could you say such a thing? Maybe I do tell you fibs now and then, but not lies. I couldn't keep anything vital from you—it would give me too much pain. These little things . . . these fibs . . I make them up because I don't want to hurt you There are situations sometimes which are so sordid that, even to relate them to you, I feel would soil you. It doesn't matter what happens to *me*. I'm made of coarser fibre. I know what the world is like. You don't. You're a dreamer. And an idealist. You don't know, nor will you ever suspect, much less believe, how wicked people are. You see only the good side of everyone. You're pure, that's what. And that's what Claude meant when he said you were one of the few. Ricardo is another pure soul. People like you and Ricardo should never be involved in ugly things. I get involved now and then—because I'm not afraid of contamination. I'm of the world. With you I behave like another being. I want to be what you'd like me to be. But I'll never be like you, never.'

'I wonder now,' said I, 'what people would think—people like Kronski, O'Mara, Ulric, for example—if they heard you talking this way.'

'It doesn't matter what other people think, Val. I know you. I know you better than any of your friends, no matter how long they've known you. I know how sensitive you are. You're the tenderest creature alive.'

'I'm beginning to feel frail and delicate, with all this.'

'You're not delicate,' said she feelingly. 'You're tough—like all artists. But when it comes to the world, I mean *dealing with the world*, you're just an infant. The world is vicious through and through. You're in it, all right, but you're not of it. You lead a charmed life. If you meet with a sordid experience you convert it into something beautiful.'

'You talk as if you knew me like a book.'

'I'm telling you the truth, am I not? Can you deny it?'

She put her arm around me lovingly and brushed her cheek against mine.

'Oh Val, maybe I'm not the woman you deserve, but I do know you. And the more I know you the better I love you. I've missed you so much lately. That's why it means so much to me to have a friend. I was really getting desperate—without you.'

'O.K. But we were beginning to behave like two spoiled children, do you realize that? We expected everything to be handed to us on a platter.'

'I didn't!' she exclaimed. 'But I wanted you to have the things you craved. I wanted you to have a good life—so that you could do all the things you dream about. You can't be spoiled! You take only what you need, no more.'

'That's true,' I said, moved by this unexpected observation. 'Not many people realize that. I remember how angry my folks got when I came home from Church one Sunday morning and told them enthusiastically that I was a Christian Socialist. I had heard a coal miner speak from the pulpit that morning and his words had struck home. He called himself a Christian Socialist. I immediately became one too. Anyway, it ended up with the usual nonsense . . . the folks saying that Socialists were concerned only with giving away other people's money. "And what's wrong with that?" I demanded. The answer was: "Wait till you've earned your own money, than talk!" That seemed to me a silly argument. What did it matter, I asked myself, whether I earned money or didn't earn money? The point was that the good things of life were unjustly distributed. I was quite willing to eat less, to have less of everything, if those who had little might be better off. Then and there it occurred to me how little one really needs. If you're content you don't need material treasures. . . . Well, I don't know why I got off on that! Oh yes! About taking only what I need. . . . I admit, my desires are great. But I also can do without. Though I talk a lot about food, as you know, I really don't require much. I want just enough to be able to forget about food, that's what I mean. That's normal, don't you think?'

'Of course, of course!'

'And that's why I don't want all the things you seem to think would make me happy, or make me work better. We don't need to live the way we were. I gave in to please *you*. It was wonderful while it lasted, sure. So is Christmas. What I dislike more than anything is this perpetual borrowing and begging, this using people for suckers. You don't enjoy it either, I'm sure of it. Why should we deceive each other about it, then? Why not put an end to it?'

'But I have!'

'You stopped doing it for me, but now you're doing it for your friend Anastasia. Don't lie to me. I know what I'm saying.'

'It's different in her case, Val. She doesn't know how to earn money. She's even more of a child than you.'

'But you're only helping her to remain a child—by aiding her the way you do. I don't say that she's a leech. I say this—you're robbing her of something. Why doesn't she sell her puppets, or her paintings, or her sculpture?'

'*Why?*' She laughed outright at this. 'For the same reason that you can't sell your stories. She's too good an artist, that's why.'

'But she doesn't have to sell her work to art dealers—let her sell direct to individuals. Sell them for a song! Anything to keep afloat. It would do her good. She'd really feel better for it.'

'There you go again! Shows how little you know the world. Val, you couldn't even *give* her work away, that's how things are. If you ever get a book published you'll have to beg people to accept copies gratis. People don't want what's good, I tell you. People like you and Anastasia—or Ricardo—you have to be protected.

'To hell with writing, if that's how it is. . . . But I can't believe it! I'm no writer yet, I'm nothing but a tyro. I may be better than editors think I am, but I've a long way to go yet. When I really know how to express myself people will read me. I don't care how bad the world is. *They will*, I tell you. They won't be able to ignore me.'

'And until then?'

'Until then I'll find some other way of making a living.'

'Selling encyclopaedias? Is that a way?'

'Not much of a one, I admit, but it's better than begging and borrowing. Better than having your wife prostitute herself.'

'Every penny I make I earn,' said Mona heatedly. 'Waiting on tables is no cinch.'

'All the more reason why I should do my share. You don't like to see me selling books. I don't like to see you waiting on tables. If we had more sense we'd be doing other things. Surely there must be some kind of work that isn't degrading.'

'Not for us! We weren't cut out to do the work of the world.'

'Then we ought to learn.' I was getting carried away with my own righteous attitude.

'Val, this is all talk. You know you'll never hold down an honest-to-God job. Never. And I don't want you to. I'd rather see you dead.'

'All right, you win. But Jesus, isn't there something a man like me can do without feeling like a fool or a dolt?' Here a thought which was forming itself on my lips caused me to laugh. I laughed good and hard before I got it out. 'Listen,' I managed to say, 'do you know what I was just thinking? I was thinking that I might make a wonderful diplomat. I ought to be an ambassador to a foreign country—how does that strike you? No, seriously. Why not? I've got brains, and I know how to deal with people.

429

What I don't know I'd make up for with my imagination. Can you see me as ambassador to China?'

Oddly, she didn't think the idea so absurd. Not in the abstract, at any rate.

'Certainly you would make a good ambassador, Val. Why not, as you say? But you'll never get the chance. There are certain doors that will never be opened to you. If men like you were directing the world's affairs we wouldn't be worrying about the next meal—or how to get stories published. That's why I say you don't know the world!'

'Damn it, I do know the world. I know it only too well. But I refuse to make terms with it.'

'It's the same thing.'

'No it isn't! It's the difference between ignorance—or blindness—and aloofness. Something like that. If I didn't know the world how could I be a writer?'

'A writer has his own world.'

'I'll be damned! I never expected you to say that! Now you've got me stumped. . . .' I was silenced for a moment.

'It's dead true what you say,' I continued. 'But it doesn't obviate what I just said. Maybe I can't explain it to you, but I know I'm right. To have your own world, and to live in it, doesn't mean that you are necessarily blind to the real world, so-called. If a writer weren't familiar with the every-day world, if he hadn't been so steeped in it that he revolted against it, he wouldn't have what you call his own world. An artist carries all worlds within him. And he's just as vital a part of *this* world as anyone else. In fact, he's more thoroughly of it and in it than other people for the simple reason that he's *creative*. The world is his medium. Other men are content with their little corner of the world—their own little job, their own little tribe, their own little philosophy, and so on. Damn it, the reason why I'm not a great writer, if you want to know, is because I haven't taken the whole wide world unto me yet. It isn't that I don't know about evil. It isn't that I'm blind to people's viciousness, as you seem to think. It's something other than that. What it is I don't know myself. But I *will* know, eventually. And then I'll become a torch. I'll light up the world. I'll expose it down to its very marrow. . . . But I won't condemn it! I won't because I know too well that I am part and parcel of it, a significant cog in the machinery.' I paused. 'We haven't touched bottom yet, you know. What we've suffered is nothing. Fleabites, that's all. There are worse things to endure than lack of food and such things. I suffered much more when I was sixteen, when I was only *reading* about life. Or else I'm deceiving myself.'

'No, I know what you mean.' She nodded thoughtfully.

'You do? Good. Then you realize that, without participating

in life, you can suffer the pangs of the martyrs. . . . To suffer for others—that's a wonderful kind of suffering. When you suffer because of your own ego, because of lack or because of misdeeds, you experience a kind of humiliation. I loathe that sort of suffering. To suffer with others, or for others, to be all in the same boat that's different. Then one feels enriched. What I dislike about our way of life is that it's so restricted. We ought to be up and about, getting bruised and battered for reasons that matter.'

I went on and on in this vein, sliding from one subject to another, often contradicting myself, uttering the most extravagant statements, then brushing them aside, struggling to get back to terra firma.

It was beginning to happen more and more frequently now, these monologues, these harangues. Perhaps it was because I was no longer writing. Perhaps because I was alone most of the day. Perhaps, too, because I had a feeling that she was slipping out of my hands. There was something desperate about these explosions I was reaching out for something, something which I could never pin down in words. Though I seemed to be censuring her I was really upbraiding myself. The worst of it was that I could never come to any concrete resolution. I saw clearly what we ought not to do, but I could not see what we *should* do. Secretly, I relished the thought of being 'protected'. Secretly I had to admit that she was right—I would never fit in, never make the groove. And so I let it out in talk. I rambled backwards and forwards, rehearsing the glorious days of childhood, the miserable days of adolescence the clownish adventures of youth. It was all fascinating, every iota. If only that man McFarland had been present, with his stenographer! What a story for his magazine! (Later it occurred to me how strange it was that I could talk my life out but could never get it down on paper. The moment I sat down before the machine I became self-conscious. It hadn't occurred to me at that time to use the pronoun I. Why, I wonder? What inhibited me? Perhaps I hadn't yet become the 'I of my I'.)

I not only intoxicated her with these talks, I intoxicated myself. It would be almost dawn before we would fall asleep. Dozing off I had the feeling that I had accomplished something I had gotten it off my chest. *It!* What was that *it?* I couldn't say myself. I knew only this, and from it I seemed to derive an unholy satisfaction: I had assumed my true role.

Perhaps, too, these scenes were just to prove that I could be as exciting and 'different' as that Anastasia whom I was getting tired of hearing about. Perhaps. Possibly I was a wee bit jealous already. Though she had known Anastasia only a few days, you might say, the room was already full of her friend's things. All the latter needed to do now was to move in. Over the beds were two stunning Japanese prints, a Utamaro and a

Hiroshige. On the trunk was a puppet which Anastasia had made expressly for Mona. On the chiffonier was a Russian ikon, another gift from Anastasia. To say nothing of the barbaric bracelets, the amulets, the embroidered moccasins, and so on. Even the perfume she was using—a most pungent one!—Anastasia had given her. (Probably out of Mona's own money.) With Anastasia you never could tell what was what. While Mona was worrying about the clothes her friend needed, the cigarettes, the art materials, et cetera, Anastasia was getting money from home and doling it out to her hangers on. Mona saw nothing incongruous in this. Whatever her friend did was right and natural, even if she stole from her purse. Anastasia did steal now and then. Why not? She stole not for herself but to aid those in distress. She had no scruples or compunctions about such matters. She wasn't a *bourgeoise*, oh no! This word '*bourgeois*' began to pop up frequently now that Anastasia was on the scene. Whatever was no good was '*bourgeois*'. Even caca could be '*bourgeois*', according to Anastasia's way of looking at things. She had such a wonderful sense of humour, when you got to know her. Of course, some people couldn't see it. Some people are just devoid of humour. To wear two different shoes, which Anastasia sometimes did absentmindedly—or did she do it absentmindedly?— that was screamingly funny. Or to carry a douche-bag through the streets. Why wrap such things? Besides, Anastasia never used one herself—it was always for a friend who was in trouble.

The books that were lying around . . . all loaned her by Anastasia. One of them was called *Down There*—by some 'decadent' French writer. It was one of Anastasia's favourites, not because it was 'decadent' but because it told of that extraordinary figure in French history—Gilles de Rais. He had been a follower of Jeanne d'Arc. He had murdered more children— he had depopulated whole villages, in fact. One of the most enigmatic figures in French history. She begged me to glance at it some time. Anastasia had read it in the original. She could read not only French and Italian but German, Portuguese and Russian. Yes, in the convent school she had also learned to play the piano divinely. And the harp.

'Can she blow the trumpet?' I asked derisively.

She gave me the horse laugh. Then followed this revelation: 'She can play the drums, too. But she has to be a little high first.'

'You mean drunk?'

'No, hopped up. *Marijuana*. There's no harm in it. It's not habit forming.'

Whenever this subject came up—drugs—I was sure to get an earful. In Mona's opinion (probably Anastasia's) everyone ought to become acquainted with the effects of different drugs. Drugs weren't half as dangerous as liquor. And the effects were more interesting. Yes, she was going to try them someday. There were lots of people in the Village—respectable people, too—who had drugs. She couldn't see why people were so afraid of drugs. There was that Mexican drug which exalted the sense of colour, for example. Perfectly harmless. We ought to try it sometime. She'd see if she couldn't get some from that phoney poet what's-his-name. She loathed him, he was filthy, and so on, but Anastasia maintained that he was a good poet. And Anastasia ought to know. . . .

'I'm going to borrow one of her poems one day and read it aloud to you. You've never heard anything like it, Val.'

'O.K.' I said, 'but if it stinks I'm going to tell you so.'

'Don't worry! She couldn't write a bad poem if she tried.'

'I know—she's a genius.'

'She is indeed, and I'm not joking. She's a *real* genius.'

I couldn't resist remarking that it was too bad geniuses always had to be freaks.

'There you go! Now you're talking just like everyone else. I've explained to you again and again that she's not like the other freaks in the Village.'

'No, she's a *genuine* freak!'

'She's mad maybe, but like Strindberg, like Dostoievsky, like Blake. . . .'

'That's putting her rather high, isn't it?'

'I didn't say she had their talent. All I mean is that if she's queer she's queer in the same way they were. She's not insane—and she's not a fraud. Whatever she is, it's real. I'll stake my life on it.'

'The only thing I have against her,' I blurted out, 'is that she needs so damned much looking after.'

'That's cruel!'

'Is it? *Look* . . . she got along all right until you came along, didn't she?'

'I told you what a condition she was in when I met her.'

'I know you did, but that doesn't impress me. Maybe if you hadn't nursed her along she would have picked herself up and stood on her own two legs.'

'We're back where we started. How many times must I explain to you that she simply doesn't know how to take care of herself?'

'Then let her learn!'

'How about yourself? Have you learned yet?'

'I was getting along all right until you came along. I not only took care of myself, I took care of a wife and child.'

'That's unfair of you. Maybe you did take care of them, but at what price! You wouldn't want to live that way forever, would you?'

'Of course not! But I'd have found a way out—eventually.'

'*Eventually!* Val, you haven't got too much time. You're in your thirties now—and you have yet to make a name for yourself. Anastasia's just a girl, but see what she's accomplished already.'

'I know. But then she's a genius. . . .'

'Oh, stop it! We won't get anywhere talking this way. Why don't you quit thinking about her? She doesn't interfere with *your* life. why should you interfere with hers? Can't I have *one* friend? Why must you be jealous of *her*? Be just, won't you?'

'All right, let's drop it. But stop talking about her, will you? Then I won't say anything to hurt you.'

Though she hadn't explicitly asked me not to visit The Iron Cauldron I kept away out of consideration for her wishes. I suspected that Anastasia spent much of her time there daily, that during Mona's swings the two were always together somewhere. In roundabout ways I would hear of their visits to the museums and art galleries, to the studios of Village artists, of their expeditions to the waterfront, where Anastasia made sketches of boats and skyline, of the hours they spent at the library doing research. In a way the change was good for Mona. Gave her something new to think about. She had little knowledge of painting, and Anastasia apparently was delighted to act as her mentor. There were veiled references occasionally to the portrait Anastasia intended to make of Mona.

She had never done a realistic portrait of anyone, it seems, and she was especially reluctant to do a resemblance of Mona.

There were days when Anastasia was incapable of doing a thing, when she was prostrate and had to be nursed like an infant. Any trifling event could bring them on, these fits of malaise. Sometimes they occurred because Mona had spoken foolishly or irreverently of one of Anastasia's beloved idols. Modigliani and El Greco, for example, were painters about whom she would allow no one, not even Mona, to say the wrong thing. She was very fond of Utrillo, too, but she did not venerate him. He was 'a lost soul', like herself: still on the 'human' level. Whereas Giotto, Grunewald, the Chinese and the Japanese masters, these were on a different level, represented a higher order. (Not so bad, her taste!) She had no respect whatever for American artists, I gathered. Except for John Marin, who she described as limited but profound, What almost endeared her to me was the discovery that she always carried with her *Alice in Wonderland* and the *Tao Teh Ching*. Later she was to include a volume of Rimbaud. *But of that later.* . . .

I was still making the rounds, or going through the motions. Now and then I sold a set of books without trying. I worked at it only four or five hours a day, always ready to knock off when dinner time came. Usually I would look over the cards and choose a prospect who lived a good distance away, in some run-down suburb, some bleak and barren hole in New Jersey or out on Long Island. I did this partly to kill time and partly to get completely off the track. Always, when heading for some dingy spot (which only a dotty book salesman would think of visiting!), I found that I would be assailed by the most unexpected memories of dear, beloved places I had known as a boy. It was a sort of inverse law of association at work. The more drab and commonplace the milieu, the more bizarre and wonderful were these unbidden associations. I could almost wager that if I headed of a morning for Hackensack or Canarsie, or some rabbit hole on Staten Island, by evening I would find myself at Sheepshead Bay, or Bluepoint, or Lake Pocotopaug. If I didn't have the carfare to make a long haul I would hitch-hike, trusting to luck that I would run into someone—'some friendly face' —who would stake me to a meal and the fare back. I rode with the tide. It didn't matter where I ended up nor when I got home, because Mona would be sure to arrive *after* me. I was writing things down in my head again, not feverishly as before but calmly, evenly, like a reporter or correspondent who had oodles of time and a generous expense account. It was wonderful to let things happen as they would. Now and then sailing along on even keel, I would blow into some outlandish town, pick a shop at random—plumber or undertaker, it made no difference—and launch into my sales talk. I hadn't the least thought of making a sale, nor even of 'keeping my hand in', as they say. No, I was merely curious to see the effect my words would have on a complete nobody. I had the feeling that I was a man descended from another planet. If the poor victim felt disinclined to discuss the merits of our loose-leaf encyclopaedia I would talk *his* language, whatever it was, even if it were nothing but cold corpses. Like that I often found myself lunching with a congenial soul with whom I hadn't a thing in common. The farther away from myself I got the more certain I was to have an inspiration. Suddenly, perhaps in the midst of a sentence, the decision would be made and off I'd scoot. Off searching for that spot which I had known in the past, a very definite, a very marvellous past. The trick was to get back to that precious spot and see if I could reconstitute the being I once was. A queer game—and full of surprises. Sometimes I returned to our room as a little boy dressed in men's clothes. Yes, sometimes I was little Henry through and through, thinking like him, feeling like him, acting like him.

Often, talking to utter strangers out there on the fringe of the world, there would suddenly leap to mind an image of the two of them, Mona and 'Stasia, parading through the Village or swinging through the revolving door of a museum with those crazy puppets in their arms. And then I would say a curious thing to myself—*sotto voce*, of course. I would say, and smile wanly as I did so: '*And where do I come in?*' Moving around on the bleak periphery, among zombies and dodoes, I had gotten the idea that I was cut off. Always, in closing a door, I had the impression that the door was locked behind me, that I would have to find another way to get back. *Get back where?*

There was something ridiculous and grotesque about this double image which obtruded at the most unexpected moments. I saw the two of them garbed in outlandish fashion—'Stasia in her overalls and hobnailed boots and Lady Precious Stream in her fluttering cape, her hair streaming loose like a mane. They were always talking simultaneously, and about utterly different things; they made strange grimaces and wild gesticulations; they walked with two utterly different rhythms, one like an auk, the other like a panther.

Whenever I went deep enough into my childhood I was no longer outside, on the fringe, but snugly inside, like a pip in the fleshy heart of a ripe piece of fruit. I might be standing in front of Annie Meinken's candy shop, in the old 14th Ward, my nose pressed against the window-pane, my eyes a-glitter at the sight of some chocolate-covered soldiers. That abstract noun, 'the world', hadn't yet penetrated my consciousness. Everything was real, concrete, individuated, but neither fully named or wholly delineated. I was and things were. Space was limitless, time was not yet. Annie Meinken was a person who always leaned far over the counter to put things in my hand, who patted me on the head, who smiled at me, who said I was such a good little fellow, and sometimes ran out into the street to kiss me goodbye, though we lived only a few doors away.

I honestly think that at times, out there on the fringe, when I got very quiet and still, I half expected someone to behave towards me exactly as Annie Meinken used to. Maybe I was running off to those far-away places of my childhood just to receive again that piece of candy, that smile, that embarrassing parting kiss. I was indeed an idealist. An incurable one. (An idealist is one who wants to turn the wheels back. He remembers too well what was given him; he doesn't think of what he himself might give. The world sours imperceptibly, but the process begins virtually from the moment one thinks in terms of 'the world'.)

Strange thoughts, strange meanderings—for a book salesman. In my portfolio was locked the key to all human knowledge. Presumably. And wisdom, like Winchester, only forty miles away. Nothing in all the world so dead as this compendium of knowledge. To spiel it off about the foramenifera, about the infra red rays, about the bacteria that lie bedded in every cell what a baboon I must have been! Naturally a Picodiribibi would have done far better! So might a dead jackass with a phonograph in its guts. To read in the subway, or on an open trolley, about Prust the founder of Prussia—what a profitless pastime! Far better, if one *had* to read, to listen to that madman who said: 'How sweet it is to hate one's native land and eagerly await its annihilation.'

Yes, in addition to the dummies, the bindings, and all the other paraphernalia which crammed my brief-case, I usually carried a book with me, a book so removed from the tenor of my daily life that it was more like a tattoo mark on the sole of a convict's left foot. 'WE HAVE NOT YET DECIDED THE QUESTION OF THE EXISTENCE OF GOD AND YOU WANT TO EAT!' A sentence like this jumping out of a book in the dreary waste-land could decide the whole course of my day. I can see myself all over again slamming the book shut, jumping up like a startled buck, and exclaiming aloud: '*Where in hell are we?*' And then bolting. It night have been the edge of a swamp where they had let me off, it might have been the beginning of one of those interminable rows of all-look-alike suburban homes or the very portals of an insane asylum. No matter—on, on, head down, jaws working feverishly, grunts, squeals of delight, ruminations, discoveries, illuminations. Because of that blitz phrase. Especially the 'and you want to eat!' part of it. It was ages before I discovered who had originated this marvellous exclamation. All I knew then, all that mattered, was that I was back in Russia, that I was with kindred spirits, that I was completely possessed by such an esoteric proposition as the debatable existence of God.

Years later, did I say? Why yes—only yesterday, so to speak, I found out who the author was. At the same time I learned that another man, a contemporary, had written thus of his nation, the great Russian nation: 'We belong to the number of those nations which, so to speak, do not enter into the structure of mankind but exists only in order to teach the world an important lesson of some sort.'

But I am not going to speak of yesterday or the day before yesterday. I am going to speak of a time which has no beginning nor end, a time moreover which with all the other kinds of time that filled the empty spaces of my days. . . .

The way of ships, and of men in general, is the zigzag path. The drunkard moves in curves, like the planets. Bu the man who has no destination moves in a time and space continuum which is uniquely his own and in which God is ever present. 'For the time being'—inscrutable phrase! he is always there. There with the grand cosmocrator, so to speak. Clear? Very well, it is day, let us say. '*And you want to eat?*' Instanter the stars begin to chime, the reindeer paw the turf; their blue icicles sparkle in the noonday sun. Whooshing it through the Nevsky Prospekt, It make my way to the inner circle, the brief-case under my arm. In my hand is a little bag of candy, a gift from Annie Meinken. A solemn question has just been propounded:

'*We have not yet decided the question of the existence of God. . . .*'

It is at this point I always enter. I'm on my own time now. God's time, in other words. Which is always 'for the time being.' To hear me you would think I were a member of the Holy Synod —the Holy Philharmonic Synod. It isn't necessary for me to tune in: I've been in tune since the dawn of time. Utter clarity is what marks my performance. I am of the order whose purpose is not to teach the world a lesson but to explain that school is over.

The comrades are relaxed and at ease. No bomb will go off until I give the order. On my right is Dostoievsky; on my left the Emperor Anathema. Every member of the group has distinguished himself in some spectacular manner. I am the only one 'without portfolio'. I am the *Uitlander*; I hail from 'the fringe', that is to say, from the trouble-bubble cauldron.

'Comrades, it is said that a problem confronts us. . . .' (I always begin with this stock phrase.) I look about me, calm, self-possessed, before launching into my *plaidoyer*. 'Comrades, let us rivet our most concentrated attention for a moment on that wholly ecumenical question——'

'*Which is?*' barks the Emperor Anathema.

'Which is nothing less than this: If there were no God, would we be here?'

Above the cries of *Rot!* and *Rubbish!* I follow with ease the sound of my own voice intoning the sacred texts buried in my heart. I am at ease because I have nothing to prove. I have only to recite what I learned by rote in off moments. That we are together and privileged to discuss the existence of God, this in itself is conclusive evidence for me that we are basking in the sunshine of His presence. I do not speak 'as if' He were present, I speak 'because' He is present. I am back in that eternal sanctuary where the word 'food' always comes up. I am back because of that.

'*And you want to eat?*'

I address the comrades passionately now. 'Why not?' I begin. 'Do we insult our Maker by eating what He has provided for us? Do you think He will vanish because we fill our bellies? Eat, I beg you. Eat heartily! The Lord our God has all time in which to reveal Himself. You pretend that you wish to decide the matter of His existence. Useless, dear comrades, it was decided long ago, before there even was a world. Reason alone informs us that if there be a problem there must be something real which brings it to birth. It is not for us to decide whether or not God exists, it is for God to say whether or not *we* exist' (*Dog!* Have

438

you anything to say?' I shouted in the Emperor Anathema's ear.)
'Whether to eat or not before deciding the issue, is *that*, I ask
you, a metaphysical question? Does a hungry man debate whether he is to eat or not? We are all famished: we hunger and thirst
for that which gave us life, else we would not be assembled here.
To imagine that by giving a mere Yes or No the grand problem
will be settled for eternity is sheer madness. We have not. . . .'
(I paused and turned to the one on my right. 'And you, Fyodor
Mihailovich, have you nothing to say?) We have not come together to settle an absurd problem. We are here, comrades, because outside this room, *in the world*, as they call it, there is no
place in which to mention the Holy Name. We are the chosen
ones, and we are united ecumenically. *Does God wish to see
children suffer?* Such a question may be asked here. *Is evil necessary?* That too may be asked. It may also be asked whether we
have a right to expect a Paradise here and now, or whether
eternality is preferable to immortality. We may even debate
whether Our Lord Jesus Christ is of one divine nature only or
of two consubstantially harmonious natures, human and divine.
We have all suffered more than is usual for mortal beings to
endure. We have all achieved an appreciable degree of emanci-
pation. Some of you have revealed the depths of the human soul
in a manner and to a degree never before heard of. We are all
living outside our time, the forerunners of a new era, of a new
order of mankind. We know that nothing is to be hoped for on
the present world level. The end of historical man is upon us.
The future will be in terms of eternity, and of freedom, and of
love. The resurrection of man will be ushered in with our aid;
the dead will rise from their graves clothed in radiant flesh and
sinew, and we shall have communion, real everlasting communion, with all who once were: with those who made history
and with those who had no history. Instead of myth and fable
we shall have everlasting reality. All that now passes for science
will fall away; there will be no need to search for the clue to
reality because all will be real and durable, naked to the eye of
the soul, transparent as the waters of Shiloh. Eat, I beg you, and
drink to your heart's content. Taboos are not God's making.
Nor murder and lust. Nor jealousy and envy. Though we are
assembled here as men, we are bound through the divine spirit.
When we take leave of one another we shall return to the world
of chaos, to the realm of space which no amount of activity can
exhaust. We are not of this world, nor are we yet of the world to
come, except in thought and spirit. Our place is on the threshold
of eternity; our function is that of prime movers. It is our
Privilege to be crucified in the name of freedom. We shall water
our graves with our own blood. No task can be too great for us to
assume. We are the true revolutionaries since we do not baptize

439

with the blood of others but with our own blood, freely shed. We shall create no new covenants, impose no new laws, establish no new government. We shall permit the dead to bury the dead. The quick and the dead will soon be separated. Life eternal is rushing back to fill the empty cup of sorrow. Man will rise from his bed of ignorance and suffering with a song on his lips. He will stand forth in all the radiance of his godhood. Murder in every form will disappear forever. *For the time being. . . .*

The moment this inscrutable phrase rose to my lips the inner music, the concordance, ceased. I was back in double rhythm again, aware of what I was doing, analyzing my thoughts, my motives, my deeds, I could hear Dostoievsky speaking, but I was no longer there with him. I was getting only the overtones. What's more, I could shut him off whenever I pleased. I was no longer running in that parallel timeless time. Now the world was indeed empty, drab, woebegone. Chaos and cruelty ran hand in hand. I was as grotesque and ridiculous now as those two lost sisters who were presumably running through the Village with puppets in their arms.

By the time night falls, and I start to trek it back, an overpowering loneliness has gripped me. It does not surprise me in the least to find, on returning to the room, a telephone message from Mona saying that her dear 'friend' is ill and that she must stay with her the night. Tomorrow it will be another story, and the day after another.

Everything is happening to 'Stasia at once. One day she is ordered to move because she talks too loudly in her sleep; another day, in another room, she is visited by a ghost and forced to flee in the night. On another occasion a drunkard attempts to rape her. Or else she is grilled by a plain clothes man at three in the morning. It is inevitable that she should think of herself as a marked woman. She takes to sleeping in the daytime and roaming the streets by night; she passes long hours at the cafeteria which never closes, writing her poems on the marble-topped table, a sandwich in her hand and a plate of untouched food beside her. Some days she is the Slav, speaking with a genuine Slavic accent: other days she is the boy-girl from Montana's snowy peaks, the nymph who must stradle a horse, even if only in Central Park. Her talk becomes more and more incoherent, and she knows it, but in Russian, as she always says it, 'nothing matters'. At times she refuses to use the toilet—insists on doing her little jobs in the chamber pot, which of course she forgets to empty. As for the portrait of Mona which she had begun, it now resembles the work of a maniac. (It is Mona herself who confesses this.) She is almost beside herself, Mona. Her friend is deteriorating under her own eyes. But it will pass. All will be well again, provided she stands by her faithfully, nurses her, soothes

440

her tortured spirit. wipes her ass, if need be. But she must never allow her to feel that she is deserted. What matter, she asks, if she has to remain three or four nights a week with her friend? Is not Anastasia the all in all?

'You trust me, don't you, Val?'

I nod a silent assent. (It's not an 'ecumenical' question).

When the tune switches, when I learn from her own lips that it was not Anastasia she spent the night with but her own mother—mothers too get ill—I know what any idiot would have known long before, viz., that there's something rotten in Denmark.

What harm, I ask myself, would there be in talking to her mother—over the telephone? None whatever. The truth is always enlightening.

So, impersonating the lumber king, I pick up the receiver and, amazed that it *is* a mother speaking to me, I inquire in the most casual tone of voice if Mona is there, if so, I would like to talk to her.

She is not there. Very definitely not.

'Have you seen her lately?' (Still the non-committal gentleman inquiring after a lady fair.)

Not a sign of her in months. The poor woman sounds distressed. She forgets herself to the extent of asking me, a perfect stranger, if her daughter could possibly be dead. She virtually implores me to inform her should I by chance get wind of her daughter's whereabouts.

'But why don't you write to her husband?'

'*Her husband?*'

There follows a prolonged silence in which nothing registers except the ocean's deep hum. Then, in a weak, toneless voice, as if addressing blank space, comes this: 'So she really did get married?'

'Why certainly she's married. I know her husband well. . . .'

'Excuse me,' comes the far off voice, followed by the click of the receiver being hung up.

I allow several nights to pass before broaching the subject to the guilty one. I wait until we are in bed, the lights out. Then I nudge her gently.

'What is it? What are you poking me for?'

'I was talking to your mother yesterday.'

No answer.

'Yes, and we had quite a long conversation. . . .'

Still no answer.

'The funny thing is, she says she hasn't seen you for ages. She thinks maybe you're dead.'

How much longer can she hold out? I wonder. Just as I am about to let out another mouthful I feel her spring to a sitting

441

position. Then comes one of those drawn-out uncontrollable fits, of laughter, the sort that makes me shudder inwardly. Between spasms she blurts out: '*My mother!* Ho ho! You were talking to my mother! Hah, hah, hah! It's too good, just too good for words. Hee, hee, hee! Val, you poor sap, my mother is dead. I have no mother. Ho ho ho!'

'Calm yourself!' I beg her.

But she can't stop laughing. It's the funniest, the craziest thing she's ever heard.

'Listen, didn't you tell me you stayed with her the other night, that she was very ill? Was it your mother or wasn't it?'

Peals of laughter.

'Maybe it was your step-mother then?'

'You mean my aunt.'

'Your aunt then, if that's who your mother is.'

More laughter.

'It couldn't have been my aunt because she knows I'm married to you. It was probably a neighbour. Or my sister maybe. It would be like her to talk that way.'

'But why would they want to deceive me?'

'Because you were a stranger. If you had said you were my husband, instead of impersonating someone else, they might have told you the truth.'

'It didn't sound to me as if your aunt—or your sister, as you say—were putting it on. It sounded thoroughly genuine.'

'You don't know them.'

'Damn it all, then maybe it's time I got acquainted with them.'

Suddenly she looked serious, very serious.

'Yes,' I continued, 'I've a good notion to run over there one evening and introduce myself.'

She was angry now. 'If you ever do a thing like that, Val, I'll never speak to you again. I'll run away, that's what I'll do.'

'You mean that you don't ever want me to meet your folks?'

'Exactly. Never!'

'But that's childish and unreasonable. Even if you did tell me a few lies about your family. . . .'

'I've never admitted anything of the kind,' she broke in.

'Come, come, don't talk like that. You know damned well that that's the only reason why you don't want me to meet them.' I allowed a significant pause to intervene, then said: 'Or may be you fear that I *will* find your real mother. . . .'

She was angrier than ever now but the word mother got her to laughing again.

'You won't believe me, will you? Very well, one day I'll take you there myself. I promise you.'

'That wouldn't do any good. I know you too damned well.

The stage would be all set for me. No sir, if there's any going I go alone.'

'Val, I warn you . . . if you dare do that. . . .'

I interrupted her. 'If I ever do it you won't know about it.'

'So much the worse,' she answered. 'You could never do that without my hearing about it sooner or later.'

She was pacing up and down now, puffing nervously at the cigarette which dangled from her lips. She was growing frantic, it seemed to me.

'Look here,' I said finally, 'forget about it. I'll. . . .'

'Val, promise me you won't do it. Promise me!'

I was silent a few moments.

She got down on her knees beside me, looked up at me imploringly.

'All right,' I said, as if reluctantly, 'I promise.'

I hadn't the slightest intention, of course, of keeping my word. In fact, I was more than ever determined to get to the bottom of the mystery. However, there was no need to hurry. I had the feeling that when the right moment came I would find myself face to face with her mother—and it would be her *real* mother.

17

'AND NOW, FINALLY, I feel urged to name once more those to whom I owe practically everything: Goethe and Nietzsche. Goethe gave me method, Nietzsche the questioning faculty, and if I were asked to find a formula for my relation to the latter I should say that I had made of his 'outlook' (*Ausblik*) an 'over-look' (*Uberblick*). But Goethe was, without knowing it, a disciple of Leibnitz in his whole mode of thought. And, therefore, that which has at last (and to my own astonishment) taken shape in my hands I am able to regard and, despite the misery and disgust of these years, proud to call *a German philosophy*.' (Blanken-burg am Harz, December 1922.)

These lines from the preface to *The Decline of the West* are to haunt me for many a year. It happens that I have taken to read-ing the book during the lonely vigils which have begun. Every evening after dinner I return to the room, make myself snug and cosy, then settle down to gnaw at this immense tome in which the panorama of human destiny is unrolled. I am fully aware that the study of this great work represents another momentous event in my life. For me it is not a philosophy of history nor a 'morphological' creation, but a world-poem. Slowly, attentively, savouring each morsel as I chew it, I burrow deeper and deeper. I drown myself in it. Often I break the siege by pacing to and fro, to and fro. Sometimes I find myself sitting on the bed, staring at the wall. I look right through the wall: I look deep into a past which is alive and fathomless. Occasionally a line or phrase comes with such impact that I am forced out of the nest, flung headlong into the street, where I wander like a somnambulist. Now and then I find myself in Joe's restaurant at Borough Hall, ordering a big meal; with each mouthful I seem to be swallowing another mighty epoch of the past. Unconsciously I stoke the furnace in order to gird myself for another wrestling bout with the omnivorous one. That I am of the borough of Brooklyn, one of the natives, seems preposterous. How can a mere Brooklyn boy ingest all this? Where is his passport to the distant realms of science, philosophy, history, et cetera? All that this Brooklyn boy knows has been acquired through osmosis. I am the lad who hated to study. I am the charming fellow who consistently rejected all systems of thought. Like a cork tossed about on an angry sea I follow in the wake of this morphological monster. It mystifies me that I should be able to follow him even distantly. Am I following or am I being sucked under by a vortex? What is it that enables me to read with understanding and delight? Whence the training, the discipline, the percipience which this monster demands? His thought is music to my ears; I recognize all the hidden melodies. Though I am reading him in English, it is as if I were reading the language he wrote in. His vehicle is the German language, which I thought I had forgotten. But I see I have forgotten nothing, not even the curricula I once planned to follow but never did.

From Nietzsche the questioning faculty! That little phrase sets me dancing. . . .

Nothing is so inspiring to one who is trying to write as to come upon a thinker, a thinker who is also a poet, a thinker who looks for the soul which animates things. I see myself again as a mere youth, asking the librarian, or the minister sometimes, to lend me certain profound works—'deep' I called them then. I see the astonished look on their faces when I mention the titles of these formidable books. And then the inevitable—'But why do you want *those* books?' to which I always rejoined: 'And why shouldn't I want *those* books?' That I was too young, that I hadn't read enough to cope with such works, meant nothing to me. It was my privilege to read what I wanted *when* I wanted. Was I not a born American, a free citizen? What did age matter? Later, however, I had to secretly admit that I did not understand what these 'deep' works were about. Or rather, I understood that I did not want the 'abscesses' whicd accompanied the knowledge they secreted. How I yearned to grapple with the mysteries! I wanted all that had soul in it and meaning. But I also demanded that the author's style match the mystery he was illuminating How many books possess this quality? I met my Waterlooo at the very threshold of life. I retained my ignorance, dreaming that it was bliss.

The questioning faculty! That I never abandoned. As is known, the habit of questioning everything leads one to become either a sage or a sceptic. It also leads to madness. Its real virtue, however, consists in this, that it makes one think for himself, makes one return to the source.

Was it so strange that in reading Spengler I began to appreciate all over again what truly wonderful thinkers we were as boys? Considering our age and our limited experience of life, we nevertheless managed to propound to one another the most profound and vital questions. We tackled them manfully, too, with our whole being. Years of schooling destroyed the art. Like chimpanzees, we learned to ask only the right questions—the ones the teachers could answer. It is on this sort of chicanery that the whole social structure is reared. *'The university of life!'* Only the desperate ones choose this curriculum. Even the artist is apt to go astray, because he too is obliged, sooner or later, to observe on which side his bread is buttered.

The Decline of the West! I can never forget the thrill which ran up my spine when I first heard this title. It was like Ivan Karamazov saying—'I want to go to Europe. Maybe I know that I shall go only to a cemetery, but it will be to the dearest of cemeteries.'

For many years I had been aware that I was participating in a general decline. We all knew it, all felt it, only some succeeded in forgetting about it more quickly than others. What we hadn't understood so clearly, most of us, was that we were part of this very 'West,' that the West included not only Europe but North America. To us America had always been a chancy place—one day hot, one day cold, one day barren, one day fertile. In short, according to how you struck it, it was either all myrrh and frankincense or plain undiluted horse manure. It was not our way to think in terms of historical destiny. Our history had begun only a few years back—and what there was of it was dull and boring. When I say 'we' I mean we boys, we youths, we young men who were trying to sprout long pants under our skirts. Mamma's boys, all of us, and if we had a destiny it was to become cracker-jack salesmen, cigar store clerks or chain store managers. The wild ones joined the Army or Navy. The incorrigible ones got themselves safely stowed away in Dannemora or Sing Sing. No one pictures himself as a plodding engineer, plumber, mason, carpenter, farmer, lumberman. One could be a trolley car conductor one day and an insurance agent the next day. And tomorrow or the day after one might wake up and find himself an alderman. Order, discipline, purpose, goal, destiny? Unknown terms. America was a free country, and nothing one did could ruin it—ever. That was *our* world outlook. As for an *'Uberblick'*, that led to the bughouse. *'What are you reading, Henry?'* If I showed the book to my questioner he was sure to say: 'You'll go nuts reading that sort of junk.' This 'junk', incidentally, was usually the world's choice literature. No matter. To 'them' or 'us' such books were of prehistoric vintage. No, no one was thinking consciously and deliberately in terms of a world decline. The decline was nonetheless real, and it was hollowing us out. It revealed itself in unsuspected ways.

For example, nothing was worth getting excited about. Nothing. Or, one job was as good as another, one man the equal of another. And so on. All boloney, naturally.

Nietzsche, my first great love, hadn't seemed very German to me. He didn't even seem Polish. He was like a fresh-minted coin. But Spengler immediately impressed me as being German to the core. The more abstruse and recondite his language ,the easier I followed him. A pre-natal language, his. A lullaby. What is erroneously called his 'pessimism' struck me as nothing more than cold Teutonic realism. The Teutons have been singing the swan song ever since they entered the ranks of history. They have always confounded truth with death. Let us be honest. In the whole metaphysic of Europe has there ever been any truth but this sad German truth which, of course, is a lie? Suddenly, thanks to this historical maestro, we glean that the truth of death need not be sad, particularly when, as happens, the whole 'civilized' world is already part of it. Suddenly we are asked to look into the depths of the tomb with the same zeal and joy with which we first greeted life.

'*Alles Vergangliche ist nur ein Gleichnis.*'

Try as I might, I could never finish a chapter without succumbing to the temptation to glance at the succeeding chapters. The headings of these chapters obsessed me. They were enchanting. They belonged to a *grimoire* rather than to a philosophy of history. The Magian World: Act and Portrait: On the Form of the Soul: Physiognomic and Systematic: Historic Pseudomorphoses. . . . And the last chapter of all, what else could it be but MONEY? Had anyone ever written of Money in this fascinating language? The modern mystery: MONEY.

From 'The Meaning of Numbers' to 'Money'—a thousand large, dense pages, all written out in three years. A bomb that failed to go off because another bomb (World War One) had blown the fuse.

And what footnotes! To be sure, the Germans love footnotes. Was it not about the same time that Otto Rank, one of the twelve disciples of Freud, was busy appending his fascinating footnotes to his studies of the Incest Motif, Don Juan, Art and Artist?

Anyway, from the footnotes to the index in the back of the book—like a journey from Mecca to Lhasa, *on foot*. Or from Delphi to Timbuctoo, *and back again*. Who but Spengler, moreover, would have grouped such figures as Pythagoras, Mohammed and Cromwell? Who other than this man would have looked for homologies in Buddhism, Stoicism and Socialism? who had dared to speak of the glorious Renaissance as a '*contretemps*'?

Wailing the streets, my head spinning with all the dazzling references, I get to thinking of similar periods, periods in the distant past, it now seems, when I was completely absorbed in books. One period especially comes back to me vividly. It is the period when I first got to know Maxie Schnadig. There he is, dressing the show window of a haberdashery store not far from Kosciusko Street, where he lived. *Hello Dostoievsky! Hoorah!* Back and forth through the winter snows—with Dostoievsky, Pushkin, Tolstoy, Andreyev, Chekov, Artzibashev . . . *And Oblomov!* A new calendar of time for me. New friends, new perspectives, new sorrows. One of these new friends proves to be none other than Maxie's cousin. He is a man much older than us, a physician from Novgorod. That is to say a Russian Jew, but a Russian just the same. And because he is bored with family life he suggests to us that we form a little study group, the three of us, to while the evenings away. And what do we choose to study? The sociology of Lester F. Ward. But Lester F. Ward is only a spring-board for the good doctor. He literally bounces into those subjects which represent the missing links in our lamentable scheme of knowledge—magic, symbols, herbology, crystalline forms, the prophets of the old Testament, Karl Marx, the technique of revolution, and so on. A samovar always on the boil, tasty sandwiches, smoked herring, caviar, fine teas. A skeleton dangling from the chandelier. He is happy that we are acquainted with the Russian dramatists and novelists, delighted that we have read Kropotkin and Bakunin, *but*—do we know the real Slavic philosophers and thinkers? He reels off a string of names which are utterly unknown to us. We are given to understand that in all Europe there never were such daring thinkers as the Russians. According to him, they were all visionaries and Utopists. Men who questioned everything. Revolutionaries all of them, even the reactionary ones. Some had been fathers of the Church, some peasants, some criminals, some veritable saints. But they had all endeavoured to formulate a new world, usher in a new way of life 'And if you consult the Encyclopaedia Britannica,' I recall him saying, 'you will discover nothing about them. They are not even mentioned.' What these Russians were striving for, he emphasized, was not the creation of a rich cultural life but 'the perfect life'. He would discourse at length about the great wealth of the Russian language, how superior it was even to the language of the Elizabethans. He would read Pushkin aloud to us in his own tongue, then throw the book down with a sigh and exclaim: 'What's the use? We're in America now. A *kindergarten.*' He was bored, supremely bored with the American scene. His patients were nearly all Jewish. but American Jews, and he had little in common with them. To him America meant apathy. He missed the talk of revolution. To be truthful, I think he also missed the horrors of the pogrom. He felt that he was rotting away in the hollow tomb of democracy. 'Sometime you must ask me about Fedorov,' he remarked once. But we never got that far. We got bogged down in Lester F. Ward's sociology. It was too much for Maxie Schnadig. Poor Maxie was already poisoned by the American virus. He wanted to go ice-skating, wanted to play hand-ball, tennis, golf. And so, after a few months the study group dissolved. Never once since have I heard mention of Lester F. Ward. Nor have I ever again seen a copy of this great work. As compensation, perhaps, I took to reading Herbert Spencer. More sociology! Then one day I fell upon his *Autobiography*, and I devoured it. There was indeed a *mind*. A lame one, but it served its purpose. A mind dwelling alone on an arid plateau. Not a hint of Russia, of revolution, of the Marquis de Sade, of love. Not a hint of anything but problems. 'The brain rules, because the soul abdicates.'

'As soon as Life is fatigued' says Spengler, 'as soon as a man is put on to the artificial soil of great cities—which are intellectual worlds to themselves—and needs a theory in which suitably to present Life to himself, morale turns into a *problem*.'

There are phrases, sentences, sometimes whole paragraphs from *The Decline of the West* which seem to be engraved in my brain-pan. The first reading went deep. Since then I have read and re-read, copied and re-copied the passages which obsess me. Here are a few at random, as inexpungible as the letters of the alphabet. . . .

'To bring up, out of the web of world-happening, a millenium of organic culture-history as an entity and person, and to grasp the conditions of its inmost spirituality—such is the aim.'

'Only the insight that can penetrate into the metaphysical is capable of experiencing in dates the *symbols* of that which happened, and so of elevating an Incident into a Destiny. And he who is to himself a Destiny (like Napoleon) does not need this insight, since between himself as a fact and the other facts there is a harmony of metaphysical rhythm which gives his decision their dreamlike certainty.'

'To look at the world, no longer from the heights as Aeschylus, Plato, Dante and Goethe did, but from the standpoint of oppressive actualities is to *exchange the bird's perspective for the frog's*.'

'The classical spirit, with its oracles and its omens, wants only to *know* the future, but the Westerner would *shape it*. *The Third Kingdom is the Germanic ideal*. From Joachim of Floris to Nietzsche and Ibsen . . . every great man has linked his life to an eternal *morning*. Alexander's life was a wonderous paroxysm, a dream which conjured up the Homeric ages from the grave. Napoleon's life was an immense toil, not for himself nor for France, but for the Future.'

'From the high and distant standpoint it matters very little what "truths" thinkers have managed to formulate in words within their respective schools, for, here as in every great art, it is the schools, conventioned and repertory of forms that are the basic elements. Infinitely more important than the answers are the *questions*—the choice of them, the inner form of them. . . .'

'With the Name comes a new world-outlook. . . . The Name grazes the *meaning* of consciousness and the *source* of fear alike. The world is not merely existent, a secret is felt in it. . . . Man names that *which is enigmatic*. It is the beast that knows no enigmas. . . . *With the name the step is taken from the everyday physical of the beast to the metaphysical of man*. It was the greatest turning-point in the history of the human soul.'

'A true system of thoughts emphatically cannot exist, for no sign can replace actuality. Profound and honest thinkers are always brought to the conclusion that all cognition is conditioned *a priori* by its own form and can never reach that which the words mean. . . . And this *ignorabimus* is in conformity also with the intuition of every true sage, that abstract principles of life are acceptable only as figures of speech, trite maxims of daily use underneath which life flows, as it had always flowed, onward. Race, in the end, is stronger than languages, and thus it is that, under all the great names, it has been thinkers—who are personalities—and not systems, which are mutable, that have taken effect upon life.'

'For the sake of the machine, human life becomes precious. Work becomes the great word of ethical thinking: in the eighteenth century it loses its derogatory implication in all languages. The machine words and forces the man to co-operate. The entire Culture reaches a degree of activity such that the earth trembles under it. . . . And these machines become in their forms less and ever less human, more ascetic, mystic, esoteric. . . Man has felt the machine to be devilish, and rightly. It signifies in the eyes of the believer the deposition of God. It delivers sacred Causality over to man and by him, with a sort of foreseeing omniscience, is set in motion, silent and irresistible. . . .'

'*A power can be overthrown only by another power*, not by a principle, and no power that can confront money is left but this one. Money is overthrown and abolished only by blood. *Life* is alpha and omega, the cosmic onflow in microcosmic form. It is *the* fact of facts within the world-as-history. . . . Ever in History it is life and life only—race-quality, the triumph of the will-to-power—and not the vistory of truths, discoveries, or money that signifies. *World-history is the world court*, and it has ever decided in favour of the stronger, fuller, and more self-assured life—decreed to it, namely, the right to exist, regardless of whether its rights would hold before a tribunal of waking-consciousness. Always it has sacrificed truth and justice to might and race, and passed doom of death upon men and peoples in whom truth was more than deeds, and justice than power. And so the drama of a high Culture—that wondrous world of deities, arts, thoughts, battles, cities—closes with the return of the pristine facts of the blood eternal that is one and the same as the ever encircling cosmic flow. . . .'

'For us, however, whom a Destiny has placed in this Culture and at this moment of its development—the moment when money is celebrating its last victories, and the Caesarium that is to succeed approaches with quiet, firm step—our direction, willed and obligatory at once, is set for us within narrow limits, and on any other terms life is not worth the living. We have not the freedom to reach to this or to that, but the freedom to do the necessary or to do nothing. . . .'

'What really signifies is not *that* an individual or a people is "in condition", well-nourished and fruitful, but *for what* he or it is so. . . . It is only with the coming of the Civilization, when the whole form-world begins to ebb, that mere life-preserving begins to outline itself, nakedly and insistently—this is the time when the banal assertion that 'hunger and love' are the driving forces of life ceases to be ashamed of itself; when life comes to mean, not a waxing in strength for the task, but a matter of "happiness of the greatest number", of comfort and ease, of "panem et circenses"; and when, in the place of grand politics, we have economic politics as an end in itself. . . .'

I could go on and on, do as I have done time and again—quote and quote until a veritable handbook accumulates. Almost twenty-five years since I made the first reading! And the magic is still there. For those who pride themselves on being always in the van, all that I have quoted, as well as that lies between the quotes, is now 'old hat'. What matter? For me Oswald Spengler is still alive and kicking. He enriched and uplifted me. As did Nietzsche, Dostoievsky, Elie Faure.

Perhaps I am somewhat of a juggler, since I am able to balance such incongruous ponderables as *The Decline of the West* and the *Tao Teh Ching*. The one is made of granite or porphyry and weighs a ton; the other is light as a feather and runs through my fingers like water. In eternity, where they meet and have their being, they cancel one another out. An exile like Hermann Hesse understands this sort of juggling perfectly. In the book called *Siddhartha* he presents two Buddhas, the known and the unknown. Each perfect in his way. They are opposites—in the sense of Systematic and Physiognomic. They do not destroy one another. They meet and part. Buddha is one of those names which 'grazes the *meaning* of consciousness'.' The real Buddhas are without name. In short, the known and the unknown balance perfectly. Jugglers understand. . . .

When I think of it now, how remarkably this '*Untergang*'

music corresponded with my 'underground' life! Strange, too, that virtually the only person with whom I could then speak of Spengler was Osiecki. It must have been in Joe's restaurant, during one of my *promenades nocturnes*, that we met again. He had not lost that weird gnomic grin—the teeth all loose and rattling louder than ever. As far as 'actualities' went he was still off the beam. But he could take in the Spenglerian music with the same ease and understanding as he did the music of Dohnanyi for whom he had conceived a passion. To while away the long, weary nights he had taken to reading in bed. All that related to the driving number, engineering, architecture (in Spengler) he had swallowed like pre-digested food. And *money*, I should add. Of this subject he had uncanny knowledge. Strange to what ends the 'unfit' develop their faculties! Listening to Osiecki, I used to think how sweet it would be to be locked up in the bug-house with him—and Oswald Spengler. What marvellous discussions we would have held! Out in the cold world all this grand music went to waste. If critics and scholars were interested in the Spenglerian view of things it was not at all in the way we were. For them it was but another bone to gnaw at. A juicier bone than usual, perhaps, but a bone nevertheless. To us it was life, the elixir of life. We got drunk on it every time we met. And of course we developed our own mutual 'morphological' sign language. With each other we could cover huge tracts of thought in jig time, because of this code language. As soon as a stranger entered the discussion we got bogged down. To him our talk was not only unintelligible, it was sheer nonsense.

With Mona I developed another kind of language. By dint of listening to my monologues she soon picked up the glittering tag ends, all the (to her) 'fantastic' terminology—definitions, meanings, and, so to speak, 'morphological excreta'. She often read a page or two while sitting on the stool. Just sufficient to emerge with a mouthful of phrases and outlandish references. In short, she had learned to bounce the ball back to me, which was pleasant and (for me) stimulating. All I ever required of a listener, when wound up, was a semblance of understanding. Long practice had developed in me the art of instructing my listener in the fundamentals, of giving him just enough of a stance to permit me to wash over him like a fountain. Thus at one and the same time I instructed or informed him—and mystified him. When I sensed that he felt himself on firm ground I would sweep the ground away from him. (Does not the Zen master endeavour to rob his disciple of every foothold he has ever had—in order to supply him with one that is really no foothold?)

With Mona this was infuriating. Naturally. But then I would have the delicious opportunity of reconciling my contradictory statements; this meant expansion, elaboration, distillation, condensation. In this wise I stumbled on some remarkable conclusions, not only about Spengler's dicta but about thought in general, about the thought process itself. Only the Chinese, it seemed to me, had understood and appreciated 'the game of thought'. Passionate as I was about Spengler, the truth of his utterances never seemed so important to me as the wonderful play of his thought. . . . Today I think what a pity it is that, as a frontispiece to this phenomenal work, there is not reproduced the horoscope of the author. A clue of this sort is absolutely requisite to an understanding of the character and nature of this intellectual giant. When one thinks of the significance with which Spengler weights the phrase—'man as intellectual nomad'—one begins to realize that, in pursuing his high task, he came close to being a modern Moses. How much more frightful is *this* wilderness in which our 'intellectual nomad' is forced to dwell! No Promised Land in sight. Nothing on the horizon but empty symbols.

That gulf between the dawn man, who participated mystically, and contemporary man, who is unable to communicate except through sterile intellect, can only be bridged by a new type of man, the man with a cosmic consciousness. The sage, the prophet, the visionary, they all spoke in Apocalyptic terms. From earliest times the 'few' have been attempting to break through. Some undoubtedly have broken through—and will remain forever outside the rat trap.

A morphology of history, valid, exciting, inspiring though it may be, is still a death science. Spengler was not concerned with what lies beyond history. *I am. Others are.* Even if Nirvana be only a word, it is a pregnant word, it contains a promise. That 'secret' which lies at the heart of the world may yet be dragged into the open. Even ages ago it was pronounced to be an 'Open' secret.

If the solution to life is the living of it, then let us live, live more abundantly! The masters of life are not found in books. They are not *historical* figures. They are situated in eternity, and they beseech us unceasingly to join them, in eternity.

At my elbow, as I write these lines, is a photograph torn from a book, a photograph of an unknown Chinese sage *who is living today*. Either the photographer did not know who he was or he withheld his name. We know only that he is from Peking: that is all the information which is vouchsafed. When I turn my head to look at him, it is as though he were right here in my room. He is more alive—even in a photograph—than anyone I know. He is not simply 'a man of spirit'—he is all spirit. He is Spirit itself, I might say. All this is concentrated in his expression. The look which he gives forth is completely joyous and luminous. It says without equivocation: 'Life is bliss!'

Do you suppose that from the eminence on which he is poised—serene, light as a bird, with a wisdom all-embracing—a morphology of history would mean anything to him? No question here of exchanging the perspective of the frog for that of the bird. Here we have the perspective of a god. He is 'there' and his position is unalterable. Instead of perspective he has compassion. He does not preach wisdom—*he sheds light*.

Do you suppose that he is unique? Not I. I believe that all over the world, and in the most unsuspected places (naturally), there are men—or gods—like this radiant being. They are not enigmatic, they are transparent. There is no mystery about them whatever: they re out in the open, perpetually 'on view'. If we are removed from them it is only because we cannot accept their divine simplicity. 'Illumined being,' we say, yet never ask with *what* it is they are illumined. To be aflame with spirit (which is life), to radiate unending joy, to be serene above the chaos of the world and still be part of the world, *human*, divinely *human*, closer than any brother—how is it we do not yearn to be thus? Is there a role which is better, deeper, richer, more compelling? Then shout it from the roof-tops! We want to know. And we want to know immediately.

I do not need to wait for your response. I see the answer all about me. It is not really an answer—it is an evasion. The illustrious one at my elbow looks straight at me: he fears not to gaze upon the face of the world. He has neither rejected the world nor renounced it: he is part of it, just as stone, tree, beast, flower and star are part of it. In his being he *is* the world, all there can ever be of it. . . . When I look at those around me I see only the profiles of averted faces. They are trying not to look at life—it is too terrible or too horrible, too this or too that. They see only the awesome dragon of life, and they are impotent before the monster. If only they had the courage to look straight into the dragon's jaws!

In many ways what is called history seems to me nothing more than a manifestation of this same fearsome attitude towards life. It is possible that what we call 'the historical' would cease to be, would be erased from consciousness, once we performed that simple soldierly movement of 'Eyes Front!' What is worse than a backward glance at the world is an oblique one.

When we speak of men 'making history' we mean to say that they have in some measure altered the course of life. But the man at my elbow is beyond such silly dreams. He knows that man alters nothing—not even his own self. He knows that man can do one thing only, and that that is his sole aim in life—open the eyes of the soul! Yes, man has this choice—to let in the light or to keep the shutters closed. In making the choice man acts. This is his part vis-a-vis creation.

Open the eyes wide and the stir must die down. And when the stir dies down then commences the real music.

The dragon snorting fire and smoke from his nostril is only expelling his fears. The dragon does not stand guard at the heart of the world—he stands at the entrance to the cave of wisdom. The dragon has reality only in the phantasmal world of superstition.

The homeless, homesick man of the big cities. What heartrending pages Spengler devotes to the plight of 'the intellectual nomad'! Rootless, sterile, sceptical, soulless—and homeless and homesick to boot. 'Primitive folk can loose themselves from the soil and wander, but the intellectual nomad never. Homesickness for the great city is keener than any other nostalgia. Home is for him any one of these giant cities, but even the nearest village is alien territory. He would sooner die upon the pavement than go "back" to the land.'

Let me say it unequivocally—after a 'reading' nothing in the world of actualities had meaning or importance for me. The daily news was about as remote as the dog star. I was in the very centre of the transformative process. All was 'death and transfiguration'.

There was only one headline which still had power to excite me, and that was—THE END OF THE WORLD IS IN SIGHT! In that imaginary phrase I never sensed a menace to my own world, only to 'the' world. I was closer to Augustine than to Jerome. But I had not yet found my Africa. My point of repair was a stuffy little furnished room. Alone in it I experienced a strange sort of peace. It was not the 'peace that passeth understanding'. Ah no! It was an intermittent sort, the augur of a greater, a more enduring peace. It was the 'peace of a man who was able to reconcile himself with the condition of the world *in thought*.

Still, it was a step. The cultured individual seldom gets beyond this stage.

'Eternal life is not life beyond the grave, but the true spiritual life, said a philosopher. What a time it has taken me to realize the full import of such a statement! . . . A whole century of Russian thought (the nineteenth) was preoccupied with this question of 'the end', of the establishment on earth of the Kingdom of God. But in North America it was as if that century, those thinkers and searchers after the true reality of life, had never existed. True, now and then a rocket exploded in our midst. Now and then we did receive a message from some distant shore. Such events were regarded not only as mysterious, bizarre, outlandish, but as occult. This last label meant that they were no longer serviceable or applicable to daily life.

Reading Spengler was not precisely a balm. It was more of a spiritual exercise. The critique of Western thought underlying

455

his cyclical pattern had the same effect upon me as the Koans have for the Zen disciple. Again and again I arrived at my own peculiar Western state of *Satori*. Time and again I experienced those lightning flashes of illumination which herald the breakthrough. There came excruciating moments when, as if the universe were an accordion, I could view it as an infinitesimal speck or expand it infinitely, so that only the eye of God could encompass it. Gazing at a star outside my window, I could magnify it ten thousand times; I could roam from star to star, like an angel, endeavouring all the while to grasp the universe in these super-telescopic proportions. I would then return to my chair, look at my fingernail, or rather at an almost invisible spot on the nail, and see into it the universe which the physicist endeavours to create out of the atomic web of nothingness. That man could ever conceive of 'nothingness' always astounded me.

For so long now the *conceptual* world has been man's whole world. To name, to define, to explain. . . . Result: unceasing anguish. Expand or contract the universe *ad infinitum*—a parlour game. Playing the god instead of trying to be as God. Godding, godding—and at the same time believing in nothing. Bragging of the miracles of science, yet looking upon the world about as so much shit. Frightening ambivalence! Electing for systems, never for man. Denying the miracle men through the systems erected in their names.

On lonely nights, pondering the problem—only one ever!—I could see so very clearly the world as it is, see what it is and why it is the way it is. I could reconcile grace with evil, divine order with rampant ugliness, imperishable creation with utter sterility. I could make myself so finely attuned that a mere zephyr would blow me to dust. Instant annihilation or enduring life—it was one and the same to me. I was at balance, both sides so evenly poised that a molecule of air would tip the scales.

Suddenly a most hilarious thought would shatter the whole set-up. An idea such as this: 'However deep one's knowledge of abstruse philosophy, it is like a piece of hair flying in the vastness of space.' A Japanese thought, this. With it came a return to a more ordinary sort of equilibrium. Back to that frailest of all footholds—solid earth. That solid earth which we now accept as being as empty as space.

'In Europe it was I, and I alone with my yearning for Russia, who was free,' said Dostoievsky somewhere. From Europe like a true Evangel, he spread the glad tidings. A hundred, two hundred years hence, the full import of this utterence may be realized. *What is to be done meanwhile?* A question I propounded to myself over and over.

In the early pages of the chapter called 'Problems of the

Arabian Culture, Spengler dwells at some length upon the escatological aspect of Jesus' utterances. The whole section called 'Historic Pseudomorphoses' is a paean to the Apocalyptic. It opens with a tender, sympathetic portrait of Jesus of Nazareth vis-a-vis the world of his day. 'The incomparable thing which lifted the infant Christianity out above all religions of this rich Springtime is the figure of Jesus.' So begins this section. In Jesus' utterances, he points out, there were no sociological observations, problems, debatings. 'No faith yet has altered the world, and no fact can ever rebut a faith. There is no bridge between the *course* of history and the *existence* of a divine world-order. . . .'

Then follows this: *Religion is metaphysic and nothing else*—'*Credo quia absurdum*'—and this metaphysic is not the metaphysic of knowledge, argument, proof (which is mere philosophy or learnedness), but *lived and experienced* metaphysic—that is, the unthinkable as a certainty, the supernatural as a fact, life as existence in a world that is non-actual, but true. Jesus never lived one moment in any other world but this. He was no moralizer, and to see in moralizing the final aim of religion is to be ignorant of what religion is. . . . His *teaching* was the proclamation, nothing but the proclamation, of those Last Things with whose images he was constantly filled: the dawn of the New Age, the advent of heavenly envoys, the Last Judgment, a new heaven and a new earth. Any other conception of religion was never in Jesus, nor in any truly deep-feeling period of history. . . . "My kingdom is *not* of this world", and only he who can look into the depths that the flash illumines can comprehend the voices that come out of them.'

It is at this point that Spengler voices his scorn for Tolstoy who 'elevated primitive Christianity to the rank of a social revolution'. It is here he makes a pointed allusion to Dostoievsky who 'never thought about social ameliorations'. ('Of what profit would it have been to a man's *soul* to abolish *property*?')

Dostoievsky and his 'freedom'. . . .

Was it not in that same time of Tolstoy and Dostoievsky that another Russian asked—'Why is it stupid to believe in the Kingdom of Heaven but intelligent to believe in an earthly Utopia?'

Perhaps the answer to this conundrum was inadvertently given by Belinsky when he said: 'The fate of the subject, of the individual, of the person is more important than the fate of the whole world and the well-being of the Chinese Emperor.'

At any rate, it was definitely Fedorov who quietly remarked: '*Each person is answerable for the whole world and for all men.*'

A strange and exciting period in 'the land of holy miracles' nineteen centuries after the birth and death of Jesus the Christ!

One man writes *The Apology of a Madman;* another writes a *Revolutionary Catechism;* another *The Metaphysics of Sex.* Each one is a revolution in himself. Of one figure I learn that 'he was a conservative, a mystic, an anarchist, an orthodox, an occulist, a patriot, a Communist—and ended his life in Rome as a Catholic and a Fascist'. Is this a period of 'historic pseudo-morphosis'? Certainly it is an Apocalyptic one.

My misfortune, *metaphysically speaking,* is that I was born neither in the time of Jesus nor in holy Russia of the nineteenth century. I was born in the megalapolis at the tail-end of a great planetary conjunction. But even in the suburb of Brooklyn, by the time I had come of age, one could be stirred by the reper-cussions of that Slavic ferment. One World War had been 'fought and won'. Sic! The second one was in the making. In that same Russia I speak of Spengler had a precursor whom you will scarcely find mention of even today. Even Nietzsche had a Russian precursor!

Was it not Spengler who said that *Dostoievsky's* Russia would eventually triumph? Did he not predict that from this ripe soil a new religion would spring? *Who believes this today?*

The Second World War has also been 'fought and won' (! ! !) and still the Day of Judgment seems remote. Great auto-biographies, masquerading in one form or another, reveal the life of an epoch, of a whole people, aye, of a *civilization.* It is almost as if our heroic figures had built their own tombs, described them intimately, then buried themselves in their mortuary creations. The heraldic landscape has vanished. The air belongs to the giant birds of destruction. The waters will soon be ploughed by Leviathans more fearful to behold than those described in the good book. The tension increases, increases, in-creases. Even in villages the inhabitants become more and more, in feeling and spirit, like the bombs they are obliged to manufacture.

But history will not end even when the grand explosion occurs. The historical life of man has still a long span. It doesn't take a metaphysician to arrive at such a conclusion. Sitting in that little hole in the wall back in Brooklyn twenty-five years or so ago I could feel the pulse of history throbbing as late as the 32nd Dynasty of Our Lord.

Nevertheless, I am immensely grateful to Oswald Spengler for having performed this strange feat of skill—describing to a nicety the unholy atmosphere of arteriosclerosis which is ours, and at the same time shattering the whole rigid thought-world which envelops us, thus liberating us—at least *in thought.* On every page, virtually, there is an assault upon the dogmas, con-ventions, superstitions and mode of thinking which have characterized the last few hundred years of 'modernity.'

Theories and systems are battered about like nine-pins. The whole conceptual landscape of modern man is devastated. What emerges are not the scholarly ruins of the past but freshly recreated world in which one may 'participate' with one's ancestors, live again the Spring, the Fall, the Summer, even the Winter, of man's history. Instead of stumbling through glacial deposits one is carried along on a tide of sap and blood. Even the firmament gets reshuffled. This is Spengler's triumph—to have made Past and Future live in the Present. One is again at the centre of the universe, warmed by solar fires, and not at the periphery fighting off vertigo, fighting off fear of the unspeakable abyss.

Does it matter so much that we are men of the tail end and not of the beginning? Not if we realize that we are part of something in eternal process, in eternal ebullition. Undoubtedly there is something far more comforting for us to apprehend, *if we persist on searching*. But even here, on the threshold, the shifting landscape acquires a more pregnant beauty. We glimpse a pattern which is not a mould. We learn all over again that the death process has to do with men-in-life and not with corpses in varying stages of decomposition. Death is a 'counter-symbol'. Life is the all, even in the end period. Nowhere is there any hint of life coming to s standstill.

Yes, I was a fortunate man to have found Oswald Spengler at that particular moment in time. In every crucial period of my life I seem to have stumbled upon the very author needed to sustain me. Nietzsche, Dostoievsky, Elie Faure, Spengler: what a quartet There were others, naturally, who were also important at certain moments, but they never possessed quite the amplitude, quite the grandeur, of these four. The four horsemen of my own private Apocalypse! Each one expressing to the full his own unique quality: Nietsche the iconoclast; Dostoievsky the grand inquisitor; Faure the magician; Spengler the pattern-maker. What a foundation!

In the days to come, when it will seem as if I were entombed, when the very firmament threatens to come crashing down upon my head, I shall be forced to abandon everything except what these spirits implanted in me. I shall be crushed, debased, humiliated. I shall be frustrated in every fibre of my being. I shall even take to howling like a dog. But I shall not be utterly lost! Eventually a day is to dawn when, glancing over my own life as though it were a story or history, I can detect in it a form, a pattern, a meaning. From then on the world defeat becomes meaningless. It will be impossible ever to relapse.

For on that day I become and I remain one with my creation.

On another day, in a foreign land, there will appear before me a young man who, aware of the change which has come over

459

me, will dub me 'The Happy Rock', That is the monniker I shall tender when the great Cosmocrator demands—'*Who art thou?*'

Yes, beyond a doubt I shall answer: 'The Happy Rock!'

And if it be asked—'Didst thou enjoy thy stay on earth?'—I shall reply: 'My life was one long rosy crucifixion.'

As to the meaning of this, if it is not already clear, it shall be elucidated. If I fail then am I but a dog in the manger.

Once I thought that I had been wounded as no man ever had. Because I felt thus I vowed to write this book. But long before I began the book the wound had healed. Since I had sworn to fulfil my task I reopened the horrible wound.

Let me put it another way.... Perhaps in opening the wound, my own wound, I closed other wounds, other people's wounds. Something dies, something blossoms. To suffer in ignorance is horrible. To suffer deliberately, in order to understand the nature of suffering and abolish it forever, is quite another matter. The Buddha had one fixed thought in mind all his life, as we know. It was to eliminate human suffering.

Suffering *is* unnecessary. But one has to suffer before he is able to realize that this is so. It is only then, moreover, that the true significance of human suffering becomes clear. At the last desperate moment—when one can suffer no more!—something happens which is in the nature of a miracle. The great open wound which was draining the blood of life closes up, the organism blossoms like a rose. One is 'free' at last, and not 'with a yearning for Russia', but with a yearning for ever more freedom, ever more bliss. The tree of life is kept alive not by tears but the knowledge that freedom is real and everlasting.